HEALING THE BROKEN

A BRIDES OF THE KINDRED CHRISTMAS NOVEL

Evangeline Anderson

PUBLISHED BY:

Evangeline Anderson Books

Healing the Broken

Copyright © 2017 by Evangeline Anderson

License Notes

This book is licensed for your personal enjoyment only. This book may not be re-sold or given away to other people. If you would like to share this book with another person, please purchase an additional copy for each person you share it with. If you're reading this book and did not purchase it, or it was not purchased for your use only, then you should return to the book retailer of your choice and purchase your own copy. Thank you for respecting the author's work.

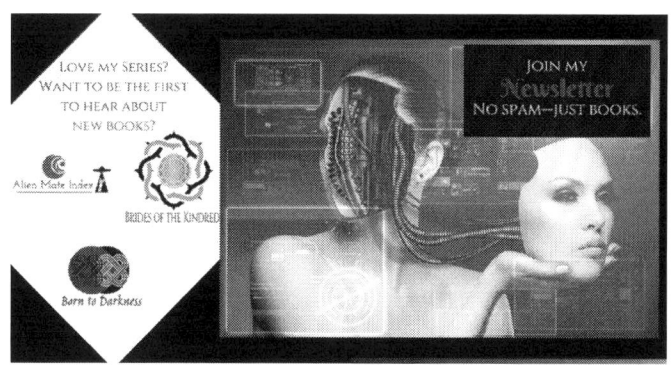

To be the first to find out about new releases join my newsletter at www.EvangelineAnderson.com.

Author's Note

This is my first ever Kindred Christmas novel and I'm so excited to share it with you. I hope you enjoy reading it as much as I enjoyed writing it!

Hugs and Happy Reading!
Evangeline 2017

Table of Contents

Chapter One 1

Chapter Two 7

Chapter Three 21

Chapter Four 45

Chapter Five 53

Chapter Six 67

Chapter Seven 75

Chapter Eight 91

Chapter Nine 101

Chapter Ten 109

Chapter Eleven 133

Chapter Twelve 153

Chapter Thirteen 163

Chapter Fourteen 179

Chapter Fifteen 199

Chapter Sixteen 215

Chapter Seventeen 229

Chapter Eighteen 241

Chapter Nineteen 247

Chapter Twenty 259

Chapter Twenty-one 265

Chapter Twenty-two 285

Chapter Twenty-three...289

Chapter Twenty-four...297

Chapter Twenty-five 311

Chapter Twenty-six...323

Chapter Twenty-seven 329

Chapter Twenty-eight...339

Chapter Twenty-nine 345

Chapter Thirty 363

Epilogue...369

Also by Evangeline Anderson 379

About the Author 382

Chapter One

"He wanted to bite me. He actually wanted to *bite me!* Can you believe that?" The slender blonde girl dressed in an expensive looking professional gray suit sounded both incensed and incredulous. "I mean, who's going to take the position when *being bitten* is one of the job requirements?"

Me, thought Sarah grimly. *I will. Because I don't have a choice. Because I need this job too badly to turn it down for any reason.*

She looked down at herself, contrasting her ratty, ill-fitting black skirt and faded blue blouse with the blonde's professional attire. One of the volunteers at the women's shelter had kindly loaned Sarah a black blazer to wear with her outfit but it didn't fit right, bulging oddly over her too-large breasts.

In fact, all of Sarah was too large—she was definitely what could kindly be called "plus sized." But that was all right with her. It was better to be bigger, safer to be overweight at the Compound. Father Caleb was far less likely to notice you that way. In fact, Sarah had managed to be overlooked for years until—

She pushed the image out of her mind. Better not to think of that right now. She'd gotten away from the Compound and no one from The Brotherhood could find her—at least they hadn't found her yet. And maybe, just maybe if she could get this job on the Kindred Mother Ship, they would never be able to find her again.

"Sarah Michaels," called the bored voice of the attendant.

Sarah started at the sound of her name. She'd thought about giving a fake one but she had to have *something* real to put on her resume, which contained no actual work experience except for the secretarial duties she'd done in The Brotherhood's home office.

She patted her thick chestnut hair, rolled into a bun at the nape of her neck, and adjusted her round glasses nervously on the bridge of her nose. The glasses were another part of her act—her camouflage. The lenses were clear, non-prescription glass—a pair she'd found in the drugstore years ago when her mother had first entered The Brotherhood, dragging Sarah and her father along with her. Sarah didn't need them to see but they, along with her frumpy clothes and the extra weight she'd put on, kept her from being of interest to men.

Especially to The Prophet, Father Caleb.

Several strands of hair had escaped from her bun and she pushed them back impatiently, wincing at the small pain in her palm as she did so. She'd cut her hand somehow, on the steel side of the seat in front of her on the bus. The small wound had mostly stopped bleeding but she hadn't been able to get a band-aid to cover it. Surreptitiously, she blotted it one last time on the underside of her rusty black blazer, glad that the blood stain wouldn't show.

"Sarah Michaels?" said the attendant again. She was a slim brunette seated at a gray metal desk. It matched the gray couches scattered around the large lobby of the Tampa Human Kindred Relations building, where the interviews were being held. Beside her was a twelve foot tall Christmas tree, decorated with red and gold ornaments and tinsel. It was incongruously colorful in the bland surroundings and it didn't match the weather either—which was hot.

Of course in Tampa, it was *always* hot.

"I'm here," Sarah said, in a voice that trembled only a little. "I'm ready."

She hoped.

"All right—go in through the double doors. Commander Sazar is in the second office on the left. He already has your resume."

"Thank you." Sarah bobbed her head nervously. "So…I'm interviewing with him exclusively? I mean, there aren't any other, uh, supervisors or—"

"Commander Sazar doesn't let anyone else help make his decisions," the attendant said briskly. "He's very particular about who he hires and he won't allow anyone else to have a say in it."

"Oh…okay. So I'm going to be in there alone with him?" Sarah asked.

The attendant must have seen the look of uncertainty on her face because the bored indifference of her own expression softened a little.

"Hey, don't worry—he doesn't bite unless you give permission first. He's a Blood Kindred—not a monster."

So the blonde applicant who had stalked out of her interview in a huff had been telling the truth—Commander Sazar *did* bite. Or at least he *wanted* to bite. Oh God, what had she gotten herself into?

I haven't gotten into it yet and I need this job, Sarah reminded herself grimly. *I need to get away from Earth and hide somewhere The Brotherhood and Father Caleb can never find me.*

She could still remember the last girl who had run away from the Compound—Jennifer Hastings—that had been her name though everyone called her Sister Jenny.

Sarah remembered how the Controllers had found her and brought her back, tied and gagged in the back of a van. The way she had screamed and struggled. And later, the drugged, dazed look on her bruised face when she stood before the alter to become a Bride of the Prophet, as all young women in The Brotherhood were expected to do so they could bear holy children to replenish the Compound…

Sarah pushed the memory away and gripped her tattered brown handbag firmly. Inside it was a cheap comb, a little tube of clear lip gloss she'd gotten as a free sample at the drugstore, and her birth certificate, which she'd managed to steal from the files of The Brotherhood before she ran. That was important because she didn't have a driver's license—women in The Brotherhood weren't allowed to drive. She didn't even have bus fare for a ride back. If she failed this interview, she'd be walking back to the shelter.

Well then, I'd better not fail.

Taking a deep breath, she lifted her chin and pushed through the double doors to go meet Commander Sazar—the man, or rather Kindred, she hoped would be her new boss.

* * * * *

Sazar looked up in irritation as the final applicant knocked timidly at his door. None of the other applicants had been right and the last one had been the worst of all—slim and blonde which reminded him entirely too much of Malinda.

The thought of his dead wife's name caused a dull ache to rise in his heart. She had been his mate for just three years before she had been taken from him leaving only the boy behind. The boy who looked so much like her with his golden blond hair and large blue eyes…

He pushed the thought of his son away guiltily. He ought to go and see the boy—he knew he should. But work kept him so busy and every time he saw Tsandor it was as though Malinda was looking at him through those crystal blue eyes…

"Commander Sazar?" The girl had a soft, low voice he found oddly soothing. Her appearance was soothing too—nothing at all like Malinda, he saw with satisfaction.

She was plump and short—she wouldn't even reach his shoulder, Sazar estimated, taking her in with his sharp, pale eyes. She had a soft, pretty face and her hair was dark brown. Her eyes, somewhat obscured behind round lenses, were an indeterminate shade of hazel. Perfect—she didn't resemble his lost wife in any way.

Then her scent hit him.

He stiffened a little as she walked into the temporary office he was using for Earth-side interviews. Gods, that *scent*. It was light and fresh and feminine but there was a deeper note underneath—a sweet, coppery aroma.

The scent of fresh blood.

Haven't smelled blood that sweet since Malinda!

As a Pitch-Blood Kindred, Sazar had what other Blood Kindred considered a disability. Instead of biting only to heal or pleasure his mate, he actually *needed* blood. Not a lot of it and not often but it had to be from a willing female and right now it had been *days* since he'd had a female willing to let him bite her.

He could still remember his last executive assistant—her big, frightened eyes and the way she'd trembled when she allowed him to bare her wrist for his fangs. The way she'd fainted from the pain when he pierced her…

Sazar had let her go after that, much to her obvious relief. He couldn't help it that his bite was so painful—it would hurt any female who wasn't either his mate or at least reasonably compatible with him. There were ways to make it hurt less but he couldn't engage in *that* kind of activity with a female who worked for him. He couldn't help needing blood but he refused to take advantage in that way.

"Commander Sazar?" the girl said again and he realized he'd been sitting there, staring at her—*More like smelling her,* whispered a sarcastic little voice in his brain—and not saying a word.

"Ms..." He looked down at the resume in his hands—which had hardly anything on it.

"Michaels," she finished for him. "Sarah Michaels." She walked up to the desk and held out her hand.

Sazar started to take it, then realized this was where the scent of fresh blood was coming from. *Gods*, it smelled good! So fucking tempting he wanted to drag her across the desk and bury his double set of fangs—which were growing longer and sharper by the minute—in the ivory skin of her throat.

No! He pushed the impulse away harshly. Yes, her blood smelled good—incredible to be honest—but that was only because he'd gone without for far too long. He would ignore his darker instincts and conduct this interview in a professional manner.

He had no choice.

Chapter Two

Commander Sazar, like all Kindred warriors, was absolutely *huge.*

His shoulders, under the wine-red uniform shirt he was wearing, were probably twice as broad as Sarah's own and she guessed that if he was this tall sitting down, he would probably be nearly seven feet tall standing. He had pitch-black hair—so shiny and dark it reminded Sarah of a crow's glossy feathers—and eyes that were a sharp, pale color which was almost white. She couldn't decide if they were pale gray or pale blue—it was impossible to tell. The look on his chiseled features was stern without even a trace of humor.

Not a man to mess with, Sarah decided.

"I'm pleased to meet you," she said, still holding out her hand.

Ignoring her offered hand, the huge Kindred nodded brusquely at the chair across from his desk—a straight backed wooden one which looked singularly uncomfortable.

"Please, have a seat." His voice was a low rumble which seemed to vibrate Sarah's bones.

Well, maybe Kindred didn't shake hands.

Feeling stupid, Sarah withdrew hers and sat on the edge of the wooden chair which was every bit as uncomfortable as it looked. Had she already blown the interview? God, she hoped not.

"Your resume is very…sparse." Sazar looked at the mostly

blank sheet of paper, frowning.

"I know there isn't much there," Sarah said quickly. "I've, uh, been with the same, er, employer for the past five years."

"It says here that you're twenty-three. So you've been working for this...organization since the age of eighteen?"

She nodded. Yes, eighteen was the age she'd been promoted to The Brotherhood's main office. At first she'd been an assistant to Sister Hope, the lovely, blonde secretary to Father Caleb.

Because Sister Hope was slim and pretty, Sarah had been able to blend into the background. And even though she ended up doing more and more of the actual work while Sister Hope "serviced" Father Caleb, Sarah hadn't minded. She liked scheduling appointments and booking interviews just fine—it was much better than disappearing into the closed executive suite in order to "relieve The Prophet's needs" as Sister Hope called it.

But then Sister Hope had started getting sick in the mornings and her belly had begun to swell...Her thickening waistline and the dark circles beneath her eyes had made her less appealing to Father Caleb, even though it was presumably his baby inside her that was causing the problems. That was when he began to turn his eyes toward Sarah...

No, she told herself, trying not to shiver. *No, I won't think about that now—I won't! I have to concentrate on getting this job.*

"I know I haven't got much experience," she told Commander Sazar, who was still studying the mostly blank page in his big hand with a frown. "But I'm very good at what I do. I'm proficient in SharePoint, Microsoft Publisher, and Excel. I can juggle your appointments with ease and make sure you're at the right place at the right time. You'll never miss an important interview or meeting while I'm backing you up and I can give the rest of the staff as much or as little access to you as you want."

"As it happens, your technical skills aren't as useful to me as your interpersonal ones," Sazar drawled in that deep, dark voice of his. "Do you know what I do for the Kindred, Ms. Michaels?"

"I...I assumed you were one of their top executives," Sarah said hesitantly. She felt foolish. After assuring him she was the perfect candidate for the job, now she had to admit she didn't even know exactly what it was he did.

"I am more than just an executive—I am a diplomat to high-level societies outside this solar system," he said, frowning. "I need an assistant who can not only keep track of my paperwork and files, but who is also willing and able to come with me on intergalactic diplomatic missions and pose as my partner if necessary."

"You mean...I would pretend to be...to be your wife?" Sarah couldn't keep the incredulity out of her voice.

"Yes." He nodded, as though it was no big deal.

"I mean but why...why would someone like *you* marry someone like *me?*" Sarah couldn't stop herself from asking. "I mean, look at you. You're so big and tall and muscular and I...I'm..."

She stopped, feeling more like an idiot than ever. She shouldn't point out the obvious physical disparity between them. Not if she wanted the job. But still, he looked like a male model with his muscular physique and chiseled jaw while she was just plain, dumpy little Sarah. Which was of course, the image she'd cultivated for herself for years. But she'd been hiding behind her glasses and baggy clothes and plump figure for so long, she didn't know how to be anything else.

"Are you implying that I wouldn't pick you as my mate? Or that *you* wouldn't choose *me* for yours?" Sazar's deep voice sounded more stern than ever.

"Neither," Sarah said miserably. "I just…I was surprised, that's all."

"All right. As I was saying, I need a female—an unattached female—to come with me and pose as a mate as well as keeping my schedule and notes in line," he said. "And I need one soon. I'm scheduled to depart for Alquon Ultrea in the Triangulum Galaxy in a few days time. As they are a people who are always in pairs, I must have an assistant before I leave."

"I can do that," Sarah said, trying not to sound too eager. "I can go with you. I don't have any attachments here."

"All right. And may I call your last employer?" He tapped the resume. "I don't see a phone number listed."

"Oh, uh…" Sarah swallowed hard. How could she explain that if she gave Commander Sazar the phone number to the Compound it would bring The Brotherhood straight to her? Father Caleb had chosen her to be one of his brides and if he found her…

"I don't even think I've heard of them—The Brotherhood of Peace?" Sazar frowned. "Are they some kind of religious organization?"

"That…that's how they, um, present themselves to the world," Sarah said, choosing her words carefully. "Our leader, I mean *their* leader, Father Caleb, is respected in the business and philanthropic communities. He was able to get The Brotherhood declared a church. They have tax exempt status and everything."

"I see. And how long have you been with them?" Sazar raised an eyebrow at her.

"I've been working in the main office since I was eighteen," Sarah said. "But I've been living in the Compound since I was twelve when my parents joined and took me with them. My father left but my mother stayed and I…I stayed with her. I didn't have a choice."

"I see," he said again and Sarah wanted to shout that he didn't see—that he could never see or understand what it had been like. Living in dread that she would be called as a Bride of the Prophet, camouflaging herself for years, arguing with her mother who was so brainwashed by The Brotherhood she refused to listen to reason...

"...living now?" Commander Sazar asked and Sarah realized she had missed a question.

"I'm sorry?" she asked, leaning forward.

"I said, where are you living now?"

Sarah swallowed hard.

"In a women's shelter. I...left the Compound a couple of weeks ago." Left—that was a laugh. More like slipped out in the dead of night after weeks of planning.

She'd been sneaking pieces of bread and scraps of meat—everything she could spare from her dinner—to Zeus, the fierce Doberman who guarded the front gates of the Compound for ages, trying to make friends with him. He'd still growled a little when she slid by him the night of her escape and Sarah had been so afraid he would start barking and howling—setting off the alarm. But she'd given him a piece of greasy, delectable bacon she'd saved from breakfast and he had stopped growling and remained mostly silent as she slipped away.

The tears of relief had been caught like a lump in her throat—tears she hadn't dared to shed until she finally found her way to the shelter after two days and nights of walking and hiding in the tangled overgrowth at the side of the road.

Sarah had known she was taking a risk in leaving—she remembered what had happened to Sister Jenny. But she couldn't wait any longer—she was to become a Bride of the Prophet the very next day. And the thought of Father Caleb's liver-spotted hands sliding all over her body as he "gave her his seed" to form a "holy child" made her flesh crawl.

Never, she thought. *I'll never go back! If I don't get this job, I'll find another. I'll stay in the shelter as long as I can. Until I find a place I can go.*

Unless they found her.

The Controllers were very good at tracking down runaways. They were a special squad of men, handpicked and trained by Father Caleb himself. They always seemed to know where to find the girls who managed to make it out of the Compound and bring them back before messy secrets and dirty stories about The Brotherhood could get out.

Not that anyone would believe me if I tried to tell them, Sarah thought bitterly. Even the shelter people thought she had just run away from an abusive husband. She didn't dare to tell them the truth.

Father Caleb had everyone fooled with his blinding televangelist smile and down-home, folksy way of speaking. He helped out in local police fundraisers too, making sure to keep Tampa's finest on his side. People from all over the world donated to The Brotherhood of Peace, thinking they were funding good works and charity.

And the Brotherhood *did* do charity—or appeared to. They were always there, on the front lines working hard after natural disasters or handing out baskets of food to the poor at Christmas. Nobody would believe that such a fine, upstanding organization hid a rotten heart—like a beautiful red apple with a putrid center. No one would believe that the Compound wasn't just a religious retreat but also a prison for the young girls who couldn't get out of it…

But I got out, Sarah told herself fiercely. *I got out and I'm not going back. I won't end up like Sister Jenny – I won't!*

"Would you rather I *didn't* call your former employer, Ms. Michaels?" Commander Sazar was giving her a penetrating look from those pale eyes.

"I…" Sarah swallowed hard. "That would…probably be better. I realize it doesn't give you much to go on for my past employment but I can give you the name and number of the woman who runs the shelter where I'm staying. She hasn't known me long but she can tell you I'm honest and a hard worker. I've been helping out in their office while I stay there."

That was all true. And she was pretty sure the shelter director, Benita Sanders, would give her a good reference—if the huge, intimidating Kindred sitting across the desk from her would only take it.

Sarah held her breath as he narrowed his eyes, apparently considering her offer. She felt like she had during those tense moments at three o'clock in the morning as she stood just inside the gate of the Compound and offered Zeus her last slice of bacon. Would he give her a chance?

At last, Sazar nodded.

"All right, I'll agree to call the shelter you're staying at instead of The Brotherhood," he said. "But…you may not want me to bother when you hear the requirements of your new position."

Sarah's heart jumped. He was talking like she already had the job! *Your* new position—he'd actually said *your* new position!

Then she remembered what the blonde applicant had been complaining about.

"Is it the biting thing?" she asked flatly, trying to keep her tone cool and businesslike.

His eyebrows shot up.

"The *biting* thing?"

"Oh, uh..." Yet again, Sarah felt like a fool. "I just thought...I mean, the girl who interviewed before me said..."

"I am a Pitch-Blood Kindred," Commander Sazar said in a dry, level voice as detached as hers had been. "Which means I need to consume blood. Not a lot of it and not very often but I *do* need it. And if you take this job and come with me to Alquon Ultrea, you must be willing to provide it to me."

Sarah squared her shoulders and took a deep breath.

"Will it hurt?" she asked directly.

"Yes." His tone was clipped, frigid. "I apologize but I cannot make the experience pleasurable for anyone save my mate. And since I have no mate at the moment—"

"Where would you bite me?" Sarah interrupted. "I mean...what I'm trying to ask is: is this some kind of a sex thing?"

He stiffened, his broad shoulders going absolutely rigid as a muscle tensed in his jaw. For a moment Sarah thought she'd gone too far but damn it, she'd *had* to ask! She hadn't gone to the trouble of running away from The Brotherhood and Father Caleb just to land herself in another position where she would be abused or molested. Although she had to admit, the idea of being touched by the tall, muscular Commander Sazar was a lot more appealing that picturing the same thing with the aging, oily Father Caleb...

"Taking blood from a mate *can* be part of the sexual experience for a Pitch-Blood Kindred," Sazar answered at last. "I tell you this in the interest of honesty and complete discloser. *However*, taking blood from you would not be in any way sexual. You are not my mate and I am not yours. I would not be seeking to pleasure you—I would only be taking a small amount for sustenance."

Sarah studied his stern, earnest face, which might have been handsome if he smiled, and decided she believed him.

"All right," she said at last. "But you never told me where you would bite me."

"The wrist. Perhaps the crook of your elbow—both areas offer easy access to veins." He spoke dryly again, the stiff irritation gone from his deep voice.

"Not...not my neck?" In every book or movie she'd ever seen featuring vampires, they always went for the neck.

He raised an eyebrow at her.

"I can call a vein for drinking from almost any area in your body—that is one of my abilities as a Pitch-Blood. But I would not...bite you there. It would be...too intimate and this is not, as you put it, 'a sex thing.' It is strictly about sustenance and survival."

"I see." Sarah was surprised at the slight feeling of disappointment she felt. The idea of the huge Kindred gathering her into his arms and pressing those cruel, sensual lips to her throat was darkly exciting.

But what was she thinking? She most definitely *didn't* want any kind of intimacy with her employer—it was the main reason she'd run away from the Compound in the first place!

"Do you think you could handle my need for blood?" He raised an eyebrow at her. "I have had...several assistants who could not. I wouldn't care to get all the way to Alquon Ultrea and find that you're too squeamish to fulfill the requirements of this job."

"Too squeamish to let you bite me, you mean," Sarah said bluntly. She'd had enough of euphemisms and double talk to last her a lifetime. She needed this job but she was going into it with her eyes open and all the cards on the table.

Commander Sazar's pale eyes sharpened but he nodded his head curtly.

"To let me bite you, yes."

"Well, let's find out, shall we?" Sarah stood on shaky legs and walked around his desk. Boldly, she stuck out her arm and pulled up the sleeve of her blazer, baring her wrist. "Go on," she said, "Drink."

Part of her couldn't believe she was doing this—how had she gotten so bold? But she had a hunch it was the right thing to do—a gut instinct she couldn't ignore.

Had any of the other applicants for this position offered to let the big Kindred drink from them? Sarah was betting they had not. What better way to seal the deal and get the job for herself than to give her prospective boss a literal taste of her abilities?

Commander Sazar's pale eyes widened but he didn't move from his position behind the desk. He looked at Sarah in complete silence for a moment—such a long moment, indeed, that she began to think she shouldn't have listened to her instincts after all.

Then he took her hand in his much larger one and turned it over.

Sarah tensed herself for a bite. But instead if sinking the long set of double fangs she could now see lurking just under his sensuous upper lip into her wrist, he did something completely unexpected—he licked her.

Sarah couldn't help herself—she gasped in surprise. His tongue was warm and wet and a total shock. It slid over the heel of her hand and sent shivering tingles through her entire body, making her catch her breath in surprise.

"What...what are you doing?" she whispered through numb

lips.

"You have a small cut on your hand—I noticed it the moment you walked in." His voice was a soft, purring growl. "I just healed it for you."

He released her hand with obvious reluctance and Sarah stared at it. Sure enough, the place where she'd cut herself on the sharp metal seat of the bus was completely healed—not even a scar was left to show where the injury had been.

"How…how did you do that?" she asked in a trembling voice.

He shrugged, his broad shoulders rolling beneath the wine-red uniform shirt.

"A talent of my kind. I wanted to reward your courage—to show you that even when I bite you, I can also heal you."

"Thank you," Sarah said uncertainly. "But…do you want to bite me now?"

His pale eyes were suddenly half-lidded and Sarah felt like she might burn up just from the way he was looking at her. But all he said was,

"No. Not now."

"All right." Suddenly being so close to him was too much—too intense. He had a scent about him—something sharp and dark and spicy that made Sarah feel warm and helpless, like she might do something foolish or submissive or both.

She had a brief image in her head—herself, half naked in his arms with her hair pulled back and her throat exposed. *Drink from me—I want you to.*

For a moment the image was so sharp she was certain she'd either seen it or lived it somehow before—maybe in a dream…

She took a step back, her heart thudding in her chest.

"Should…" Her voice came out in a squeak and she had to clear her throat and start again. "Should I wait for your call or…"

"If you'll give me the number of the shelter you're staying at, I'll call the supervisor there and verify what you've told me is true," he said. His tone was brisk again and some of the intensity had leaked from his pale eyes. "If the call goes well, you'll have the job and I'll expect you to take a shuttle with me immediately to the Mother Ship."

"Oh…" It was exactly what Sarah had hoped for and yet, she still felt like her heart was in her throat. "All right. Thank you. It's 813-558…" She gave him the phone number and watched as he wrote it down in tiny, precise handwriting. "Will…will we be going to, uh, Alquon Ultrea right away?" she asked as he finished.

"We'll have a day at least for you to get oriented. I'll have errands for you to run. And I'll put you on my expense account…" His sharp, pale eyes flickered over her rusty black blazer, faded blouse and ill-fitting skirt. "So you can get some suitable clothing."

Sarah felt her cheeks get hot with shame but what could she say? She knew her interview clothes were a pretty sad affair but the shapeless dark dress she'd always worn at the Compound had been torn and stained in her desperate flight. Still, she didn't like to accept charity.

She lifted her chin and looked him in the eyes.

"I appreciate your kindness, Commander Sazar, and I'll accept it—for now. But I want you to know I'll pay you back for every article of clothing out of my first paycheck."

For the first time she saw a hint of a smile twitching the corner of his sensuous mouth.

"Proud little thing, aren't you?"

"I just don't like taking charity," Sarah said stiffly. "I can pay my own way if you'll just give me a chance."

"If your information checks out, I will."

"It will," Sarah said confidently. "I'll be going with you to the Mother Ship." *Going to the Mother Ship and from there, right out of this solar system – right out of this galaxy.*

She was going somewhere The Brotherhood and Father Caleb could never reach her.

For the first time since she'd slipped past the softly growling Zeus and run from the Compound, Sarah permitted herself a sigh of relief.

Then she looked at her future employer's sharp eyes and even sharper teeth and wondered if she was really doing the right thing. Would she be any safer with this huge Kindred warrior than she'd been at the Compound?

Sarah wasn't sure but she decided she was going to find out.

What other choice did she have?

Chapter Three

Sazar couldn't help watching her from the corner of his eye as he piloted the small shuttlecraft upward.

Sarah Michaels was such a tiny little thing—at least compared to himself—but she had immense courage in that soft, curvy little body. She didn't cry out or gasp as the shuttle left the embrace of Earth's gravity. In fact, the only sign of possible distress was the way her knuckles whitened as she grasped the restraining straps he'd fastened around her. Her hazel eyes behind their lenses—he couldn't decide if they were more brown or green—widened as she watched her home planet drop away on the viewscreen but she said nothing and he could see by the firm set of her jaw that she meant to keep silent.

She's determined to bear anything to have this job – to come with me. Why?

His conversation with the director of the shelter for battered women had shed at least a little light on the situation. At first Benita Sanders refused to speak to him, clearly thinking that Sazar was an abusive mate, trying to find Sarah. But after hanging up and calling the HKR building to reach him, she had apparently believed he was who he said he was and had been willing to talk to him.

Once her guard was down, the shelter director had given Sarah an excellent recommendation. She'd also spoken of how Sarah had come to the shelter, shivering and frightened in the middle of the night—it was clear she wanted to be certain she would be protected.

"She's a good girl—helpful and kind. Wonderful with the children and a whiz on the computer," she'd told Sazar. "So just you be good to her, Commander Sazar, you hear me?"

"I will," Sazar had promised, touched almost against his will at this outsider's perspective of his new assistant.

"She came to us from a bad situation—I don't know the details exactly because she didn't want to talk about it," Benita Sanders continued. "But whatever it was, she needs to steer clear of her past life as much as possible."

"She will be accompanying me to the Kindred Mother Ship," Sazar had said dryly. "I don't think she can get much further from her past life than to leave the planet."

"Good, that's good." The shelter director sounded approving. "But I'm just saying—I know you Kindred are supposed to be all about honoring women and keeping them safe. You do that for little Sarah—I want your word right now that you will."

Bemused by her demand, Sazar had sworn his oath.

"I swear upon my life that Sarah will be safe with me. Any who seek to harm her, I will strike down in fury. My body will be her shield, my strength her shelter. May every bit of my own blood be shed before even a drop of hers is spilled."

"*Well…*" There had been silence on the other end of the phone for a long moment and for some reason Sazar got the mental image of the woman fanning herself.

"Is that enough to satisfy you?" he asked dryly. "I know of no other stronger oath I may swear."

"No, no…that's good. That will do." Benita Sanders had sighed in his ear. "I just wish human men were like you Kindred. We wouldn't need shelters if they were."

"It is true, places of refuge where females can hide from males are not needed in Kindred society," Sazar had told her. "But then, we worship the Goddess who is the Mother of All Life. She dictates that we have reverence for females."

A Goddess he still believed in, though he was bitter at the way she had taken his Malinda.

He had wrapped up the call with the shelter director shortly after and had opened the door to find Sarah waiting for him. She'd shown a controlled excitement and something else—could it be relief?—when he'd informed her she was hired. And after signing the papers on her new contract of employment, he'd led her to the waiting shuttle and fastened her into the passenger seat, trying not to notice how good she smelled as he did so.

It was her scent that he found especially distracting now. It seemed to grow stronger in the closed cabin—so strong, in fact, that his fangs were long and sharp and eager to bite. He kept remembering that one taste of her blood he'd had when he healed her small wound—how intoxicatingly sweet it had been…

No, he told himself firmly. *No, I won't bite her—not yet. I need to get things ready for our trip before I indulge myself.*

Grimly, he ignored the Blood Hunger which had been tearing at him for days now, ever since the last few, bitter drops he'd taken from his former assistant before she had fainted and he had let her go. There would be time for feeding later—time to taste Sarah's sweet, indescribably delicious blood again once all the preparations were in place.

If he had been mated to her, he would have bitten Sarah at least once a day—sometimes more. But it was stipulated in her employment contract that he would bite her only once during each standard seven-day week. It would be better to have her blood to nourish him at the very beginning of their mission rather than a day before, when he didn't really need it.

*But you **do** really need it,* whispered the Blood Hunger. *You're half starved — hell, more than half. You haven't had a true drink since Malinda died and that was a year and a half ago.*

Thoughts of his dead mate started a fierce ache inside him which he pushed ruthlessly away. It also made him think of his son, Tsandor. The constant care facility had informed him that the boy needed new clothing. Apparently he was growing tall for his age and had outgrown the last set Sazar had sent over.

He felt a stab of guilt, as he always did when thinking of his son. He should go and visit at least, reassure the boy that he was not forgotten. But somehow he couldn't face those eyes, so much like Malinda's, or bear to answer questions about how she had died…

"What happened to Mamam? Where is she? When is Mamam coming home?"

The questions Tsandor had asked over and over when Malinda had first passed over to be with the Goddess were unanswerable, unendurable. He had been so young when it happened. He was still young, still vulnerable…

I'll send Sarah, Sazar thought, casting a glance at his new assistant. *It can be her first assignment — to shop for new clothing for herself and the boy and to bring it to him at the constant care house.*

It seemed the perfect solution. The shelter director had said that Sarah was excellent with children, after all. Maybe Tsandor would like her and be comforted. Sazar hoped so — he had no comfort to give right now and he didn't know when he ever would again. His heart was a stone since his mate had passed — he had no feeling left inside but the deep, bitter ache and he knew he never would again.

Guilt slightly assuaged, he guided the shuttle towards the huge white bulk of the Mother Ship which was orbiting the Earth's moon. Time to get ready for his diplomatic visit with the dignitaries on Alquon Ultrea. They could be valuable genetic trade partners and allies against the Hive—the insectile race which threatened Earth and the Kindred who protected it—if Sazar did his job correctly.

Can't allow myself to be bogged down in sentiment, he told himself sternly. *I have a mission to complete and I must and will complete it for the good of my people.*

He would do his job, no matter how the Blood Hunger tore at him. After all, now that his love was dead, honor and duty were all that remained to him.

* * * * *

"Hey, doll—you look lost."

The voice belonged to a pretty auburn-haired girl who was as curvy as Sarah was herself, though the stranger was considerably taller.

"I *am* lost," Sarah confessed. She'd been standing in the main terminal aboard the Kindred Mother Ship for fifteen minutes, trying to decipher the map which would hopefully lead her to the clothing stores she was supposed to visit, but so far she couldn't make heads or tails of it.

The Mother Ship was a huge place, compared to the Compound. Kindred warriors and human women rushed back and forth, getting on and off the trams which pulled soundlessly up to the platforms and rushed off again just as fast.

It felt vast and impersonal and frightening after living much of her life in a controlled environment and Sarah was beginning to feel like an ant on a leaf, watching as the waters rose and swirled around her, just trying not to drown. This auburn-haired girl was the first person to stop and talk to her and she felt incredibly grateful for her kindness.

"Well, tell me where you're supposed to go and I'll help you get there," the girl said. "My name is Kat, by the way. I'm mated to Twin Kindred. How about you? What kind of Kindred did you get? Oh, and what's your name?" She laughed. "Sorry, guess I should have asked that first."

"I'm Sarah Michaels." Sarah held out a hand and the other girl shook it warmly with a smile. "But I'm not mated to any of the Kindred—I'm a personal assistant to one and I'm supposed to be doing some errands for him." She shrugged helplessly. "Only I don't know where I'm going. I just came up to the Mother Ship about an hour ago and I'm really lost."

"What? You mean he brought you up here and dumped you and just expects you to find your way around?" Kat sounded indignant. "What a jerk! What is he—a Dark Kindred? They don't understand emotions so it sounds like something one of them might do."

"No, he's a Blood Kindred," Sarah explained. "And he didn't just dump me—he actually gave me a way to call him if I get lost." She rummaged in her battered brown leather handbag and brought out the thin silver circle Sazar had given her before pointing the way to the terminal and going the opposite direction himself. "He said to put this around my head like a crown and *think* to him if I needed help."

"Wow—he gave you a think-me?" Kat's auburn brows rose in apparent surprise. "He must have known you a while to ask you to bespeak him. That's a pretty intimate form of communication."

"No, actually—he just hired me today," Sarah said. "Which is why I don't want to use this, uh, think-me thing." She lifted her chin. "I need to prove I'm a competent assistant and calling for help every five minutes doesn't look very competent, does it?"

"I guess not." Kat smiled cheerfully. "Which is why it's good for you that I'm nosey. I saw you standing here with that look on your face and just *had* to know what was going on with you."

"I'm glad you're nosey." Sarah smiled at her, feeling like she'd known the other woman all her life. "If you could just direct me to some clothing shops. I need to get some new clothes for myself and for a little boy around four and a half years old."

Kat's eyes practically glowed with interest.

"You're in luck, doll—I just happen to be taking a little shopping day myself. And since you and I are both pleasingly plump, you can tag along. Come on."

She led Sarah to a platform and then onto a whisper-quiet tram with clear glass sides which allowed a view of the different areas of the Mother Ship as they rushed past.

"Wow—it's really fast," Sarah remarked. "I have to stop looking—it's making me dizzy."

"You're lucky to ride it," Kat informed her. "The Kindred only installed it recently, you know. When I first came aboard the Mother Ship, you could either go up and down in these fast, cramped little tubes or you had to ride this two-headed animal called a Take-me." She made a face. "Believe me—neither option was any fun." She leaned casually against a pole, her eyes sharp. "So tell me more about this boss of yours…"

Kat was easy to talk to and by the time she'd led Sarah past the huge park-like common area and into the shopping district, Sarah felt like she'd known her forever. She was cautious about explaining her past—even though she was far past the reach of The Brotherhood, she still didn't like speaking about them and her life in the Compound. But she didn't mind telling Kat about her new employer and the mission she was going to accompany him on.

"So your new boss is Commander Sazar—the Pitch-Blood Kindred diplomat?" Kat asked as they tried on clothing at a store which catered to the plus sized body type. In fact, most of the stores aboard the Mother Ship seemed to have a good selection of plus sized clothing, unlike the stores down on Earth. Kat had explained that many Kindred warriors found "fluffy" girls appealing which was surprising to Sarah. Larger girls were considered inferior at the Compound, which was one reason she'd escaped Father Caleb's notice for so long.

"Yes, he is—do you know Commander Sazar?" Sarah stepped out of the dressing room and looked at the outfit she'd picked from the rack. It was difficult to know her size since all her clothing from the age of twelve had been hand-sewn by her mother and the other Sisters in the Compound.

"I know *of* him. His little boy goes to nursery school at the same place my three little guys do. In fact my son Shad is especially good friends with him—he talks about him all the time."

"So he's friends with Tsandor—Commander Sazar's little boy?" Sarah asked.

"Uh-huh. Oh no, doll—you can't wear *that*. It's way too big for you!" Kat was frowning in distaste at the shapeless sweater and baggy slacks Sarah had pulled on. "Here—let me find you something." She hunted among the racks for a few minutes and came back with an armful of clothing. "Try these."

"Well…all right." Sarah looked doubtfully at the jewel-toned colors in the heap of garments. She hadn't been allowed to wear anything but gray, navy blue, black, and occasionally tan since her parents had joined The Brotherhood when she was twelve. It seemed strange to be trying on an emerald green sweater which hugged her breasts and tight-fitting jeans which emphasized her hips and behind rather than obscuring them.

"Now *that's* more like it!" Kat exclaimed when she came out of the dressing room. "Show off those curves, girlfriend. Don't try to hide them."

"I don't know…" Sarah looked at her reflection uncertainly. "These seem so…form fitting. So immodest."

"Immodest?" Kat laughed. "But just about every inch of your skin is covered."

"Yes but…these show so much of my shape." Sarah couldn't seem to let go of her habit of camouflage. These clothes would have gotten her punished at the Compound—and they would have drawn unwanted attention.

"Well, you have a *nice* shape," Kat countered. "Look, you're shaped like me—a really full hourglass. You have big boobs and plenty of junk in the trunk but your waist is narrow—you need to show that off."

"But…what will Commander Sazar say?" Sarah asked, biting her lip. "Are these the kind of clothes I'm supposed to wear on Alquon Ultrea?"

"Probably not," Kat said cheerfully. "But it's not like you're moving there for life—you're just going on a diplomatic mission for a little while. You need clothes you can wear here on the Mother Ship."

"But the mission—"

"Will be fine. Look here, doll—I'll do some research into the Alquon culture and have my clothing pattern replicator print you out some outfits that will work over there. They won't last nearly as long as clothes you'd buy in a store but they'll work for the mission, okay?"

"You'd do that for me?" There was a lump in Sarah's throat. "But…you just met me. You don't even know me."

"I know I like you—you seem like a sweet girl." Kat smiled. "And I have a friend who's going to be very eager to meet you. She's extremely interested in Commander Sazar's little boy because she teaches him art at the day care. You can meet her when we bring the clothes for the little guy."

Kat was a big help in picking out clothing for a four-going-on-five-year-old and Sarah found she was much more comfortable with those than some of the choices her new friend had talked her into for herself. She still felt uncomfortably exposed, even wearing the sleek black business suit Kat had talked her into.

The pencil skirt clung too tightly to her full hips and the white blouse and blazer that went with it conformed to her curves more closely than she liked. But Kat assured her that she looked fabulous—svelte and sexy. Sarah had to admit her new suit was a big improvement over the interview clothes she'd been able to get at the shelter.

Before she knew it, they were on their way to the daycare center with new clothes for Commander Sazar's little boy and a few toys which Sarah had picked out as well. She felt sorry for the little boy, living away from his father—it reminded her of how her own father had abandoned her to her fate at the Compound when he had chosen to leave The Brotherhood of Peace.

They went up several levels and Kat led her into a gorgeous

play area with a reading corner, jungle gym, ball pit, and so many other toys and games it looked to Sarah like a kid's idea of paradise.

She couldn't help contrasting it with the raggedly mown back lawn and the broken tire swing which had been the play area at the Compound. There had been a sand pit too but it was usually crawling with sand fleas which meant multiple itchy bites. The sand box here on the Kindred Mother Ship was filled with clean sand in every brilliant color of the rainbow and the children playing in it were likewise clean, happy, and obviously well cared for.

"Oh, there she is—there's my friend, Sophie," Kat said, leading Sarah past the happily playing children to a back area which was obviously dedicated to art. At the moment, it was set up with about a dozen miniature easels fitted out with long sheets of paper and paint pots filled with bright, primary shades. Little artists wearing protective smocks over their clothing were dabbing with brushes, each creating their own version of a Christmas tree.

"Hello." Sarah nodded shyly at the pretty woman with long brown hair and big green eyes. She was wearing a paint-daubed apron herself and smiling as she went around, supervising her young artists.

"This is Sarah," Kat explained. "I thought you might like to meet her since she's working for Commander Sazar—you know—Tsandor's father?"

"Oh, you are?" Sophie turned bright, inquisitive eyes on her. "I've been hoping to meet him in person but he almost never comes here. Did you come to take Tsandor home to be with his father? Are you his new nanny or something?"

"Um, actually I'm just here to drop off clothes for him," Sarah said apologetically. "I do work for Commander Sazar but as his executive assistant—not a nanny."

"That's too bad." Sophie looked genuinely upset. "I was so hoping you were coming to take him home. That poor little boy is starved for love and affection and his father *never* comes around."

"I think that maybe he's, uh, very tied up with his job," Sarah said awkwardly, feeling that she had to defend her new employer. "We're getting ready to go on a mission to Alquon Ultrea in a whole other galaxy in a day or so."

"Well if he's going off on a long mission, all the more reason to come see his son himself instead of sending you," Sophie exclaimed. "How can he be so cold hearted? Did he give you any explanation at all as to why he couldn't come?" she demanded.

Sarah took a step back. "No, but he only hired me today so he hasn't told me much of anything," she admitted. "Actually, I was really surprised to learn he has a son at all. He seems like such a…such a solitary man."

That was the main impression she got from the big Kindred—a sense of solitary loneliness—like a bubble around him that couldn't be breached.

"Take it easy on poor Sarah," Kat told Sophie. "She doesn't know why Commander Sazar won't come to see his own kid—she's just doing her job."

"Well do you at least know how his wife died?" Sophie asked. "I've asked my husband, Sylvan, about it but her death seems to be shrouded in mystery."

"I'm afraid not." Sarah shook her head regretfully. "He didn't volunteer any information—just told me I was to bring some clothes for Tsandor."

She could still remember the cool, collected way Commander Sazar had given her this first assignment…

"You're to go to the clothing shops and buy suitable clothes for both yourself and a young male about four and a half cycles old," he'd said to her as he landed the shuttled they'd flown up on in the docking bay.

"I'm sorry…" Sarah cleared her throat. "A young male?"

Sazar made an impatient gesture with one hand. "What your people would call a 'little boy' I believe. He is housed in the constant care facility on the twenty-second level, east wing of the Mother Ship. Buy him four or five outfits and anything else you think necessary."

"Wait—you want me to shop for a little boy?" Sarah had been surprised. There had been nothing about this in her interview. "What little boy? Whose little boy?"

"His name is Tsandor and he is my son." Commander Sazar had stared straight ahead, studying the viewscreen as he spoke, his pale eyes never meeting hers.

Sarah had felt a funny twitch in her midsection. A son…he had a son. Which meant he must have had a wife at one time. Or maybe he still had one and they were divorced or separated. Was that why he needed to take blood from Sarah instead of from his own mate?

"Your son?" she asked hesitantly. "Is his mother—"

"His mother is *dead*." His deep voice had crackled like lightning in the small, confined shuttle, making her wince. And still he looked straight ahead, refusing to meet her gaze.

"I…I'm sorry," Sarah had faltered.

"Don't be. And don't speak of her again," Sazar snapped. "You have your first assignment—can you handle it or not?"

Sarah had lifted her chin. "I can handle it."

"Good. I've placed you on my expense account so you should have no problems. I'll expect to see you in my quarters at nineteen hundred hours so that I can brief you on the details and timeline of our mission. You're excused Ms. Michaels." And he had let her out of the shuttle and pointed the way to the tram station with hardly another word...

"So I really don't know any more than you," Sarah told Sophie, as she finished recounting the way Commander Sazar had given her the assignment. "I've never even shopped for a little boy before so I was lucky to run into Kat, here, who helped me out." She held up her shopping bag. "I have the clothes right here along with a toy or two I picked out for Tsandor. Can I give them to you?"

Sophie's pretty green eyes softened a little.

"I'll take the clothes and make sure they get to the constant care house. But why don't you give Tsandor the toys yourself?"

"Oh...well, if you think that would be all right," Sarah faltered.

"Of course it will be all right. Look, he's right over here, painting a Christmas tree with the others."

She took the bag from Sarah and gestured to a little boy with curly, golden blond hair who was bent studiously over a surprisingly good painting of a Christmas tree.

Feeling awkward, Sarah tucked the toys she'd bought under one arm and approached the little boy. He was taller than the rest and looked nothing at all like Commander Sazar in coloring, although his finely molded features were very like his father's.

What gorgeous blond hair — he must take after his mother, Sarah thought. She watched quietly for a moment as he worked with fierce concentration, the tip of his tongue poking out from the corner of his mouth. She couldn't help noticing all the other children were painting green Christmas trees but Tsandor's was a defiant teal color with purple and yellow ornaments.

"Hello, Tsandor," she began in a soft, low voice.

"Hi." He dabbed a final blob of purple paint on his turquoise Christmas tree and then turned his face up to hers. His beautiful crystal blue eyes widened as he took her in.

Sarah thought he must be afraid because she was a stranger.

"Hi Tsandor," she said again. "Your father sent me. I'm Sarah and—"

"Sarah! Sarah!" To her surprise, he dropped his paintbrush and rushed into her arms, grabbing her around the waist and pressing his face eagerly to her midsection.

"Oh!" gasped Sarah. He was quite big for his age—no doubt he got his size from his father—and he nearly bowled her over.

"I was waiting for you to come!" He looked up at her with shining eyes. "Shad said it wouldn't be long. He said the Goddess told him so—she talks to him sometimes. Isn't that nice?"

"I…I guess…yes, it certainly is," Sarah said, uncertain what else to say. "But…how do you know me?"

"Shad told me all about you," he said impatiently. "He said you'd be coming to be with me and my daddy now that my mommy is with the Goddess."

Sarah looked helplessly at Kat and Sophie who were watching with wide eyes.

"Shad…told you?" she asked.

"Shad is my little boy," Kat said, nodding at a child with white-blond hair and big dark eyes. He was watching as Tsandor hugged her with a strangely knowing expression on his young face. "He…knows things sometimes."

"The prophesy," Sarah heard Sophie whisper to Kat. "Remember what Dani told us the Goddess told her in the Sacred Grove?"

"How could I forget?" Kat murmured back.

Sarah wanted to ask what they were talking about but she still had an armful of eager four-almost-five-year-old and found she couldn't easily extricate herself. Not that she wanted too—the excited, hopeful expression on Tsandor's sweet face tugged at her heart. She'd always liked children and there was something about this little boy that seemed to call to her.

"Hey," she said and gently hugged him back. "I'm really glad to meet you, Tsandor."

"I'm so glad you're finally here." He nuzzled against her, leaving a smear of paint on her new suit jacket but Sarah found she didn't even care. "I dreamed about you, you know. I've been waiting for so long to meet you."

"Well...I've been waiting to meet you too," Sarah said, smiling at him. "I brought you some new clothes—and some toys. Would you like to see them?"

"Sure!" He eased his grip on her and Sarah was able to crouch down beside him, to get on his level.

"Well, let's see," she said, pulling out the first toy. "How do you like this? It's a model of the Mother Ship—I thought it was really neat when I saw it."

"Cool!" Tsandor's eyes shone as he carefully took the tiny scale model from her. It was the size of a Matchbox car—about as long as his hand. "Look, you can see the docking bay and everything," he exclaimed, pointing at the toy. "Thanks!"

"You're welcome—thank you for your good manners," Sarah said, smiling. "I do have one more thing but, well, I'm not sure if you'll like it or not."

"What is it?" He slipped the scale model of the Mother Ship carefully into his front pocket. "Can I see?"

"It's this." Sarah pulled out a small stuffed elephant and showed it to him. "I had a stuffed animal like this when I was little—I called him Mr. Nosey."

Tsandor started at the stuffed animal in obvious confusion.

"What is it?"

"It's an elephant," Sarah said, rather surprised. "Haven't you ever seen an elephant? Maybe at the zoo or in a video?"

Tsandor shook his blond curls.

"Uh-uh. Is it an Earth animal? My daddy and I came from Tranq Prime—we didn't have any ef… efulumps there."

"*Elephants*," Sarah corrected gently. "This one is small but the real ones are *huge*. Bigger than your daddy."

His crystal blue eyes widened.

"Wow—really? Is it as big as a *vranna?*"

It was Sarah's turn to frown in confusion.

"What's a *vranna?*"

"Um…it's kinda hard to explain." His face brightened. "I made one out of clay the other day—it should be dry by now. Wanna see?"

"Well, sure." Bemused, Sarah allowed him to take her hand and lead her into a small structure where the art supplies were stored. There was a shelf which he could reach by standing on tiptoes which contained several "sculptures" made of Play-Doh.

Carefully, Tsandor brought his down—a turquoise and purple collection of lumps which looked a little like an animal. At least, it had a body, a head, and four long appendages.

"See?" he said proudly. "I made it for my daddy. Do you want to bring it to him?"

"I'll be happy to." Sarah took the lumpy sculpture from him carefully. "This is great—I'm sure he'll love it."

"I wish I could give it to him myself, though." Tsandor's big eyes were suddenly wistful. "Are you going to take me away with you now?" he asked hopefully. "So I can live with you and daddy?"

"Well…I'm afraid I'm not here to take you away," Sarah said as gently as she could. And added, "Not yet, anyway," because she couldn't stand to see the broken hope on his little face. "First your daddy and I have to go on a, uh, top secret mission to another planet. Okay?"

He sighed. "Okay. But you'll be back soon, right? And then we'll all live together?"

"Um, well…*maybe* so," Sarah said cautiously. She still had no idea how long the diplomatic mission to Alquon Ultrea would last and she didn't want to give the little boy false hope.

False hope? exclaimed a little voice in her head sarcastically. *What do you think you're doing by letting him think he's going to live with you and Commander Sazar? As if the three of you would be some kind of a family?*

The idea was laughable. The big, handsome Kindred commander would never want anything to do with dowdy, plus-sized Sarah. He might be willing to take her as an assistant and drink her blood every so often *(once a week, as specified by the contract,* she reminded herself,*)* but that didn't mean he would ever want any kind of romantic attachment with her.

She tried to push away the shiver she felt at the idea of romance with her new boss.

*Your **boss**, that's all he is,* she reminded herself. *And that's the* *way it's going to stay, no matter what strange ideas Tsandor has somehow cooked up in that funny little head of his.*

"So tell me more about *vrannas*," she said, trying to change the subject.

"Okay." The tousled blond head nodded. "If you'll tell me more about efulumps."

Sarah wound up staying at the day care center for hours—talking and playing with Tsandor, getting to know the little boy who already seemed to know a startling amount about her. He told her about the strange and ferocious beasts on his native world of Tranq Prime and she tried to explain about elephants and other Earth animals.

Finally she found a book about zoo animals in the reading corner and they sat with their heads together, studying it as she pointed out plant eaters and predators, much to his intense interest. He was smart as a whip—she could tell that. He asked surprisingly astute questions and was already reading in English though she knew it wasn't his native language.

She even stayed for supper, when Sophie invited her to, and got to meet with the caregivers who staffed the constant care facility. Every one of them talked about what a sweet little boy Tsandor was…and how much he missed his father.

"I wish he would come around more," Lola, the girl who watched over Tsandor most told her. "That little boy just pines for his daddy day and night. In fact, he's been sad and withdrawn for days—until you showed up." She smiled. "I've never seen him light up for anyone but Commander Sazar the way he lit up for you. Did you know him before, on Tranq Prime?"

"No," Sarah admitted. "Honestly, I just met him for the first time today."

But somehow that didn't feel right. She had the strangest feeling that she'd seen Tsandor before—maybe in a dream? It seemed silly but the nagging notion wouldn't leave her, though she told herself she was being ridiculous. Still, how could she explain the way that Tsandor had instantly known her?

I dreamed about you, he had said. And he'd also claimed that Kat's little boy had told him she would be coming. But how could any of that be true? Unless the Kindred Goddess was more than just an abstract idea—more than just a false deity.

Sarah didn't believe in God or gods or goddesses. At least, not the God she was taught about during her time at the Compound. According to Father Caleb, God insisted that women should serve men and do as they were told. Sarah knew she was little and unimportant but she rejected the idea of a deity who insisted she was less just because of her sex. A deity who commanded her to submit herself to The Prophet and let him "plant his seed" in her.

Ugh—don't think of it, she ordered herself. *Just enjoy being here with Tsandor. You're away from the Compound and The Brotherhood now—they'll never be able to find you here. You're safe—try to enjoy yourself and forget the past.*

So enjoy herself she did. After supper, she read Tsandor a few more books and then it was bedtime.

"Would you like to tuck him in?" Lola asked, with a smile when Tsandor came out in his pajamas with his face washed and his teeth brushed. "You two seem to have really hit it off."

"Yes, yes—please Sarah! Please tuck me in!" Tsandor begged.

Sarah couldn't keep a smile from tugging at the corners of her mouth.

"With an invitation like that, how can I refuse?"

"Goody!" Tsandor took her by the hand and led her through

the long hallway of the constant care house to his own small dormitory, where he slept in a small bed. There were five other little beds in the room as well, with boys already asleep in them.

She watched as Tsandor climbed into bed and then tucked the coverlet up to his chin as he cuddled the toy elephant she'd given him—which he had named "Lump-lump"—short for Efulump.

"Good night…Sarah," he murmured with a yawn.

"Good night, Tsandor." She stroked his blond curls away from his forehead and felt a rush of love for the little face looking sleepily back at her. What was it about this little boy that tugged at her heart so?

"Promise you'll come back soon," he ordered her, even as his eyes grew heavy. "Promise…" he yawned. "Promise you'll come back and you and me and daddy will all live together."

"I promise to come back," Sarah said softly. Her heart ached for him—how she wished she could give him what he really wanted—the promise of a real family to come home to. But that could never be, she was certain. Commander Sazar should be dating some kind of super model—not a runaway from the Compound who was short and dowdy and not exactly thin.

"You remind me…remind me of my mommy," Tsandor told her, still yawning. "You don't look like her but you act like her."

"Thank you, Tsandor—that's a beautiful compliment. But…what happened to your mommy?" she asked gently. She didn't want to push but it would be nice to know.

He shook his head sleepily.

"Don't know. One day she fell down when she was making me lunch. Then daddy called the healer and she had to go away and then…" His half-closed eyes grew suddenly bright with tears. "And then she never came back any more. For a long time daddy said she was just sick but then, after we got here…" He sniffed. "Then they told me she went to be with the Goddess. I miss her," he added in a small voice. "But you remind me of her. You smell so nice and you're soft to hug." A tear rolled down his flushed cheek and he buried his face in the soft gray plush of the stuffed elephant.

Sarah felt like she might start crying herself. She knew what it felt like to lose a parent, if not by death then by abandonment. Her own father had left her to the tender mercies of The Brotherhood and her mother was lost to reason—lost to anything but the words of The Prophet, Father Caleb whom she considered to be divine and beyond judgment.

"I'm so sorry, Tsandor," she whispered, leaning down to kiss his hot little cheek. "I know you miss her."

"I do." His voice was muffled. "But it's okay because you're here now. When I told Shad about my dream of you, he said you were coming to fix daddy and me. To…to…heal us." One crystal blue eye peeked out from behind Efulump's furry side. "I don't know why he said that though. We're not sick but I'm awful glad you're here anyway."

"I'm glad I am too," Sarah whispered, and really meant it. "Goodnight, sweetheart."

"G'night." Tsandor yawned again. Apparently he was all worn out. "I'll see you soon, right?"

"As soon as I get back," Sarah promised him. She made a promise to herself too—she would come and visit this lonely little boy as often as she could while she lived here on the Mother Ship. She might not be able to offer him the family he so desperately desired but she could at least give him the love he was lacking.

Why is he lacking it though? Why won't Commander Sazar comes see him? She had no answer for that question. It was true that Sazar seemed like a cold and withdrawn person—was he unable to love his son? Or was there some other reason—something else that was holding him back?

Well, I just met him—it's not my place to ask, Sarah told herself. But there was one thing she could do—she still had the Play-Doh sculpture of the *vranna* wrapped carefully in tissues in her battered handbag. She could at least give that to Commander Sazar and give him Tsandor's love.

"I'm afraid I have to ask you to leave now," Lola, who had come in the room to check on the sleeping boys, whispered in her ear. "Lights out at seven o'clock sharp, you know. They need a lot of sleep at this age."

"Seven o'clock?" Sarah looked at her watch—a scratched Timex which had been her mother's before they entered The Brotherhood. "Oh no—seven o'clock—nineteen hundred hours!" she gasped.

"Well, yes—if you want to give it in military time." Lola looked confused. "Is everything okay?"

"I'm afraid not." Sarah was already rushing out the door. "I was supposed to meet with Commander Sazar—Tsandor's father—fifteen minutes ago."

Chapter Four

She was late. Late, Goddess damn it! What in the Seven Hells was wrong with her? She'd had hours to complete the few simple errands he'd given her and where was she?

Maybe you shouldn't have set her lose on the Mother Ship with no one to guide her when she's never been here before, whispered the voice of guilt in his head. *Are you sure she's all right? What if something's happened to her? Something could, you know – people can die at any time for no outward reason. You know that.*

Yes, he knew it from bitter personal experience but he refused to dwell on it now.

Irritably, Sazar pushed his guilt and worry away. The Mother Ship was a big place but it was also a safe place, even for a female alone. Sarah would be all right. He was *almost* sure of it.

If she's all right then why is she late? Where is she? Why hasn't she used the Think-me and bespoken you yet? the voice in his head demanded. Damn it, why wouldn't the fucking thing just *shut up?*

He supposed he could use a Think-me himself and call her but he'd given her his only one and he would have to go find another. Maybe he should do that? Then again, why was he so worried about her? She was only a little human assistant—he shouldn't be getting so worked up—should he?

The Blood Hunger gnawed at Sazar, making everything worse. His head throbbed and his fangs ached. His throat felt as dry as a

Karnethian desert.

Gods, what if something *had* happened to her? What if she'd fallen on the tram tracks and been run over? Or what if she'd wandered into the Unmated Males area by accident—now *there* was a pleasant thought. As safe as most of the Mother Ship was, the Unmated Males section was the definite exception to that rule. If she'd somehow gotten in there…

He started up from his chair to go get a Think-me when a sudden rapping at the front door of his suite interrupted his guilty, worried thoughts. Sazar's big hands clenched into fists.

"Come!" he called harshly, his voice coming out strained and dry.

The door slid open, revealing a flushed and panting Sarah. She had a bag over her arm and something wrapped in a wad of tissues clutched in her hand.

"I'm so sorry, Commander Sazar," she exclaimed. "I know I'm late. I—"

"Where were you?" Before he could stop himself, Sazar was across the room in front of her. He took her by the shoulders and shook her once, hard.

The plain, round framed glasses she wore fell off and hit the floor with a flat *crack* and her hair, which was coming loose from its bun at the nape of her neck, tumbled down in a profusion of silky brown waves.

"I…I'm sorry," she gasped, looking up at him. "I didn't mean—"

"I was worried about you," Sazar heard himself admitting. Although he didn't know why he should be. He hadn't even known the little human for twenty-four Earth hours yet but already the idea of losing her—of her being hurt or injured in any way—made his protective instincts rise.

"I'm sorry," she said for the third time. "I just...lost track of time when I was playing with your son. And then I got on the wrong tram trying to get back to this level. But I never thought—"

"No, you *didn't* think, did you?" Sazar forced himself to let her go and take a step back.

The Blood Hunger was too close to the surface and this little human was entirely too appealing. He could still remember the one sweet taste of her blood he'd gotten when he healed her. It made him ache to sink his fangs into her vulnerable throat but he restrained himself sternly.

"Why didn't you use the Think-me to call and let me know you were all right?" he demanded.

Her cheeks flushed. Without the round lenses her eyes were big and starry, fringed thickly with dark lashes. They were more green than brown, Sazar decided—the color of a quiet forest pool, reflecting the leaves of the trees overhead.

"I should have used the, uh, Think-me," she admitted quietly. "To be honest, I forgot all about it. And...I didn't think you'd be so worried about me. Isn't the Mother Ship safe?"

"It is," Sazar admitted grudgingly. "Except for the Unmated Males section. You should never go there without the scent of a male on you to protect you."

"Uh...okay."

Clearly she didn't understand. To be honest, Sazar didn't understand himself. Why was he getting so worked up about his new assistant? He'd had five or six assistants since moving from Tranq Prime to take this position aboard the Mother Ship. He hadn't worried about any of them—other than the fact that taking blood from them was a problem. So why was he so worried about Sarah?

He took another step back and the heel of his boot crunched on something. Looking down, he lifted his foot and saw the mangled metal frames of the round glasses she always wore.

"Goddess damn it!" he swore, bending to retrieve them.

"Oh!" Sarah took them from his hands, looking with an unreadable expression on her face at the twisted wire and broken glass.

"Forgive me," Sazar growled. "I'll have these replaced at once, of course. Or if you'd rather, I believe there is a Tolleg surgeon onboard who can fit you with permanent lenses that will correct your eyesight."

"No, no…that's okay. I…" She cleared her throat and her creamy cheeks got a shade darker. "I don't really need them. So you don't have to replace them."

"Don't need them?" Sazar exclaimed. "Then why would you wear them?"

"I…" She looked up, her eyes huge and uncertain. "I have something for you. Here—look."

It was obvious she was changing the subject and Sazar wondered what was going on with her. Why would any female wear oculars she didn't need? Was it some kind of a fashion statement? But she actually looked *better* without the round lenses. In fact, with her thick brown hair down and her large, dark eyes naked without the glasses, she looked…

Beautiful. In fact, she's Goddess-damned gorgeous. Why didn't I see that before?

He pushed the thought away quickly—it was unprofessional to be thinking that way about his new assistant. Instead, he concentrated on what she was holding out to him—which appeared to be a wad of paper tissues.

"What—" he began.

"It's a *vranna*. At least I *think* that's what Tsandor called it." She unfolded the tissues carefully, as though they held an incredibly valuable treasure. Inside was a lumpy figure made of teal and purple clay which had dried.

Sazar felt guilt pierce him like a knife.

"Yes," he said dryly. "A *vranna*. It's a large carnivorous beast from our home planet of Tranq Prime."

"He wanted you to have it." Sarah held the clay figure out to him but Sazar didn't take it. "He…I think he misses you," she said in a low voice.

Guilt turned to anger—a fury as icy as the depths of a Tranq Prime winter.

"I sent you to bring the boy some clothing, *not* to meddle in my personal affairs."

Sarah blanched but then a determined light came into her eyes and she lifted her chin.

"Commander Sazar, he's *lonely*. If you would go see him just once before we leave—"

"I told you, my personal life is *none of your business!*" His voice rose to a roar and Sarah flinched back, one arm half raised as though she expected a blow.

Her protective stance made Sazar hate himself all the more. Gods, had it come to that? Did she fear him as she feared the abusive past she'd run away from? What was *wrong* with him?

He turned away from her abruptly, unable to face the fear on her lovely features. Fear that *he* had put there. The Blood Hunger clawed at his throat, making his voice come out husky and strained.

"Go to your quarters. You have the suite right beside mine.

Simply press your palm to the metal pad outside and the door will admit you."

"All...all right." Her voice was quiet and shaken. He'd really frightened her, hadn't he? Gods, he was a monster.

He didn't watch her go. He kept his back turned as he listened to her cross the floor and the door to his suite *swooshed* shut behind her. Only when he was certain she was gone did Sazar turn around and see that she'd left him something.

Lying on the arm of the chair, still half wrapped in the protective tissues, was the lumpy clay figure of the *vranna*.

Sazar took it gently in his big hand and collapsed into the chair. He wanted to weep but his eyes were dry.

The ache was too deep for tears.

* * * * *

Oh God, what have I done? He hates me now — he's going to fire me. What am I going to do?

Sarah paced back and forth on the plush carpet of the guest suite she'd been assigned. Had she just lost her job — the only thing that was keeping her safe, keeping her on the Mother Ship instead of down on Earth where the Brotherhood could find her?

What's wrong with me? Why didn't I keep my mouth shut?

But she knew why — she couldn't stand by and be silent when she'd seen Tsandor's pain and longing for his father. Why didn't Sazar go to him?

Because he's in pain too.

The voice seemed to come from outside herself somehow, though Sarah heard it in her mind. She looked around the room but she was alone.

Must be hearing things. But it made her think. Kindred were said to be devoted to their mates so Commander Sazar must be as broken as his son, though it was clear he tried to hide his wounds as much as he could.

It's a sensitive subject and I put my foot right in it, Sarah thought ruefully. *He didn't need a lecture from me. He needs…*

She paused. What did he need?

A picture popped into her head—a memory from when she was only nine or ten, well before her mother had gotten involved in The Brotherhood and dragged Sarah into a life she'd never wanted.

Her father, coming home from work in an awful temper. It was something to do with his supervisor—Sarah wasn't sure what. She only remembered being frightened by the way he shouted and slammed things around. Her mother had found her later, crying in her room and had comforted her.

"Don't you worry, sweetpea," she'd said, wiping Sarah's eyes with a tissue. "Your daddy isn't mad at you or me. He just had a bad day and he missed lunch—he's hungry. Most men get grouchy when they need to eat, that's all."

Sarah stopped pacing, her eyes wide. In her mind's eye, she saw Commander Sazar, his eyes blazing. There were dark shadows around those pale eyes and a strained look on his face. His high cheekbones stood out starkly and his chiseled features looked too sharp—too prominent somehow. It was the haggard look of a man who hasn't gotten enough nourishment for days—possibly weeks.

He's hungry, Sarah realized. *Or in this case, **thirsty**!*

She took a deep breath and smoothed her hair. All right, she shouldn't be surprised. After all, her new boss was a vampire—well, a Pitch-Blood Kindred, which amounted to the same thing. Just because he could go out in daylight and wasn't allergic to garlic (that she knew of) didn't change the fact that he needed blood to survive.

The contract she'd signed had been very specific in spelling out how much blood he could take from her (not much) and how often he could take it (not more than once a week.) Sazar had also informed her that he would let her know where and when he wanted to drink from her and he hadn't said anything to her yet. If he was in dire need of blood, why not just tell her?

Maybe because of the way his past assistants reacted, Sarah thought. She remembered the disgusted, incredulous look on the blonde applicant's face after her interview earlier that day.

"He wanted to bite me — can you believe that? He actually wanted to bite me! Whose going to take a position where one of the job requirements is getting bitten?"

Me, thought Sarah grimly. *I took the job and I was lucky to get it. It saved me from the Controllers of The Brotherhood. The least I can do is fulfill my duties.*

A good personal assistant anticipated her boss's needs and met them, even before he asked, she told herself. Now her boss needed blood.

So what was she going to do about it?

Chapter Five

It seemed to take Sazar a long time to open the door this time. Or maybe the minutes just seemed to stretch out like taffy because Sarah's heart was beating so hard.

She'd taken the time to change out of the paint-stained suit—Lola had assured her the water-based paint would come out at the dry cleaners—and into something she hoped was more suitable.

But what was suitable attire for offering yourself as a blood sacrifice?

Sarah didn't know. She had agonized about the decision for some time and decided at last on the jeans Kat had talked her into and a silky top of deep crimson. It had a V neck and flowing sleeves edged with lace of the same color as the blouse which could be pushed up easily to show the veins of her wrists or elbows. Sarah hoped the big Kindred went for the elbow—in her experience it hurt less to be poked by a needle there and she assumed it would be the same for fangs.

Despite the fact that she knew her choice of clothing would be viewed as perfectly modest and conventional aboard the Mother Ship, she couldn't avoid the feeling that she was totally exposed. It was hard to come out of the protective shell she'd worn so long at the Compound. But now that her glasses were broken, it seemed like she might as well try to get used to her new look.

I look fine, she tried to reassure herself. *Just because these clothes would be forbidden in the Compound doesn't make them bad. I have to get away from the past, away from that way of thinking and learn to find my own style, like Kat said.*

She was about to knock again when she heard a deep, weary voice say, "Come," and the door slid open.

Commander Sazar was sitting in a large leather chair in front of the fireplace which seemed to be standard in all Kindred suites. He cupped the little clay *vranna* carefully in one hand, cradling it as though it was something precious. When he saw it was Sarah standing there, he put it down gently on a side table.

"So," he said heavily, not bothering to get up. "You've come to offer your resignation. Can't say that I blame you—you lasted longer than some of the assistants I've had."

Sarah was taken aback by his appearance. Had she thought he looked tired and malnourished before? Now he looked beyond weary—almost ready to collapse. Not only that, his pale eyes had turned a dull red—was that also an indication of his thirst?

Her heart went out to him in a sudden flood of compassion—a deep welling of emotion, just as she'd had when she'd first seen Tsandor.

"No," she said, striding purposefully over to him. "I didn't come to give you my resignation. I came to offer you something else—something you need."

"What are you—" The words died on his lips as she pulled back the full, trailing sleeve of the crimson blouse and offered him her arm.

"Drink," she said simply.

His eyes blazed a deep, hungry red.

"You don't know what you're offering me. You don't know how thirsty I am right now."

An icy finger of fear slid down Sarah's spine but she refused to give in to it. So her instincts had been right—he *was* thirsty. So thirsty he was barely controlling himself.

"Drink," she repeated, not trusting herself to say anything else.

He took her arm in his big hands and for the first time she felt his warmth—a heat that radiated from his muscular body, the need like a flame blazing inside him. His warm, spicy scent surrounded her, making her feel dizzy.

"I can't make it pleasurable for you," he warned in a hoarse voice. His double set of fangs, placed where a human's canine teeth would be, had grown long and incredibly sharp. "This will hurt—badly."

"I've never been afraid of shots or needles," Sarah said, trying to keep her voice from trembling. "Go ahead—do it."

It seemed Sazar had exhausted the last of his willpower. With a low noise somewhere between a groan and a growl, he sank his fangs deep in the flesh of her inner elbow.

The pain was, as he had promised, intense.

Sarah bit her lower lip until she tasted blood when his fangs first dug into her sensitive flesh. But after the initial wound was made, she found that the pain was easing somewhat. Maybe it was because he had withdrawn his fangs and was just sucking now—drawing from her in deep, thirsty draughts.

This isn't so bad, Sarah told herself. *Now that his fangs are out it actually just feels like giving blood at the doctor.*

Only somehow, it felt like more than that.

To Sarah's intense discomfort, the sucking sensation seemed to spread from her arm to other, much more sensitive parts of her anatomy. When Sazar drew blood from her arm, she felt a deep pulling sensation not only in the inner crook of her elbow but also at the tips of her breasts and between her legs.

What's happening? she wondered nervously. *Is this normal? Why am I feeling like this?*

She had no answers, only the growing pleasure which made her clench her free hand into a fist and press her thighs together tightly, trying to fight the pleasurable ache that grew inside her with each mouthful of blood Sazar took from her.

What is he doing to me? What…how…

Her thoughts seemed to be growing hazy and suddenly the room was spinning. Sarah felt light-headed and weak and then she was falling…

"Careful!" Strong arms caught her just before the world went dark.

* * * * *

An unknowable length of time later, her eyelids fluttered. Sazar breathed a sigh of relief as he cradled her limp body in his lap. The Blood Hunger had overcome him and he had taken too much from her. She was so little to begin with, he might have drained her dry.

He didn't usually require so much blood but it had been so long, so very long since Malinda…

Sazar pushed the thought of his dead mate aside along with the lingering ache that came with it. He had to concentrate on Sarah now—had to be certain he hadn't done her any lasting damage.

Her eyelids fluttered again, the lashes like dark fans on her pale cheeks.

"What…where am I?" she murmured thickly.

"Here in my suite, with me," Sazar answered. "How do you feel?"

"Dizzy." She tried to sit up but he held her down, cradling her against his chest. Gods but she was soft and curvy in his arms and her scent was *amazing*.

Not that he should notice such a thing about his assistant.

"Don't try to move just yet. I took too much from you. For that I must ask your forgiveness."

"What? I don't…Oh!" Her hazel eyes went wide with sudden remembrance and understanding. "Am I…will I be okay?"

"I believe so, yes, since you're talking and apparently thinking clearly," Sazar said dryly. "Here, drink this." He held the cup he'd gotten from his food delivery chute to her lips.

She started to sip and then winced away.

"Ouch!"

"Is something wrong?" Sazar drew the cup away, concerned.

"Nothing," she said sheepishly. "I just…I think I bit my lip when you, uh, sank your fangs into me."

"Ah, I see." He looked at her lush pink mouth—there did seem to be a small wound on her bottom lip he hadn't seen before. "Do you wish me to heal you?" he asked. "As I did your arm after I drank from you?" He nodded down at the crook of her elbow and Sarah looked there too, her eyes wide. Her pale skin was smooth and unbroken, as though he had never pierced her flesh at all.

"I'm still amazed you can heal me like that," she murmured dreamily. To Sazar she still sounded only half conscious.

"It's only fair considering that I am the cause of your wound. Will you allow me to heal you now?" he asked.

"I…I guess so," she murmured dreamily.

Gods, shouldn't want to do this so much…but he did.

Setting down the cup, he cupped her cheek in his free hand and tilted her mouth up to his. Bending down, he sucked her lower lip gently into his mouth and laved it carefully with his tongue.

Sarah gave a soft, low moan and suddenly the healing turned into a kiss. She threw her arms around his neck and Sazar found that for a brief moment, he was tasting her fully.

Lust filled him—a desire to own and possess—a need to claim her as his own so strong it nearly overloaded his system. Once more his fangs sharpened, ready to bite at the moment of claiming and he crushed her to him, eager for more of her sweetness.

Then Sarah stiffened abruptly and pulled away. With a great effort of will, Sazar let her.

"I…I'm sorry," she gasped. "I don't know what came over me. I think…I thought I was having a dream. I just…I don't…"

"It's all right." He saw that she was flustered and embarrassed. He was ashamed himself—he shouldn't be taking advantage of a subordinate, especially not in her vulnerable state. What was wrong with him? He'd never had any desire to kiss from any of his other assistants. In fact, he hadn't even wanted to take blood from any of them, though it was a necessity. None of them attracted him but Sarah, well…this curvy little human was a different case.

Trying to cover his own confusion as well as hers, he offered her the cup again.

"Here—you need sustenance."

Sarah swallowed obediently several times.

"Orange juice," she said with a weak laugh when he took the cup from her lips. "Isn't that what they give you when you donate blood? But where are my cookies? I'm supposed to get some of those too, right?"

Sazar frowned. "I asked my computer operating system for a

natural Earth liquid full of potassium and sugar to revive you after your recent blood loss and this is what it recommended. Should you also require something else such as these 'cookies' whatever those may be, I can have them sent up the food delivery chute as well."

It was Sarah's turn to frown.

"You don't know what cookies are? And I thought *I* led a sheltered life. Even in the Compound we had cookies. Mostly only Father Caleb got to eat them but sometimes we could sneak one or two…" She trailed off when she saw him watching her.

"What is the Compound?" Sazar asked softly. "Is that the place you ran away from? Is it a facility run by The Brotherhood of Peace?"

Her eyes flickered nervously away from his face and he sensed she didn't want to talk about it.

"I'm just saying you ought to know about cookies, that's all. Look, the orange juice worked — I'm not a bit dizzy anymore. Let me sit up."

She struggled against him and Sazar helped her up obligingly. But the moment she got to her feet, she started to wobble and he had to reach out quickly to catch her and pull her back into his lap.

"Just relax," he ordered her. "Sip some more of this juice of the orange and try to regain your strength."

"Orange juice — it's orange juice, not juice of the orange," she mumbled as he put the cup to her lips again.

She finished the liquid this time but Sazar wouldn't let her up again — not yet. He told himself he didn't want her to faint and hurt herself but far in the back of his mind he couldn't help thinking how long it had been since he'd held a female in his arms. Especially such a soft, curvy, delicate little female. The scent of her hair and skin drifted up to him like the warm aroma of some exotic flower and the taste of her mouth was still on his tongue.

Her kisses were as sweet as her blood—he wanted more.

Well, you can't have more, he lectured himself. *It's not right—it should never have happened in the first place!*

Still, he couldn't help holding her close and telling her to be still.

"This isn't right, you holding me like this," she protested weakly. "You're my boss. This isn't…isn't in the contract."

"I'm only holding you until I'm sure you won't get dizzy and fall over," Sazar remarked. "And as for our contract, I'm afraid I have already violated it. I took much more of your blood than was legally mandated."

Her large eyes turned up to his looking vulnerable and uncertain.

"Will you always need this much? I mean, I'm just asking because I might need to start taking iron supplements or something…"

Sazar shook his head.

"I should never need so much blood from you again. I was…exceptionally thirsty when you offered yourself. I had been in a state of semi starvation ever since…" He cleared his throat, looking away. "Ever since my mate died."

"I'm sorry." The compassion in Sarah's voice caught him off guard and he looked back at her.

"Sorry for what?"

"Sorry for your loss. Sorry that I…pushed you earlier." Her eyes flickered over to the clay *vranna*. "I haven't known you long enough to, uh, lecture you. I don't know your past. I shouldn't have presumed."

"I don't know your past either—not much of it," Sazar pointed out. Although he certainly wanted to learn more. The few tidbits she'd dropped intrigued him. What or who was she running from at The Brotherhood of Peace? What had made her so desperate to take this job with him, even knowing she would have to give him her blood?

Sarah's eyes flickered again and he sensed she didn't want to answer his unspoken question.

"Tell you what," she said. "Let's let the past be the past. I won't bother you about yours if you don't bother me about mine."

"For now," Sazar agreed gravely. "But to answer your earlier question, no, giving me your blood will not always be like it was tonight. I'm afraid there will still be pain—"

"It's not the pain I'm asking about—it's the pleasure," Sarah exclaimed.

Sazar raised his eyebrows at her.

"Pleasure?"

"You know…" Her pale cheeks were getting pink, though she'd given him too much of her blood for them to grow truly red. "The way I felt when you were…were sucking from me. I mean I didn't just feel it in my arm. I felt it in…well…"

She gestured with one hand, waving vaguely to her breasts and the area between her thighs.

Sazar couldn't have been more shocked if she'd slapped him. For a moment he was speechless, trying to collect his thoughts. Could it be that this little human female had experienced the Blood Pleasure when he drank from her, even though they had no prior physical connection? But that was something only a Fated Mate would feel!

Not even Malinda, as much as he had loved her, had felt the Blood Pleasure when he bit her to feed from her. She had only been able to experience ecstasy from his bite when he bit her during bonding sex and injected his essence—something which was impossible during feeding.

"Tell me more about what you experienced," he said urgently. "Describe it exactly—I need to know."

Her cheeks went even pinker.

"Never mind. I must have imagined it. Look, can I please get up now, Commander Sazar?"

So she was returning to their formal relationship—it was definitely a hint for him to let her go.

Reluctantly, Sazar helped her get on her feet again. She wobbled for a moment but this time she didn't fall over.

"Sarah," he said gravely. "Do you still want to work for me? I know tonight as been…traumatic. I shouted at you and nearly drained you dry. I violated our contract. For that I am truly sorry."

She lifted her chin.

"Yes, I'll still work for you. You don't know what—" She bit her lip and he got the sense she was choosing her words carefully. "This job saved me," she said at last. "Being up here in the Mother Ship away from Earth—it's the best possible place for me."

"So it's better to be with a superior who shouts at you and drinks your blood than to be back down on Earth?" Sazar asked quietly. "Who are you running from, Sarah?"

"I…I don't want to talk about it…Sir," she added. "I should just…I need to go to bed."

"Very well." Sazar would let her keep her secret—for now. He was fairly certain it had something to do with The Brotherhood of the Peace, for which she had worked for five years. But they were supposed to be a religious organization devoted to peace and self sacrifice. How could that be a bad thing?

"I guess I'll see you in the morning?" Sarah asked.

He nodded thoughtfully.

"Indeed. I'll expect to see you after mid-meal—what your people call lunch. We'll have a short briefing and then we'll be on our way to Alquon Ultrea."

"Really?" Her eyes widened. "So soon?"

"Is that a problem?" Sazar asked her. "I thought you wanted to be far from Earth. You can't get much farther than going to a whole different galaxy."

She lifted her chin—he was quite beginning to like that defiant little gesture.

"No, that's fine with me. I was just…surprised, that's all. But I'll be ready—I met a new friend today—Kat. She's married to the Twin Kindred officers Deep and Lock. She's going to make us some Alquon clothes."

"That's very good." Sazar was pleased at her forethought. "I appreciate you taking steps to see that we're prepared for our mission."

"I'll make sure we're ready for anything," Sarah promised. "See you after lunch tomorrow."

"All right. And Sarah?"

She had been making her way to the door but she turned back.

"Yes, Commander Sazar?"

"Be certain you eat enough to replenish your strength," Sazar ordered.

She paled a little.

"Okay. Are you, um, going to drink from me again?"

He frowned. If she had really experienced the Blood Pleasure, she would be eager for him to drink again, not frightened or worried. Perhaps she had simply been imagining whatever sensations she'd felt after all.

Well, that was disappointing but hardly surprising. Coming across a Fated Mate was a rare occurrence for a Pitch-Blood. So rare that not one male in ten thousand would ever find such a female in their lifetime.

"No," he said, answering her anxious question. "I'm not going to drink from you again for an entire week—as per our agreement. I simply want you to replenish what you have lost. I don't want you to be too weak to function on Alquon Ultrea."

That defiant chin tilt again.

"I'll be fine, Sir—don't worry about me."

"All right," Sazar said simply. "I won't." But that didn't mean he wouldn't think about her. About how sweet her blood was, how delicious her scent, how soft and curvy she'd been in his arms—how good her mouth had tasted in that one moment she'd kissed him back. Gods, just thinking of it made his shaft hard!

Which was plainly unacceptable.

Have to stop this now, he told himself grimly. *She's your assistant. The humans have a name for acting on such feelings—it's called sexual harassment.*

Sarah wobbled a little and for a moment he thought she would fall—then she righted herself and continued towards the door. Though he wanted to jump up and go sweep her into his arms so that he could carry her to her suite, Sazar restrained himself. He had to reign in his emotions—had to get this relationship back onto a professional track.

"Good night, Ms. Michaels." Deliberately, he made his voice cool and impersonal. "I'll see you tomorrow after mid-meal."

"After lunch…Sir," she agreed. She gave him a little nod of her head and then she went through the door and it *whooshed* shut behind her.

Sazar sat staring after her for a long time.

He had a bad feeling that his little human assistant had gotten firmly under his skin and he would have a Goddess damned hard time dislodging her.

Chapter Six

Oh my God, what was that all about? He held me — held me like a baby! And not only that, he wouldn't let me go! And he kissed me — or I kissed him! I can't believe I did that — I can't believe I kissed my boss! It's so embarrassing!

Embarrassing yes, but it had felt *incredible*. And completely different from what she was used to.

Sarah could still remember the way her skin had crawled every time Father Caleb had touched her. He hadn't forced her to "meet his needs" as Sarah knew he forced others at the Compound. But he had strongly hinted that it was the proper thing for her to do. And when Sarah had persisted in not taking his broadly dropped hints, he had declared that it was time she became a Bride of the Prophet in order to have a "holy child."

Ugh! She pushed the thought away. Being held by Commander Sazar had been nothing like that. When he'd held her close to his broad, muscular chest she felt small and cherished and when he kissed her — or she kissed him, it was hard to tell which had actually happened — it seemed like her whole body was on fire with yearning for him.

Just the memory of it made the tips of her breasts throb and the spot between her legs felt hot and achy.

Sarah bit her newly healed lip and tried to ignore the feelings. She had been raised to believe that there were places on a woman's body she shouldn't touch. Forbidden places, meant only for the Prophet...or for her husband if one of the men of The Brotherhood decided to add her as a second or third wife or concubine.

But I'm not letting them tell me how to dress anymore, Sarah told herself defiantly. *The Controllers aren't here and neither is Father Caleb. So why should I let what they taught me dictate my other actions?*

Why indeed?

Walking into the bedroom of her guest suite, she pulled off her clothing and folded it neatly on the dresser. There was a lovely nightgown Kat had talked her into getting—a silky deep blue which showed up the auburn highlights in her chestnut hair.

Sarah slipped it on and then, since she still felt a little dizzy from blood loss, she lay back on the bed. She started to run a hand over her breasts, bare beneath the nightgown, but a harsh voice intruded in her head.

You must never touch yourselves in the forbidden areas, girls, lectured the voice of Sister Sylvia, the elderly matriarch who had ruled over the women of the Compound with an iron fist. *It is wrong and disgusting. Only your husband or The Prophet may touch you there.*

Sarah stopped, her hand curling into a fist of pure frustration between her breasts. Damn it—why did her past keep intruding on her present?

Only the hand of your husband should touch you there! Sister Sylvia insisted in her head.

Well, what if...what if Commander Sazar was my husband?

The naughty little thought brought a whole flood of fantasies with it. She could imagine him cradling her in his arms, just as he had when she'd fainted. But this time he wouldn't just kiss her, he would touch her, his big hand moving over her body, teasing her nipples…stroking between her legs…

As she pictured it, her own small hand copied what she saw in her mind's eye. It glided over the silky nightdress, circling her puffy nipples gently until she moaned with surprised pleasure.

God, that felt *good*! She'd known she was sensitive there but she'd never dared to touch herself deliberately before. She tugged lightly at her tender buds, imagining her fingers were Commander Sazar's.

"Oh, Commander Sazar," she moaned softly. Pleasure zinged through her, electrifying…a revelation. It reminded her of the sensations she'd experienced while he'd fed from her.

Another stray thought crossed her mind.

He said he could call a vein from anywhere on my body. Could he call one here?

She imagined the big Kindred bending over her, taking one tight pink nipple in his mouth. It would hurt when his fangs pierced her flesh but then after that, the deep sucking sensation that shot sparks of pleasure through her entire body would begin.

"Oh! Commander Sazar," she gasped as she imagined the forbidden sight of his sensuous lips wrapped around her nipple. "Oh! Do you really want to drink from me *there*?"

Unbidden, one of her hands found its way lower, slipping between her thighs. The silky nightgown was still in the way but that didn't stop the good feelings from coming when Sarah dared to press her fingers against the soft curls of her mound.

More even than her nipples, this place was sensitive and extremely prone to pleasure.

Pussy…The forbidden word formed in her head and she imagined Commander Sazar whispering to her.

"I want to touch your pussy, Sarah. I want to taste you...to drink from you here."

Oh God, could he do that? Would he be able to drink from such a delicate area? Would it hurt? Or would it feel so good she couldn't stand it?

Sarah squeezed her thighs together, still pressing rhythmically with her hand.

"Commander," she whispered. "Oh Commander Sazar...*Sazar*..."

His name rose like a prayer on her lips and she didn't realize she was getting louder and louder. Pleasure shot through her, building and building. It felt incredible but somehow it seemed there should be *more*.

It felt as though she was climbing a mountain—trying to reach a peak but something was always in the way. Sarah pressed harder, feeling almost desperate.

*Why can't I reach it? I want to reach it. I **need** to!*

But she couldn't get there.

It was disappointing and frustrating, especially since Sarah had the feeling that if she could only reach that elusive peak of pleasure once, she would always be able to reach it in the future. But her body wouldn't cooperate—maybe because she could still hear the disapproving voice of Sister Sylvia speaking in her ear, telling her what a dirty thing it was for a girl to touch herself and how only nasty girls did that—nice girls waited for their husband or the Prophet...

*But I didn't even take off my gown! It's not like I'm touching myself **bare**.* The very thought made her shiver, it was so forbidden. But the fact that she wasn't committing the ultimate sin didn't seem to make any difference—she could feel the pleasure slipping, fading away.

It wasn't just the voice of Sister Sylvia either—it was the guilt she felt about using her new boss as fantasy material. How could she look him in the eye again after imagining him doing such indecent things to her?

I really need to control myself better.

With a frustrated sigh, Sarah gave up. Well, she had been at the Compound for nearly half her life. It would take time to get over all she had learned there—time to change herself and her worldview.

I have time, she thought, trying to feel better about her failure to reach the peak. *I have plenty of time. And I'll be far away – where no one from The Brotherhood can ever reach me again. I'll get there.*

Eventually…she hoped.

* * * * *

Had he really heard her cry his name? Sazar turned over in bed, getting closer to the thin wall which connected their sleeping chambers.

At first he'd thought she must be in trouble and was crying out for him. He'd been halfway to the door when he heard her again…and identified the soft, husky tone in her voice.

Sarah wasn't crying out in pain or fear…she was crying out in pleasure.

Gods, is she thinking of me? Picturing me the way I've been picturing her?

He lay back down on the bed and listened again.

"Oh!" he heard her moan softly. "Do you…do you really want to drink from me *there?*"

Immediately his shaft was almost painfully erect. Gods, was she imagining what he *thought* she was imagining? A picture formed in his mind—the image of his own hand pulling off the deep red shirt she'd been wearing, baring her full, lush breasts for his mouth…for his fangs.

Calling a vein to drink from such a delicate area wasn't often done. His mate, Malinda, hadn't liked it very much—saying it was uncomfortable and too intense—though she had loved it when he bit her neck and injected his essence during the peak of passion.

Regular Blood-Kindred were able to give pleasure with their bite when they bit at a conventional spot—like the neck or the inner thigh. That was because they were injecting their essence when they bit—a chemical compound which brought intense pleasure and marked a female as that Kindred's own.

Pitch-Blood Kindred, however, were biting to feed, not to pleasure. Without the injection of essence, their bite could be extremely painful during the feeding process unless they were also touching a female sexually. Only during Bonding Sex were they able to inject essence because that activity was linked to claiming and bonding, not feeding. It was one reason Sazar's own peculiar sub-set of Blood Kindred were considered to have a disability by the rest—the fact that they could not make their bite pleasurable all the time.

Pitch-Blood *did* have one special ability that normal Blood Kindred did not, however—the ability to give a deep sexual pleasure—the Blood Pleasure it was called—when piecing the most delicate spots on a female's body with their fangs. But this was only possible with a Fated Mate. As much as he had loved Malinda, she hadn't been a Fated Mate—so when he'd tried drinking from her breasts, she hadn't enjoyed it.

Now he wondered—would Sarah be able to draw pleasure from his bite in such an intimate area? And was that what she was picturing as she…what? Touched herself? Yes, it must be that — as she touched herself on the other side of that wall which separated them.

The thought set him on fire and he couldn't help himself — he pulled down his black sleeping trousers and fisted himself in one large palm. Gods, the idea of biting her *there*…of drinking from one of her tender pink nipples or even the soft, sweet spot between her thighs…

He could imagine how it would be…spreading her pussy lips open to reveal her swollen, wet folds…lapping and sucking her, circling the throbbing button of her clit with his tongue and then…

"Ah…*Gods!*" He managed to muffle his cry in a pillow at the last instant as the pleasure arched through him like a bolt of lightning. Hot cum spurted from the tip of his cock, the shaft pulsing in his hand as he came again and again. It wet his belly with its profusion — Gods there was so *much* of it.

It made him realize he was hungry for more than just blood. How long had it been since he'd had any kind of sexual contact?

Since Malinda died, he thought and felt a fresh wash of sorrow. Perhaps he shouldn't be thinking of another female this way. Was he being unfaithful to the memory of his dead mate?

Even if you aren't, you damn sure shouldn't be thinking of your assistant that way, he told himself sternly as the pleasure ebbed. *Sexual harassment, remember? You don't want to be guilty of that.*

But Sarah had been thinking of *him* that way — at least, he *thought* she had been. How else to explain the hot little sounds coming from her side of the wall? The way she had been calling his name?

Don't think of it — don't think of any of it, he ordered himself. *You have a mission to conduct — an important one. Just go to sleep so you can be well rested when you meet with the Alquons tomorrow.*

Deliberately, he turned his back to the wall and closed his eyes. But in his mind's eye, he continued to see himself with Sarah, baring her sweet luscious body and taking her ripe nipple deep in his mouth as he prepared to give her the Blood Pleasure again.

Chapter Seven

"Now these are the clothes I made on the replicator," Kat said as a large pink cube was loaded into the sleek silver, long-range shuttle Commander Sazar was going to fly them to Alquon Ultrea in. "Of course, I only had a few vids to go on," she told Sarah apologetically. "And they were almost all just a bunch of old guys talking so Commander Sazar's clothes might be slightly more authentic than yours."

"I'm sure it will be fine," Sarah said warmly. "Thank you so much for taking the trouble! And I'm sure Commander Sazar will be thankful that you made some for him too."

"Well, I did my best. And this is my friend Liv—she's a nurse. She's also the twin sister of Sophie, who you met yesterday," Kat said.

"Oh, hello." Sarah held out her hand to the pretty blonde girl with silvery gray eyes. She looked so much like Sophie in the face it was clear to see they were twins, although identical or fraternal it was impossible to tell. "It's nice of you to come and see me off," she said smiling.

Liv smiled back.

"Oh, I didn't just come for the fun of it—I have something for you."

"More clothes?" Sarah asked. "But Kat already packed me more than I'll ever be able to wear!" She wished she could have had a look into the large pink cube Kat had packed the clothes in but there was no time—Commander Sazar had told her sternly that they needed to get going as soon as possible

"Not clothes—something that's going to help you deal with your new boss." Liv nodded at Sazar, who was speaking to a tall, blond Kindred he had called Commander Sylvan. Kat had informed her that this was Sophie's husband and he was also a Blood Kindred, although apparently a different kind than Sazar.

"Really? What is it?" Sarah dropped her voice uncertainly. What in the world could Liv have for her?

"It's something Commander Sylvan developed—he's also a doctor in addition to being the head of the Kindred High Council," Liv told her. "Here."

She handed Sarah a small packet filled with blood red capsules.

"Um, thank you," Sarah said, frowning. "But I don't know how Commander Sazar would feel about taking medicine without going to see a doctor first."

"Oh, it's not for him, hon!" Liv exclaimed, laughing. "It's for *you*."

"For me? But…what are they?" Sarah frowned at the baggie of blood red capsules. "What's in them?"

"They're a compound Sylvan developed especially for the prospective mates of Pitch-Blood Kindred," Liv explained. "They're blood replenishers—the chemicals in each pill will encourage your body to make more red blood cells and more blood in general. This way Commander Sazar can bite you and feed from you as often as he needs to." She made a face. "I mean, if you *want* him to. Sylvan did tell me that a Pitch-Blood Kindred's bite can be much more painful than the bite of a regular Blood Kindred because they're biting to feed so they're not injecting their essence."

Sarah thought of the intense first pain of the big Kindred's fangs sinking into her arm...and the deep, pulling pleasure that had followed and spread throughout her body.

"It's...not so bad," she said in a low voice. "It hurts at first but then it gets better. But..." She cleared her throat. "I don't really think I'll need these. Commander Sazar took a very, uh, deep drink last night and he doesn't anticipate needing any more for quite some time."

"Take them anyway, just in case," Liv said, pressing the baggie with the pills back into her hand when Sarah would have given it back. "In fact, why don't you take one now? You're pale as paper."

"She's right, doll," Kat said. "You look like you're about a quart low."

"Well...all right." It was true, Sarah told herself—she *did* still feel quite weak, despite eating a good breakfast and lunch and drinking even more orange juice to replenish herself. She popped one of the capsules in her mouth and dry swallowed it. "There—now I should be all ready to go."

"Almost." Liv smiled and produced yet another pill—this one bright pink and considerably larger.

"What is that—to help me make more white cells or something?" Sarah asked frowning.

"Nope—translation bacteria. Take this and they'll make sure you can understand every word spoken on the new planet you're going to." She shrugged. "Sorry it's so big—I think you'll need some water to swallow this one down."

"Here, have some of my mango smoothie." Kat held out a plastic cup filled with bright orange liquid and Sarah took it, along with the big pink pill.

"Just for me?" she asked, after she'd swallowed it with some difficulty. "Doesn't Commander Sazar need one too? I don't think he's ever been to Alquon Ultrea before, although he told me he had been studying some of their videos and culture."

"If he's been studying their vids, that's all he needs," Liv said confidently. "Kindred are incredibly quick at learning new languages—it's part of being genetic traders. They have to be able to communicate almost instantly with any new people that they meet."

"Oh….all right. Well thank you." Sarah took one more sip of the tart, sweet smoothie and handed the glass back to Kat. "Mmm, that's really good."

"You better keep it, doll." Kat gave it back to her. "You never know what you're going to end up eating on a strange new planet. This might be the last yummy thing you taste for a while."

"But for how long?" Liv wanted to know. "Do you know if you guys will be back in time for Christmas? Sophie wanted to me to ask—she wants to have Commander Sazar's son, Tsandor, over to her place for Christmas if not."

"What, so he can go bobbing for *tan-tans* in the living slime?" Kat asked, making a face.

"What?" Sarah frowned. "What are you talking about?"

Liv laughed. "Oh, it's a Kindred thing. See, they don't have Christmas where they come from—I mean, obviously not, that's an Earth thing. But they *do* have a Winter Solstice holiday. And some of their, er, traditions have kind of gotten mixed up with our own. It makes for a really unique holiday experience."

"We usually have a big multi-family get together on Christmas Day in the afternoon," Kat added. "If you *do* come back on time, you and Commander Sazar are totally invited. And Tsandor too of course."

"But if you're going to be stuck on your mission, please just see if Tsandor can at least spend Christmas morning with Sophie," Liv said. "She's already gotten him presents and everything."

"I don't know." Sarah bit her lip. "I don't *think* Commander Sazar would mind, but I don't know if now is the time to ask him. He seems really busy." She nodded at her new boss, who was in an apparently private and intense conversation with Commander Sylvan.

"That's okay—you can ask him while you're on your mission," Kat said brightly. "That'll give you time to soften him up. And if he's okay with it and it looks like you guys will be spending Christmas on Alquon Ultrea, you can send a message back letting us know."

"I'll do my best to convince him," Sarah promised. The idea of sweet little Tsandor spending Christmas in the constant care house without his father or any other family made a lump form in her throat.

I'll make his Christmas special if I get back here on time, she vowed to herself.

"You're going to do great." Kat smiled at her. "Be sure you let me know how you like the clothes I made for you on my clothing pattern replicator."

"I will. Thank you for everything." Overcome by the kindness she'd been shown, Sarah reached for Kat and gave her a big hug. "You're so kind to me," she whispered in the other girl's ear. "I don't know what I would have done if you hadn't said hello to me and helped me in the tram station."

"We like to help the new girls out." Kat squeezed her back affectionately. "The new brides, right, Liv?"

"But I'm not a bride—I'm just a glorified secretary," Sarah

protested.

"Really? We'll see." Liv gave her a mysterious smile. "You better get going—your, uh, *boss* is waving at you."

"Oh!" Sarah looked up to see that indeed, Commander Sazar was beckoning her over to the sleek, silver long-range shuttle. "Okay—I'd better go."

"Have a good time, hon," Liv told her.

"And don't forget to call us." Kat smiled and blew her a kiss.

"See you later—hopefully before Christmas," Sarah told them. With a wave, she headed for the shuttle. But she couldn't help wondering how she would broach the subject of where Tsandor would spend the holiday when Commander Sazar's son was obviously such a sensitive topic.

* * * * *

"So tell me about Alquon Ultrea," Sarah said after the shuttle cleared the fold in space and entered the Triangulum Galaxy. "What do I need to know? And what should I do to fit in once we get there?"

Sazar cast her a glance. His assistant was dressed in her new black suit with a spotless white blouse and her hair was up in a bun at the back of her neck, just as it had been during their interview. Despite the fact that her glasses were gone, she somehow managed to convey the impression that she was still wearing them. She looked studious and professional—all business today—as though their interlude of the night before had never happened.

Of course, he was acting extremely businesslike himself—it was only proper. But he couldn't help remembering the soft cries he'd heard through the wall the night before or the way she'd moaned his name…

*Sazar...do you really want to bite me **there**?*

Stop it, he told himself sternly. *This is an important mission – there is absolutely no place for inappropriate thoughts or feelings here.*

So then why couldn't he stop having them?

"I'll tell you what I can," he said, endeavoring to push back the memory of holding her curvy body close and tasting her sweet blood the night before. "But the Alquons are an intensely private, formal, and easily offended people, from what I've been able to gather by speaking to their representative and studying the transmissions he sent me. Look."

He reached forward and pressed a button on the console. The viewscreen lit up, showing one of the vids the Alquon Minister of Cultural Studies, who was his contact on that world, had sent him.

It was a somber affair—a group of Alquon males standing in a circle and speaking in deep, sonorous voices that were almost musical. They had pale green skin tones, mottled with blue or purple spots and their hair reminded Sazar of the kelp which floated in the Earth's oceans.

The males wore long loose trousers and flowing robes which draped over the shoulders and were open at the front. Some were bare-chested beneath the robes and others had tight shirts which seemed to cling to them, as though they were wet. Dark green ridges almost like fins protruded from their elbows and ran down the length of their forearms. Gill slits creased the sides of their necks and their fingers were webbed.

"Huh," Sarah remarked, staring at the viewscreen. "They look almost like...mermaids or something. If they had fish tails it would be perfect."

"Excuse me?" Sazar frowned. "I have been speaking English for over a year now but I don't understand the term 'mermaids.'"

"Oh, it's an Earth legend." Sarah waved a hand in an embarrassed way. "About people who are half human and half fish. Homesick sailors used to imagine beautiful mermaids singing to them in the ocean—that kind of thing."

"Well, 'that kind of thing' is exactly what the Alquons are—so the idea of them being mermaids is an extremely astute observation." Sazar was pleased with her quickness.

"What? They're half fish?" Sarah frowned.

"Not exactly but they live on a planet which is completely submerged in water—an endless ocean with no dry land at all."

"Really?" Sarah had turned suddenly pale. "Because I have to tell you, Commander Sazar—I haven't been swimming in years. They wouldn't let us at the Compound—it was called mixed bathing and The Prophet, I mean Father Caleb, forbid it."

"The Prophet?" Sazar frowned. "Who—"

"Never mind." Sarah seemed to think she had given too much information. "I shouldn't have said all that. It's just…the idea of being thrown in a big endless ocean…well, it makes me nervous."

She looked so pale Sazar wished he could gather her into his arms and comfort her but he suppressed the unprofessional impulse sternly.

"I would never put you in danger," he told her quietly. "And please don't worry about your lack of swimming ability. We will be staying in the Alquon's indoor facilities—they know we are not adapted to both ocean and land as they are."

"Oh, good." Sarah looked immensely relieved. She frowned. "But…why do they have indoor facilities at all if they're able to live in the ocean? I mean…" She gestured at the long, boring vid which was still playing. "They seem to have some kind of gills on the sides of their necks and their hands are webbed. If their whole world is ocean, why would they ever come indoors?"

"From what I am able to gather, their world wasn't always as it is now," Sazar said gravely. "Many millennia ago, it had the same composition of your own Earth—with huge polar icecaps which locked much of the water away and only two thirds of the planet covered in ocean."

"Really?" Sarah's eyes widened. "What happened?"

"They grew too quickly and used resources which harmed their environment," Sazar told her. "Those in power were warned but they were greedy and willfully ignorant. They refused to take heed until it was too late. Eventually their world reached a point of no return—their ice caps melted and the entire planet was submerged."

"So…they evolved to live in the water? Wouldn't that take time?" Sarah frowned again.

"This was not a natural evolution." Sazar gestured at the males on the vid. "Their scientists developed a gene therapy which allowed them to draw oxygen from the water much in the same way fish do. They were able to survive in their new environment both on land and in the sea."

"Wow, *amazing*." Sarah's lovely hazel eyes shone with excitement. "You know, I used to go to the library and read books about different cultures and exotic people but I never thought I'd get to meet anyone outside my own little circle in the—." She stopped abruptly.

"In the Compound?" Sazar raised an eyebrow at her. Little by little she was letting tidbits about her past drop. It sounded extremely restrictive—who ever heard of a religion where swimming was forbidden? He wondered if she'd had to sneak away to the library—it didn't sound like this Compound place where she'd been would allow or encourage the seeking of knowledge.

Sarah flushed, her pale cheeks getting pink.

"Well, yes. So do the Alquons live underwater most of the time?" she asked quickly. "Or do they spend more time in their indoor dry areas and just go out into the ocean occasionally?"

"As to that, I'm not entirely certain. I only know that the Alquon Minister of Cultural Studies has promised me that we will be given dry facilities to stay in."

"Okay, that's good enough for me." Sarah nodded. "So where are the women—the females?" she asked, nodding at the vid. "Do they look like mermaids too?"

Sazar shook his head. "I'm not sure what they look like. The only vids I was sent are all like these. They appear to be prominent males discussing Alquon culture and laws."

Sarah remembered that Kat had also complained the only vids she could get of Alquon fashion were all males and no females.

"Discussing it for hours on end, huh?" she murmured. "Not exactly must-see TV is it?"

"It's not very exciting," Sazar admitted. "But I couldn't exactly ask for their most salacious entertainment—I had to take what was given."

"Oh no—it's fine," Sarah said quickly. "I just wish we could see their version of a soap opera or a drama with both men *and* women. It would be nice to know what I'm supposed to act like once we get there."

"You'll act as though you were my mate or my pair partner as they are called on Alquon Ultrea," Sazar told her. "The Minister specified that they do not allow singles to visit their communities—obviously this is something I hope to change their mind about if we are to make a genetic trade with them. A single Kindred male cannot call a female from a society where he is forbidden to come alone to see her."

"That *would* seem to pose a problem," Sarah mused. "So is that the only reason we're going—so the Kindred can, uh, do a trade with them?"

"No—I'm also hoping to see if they have any technology or weapons we can copy to use against the Hive. Have you heard of them?"

"Kat told me a little." Sarah's face was pale. "Giant insects who want to abduct Earth girls and do awful things to them, right?"

"Essentially," Sazar said grimly. "Any new weapon we can find to use against them will help."

"Then we have to make sure we don't blow our cover," Sarah said firmly. "And for now we're pretending we're a, uh, a couple, right?"

Sazar nodded. "On Alquon, almost everyone is paired off at a very young age. It is imperative that they believe you are my partner."

Sarah's cheeks got pink again but she nodded.

"Yes, Commander."

Sazar frowned. "You'll have to stop calling me by my title, I'm afraid. You will call me simply 'Sazar' and I will call you 'Sarah.' Is that acceptable?"

"It's…" She got even pinker. "It's just fine. It'll feel kind of funny to call my boss by his first name but I can manage…Sazar."

Hearing her name on his lips did something strange inside his chest. No one had called him by his first name without 'Commander' in front of it in so long…so very long. It felt right to hear Sarah speak his name. It was…intimate.

Sazar wished he could take her hand or pull her into his lap again as he had the night before but she wasn't dizzy so he had no excuse to hold her.

He contented himself with reaching over and brushing a strand of her long brown hair which had escaped from her bun out of her eyes. Her cheek was hot against his fingertips and he couldn't miss the way her breathing suddenly quickened but she didn't pull away. In fact, for just a moment, she nuzzled against him and her big eyes turned up to his.

Gods… Sazar found he couldn't stop looking at her—their eyes were locked and he was aching to taste her sweet lips again. He knew Sarah felt the same—he could tell it by the way the warm, feminine scent of her desire suddenly filled the small cabin of the shuttle.

She feels it too. Last night wasn't just a fluke. She desires me as I desire her.

He had to shift in his seat as his shaft hardened in his flight leathers.

"Commander…I mean, Sazar," she whispered, nibbling her lush lower lip indecisively. "I…I'm supposed to ask you something but I don't know how to do it."

"You are?" he murmured, picking up on her uncertainty. "What is it, Sarah? Just ask."

"It…it has to do with another Earth legend. Like the mermaids?"

The idea of the half human-half fish people she'd talked about turned his attention back to the Alquons and the mission they were supposed to be on. The one which didn't allow for personal feelings or inappropriate contact with his subordinate.

Sazar had been leaning over, cupping Sarah's cheek. Now he straightened up and cleared his throat.

"You do seem to have a lot of legends. Which one is this?" he asked, trying to sound more businesslike again.

"It's…about Christmas," she said hesitantly. "Do you think we'll be back in time to celebrate it on the Mother Ship?"

"Christmas?" Sazar shook his head. "I'm not sure, to be honest. That's your festival of giving, correct? Somewhat analogous to the Kindred Winter Solstice celebration?"

"It's more than that," Sarah said earnestly. "It's a religious holiday that celebrates the birth of Christ. But there are also many legends and traditions associated with it. Like Santa Clause."

"Santa Clause? What is that?" Sazar shook his head. "I moved to the Mother Ship just after the Christmas festival concluded last cycle so I'm afraid I'm not well acquainted with your holiday customs."

"Not what—*who*. Santa Clause is this fat, jolly old man who dresses up in a red and white fur suit. He comes around on Christmas Eve, goes down the chimney, and leaves presents for all the good girls and boys of the world as they sleep. When they wake up on Christmas morning, they come downstairs and rip into the packages he leaves to see what they got."

"Hmm…" To Sazar it sounded bizarre and not remotely logical. "How can one elderly overweight male get to every house in the world to leave presents in a single night?" he demanded. "Also, if he is overweight, how does he fit down the chimneys of the respective houses? And what about the domiciles which have no chimneys?

"He flies through the sky in a sleigh pulled by eight tiny flying reindeer," Sarah said, with a completely straight face. "And don't worry about the chimney thing—he manages."

"This legend gets stranger and more implausible all the time," Sazar complained. "How are the deer able to fly? Are they somehow genetically modified to take flight? Or is there some kind of motor in the sleigh?"

"No, no—it's *magic*." Sarah was laughing now and Sazar found that the corners of his own mouth were twitching though he didn't really understand why.

"Magic? There is no such thing," he said, trying not to laugh.

"There is at Christmas. Look—I know it sounds crazy but it's all part of our legend and traditions."

"And everyone on Earth believes in this 'Christmas magic?'" Sazar demanded.

"Well, almost every country has some version of Christmas and their own way of celebrating but I'm telling you about what I grew up with. There's so much that goes into it—trimming a Christmas tree…stuffing stockings…drinking eggnog… baking Christmas cookies, and oh…so many other things."

Her eyes lit up at what Sazar thought must be memories of Christmases past and he couldn't help thinking again how devastatingly lovely she was. She was made all the more beautiful by the fact that she clearly didn't understand her own appeal.

"It sounds…enjoyable, if somewhat strange," he admitted. "So I take it you do not wish to miss this celebration and you're hoping our mission will end in time for us to get back to the Mother Ship so you can celebrate there?"

"Well, not exactly…" She bit her lower lip again. "I don't mind being away for Christmas—I haven't had a really good one since I was a kid before my parents entered The Brotherhood and we went to live at the Compound but—"

"Wait." Sazar held up a hand to stop her. "You told me you worked for The Brotherhood of Peace from the age of eighteen, correct?"

"Yes." She looked away. "But my parents actually joined The Brotherhood when I was twelve. My best memories of Christmas are before that." She smiled. "My dad used to dress up like Santa and let me 'catch' him leaving presents out on Christmas Eve. And Mom and I always had to make double chocolate chip cookies to leave out for Santa because those were my dad's favorite."

Sazar sensed that yet again she was changing the subject but he decided to let her…for now.

He frowned. "I thought Santa was a mythical person. Why did your father dress up like him?"

"Because Christmas is for kids," Sarah said earnestly. "And that's what I really wanted to ask you about. See…" She cleared her throat but just then a voice from the viewscreen interrupted her.

"Commander Sazar of the Kindred, this is Alquon Ultrea Landing Control. We have your ship within tracking distance of our planet."

"Yes, of course." Sazar quickly turned off the Alquon vid which had been playing all this time, allowing the speaker to be seen on the viewscreen instead. A male—younger than the ones they had been watching—was speaking to them. He had vivid aquamarine eyes which almost seemed to glow.

"You are cleared for landing. A platform is being raised for your ship on the southeast quadrant of the planet," the male said. "Minister Obglod will meet you and escort you to your quarters."

"We will be there momentarily," Sazar promised.

"Understood." The male's glowing eyes flickered from Sazar to Sarah and a slight frown creased his pale green features. "Forgive me for asking, but are these the clothing you and your pair partner intend to wear?"

"Well...we do have Alquon clothing with us," Sarah said, answering since the male on the viewscreen was looking at her. "We can change before we go out to meet the Minister."

"I recommend you do so. Proper attire is of the utmost importance—especially if you are to meet our ruler, The Lord Magnate. And I do believe you might have that honor."

"Duly noted. Thank you for taking the time to tell us. Under no circumstances do we wish to give offense," Sazar said.

The male nodded shortly.

"Alquon Ultrea welcomes you."

Then the screen went abruptly blank.

"All right." Sarah took a deep breath. "I guess it's time to see what Kat packed us. If it looks anything like what those guys were wearing on the video you showed me, you're going to look spectacular and I'll look like a bundle of old clothes."

"I very much doubt that," Sazar murmured. Though her interview outfit of the day before hadn't been very becoming, he now believed that no clothing, no matter how unsuitable, could hide her beauty. He still wondered how he could have missed it before...and he wished he could stop thinking about it now.

Keep your mind on the mission, he told himself. *That's what matters now. Do your job and forget about this inappropriate attraction.*

He just hoped he could take his own advice.

Chapter Eight

I was right, Sarah thought, eyeing the big Kindred appreciatively. *He looks amazing in the Alquon clothes. But then, he'd probably look amazing in anything.*

Sazar was dressed in a pair of loose, silky black trousers and a long, flowing robe of the same color that opened at the front, leaving his muscular chest bare. There was an edge of deep red trim around the robe, almost the same color as the uniform shirt he usually wore, which made his tan skin seem to glow and set off his pale eyes perfectly.

Sarah couldn't help thinking of how close she'd been pressed to that broad, bare chest last night—how he'd held her to him and cradled her tenderly until he was certain she could walk. That memory led to the thought of how he'd cupped her cheek earlier when they were speaking—for a moment she'd been sure he was going to kiss her. And God, she certainly wouldn't have pushed him away!

Could it be that such a big, gorgeous man could be interested in plain little her? She had to be imagining it, didn't she? But the way he had looked at her…

Stop it, Sarah—stop thinking like that! He's your boss! she lectured herself.

Besides, he certainly wouldn't be attracted to her in the clothing she had on now.

Her own version of the Alquon outfit was white and blue instead of black and red but it seemed to bunch and bulk in all the wrong places. The loose trousers looked baggy and made her too-large hips even bigger and the robe hung oddly from her shoulders. She *did* at least have a blue shirt to go on under it, but the material was too thin and clearly showed the outline of her bra.

Too bad though, Sarah thought. *Because I'm sure not taking off my bra!* If she did, the shirt was so thin that the outlines of her nipples would be clearly visible.

The effect of the entire outfit made Sarah feel like she was wearing her pajamas and bathrobe to a solemn occasion where she should have been dressed up. But what could she do? Kat had done her best copying the Alquon fashions. If this was how people dressed here, she would just have to put up with it.

At least I don't have to be half-naked or anything, Sarah told herself. She didn't know how her Compound-trained sense of modesty would be able to bear something like that. Though the shirt was thin, at least all her skin was covered and besides, all eyes would most likely be on Commander Sazar, not her.

Sazar—just call him Sazar, she reminded herself. *We're pretending to be a couple—can't screw that up.*

"Are you ready?" Sazar's big, well-formed hand was poised on the latch that opened the door of the shuttle.

"Yes." Sarah took a deep breath and straightened her shoulders. "Yes, I am. Let's go."

He turned the latch and swung open the door. Making a sweeping gesture with his free hand he said, "After you."

"Thank you." Pleased by the courtly gesture, Sarah smiled at him as she stepped out of the ship…and then she gasped in awe.

The Kindred shuttle was perched on a long, thin metal platform barely wider than the ship itself. Surrounding it on all sides was an ocean—but *what* an ocean!

Sarah had grown up in Florida and had gone to the beach with her parents before they entered The Brotherhood where things like wearing swimsuits and swimming were forbidden, but this was an ocean like nothing she had ever seen.

The waters were so pale and translucent they almost seemed to glow in the pale, bright sunlight. The waves lapped quietly at the platform the ship was perched on, a dazzling shade of turquoise with patches of light green and delicate purple in places. Sarah thought these must be undersea plants. She could see the darting, jewel-like bodies of what seemed to be fish moving among the green and purple plants—the waters had a crystal-clear quality that made them easy to spot. They made little plops when they splashed out of the water and the air was filled with the salt tang of the sea.

Sarah thought it was the most amazing and beautiful thing she'd ever seen.

"Sarah? Are you all right?"

Clearly Sazar had heard her gasp and was concerned. He came out into the brilliant sunlight wincing, his pale eyes narrowed against the blinding rays.

"It's...very bright out here," he muttered.

"It's beautiful," Sarah breathed. Being a Florida girl, she was used to bright sunlight. "But where are we supposed to go?" she added, dragging her eyes away from the mesmerizing sight of the vast, limitless ocean. "I don't see anything but this platform we landed on. Where are the houses and buildings?"

"Down below, under the water of course," a new voice said.

Sarah spun around with a gasp and nearly fell off the platform. Only Sazar's big hand on her arm kept her from going over the edge. He pulled her to his side and then stepped out in front of her protectively as a stranger approached.

He had come up behind them as they stood looking over the ocean and all Sarah could think was that he must be about a hundred years old.

The stranger had the pale green, purple-mottled skin they had seen on other males on the Alquon video but it was a mass of seams and wrinkles. He was bald but he had a long white beard, which hung in thick, kelp-like strands from his chin. His shoulders were stooped but it was clear he must have been a tall man at one time — maybe almost as tall as Sazar.

"Minister Obglod?" Sazar asked.

"Indeed, indeed, yes. Obglod, Minister of Cultural Studies at your service. I'm gratified to finally meet you in person, Commander Sazar." He bowed deeply, a gesture which Sazar returned gracefully.

Sarah bowed as well, feeling slightly awkward. Was this how women were supposed to behave on this planet? Should she be bowing or would it be better to try and do a little curtsy? Not that she knew how to curtsy but still, she would try if someone would only tell her what to do and how to react. She remembered Sazar saying that the Alquons were extremely easily offended and prayed she wouldn't be the one to do the offending.

I just don't want to mess this up, she told herself. *I don't want Sazar to be sorry he hired me.*

"But who is this you have with you?" Minister Obglod asked, raising his head and peering at Sarah with faded, light blue eyes.

"This is my pair partner, Sarah." Sazar pulled her to him and put an arm firmly around her shoulders.

"Hello, Minister. I'm very pleased to meet you." Sarah smiled in what she hoped was a pleasant and non-offensive way.

Unfortunately, she must have said something wrong because the minister was directing a stern and unforgiving frown at her. Oh God, what was wrong? Why was he looking at her that way? Sarah felt her cheeks getting hot.

"What blasphemy is this?" the old man demanded, speaking to Sazar while staring disapprovingly at Sarah. "If this is a female, then *why* is she dressed as a male?"

"We beg your pardon, Minister Obglod," Sazar said swiftly, before Sarah could start making excuses. "We had nothing but the vids you sent me to guide us when it came to your methods of dress."

"Well, she cannot go before The Lord Magnate looking like *that*," Obglod exclaimed. "She must be changed into proper female attire."

"If you have some, I'd be happy to put it on," Sarah volunteered quickly.

"You cannot put it on yourself—not all of it, anyway," the minister snapped, clearly annoyed. "You must have the help of your pair partner."

"Then I will assist her," Sazar said smoothly. "Please, Minister, if you will just let us know where we can get a proper outfit for Sarah…"

"I know where you can get one but it's going to throw off the schedule terribly. The Lord Magnate is waiting to see you!" the old man groused. "Still, I suppose there's no help for it. Come with me. As you are unable to tolerate the ocean, we will descend in the *tuve*."

Huffily, he turned and led them towards the end of the long, narrow platform. Sarah now saw that there was a tall metal doorway at the far edge. Was it some kind of elevator? Was that what a *tuve* was? It seemed to be a word the translation bacteria she'd taken couldn't quite translate.

"Come," Sazar murmured, taking her by the hand. "We'd better follow."

"Do you think I offended him?" Sarah asked in a low, worried voice. "I know you said they're very easily offended but I don't see how we could have known how I was supposed to dress by the vids they sent."

"Don't worry about it." He gave her fingers a comforting squeeze. "I've been on many diplomatic missions. The only thing you can do is apologize sincerely for whatever blunder you've made, correct the situation, and move on. We've already apologized and now we're going to get you changed and then go meet their ruler. All will be well."

"I hope so," Sarah murmured back as they reached the tall metal door. "I don't want to be the reason the whole mission is messed up."

"You won't be. Don't worry. I'll be here with you every step of the way," he promised. "And I wouldn't have brought you with me if I couldn't protect and guide you."

Sarah felt a warm rush of gratitude for the big Kindred and squeezed his fingers back. Sazar seemed so calm and collected—so sure of himself. It was comforting to see that her apparent social gaff hadn't rattled him a bit.

"Thank you," she whispered and then they reached the metal door.

Minister Obglod snapped his fingers and the thin silvery metal suddenly started folding in on itself. It folded itself smaller and smaller, into concentric patterns of diamonds and squares until it disappeared completely like a magic trick, and the opening of a vast, clear tube was revealed.

"What is *that?*" Sarah breathed, forgetting she was trying to be quiet and inoffensive. It looked like a dark tunnel that led straight down into blackness.

"The *tuve* of course," the old minister said peevishly. "Do your people not have ways of traversing long distances quickly?"

"Well, we have elevators and escalators," Sarah said. "But—"

"But nothing quite like your *tuve*," Sazar finished for her, smoothly. "Would you be kind enough to explain how it works, Minister Obglod?"

"How it works? You get in it and it takes you down," the old man exclaimed impatiently. "How else would it work?"

"So…we're supposed to jump in a hole that leads to the bottom of the ocean?" Sarah could feel the fear of deep water crawling up her spine like an icy hand. The waters around the platform seemed shallow and clear—almost as though she could step right off the platform and wade in their warm, tropical depths. But farther out she could see a much deeper blue, shading to black. Clearly there were depths to this ocean—vast trenches where the pale brilliant sunlight never shone and who knew what dark things swam there?

She wasn't anxious to go jumping into a hole that might lead to a place like that—not a bit.

"My pair partner has, alas, never learned to swim," Sazar told Minister Obglod who was frowning thunderously at her, his kelpy eyebrows drawn low over his faded eyes. "So it is important for us to know that this tunnel—this *tuve* – doesn't lead into deep waters."

"Cannot swim? You mean she is wholly unable to get around in a wet environment?" Obglod looked at her in apparent surprise.

"It was against her religious beliefs," Sazar said swiftly. "Her planet is much different from this one. They still have dry land which is not submerged."

The old minister made a sound like, *hmph* but his tone gentled a little as he turned to Sarah.

"The *tuve* leads to our dry facilities—to the famous city of Idd, jewel of our ocean. No harm will come to you there."

"Our luggage," Sarah protested, thinking of another problem. "I have a pink carry-all cube and Sazar—"

"I'll send an attendant to deal with your luggage," the old man said peevishly. "Now come."

And with surprising swiftness for such an ancient creature, he jumped nimbly into the dark round opening. With a sound like a huge vacuum cleaner sucking up a large object, he was whisked out of sight, into the long dark tunnel which led only down as far as Sarah could see.

"Oh!" she gasped because it really was a very surprising sight.

"Are you all right?" Sazar asked, frowning with worry.

"I'm fine." Sarah shook her head. "It's just…you don't see a little old man get sucked down a long tube every day of the week. You know?"

A slight smile twitched the corners of his mouth.

"You get used to seeing strange things when you're a diplomat to other cultures and planets. Although I grant you, this is the most unusual mode of transportation I've run across in some time."

"Do you think it's safe?" Sarah asked uncertainly.

"I don't think Minister Obglod would have jumped into it if it wasn't," Sazar said gravely. "However, I will go first if it would make you feel better."

Sarah lifted her chin. "I'm not afraid. I was just…startled, that's all. I can go first."

"No." He frowned. "Your safety is my responsibility. Let me jump and then you follow. All right?"

Sarah wasn't unwilling to let him persuade her. She didn't want him to think she was a coward but she wasn't anxious to be sucked into that long, dark tube either.

"Well, all right," she said. "But I'm coming right after you. I don't like the idea of being out here by myself with nobody but the crabs and the fishes. If there *are* crabs and fishes on this planet."

"I'm sure there are—or some approximation of them," Sazar said dryly. "Very well, I'll go first and you follow directly after."

He walked nonchalantly to the vast, dark *tuve* and then, without a hint of fear, stepped over the edge.

Immediately there was the giant sucking sound again and he was gone, whisked away as suddenly and completely as Minister Obglod before him.

Sarah couldn't give herself time to think—she had to do this now or she wouldn't do it at all.

Just do it, she told herself grimly. *Do it now before you lose your nerve, Sarah!*

Taking a deep breath, she ran to the edge, closed her eyes, and jumped.

Chapter Nine

A cool wind seemed to envelope Sarah's entire body—a wind that felt almost like a hand, pulling her downward on a cushion of air. The sides of the tunnel looked slick but it was hard to tell because she never touched them—she was at all times surrounded by the invisible air shield. Which only made her feel more than ever like she was falling.

Before her parents had joined The Brotherhood, they had taken her to Busch Gardens every summer where the three of them had ridden all the roller coasters together. The breathless rush and the feeling that she'd left her stomach somewhere far behind her reminded Sarah of riding the coasters. It was the sensation she felt while traveling down the *tuve*.

I wonder how we'll ever get back up again? she thought as she struggled to control the scream that wanted to rise in her throat. *Does the wind suck both ways?* It seemed to go on and on, not straight down but making twists and turns and loops and spirals until she was really, *really* glad it had been a long time since lunch.

The ride ended abruptly when the last few feet of the dark *tuve* grew suddenly light and dumped her out. She landed on something hard and warm, eliciting a gasp of air and a harsh exclamation.

Sarah blinked in the sudden brilliance, trying to get her bearings but her eyes were still adjusted to the darkness inside the *tuve* and she felt half blind.

"Here—be careful! Hold still," a deep, familiar voice ordered as she struggled to sit up. Warm arms like steel bands encircled her and Sarah realized she'd landed directly on Sazar's big body and was currently pressed right up against him, chest to chest and groin to groin.

"Oh...I'm sorry," she gasped, trying to get up again.

"Just hold still, I said!" he commanded again. "Let your eyes get adjusted to the light—I think it's even brighter than outside."

His own pale eyes were narrowed into a wince and Sarah thought she saw a look of pain cross his face as she stopped struggling and allowed her eyes to adjust to the brilliant illumination around her.

Does the bright light bother him more than me? she wondered, trying not to notice how big and hard and warm he was, pressed against her body. She had a flicker of a thought—something about how vampires can't stand sunlight. But that was silly, wasn't it? Just because Sazar drank blood from time to time didn't make him an actual vampire. Still, he did seem more sensitive to the brilliance than she was—her eyes were already adjusting. Although the harsh light wasn't very pleasant, she *could* function.

Looking around, she saw that they had landed on a vast thick purple cushion like a three-foot-thick mattress. It seemed to have a cushy, giving surface something like memory foam. Sazar was lying on his back on it and she was lying on her stomach on top of him.

Oh dear.

Since he had told her twice not to move, Sarah obediently put her head on his broad shoulder and waited until they could disentangle themselves. God, he smelled so *good*. Spicy and dark and masculine, his scent seemed to fill her senses and she inhaled deeply, wishing she could stay right where she was forever even though part of her was really embarrassed to be pressed so intimately against him.

"Don't you have any idea of proper *tuve* travel?" Minister Obglod's cracked and disapproving voice exclaimed above them, breaking her pleasant fantasy. "You must always, *always* wait five deep breaths before jumping into a *tuve* to allow the last passenger before you to clear the landing area. Even the youngest child knows that!"

"Forgive us," Sazar said, squinting up at the old man. "We are not used to your modes of transportation."

"Well, come on," Obglod said impatiently. "We must get your pair partner properly attired before you have your interview with The Lord Magnate. I've called for help which will be here shortly."

Sazar rolled over carefully and for just a moment he was above Sarah and she felt his big body pressing hers into the mattress. There was something hot and hard rubbing between her thighs and she gave a little gasp as she realized it must be his shaft. Had being pressed together so intimately affected him as much as it had her?

"Sorry," he said roughly. "Here, I'll get up first and give you a hand."

He levered himself off her and stood gracefully, then held out a hand to her.

Sarah took it and he pulled her to her feet. Looking around, she noticed the thick purple mattress wasn't the only one in the room. In fact, there were dozens of mattresses with the ends of *tuves* poised over them. Was this some kind of hub? Like a bank of elevators in a busy building? Or maybe more like a bus station or an airport hub where many terminals met at the same spot?

Her speculation was cut short when a young woman who looked to be about her own age slid out of a nearby *tuve* and landed gracefully on one of the thick purple mattresses.

She had pale green skin mottled with blue and purple splotches, just like the males they had seen in the Alquon vids, and her long purple hair was in thick kelp-like ribbons which reached her narrow waist—but that was where the similarities ended.

Her outfit was…well those in The Brotherhood would have called it obscene.

A short, ruffled top ran around the girl's chest but the ruffle didn't quite cover her perky breasts. They peaked out from under the bright pink fabric enticingly. They were pale green like the rest of her skin and she had deep purple nipples, Sarah saw. Both were pierced with delicate gold rings and a silver chain ran between them.

Down below, her outfit wasn't much better. She was wearing a long skirt which started at her hips and brushed the ground at her dainty bare feet which had webbed toes. But there was a wide, triangular slit up the middle which clearly flashed her dark purple mound of curls.

Oh my goodness! Sarah tried not to stare as the girl bounced gracefully up off the mattress and came over with a smile.

"Well Chandra, *there* you are," Minister Obglod said querulously. "I was just wondering what was taking you so long. These are Commander Sazar of the Kindred and his pair partner Sarah. As you can see, we have *quite* a situation."

He pointed at Sarah who blushed and tried again not to look at the Alquon girl's goodies, which were completely on display.

"Oh my, yes I see," the girl named Chandra said, smiling frankly. "Why are you dressed like a male?" she asked Sarah.

"We weren't sure how females on your planet dressed," Sazar growled. He was keeping his eyes fixed firmly on the girl's face,

Sarah noticed. He must have iron control not to take a leisurely visual tour of her exposed assets. Sarah was having a hard time not doing it and she wasn't even attracted to other women!

"Well, come with me," Chandra said, smiling. "I have access to a good, private clothier in this district. They do all my formal outfits for when I visit the court of the Lord Magnate—I'm sure they'll be able to help you out."

"Thank you," Sarah said, though she really, *really* hoped she didn't have to wear something as revealing as Chandra's outfit. Maybe the formal clothes she was going to be wearing would cover more? *Oh God, I hope so!*

"You're very welcome. Hello, Minister." She walked over to the old man who did something that shocked Sarah even more than Chandra's outfit.

"You're late," he said. Casually he took the silver chain which connected her pierced nipples and tugged it, making her gasp. But not in surprise, evidently because she just smiled and kissed him on his wrinkled cheek.

"I'm sorry. Kendro didn't want to stop making love to me. He gets so cranky when he's interrupted—he wouldn't even let me put my panties back on—see?"

She opened the slit in her skirt wider, flashing her pussy as casually as someone else might show off a new pair of shoes. A pair of delicate silver chains which matched the one between her nipples were dangling from between her puffy nether lips which were a dark purple. Was she pierced *there* too?

"He promised he'd finish filling me later." Chandra giggled as though it was funny.

Sazar cleared his throat and looked deliberately over the girl's left shoulder while Sarah also tried to avert her eyes. It was hard though—she'd never seen such a frank display of sexuality.

Minister Obglod, however, seemed to take it in stride.

"Chandra, my dear, I'm glad you were free," he said. "And tell that pair partner of yours I want to see him soon—we have business to discuss."

"Of course, Minister." The girl smiled again and then beckoned to Sarah. "Come on—let's get you dressed." Turning, she led the way and now Sarah could see she had a slit up the *back* of her skirt too which clearly showed most of her pert behind.

Oh please, she thought. *Please don't make me have to wear something like that! I would **die** of embarrassment.*

But of course, she couldn't ruin the mission just for the sake of her own modesty. Only how was she going to manage if she had to show off her body like that?

Sarah had a very unhappy feeling she was going to find out soon enough.

* * * * *

The females here dressed in a very revealing manner. Sazar did his best not to look out of respect not only for the females in question, but also for Sarah who was supposed to be his pair partner. But as they passed out of the *tuve* room and into a busy corridor it was difficult not to notice all the flashes of feminine flesh which were visible everywhere around them.

The men were dressed as he was with loose trousers and long, open robes but the females' outfits were much less modest. Everywhere dark green and purple nipples peaked from under brief tops and skirts were slit to show undergarments or in some cases, like Chandra's, just bare flesh.

Sazar winced in the brilliant light which bathed the corridor and tried not to stare.

Why did the old fool only send me vids of males? he wondered, glaring at the old Councilor's back. *I never would have brought Sarah if I'd known this was the way she would have to dress. How will she deal with this?*

He knew that she'd been raised in an extremely restrictive environment—the fashions of Alquon Ultrea probably seemed shocking and deviant to her. However, she said nothing but only stayed by his side, following obediently behind Minister Obglod and Chandra.

Sazar wished he could close his eyes and find his way by touch instead of sight. Not just because it would be easier not to look at all the exposed female flesh but because the brilliant light was giving him a blinding headache and sapping his strength. Pitch-Blood Kindred had a sensitivity to sunlight or intense UV radiation which made functioning in it difficult. His throat felt dry and even though he had slaked his thirst with Sarah's blood only the night before, he again felt the Blood Hunger clawing at him.

He supposed the Alquons kept their undersea environment lit brightly to emulate the surface levels of sunlight which they had been used to before their world became submerged. But it was extremely unpleasant. How was he going to function when the environment around him aroused his thirst and sapped his strength?

Sazar sighed inwardly. Well, he would just have to do his best—there was no other possible course of action.

Chapter Ten

"Here we are! This is the clothier I was talking about," Chandra said brightly. She pointed at a small tunnel with a sign over it up ahead on their left.

"Oh good," Sarah said, trying to smile. She certainly hoped the shop they would be visiting would be a little less brightly lit than the street area. The long, underwater tube which housed the part of the city of Idd they were walking in was brightly lit from both above and below. Outside its glass walls, Sarah sometimes caught glimpses of what she assumed was the ocean but the bright illumination inside made it difficult to tell.

It wasn't just that the bright light was annoying, although it certainly was— but the blazing illumination was also making her worried about Sazar. The big Kindred strode along with a stoic look on his face but Sarah thought he looked paler and his eyes were narrowed in apparent pain. And had she seen them flash red—the same dull, almost-maroon color they'd turned the night before when he was so thirsty?

This light really isn't good for him, she thought anxiously. *He's beginning to look like he did when he needed blood so badly.*

Would she have to feed him again? The thought gave her a strange shiver in the pit of her belly. She was glad that Kat and Liv had given her the blood replenishment pills. If Sazar needed to bite her again he could without fear of draining her—she would be able to slake his thirst as often as she needed to.

*But **where** will he bite me?* She couldn't help dreading that initial moment of pain. Would it hurt less on the neck? Or maybe—

Her thoughts were cut off as they entered the small side tunnel which dead-ended in a round bubble of glass that housed a cool, dim shop. Beside her, Sarah heard Sazar breathe a sigh of relief. She couldn't help feeling relieved herself. It was like stepping out of the brilliant sunshine of a Florida day into a cool, dim, air-conditioned house.

But not everyone liked the change.

"My goodness, it's so dark in here I can hardly see a thing!" Minister Obglod complained.

"That's just because the proprietor, Lemesh, has light sensitivity," Chandra explained. "She spends most of her non-work hours in the depths. Don't worry, Minister. We won't be here long." She raised her voice and called, "Lemesh? Oh, Lemmy—I have some customers for you here."

Her call brought a girl to the front of the shop, which was crowded with hanging swaths of fabric in every conceivable color. Like all the other females they had seen, she was dressed in a manner which showed off her assets, though her clothing wasn't quite as bright as Chandra's. Her skin was also a darker green and Sarah thought the gill slits at the sides of her neck looked much more pronounced. Chandra had said she spent a lot of time "in the depths"—did that mean swimming out in the dark ocean, which was much more visible in the dim bubble of the shop, than it had been in the brightly lit outer tunnel?

"Hello, my dear." Lemesh flowed forward with a graceful gesture that was almost like swimming and hugged Chandra, pressing her cheek to the other female's for a moment. "What can I do for you? The Breeding Ball isn't until tomorrow night and I thought you had your outfit all ready. Do you need to make an alteration?"

"Oh, I'm not here for me, Lemmy dear," Chandra said. "These nice people are Sarah and her pair partner Commander Sazar of the Kindred. They have come to visit us all the way from another galaxy." She motioned to Sazar and Sarah who smiled and nodded politely. "Minister Obglod here is their host and he's anxious that they should be, um, properly dressed for their meeting with The Lord Magnate."

"Oh my, another galaxy? Well, that's certainly interesting. I just..." The clothier stopped short, her eyes flickering over Sarah. "Oh my dear — *why* are you dressed like a male?"

"We, uh, didn't know how females dressed here," Sarah said, feeling her cheeks get hot. "I'm really very sorry — the only videos we had showed men, er, *males* only."

"I sent you very proper vids of our most famous law-making sessions," Minister Obglod said, frowning. "If you had listened correctly, you would have heard our law about how males and females are to dress appropriately at all times with no exceptions."

Sarah wanted to exclaim indignantly that if he thought they had time to listen to hours and hours of old men droning on about laws he had another think coming but Sazar spoke before she could say anything.

"Forgive me, Minister. The fault was mine — I did not interpret your laws correctly," he said smoothly. He seemed much more at home in the dim shop and she noticed with relief that his handsome features had lost their strained expression and his eyes were no longer red.

"Well, well, it can't be helped," Obglod grumbled. "Let's just hope Chandra and her friend can make your female presentable."

"Oh, I'm certain I can. What lovely, unusual skin coloration," Lemesh remarked, coming closer and tilting her head to one side as she studied Sarah.

"Um…thank you. I think your skin is lovely too," Sarah said with a smile.

"Oh no," the clothier protested. "My skin is too green—my coloration is dark because of my blood." She smiled at Chandra. "But we can't all have such pure blood as my lovely friend here."

"Oh, Lemmy…" Chandra made a shooing motion.

"Well, it seems you have the matter in hand," Minister Obglod announced, clearly bored of the female chatter. "I must go make some excuses as to the delay of our party to the palace." He pointed at Chandra. "I'll be back soon. See that she's properly arrayed when I return."

"Of course, Minister." She kissed him affectionately on the cheek and he tugged at the chain between her breasts almost absently and then left the shop in a fast, shuffling walk.

"Well, you heard the Minister—we need to get moving," Chandra said briskly. "What can you do for us, Lemmy?"

The clothier was still staring at Sarah thoughtfully.

"I think perhaps some lovely gold netting to set off the rings in her breasts—or maybe silver. Tell me dear, what color are your piercings?"

"Oh…" Sarah felt the blood drain from her face. "I…I don't have any, uh, piercings," she admitted. And she *really* hoped she didn't have to get any either! The idea of someone poking a needle in her nipples was *not* appealing.

"What? No piercings? Let me see your breasts!" Lemesh demanded.

"Um...uh..." Sarah stuttered, casting a glance at Sazar. She couldn't just start stripping in front of her boss, could she?

Sazar clearly saw the uncertainty on her face because he considerately turned around, putting his broad back to her and the other two girls.

Sarah felt somewhat relieved but she still didn't like getting undressed in front of strangers, even if they were female. Still, what else could she do? Alquon Ultrea could represent an important alliance with the Kindred—she couldn't screw that up just because she was shy.

Taking a deep breath, she dropped the bulky robe and pulled the tight blue shirt over her head, revealing her bra.

This garment, which Sarah had bought yesterday, was a nice, new black one with plenty of support for her too-large breasts. It immediately provoked a lot of interest from both of the Alquon girls.

"But what is *this?*" Lemesh fingered the black elastic straps with interest. "What can be the meaning of covering your breasts with a top and then covering them again with this strange thing?"

"It's a foundation garment," Sarah tried to explain. "It...gives you support. Especially if your breasts are on the, uh, large size," she added in a low voice. "We're not all as perky as we'd like to be." She nodded at Chandra's tea-cup sized breasts which were small and perfectly formed.

"She *does* have extremely large breasts," Chandra remarked. "I don't think I've ever seen such big ones." She giggled. "You're going to be *quite* the center of attention once we get your outfitted properly!"

"I'm a triple D," Sarah said, trying to keep her voice low. "But that's not *that* unusual back on my home planet of Earth." She knew for a fact that there were women with bigger boobs than hers. Mostly porn stars, not that she ever watched porn, but still...

"I still don't understand the use of this garment." Lemesh was frowning at Sarah's bra. "If you need support, why do you not simply wear a float dot under each breast? So much easier and they don't hide your lovely breasts like this ugly thing does." She plucked at the elastic strap again disdainfully. "Ugh."

"Float dots? What are those?" Sarah asked.

"Lemmy will show you. Come on— take that that nasty black thing off," Chandra commanded. "Hurry—the Minister doesn't like to be kept waiting and The Lord Magnate likes it even less."

There was no choice. With trembling fingers, Sarah unhooked her bra and let it slide down her arms. She cast a nervous glance over her shoulder but to her relief, she saw that Sazar was still facing away, although she could tell by the set of his shoulders that he was listening to everything they said.

"Oh, you *do* have large breasts," Lemmy exclaimed. "*Very* large. My—we might need two float dots under each one."

"They're nicely shaped though," Chandra remarked. "And I don't think I've ever seen *pink* nipples before—how unusual. Lovely, though." She spoke in the conversational tone someone complimenting a new pair of shoes might use.

Sarah did her best to take their remarks in stride although she couldn't help wondering what Sazar was thinking of all this.

"Um, thank you," she said. "Pink isn't an unusual color for my people."

"Oh no? What a strange planet you must live on," Chandra mused.

Lemesh, however, was all business.

"Now then—you've never been pierced at all?" she demanded.

"No, and I *really* don't want to be if I can avoid it," Sarah said quickly. "I mean if it would give offense not to, I'll do it, but—"

"Don't worry my dear—I'm not set up for piercing here," Lemesh told her comfortingly. "I'll tell you what—let's just get your outfit settled first and then we can see about nipple jewelry. I think I have some non-piercing sets for clients with sensitive skin in the back. But of course we'll need the help of your pair partner to put it on."

Sarah had no idea why Sazar's help would be required but before she could ask, Chandra was already holding swaths of cloth up to her front, looking for the perfect color while Lemesh took her measurements using a tiny hand-held machine which pricked her skin lightly without drawing blood wherever it touched and beeped intermittently.

Before she knew it, Sarah had been fitted for several outfits which were, unfortunately, every bit as revealing as the ones Chandra and Lemesh were wearing. One was a stretchy, gold lame' material which molded itself to the tops and sides of her breasts while leaving her nipples bare. The skirt that went with it was of the same fabric and clung to her hips and behind with a slit up both the back and the front. Lemesh had apparently made it for another client who decided to wear something else so it was all ready to go.

"That one is for the Breeding Ball," she explained as she had Sarah try it on. "I'm assuming you'll be invited since you're important guests of the Minister and you're visiting the palace today."

"She'll need the right undergarments too," Chandra reminded her friend.

"So she will. I'll pack them with the dress when I wrap it up for you," Lemesh promised Sarah.

"Undergarments? But I thought…thought you didn't wear, uh, bras here?" Sarah asked in confusion.

"You mean that ugly breast-hider thing you were wearing? No, of course we don't! We show off our assets as is right and proper and feminine," Lemesh exclaimed. "But you'll need the proper breeding panties—it isn't good etiquette not to wear them during public breedings, especially in a formal setting like the palace."

"While you're…breeding?" Sarah heard the tone of uncertainty in her own voice but Lemesh was already moving on to other things.

"Now, as for your outfit for today, I think something a little less formal but still eye-catching. I have a gorgeous deep, sea green I've been dying to use but it didn't quite match any of my client's nipples."

"It won't match Sarah's either—they're pink," Chandra pointed out.

"It won't match but it will *accentuate*," Lemesh said. "Here, let me show you."

She went to the back of her shop and returned with a bolt of deep green, silky fabric. Holding the same machine she'd used to take Sarah's measurements, she ran it over a length of the fabric and several pieces of pre-made clothing simply fell out of the cloth.

"Wow! That was *fast*." Sarah marveled at how quick and efficient the process was. She couldn't help remembering how laborious making clothes was back home—how her mother and the other women of the Compound had labored for hours cutting and using their sewing machines. Sarah had helped too until she had been promoted to working in the office—sewing was something she hated with a passion but with a tool like Lemesh's, it would be a breeze.

"Yes, the measure-maker really does come in handy. Don't you have anything like it on your planet?" Lemesh asked.

"No—I wish we did," Sarah said as the other woman pulled the top over her head.

"Maybe we can get you one while you're here," Chandra remarked. "Oh Lemmy, you were right—that color is just stunning against her pale skin!"

Sarah had to agree they were correct—the deep green looked wonderful with her ivory skin tones. The material was silky and cut in an inverted V neck which started at the hollow of her throat and then sloped down and away, framing her full breasts beautifully. If the top hadn't exposed her so much, she would have really liked it. As it was, though, Sarah couldn't believe she had to wear it out in public. Had she thought she felt exposed before when she'd been wearing the close-fitting clothing Kat had talked her into? Well this was a hundred times worse and there was no way to get out of wearing it!

The one thing she didn't like was that her breasts weren't as perky as Chandra's or Lemesh's or really as any of the Alquon girls she'd seen. The Alquon people seemed to tend towards small breasted women and there was no denying that small, tight breasts looked better in this particular style than her own full to overflowing type of bosom.

Lemesh seemed to see the problem too because she announced, "Time to get out the float dots!"

Before Sarah could ask again what they were, she produced a small black box and opened it to reveal tiny red jewels that looked like rubies.

"Here we go," she said, picking one out carefully with her fingertips. It made a slight humming sound and Sarah bit her lip as the Alquon clothier lifted her right breast in a professional manner and placed the tiny ruby-looking thing directly on the crease where the bottom of her breast met her chest wall.

At once she felt a soft vibration and her breast began to lift. Not in a strange, unnatural way—it was as though some invisible hand was cupping her from underneath and giving her support.

"Hmm, another I think," Lemesh said, looking critically at the result. She added another float dot to the underside of Sarah's right breast and then two to the underside of the left. When she was finished, Sarah's too-large breasts looked every bit as perky as Chandra's teacup-sized ones and the deep green top fit perfectly as it molded to the sides of her breasts without covering the undercurves or nipples.

"Wow, that's...amazing." Sarah looked down at herself. No wonder nobody wore a bra here—the float dots did a perfect job of support without the need of tight elastic straps or uncomfortable bands. "How long will they last?" she asked Lemesh.

"Hmm? Oh, as long as you keep them on, my dear," the clothier assured her. "I'll give you a special box to keep them in—you have to keep them charged up of course, and that's what the box does. But once you put them on, they draw power from the warmth of your skin."

"So you can wear them multiple times?" Sarah asked.

"As often as you want." Lemesh smiled brightly. "Many of my clients wear them all the time and just never take them off. They work so well."

"They certainly do." Sarah regarded her breasts which, now that the effects of gravity had been removed, suddenly looked like she'd had a boob job. They jiggled when she moved but they stayed full and firm no matter what she did, apparently immune to gravity.

"Now the skirt fits nicely too," Lemesh remarked, smoothing it over Sarah's full hips. She and Chandra had gotten Sarah to take off the baggy trousers, but Sarah was still wearing her nice cotton flower-print panties. "But those won't do at all," she added, frowning.

Sarah saw she was staring at her underwear and pressed her thighs together protectively. "I'd rather not take those off. My people don't, uh, believe in going around without underwear."

"We'll give you some to take their place," Chandra promised her. "But you absolutely *cannot* wear those to the palace! They don't match at all—they ruin the look of the entire outfit."

"Here—these are perfect for the palace." Lemesh had brought out something which looked a little like a thong but instead of fabric in the back, it had a double strand of exotic-looking black and green pearls of all different sizes, from the circumference of a ball bearing to the size of a gumball.

"Really?" Sarah looked at the strange garment uncertainly as she reluctantly shed her own panties. "But if I wear that, won't the uh, pearls go right up my behind?" The pearls in question were in a kind of long loop, she saw, making a kind of oval of little green and black spheres which was certain to be uncomfortable if it got into the wrong crevice.

"Up your behind?" Chandra started laughing. "Oh my dear," she exclaimed as Lemesh helped Sarah step into the new underwear. "The honey pearls don't go in the back—they go up the *front.*"

To her dismay, Sarah saw it was true. The double strand of

pearls nestled in the center of her pussy slit against her outer lips. She was glad she kept her curls neatly trimmed into a small triangle because the new panties did nothing to hide her mound at all.

Well, at least they're not up inside me, she thought and then Lemesh said,

"Wait, it's a little too loose."

"And you forgot to turn the honey pearls on," Chandra added.

"Silly me—how could I forget?"

The Alquon clothier reached under the slit of Sarah's gown and did something to the panties. Suddenly there was a slight humming sound and the double string of multi-sized black and green pearls cinched inward, sliding between Sarah's outer pussy lips and coming to rest against her inner folds.

"Oh!" she exclaimed, shifting her hips quickly but that only made things worse. The pearls were vibrating—not a lot—but enough to cause a tingling sensation right against the pink button of her clit that made her feel like she suddenly had ants in her pants. There was one pearl on each side of her button and the strands seemed to be moving up and down as the pearls spun in circles, creating a double sensation that began driving her crazy in short order.

Suddenly Sarah felt like she had the night before when she'd been touching herself and trying to reach that elusive peak. She didn't think the faint vibrations of the honey pearls would be enough to help her get to that peak or push her over, but they were certainly enough to make her uncomfortably aroused.

"Just perfect for the palace," Chandra exclaimed. "Now all she needs is some nipple jewelry!"

"But...but..." Sarah stammered. "How, uh, what if I want to

turn them off?"

"Why would you want to do that? They feel nice, don't they?" Chandra giggled. "I love to wear my honey pearls! My pair partner, Kendro, says they make me so wet for him. Sometimes he fills me while I'm wearing them—won't even let me take them off." She winked at Sarah. "I bet your partner will feel the same."

Mention of her "partner" made Sarah realize that she'd almost forgotten Sazar was standing behind her, waiting patiently for this whole process to be finished. Suddenly she remembered all over again that he was going to have to see her in this extremely revealing get-up and she felt herself blushing. What would he think of her? The clothing fit well, showing off her curves to the best advantage and the float dots made her full breasts perfectly perky, but it was all so *revealing*. And the honey pearls wouldn't stop stimulating her, no matter how she shifted around. In fact, shifting her hips seemed to make their effects *worse*.

"Here we are!" Lemesh came back carrying a broad, flat black lacquered box. "I knew I had some non-piercing ones."

She opened the box, revealing several sets of tiny gold and silver bands joined by chains, just like she and Chandra were wearing.

"Go ahead, pick a set," she told Sarah. "I'd recommend gold because it will match with both outfits."

"All right." Feeling a sense of disbelief—as though she was trapped in a bizarre dream and couldn't wake up from it—Sarah pointed to a set with a thin, filigreed golden chain attached to two thick gold bands. She had an idea that the thick bands might hurt less wrapped around her nipples than the tiny thin wire ones she also saw in the box.

"Excellent choice!" Chandra said. "Now we just need your pair partner to help put them on."

"Oh, I...I can put them on myself, I think," Sarah said quickly but Lemesh and Chandra only laughed at her.

"Now how can you do that? How are the bands going to adhere to your peaks without the help of your pair partner's mouth?"

"What?" Sarah exclaimed but Chandra was already tugging on the back of Sazar's robe, telling him to turn around.

The big Kindred didn't move.

"Sarah?" he said, making her name a question and Sarah knew he was asking if she wouldn't mind him seeing her in her present state of dress—or rather *un*dress.

As it happened, she *did* mind—a lot—but again she reminded herself that she couldn't scuttle the entire mission just because of her own personal sense of modesty.

I'm dressed like everyone else here, she reminded herself. *Well, everyone else who's female, anyway.*

"Yes," she said aloud in a voice that trembled only a little. "You...uh, you can look."

Sazar turned slowly and Sarah bit her lip, waiting to hear what he would say. He was silent at first but his pale eyes widened as he took her in from head to toe, lingering briefly on her exposed breasts and the string of honey pearls nestled between her pussy lips. Finally he breathed a single word.

"Beautiful."

"She is, isn't she?" Lemesh smiled. "That dress really sets off her pink nipples, don't you think, Commander Sazar?"

Sazar cleared his throat, his eyes drawn downward to Sarah's bare breasts again.

"Indeed," he said at last in a somewhat choked voice. "They are...lovely. Very full and ripe."

For a moment Sarah thought she saw his eyes flash red again. Was that a sign of lust as well as a sign he was needing blood? Did it signal a different kind of hunger? The thought made her feel flushed and hot in all the wrong places and she wished she could cover herself with her hands but she knew that would look wrong. She and Sazar were supposed to be mated partners—she wouldn't cover herself from her own husband, would she?

I guess not, Sarah thought, shifting her hips and wishing the honey pearls wouldn't vibrate so much.

"All right, now that your partner has had time to admire you, we need his help getting this jewelry on," Lemesh said briskly. She produced a small round bottle with a long thin tube attached to it which reminded Sarah weirdly of an old-fashioned perfume atomizer. Unscrewing the top, she pulled out a long, thin silver pin and motioned to Sarah. "Give me your finger please."

"What? Why?" Sarah asked even as she held out her finger.

"I need a drop of your blood for the compound," the clothier said. And before Sarah could protest, she stuck the pin into the pad of her right index finger.

"Ouch!" Sarah exclaimed, jumping.

Sazar came forward, his face like a thundercloud.

"I don't appreciate you hurting my mate without getting her permission first," he growled. "I have sworn not to allow even a single drop of her blood to spill."

"Please don't worry, Commander Sazar," Chandra told him soothingly as Lemesh held Sarah's bleeding finger over the black bottle and squeezed gently. "One drop is all it takes and we promise she will be well taken care of."

"I need a drop of yours too," Lemesh told him briskly. "Please give me your hand."

"First I will heal my mate." Stepping up to Sarah, Sazar took her wounded finger and sucked it gently into his mouth.

"Oh," Sarah whispered as a tingle ran through her. God, it felt good when he healed her! And the intense way he was looking at her made her feel weak in the knees. His eyes flashed red again as he held her gaze.

"Your blood, Commander Sazar," Lemesh reminded him impatiently.

"All right." Sazar released Sarah's hand and frowned as he extended his right index finger for the clothier.

"What is the purpose of this? Why do you need our blood?" he asked.

"Because..." Lemesh pricked his finger and allowed a drop of his blood to fall into the small black bottle. "It's the only way to activate the adhesive compound," she finished, releasing his hand and screwing the top back on the bottle.

"Adhesive?" Sarah asked. "What do you...Oh!" Her last word ended in a gasp because the Alquon clothier had sprayed her right nipple with the contents of the black bottle and it was some of the coldest liquid she'd ever felt in her life.

Her right peak, already hard from the cool air in the room and the embarrassment of exposure, tightened even more until it ached. Lemesh did the same to the left nipple before Sarah could protest and then nodded at Sazar.

"All right, suck them, Commander. Hurry or I'll have to spray her again."

"Excuse me?" Sazar frowned as though he was certain he'd misunderstood her. "I'm sorry but *what* did you say?"

"Suck them—suck her nipples." Lemesh sounded impatient. "It's the only way to finish the reaction started by the compound and make the jewelry stay in place. Hurry or I'll have to spray her again."

"I...I don't understand," Sarah said faintly. "You want him to, uh, suck my...um..."

Lemesh frowned. "Why are you acting as though this is hard to understand? The compound keeps the nipple jewelry in place but only if it's activated first by the saliva of your partner."

"And...it won't stay on otherwise?" Sarah looked doubtfully at the small golden bands which were supposed to encircle her tender peaks.

"Not at the right tension," Chandra said, jumping in to help explain. "You see, the jewelry automatically tightens to just the right amount to keep your nipples hard and erect without cutting off the blood flow. Without the chemical compound, which is tailored to both of your bodies by the drops of blood you just gave, the metal will either be too loose and slip off—which is terribly embarrassing and unacceptable, especially in front of the Lord Magnate..."

"Or it can tighten too much and cut off the blood flow, causing permanent damage to the sensitive nerves of the nipple," Lemesh finished for her. "You don't want that, do you?"

"No, I...I guess not," Sarah said. "But..."

"It's either this or get your nipples pierced," Lemesh pointed out. "And you don't want that either, do you?"

"No," Sarah said fervently. "No, I really don't." If she had to choose between the embarrassment of having her boss put his mouth on her nipples and the pain of having a needle shoved through them, she would take the embarrassment every time.

Sazar was still frowning. "Are you *certain* this jewelry is necessary for Sarah? Can't she simply go without it?"

"What? Go out in public without her nipple jewelry?" Chandra looked shocked. "Why, that's indecent! She might as well go outside naked!"

Like I'm not half naked already, Sarah thought dryly. God, it looked like there was no way around it—she was going to have to let her boss suck her nipples. But how would Sazar feel about it? Did he *want* to suck her nipples?

A look at his eyes, which had turned that maroon-red color again and the prominent lump rising in the crotch of his loose black trousers gave Sarah her answer. Sazar wasn't opposed to it—he was probably just worried that *she* was.

"Now just look," Lemesh said impatiently. "The compound has dried and I'll have to spray her again. I don't see why something as simple as nipple jewelry is causing such a problem!" She sprayed Sarah's tight peaks with the achingly cold compound again, causing her to hiss and flinch. Then she motioned to Sazar. "Come on!"

"Please hurry," Chandra begged. "The Minister will be back very soon and we need to be ready to go to the palace!"

Sarah bit her lip and looked up at Sazar. He was looking at her with uncertainty stamped on his chiseled features and she knew it was up to her to give him permission to do this—he was too honorable to take advantage of her.

"Please," she whispered. "I...I don't want her to have to spray me again. That stuff is really *cold.*"

It was apparently all he needed to hear.

"As you wish," he said hoarsely and dropped to his knees before her.

He was so tall that the new position put his lips exactly opposite her breasts. Looking Sarah in the eyes, he opened his mouth slowly and lapped upward, dragging his hot tongue up and over her aching peak, making her gasp with sudden need and pleasure.

"Sazar," she whispered and put her hands on his broad shoulders. "Oh God that feels…feel so *good.*"

He gave a soft growl in the back of his throat and sucked her stiff peak deep into his mouth. Sarah gasped again and gave a little moan when she felt the sharp points of his fangs bracketing her tender nipple as he sucked her hard and long. She found that her hands had somehow gotten buried in his thick black hair and she was pressing forward, trying to get more of her breast in his mouth.

She had a hazy thought, wondering again if he could drink from her here, and then Lemesh was saying, "All right now—that's quite enough. We're not at the Breeding Ball, you know."

Reluctantly Sazar allowed Sarah's stiff, aching nipple to slip from between his lips and sat back.

Quickly and efficiently, the Alquon clothier slipped one of the golden rings over the throbbing peak and Sarah felt it tighten at once to just the right amount.

"Good," Lemesh said. "That's one down—now do the other."

Wordlessly, Sazar leaned forward and took her other stiff nub in his mouth, sucking and licking until Sarah started to wonder if she could reach that elusive peak she'd been seeking just from having him suck her nipple.

Once more Sazar held her gaze with his, his eyes burning red, and once more she found she couldn't look away. This definitely wasn't what she'd had in mind when she walked into the interview room with him but she found she was having a hard time thinking of him as her boss right now—especially while his sharp fangs pricked her lightly and his hot tongue drew circles around her swollen peak. He never drew blood but Sarah couldn't help wondering if he wanted to…and if he could from this sensitive area.

Finally, again at Lemesh's orders, he withdrew, releasing her peak with a last, soft kiss, and the Alquon clothier was able to fit the other golden ring on Sarah's left nipple. It tightened just as the other one had and the golden filigreed chain hung between her breasts enticingly.

"So beautiful," Sazar growled softly as he rose smoothly from his kneeling position. "Do they feel all right?" he asked, indicating the golden rings now encircling her tight pink nubs.

"I…I think so," Sarah murmured. She looked at Lemesh. "But…how do I get them off when…when I want to go to sleep at night?"

"The same way you put them on." The Alquon clothier smiled.

"You mean use the spray again—the compound?" Sarah asked, nodding at the bottle.

"Oh no, my dear—that's only for putting them *on*. To get them off again, your pair partner must get them nice and wet with his mouth—that will dissolve the compound and release the rings until the next time you want to wear them."

Oh God, this situation just got more and more embarrassing!

"So every time I want to take these off or put them on…" Sarah began.

"Your pair partner has to help you," Chandra said brightly. "Which is sure to lead to lots of fun. I know it always does with my partner Kendro when I wear the non-piercing kind of jewelry—sometimes I do it on purpose just for that reason." She giggled.

"Oh, uh…" Sarah wasn't sure what to say to that. She glanced up at Sazar who was still looking intently at her. What did he think about this arrangement?

There was no time to ask him because just then Minister Obglod reappeared.

"Well, there you are. And looking much better I'm sure!" he exclaimed, looking Sarah over. He reached forward, as though to grab for the chain between her breasts but Sarah took a quick step back and wrapped her arms over her exposed assets. She couldn't fight the instinctive urge to cover herself. She had gotten somewhat used to being half naked in front of Lemesh and Chandra and even Sazar but she just couldn't let some man she barely knew ogle her bare breasts—she *couldn't.*

"What's wrong, my dear?" Obglod asked, frowning. "Does your jewelry pain you?"

"She's just not used to it yet," Chandra said quickly. "Come Minister—we are all ready for a trip to the palace!"

"Excellent—we have kept The Lord Magnate waiting long enough. Come this way."

He started to lead the way out of the small, dim shop but Sarah said, "Wait!"

"What is it now?" The elderly minister turned on her with a fierce scowl. "We need to go!"

"I just...I was wondering if you had any sunglasses, er—dark lenses—my partner could use to shield his eyes," Sarah said, speaking to Lemesh rather than the minister. "He has a sensitivity to light which makes the brightness of your main corridors very uncomfortable."

Sazar was giving her an unreadable look, which she hoped wasn't anger or irritation. But she didn't want him going out in that bright light again without any protection. *A good assistant anticipates her boss's needs,* she told herself. And the last thing Sazar needed was to be exposed to that painfully bright light again.

"Oh, of course!" Lemesh exclaimed. "I am light sensitive myself, you know. I'm sure I have an extra pair of blockers…"

She ran to the back of her shop and returned with a strange contraption which looked like a long, rounded metal wire with a black square attached to either end.

"Look, you wear it like this—if you'd just lean down…" She motioned to Sazar.

The big Kindred leaned over obligingly and Lemesh looped the wire around the back of his neck. Then she brought it up and pressed the black squares together to form a long, dark rectangle which fit over his eyes.

"There—that should work." She nodded approvingly.

"I thank you," Sazar rumbled but he was looking at Sarah as he spoke.

"My pleasure," Lemesh said, smiling.

"Yes, thank you, Lemmy—you're a lifesaver." Chandra gave the other girl a hug and they pressed their cheeks together briefly.

"We really do appreciate your help," Sarah said, smiling at the Alquon girl. Though it was going to be excruciatingly embarrassing to walk out in public completely exposed, the clothier really had done her best for them. She was good at her job—Sarah just hoped she could be as good at hers.

"You're welcome, my dear." Lemesh smiled back warmly. "I'll have the other clothes and the bottle of compound packed up and sent over to your guest quarters."

"Thank you, Sazar said gravely. "And now it appears the minister is eager for us to go."

"Yes, yes—hurry up, won't you?" Obglod exclaimed impatiently. "We cannot keep the Lord Magnate waiting for one moment longer unless you wish us all to be thrown to the *grike.*"

Sarah wasn't sure what a *grike* was and she certainly didn't want to find out.

"We'd better go," she said. Waving at Lemesh, she followed Minister Obglod and Chandra out of the small dark shop and back into the brilliant corridor. She immediately wished she'd asked for a pair of the sunglasses herself but it was too late now. They were going to the palace to meet the Alquon ruler and she would be squinting all the way. She was also going to have to fight the urge to cover herself again once they got into public.

God, whoever would have guessed when she took this job that she'd be walking around bare-breasted on an alien planet? What had she gotten herself into?

And yet, when she stole a glance at Sazar, striding along beside her, she couldn't feel sorry about the strange turn her life had taken…and she also couldn't help remembering how hot his mouth had felt on her breasts or the intense way he looked at her when he'd sucked them.

Was she falling for the big Kindred?

You'd better not be, whispered a stern little voice in her head. *He's your boss and this is still a professional relationship — don't forget that, Sarah!*

But somehow it was hard to remember when her nipples were still tingling from his mouth and her body was on fire from his touch.

Chapter Eleven

The light blockers helped a lot, though the brilliant radiance still sapped his strength. At least he could see, however—in fact, Sazar had to admit to himself, maybe he could see *too* well. With the dark lenses shielding his eyes, it was obvious exactly how many males were staring at Sarah in open admiration.

Sazar tried to tell himself that some of their interest in her was doubtless because she was alien to their planet with different skin and hair tones than the Alquons were used to. But some of the attention she was getting was undoubtedly lust.

It's her breasts, he thought, frowning as the eyes of the Alquon males followed his little human assistant's every movement. *They're so large—much larger that the Alquon females' endowments.*

In fact, they were larger than he was used to himself—Malinda had been quite small up top. Sazar had loved her to distraction—breast size wasn't an issue with him. But he had to admit his new assistant's assets were definitely distracting.

So big and soft and sweet, he couldn't help thinking. His hands itched to cup them again and he couldn't help remembering how good her nipples tasted or the soft little moans she made when he sucked them.

The Blood Hunger tortured him and his fangs were long and sharp, longing to pierce her there and drink from an area where only a Pitch-Blood Kindred could call a vein. But he didn't want to hurt her and there was no doubt taking blood from such a sensitive area would be painful unless he pleasured her first.

Not if she's your Fated Mate, whispered a little voice in his head. *Then it would be nothing but pleasure for her, were you to drink from her breasts or between her thighs.*

But Sazar couldn't take that chance. Fated Mates were rare and his idea that Sarah might be his was probably just wishful thinking.

I can't drink from her there, he told himself. *In fact, I can't drink from her **anywhere** for at least a standard week. I'll just have to keep the Blood Hunger in check and concentrate on doing my job.*

And right now his job was to make contact with the ruler of Alquon Ultrea — The Lord Magnate.

"Now you can tell we're entering the territory around the palace because of the light," Chandra said, looking back at him and Sarah. She had been playing the tour guide as they moved through the busy tunnels that housed the city streets, pointing out various landmarks, businesses, and the private residences of leading citizens, but Sazar had been paying scant attention to her.

Sarah, however, was looking all around her with wide-eyed awe. Sazar reminded himself that this was the first time she'd been off her own little planet. This was just another diplomatic mission to him but to her, it was all new and fascinating.

"How can we tell? What about the light?" she asked Chandra.

"Well, it's *golden* — can't you tell, my dear?" The Alquon girl's big purple eyes widened dramatically. "Everything around The Lord Magnate must be golden — even the light. His plates and cups and utensils are all gold." She dropped her voice. "Some say even the pot he does his business in his gold and I believe it!"

"Wow," Sarah said. "That's, uh, really something."

"Yes, isn't it?" Chandra giggled. "Now here we are — the Palace of Idd."

She threw out a hand and Sazar saw that they were indeed approaching a tall structure with many towers and turrets, all of which gleamed in the golden light. They approached a tall gate made of golden bars and two guards dressed in golden armor shaped like interlocking fish scales stopped them.

"Open in the name of Minister Obglod," the old minister snapped at the guards, who were pointing golden trident-like weapons at him. "The Lord Magnate is expecting us."

"Yes, Minister." The tridents were withdrawn and the golden gates opened. Inside Sazar noticed that even the plain path they had been walking on had become gold-plated. He wondered if gold was less rare here than it was in other parts of the universe. There was known to be miniscule amounts of it in the seawater of Earth—perhaps the Alquons had found a way to process the waters of their home world and extract it.

"This is…quite a palace," he remarked to Minister Obglod as they walked up the solid gold-plated path to the golden castle rising before them.

"Yes, isn't it? But it's all the work of the late Lord Magnate—the father of the male who now sits the throne of Idd," Obglod informed him.

"He was a proud male who sought status above all else," Chandra said in a low voice. "Nothing like his son who is the soul of sweetness and generosity. Why, he's always having balls and helping young women find their place in society. He helped me find mine and I'll always be grateful." She smiled.

"He sounds really…nice," Sarah said but Sazar thought there was a peculiar flat tone in her voice. "So do we just go right into the palace to meet him or what?" she asked, motioning to the tall double doors of the castle which were, of course, solid gold.

"One of his Privy Council will be coming out to bring us in and announce us," Obglod answered. "Ah—here he is now. Councilor Rando—how nice to see you! Thank you for making our abject apologies to The Lord Magnate for our tardiness."

"It will cost you later," said Councilor Rando—a small, oily looking male with a thin face and beady eyes like a weasel's, Sazar thought. His lank, black, kelp-like hair was greasy, as though it hadn't been washed in a long while. "So who have you brought to meet The Lord Magnate?" he asked, coming up to Sarah and Sazar. He spoke to Minister Obglod but his eyes were glued to Sarah's breasts.

"This is Commander Sazar and his pair partner, Sarah," Obglod said, nodding at them.

"Pleased to meet you both," Rando said, but he had eyes only for Sarah. "And you, my dear—aren't you *lovely*. You have such large...*assets*."

He reached out and grasped the golden chain swinging between her breasts. Before Sazar could stop him, he gave the chain a hard tug, eliciting a startled gasp from Sarah who moved at once to get away from him. But she couldn't get far—she was tethered by the breast chain which Rando still gripped firmly in one hand.

Sazar felt a blinding rage come over him as quickly as though someone had dropped a red curtain across his vision. With a low growl, he caught Councilor Rando's wrist and squeezed until the weasely little male released his hold on Sarah's breast chain and shrieked in pain, his face going pasty pale.

"Here now, stop that! What do you think you're doing?" Minister Obglod exclaimed.

"Sarah is *mine*." His words came out in a low, possessive

growling tone that was completely different from the calm, diplomatic voice he usually spoke in while on a mission. Part of him knew this wasn't right—wasn't the way he ought to handle this situation at all—but Sazar found himself completely beyond reason. A deep, possessive voice inside him insisted that his female was being hurt or molested and he had to put an end to it *right now*.

"Oh Commander Sazar, please—you'll break his arm!" Chandra gasped.

"Stop at once! You cannot treat a member of the Privy Council like this," Obglod declared.

Sazar didn't give a damn for either of them or for the squealing Rando who's face had gone a strange mint-green color. He could have broken the male's wrist or at least several of his fingers and enjoyed it thoroughly but there was one soft voice which got through to him.

"Sazar please," Sarah pleaded with him. "Please—the mission! Don't forget our *mission*."

That's right, we're here on a mission. I must conduct myself professionally...diplomatically.

And the way he was acting right now was anything but diplomatic.

Abruptly he dropped Rando's wrist and wiped his palm on his robe, feeling he had touched something dirty.

The Privy Councilor whimpered, holding his wounded hand to his skinny chest.

"You cannot do this to me! I am a member of The Lord Magnate's inner circle! How dare you treat me so?"

"My...apologies," Sazar said, struggling to keep the angry growl out of his voice. "But you cannot manhandle my mate. Sarah is mine and I will allow no other male to touch her."

"But tugging on a breast chain is just a standard greeting between a male and a female," Chandra protested. "It wasn't as though Councilor Rando bent Sarah over and tried to breed her!"

The very thought of anyone doing such a thing to Sarah brought a fresh rage which Sazar had to struggle to control.

"We didn't know that," Sarah said soothingly. "Tugging, uh, someone's breast chain would be considered extremely rude back on the Kindred Mother Ship or on my planet of Earth."

"Well you are not on the Kindred ship or on Earth—you are on Alquon Ultrea," Rando snapped.

"Exactly! And while you are here as my guests, I must *insist* that you act in a civilized manner!" Obglod exclaimed.

"Agreed." Sazar straightened his robe, still trying to regain control. "But no other male must touch or approach Sarah. She is mine and I refuse to allow her to be molested, no matter what your customs are here."

"*Molested?*" Minister Obglod looked incensed but Chandra stepped up and touched him timidly on the arm.

"It's all right, Commander Sazar—we can tell how deeply you love your pair partner and I'm sure we can accommodate your customs," she said quietly. "Just keep Sarah at your back and I'll walk behind her and run interference to make certain no other male tries to, er, greet her."

"It's her breasts," Rando complained, still nursing his sprained wrist. "Why did you bring a female with such large and enticing breasts if you didn't intend to let any other male greet her or taste her favors?"

"Taste her *favors?*" Sazar glared at the other male and the Privy Councilor flinched and edged away from him.

"It's not an unusual request from one male to another! I don't know what kind of backward culture you come from but in civilized places males *share*."

Sazar frowned. Was this something the Alquons did? Did they trade partners or allow other males to use their females sexually? He had heard of such things happening on Earth but to him the very idea was repugnant. Kindred warriors mated for life and were intensely loyal to the females they claimed. A Kindred would no sooner allow another male to take his female sexually than he would cut off his own hand.

"I repeat," he growled, glaring at Rando. "Sarah is *mine*. I refuse to 'share' her in any way."

"Come," Chandra said, apparently still trying to defuse the situation. "We really must go. The Lord Magnate is still waiting."

"Go in yourself then," Rando sneered. "See how far you get without someone to introduce you."

"But Councilor Rando, you promised you would make the formal introduction of the Commander and his pair partner to the Lord Magnate yourself," Obglod protested. "You said—"

"That was *before* I had a broken wrist to deal with," Rando sniffed. "I must go seek medical attention at once. You are on your own."

And he spun on his heel and flounced off in a huff.

"Well, now I don't know what to do!" Obglod exclaimed. "Everything is ruined—just *ruined*. We cannot appear before The Lord Magnate without a formal introduction and since he's already expecting us, we will get into terrible trouble when we don't appear at all. Either way it will be an affront to the palace and we'll all be thrown to the *grike!*"

"No, we won't. Calm down, Minister dear." Chandra patted his stooped shoulder soothingly. "Everything will be all right."

"Why can't we introduce ourselves?" Sarah asked.

"What? Impossible!" Obglod sputtered. "You must be introduced by a person well known to The Lord Magnate."

"Don't *you* know him?" Sazar asked.

"Of *course* I do! But I am *sponsoring you.*" Obglod wrung his withered hands in exasperation. "You cannot be introduced by your sponsor—it simply isn't done?"

"What about Chandra?" Sarah asked. She turned to the Alquon girl. "Didn't you tell me The Lord Magnate gave you your start in society?"

"Well, yes…" Chandra preened nervously. "But the introduction is usually made by a male…"

"Is that a hard and fast law?" Sarah demanded.

"Well, no…" Chandra said slowly. "You know, I suppose I *could* introduce you. I was always a favorite of The Lord Magnate's." She drooped her voice to a low, confiding tone. "He even bred me once *and* gifted me with his seed. If it had given me a big belly, I would have remained in the palace as a concubine." She dropped her voice even lower, speaking to Sarah. "Don't tell anyone but I was rather glad it didn't. I love my partner Kendro too much to want to leave him."

"So you'll introduce us?" Sazar asked, impatient with the Alquon girl's gossip.

"Yes." Chandra nodded decisively. "Yes, I will." She took Minister Obglod, who was still protesting loudly, by the arm and tugged at him gently. "Come on Minister—everything is going to be all right. You won't end up in the belly of the *grike.* Not today, anyway."

* * * * *

Sazar kept Sarah protectively behind him although, as Chandra was leading the way, there was no one to run interference from behind as the Alquon girl had originally suggested. Sarah made sure to stay close to the big Kindred—she didn't want a repeat of the "greeting" she'd gotten from the oily little Councilor Rando. Her nipples were still sore from his vigorous tugging.

And it was clear from the way the men they passed in the palace halls were looking at her that they would have been happy to literally yank her chain. Sazar stared them all down, though—a low, warning growl rising in his throat so that males who came forward as though to speak to them or greet Sarah soon had second thoughts and wandered off in the other direction.

It's my breasts, Sarah thought unhappily. They were still causing her problems, just as they had at the Compound. She'd been able to hide them for years under the shapeless, baggy garments she'd worn but after Sister Hope had gotten pregnant, Father Caleb had turned his eyes to her and had noticed how enticing her larger than average bosom was.

I should get a boob job, Sarah thought savagely. *I should get a reduction done. Anything to stop this kind of attention! I hate it!*

You didn't mind it when Sazar was paying you attention, a little voice in her head remarked. *In fact, you loved it. And what was the deal with him going all caveman with that Rando guy?*

She could still remember the deep shiver that had gone through her entire body when she'd heard him claim her. *"Sarah is **mine**,"* he'd growled and that was the right word for it—*growled.* Like a wolf or a bear or some other predator prepared to fight to the death to protect its mate.

Sarah had never heard her new boss sound so animalistic—not even the night before when he'd been feeding on her blood. Did he actually feel something for her? Or was he just defending her honor?

Sarah wished she knew but she didn't have much time to ponder the situation. Before she knew it, they had come to another set of golden double doors—even finer than the front doors—with diamonds embedded in curling patterns on them.

Chandra gave their names to the guard standing at stiff attention outside and the doors swung open, admitting them to what Sarah supposed must be the throne room.

Inside it was just as grand as the rest of the palace with golden floors polished until Sarah could see her reflection in them and a large golden throne with diamonds and rubies embedded along the back and arms. A vaulted ceiling soared overhead, at least a hundred feet above them, and a massive chandelier which seemed to be made of liquid blobs of light hung from the central arch.

Despite the throne room's richness, there wasn't any other furniture besides the throne. The room was bare except for the incredibly tall, floor-to-ceiling windows which dominated the left side of it.

Standing by one of the windows, gazing thoughtfully out at the golden parkland beyond the palace, was a male who looked to be about twenty years younger than Minister Obglod.

Which still puts him somewhere in his sixties, Sarah thought.

But despite his age, the man—who must be The Lord Magnate—was tall and straight with a regal bearing and sharp aquamarine eyes when he turned to look at them. He was wearing a plain white robe and trousers with no trim, which contrasted oddly with the rich gold all around him.

There was something else that was odd about him, Sarah thought—he had no gill slits at all and his fingers, unlike the other

Alquons, weren't webbed. His skin was much closer to tan than it was to green, too. Why was he so different from his people?

Before she could ponder any more, he spoke.

"Well now, who is this?" he asked in a warm, friendly tone which Sarah didn't trust a bit.

"My Lord Magnate," Chandra began timidly. "It is I, Chandra, pair partner to Kendro of the thirteenth house of the Sketty-moors of Idd. Do you remember me?"

For a moment The Lord Magnate frowned, as though trying to place her. Then his aristocratic features broke into a sunny smile.

"Why Chandra my dear! Of course! You used to play in the palace halls as a child when your mother brought you to court. You were such a happy little girl."

But didn't Chandra say he "bred" her once? Sarah thought. Did that mean the Lord Magnate had known her as a child and still decided to have sex with her when she became an adult?

She tried to hide the look of disgust that wanted to form on her face. It reminded her entirely too much of the way Father Caleb operated back at the Compound. He sometimes didn't even wait for girls to reach legal age before declaring that they were ripe to become a "Bride of the Prophet."

"Yes, my Lord Magnate—that was me." Chandra came forward and kissed him on the cheek.

The Lord Magnate smiled warmly at her and tugged her breast chain, admiring her nipples. "Look at you—all grown up!"

Chandra bowed her head. "Yes, my Lord Magnate."

He snapped his fingers. "Wait, I remember now—you were almost one of my concubines!" He drew Chandra to him and cupped her breast in one hand, fondling her familiarly. "But somehow you got away."

"Not for lack of trying on your part, My Lord." Chandra giggled. "You did your very best to give me a big belly, as I recall."

"So I did." The Lord Magnate let her go with a final tweak of one pierced nipple and turned to the rest of them. "So, Obglod," he remarked. "Who have you brought me today?"

"These fine people are Commander Sazar of the Kindred and his lovely pair partner Sarah," Chandra said quickly. "Minister Obglod is sponsoring them and he asked me to make their introductions to you, my Lord Magnate."

"I see, well—it's a pleasure to meet you." The Lord Magnate nodded at them which appeared to be their cue to step forward.

They did so but Sarah made sure to stay behind Sazar, well out of fondling range. She didn't care what strange customs the Alquons had—the casual display she'd witnessed between Chandra and the Magnate, who was old enough to be her grandfather, had sickened her.

More and more the Alquon ruler reminded her of Father Caleb…of the way he would brush against her in the halls and try to find reasons to touch her inappropriately. She could never bend over if she thought he was anywhere around—he would be sure to snake a liver-spotted hand up her skirt. Or he would pin her to the desk and grind against her, telling her it was her duty to help "Slake the Prophet's Needs" now that Sister Hope was no longer able to do her duty…

"My Lord Magnate, it is a pleasure to meet you," Sazar said smoothly, interrupting her distressing memories. Apparently he had regained his diplomatic composure because he looked cool and collected as he bowed to the Alquon leader.

"Commander Sazar, how very good to meet you. We have

heard of the Kindred, I believe. Genetic traders, aren't you?"

"Indeed yes, My Lord Magnate." Sazar nodded. "I have come to see if your people might consider a genetic trade with mine. And I am also seeking new weapons technology to help in our war against the Hive—a race of insectile beings who threaten our very existence at the moment."

"Well, I'm afraid we won't be much help in a fight against insects," The Lord Magnate remarked. "We have none since our world became completely submerged." He chuckled. "It's one of the benefits of having a completely underwater society."

"I can see how that would be so," Sazar said dryly.

"But as for a genetic trade…let me think on it." The Lord Magnate rubbed his chin thoughtfully. "I must get to know you a bit better before I can determine if our peoples would get along."

"Of course—such decisions cannot be rushed." Sazar nodded.

"And I want to get to know this enchanting creature as well—much better." To her dismay, Sarah saw The Lord Magnate was eyeing her hungrily. "Come out my dear," he said, beckoning to her. "Don't be shy."

A low growl began to rise in Sazar's throat and Chandra, obviously seeing the problem, hurried to The Lord Magnate's elbow.

"Sarah and Commander Sazar are very close, My Lord," she said softly. "And their culture does not allow the, uh, sharing of females. In fact," she added hastily as The Lord Magnate began to reach for Sarah's breast chain. "Even our forms of greeting are against their cultural dictates."

"Is that right?" The Lord Magnate raised one pure white eyebrow which wasn't kelpy at all, Sarah thought. In fact, his hair looked like, well…*hair* instead of some kind of sea plant. She wondered again why he was different.

"I'm afraid so, My Lord," Chandra said humbly. "There was a...slight misunderstanding with Councilor Rando on the way in so I wanted to be certain My Lord knew the customs of our guests."

"Indeed. We must at all costs treat our guests with respect," The Lord Magnate said but Sarah couldn't help noticing his jewel-toned eyes were trained on her bare breasts. Having him look at her like that made her skin crawl—it was exactly the way Father Caleb had eyed her after Sister Hope had gotten pregnant.

"You have a beautiful palace," she said, trying to shift his attention away from her exposed chest. "I don't think I've ever seen so much gold in one place in my life."

"Ah yes—that was the wish of my sire." The Lord Magnate lifted his eyes eloquently to the vaulted ceiling. "One cannot speak ill of the dead, of course, but I will say his tastes were rather...extreme. I am a simple male myself." He motioned at his unadorned white robe and trousers.

"Maybe you ought to let your wife—er—pair partner redecorate," Sarah suggested.

For some reason her words caused Minister Obglod to exclaim and Chandra to blush.

"I'm sorry," she said uncertainly. "Have I said something wrong or offensive?"

"Oh no, my dear—not at all." The Lord Magnate laughed. "It is just that, I alone among all the people of Alquon Ultrea have no pair partner."

"And why is that, may I ask My Lord Magnate?" Sazar asked. His deep voice was still close to a growl—clearly he didn't like the way the Alquon leader was still staring at Sarah's chest.

"You may certainly ask, my dear Commander." The Lord

Magnate nodded genially. "It has to do with the sad history of our race. You see, we used to look…well, very much like *you*, my dear," he said, turning to Sarah. "You have the most lovely skin I've ever seen—such a creamy ivory."

"Um…thank you," Sarah murmured, feeling more creeped out than ever.

"But when it first became clear that our entire planet would be submerged in the waters of our ocean, our scientists were forced to genetically alter 99% of our population to enable them to survive in water as well as in air. The other 1%—my ancestors and the Lord Magnates who came before me—were spared this alteration and put into the first glass submersible underwater air habitat. That, of course, was the forgoer to our modern pressurized glass enclosures which keep our entire city of Idd dry.

"We soon had the technology to keep everyone dry but alas, once our population was altered, it was impossible to go back and undo what had been done." The Lord Magnate made a sad face. "And so, as one with superior genes, it is my responsibility to spread my seed as widely as possible—to dilute the genetically altered blood and try to get our people back to normal."

"That's…very sad for you," Sarah said, trying to sound sincere. But inwardly her skin was crawling. *It's just like Father Caleb all over again!* she thought. *Thinking it's his right to sleep with any woman he wants because he's somehow superior!*

The thought made her sick but she did her very best to keep the emotion off her face.

The Alquon ruler sighed heavily. "It is a difficult life and I am sorry not to have a pair partner at my side as all the rest of my people do, but as Lord Magnate I cannot shirk my duty."

"He certainly doesn't shirk it, either," Chandra giggled.

"Oh, are you remembering how I bred you again, my dear Chandra?" The melancholy look left the Lord Magnate's handsome face and he chuckled.

"It was quite vigorous, as I recall." She fluttered her eyelashes at him and thrust out her breasts enticingly.

"Well, speaking of breeding, can I count on your attendance at our annual Breeding Ball tomorrow night?" The Lord Magnate asked, turning to Sazar.

"Of course they'll come!" Chandra exclaimed. "Why, we already got Sarah an outfit and some breeding panties!"

"That's excellent then—excellent." The Lord Magnate nodded and clapped his hands together in approval.

"We would be pleased to attend but I would appreciate knowing more about what exactly will be required of us," Sazar said carefully. "What exactly takes place at this, er, breeding ball?"

"Well, breeding of course, Commander Sazar!" Chandra exclaimed, giggling.

"It is the time when all of the blood rolls are called," Minister Obglod said, frowning. "When those of the purest blood are put together for breeding purposes, hoping to spread the Lord Magnate's pure bloodlines throughout the population and rid ourselves of the genetic taint we were forced to take so many years ago."

"So...we would not be expected to participate?" Sazar asked, raising an eyebrow.

"Really! To be invited to the Breeding Ball and to refuse the honor of participating? That is just *outrageous*—" Minister Obglod began but The Lord Magnate held up a hand for silence.

"Mix your blood with ours? A most intriguing concept," he remarked. "The idea requires careful consideration—as does the idea of a genetic trade. But no, at this particular ball you would not be required to interbreed with my people."

"Then we accept your invitation with our thanks," Sazar said formally. "And I hope that our peoples can come to an understanding soon. The Kindred are always interested in trading with intelligent sentient races."

"Of course, it will be my first item of consideration and I will give you my decision soon. In the meantime, please enjoy your time in our beautiful city." The Lord Magnate inclined his head to Minister Obglod. "I hope, Obglod, that you've put them in only the finest guest quarters?"

"But of course, My Lord Magnate." Obglod bowed obsequiously. "They are in the Courtly Row, close to the First Form *tuve* station."

"Very good. Only the breast…er, *best* for our esteemed guests from another galaxy."

As he spoke, The Lord Magnate's eyes found Sarah's breasts again and there was a hungry look on his face that made her distinctly uncomfortable. She thought she had never wanted so badly to cover herself in her life but she forced herself to keep her arms by her sides, though her hands curled into fists with the effort of not shielding herself from his view.

Sazar seemed to see where the Alquon ruler was looking because he stepped pointedly between Sarah and The Lord Magnate, blocking the other male's view.

"We thank you again," he said formally. "And we will see you tomorrow evening for the ball."

"Until then." But the genial smile on The Lord Magnate's kindly face didn't quite reach his eyes. Sarah wondered if he was irritated that Sazar was blocking his view of her breasts. If so, he didn't say anything about it. He simply nodded and waited while all of them bowed before turning back to his place at the window.

*****

"Wasn't that exciting?" Chandra squealed when they were safely outside the throne room with the double golden doors closed behind them.

"Extremely," Sazar said dryly. In fact, the encounter had been a bit *too* exciting for him—he'd been working hard to keep his temper from boiling over during the entire interview. Though the Alquon leader hadn't been nearly as overt in his attentions to Sarah as Councilor Rando had been, Sazar hadn't liked the way The Lord Magnate had been eyeing his little human assistant one bit.

She isn't safe here unless I'm with her, he thought, frowning. *Her beauty and her breasts attract too much attention.*

Silently he promised himself he would never be parted from her as long as they were on Alquon Ultrea. He had vowed to see to her safety and he didn't intend to break that vow.

Oh, your vow? Is that the only reason you want to keep her near you? whispered a sarcastic little voice in the back of his head. *Or could it be that you're beginning to have feelings for the little human?*

Sazar told himself it was impossible and even if he *was* starting to have feelings for her he had to keep them strictly private. Still, he knew himself—he had no interest in females until the right one came along. When that happened, he fell hard and fast. He had met Malinda and had asked her to be his mate only two days later. And besides his late mate, he had never had such protective instincts for any female as he felt for Sarah now.

I really think I was going into Rage when that slimy little bastard

Rando touched her, he thought, casting a sidelong glance at Sarah. Rage was a state of intense, berserker fury a Kindred warrior went into when he thought his chosen female was threatened. That had never happened to Sazar before—not even when he had been mated to Malinda.

What was happening to him? What was he becoming?

"Well, I am *completely* exhausted by the fracas we've been through today," Minister Obglod announced when they exited the palace. "Chandra dear, would you be kind enough to conduct Commander Sazar and his pair partner to their quarters?"

"Of course Minister! I'm always happy to help." She dropped an affectionate kiss on the old male's withered green cheek.

"Thank you, Chandra. You're a good girl." Absently, Obglod tugged at her breast chain, making her giggle with apparent delight. He turned to Sazar. "See that you're at the palace dressed in proper breeding attire tomorrow evening in time for the ball and kindly behave yourselves in the interim. Remember, I am your sponsor so anything you do reflects directly on me."

It was an insulting speech to direct at a grown male—especially a foreign diplomat—but Sazar only nodded politely. It occurred to him that he perhaps hadn't been acting as diplomatically as he normally would have. His protective instincts toward Sarah seemed to have squeezed out the tactful impulses which normally ruled his dealings with a new culture.

"Come on you two," Chandra said, taking Sarah by the arm. "It's getting late—let's take the *tuve* to your room. You're just going to *love* the Courtly Row. I know the manager there—he's a darling."

"Will there be anything to eat there?" Sarah asked hesitantly. "I don't mean to be a bother but we haven't eaten since before we left our own galaxy and that was *hours* ago."

"Oh, you poor dear! You must be positively *starving*," Chandra exclaimed. "Yes, of course we'll feed you. You're going to be on the Minister's expense account while you're here and I can recommend a *lovely* little eatery not far from your accommodations. It has the *freshest* seafood around."

"That sounds delicious," Sarah said, smiling.

"Yes, some food would be good," Sazar said. *Some fresh blood would be even better,* the voice of the Blood Hunger growled at him but he ignored it. Better to satisfy his hunger for food and try not to think about his thirst for blood, which could not be quenched for at least a week anyway. If only the lights in the main tunnels weren't so damnably *bright*.

"You've been so good to us, Chandra," Sarah said, drawing him out of his thoughts. "Thank you so much for all you've done today. Commander Sazar and I really appreciate all your help."

The Alquon girl blushed with pleasure but waved off the compliment.

"Oh, it's nothing really! I just love to help out the Minister. He's my mother's brother once removed and family is important to us here."

"I can see that it is but Sarah is right—we have much to thank you for," Sazar said, nodding gratefully at Chandra.

The Alquon girl affected the outward appearance of being what humans would call "ditzy" but in reality, she had proved to be a much more competent guide and host than Minister Obglod had been. He was grateful for the assistance she had offered them, even though he really could have done with less intimate information about her private life.

"You are more than welcome." Chandra smiled at him and Sarah both. "Come on then—this way to the *tuve* and your seafood supper," she exclaimed perkily and led them into the brilliant lights of the main tunnel once more.

Chapter Twelve

The Courtly Row was off the main tunnel and was indeed a row of large glass bubbles, each housing a separate accommodation. Sarah and Sazar had been given one on the very end which seemed slightly larger than the rest and was as brilliantly lit as the outside tunnel.

The first thing Sazar did when they got in and shut the door—which appeared to be both air and water-tight—was to find the lighting controls and turn the illumination down to low.

Sarah breathed a sigh of relief as soon as the relentless brilliance dimmed.

"Whew—they sure do like to keep it bright, don't they?" she remarked.

"Yes, unfortunately," Sazar growled. Despite the dark light blockers he wore, he was looking a little peaky, Sarah thought. She wondered again if he needed blood. Should she ask him? But the thought of walking boldly up to him and offering herself as she had the night before was now considerably complicated by the outfit she was wearing.

I don't know why you're hesitating to offer him your blood just because your boobs are out, whispered a sarcastic little voice in her head. *After all, you're going to have to ask him to suck them again eventually if you want to get the nipple jewelry off.*

But Sarah didn't want to think about that—it was too

embarrassing. Too…stimulating. And with the honey pearls still rotating and vibrating between her legs, she didn't need anything else to get her going. She wondered if now would be a good time to try and turn the darn things off—surely there must be a way! She would just slip into the bathroom, if they had one here, and do her best to find the off switch before they went to dinner.

She looked around, searching for a restroom and ended up studying the room itself instead.

Now that her eyes were adjusted to the dimness, she saw that the bedroom walls were clear glass but mostly obscured by hangings and tapestries depicting scenes of Alquon people both swimming and walking. Some of the water scenes made it look like they had pets with them—crab and lobster like creatures that swam along beside them on long leashes.

Sarah studied them with interest—she'd never thought of having a crustacean for a pet although she supposed it would be much more practical than a dog or a cat if you lived in the water half the time.

The tapestries and wall hangings were gorgeous and interesting but Sarah couldn't help wondering why the Alquons would block out the view of the ocean, which she could catch little tantalizing glimpses of through the walls now that the lights were dimmed. She saw multicolored plants swaying in the currents and schools of jewel-bright fish darting around rocks and coral as well as some creatures that didn't look much like fish at all. Sarah saw one that looked a little like a flying squirrel but covered in scales and another that looked like a cross between a sea turtle and a giraffe.

She wished she could get a better look at all this but the walls and ceiling were too obstructed. Well, maybe she could get a better view from the bathroom when she found it.

There was a large, round bed in the center of the room covered by a satiny aquamarine coverlet that seemed to ripple like waves in the sea. Beside it was a tall white set of double doors that Sarah at first thought must lead to the bathroom she was seeking. But when she pulled it open, she found it was a kind of free-standing closet.

Inside someone had thoughtfully placed her pink carry-all cube and Sazar's luggage as well. Her anonymous benefactor had also hung her gold lame' outfit so it wouldn't wrinkle. On a shelf beside it were the black atomizer bottle containing the compound for applying her nipple jewelry, a small box with more float dots in it, and a pair of strange looking, stretchy gold lame' panties which appeared to match her ball outfit. Sarah picked them up and studied them with a frown.

What's the deal with these things? They have too many holes. One for the waist and two for the legs but…what's this last one for?

"Is everything all right?" Sazar asked from right behind her.

"What? Oh, yes—yes just fine. I…I was looking for the, uh, the bathroom but I think this is just the closet." Blushing, Sarah hastily pushed the gold lame' panties with their extra hole back onto the shelf and shut the doors.

"I think it's over there—behind that large tapestry." Sazar nodded his head at a colorful depiction of Alquons playing what appeared to be some sort of underwater game using giant chess-type pieces as large as themselves on a green and blue and red checkered board.

"Oh, thank you." Sarah nodded gratefully and ducked behind the tapestry. Sure enough, she found a small door leading into an even smaller glass bubble which connected to the main room bubble.

Now this is more like it! she thought as she looked around. The bathroom's walls were clear and unobstructed by hangings or pictures. She could see right out into the lovely depths of the ocean.

She didn't admire the darting fish and swaying plants for long though, because the honey pearls were really driving her crazy. She reached into her split skirt and felt along the fine, silky ribbon-like fabric which made up the sides and back of the buzzing panties but nothing but smooth material met her fingers. All right—maybe the switch was somewhere on the double strand of black and green pearls themselves?

But try as she might, Sarah couldn't find any way to turn the pearls off there either. She shifted her hips and tried wiggling out of the annoying undergarment but it was on her too tightly. She was getting desperate—maybe she ought to tear the panties off? Snap one of the sides and slither out that way?

But no matter how she tugged, the fabric stayed firm. Sarah considered trying to break the strand of pearls instead but they seemed really expensive. What if Sazar had to pay the equivalent of thousands of dollars for them?

Reluctantly Sarah admitted defeat…for now. She would try again before bed to get out of the vibrating pearl panties. If she still couldn't find the switch to loosen and deactivate them, she would have no choice but to break them after all.

Sighing, she started to leave the bathroom. But then her curiosity got the better of her—she couldn't go before examining the Alquon facilities.

There was something that might have been a shower—although the nozzle looked much too low and the bathtub was much too deep with very high sides. How would you even climb into the strange contraption? And once you were in, how would you get out again, Sarah wondered. It also had buttons instead of any kind of knobs—*lots* of them in several different colors. Weird.

Beside the strange shower was something vaguely resembling a toilet—at least, it appeared to be a low black bench with a lid. Sarah wondered if the Alquons flushed their waste right out into the open ocean. She hoped not since many of them spent a lot of time swimming out there. It wouldn't be very agreeable to swim outside of Idd if everyone who lived there was flushing their toilet into the sea around the city.

Curiously, she opened the lid and peered in. She jumped back with a frightened gasp, nearly falling ass-first into the shower. About a foot and a half down, where an Earth toilet would have held water, was a writhing mass of long, slender black bodies which glistened in the dim light.

"Sarah? Are you all right?" Suddenly Sazar was at the door.

"I...there..." Sarah tried to clear her throat and found she could barely get the words out. "There are snakes in the toilet!" she managed at last. "A *lot* of them."

"What? I'm coming in."

Sarah hadn't locked the door—mainly because she hadn't seen any way to lock it—so the big Kindred was able to push his way into the bathroom easily.

"*What* did you say was in the waste facility?" he asked, raising an eyebrow at her.

"Snakes," Sarah whispered. "Or eels or *something*. I know it sounds crazy but there is something alive down inside the toilet—or some*things*. Look for yourself."

Sazar opened the lid and gave a low curse when a slender, snake-like head raised up to look at him with unblinking yellow eyes. He slammed the lid back down and frowned.

"Some sort of infestation. I'll go and tell the manager of the property at once. Are you…"

He said something else but Sarah barely heard him—she was too busy looking at the scene outside the clear glass wall of the bathroom bubble in utter dismay and terror.

There was a creature outside—a *huge* creature with long red and black tentacles and an eye as big as her head. Sarah knew because that eye was currently pointed right at her. It looked like an undersea monster—a kraken or a giant squid or something.

The kraken, or whatever it was, was staring in at her like a little girl might stare into the window of a doll house—that was how great the size discrepancy was.

But I don't know any little girls with dinner-plate sized eyes and eighty-foot-long tentacles, Sarah thought numbly. The tentacles were pulsing with light now—red dots glowing up and down their length—strobing like a neon sign in a bar window.

"Sazar." Had Sarah thought her voice was hoarse before? Now it came out in a rusty squeak, like a hinge that needed oiling. She cleared her throat and tried again. "Sazar…outside…"

"Outside what?" he asked impatiently.

"I…I think we ought to get out of here," Sarah whispered. "I…we…"

His eyes finally lifted to where she was looking and he gave a low curse.

"Seven Hells, what *is* that monster?"

"I don't know," Sarah moaned softly. "But it's *looking* at me. Sazar, let's get out of here—please?"

"At once. Out—now—move!" He grabbed her by the arm and

pushed her out the door ahead of him.

Once she was out of the bathroom Sarah's heart slowed a little but she still didn't feel safe. That thing outside the bathroom had been so huge it would certainly be able to encompass their bedroom bubble easily with its tentacles. They had to get out of there!

Sazar seemed to feel the same way because he guided her quickly to the room door. But when he opened it, their way was blocked. The round-faced manager of the Courtly Row whom Chandra had introduced as "Blorg" before she had left them, was standing there looking as though he had been about to knock.

"Out of the way," Sazar growled. "We must get out of this room at *once*."

"What? What's wrong?" Blorg had very prominent gill slits and they flapped open now in apparent distress, making him look like his neck was growing bizarre green wings.

"What's wrong?" Sarah fought back a hysterical laugh. "Oh nothing if you don't count the snakes in the toilet and the giant Kraken about to break into the bathroom."

"The which and the what?" Blorg raised kelpy green eyebrows in confusion.

"There appears to be some kind of large sea creature with long tentacles and huge eyes about to break in to the fresher facilities," Sazar told the manager.

"Oh, you mean you saw a *tizen?*"

"A what?" Sarah asked.

"A *tizen*. They're big but they're peaceful. And real curious. Here, let's go have a look."

He walked without fear back into the bed chamber they'd been given. Sazar followed him and after a minute of not hearing any sounds of screaming or glass shattering, Sarah followed as well.

"Yep—just a *tizen*," Blorg was saying as he tapped on the glass wall of the bathroom, right where the giant eye was still peering in. "And I see the problem—you got the lights set too low. Either turn 'em all the way up where they're s'posed to be or turn the lights off completely. Anything else makes these big fellahs curious."

He tapped the glass again and the huge eye slowly blinked, the lid coming down like a pull shade over a lighted window. Then the *tizen* swam swiftly off as suddenly as it had come, leaving nothing but a trail of bubbles in its wake.

"See?" Blorg said. "Ain't no harm in a *tizen*. They're just nosey."

"All right, so maybe we overreacted about that," Sarah said, feeling irritated. At least now she knew why the Alquons kept their clear glass walls obscured—they didn't want nosey giant squids staring in at them! "But what about the snakes in the toilet?"

Blorg walked over to the black rectangular bench, lifted the lid, and peered in casually. Several long, slick, black heads rose up to regard him but he didn't slam the lid down as Sarah had done or curse like Sazar. He just shrugged his shoulders and looked at them.

"Is this what you were getting all upset about?"

"Well *yes* we were upset about it!" Sarah exclaimed. "I mean, the toilet is *full* of those things."

"Those are just *yeechees*," Blorg said patiently. "They eat up the waste you send down to them and don't make hardly any of their own. It's a real useful arrangement. They get fed and we don't pollute our oceans."

"So...so I'm supposed to sit there and...and do my business right down on their heads?" Sarah could hardly believe it. Surely

Blorg was joking!

But the heavy-set Alquon was nodding his head.

"Now you got the idea, little lady."

"But...but what if they bite me?" Sarah asked.

"Oh *yeechees* don't bite."

"Good!" Sarah felt a wave of relief.

Of course, they might nip you from time to time if they get impatient."

"What?" Sarah did *not* like the idea of being "nipped" in any area that was exposed while she was using the bathroom.

"Yeah." Blorg shrugged casually. "Best advice I can give you is don't sit down until you're really ready to go—you know? The faster you do your business, the happier the *yeechees* will be and the less likely you are to get nipped."

"But I don't want to be nipped *at all,*" Sarah protested.

The manager shrugged again.

"Better do your business fast then, little lady." He straightened up. "Now, is there anything else I can help you folks with?"

Sarah thought it might have been a good idea to ask how to use the high-sided, insanely complicated looking shower but Sazar spoke before she could say anything.

"We are fine now. Thank you for your assistance."

"All right then. Anything else, just let me know." He gave them a friendly grin and then, gill slits still flapping, left the room.

Sarah looked at Sazar.

"I don't know about you, but I need to get out of here."

"Agreed." He nodded. "But before we go...this is the first moment we've had alone and I need to apologize to you, Sarah."

"Apologize? Why?" Sarah was mystified. "What for?"

"For what you've been through." He cleared his throat and gestured at her exposed breasts. "I had…no idea what would be involved in this mission or I would not have asked you to come with me."

"Oh…" Sarah fought the urge to cover herself. She was getting used to being exposed but it still wasn't comfortable. "I…I have to admit being dressed this way—or undressed—isn't my idea of a good time. But you couldn't have known about the Alquons' weird fashion sense or the fact that they have snakes in their toilets and monster squids looking in through their walls."

The corners of Sazar's mouth twitched.

"No. If I had known all that, I am not sure I would have come myself."

"Let's go get something to eat," Sarah suggested. "Everything will look better on a full stomach."

"Let's hope you're right." Sazar sighed. "Do you wish to try the seafood eatery Chandra recommended?"

"Oh yes, I'm a Florida girl. I love seafood."

Sarah could already feel her stomach growling at the thought. She wondered if the Alquons had anything resembling coconut battered fried shrimp? She certainly hoped so although even if they didn't, she thought she would probably eat anything that was put in front of her. She was *starving*.

"Come on," she said, daring to take Sazar's hand. "Let's go."

Chapter Thirteen

The restaurant was one of the strangest Sarah had ever seen. Not so much in the seating arrangements—there were rows of dark booths along two long walls which looked like they could have been pulled out of any chain restaurant on Earth. But running across the tables of the booths and indeed, through the booths themselves, was what looked like a single long, narrow fish tank.

The tank was only about a foot and a half wide but it ran the entire length of the restaurant on each side. It appeared to be open on both ends so that it connected through the walls of the restaurant—which was called Fresh Catch—to the open ocean beyond.

Sarah watched with interest as various fish and other creatures swam through the long tank from one side of the restaurant to the other. Did Fresh Catch lure them in using bait somehow so that the patrons had a constant view of an ever-changing aquarium from their own seats? It was an interesting idea.

The waiter, upon hearing they were guests of Minister Obglod from a different galaxy, immediately led them to a seat of honor—the most centrally located booth in the restaurant. Sarah wished he hadn't—she felt even more put on display by the way every other patron of Fresh Catch was staring at them. But she tried to put it out of her mind and concentrate on the hope that there might be something like fried shrimp on the menu.

"Now then, welcome esteemed and honored foreign guests. I'm Toodles and I'll be seeing to your every need this evening." Their waiter smiled widely at them. He was a thin Alquon male with deep green skin and purple mottling over his eyes which made him look strangely as though he was wearing glasses. "Have you ever dined with us before?"

"Never," Sazar said and Sarah added,

"I hope you can teach us to use all these, uh, utensils."

She motioned to the wide array of strange instruments which were laid in neat rows on the table, where a knife, fork, and spoon would be on Earth.

"Oh, these are your fishing tools," Toodles the waiter explained brightly. "At Fresh Catch we promise you will have the freshest seafood experience anywhere in Idd. And you will—provided you're a reasonably good fisherman!" He laughed at his own joke.

"So…we're supposed to catch our own dinner?" Sarah looked at the tools on the table in dismay. There were sharp metal hooks, a long-handled net, and something that looked like a miniature harpoon as well as a shiny pair of metal tongs.

"Catch it *and* cook it," Toodles said, nodding. "Here is your cooking medium."

He pressed a button on the end of the booth and a round pot filled with some kind of bubbling dark blue liquid suddenly rose up into the middle of the table.

"Is that some kind of oil?" Sarah asked, quickly covering her exposed breasts. She didn't want her nipples to be flash fried by popping oil droplets!

"Oh, no! This is our own private broth recipe here at Fresh Catch—anything you cook in it will be *delicious,* guaranteed." Toodles grinned toothily at them.

"So…we just start fishing and throw what we catch in the pot?" Sazar asked.

"I guess so," Sarah murmured, picking up the long thin net and wondering if she could catch anything in it. It seemed better than spearing a live fish with the harpoon looking thing—more humane. Although if she caught something live in the net and threw it in the pot, she would be boiling it alive. Either way the coming meal seemed less and less appealing.

"Oh, you can't catch your meal without some help!" Toodles looked shocked. "Let me fetch your *catchems.*"

He disappeared for a moment and returned with a box which reminded Sarah of a small pet carrier. And indeed, when he opened the wire door, four creatures about the size of large mice or hamsters scuttled out.

But these were no hamsters, Sarah saw with a shiver. They looked to be part crab and part lobster—at least their bodies did. Their faces looked strangely cat-like with large luminous eyes, pointed ears, and long whiskers. They were a dull, gleaming silver all over except for the glowing eyes which appeared greenish-blue.

"What are those?" Sazar asked flatly as two of the creatures sidled over to him and stood at attention by his plate.

"Why, the *catchems,* of course. Some people call them "silver fingers"—because of their coloration, you know. Here at Fresh Catch we pride ourselves on having the best trained *catchems* in Idd."

"How…how exactly do they work? I mean, what are they trained to do?" Sarah was keeping her distance from the two crab-cat creatures who had scuttled over to stand by her own plate. They seemed to be staring up at her with interest in their huge blue-green eyes and she wondered exactly how intelligent they were…and how much it would hurt to be pinched by one of their disproportionately large claws.

Inwardly she winced. A hot pot full of boiling liquid and crab creatures crawling on the table—could she have *picked* a worse time to be basically topless with her large breasts out and vulnerable? She wished she had tiny breasts, like most of the Alquon women she saw in the booths around them. Many of them were almost flat—in no danger from the *catchems* or the boiling pot of broth. Sarah's breasts, on the other hand, were large enough that if she leaned forward even a little they would rest right on the table. Not good.

"They're very well trained," Toodles repeated. "Just tap them on the back with your wand…" he picked up a long silver knitting-needle looking instrument, "And they'll go to the tank and catch you some delicious, fresh seafood."

"If the, uh, *catchems* do all the work, what are all these items for?" Sarah wanted to know, pointing at the various implements on the table.

"Oh, you can have the *catchems* help as much or as little as you like," Toodles explained. "Tap them once to simply have them hold an item for you to spear or net yourself. Tap twice if you want them to dispatch the creature so you can scoop it up in your net. Or, if you're feeling lazy, tap them three times to have them catch, kill, and bring your fresh, delicious catch directly to the pot for you."

That sounded like the way to go for Sarah but she still had questions.

"What about when we're full?"

"Just wave your hand in the air and I'll come take them away. No muss, no fuss. Any other questions?" Toodles was already eyeing a large, rowdy party of Alquons who had just come in the door. He was clearly eager to get away.

"I think that about covers it," Sazar said dryly.

"Good! Well, enjoy your meal!" And the waiter hurried away to seat the large party.

"Well…this isn't exactly what I pictured when Chandra said this place had fresh seafood but you have to admit it's different," Sarah remarked.

"Different indeed," Sazar growled. "This seems like a lot of work for a meal of dubious quality. Do you want to go someplace else?"

"I don't see how we can," Sarah objected. "We already let it be known we're being sponsored by Minister Obglod and, uh, Toodles put us where everyone can see us. We're representing the Kindred and Earth, right?"

"We are." Sazar nodded. "But if you're uncomfortable we will leave. I see no reason to put you through any more traumatic experiences today."

Sarah was touched that he was putting her feelings before the mission but it only made her more determined not to give up.

"No," she said lifting her chin. "I'm fine—I like the kind of place where you cook your own food. Before my parents joined The Brotherhood, we used to go to the Melting Pot all the time for special occasions."

"The Melting Pot? What's that?" He frowned.

"A fondue restaurant. Basically you have a pot on the table—a little like this…" She indicated the bubbling pot of dark blue liquid. "And you dip things in it or cook things in it. Like, they bring you a big pot of cheese and you dip bread and apples and carrots into it. And for the second course they bring you meat and veggies and you can either cook in broth or oil. And the third" She closed her eyes briefly, remembering. "Oh God, the third is the *best*."

"What is it?" Sazar sounded really interested.

"Chocolate—a big pot of melted chocolate." The memory made Sarah's mouth water. "It's *sooo* good. You can pick white or dark or milk chocolate or a mixture and they give you fruit and brownies and pound cake to dip in it…" She trailed off. "Well, I'm going on about it too much. I just really loved to go there when I was younger."

"Before you went to live at the Compound," Sazar said quietly.

"Yes," Sarah murmured. "Before that." She wondered if he would push for more information. Part of her wanted to keep her past at the Compound a secret but part of her wanted—no *needed*—to talk about it. She hadn't felt that way before but somehow she did now.

The big Kindred only smiled though.

"Well, I think this Pot that Melts sounds delightful."

"Melting Pot," Sarah corrected. "And it is! It's really nice. We'll have to go there sometime when we get back to Earth." She bit her lip, realizing what she was saying. "Uh, I mean, if you want to," she finished lamely.

Oh my God, screamed a little voice in her head. *Did you just ask your boss out on a date? Did you really?*

But Sazar's smile hadn't faded. Sarah remembered thinking that he would be handsome if he smiled and damn, had she been right! The sharp-edged features were softened by his expression and his pale eyes seemed warmer too.

"I'd like that," he said quietly. "It would be nice to go out together when we're not on a mission."

Sarah's heart seemed to miss a beat. Could she really believe that her gorgeous Kindred boss wanted to go out with her?

"I...I'd like it too," she nearly whispered. "They, uh, have a special Christmas menu—if we get back in time." This made her remember she was supposed to ask about Tsandor spending Christmas with Sophie and her family but somehow now didn't seem the right time.

"Then we'll go," Sazar murmured. He reached across the table and took her hand in his large, warm one. "I look forward to it."

"All right..." Sarah felt she was in danger of falling into those pale eyes of his and never getting out again. If she didn't do something soon she was going to start babbling. "Um...I guess we should, uh, start fishing," she murmured, tearing her gaze from his.

"I guess so." Sazar sighed and picked up the knitting-needle type implement which Toodles had called a "wand." Carefully, he tapped each of the *catchems* three times on their dull silver shelled backs.

At once the two hamster-sized creatures scuttled over to the narrow glass tank, easily scaled the steep sides, and plopped into the running water.

The bottom of the tank was filled with grayish shells and pebbles and the *catchems* blended into their surroundings beautifully, their dull silver carapaces offering natural camouflage.

Soon a bright red fish about as big as Sarah's palm swam through the long narrow aquarium. The *catchems* crouched at the bottom of the tank and the moment it swam into range, their big claws shot out to catch it.

One *catchem* caught the fish by its tail and held it, struggling in the swift current. The other *catchem* cut off its head with a quick snip of its silver claws and shoved it, bulging eyes, gaping mouth and all, into its own kittenish maw. Its long whiskers twitched while it chewed.

The first *catchem* now cut off the tail and ate it, then ripped open the fish's belly and pulled out the entrails which the two creatures shared.

"Wow," Sarah remarked uneasily. "Their claws must be *really* sharp."

"Indeed," Sazar murmured. "I guess now we know why they are so well trained—they get a bit of everything they catch for their own dinner."

They watched as the *catchems* climbed out of the tank, bringing the fish's decapitated and gutted body with them. Sarah remembered Toodles saying they would even throw it in the pot and wondered how they would reach it. The metal surface of the boiling pot was too hot to climb and it was almost twice as tall as the diminutive *catchems*.

But she hadn't counted on their ingenuity. Holding the dead fish, one *catchem* climbed up onto the other one's back. The one on the bottom crawled as close as was apparently comfortable to the pot and the one on the top tossed the fish into the bubbling liquid. Then the two of them scuttled back to Sazar's plate and looked up at him expectantly.

"Wow," Sarah breathed, amazed at the little creatures. "I can't believe they just did all that. They must be really smart."

At her words, the *catchems* standing by her own plate got a little closer and started making a low humming sound.

Wait a minute—they're not humming, Sarah realized. *They're purring. Do they know I just called them smart? Or is this the way they beg to go catch fish?*

Whatever the reason, she found her unease at the cat-crabs was considerably eased. She didn't care much for the crab part of them but their kitten-like faces really *were* adorable. Sarah had always been a cat person and she especially loved kittens.

"Hey, little fellas," she murmured, daring to use one fingertip to stroke the fuzzy tops of one of the *catchems'* heads. "Hey, you're kinda cute, aren't you? In a weird half-crab kind of way."

"I'm not sure you ought to do that," Sazar remarked. He had already sent his own *catchems* back for another fish. "They're not meant to be pets, I don't think."

"But they *like* being petted, don't you fellas?" Sarah crooned, stroking the head of the other one. It sniffed her and rubbed its cheek against her finger, exactly like a cat. "Aww…see? He really likes me. He—oh!"

Her words ended in a gasp because the *catchem* she'd been petting suddenly skittered up her hand and onto her arm. From there it ran right up to perch on her shoulder and rubbed its furry cheek against Sarah's own.

"Clearly he does indeed like you," Sazar remarked dryly. "I think you have a new friend, Sarah."

"This isn't funny," Sarah exclaimed, seeing that he was laughing at her—or smiling anyway. "I don't think—oh!" she gasped because the other *catchem* had run up her other arm and was sitting on her other shoulder.

"Well, you've certainly charmed them," Sazar said.

"I didn't *mean* to though," Sarah wailed. She had been all right with petting the little creatures but she didn't know how she felt about having them sitting on her shoulders, purring in her ears. Their faces might be as cute as kittens but their bodies were still chitinous and crab-like. She could feel their little claws pricking her bare skin sharply.

"Well, I don't think—" Sazar began but just then, his own two *catchems*, who had been hauling another decapitated fish to the pot, suddenly abandoned the piscine carcass and also ran up to Sarah.

"Oh no," Sarah told them. "No, not you guys too! You're *wet!*"

But her protest was to no avail. Sazar's *catchems* also ran up her arms and since her shoulders were taken, these perched on the top slopes of her breasts like bizarre silver jewelry.

Sarah was painfully aware that the sharp-clawed creatures were dangerously close to her exposed nipples. What would she do if they decided they were hungry and her enticing pink peaks looked like food?

"Sazar," she moaned softly. "Sazar, I *really* don't like this."

"I don't blame you. All right—that's enough," he said, reaching out to pluck the *catchems* from her breasts. He put them down on the table and reached for the other two on her shoulders. But the moment he let the first pair down, they scrambled right back to Sarah's side of the table. As fast as lightning, they skittered up her arms again, this time perching in her hair.

"Hey, no—no!" Sarah gasped. Then she felt something crawling on the back of her neck. Was it one of the *catchems*? But no—she had two *catchems* on her shoulders and two in her hair, so what was it?

"Excuse me," an indignant voice from the booth behind her said. "But there's no need for you to take our *catchems*. Ask your server for new ones if you don't like the ones you were given."

"Oh, *no*," Sarah moaned as she felt two new *catchems* climbing all over her back. These were wet too and she could feel the cool, ticklish trails of water they were dripping down her shoulders and spine.

"Hey, what's going on?" someone demanded. "Where are they

all going?"

Sarah looked up and saw to her horror that more *catchems* were on the way. Their big blue-green eyes were wide, their mouths open in eager mews. And at least a dozen were headed straight for her. The diners whose tables they had left were staring angrily at her and pointing as though they thought she had lured them away on purpose.

Which is ridiculous, Sarah thought wildly. *Who would voluntarily have dozens of cat-crabs crawl all over them? And how am I ever going to get them off?*

She didn't want to hurt the *catchems* but to be honest, she was even more concerned that one of them might hurt her. She had at least seven or eight clustered together on the tops of her breasts now and she was afraid any minute one of those deadly claws was going to grab one of her exposed, vulnerable nipples.

"Help!" she gasped. "Please, how do I get them off me?"

"The prophesy," she heard someone say. "You know—the one about silver and ivory?"

"You think?" someone else asked. "Really?"

"Yes, I do. Just look—" But the rest of the strange conversation was drowned out in a sea of voices.

All this time Sazar had been alternately plucking *catchems* off Sarah and waiving for their waiter, who was busy serving another group and either couldn't see the big Kindred's waving hand or was ignoring it. Now Sazar had apparently had enough. He stood to his full height and bellowed to be heard over the rowdy crowd.

"Toodles, come here *now* before I rip your fucking throat out!"

This, of course, got the attention of both their errant waiter *and* the entire restaurant. If everyone inside Fresh Catch hadn't already been staring at them before, they certainly were now.

Toodles came rushing over and when he saw Sarah's predicament, his eyes grew wide.

"Oh my goodness gracious me!" he exclaimed. "*What* are you doing to the *catchems?*"

"It's what the *catchems* are doing to Sarah," Sazar growled. "Just *look* at her!"

"But how did this happen?" Toodles gasped.

"I don't know and I don't fucking care," the big Kindred snapped. "All I know is you'd better get them off her *now.*"

"But…I don't know…" Toodles dithered.

Sazar took him by the shoulders and glared him in the eyes. He bared his teeth at the waiter, letting the other male see exactly how long and sharp his fangs were.

"I said, *now,*" he growled. "You say you've got the best trained *catchems* in the whole city? Well fucking *prove it.*"

Toodles went extremely pale.

"Yes," he muttered, his eyes wide. "Yes, of course. I'll see to it at once."

He rushed away and was lost in the crowd that was beginning to gather around their table. They all seemed fascinated by what was happening to Sarah but no one but Sazar was even trying to help.

"Just hold on, sweetheart," he growled, picking the *catchems* off her and tossing them into the long, thin aquarium, which they promptly crawled out of and came running back to her. "Hang in there. We're going to get all these off you."

"Please, *please* do!" Sarah felt almost frantic by now but she knew she had to hold still. If she started thrashing around—which was what every nerve in her body was screaming to do—she might startle the *catchems* into attacking her instead of just crawling and clinging to every inch of her they could find while purring and meowing in her ears.

Why did I ever pet them? Sarah thought in despair. *And how am I ever going to get them off me?*

She had the same awful feeling she'd had once as a child when a palmetto bug — one of the huge flying roaches native to her home state of Florida — had landed on her arm. The crawling sensation of the disgusting thing had made her scream and flap her arm wildly to get it off. That was the way she felt now with the *catchems* all over her but she knew she couldn't give in to the impulse. She just had to sit there and deal with it.

Still the crawling sensation was almost more than she could bear.

Shouldn't have thought about the palmetto bug — shouldn't have thought about roaches, she thought miserably. The awful memory made everything worse and the feeling of being climbed all over by many, tiny, chitinous claws was maddening. *I'll go crazy if I don't get them off soon,* Sarah thought wildly. *Completely crazy!*

Suddenly Toodles was back, shoving his way through the gathering crowd. He was pushing a rolling silver cart and on top of it was a cage like the one he'd originally used to bring out the *catchems* for their table — only this one was much bigger. It looked big enough to hold dozens if not hundreds of the little cat-crab creatures.

Sarah eyed it skeptically.

Great. So there's the cage — now how is he going to get them back in it?

Her question was answered when the waiter put a silver whistle to his lips and blew three, short, sharp blasts on it. He was quite close to Sarah when he did it and the noise was deafening—but at least it had the desired effect.

The *catchems* began climbing off her as fast as they had climbed on. Dozens of them jumped off her breasts and onto the table—using her almost like a human trampoline. At least that was the half-hysterical image that filled Sarah's mind. But at this point she didn't care how they were leaving as long as they just *left*.

Soon all but a few of the cat-crab creatures had skittered across the table and jumped into the large wire cage. The ones that were left were mewing hysterically and tangled in Sarah's long brown hair, which had long ago come down from its bun.

"Hold still, sweetheart," Sazar murmured as he picked the distressed creatures carefully off her, untangling their flailing legs from the strands of her hair. "All right now—I think that's all of them."

"Are you sure? I swear I can still feel them on me…all over me!" Sarah rubbed her arms, trying to get rid of the awful crawling sensation which still lingered even though the *catchems* seemed to be gone. She wanted to get up and leave the restaurant but there was too much of a crowd around them. It seemed that the Alquons were almost as nosey as the giant *tizen* which had been staring in the bathroom at her. They wouldn't move an inch, even when Toodles begged them to.

"Please, would all guests return to their seats?" he asked, trying again to make his thin, reedy voice heard above the babble. "Please, there is nothing to see here. Please go back and leave these fine people alone."

Nobody budged and Sarah saw lots of them had little flat black squares they were pointing at her. Was that the Alquon version of a cell phone or a camera? Was she going to be plastered all over their social media as the girl who was attacked by cat-crabs?

"Please," she whispered desperately. "Please, I just want to *go home.*"

"Enough of this," Sazar growled. He moved from his side of the booth, pushing the shorter Alquons physically out of the way when they wouldn't step aside, and reached for Sarah.

Before she could say a thing, he had swept her up and was holding her to his chest, above the babbling crowd.

"Out of the way," he roared, making her wince and put her hands to her ears. "Fucking *move!*"

But his deep, base voice had the effect that their waiter's exhortations to the crowd hadn't. The Alquons looked at the big Kindred uncertainly and began to clear a path.

"That's more like it," Sazar growled. Holding Sarah close, he left the milling crowd behind and at last, to Sarah's intense relief, got them out of the restaurant.

She took a deep breath and it came out in a shuttering, shaking sound that was too much like a moan. Sarah clamped her lips shut before more moans followed. Her nerves felt as though they had been strung as tight as harp strings and some cruel musician had been plucking them for hours.

The *catchems* crawling all over her, the pressing, babbling crowd, the feeling of being vulnerable and exposed…it was too much. Just too, too much. She put her head against Sazar's broad chest and shook silently, feeling like her whole body was going into overload.

Feeling like she would never feel normal again.

Chapter Fourteen

Sarah seemed shaken and silent after their escape from the ill-fated dinner and Sazar didn't blame her a bit. The poor little human had had one traumatic experience after another from the moment they'd gotten here.

First she'd been forced to show much more of her body than she was comfortable with, then she'd been ogled by every male that came near them and she'd been nearly assaulted by that bastard Rando, not to mention mentally molested by the perverted Lord Magnate. After arriving at their nighttime accommodations she had been confronted by both snakes—or something that looked very like snakes—in the fresher facilities, and a giant creature with an eye bigger than her own head staring in at her.

All that was a heavy load even *before* the incident with the *catchems*. Sazar was inclined to think his little human had probably had much more than she could bear.

And it was all his fault for dragging her here in the first place.

He carried her silently through the streets back to their room at the Courtly Row. When he got her inside he said, in the softest voice he could manage, "Sarah...sweetheart—"

"Don't..." She was shivering and her teeth were chattering. "Don't talk about it. I just...just want to take a shower. They were all *over* me. Please—I need a shower!"

"As you wish," Sazar said quickly. He put her in a chair and gave her a drying blanket, then went into the fresher to try and figure out the strange shower device. Luckily Kindred were almost as good with machinery as they were with languages. He was able to get the complicated array of buttons to give him a hot flow of steaming, sweet-scented water in a short time.

He came back to find that Sarah had stripped and was holding the drying blanket wrapped around herself.

"It's ready," Sazar told her.

"I...is it? Good." She tried to stand and nearly fell over.

She's in some kind of overload. In shock, he thought as he caught her.

"Sarah, maybe you should just lie down a moment—" he began.

"No!" She began to struggle in his arms. "No, I need a shower *now.*"

"All right," Sazar said grimly. "You'll have your shower but not alone."

He carried her into the bathing area and leaned her against him while he stripped off the long robe he was wearing and toed off his boots. He left his trousers on for propriety's sake. Then he unwound the drying blanket from around her shoulders and lifted her again.

"W-wait," Sarah tried to protest, her teeth still chattering. "Wh-what are you d-doing? I...I'm n-naked! I can take a shower b-by myself."

"Not in this state you can't," Sazar growled. "I won't have you slipping and falling in the tub. Besides, you're not naked—you still have on your underthings and your, er, jewelry."

He nodded at the tiny, skimpy panties she was wearing which honestly were just strings and the double strand of pearls. She was still wearing the nipple rings and breast chain too but he would worry about that later.

"But—" she began again.

Sazar ignored her. Carefully, still holding her close to him, he climbed over the high side of the tub. When he got her into the shower, which was the kind that rained straight down from above, he leaned her against him again and reached for a puffy white thing he was fairly certain was a bath sponge.

The sponge had one soft side and one abrasive side and emitted a flood of floral-scented bubbles when he held it under the water and squeezed. Sazar used the abrasive side to scrub Sarah's skin, making sure to clean everywhere he thought the *catchems* might have crawled.

At first she just stood there shivering, allowing him to scrub her. Then, after a moment, she leaned her head against his chest and her shoulders began to shake with low, almost inaudible sobs.

Sazar felt as though she'd reached into his chest and squeezed his heart in her soft little hand.

"Sarah…oh, sweetheart," he murmured, putting his arms around her and holding her close. "I'm sorry…so sorry…"

Slowly her arms came up and wrapped around his waist. She pressed her face to his chest and held on while she continued to cry. Sazar stroked her shoulders and murmured softly into her ear. He wasn't even sure what he was saying or if she could hear it over the sound of the shower but he didn't care—it was instinct to comfort his female, instinct to hold her close and let her cry if she needed to. And she felt so right in his arms—so soft and small and perfectly curved.

"Sweetheart," he whispered, stroking her trembling shoulders. "*Ladara.*" It was a term of endearment in his own dialect—the language of the Pitch-Bloods. A name used for a lover, but that didn't even occur to Sazar. He just knew it felt right to call Sarah that—as right as it was to stroke and comfort and hold her.

At last Sarah stopped crying and gave a long, trembling sigh. When she looked up at him, her eyes were wet but her face was calm.

"I...I think I'm okay now," she said. "Can we get out?"

"Of course." Sazar lifted her out and wrapped a drying blanket around her. He made certain she was steady on her feet before turning his back and shucking down the sodden trousers. He toweled off quickly and wrapped a similar blue blanket around his waist before turning back to her.

"Feeling better?"

"Yes, thank you." Sarah nodded.

"Good. Then let's get dressed. I'm taking you home."

* * * * *

"What?" Sarah's heart seemed to drop down to her toes. "No—you can't," she exclaimed. "I know I got all emotional and I freaked out at the restaurant but I swear I'll do better, Sazar. Please don't fire me!"

"Fire you?" He stared at her blankly. "Whatever gave you that idea?"

"I just thought...I know I probably ruined the mission or at least gave the Alquons a bad view of us. But I just...I couldn't help it. When those things started crawling all over me..." Sarah shivered. "Look, can't we just not go back to that restaurant and *try* to go on with the mission?"

His pale eyes got wide. "You want to keep going? You want to *stay here?* After the day you've had?"

Sarah nodded. "I swear I'll do better."

"Sweetheart…" Sazar cupped her cheek in a gesture of tenderness that nearly undid her. "I was going to cancel the mission and take you home because all of this is just too much—too hard on you. But I certainly wouldn't fire you over it. If anything you've withstood much more than any other assistant I've ever had and you've kept your composure beautifully."

"I haven't, though," Sarah whispered. "I…I just had a mini-nervous breakdown in the shower."

"And you had every right to," he said firmly. "After everything you've been through today I would be surprised if you *weren't* upset."

Sarah's heart, which had been skittering around her chest in fear, began to beat a regular rhythm again.

"So you're not mad at me? You're not going to let me go?"

Sazar stroked her cheek again.

"I never want to let you go, Sarah," he rumbled softly. And somehow, she got the feeling that he wasn't talking about her employment with him. But that was crazy, wasn't it? She wondered again if he was having feelings for her…because she couldn't help herself, she was certainly having all kinds of feeling for him.

"Th-thank you," she stuttered and dropped her eyes. His pale gaze was simply too intense.

"You're welcome. Now that we've established I'm not going to fire you, let's get dressed—in our proper clothing—and get out of here."

"What?" Sarah looked up quickly. "You still want to go? Why?"

"Because of what you've gone though. We can't stay in a place where you're constantly exposed to degradation and danger."

"I'm fine," Sarah insisted. "I don't want you to scrap the mission because of me."

He raised his eyebrows. "You're certain about that? You want to stay?"

"Positive." Sarah lifted her chin. "You said yourself you might be able to make some valuable exchanges with the Alquons. I don't want the Kindred to lose their chance to trade with these people all because I was too squeamish to do what was expected of me."

"Sarah... *Ladara*," he murmured. "No one expects you to put up with the things you've been dealing with today—least of all me. I promise I won't be upset with you and I absolutely won't fire you if you want to go."

"But I *don't* want to," Sarah insisted. She wasn't sure why she was so determined to stay. Sazar was right, she'd really been through some rough experiences today.

But as unpleasant as some of it was, it was also new and exciting and *real.* She'd spent years reading about foreign, far off places and researching them on the computer, when she could use it for something other than work, although any "questionable" websites had been blocked, of course. But she'd never in her wildest dreams expected to get outside the Compound and actually experience other cultures herself.

And there was another reason she wanted to stay, if she was being honest with herself. Being here with Sazar, when they had no one but each other to look to for support, was definitely drawing them together. She couldn't imagine any scenario on Earth or even on the Mother Ship that would have ended with the big Kindred bathing her so gently and holding her while she cried. She would probably just be filing paperwork and making appointments for him if they went back now.

Sarah didn't want that. As uncomfortable and downright scary as some of the experiences she'd had today had been, she didn't want to stop…didn't want to leave as long as it meant she'd get to be closer to Sazar.

I'd rather stay in a place where I have to show my breasts and they have snakes in the toilet than leave, just because I want to be with my new boss, she thought. *That's crazy, right?*

But it didn't feel crazy—it felt *right*.

"I want to stay, Sazar," she repeated. "Please."

He sighed deeply. "All right. But if we do, you have to promise to be near me at all times. Your beauty attracts much too much attention here." His voice dropped to a growl. "I don't like the way the Alquon males look at you."

"The way they look at my boobs, you mean," Sarah muttered and then blushed. Why had she said such a thing?

"Your boobs?" He raised his eyebrows quizzically. "You mean your breasts?"

"Well, yes," Sarah admitted.

"They are…quite large. Especially compared to those of the Alquon females," Sazar remarked in a low voice.

"They've always been too big. I *hate* how big they are," Sarah said passionately.

Speaking of her breasts, they were feeling extremely uncomfortable now that the thin towel-like blanket he'd wrapped her in was rubbing against them. It occurred to Sarah that she'd had the damn golden bands on for hours and her nipples were throbbing. She wondered uneasily if she was losing blood flow.

Was it bad to wear the jewelry and breast chain too long? What if it was doing permanent damage?

This is bad, she thought, nibbling her lower lip. *But what can I do about it? I know the only way to get the chain and bands off is to have Sazar help me but I can't just ask him to suck my nipples, can I?*

She had the sudden feeling she was being watched and looked up to see Sazar staring at her, a frown on his chiseled features.

"Sarah," he murmured. "I can tell that something's bothering you."

"You can?" Surprise and a feeling of guilt came over her, as though she'd been hiding things from him she shouldn't have been hiding. "How?" she managed to ask.

"The way you're shifting from foot to foot for one thing…and I've also noticed when you bite your lower lip you're feeling anxious or uncertain about something. Why don't you tell me what it is?"

"I…I don't know." Sarah shifted again. They were still in the bathroom with the open ocean clearly visible through the glass wall. "I can't talk in here," she said. "What if another giant nosey kraken comes along? Can we please go in the bedroom? I…I can walk," she added when he started to pick her up again. "I feel fine now."

"Of course. Come." Sazar led the way into the bedchamber and Sarah couldn't help admiring him as she trailed behind him. He was so big and his ass was extremely firm and muscular under the blue bath-sheet he had wrapped around his trim waist. Hi broad, bare shoulders were beaded with water from their shower. She found herself wishing she could lick it off and scolded herself for the naughty thought.

He's your boss, Sarah! Stop acting like he's your boyfriend and behave yourself.

But no matter how she berated herself, she couldn't disguise or ignore the fact that she needed help—intimate help—and Sazar was the only one who could give it to her.

The big Kindred went and sat on the edge of a tall, armless chair with cushions patterned in the same aquamarine blue as the bedspread. He motioned for Sarah and she came to stand before him, still nibbling her lower lip.

"Now," he said. "What is it?"

"I…my…my breasts are starting to hurt," she blurted out. "I just…I need to get these bands off. I'm starting to get worried about the long-term effects of the, uh, jewelry."

"Of course. Why didn't you say so before?" Sazar asked calmly.

"Because it's really freaking embarrassing." Sarah hunched her shoulders. "I mean, you're my boss. How can I ask you to…"

"To help you? To suck your nipples?" he suggested in that deep voice of his that sent shivers through her.

"Yes," Sarah whispered. "It just…seems wrong."

"I sucked them to help you put the rings *on*," he reminded her.

"I know but…but we didn't have a choice. I didn't know how…how you actually felt about it." Her voice came out in a whisper and she couldn't meet his eyes.

"Sarah…" He lifted her chin and looked at her steadily. "You're beautiful—your breasts are beautiful," he murmured. "I know I shouldn't say this because it's not in any way professional but I didn't mind helping you with the jewelry. In fact…" He cleared his throat. "I very much enjoyed it."

Sarah could feel her cheeks getting hot but she felt a pleased kind of embarrassment. He thought she was beautiful—plain, dowdy little Sarah—beautiful. Her heart skittered in her chest.

"So...you don't mind helping me again?" she whispered.

His pale eyes were suddenly maroon red.

"Drop the towel," he said quietly.

Taking a deep breath, Sarah did as he said. She let the long blanket-towel fall around her feet, leaving herself naked—or mostly naked—before him. She still had on the nipple jewelry and breast chain and the irritatingly pleasurable honey pearls were still rubbing between her legs, but other than that she was bare.

For the first time, she didn't feel ashamed of her body—or not *as* ashamed as she'd been taught to feel at the Compound, anyway. Yes, she was curvy and full figured but Sazar didn't seem to mind—at least if the way he was looking at her was any indication. And it didn't seem shameful to be naked in front of him—although it *was* still a little embarrassing.

"So beautiful," Sazar murmured, his pale eyes roving over her exposed body. "I'm going to suck your breasts now, Sarah—going to suck your nipples. Let me know when you feel like the gold bands are loose enough to slip off."

"All right," she whispered, not knowing what else to say. His seated position put his mouth on the level of her breasts and the float dots were still working, keeping her full mounds high and her nipples pointed right at him.

Sazar drew her closer and cupped her right breast in his big, warm hand before sucking her nipple gently but fully into his hot mouth.

"*Oh,*" Sarah couldn't help the soft moan that was drawn from her lips as she felt the hot, gentle suction and the way his warm, wet tongue was sliding over her tender peak. The sensation sent sparks of pleasure from her aching nipple down to the spot between her thighs and the honey pearls, which she'd almost begun to ignore, suddenly seemed to vibrate faster.

She began to get that feeling again—the feeling of climbing a mountain and trying to reach the summit. But before it could get really intense, she felt the golden ring come off her nipple and Sazar pulled back, holding it in his hand.

"There," he said thickly. "One down…one to go."

"Oh. Um, thank you," Sarah tried to sound grateful—and she was—but she was also disappointed by how quickly the band had come off. She'd been hoping to feel the big Kindred's mouth on her breasts for more than just a few moments.

Sazar must have been thinking the same thing because he drew out the process of removing the golden band on her left breast for much longer.

He leaned forward and Sarah assumed he would suck her again. Instead, he put out his tongue and twirled it slowly around her aching left nipple, making her moan and grasp his shoulders as he gently bathed her aching bud.

"Sazar," she whispered, pressing her breast forward. "God, that feels so *good*."

"Do you like it, *Ladara?*" he murmured, pulling back for a moment. "Does it give you pleasure when I lick and suck your peaks?"

"Yes," Sarah whispered, ashamed to admit it but unable to lie. "I know…know you're only doing it from necessity but, well…I *really* like it."

"I like it too." His voice was a low growl and his eyes were the darkest red she'd ever seen them as he sucked her left nipple deep into his mouth. She felt the sharp prick of his fangs, bracketing her tender nub and wondered hazily again about his need for blood. Then the deep suction of his hot mouth on her flesh, drove all rational thought from her mind.

At last, much to her disappointment, the second ring came off and Sazar sat back, panting a little. His eyes were dark and his fangs were long and there was a definite bulge under the towel which was still wrapped around his waist.

Sarah felt a shiver go through her. God, he looked hot! And he smelled so *good* — that dark, spicy, masculine musk was rising from him, invading all her senses, making her want more — making her want *him*. Sarah shivered, her bare and newly freed nipples feeling incredibly sensitive to the cool breeze in the room. She didn't want this to end and she had the distinct feeling Sazar didn't want it to either. But he was her boss and she was his assistant — neither of them could think of a reason to keep it going.

"Sazar?" she murmured, making his name a question.

"Yes, *Ladara*?" His voice was a soft growl and she felt certain the strange word her translation bacteria seemed unable to translate was an endearment of some kind.

Sarah opened her mouth, uncertain what would come out.

"I…I wonder if you can help me with something else," she heard herself say.

"Anything." He stroked her cheek with the backs of his knuckles, sending another shiver through her. "Just ask it."

"I…I wonder if you could help me, uh, get these freaking panties off."

Sarah shifted from foot to foot. The vibrations of the honey pearls had *definitely* gotten stronger while he was sucking her nipples and now she felt like they were about to drive her crazy.

"I mean, I tried to get out of them myself earlier," she hurried to explain. "Or at least find the off switch. But I couldn't do it and they're driving me insane."

He raised an eyebrow at her. "The *off* switch?"

"They're buzzing—vibrating," Sarah explained, feeling her cheeks get hot. "Lemesh turned them on somehow when she helped me get into them but now they're too tight to get out of and I can't seem to turn them off. It's really…uncomfortable."

"I can imagine," he said dryly. "Here, let me have a look."

He turned her from side to side, examining the thin but incredibly strong straps that held them in place. Grasping one he tested it, trying to break it just as Sarah had. After a moment he gave up, frowning.

"I think there must be some kind of metal wire woven into this fabric. It's unbreakable."

"Oh no!" Sarah was beginning to feel desperate. "Isn't there *any* way to get them off?"

"Well…" Sazar cleared his throat and looked up at her. "I haven't looked at the string which holds the pearls in place yet."

"Oh…um…" She could feel her entire body getting hot. The string he was talking about started right at the top of her pussy slit and then disappeared into her inner folds where the humming pearls were torturing her clit. "I…do you think it might be weaker than the straps?" she asked at last.

"Possibly." Sazar's deep voice was neutral but his eyes were red and half-lidded. "Would you like me to take a look?"

"I…I guess so," Sarah whispered.

"All right. Here, switch places with me." He put her in the chair and knelt in front of her, his hands on her knees. "All right now—let me see."

Sarah wiggled in the chair uncomfortably. God, this was *embarrassing*. What had she been thinking? But it seemed too late to stop now. Squeezing her hands into fists at her sides, she forced herself to spread her thighs.

"Hmm...." He was frowning again.

"What?" Sarah asked, feeling breathless with embarrassment and some other emotion she couldn't name. "What do you see?"

"Well...not as much as I need to." He looked up at her. "The string is...somewhat obscured." He looked up at her. "Sarah, I need permission to spread you—to open your pussy lips so that I can get a better look."

Sarah felt like she might die of mortification but she couldn't deny that his big, warm hands on her inner thighs felt good—felt amazing if she was being honest with herself.

"All...all right," she whispered, nodding. "Do what you have to do."

"Thank you for trusting me," Sazar said gravely. Then his long fingers were spreading her open, revealing the double row of pearls and the way they encircled the pink, swollen nub of her clit.

Sarah bit back a little moan and her heart thumped in her chest. Oh God, it was bad enough to have him looking at her here but what made it even worse was how wet and shiny she was. Her juices were leaking out, coating her folds and her clit and even her inner thighs. Was it just because of the honey pearls? Or did her extreme reaction have to do with the gentle way Sazar was touching her.

"Gods," he breathed softly. "*Numalla*..." Another word her translation bacteria couldn't translate but somehow it seemed to be a good thing.

"What?" Sarah asked.

"*Numalla*—liquid pussy." Sazar looked up at her. "It's a word my people have for a female who makes a lot of honey. It's beautiful," he added, making Sarah breathe a sigh of relief. "But I can see how the pearls must be bothering you…stimulating you. Here…and here."

One long finger traced over the humming pearls on either side of her swollen clit and Sarah jumped and gave a little gasp.

"May I have your permission to examine the string?" Sazar asked her. "I might touch you in a rather intimate area as I do—I won't be able to help it."

"That…that's okay," she whispered, her heart thumping so hard she could feel it in every part of her body at once. Could this really be her? Frumpy little Sarah, naked with her legs spread and a gorgeous Kindred male between them, asking if he could touch her?

He's only asking so he can help you, pointed out a little voice in her head.

I don't care, Sarah told it. *I'll take it—I'll take him any way I can get him.*

"Yes," she said again. "Do it…do what you have to do."

"Thank you," he murmured again and knelt closer to her—so close that Sarah could feel his warm breath blowing across her inner thighs and open pussy.

His long fingers traced the buzzing pearls, stroking over her swollen clit in the process, making her gasp and bite her lip to keep from moaning. God, it felt good!

"Hmm…" Sazar was frowning again. He looked up at her. "I *think* I can bite through the string with my fangs but you'll have to hold very, *very* still. I wouldn't want to cut you."

"You…" Sarah could hardly believe her ears. "You want to put your mouth…"

"Near your pussy?" He gave her a lazy smile. "Oh yes, Sarah.

Unless you object?"

"No," she whispered. "No, not…not if you don't mind."

"Not at all," he assured her. "Now hold still… It might take me a minute to get the string in the right position to bite…"

He leaned forward and this time Sarah couldn't hold back a moan as his hot, wet mouth connected with her open pussy. He tugged at the string with his fingers, trying to get it into a good position between his fangs and she swore she felt the wet heat of his tongue swiping briefly over her clit.

Then there was a quick movement, a hard yank, and black and green pearls went rolling everywhere. The strap around her waist parted at the same time and she was finally free of the panties. The buzzing vibration stopped abruptly but Sarah didn't feel any less stimulated.

Sazar sat back, licking his lips but she couldn't help noticing that he didn't withdraw his hands. In fact, he was still holding her pussy lips open and frowning a little.

"What…what is it?" she asked breathlessly. "Is there something else—some other problem?"

"I think there might be. The pearls seemed to have made some marks on you. Look." He motioned for her to bend down. "Here…and here," he murmured, stroking on either side of her clit.

Sure enough, Sarah saw, there were red marks there as though the constant buzzing of the honey pearls had nearly rubbed her raw. She winced a little as Sazar touched her there lightly. Now that he had pointed it out, it really *hurt*.

"Ouch—that's awful," she exclaimed. "Those damn things—Lemesh should have showed me how to turn them off."

"Yes, she should have. You're wounded."

"I guess so." She winced again, feeling increasingly uncomfortable.

Sazar looked up at her, his eyes drowning deep.

"I can heal you," he said quietly. "As I healed the wound on your hand and the wounds on your arm when I fed from you."

"You...you can? With...with your mouth, you mean?" Suddenly her own mouth was as dry as a desert.

Slowly, he nodded. "Oh yes. With my mouth."

"But...you...you want to do that? I mean, biting the pearls was one thing but..."

"I want to do it, Sarah." His deep voice was hoarse now. "Gods, how I want to do it. To taste you...to heal you. I haven't tasted a female in...Gods, so long."

So he really *did* want to do it. Sarah could hardly believe it. She'd fantasized briefly about him biting her here but she'd never dreamed he would want to taste her just for the fun of it.

He's not though—he's just going to be healing me, she told herself sternly. And as long as the big Kindred was just healing her, there was no harm in it, right?

"All right," she whispered. "I don't mind. I guess you can."

"I'll need to lick you where you're injured," he murmured. "I may even need to take the whole area in my mouth to give it my full attention."

God, he was talking about sucking her throbbing clit into his mouth and licking all around it!

"Yes," Sarah breathed, trying to keep the need and eagerness out of her voice. "Yes, I understand. Please..."

"Gods, Sarah...so beautiful. So hot and wet..." His voice was a low, hoarse growl as he leaned forward once more and buried his face between her thighs.

She cried out as she felt the warm, wet tip of his tongue tracing over the places where the vibrating pearls had rubbed her. And then, somehow, her fingers found their way into his thick black hair and she was pressing her hips up to meet him.

Her enthusiasm seemed to make him even more eager. Pulling her back, he hooked his big arms around her thighs, splitting her wide, as he pressed his mouth to her open pussy.

Sarah had never felt so open…so vulnerable…or so hot. Once more the feeling that she was trying to reach some pinnacle overcame her. The hot, wet lapping of his tongue over her tender clit was pushing her higher, taking her there. She was beginning to think she was finally going to reach that elusive peak.

"Sazar," she moaned, tugging hard on his hair as she thrust up to meet him. "Sazar, oh God, *please…*"

He looked up, a teasing light in his hot, red eyes.

"I think you're healed now. Do you want me to stop?"

Sarah could have sobbed with frustration.

"No!" she exclaimed. "No, please. I…I feel like I'm close to…" She groped for words. "Close to *something*," she said at last. "I don't know what it is but if you'll just lick me a little more…"

His eyes widened. "Close to an orgasm, you mean? Have you never come before, sweetheart?"

"I don't know…I don't think so. We weren't…weren't supposed to touch ourselves in…at the Compound," Sarah explained brokenly. "I…I've tried before but I can never quite…*get* there. Wherever there is."

"I know where it is," Sazar growled softly. "And I know what you need. Just relax, sweetheart and I'll take you there."

Before Sarah could answer, he had fastened his mouth on her pussy again and was lapping her hungrily, dragging the flat of his hot, wet tongue over her open folds and throbbing clit.

The feeling, which had begun to wane as they were talking, came back in full force. Moaning, Sarah bucked her hips upwards, giving herself completely to the amazing sensations he was causing inside her…giving herself utterly to the relentless tide of pleasure which would either lift her to the highest peak…or drown her. She didn't know which and she no longer cared.

* * * * *

Sazar felt her pussy quivering under his tongue and heard the soft, helpless, broken sounds that came from her as he lapped and sucked her sweet folds. Gods, she tasted good! All Kindred have an innate need to taste their females and give pleasure with their mouths and he hadn't been with a female for well over a year. In a way, he had been as thirsty for this as he had been for blood. And Sarah was giving it to him…giving as freely and as openly as she gave her blood. Gods, what a female!

Mine, he thought as he circled her tender clit with his tongue, being careful not to cut her with his fangs. *She's mine and I'll never let her go!*

Then Sarah cried out sharply and her inner walls began to contract and quiver. Sazar tasted fresh wetness from her sweet folds and her fingers in his hair tightened.

He lapped her honey up eagerly, savoring her secret flavor, loving the way she pulled at his hair and bucked up to meet his tongue. If this was truly her first orgasm, it was an incredibly strong one. She couldn't seem to stop moaning and her body was writhing all over the chair so much he had to hold her in place with his arms or she would have fallen off and landed on the floor.

At last, however, she stopped her restless movements and lay back, panting her lovely hazel eyes closed as if from exhaustion.

"Oh Sazar…" she whispered, turning his name into a prayer. "Sazar that was amazing…just *amazing*."

"*You're* amazing, sweetheart." He placed one last gentle kiss on her swollen clit and rose to gather her into his arms. Now that her pain and her pleasure both were over, she seemed exhausted and could hardly keep her eyes open. Well, it had been an extremely long day.

Poor little human.

He cuddled her close to his chest, feelings of protective possessiveness rising so fast they nearly drowned him. Gods, she was so beautiful. And she was his—all his.

"Thank…you," she whispered and yawned. "I've never…never felt anything like that before. So good…" She yawned again.

"It's time you got to bed," Sazar murmured. With one hand he pulled back the aquamarine coverlet, revealing soft pale blue sheets beneath. He slid Sarah gently between them and she barely protested at all. All the emotion of the day had worn her out.

He kissed her gently on the lips, sharing a bit of her secret flavor with her, and then pulled the coverlet up to her shoulders. His shaft was still throbbing between his thighs but he could take care of that later—and he fully intended to while he relived the experience of tasting Sarah's sweet pussy and feeling her come all over his face.

Mine, he thought again, reaching down to stroke her flushed cheek. *You're mine, Sarah and I'll never let you go…*

Chapter Fifteen

Sarah woke up from the strangest, most embarrassing dream. Something about her boss biting her panties off and then licking her between her legs…

Just a dream she told herself uneasily. *It was just a dream…right?*

She stirred and found that she was in a strange bed, not at all like the sagging cot she'd slept in at the Compound. It didn't feel like the hard, narrow bed she'd been given at the shelter either, though. It was soft and squishy and warm but not wet—just jiggly.

It's like I'm sleeping on Jell-o, Sarah thought sleepily. She rolled over and found that the Jell-o bed gave alarmingly, moving like a wave in the ocean. Her momentum pitched her into the broad, bare back of the man sleeping beside her.

Wait a minute—*man?* Who was she sleeping with? And how had they ended up in bed together?

Then a warm, spicy scent hit her nose and everything came rushing back.

It's Sazar! And we're in bed together because we're pretending to be a couple here on Alquon Ultrea.

Sarah was fully awake now and she became aware of something else—she was completely naked. Naked and plastered to her boss's back with her bare breasts pressed against him and her crotch cupped against his extremely firm ass.

Oh God…oh no! She struggled to push away from him but the

Jell-o bed kept pulling her back down with its odd wave-like motions. They were lying together in a big dip now, right in the middle of the strange mattress and there didn't seem to be any way to extricate herself.

"Sarah?" a deep rumbling voice said, sounding sleepy and annoyed. "What in the Seven Hells are you doing?"

"Trying to get up." She managed it at last and struggled to her feet just as he turned over.

Reflexively, she tried to cover herself with her hands. There was a dim light coming through the clear glass of the walls—not much, but enough to see by and she was suddenly ashamed.

He rolled over and regarded her, one black eyebrow raised quizzically.

"Why are you hiding yourself from me, sweetheart? I saw all of you last night. I *tasted* all of you."

Sarah could feel her cheeks getting hot. She couldn't believe what they'd done together. It went far past the bounds of their professional relationship of boss and assistant. Plus, she barely knew the big Kindred. She'd only been working for him for two days and she'd already fallen into bed with him—*literally*. What would he think of her?

Be careful, Sarah, whispered a little voice in her head. *You know what happens to secretaries who get too familiar with their bosses.*

She couldn't help remembering Sister Hope, her belly swollen and her eyes red as Father Caleb sent her away, telling her that her "services" were no longer needed.

She needed to be careful here. Damn careful.

Sazar was still looking at her and he appeared to be about to speak.

"I...um... I have to use the restroom," she said quickly, not waiting to hear what he had to say. "Sorry." She fumbled under the wall hanging for the bathroom door and slipped inside, closing it firmly behind her.

She'd been making an excuse to get away but once she found herself in the bathroom, she realized she really *did* have to go. In fact, she thought she'd never had to pee so badly in her life.

Without thinking, she flipped up the lid of the black bench commode and sat down.

She was almost done peeing when she remembered the *yeechees*. All her muscles clenched and she stopped in mid-stream.

Then she heard a faint, angry hiss.

"Oh my God...oh no," she whispered, tensing. What was she going to do? Could the weird, snake-like animals tell she hadn't given them everything she had? Would she feel their little sharp fangs sinking into her bare behind any moment?

Quickly, she vaulted off the toilet and slammed the lid closed, panting. She could hold the rest until later, she told herself. Until she could find a toilet without snake-things in it. She wanted a shower anyway.

After about fifteen minutes of trying, she finally got the shower to work at a reasonable temperature. As she clambered carefully over the high side of the tub, she couldn't forget how Sazar had held her in the pouring water the night before, letting her sob against his chest as he stroked her shaking shoulders and murmured sweet soothing nothings into her ear.

What was that name he called me? Something with an L – Lavnana? No...Ladara. That was it. What does that mean?

He had called her that more than once and he had been so gentle with her. Did it mean anything or was her cold, prickly boss just a nice guy under his tough exterior? Did he have any kind of feelings for her? The kind she was beginning to have for him even though she knew she really, *really* shouldn't?

Sarah had no idea. She soaped herself with the white, puffy sponge which looked like a miniature cloud and then rinsed and climbed out again.

She wrapped another blue bath-sheet around herself and toweled her hair as dry as she could get it. Then she decided she couldn't stay in here, hogging the bathroom forever. After all, Sazar probably had to use it too and he was in a much better—and safer—position to pee on the toilet eels or snakes or whatever than she was.

She came out of the bathroom and found him sitting up in the bed. He was naked too but he covered himself considerately with a discarded bath-sheet when she came in.

"Um, hi." Sarah wasn't sure what to say to him.

"Hello." The big Kindred seemed uncertain as well.

"The, uh, bathroom is free if you need it." She gestured lamely at the door.

"Oh. Thank you." He rose and brushed past her, keeping himself covered as he went. Sarah breathed a sigh of something that was either relief or regret—she couldn't tell which—when it *snicked* shut behind him.

She went to the closet and opened the cube, intending to get dressed and then remembered she couldn't used the Alquon clothing Kat had packed for her or the clothes she'd bought herself on the Mother Ship.

With a deep sigh, she looked back in the closet. The gold lame' outfit was for the ball tonight but there was a new dress she hadn't noticed the night before. Had Lemesh made her an extra one and sent it along with the rest? That seemed like something the Alquon clothier might do.

It was less flashy than the other outfits she'd worn—possibly the Alquon equivalent of a little black dress. It had a black jacket with long sleeves and a rounded back. The high collar which fastened at her throat was cut in an inverted V to show her breasts.

Sarah sighed in resignation as she put the jacket on. She was just going to have to get used to exposing herself while she was on Alquon Ultrea. But after a lifetime of shapeless clothes and body shame, it was really, *really* difficult to feel good about going around basically topless.

At least the float dots are still working, she thought, looking down at her full breasts which were still as firm-looking as ever. Lemesh had given her plenty of extras too. She would never have to wear a bra again if she didn't want to.

*Only I **do** want to,* Sarah thought ruefully as she remembered the way Councilor Rando had pulled her breast chain and the creepy way The Lord Magnate had eyed her exposed assets. *I wish I could wear one right now!*

But there was no use wishing that. She had made the decision to stay here on Alquon Ultrea and she would have to deal with the consequences—one of which was walking around topless all day. With a sigh, she finished getting dressed.

She was mildly surprised to see that the bottom half of the outfit wasn't a skirt but long silky slacks made of black material which gathered in a cuff at her ankles.

"Huh," Sarah muttered to herself, putting them on. "I dream of Jeanie pants."

They *did* look like harem trousers and they would have been considerably more modest than the split skirts she'd been wearing—except for the fact that they were made of some black, translucent material which was pretty much see-through. There didn't seem to be any panties to go with them either, though Sarah checked everywhere in the closet, hoping they might have fallen down behind her pink carry-all cube.

"What are you looking for?"

Sazar's deep voice startled her so much she jumped and smacked her head on the closet's shelf.

"Oh!" she gasped, putting a hand to the back of her head.

"Are you hurt? I didn't mean to startle you. Here—let me see."

He came to her, wearing a towel around his waist and leaned over to study the back of her head, where she'd hit herself.

Sarah found herself practically in his arms with her face to his broad chest and her sensitive nipples brushing against the rock-hard plane of his abdomen.

"I...I'm fine," she tried to explain but Sazar wouldn't be satisfied until he was certain she wasn't bleeding. The warm, spicy scent of his skin invaded her senses and seemed to do strange things to her. She felt weak in the knees and every time her nipples brushed his skin electrical shocks ran through her, making her feel hot and helpless.

"Well...just a bump." At last he released her. "What were you looking for, anyway?"

"Oh nothing," Sarah said quickly. "I mean, I just thought...I was hoping..." She cleared her throat, miserably aware that she was babbling. "I was looking to see if there were any, uh, panties to go with this outfit Lemesh left me," she said at last, gesturing to herself. "But, well...there aren't."

"The Alquons certainly seem intent on exposing and objectifying their females," Sazar remarked, frowning. Then his face softened. "But you look lovely in that outfit—whatever it's supposed to be."

"Thank you," Sarah murmured, feeling her cheeks get hot at his compliment.

"You're welcome," he murmured. "Well, let me get dressed myself and I'll help you with your jewelry."

"Oh...oh of course." Somehow she'd managed to forget she wasn't completely dressed yet—she couldn't go out without her breast chain fixed firmly in place. Just thinking of how he would have to "help" her made Sarah feel hot and cold all over. Especially when she remembered the way this scenario had ended the night before.

She fixed her damp hair into a bun at the back of her neck and tried not to think about it as the big Kindred got dressed.

Sazar chose a dark blue robe and trousers edged in silver from the carry-all cube. It made his pale eyes ice blue and Sarah couldn't help thinking how handsome he was. His black hair was so thick and dark in contrast to his pale skin...wait a minute, he *was* pale—much paler than he had been. Did he need blood? Should she ask him? She'd taken her blood capsule so she ought to be well able to supply him...

Her thoughts trailed off when he sat on the chair he'd used the night before and motioned to her.

"Come, Sarah—let me help you. We need to go out and find something for First meal since we didn't get anything to eat the night before. And..."

"And I can't go out without my jewelry," Sarah murmured, finishing his thought.

"Exactly. Bring the compound too please."

"Oh, I can do that part myself."

Wincing at the icy liquid, Sarah sprayed her nipples with the black bottle of compound and then came to stand between his legs with the gold bands and breast chain clutched in one hand.

"Shall I make it quick?" Sazar raised one black arched eyebrow questioningly. Sarah realized he was trying to gauge her mood—to see what she wanted.

I want you! she thought but didn't dare to say.

"I...I don't...I mean, it's probably better if...if you go slower, don't you think?" she asked at last, stumbling over the words. "I mean it's more, uh, *thorough* that way."

"As you say...more thorough," Sazar murmured, his eyes going half-lidded with desire. "Very well—slowly then. Come here so I can reach you better."

Before Sarah could protest, he had gathered her up and she was somehow straddling his lap with her hands on his shoulders and her breasts in his face. The position spread her legs wide and she could feel her pussy lips parting which she knew would be completely visible through the see-through harem trousers.

"*Oh,*" she moaned as Sazar sucked her right nipple into his mouth. He swirled his tongue around and around her pink peak before sucking hard—so hard that points of his fangs pricked against her skin.

His fangs, she thought and suddenly she wanted to be pierced by them again. Despite the pain, she wanted it.

"Do...do you need blood?"

The words came out before Sarah could stop them. When Sazar pulled away, letting her nipple slip from between his lips, his eyes had gone a deep, pulsing red.

"What did you say?" His voice was a soft, low growl.

"I...I just thought..." Sarah wished her heart wouldn't pound so hard—it made it difficult to get a deep breath. "I could feel your...your fangs," she explained at last, haltingly. "And the lights around here are so bright and we were out in them for so long yesterday and vampires aren't good with sunlight. Not that you're a vampire," she said quickly. Oh God, she was making this worse and worse. "But I just thought..."

She trailed off, feeling miserable. Why had she brought it up anyway? Why hadn't she just let him put the nipple bands on her and ignored the prick of his fangs?

For a moment, Sazar was silent, his eyes a burning red as he looked at her.

"I drank from you only a day ago," he said at last.

"I know that," Sarah whispered. "But I thought you might need...need more."

"It's not in your employment contract to allow me to drink from you more than once a week," he pointed out.

"I know," Sarah said again. "But, well, I don't care about that."

"We're not mated so your body won't replenish itself as it would if I claimed you. You'll get depleted if you give me too much blood," he pointed out.

"No I won't. Liv—that's Olivia, Sophie's sister—is a nurse. She gave me a special capsule that helps me make blood faster."

His eyebrows shot up and he frowned.

"She did, did she? What business is it of hers?"

"She...she wasn't trying to be nosey," Sarah said quickly. "She said Commander Sylvan helped develop them. Look...the point is I can give you blood. If...if you need it."

"So you're offering?" His eyes had gone half-lidded. "Despite the pain?"

Sarah nodded. "If…if you want some…need some, then I want to give you some."

"Very well—give me your arm." He reached for her right arm but Sarah drew back.

"Wait. Can you…could you…" Her mouth went dry and she couldn't finish.

"Could I what? Tell me, Sarah—don't be afraid. I won't be angry at anything you ask," he murmured.

"Could you, uh, take it from here?" She nodded down at her right nipple, which he had been sucking so deeply. "If…if you wanted to?"

He raised his eyebrows. "I can call a vein anywhere on your body. The question is, do *you* want me to bite you here?" One long finger stroked over her nipple, making Sarah moan.

"Yes," she whispered. "Yes, I want that."

His eyes went even hotter but his voice was very soft.

"It's a very sensitive area. I can't make it pleasurable for you unless you're my—"

He stopped short and Sarah wondered what he had been about to say.

"I mean, I cannot give you pleasure as I bite you unless I am…touching you intimately."

"How," Sarah breathed. "Show me."

One big, warm hand came up to cup her pussy through the silky, transparent trousers.

"Like this," Sazar growled softly. "If I'm bringing you pleasure, you won't feel pain when my fangs pierce you here." He nodded at her breast. "If I'm not, the sensation may be…too intense for you to bear."

"I want to try it," Sarah said. She could hardly believe she was being so bold but she couldn't help herself—she wanted the big Kindred—wanted to feel his mouth and hands on her again.

"As you wish," he breathed and then his hand was slipping into her trousers to cup her bare pussy as he sucked her nipple back into his mouth.

Sarah moaned as two long, strong fingers found her pussy lips and parted them to stroke her aching clit. At the same time, she felt Sazar's fangs again, much more sharply than before.

"Oh!" she gasped and threaded her fingers through his thick hair. "Oh God, Sazar, yes!"

His fingers were strumming lightly over her swollen bud, caressing and teasing her, pushing her to that peak again—the one he'd helped her finally reach last night.

Coming...he called it coming, she thought deliriously. *I'm going to come again if he keeps this up.*

She felt a sharp pain in her breast which turned immediately to pleasure. And then, suddenly, she was there—at the peak and flying over as Sazar drank deeply from her and stroked her quivering pussy as she moaned and writhed in his lap, unable to help herself...unable to stop herself...

"Hello? You two? Commander Sazar? Sarah?"

The voice at the door of their room and the light rapping of someone knocking on their door broke through Sarah's euphoria as suddenly as though someone had dumped a bucket of ice water on her head.

"Oh no!" she gasped, wriggling in Sazar's lap. "Quick—what if she catches us?"

He let her breast slip from his mouth and licked his lips, still holding her tightly to him.

"What if she does?" he said thickly. "We're supposed to be pair partners—a couple. Remember?"

"Well, yes." Sarah shrugged uneasily. "But that doesn't mean she has to see us, uh, doing what we're doing." She nodded down to where his hand was still cupping her pussy.

"Indeed." He withdrew his fingers and, never taking his eyes from hers, sucked them clean of her juices. "Delicious." His voice was still a low, lustful growl.

Sarah felt like a thousand butterflies had just taken off inside her stomach.

"Sazar," she whispered. "I just…I think you should let me down off your lap."

"No," he murmured. "I haven't finished placing your breast jewelry yet.

"But—"

Suddenly the door burst open.

"Are you two all right?" Chandra was standing there, wide-eyed and worried. "I heard strange noises and I didn't know what to think," she explained.

Sazar frowned. "I thought I locked the door. We are perfectly fine, as you can see. I was just helping Sarah apply her breast jewelry."

"Oh, all right. Hurry up then." The Alquon girl gestured impatiently. "We have lots to get to before you come back here to get ready for the Breeding Ball."

"Lots to get to? What…what do you mean?" Sarah asked breathlessly. She couldn't help the little gasp in her voice. She was still feeling the after-shocks of her orgasm and Sazar had matter-of-factly sucked her nipple back into his mouth, as though he was simply getting her ready to wear the golden bands. God, would she ever get used to letting her boss suck her nipples as though it was no big deal? Especially while someone else was watching?

Somehow she didn't think so.

"I mean we have engagements today we didn't have yesterday. What happened at Fresh Catch last night was the talk of our social-net," Chandra said. "How *did* you manage to attract all those *catchems* Sarah? *Everyone* is talking about it!"

"I didn't do it on purpose," Sarah protested as Sazar put the first golden band in place and it tightened around her nipple. "I...I just..." She had to bite her lip for a moment because he was sucking her other nipple, deep and hard and long. "I only petted one of them," she told Chandra. "And...and then they all came running up to me. It was awful..." She shivered.

"Well some people are saying it's that old prophesy. You know—

'When the silver fingers...

Find the ivory mounds...

There you may be certain....

Pure blood abounds.'" Chandra sounded like she was quoting.

"What?" Sazar finished placing the second golden band, which tightened over Sarah's left nipple. He frowned at Chandra. "What does that verse you quoted mean?"

"You know—what The Lord Magnate was telling you yesterday," Chandra said impatiently. "About how the blood of our people was genetically altered—and how it's his duty and the duty of every Lord Magnate that came before him to try and spread his seed and his own pure blood to change it back?"

"Yes, we remember that," Sarah said, climbing somewhat awkwardly off Sazar's lap. Now that the jewelry was in place, he seemed willing to let her go and she felt embarrassed to be straddling him so blatantly for no reason. "But what about the silver fingers and ivory mounds? What is that?" she asked.

"Our waiter last night told us that the *catchems* are often referred to as 'silver fingers,'" Sazar rumbled, sounding thoughtful.

"Oh—okay. But where are the mounds? What does that mean?" Sarah asked.

"They're *there*." Chandra pointed at her chest.

"What?" Sarah looked down at herself and noticed that her nipples seemed extra red, possibly from all the sucking Sazar had been doing before he put on the jewelry. There was no sign of his fang marks, though—he must have healed her. "I still don't get it," she said.

"Ivory mounds," Chandra said impatiently. "Look at yourself, my dear Sarah! Your breasts."

"What? So *that's* what the verse means?" Sarah could hardly believe it. "But that...that's ridiculous."

"No it's not. Look." Chandra pulled out one of the flat, black squares Sarah had seen several people pointing at her in the restaurant last night. She remembered wondering if they were the Alquon version of cell phones.

When Chandra tapped the square it started to glow and soon a picture of Sarah appeared with twelve or thirteen of the little silver *catchems* clustered together on the tops of her breasts.

"See? Silver fingers on ivory mounds." Chandra tapped the square and another picture popped up—and then another and another.

"Oh, *no!*" Sarah moaned. "Are you telling me these pictures are all over Alquon Ultrea?"

"First thing I saw when I looked at my square this morning." Chandra giggled. "Don't worry—it's a *good* thing! It raises your profile—you're trending now! Lots of Alquons say they want a genetic trade with the Kindred. Of course, the final decision rests with The Lord Magnate. But you'll be seeing him tonight at the Breeding Ball—hopefully you can convince him then."

"Hopefully so," Sazar said dryly. "But in the meantime, these pictures are demeaning and embarrassing to my partner."

"Oh, she'll be fine." Chandra patted Sarah on the shoulder. "She'll just have to deal with being a minor celebrity—that's all."

"But I don't *want* to be a celebrity," Sarah exclaimed. "I'm not that kind of person! I'd rather stay in the background, behind the scenes."

"I'm afraid you can't hide from fame, my dear," Chandra told her. "But if it bothers you that much, I promise I'll take you to the *chample* farm on the most indirect *tuve* I can find."

"*Chample* farm? What's that?" Sazar asked.

"Oh, it's on the agenda Minister Obglod set up for you. He's waiting for us there, you know—we need to hurry." Chandra motioned for her. "Are you all ready to go?"

"Can we at least get some breakfast first?" Sarah asked desperately. "We didn't get anything for dinner and we're both starving." At least she knew *she* was.

"Oh you poor thing!" Chandra exclaimed. "You mean that whole incident with the *catchems* happened before you could eat?"

"We didn't get a single bite," Sarah said and then her eyes were drawn involuntarily to Sazar's fangs.

He saw where she was looking and a corner of his mouth twitched up in one of his rare smiles.

"Well, maybe *one* bite," he murmured and Sarah felt her cheeks getting hot with a blush. She really wished Chandra hadn't interrupted when the big Kindred was drinking from her. She'd had a feeling that maybe the intense pleasure she'd felt could be repeated over and over again as long as he was taking her blood and touching her at the same time. Even though he'd made her come really hard it had been only once—she still wanted more.

Don't be greedy, Sarah, she scolded herself. *And don't wish for more than you can have.*

She was still certain that a permanent relationship between them was impossible. They were only together here because he needed her to act as his wife and he needed her blood. Once they got back to the Mother Ship they would probably have a much more normal and boring boss and assistant relationship.

Sarah told herself she didn't care, though. She intended to enjoy her special time with Sazar as long as she could.

"…at the *chample* farm," Chandra was saying and she realized she'd missed the first part of the sentence.

"I'm sorry?" she said. "What did you say?"

"That you can eat at the *chample* farm—there will be samples from all the different varieties there and as the honored guests you'll get to try them all."

Alien produce samples wasn't exactly what Sarah had had in mind for breakfast but it looked like that was the best they were going to get. With a sigh, she looked at Sazar, who shrugged.

"All right," she told Chandra. "Let's go to the *chample* farm."

Chapter Sixteen

The brilliant artificial sunlight wasn't as taxing on Sazar as it had been the day before. Doubtless that was because of the sweet blood Sarah had offered him so freely.

*She actually **wanted** me to drink from her breast.* He couldn't help looking at the full mounds in question. Gods, they were beautiful — *Sarah* was beautiful. He loved touching her but he couldn't help wishing he could have tried drinking from her without pleasuring her as he did so. If she could feel the Blood Pleasure when he called a vein to her breasts or between her legs and bit her there, even without sexually stimulating her first, it would prove beyond the shadow of a doubt that she was his Fated Mate.

And what if she is? whispered a little voice in his head. *What good will it do you? She's supposed to be your assistant — not your lover. You have a proscribed relationship. It's time you remembered that and returned to propriety. You went far over the line last night and this morning as well.*

Reluctantly, he acknowledged it was so. He didn't want to take advantage of Sarah and he still wasn't sure if she might feel something for him…or if she was just innocently trying to do her best to supply his needs and be a good assistant.

Whichever it was, Sazar told himself he needed to start behaving more like a boss and less like a lover. He promised himself he would be more careful in the future.

* * * * *

Chandra led them to a little used *tuve* station and they were sucked away on a cushion of warm air to arrive in a rather rumpled state at the entrance of the *chample* farm.

Sarah wondered what in the world a *chample* was but she didn't have time to speculate for long.

"There you are!" Minister Obglod's thin, irritated voice rose to meet them as Chandra led them down a side tunnel to the entrance of a vast glass globe bigger than any underwater area Sarah had seen yet. There was a clear glass door which kept them from entering but she could see inside and she marveled at its size.

It was even taller than the globe that housed the palace and the top of it appeared to be poking out of the Alquon ocean which the rest of the city's structures were submerged in. There was a clear demarcation between water and air when she looked through the clear sides.

The vast glass globe was filled to the top with long, thin plants which seemed to sway in the air currents the way kelp sways in ocean water. The plants themselves were a dull, blue-gray but they had brightly colored clusters of some kind of fruit or vegetable near their tops. Were those the *champles?*

"We're here, sorry to keep you waiting," Chandra fluttered, running up to the minister who tugged her breast chain absently. Sarah made sure to stay out of tugging range herself.

"Hello, Minister," Sazar said, coming up beside her. "It's good to see you again."

"What is all this I hear about the two of you causing a kafuffle at one of the best restaurants in Idd?" Obglod demanded. "It's all anyone is talking about. Can't I leave the two of you alone for a moment without disaster ensuing?"

Once again Sazar had to bite his tongue at the old minister's rude words. But as long as no one was threatening Sarah, he was able to be diplomatic.

"A simple misunderstanding," he said smoothly. "I'm certain it won't happen again."

"It had better not!" Obglod exclaimed in his cracked and strident voice. "Don't forget that I'm your sponsor and when you misbehave—"

"It reflects poorly on you. Yes, we know," Chandra exclaimed. "Only they *didn't* misbehave, Minister! Sarah here is the answer to the ancient prophesy about purifying our blood."

"What?" Obglod demanded, staring at Sarah. "What nonsense are you talking?"

Chandra started to explain but just then a hearty-looking Alquon male in simple clothing came up to meet them. His kelpy hair was receding and he had an open, honest face that Sarah liked at first sight.

"Hey now, I reckon you fancy looking folk must be the group I've been expecting to tour the farm. I'm Dod."

"Hello, Dod," Chandra said brightly. "Yes, that's us! I'm Chandra, assistant to Minster Obglod here." She nodded at Obglod. "And these two fine people are visitors from another world. They've never seen *champles* before and I was hoping you could explain their importance to our people and maybe let them taste a few samples."

"Oh, I can do better than that," Dod said easily. "I'll let 'em harvest their own."

"Really?" Sarah asked, craning her neck to look up at the very tops of the immensely tall plants where the brightly colored clusters were growing. "How? I mean, if those are the *champles*, how are we supposed to get up there?"

"Those are them, all right," Dod assured her. "But don't worry—you can just jump right up there."

"I think you may be overestimating our abilities," Sazar said dryly. "Kindred are strong but I don't know a single one who can leap a hundred feet into the air."

"Maybe not in regular gravity," Dod said, still sounding quite unperturbed. "But we grow *chample* stalks in low G. They can't support the weight of their fruit otherwise. C'mon. You too, my Lady and Sir Minister, if you like," he added, nodding deferentially to Chandra and Obglod.

Minister Obglod decided to stay outside the globe, saying he was too old to be doing manual labor like harvesting fruit. But Chandra agreed to come eagerly and Sarah noticed she was clutching her little black square again, possibly intent on taking some publicity photos.

The moment they stepped inside the huge glass globe, Sarah began to feel oddly light. Her whole body seemed to have less mass and she nearly stumbled from the strange new sensation.

"Easy there," Dod, who moved with ease in the new environment, said. "It takes time to get used to low G. One little hop can send you spinning out of control so you have to be careful."

"What are we supposed to do?" Sazar asked. He also moved with confidence and Sarah wondered if he had experienced low gravity before. It would make sense—he was a diplomat and had been to plenty of different worlds. Maybe some of them had had considerably less gravity than she was used to.

"Well, I'll give you each a suction bag—here..." Dod handed out padded silver bags, about the size of a reusable shopping bags to each of them. Sarah noticed that the tops of the bags were pursed tightly shut. But when she put her hand down to touch hers, the bag opened and a strong suction pulled at her fingers. When she moved her hand, the bag stopped sucking and pursed shut again.

Weird but she supposed the design had practical value. If things bounced around so easily in the low G environment there had to be a way to secure the *champles* they picked or they would just go flying out of the bags and go everywhere.

But she still had questions.

"Please," she said as Dod was showing Chandra how the suction bag worked. "What *are champles?* We still don't know."

"Oh goodness me—I'm about to let you pick some and here I went and forgot to tell you what they are!" Dod slapped his balding forehead good-naturedly and laughed. "Well, they're one of our main food sources and the only plants we grow. We get everything else we need from the ocean around us."

"Why grow them at all if the ocean supplies your needs so well?" Sazar asked.

"Because *champles* are a link to our past—to the way things were back before our world became covered in water," Chandra explained, picking up the narrative.

"My lady is right." Dod nodded. "See, *champles* are plants genetically modified to taste like all the foods we lost when we moved permanently to the oceans."

"Really?" Sarah couldn't help being interested. "Like fruits and vegetables you can't grow anymore?"

"We could grow them," Dod said. "But it would take up valuable living space. Why bother when we can grow the *champles,* which take on the taste and texture of the lost food while delivering three times the nutrients and making plenty of oxygen to circulate through all of Idd?"

"Some *champles* also have the taste and texture of food animals we couldn't afford to bring with us," Chandra explained. "Feeding and storing animals just for food is expensive and wasteful. Plant protein from the *champles* is a much better option."

Sarah's stomach growled, reminding her that she was nearly weak with hunger. Enough with the history lesson already. She didn't care what the *champles* tasted like—she wanted to eat!

"They sound delicious," she said quickly. "Can you tell us which ones taste like what?"

"Reckon it's best if you just find out for yourself, my lady." Dod grinned at her. "Wanna try harvesting?"

"Yes, please!" Sarah exclaimed but Sazar put a hand on her arm.

"Would you be so kind as to show us first, exactly how it is done?" he asked Dod.

The Alquon shrugged. "Be glad to. Here."

He took Sarah's silver suction bag and crouched low on the spongy ground. It looked to Sarah like he only took a little hop but his momentum sent him soaring high in the air, all the way up to the top of the greenhouse globe where the clusters of *champles* grew. He grabbed one of the tall, thin plants to steady himself and twisted a bright blue *chample* off its stalk. He shoved the fruit into the silver bag before letting go to drift slowly down again, as though carried by warm air currents.

"There, see?" he asked, returning to them and handing the bag back to Sarah. "Easy as can be. Wanna try that?" he asked, when she braved the strong suction to get the bright blue *chample* out of the bag. It was about as big as a large apple and to her surprise it was cube-shaped, not round as she'd expected. "It's one of our most popular flavors—*plez-nack*," Dod added.

Sarah didn't know what *plez-nack* flavor was but it smelled delicious—kind of like a cross between watermelon, strawberries, pineapple and hot buttered popcorn. She took a bite, finding the texture both crunchy and chewy. It tasted as good as it smelled and her stomach growled again. Eagerly she took another bite and then offered it to Sazar.

"You have to try this—it's one of the best things I've ever tasted!"

Obligingly, he took a bite and chewed.

"There," Sarah said, smiling. "Isn't that the best thing you've ever put in your mouth?"

"Not quite the *best* thing I've had in my mouth." His pale eyes glowed red for a moment. "But it is very good."

Sarah felt her cheeks get hot at the way he was looking at her and her stomach fluttered. Why had she put it like that?

But before she could get any more flustered, Dod was saying it was time for them to try harvesting some of the *champles* for themselves.

"Just push off real easy," he instructed. "If you jump too hard you're going to bang your heads on the ceiling and that's never any fun. Hold on to the stalks when you get to the top and give the *chample* you want to pick a little twist. Don't forget to put it in your suction bag before you come back down. All right? Everybody ready? Then *go.*"

Sarah thought later that picking *champles* was more fun that almost anything else she and Sazar did (at least in public) while they were on Alquon Ultrea. The feeling of near-weightlessness was exhilarating although it took some time to get used to.

She watched as Sazar took off and then Chandra, who was pointing her black square at him, probably taking pictures. Sarah didn't want to be left out so she pushed off from the spongy ground too, only she pushed too hard and went rocketing up at a frightening speed.

Oh no! she thought as she saw the thick glass dome of the ceiling getting closer and closer. *I'm going to bang my head, just like Dod said! That's going to hurt!*

She tried to shield her head but Sazar, who was already holding tight to one of the long thin *chample* stalks, reached out and snagged her arm. Pulling her tight against him, he murmured in her ear,

"Be careful, *Ladara*. I wouldn't want you getting injured."

"Oh—I think I jumped too hard," Sarah said breathlessly.

"Stay with me. I've had experience in low G." He twisted two of the bright yellow, cube-like fruit from the branch and handed one to Sarah who put it in her suction bag. Then, keeping an arm wrapped firmly around her waist, Sazar let go and allowed the two of them to drift slowly back down.

They jumped up again, this time holding hands. Now that she felt safe, Sarah couldn't help laughing in sheer exuberance at the wild sensation of being nearly weightless and flying upwards. Sazar laughed too, a warm, deep chuckle she hadn't heard before but liked at once. His face was so different when he smiled, Sarah thought. So much more open and free. It made her feel close to him.

Again and again they jumped from different spots, aiming to get one of every kind of *chample* growing in the huge glass dome. They spent some time on the ground trying them, too.

"Just don't eat any of the brown ones unless you're bound up inside," Dod advised as he named and explained the various varieties they had picked.

"I'm sorry, what?" Sarah asked. "I don't understand."

"They're medicinal *champles*," Chandra said delicately. "For…digestive health."

Oh, so it must be like eating prunes or taking some kind of laxative, Sarah thought.

"They work pretty quick too," Dod put in. "So be certain you don't eat one when you're too far from a bathroom."

"We'll keep it in mind," Sazar said dryly. "I don't think we'll be trying those particular *champles* right now."

But there were plenty of the strange alien fruits that were grown simply for their flavor and texture. Sarah's favorite was a red one with yellow and green spots which she thought tasted just like a cheeseburger. Sazar favored a dark purple *chample* that had a sweet and sour flavor Sarah couldn't place. He said it reminded him of a food from his home world.

Chandra asked him if he liked it and he smiled.

"It is good but not nearly as delicious as other things I have tasted recently," he remarked, giving Sarah a meaningful look.

"Oh…" Sarah put a hand on her fluttering heart. Was he talking about the taste of her blood…or other things? She kept seeing him in her mind's eye, between her thighs healing her pussy with his tongue the night before. The memory made her feel hot and breathless.

She wished she had the nerve to kiss him again, as she had that first night in his room. But everyone was watching and Chandra was, presumably taking pictures for the Alquon version of social media. So she simply looked into those pale eyes, flickering red with desire as he looked back at her, and wished this moment could last forever.

At last Chandra remarked that it was late and they'd spent much more time at the *chample* farm than she'd intended.

"I'm afraid we don't have time to see the *yeechee* fields or the *to-ti* works either," she sighed. "We'll have to get the two of you back to your room to get changed for the Breeding Ball tonight."

"That's fine with me," Sarah remarked. She didn't know what a *to-ti* was but the *yechees* were the toilet snakes and she had no wish to have any kind of contact with them at all—let alone go visit a whole field full of them.

They thanked Dod who nodded good-naturedly and gave them some extra bags of *champles* to take home and share on the Mother Ship. Sarah hoped they would last—she had no idea of the shelf life of the alien fruit but she really wanted to share some of it with her new friends Kat and Liv and Sophie.

I wonder if they'll keep until Christmas, she thought as they made their way back to the *tuve* station. *They would make really unique gifts.* Kat, especially would love them. She struck Sarah as being kind of a foodie.

Then she thought of Tsandor—he would probably like the purple one Sazar had liked. Or maybe the bright yellow one that tasted like a mixture of lemon cookies and grape popsicles...

Her heart gave a little lurch when she thought of Sazar's son. How was he? Was he lonely? Waiting to see her again? Still hoping to have a complete family?

Sarah couldn't let her thoughts go in that direction, though—she knew things between herself and Sazar seemed really close now but once they were back on the Mother Ship, who knew what might happen?

She was aware that she needed to ask Sazar about allowing Tsandor to celebrate Christmas with Sophie's family. But again, it didn't seem to be the right time.

Christmas isn't for a little while yet, she thought. *I'll ask him later...when the time is right.*

But whatever happened, she promised herself sweet little Tsandor wouldn't have to spend the holiday alone or in the care house.

* * * * *

"So do you have your outfit for the Breeding Ball all ready to go?" Chandra asked Sarah as she walked them to the door of their room. She had hooked an arm through Sarah's and was strolling beside her in a chummy way, with Sazar on her other side. Minister Obglod had pleaded exhaustion again and returned to his own home.

Privately, Sazar thought that was best. The elderly Minister irritated him with his constant complaining and lecturing. Despite her "ditzy female" act, Chandra was much more pleasant to be around. Although if he had his preference, he would simply spend time with Sarah alone.

"Oh yes—the gold outfit. It's all ready to go," Sarah said, nodding.

"Good. Oh, and I had Lemmy make a new outfit for you too, Commander Sazar," Chandra remarked, looking up at him. "It's silver to match Sarah's gold. It's going to look *spectacular* with those pale eyes of yours."

"I thank you," Sazar said a bit stiffly. "I'm certain it will look fine."

"There is *one* question I wanted to ask you about my, uh, outfit..." Sarah's voice dropped to a confidential tone. It was clear she had no idea how sharp a Kindred's hearing was—though she spoke very softly, Sazar couldn't help catching her words. Still, since his little human obviously wanted privacy, he walked a little ahead to at least give her the illusion that her conversation could not be overheard.

"Yes, what is it?" Chandra murmured, also keeping her tone low.

"It's the panties that go with it," Sarah murmured. "They seem to have an, uh extra hole."

"What?" Chandra started to laugh. "What do you mean an extra hole?"

"*Shhh!*" Sarah hissed. "Well, they have a hole for my waist, and two for my legs but then there's another one, right in the back. They have *four* holes. That can't be right, can it?"

"They're *breeding* panties—of course they have four holes!" Chandra exclaimed, still laughing. "One for your waist, two for your legs, and one for your pair partner's shaft to enter you while he breeds you."

"Oh, uh…" From the corner of his eye, Sazar saw that Sarah's face had gone red. She glanced quickly up at him but since the topic clearly embarrassed her, he pretended not to have heard.

"I can't believe you've never worn breeding panties, before," Chandra went on. "How do they do things on your planet, anyway?"

"Well we don't…usually all, uh, breed together at a big ball," Sarah said quietly, still sounding embarrassed. "It's usually a private thing—just between a man, er a male, and a woman."

"How strange! Well, I guess you'll get a taste of the Alquon way tonight," Chandra remarked "Just remember to position yourself on the breeding couch so your breasts show to best advantage when Commander Sazar takes you. Good form is important, especially at the palace."

"Wait—what?" Sarah sounded slightly panicked now. "But Sazar and I don't have to participate—The Lord Magnate said so.

We're just going to be there to watch."

"No, that's not what he said *at all*." Chandra shook her head. "He said, you two don't have to breed with anyone else at the ball. But you *must* breed together. To attend a Breeding Ball at the palace and refuse to participate is the worst offense you can give! Why, The Lord Magnate would throw you to the *grike* if you just stood there and did nothing while everyone around you was doing their best to honor the tradition."

"He…he would?" Sarah sounded positively faint. "You know, I don't feel so well, Chandra. I…I think maybe one of those *champles* I ate disagreed with me. I'm not so sure I can go to the ball tonight."

"Oh but you *have* to!" Chandra exclaimed. "Once a royal invitation has been given and accepted, you cannot back out of it for any reason. It would be an even greater insult than attending the ball and not breeding! The Lord Magnate would have both of you thrown into the middle of the ocean without your ship and Minister Obglod told me you can't swim."

Sarah's face had gone pale—a clear sign of distress. Sazar wanted to gather her into his arms and comfort her but he wasn't sure what to say. It appeared they were in a very difficult situation.

If they didn't attend the Breeding Ball, they risked expulsion from Idd and possible death in the waters that surrounded it. If they did attend but refused to participate, they would be thrown to the *grike* – whatever that was. Possibly some kind of wild animal, Sazar speculated.

Either way they risked danger or death but the alternative—taking Sarah in the middle of a room full of strangers—was unthinkable. Not that Sazar didn't want to make love to her—he did, very much. She was beautiful and perfect and curvy and he was beginning to care for her very much—maybe even love her.

However, Sazar wanted to make love to her when she was *ready*—when he was certain she felt for him the way he felt for her. Not just because they were expected to participate in some barbaric alien ritual! How could the Alquons present themselves as a civilized people when they objectified their females the way they did and insisted on public sex?

"I'll tell you what," Chandra was saying, pulling him out of his angry thoughts. "I'll send you a few vids of past Breeding Balls—I'll have Blorg activate a screen in your room. That way you'll know what to expect. All right?"

"All right," Sarah said faintly. "I guess…guess that's good."

"It will be! This is going to be the best Breeding Ball *ever*—you'll see." Chandra smiled brightly and pressed her cheek to Sarah's. "Now you get ready to go. I'll be back for you in a bit to take you and Commander Sazar to the palace. See you soon!"

And with a final wave she left them standing in the doorway to their room.

Sazar tried to hold back a frustrated growl. They were in a damn sticky situation—what in the Seven Hells were they going to do?

Chapter Seventeen

The minute the door closed behind them, Sarah turned to the big Kindred.

"Sazar," she said, her voice trembling. "I…I have to tell you something."

"I know," he growled, to her surprise. He'd looked like he wasn't paying attention to her and Chandra whispering as they walked along.

"You…you do?" Sarah asked.

"I heard." He frowned at her. "We're expected to perform at the Breeding Ball after all. Now what in the Seven Hells are we going to do?"

"I don't know, but Sazar…" She licked her suddenly dry lips, unsure how to say what she had to say. "I…I'm a virgin," she blurted out at last. "I can't…I mean, I don't…"

"What?" His eyes widened. "You've never—"

"No!" Sarah said quickly. She looked at him shyly. "I've never wanted to. And now this…this Breeding Ball…"

"Well of course you can't have your first sexual experience in the middle of an alien orgy," he exclaimed, as though reading her mind. "That's out of the question!"

"It is? Oh, good…" Sarah was weak with relief that he understood. "I mean, not that I wouldn't like to, uh, you know, with you," she went on, stumbling over the words. "But in public like that…"

Sazar took her by the shoulders and looked into her eyes.

"Sarah," he said quietly. "I understand. Virginity is precious among my people—I won't take it from you. Your first time should be special—with a male you love and want to bond with. I'm not going to take you at the Breeding Ball."

Sarah bit her lip.

"But what are we going to do?"

"I don't know." He frowned. "We'll think of something."

Just then a knock sounded at the door and they heard the voice of the manager, Blorg.

"Hey—Chandra said you needed a screen?"

Sazar went to let him in. "Yes, Chandra is supposed to send us some, uh, instructional videos."

"Uh-huh." Blorg nodded absently. Sarah had expected him to bring some kind of screen or TV with him. Instead, he cleared a spot on the rounded glass wall across from the bed, moving a colorful wall hanging to do so. "There you go, folks," he said, tapping the clear glass several times. "Should pop up right here when she sends it."

Suddenly the clear spot on the wall darkened and loud moans began to come from it. At the same time, a picture of writhing bodies, clearly engaged in sex, showed up.

"Instructional vids, huh?" Blorg cocked an eyebrow at them.

Sarah felt like she could sink through the floor with mortification. Clearly the hotel manager just thought they wanted to watch porn together. How embarrassing!

"We can explain," she began but Sazar shook his head.

"Thank you—that's all we need," he told the Alquon manager shortly.

"All right. Pat the wall here—" he showed with his own hand, "For controls. Volume, picture…that kind of thing. Enjoy." Then he smirked and left.

When he was gone, Sazar took care to lock the door behind him and came to sit on the bed by Sarah. The mattress swayed in a rocking motion when he settled his big body beside hers.

"Well?" he asked in a low voice.

"Well, it…it's a lot of people, uh, having sex."

Sarah was so embarrassed she could hardly look at the screen. She'd never been allowed to see such things at the Compound where there was a strange double standard. On one hand, a girl was supposed to keep herself clean and never touch her body or think wrong thoughts or do or say anything sexual. But on the *other* hand, she was supposed to submit her body willingly to become a Bride of the Prophet when Father Caleb decided she was ready. After he was tired of her, she was passed to a husband and had to submit to him as well.

But she was never supposed to enjoy sex, talk about sex, or God forbid, watch sex in any format. Sex was only for the pleasure of the man—the husband or The Prophet. Never for the female who must submit to it.

So she had been taught, anyway. But the people on the wall screen certainly seemed to be enjoying it—both men *and* women.

"It's not *just* people having sex." Sazar was staring at the people on the screen intensely, as though he was seeing something Sarah wasn't. He looked at her, his eyes blazing. "It's not just porn—it's our way out of this mess. Look."

He stood up and walked to the screen, pointing to an Alquon

couple with the pale green and purple mottled skin common to just about everyone in Idd except The Lord Magnate. The male was wearing the usual trousers and open robe combination and the girl had bare breasts and was wearing a split skirt.

"Look at the way he's taking her—the way they're doing it," Sazar said. "Here, let me start from the beginning…"

He did something to the barely visible controls on the glass and the scene rewound itself to the point where the Alquon couple were just entering the vast golden throne room. Sarah recognized the tall windows and the golden light but the throne was no longer the only piece of furniture. The huge room, which had been empty when they saw it in person, had been filled with small pieces of waist-high furniture which looked like padded benches. The benches were curved down on one end and up on the other, with a large oval opening in the upward curving side.

They watched as the Alquon couple walked up and the female positioned herself lying on her stomach on the padded bench. Her bare breasts fit through the hole in the upward curving end, putting them on display and she gripped the carving handles that came off the sides almost like a pair of handlebars. Her lower abdomen and bottom were free of the bench, her feet planed firmly on the golden floor for balance.

"The breeding couch—that must be what Chandra was talking about," Sarah exclaimed.

"Exactly." Sazar was still staring intently. "Now watch what happens next."

Sarah knew what happened next—the man was going to get behind the woman and mount her. But she made herself watch anyway because Sazar seemed to be seeing something she had missed.

As they watched, the Alquon female spread her legs with her bottom half hanging off the end of the bench. The male, standing behind her, opened her split skirt to show a pair of bright blue breeding panties, much like the ones waiting in the closet for Sarah. He opened his own trousers and pulled out a long, thick shaft.

It was clear now, what the fourth hole in the panties was for. It was just wide enough to admit his cock and guide it straight into his female's pussy. Sarah nibbled her lip, her face flaming with embarrassment as she watched, waiting for him to push the thick, throbbing monster into his female's slit.

But instead of ramming himself home in his female immediately, the male Alquon waited until a person in a long white robe and white makeup approached. It was impossible for Sarah to tell if the person was male or female—he or she had very androgynous features and unlike the other Alquons, his or her entire body was covered, making it impossible to tell the sex.

The androgynous attendant in the white robe said a few words and then motioned for the male Alquon to continue. Under the attendant's watchful eyes, the male slipped his thick shaft through the hole in his female's panties and thrust forward, clearly sliding into her pussy.

The attendant nodded and watched as the male pulled out and pushed in again, making low, rough grunts of effort as he did. The female moaned and writhed beneath him and he gripped her hips hard, riding her on the breeding couch as she gasped and cried his name.

The female's bottom was hanging off the end of the bench but her panties, Sarah saw, hid most of the action. Though it was amply clear the male was indeed filling her, at least she wasn't *completely* on display.

The attendant watched for a moment then nodded and moved on. But the camera person—had it been Chandra?—stayed with the rutting couple until the male thrust forward hard and held steady, clearly pumping his female's womb full of his cum.

His seed, Sarah thought, feeling her cheeks get even hotter. *He's giving her his seed.*

She thought of Sazar doing that to her—what would it feel like? Would it hurt? The female in the video had been moaning and writhing as though she liked it. But how big was Sazar? Sarah had only caught glimpses of his equipment but it seemed really *large…*

At last the Alquon male finished. After a long moment he pulled out and whitish stuff could be clearly seen dripping from the hole in the female's breeding panties. She smiled up at him and he grinned back and slapped her exposed ass playfully. Clearly they had both enjoyed what had happened but Sarah couldn't understand how they could be so casual about it. How they could just have sex in a crowded room and think nothing of it.

Sazar paused the video and turned to her, his eyes blazing.

"Did you see that?" he demanded.

"Of course I saw it—you made me watch it!" Sarah squeezed her thighs together tightly, trying to stop the throbbing in her pussy. God, she wished she hadn't allowed herself to imagine what that would be like with her boss. What it would feel like to let the big Kindred breed her…

His voice softened a little.

"I think you're missing the point, Sarah. It was the *way* he took her that offers us an answer—a way out of this."

"What? How?" Sarah exclaimed. "He just…just stuck it in her." She wished her heart wouldn't pound so hard when they talked about this!

"Yes, he did but that's *not* what we're going to do," Sazar said. "You'll lay on the bench and get into position, just like that female did." He pointed at the female in the video. "But when I put my shaft into the hole of your breeding panties, I won't slide inside you—I'll slide *under* you."

"You mean..." Sarah was starting to get the idea.

"I'll be inside the breeding panties but not inside *you*," Sazar explained. "I'll make thrusting motions but no one will know I'm not in you—the panties will hide it all."

"Are you sure about that?" Sarah bit her lip. "I mean, there was an attendant watching them the whole time."

"We'll make it convincing." He looked at her seriously. "Do you think you can act as though I'm really sliding into you? As though I'm really breeding you?"

God, if her face got any hotter from embarrassment her hair was going to catch fire! But somehow Sarah nodded.

"I...I think so," she whispered.

"Good." He nodded decisively. "Because I think this is our only chance. We'll just have to fake it as convincingly as we can and wait until we're certain we won't cause offense by leaving."

He pressed the controls again and the scene started once more. Sarah watched as female after female was mounted and felt a throbbing between her thighs.

So she and Sazar were going to fake it. But what happened if they were caught? And what if—

Her thoughts derailed suddenly because the videographer had come to the front of the throne room where a larger, more elaborate breeding couch was set up. It gleamed gold and The Lord Magnate himself was using it.

Or he's using the girl who's on it, anyway, Sarah thought, grimacing. The girl beneath the Alquon ruler was so much younger than him it made her sick. At least she looked to be of legal age but just barely, Sarah thought. Her face was twisted in a look of agony and The Lord Magnate was riding her hard, clearly not caring that he was obviously hurting her.

Ugh! Just like The Prophet! Just like Father Caleb, Sarah thought.

"Who?" Sazar paused the scene again and turned to her. "Who is this Prophet I've heard you speak about before?" he asked. "Are he and Father Caleb one and the same?"

Sarah's mouth went dry when she realized she'd said the words aloud. She'd spent so much time hiding her past—running from it. She had the urge to run and hide again but somehow when she opened her mouth what came out wasn't another excuse or evasion...it was the truth.

"Father Caleb is The Prophet—or that's what he calls himself. He...The Lord Magnate reminds me of him. He's the leader of The Brotherhood of Peace," she added in a low voice.

"The religious organization you ran away from," Sazar said and it wasn't a question.

"Call it what it is." Sarah's throat felt tight. "It's a *cult.*"

"A theological movement with socially deviant or novel beliefs and practices usually directed at a particular figure or object," Sazar said, sounding like he was quoting from the dictionary.

"Exactly." Sarah nodded, looking down at her hands. "In the Brotherhood, at the Compound where we all lived, Father Caleb was who we—*they*—venerated."

"But not you?" he asked.

Sarah shook her head vehemently.

"Not me—never me!" she said fiercely. "I was just stuck there—stuck because my dad left me and my mom was completely brainwashed. I would have been brainwashed too if I hadn't been able to sneak off to the library and read books. I found out what The Brotherhood really was and I knew what Father Caleb wanted from us wasn't…wasn't right."

"What did he want?" There was a soft growl in Sazar's deep voice but she didn't think it was directed at her.

"What The Lord Magnate wants," she said, feeling her stomach clench. "To sleep with any girl he takes a liking to. So he made up a reason to do it—he's 'special' you see. He's The Prophet and he has to spread his seed to make 'holy babies' in as many girls as he can."

"Sarah…" Sazar reached for her but she pulled away. "Did he do that to you?" he asked in a low voice. "Did he—"

"I told you I'm a virgin, didn't I?" she snapped. "I hid for as long as I could—hid in plain sight. By wearing clothes that were too big and gaining weight. By looking as plain as I could…"

"*That* was why you wore the glasses!" Sazar snapped his fingers. "I wondered why anyone would wear oculars they didn't need. You wanted to disguise your beauty."

"Right. My beauty." Sarah gave a sarcastic laugh. "My 'beauty' is why I ran away in the middle of the night, praying they couldn't find me…" She put a hand to her eyes. "I was safe for years, you know—even working in the office. Because Father Caleb had another girl he liked—the head secretary, Sister Hope. She 'met his needs' as often as he wanted so he didn't bother me. Until…until she got pregnant."

"And then he turned his attention to you?" Sazar's voice was low and dangerous. "Did he hurt you? Did he touch you?"

"He tried…tried plenty."

Sarah swallowed convulsively, remembering the skin-crawling sensation whenever Father Caleb had snaked a hand up her skirt or tried to paw her breasts.

"I put him off and put him off," she said in a low, choked voice. "But finally he said it was time I…I became a Bride of the Prophet." The words seemed to stick in her throat. "I knew I would end up like his other secretary, Sister Hope—like every other girl in the Compound who had to 'receive his seed'—pregnant and handed off to some other man I didn't love. I knew I'd rather die than let that happen."

"So you ran away," Sazar said.

She nodded. "I ran away. I ran to the shelter and stayed for as long as I could." She looked up at him. "Then I saw the ad for a job up on the Kindred Mother Ship. I knew if I could just get there, I'd be safe. That the Controllers from The Brotherhood would never find me."

"They won't," he said in a soft, low voice. "You're safe with me, Sarah. You know that, don't you?"

She looked up at him. "Thank you, but can we please not talk about this? I shouldn't have said anything. It's just that the creepy Lord Magnate reminds me of Father Caleb. And the way he looked at me when we went to the palace…" She shivered. "Let's just say I'm not looking forward to seeing him again."

"I'll keep you away from him," Sazar vowed in a low voice. "He won't touch you, I swear it."

"Thank you." Sarah looked at him gratefully. "I feel better knowing that."

"Let's just get through this ball tonight," Sazar said grimly. "If we can give a good performance and appear to be honoring the

Alquon traditions, I think we can probably be assured of getting the Alquons to agree to a trade with the Kindred. After that our job is done and we can go home."

"Just in time for Christmas," Sarah murmured.

"Oh, yes…" He frowned distractedly. "Your upcoming festival of giving. I had almost forgotten about that. Yes, let's hope we may be back to the Mother Ship in time for you to celebrate there."

It was on the tip of Sarah's tongue to ask if they could celebrate together…but somehow she couldn't make herself say the words. They'd only known each other a few days, she reminded herself. And despite the intimacy they'd shared here on Alquon Ultrea, things might be completely different back aboard the Mother Ship.

Let's just get through the ball tonight, like Sazar said, she told herself. *Once we get through that and get out of here maybe we can talk.*

And maybe…just maybe they might have more to talk about than work. She hoped.

Chapter Eighteen

"Well, the two of you look just *perfect,*" Chandra exclaimed when Sazar opened the door to their room. "I just knew that silver outfit would do you justice, Commander!"

Sarah had to agree that the formal clothing the big Kindred was wearing did indeed do him justice. The silver material of the robe and trousers was somewhat thinner than his everyday wear and the shimmering silver fabric clung to his muscular frame and made his pale eyes stand out dramatically. But she couldn't stand there all day drooling over her boss, she told herself, dragging her eyes away from his tall frame.

"You look beautiful too, Chandra," she said, nodding at the vivid pink and purple silk outfit Chandra had on.

The Alquon girl blushed. "Oh, this old thing? I just threw it on. But that gold looks *gorgeous* on you, Sarah." She nodded at the gold lame' jacket which framed rather than covering Sarah's breasts and the long gold split skirt she was wearing.

"Thank you," Sarah smiled, trying to take pleasure in her own appearance. But though she had gotten more or less used to going out in public basically topless, she was never going to actually *like* it.

Chandra dropped her voice, a mischievous look dancing in her eyes. "And do the panties fit all right?" she murmured.

"Oh, uh, yes. Yes, of course." Sarah tried not to blush and failed. In fact, the gold breeding panties were much more skimpy than she had realized when she'd first looked at them. When she put them on, she was disturbed to see that the front border barely came higher than the top of her pussy slit. They were more like bikini panties than the high-waisted cotton briefs she was used to from years of living in the Compound.

"Well, I'm glad they're working for you." Chandra gave her a critical look. "There's only one thing missing."

"Oh, what's that?" Sarah asked uneasily.

"Formal nipple jewelry of course." Chandra produced a long, flat box and opened it to reveal new nipple bands and a brand new breast chain. The new bands were also gold but unlike the plain ones Sarah was wearing, these were studded all over with tiny diamonds. Hanging from the golden, fine-link breast chain which was strung between them were several gold and diamond charms which were no doubt meant to dangle playfully and attract attention at the same time.

"Oh," Sarah breathed. "It's beautiful, Chandra but it must have cost a fortune."

The Alquon girl made a shooing motion. "Not so much. Just consider it my gift from me to you. I want you to look right at the ball tonight. Everyone is going to be watching you so you have to be absolutely perfect."

"Wow, okay." Sarah swallowed nervously. So they were really going to be on display. She supposed she should have expected that, considering all the fuss they'd caused the night before at Fresh Catch and the crazy way the Alquon people seemed to think she was the answer to some weird "prophesy."

A new thought entered her head. She wondered uneasily if they were going to be able to pull off their fake breeding with everyone watching them. What if they got caught faking it? What would the Alquons do to them?

We just can't get caught, she told herself firmly. *We can't.*

But what if they were?

"Well…" Chandra tapped the box with the new breast jewelry in it. "Aren't you going to have your pair partner help you put it on?"

"Oh…of course." Though she knew she ought to be used it this by now, Sarah couldn't stop the pounding of her heart as she turned to Sazar for help. "Can…would you help me take the old jewelry off and put the new bands on?" she asked.

"It will be my pleasure." His voice was a low rumble and his eyes flashed red. "Come, let me sit in the chair so I can reach you better."

* * * * *

Sazar would have liked to take his time taking off the old breast bands and putting on the new ones but Chandra proclaimed that they were in a hurry and kept asking if he was almost finished. It was incredibly annoying and it set Sarah on edge as well, he could tell.

"Sazar," she breathed as he sucked her nipples gently but thoroughly to get the old bands off. "Do you really think everyone will be watching us tonight?"

"It seems likely," he murmured. "Are your breasts sore from wearing these all day?" he added, nodding at the golden bands now in the palm of his hand. "Your nipples look red."

"Maybe a little," Sarah murmured, her cheeks going warm. "Why, are you going to, uh, heal me?"

"I'll be sucking your nipples again before I put your new bands on," he remarked, examining her tight pink peaks. "I'll release a little of my essence and apply it to be certain they're in good shape before I put on the new bands."

"Th-thank you," she stuttered and looked at him shyly. "You…you take such good care of me, Sazar."

"I don't know if going to the Breeding Ball tonight qualifies as taking good care of you," he murmured wryly. "It's more like taking you into danger but I don't see that we have a choice about it."

"I was the one who wanted to…*ahhh*…the one who wanted to stay," she moaned softly as he sprayed some of the compound on her right nipple and took it deep into his mouth, spreading the essence all Blood Kindred make with their fangs to heal or pleasure a mate. "You gave…gave me the option to leave and I chose not to."

"I would not have given you the option if I'd known how dangerous this might become," Sazar said severely as he applied the new, diamond studded band to her nipple. He had to admit it looked lovely.

"That's one thing I wanted to ask," Sarah murmured. "How dangerous do you think it will get if someone figures out we're…" She cast a side-long look at Chandra who was amusing herself by playing back the orgy video of the last Breeding Ball on the wall screen. "If someone figures out we're *faking?*"

"They won't find out," Sazar assured her and sucked her other nipple into his mouth, healing it as well. Gods, he loved how stiff her peaks got when he sucked and licked them…loved the way she moaned and shifted her hips as she stood in front of him.

"But these panties…they're so tiny," she protested when she got her breath again. "What if…what if someone sees that you're not, you know, actually *in* me?"

Sazar allowed his gaze to travel down her body and saw that she was right. The tiny golden panties were so low in front he could actually see the top of her pussy slit. Their plan was for him to press his shaft into the hole at the back of her panties and conceal the fact that he wasn't actually inside her, but it seemed clear to him that the low-slung panties would never hide his shaft. He would poke out the front of them as he rubbed against her pussy rather than sliding inside it.

Seven Hells, this *was* a problem. Then he had an idea.

"I'll let the sides of my robe fall over you," he told her, placing the other diamond studded band and admiring the effect. Her nipples glittered like rainbow ice when she moved. He might never have been much for nipple jewelry before, but their time on Alquon Ultrea was turning him into quite a connoisseur—as long as the jewelry was on Sarah, anyway. "That should hide our, um, activity," he told her.

"I hope you're right." She bit her lip in that way she had when she was worried about something.

"Everything will be fine." Sazar tried to sound reassuring but to be honest, he wasn't completely certain about the security of their position.

"But what if it isn't?" Sarah persisted. "What if you have to, you know, breed me for real?"

"I won't do that to you," Sazar said fiercely. "I told you, it's *completely* out of the question."

"But what if there's no other way?"

"Sarah..." He cupped her cheek, meeting her worried hazel eyes with his own. "I won't do that to you, *Ladara*," he murmured. "Won't take your virginity that way—I swear it."

"All right." She nodded. "Thank you, Sazar."

"Are you two almost ready?" Chandra had apparently gotten bored of watching and re-watching the orgy video. "We *really* need to get going."

"We're ready." Sazar tugged lightly on Sarah's new breast chain, making her moan softly. "Aren't we, Sarah?"

"As we'll ever be, I guess." She gave that defiant little tilt of her chin he loved so well. "Let's go."

Sazar put a protective arm around her and ushered her out of the guest quarters, vowing to himself to protect his little human from everything and everyone. To keep her safe and at all costs.

She's going to remain a virgin, he told himself firmly. *I won't take her purity no matter what else happens. She'll stay intact.*

It was a vow to himself and to Sarah. He intended to keep it.

Chapter Nineteen

The palace was resplendent, glowing with golden light and filled with the upper crust of Alquon Ultrea, who had been given invitations to the Breeding Ball. According to Chandra, only the best of the best were invited and everyone they saw was of the noblest and purest blood.

"All of the Alquons here have the blood of the past Lord Magnates in their family trees," she explained to Sarah as they strolled up the golden path leading to the vast front double doors. "And for this one night, we are all paired together by the purity of our blood, with only the purest males breeding the purest females in hopes of producing even purer children. Only in this way can we remove the taint of the genetic modification we were forced to take so many years ago when our world was first covered in water."

"But…what's so wrong with your modification?" Sarah asked. She motioned at Chandra's dainty, barely-there gill slits and the slight webbing between her fingers. "It seems practical to me. And don't you enjoy being able to live in the water as well as in a dry environment?"

"*Children* enjoy playing in the water," Chandra said. "And some of us with more…*extreme* modifications find it more comfortable. Lemesh, who made your clothing, far prefers the depths to the bright lights of Idd. But most of us just wish to get back to the way we were before we were modified. Also, water messes up your hair." She tossed her own kelpy ringlets with a little sniff.

Suddenly a well dressed Alquon nobleman with perfectly coiffed green hair strolled up to them. His gill slits were more prominent than most of those in attendance although it looked to Sarah like maybe he'd applied some kind of makeup to try and minimize them.

"Hello, darling," he said to Chandra and gave her an affectionate kiss on the cheek.

"Oh, Kendro! Darling!" Chandra threw her arms around his neck and kissed him back enthusiastically. "This is my pair partner, Kendro," she said when she finally pulled away. "And Kendro, these are the Kindred diplomat, Commander Sazar, and his female, Sarah I've been telling you so much about."

"Very pleased to meet you." Kendro nodded politely. "I'm glad to finally meet the people who have been monopolizing my beautiful pair partner these last two days."

"Chandra has been invaluable to us," Sazar said seriously. "She's both considerate and knowledgeable. Forgive us for taking so much of her time."

"Oh, Kendro is just teasing you." Chandra slapped her pair partner lightly on the chest. "I'll see you after the breeding, darling. Who are you paired with, anyway?"

"Natalan Tangoo." Kendro made a face. "Her blood is a whole sixteenth less pure than mine. *So* common! I don't know how I'll bear it!"

"Now, darling..." Chandra shook a slim finger in his face. "Every little drop of purer blood helps, you know. So breed her well and do your best to give her a big belly."

He sighed dejectedly. "You know I will. Are you paired with

Jakkob again?"

It was Chandra's turn to make a face. "Yes and you know he's *so* stuffy and proud just because he's directly related to The Lord Magnate and has some of the purest blood in Idd. He acts like he's doing me a favor every time he puts his shaft inside me!"

"But think if you conceive," Kendo exclaimed. "Our child will be one of the purest in all of Idd! You have to do your best too, Chandra. Let him breed you more than once if he will."

"I'll try to convince him but Jakkob is notoriously stingy with his seed." She sighed. "Well look, darling—I really must dash. I need to get Commander Sazar and Sarah here set up with a good centralized breeding couch and show them the ropes before I go find Jakkob."

"All right. Happy breeding—I'll see you after." Kendro kissed her casually on the lips and waved as he walked off in another direction.

Sarah could hardly believe what she'd just seen. And as Chandra stopped to speak to another Alquon noble she looked up at Sazar.

"Correct me if I'm wrong," she murmured. "But…aren't pair partners like husband and wife?"

"I believe so, yes," he said in a low voice.

"But then…did I just hear them making plans to…to have sex with other people? Right in front of each other?"

"It appeared so." Sazar shrugged. "Such a thing would never be permissible in a Kindred society but I have been on missions to polyamorous cultures before."

"But how can they just…just plan to have sex with other people and then agree to meet later like it's no big deal?" Sarah exclaimed. Even in the Compound such a thing would have been frowned on and punished severely. The only male a woman was supposed to sleep with was her husband—*after* Father Caleb was done with her, of course.

"Oh, do our breeding customs upset you?" Chandra asked and Sarah realized with embarrassment that the Alquon girl had heard everything she'd said.

"They just…surprise me, that's all," she said quickly.

"Well believe me, it's not always pleasant to be bred by another male." Chandra pouted prettily. "But we do whatever we must to purify our bloodlines. And of course, The Lord Magnate has the purest bloodline of all—that's why it's such a great honor to be bred by him." She sighed, as though remembering something lovely. "I had only just come of age the year he bred me at the ball. I was *so* excited."

"I'm…sure you were," Sarah said as neutrally as she could though the idea of being "bred" by The Lord Magnate still made her skin crawl.

They entered the vast double doors along with a few other nobles and Sarah was surprised to see there was a new addition to the gold and marble entry hall.

An enormous fish bowl—bigger than a dump truck—was placed right in the center of the foyer. It was filled with pale green water that shimmered in the golden light. An enormous, shiny black lump sat like a mountain right in the middle of it.

"Oh look—they brought the *grike* inside this year!" Chandra exclaimed.

"The *grike?*" Sazar frowned and Sarah felt a stab of curiosity herself. Since the moment they'd gotten to Alquon Ultrea she'd been hearing about people getting "thrown to the *grike,*" as though it was the worst possible punishment. She'd assumed the *grike* must be some kind of wild animal but where was it?

"I don't see anything," she said to Chandra. "Other than that big black blob in the middle of the bowl. Where's the *grike?*"

"Darling, that big blob *is* the *grike.*" Chandra walked up to the fish bowl and tapped smartly on the glass side with one longer fingernail.

At first nothing happened. Then one enormous luminous white eye opened slowly on the side of the black blob. It blinked lazily and then closed again.

"Wow, it really is *gigantic,*" Sarah murmured. It reminded her of stories she'd heard about grouper who lived off the Florida coast. Rumor was that some of them grew huge in the depths—big enough to swallow a small car in a single gulp. The *grike* made her think of such a fish. It was enormous, yes, but it looked sleepy and peaceful and not very threatening.

"It's very large," Sazar remarked diplomatically. "But not very…active apparently."

"Oh, you want to see active?" Chandra smirked at him.

There was a small pedestal table sitting beside the fishbowl. It was full to the brim with some reddish-brown substance which had a strange smell. Sarah had thought it might be some kind of alien potpourri. But the minute Chandra picked up a long handled spoon from the small table and scooped it into the bowl, she saw she had been wrong. This was no potpourri—it was more like chum—the mixture of fish guts and blood fishermen use to lure in sharks.

Still smiling widely, Chandra stood on tiptoes and emptied the contents of the long-handled spoon right into the water.

At once the *grike* came to life.

The luminous white eye opened again—and then another eye and then another. Soon Sarah could see the creature had at least three pairs of eyes and none of them looked happy.

A huge mouth, wider across than Sarah was tall, suddenly gaped open in the greenish water and teeth were revealed—sharp, dagger-like fangs as long as her arm. The teeth were so long and thin they were almost translucent but somehow Sarah knew they were still horribly, incredibly strong. She had read once about an armored fish which had lived in the ancient oceans of the Paleolithic era. Supposedly it had had more bite force in its massive jaws than even the deadly Tyrannosauruses Rex.

Now that the *grike's* teeth had been revealed, it reminded her much more of that ancient, extinct fish than the sleepy grouper it had first appeared to be. Sarah was certain it could bite a person in half as easily as she could bite into a breadstick. Her stomach lurched.

"Dear God," she whispered as the jaws opened wider and wider. Now they were wider than *Sazar* was tall.

"Oh, you haven't seen anything yet." Chandra giggled. "Watch this." She dumped another spoonful of chum into the *grike's* bowl and stood back.

Suddenly the giant fish went crazy. Writhing and thrashing, the *grike* came to the surface, its massive, deadly jaws gnashing in the water as those terrible, deadly teeth sought something to bite.

"Oh!" Sarah jumped back and would have fallen if Sazar hadn't caught her and helped her stand steady.

"Don't worry," Chandra laughed again, obviously amused by her reaction. "He can't get out. The only way the *grike* can get you is if you get your self thrown in."

"Does that happen often?" Sazar demanded. "Someone getting thrown in, I mean.

"Oh, no—not usually. It's more of a deterrent than anything

else. Although there *have* been times when The Lord Magnate has ordered someone tossed to the *grike*. Usually someone who refused to participate in the ball, or refused their assigned breeding partner."

"Why would...would someone do that if you all take, uh, breeding so casually here?" Sarah asked.

"Well as I said, it doesn't happen often. It *did* happen at last year's Breeding Ball though." Chandra sounded thoughtful. "Landro Doormel refused to breed with KiiKii Doormel."

"Why?" Sazar asked.

"Oh, he thought their bloodlines were too close because they were related." Chandra waved away such incestuous concerns breezily. "But she was only his *half*-sister! Really, it was such a fuss about nothing."

Fuss about nothing? Sarah thought. *A man refuses to have sex with his sister and he's thrown to a giant man-eating fish as punishment? Oh my, how terribly dull dear!*

A hysterical laugh rose in her throat but she swallowed it back down hastily. Suddenly the stakes for being caught faking the breeding ritual were raised considerably. God, what had they gotten themselves into here?

She looked up at Sazar and saw that his face had gone grim, his lips thinned to a line and his pale eyes narrowed. Was he doubting their chances of getting away with this too?

"Well, enough about the *grike*," Chandra said casually. "I think it's time we go to the throne room and get you two settled. Just think—your first Breeding Ball!" She clapped her hands eagerly. "So thrilling! Aren't you excited?"

"Overwhelmed is probably a better word," Sarah said.

"Oh, there's nothing to be nervous about, sweetie." Chandra

patted her arm comfortingly. "You don't even have to worry what it's going to be like with a new breeding partner! You and Commander Sazar have been together already. So you're just going to be doing in public what you've been doing in private for ages."

Sarah blushed when she thought about some of the things she and Sazar had been doing in private—the way he'd sucked her nipples and healed her pussy with his tongue…but none of that had been actual sex. Now they were going to have to pretend to make love and hope no one noticed they were just faking.

She looked up at Sazar again but he was staring back towards the *grike* as Chandra led them further into the palace, towards the throne room. What was he thinking? And were his thoughts as chaotic and frightened as hers?

* * * * *

This is going to be fucking tricky, Sazar thought, staring over his shoulder at the monstrous fish which still thrashed and gnashed its dagger-sharp teeth in the immense bowl. *We can't be caught under any circumstances.*

Their position would be much simpler, of course, if he and Sarah could just perform the breeding as expected, but Sazar was absolutely determined that wasn't going to happen.

In his home world of Tranq Prime, a female's virginity was prized above everything—without it she was nothing. He refused to take his innocent little human's virginity—absolutely refused. Even if he'd been certain she felt for him as he felt for her, he would have balked at such an action in a public venue like the Breeding Ball.

Sarah was special—she deserved to be taken gently with lots of preparation—not bent over a breeding bench and unceremoniously skewered. She shouldn't have to give up the treasure of her virginity for this mission or for fear or uncertainty—she shouldn't have to give it for anything but love, Sazar told himself. And until he was certain she loved him and wanted him, he wouldn't do that to her—wouldn't take her.

Besides, she'd run away from The Brotherhood of Peace in order to get away from a forced breeding—he was determined he wasn't going to betray her trust by forcing her now.

We'll fake our breeding and make it work, he told himself fiercely. *We have to.*

They entered the throne room which looked much different than it had the day before when they'd first been introduced to The Lord Magnate. The formerly empty area had been filled with concentric rows of the same red-padded benches they'd seen on the video Chandra had sent them. They curved in a semi-circle around the dais where the golden throne had been the day before. In its place was a golden breeding couch, much larger and finer than the rest. Clearly it was for the use of The Lord Magnate himself.

"Now let me see, oh yes—as guests of honor I believe you're be assigned to this bench…here," Chandra said.

To Sazar's dismay, she led them to the center bench in the front row—directly in front of the dais.

We'll be directly under The Lord Magnate's eye. Goddess damn it—she couldn't have picked a worse spot!

Sarah seemed to be thinking the same thing because she was protesting to Chandra that this spot was much too exposed.

"Sazar and I aren't used to doing this in public," she said earnestly. "I really think we'd feel much more comfortable over on the side of the room—maybe even in the back corner."

"Shove you away in the back corner when you've got the purest blood of all—proven by the prophesy?" Chandra exclaimed.

"Heaven forbid!"

"But—" Sarah started.

"Besides," Chandra went on. "*I'm* not the one who made the breeding chart! That would be the Councilor in charge of Breeding. And your names are right here—see?" She pointed to a small tag with curving, alien script on it attached to the bench.

Sazar frowned. "We do not wish to be so prominently placed. What Councilor must we speak to in order to get our position changed?"

"Well…" Chandra hesitated delicately. "That would be Minister Rando. We met him yesterday if you remember."

Inwardly, Sazar groaned. He had nearly broken Rando's arm the day before—there was no way the male would be willing to accommodate them by moving them to a more obscure spot in the room.

"Look," here he comes now," Chandra remarked. "You can ask him if you want."

"Ask me what?" Rando snapped, coming up to them. He looked every bit as greasy and weasely as he had the day before, Sazar thought. And his beady eyes crawled just as greedily over Sarah's exposed breasts, though he made certain to keep his distance and didn't try to reach for her breast chain this time.

Sazar swallowed down the possessive growl that rose in his throat and tried to address the male in a neutral tone.

"We find that our, uh, breeding position is much more centrally located than we like," he said, looking down at the shorter male. "Such things are done in private in our culture and though we are willing to participate in your Breeding Ball ritual, we prefer to be as far out of the public eye as possible."

"Well that's too bad," Rando snapped, glaring up at him.

"Because you're stuck here—by order of The Lord Magnate himself," he added quickly, when Sazar took a menacing step toward him. "He apparently thinks you deserve the honor of this position although I can't say I agree with him." He sniffed. "So you'll have to take it up with him—if you dare. He wants to see you anyway."

"He...he does?" Sarah faltered, putting a hand to her chest. "What for?"

"How should I know?" Rando shrugged his skinny shoulders. "Something about some ridiculous ancient prophesy, I believe. Anyway, he's waiting for you in the throne antechamber—through the door at the end of the dais." He nodded the way. "Tell the guards The Lord Magnate is expecting you." He gave Sarah's breasts one more hungry look and added, "Happy breeding," before leaving abruptly.

"Sazar?" Sarah looked up at him, fear in her big hazel eyes.

"It's all right," he said with confidence he didn't feel. "Let's just go see what he wants."

"Oh, so exciting!" Chandra clapped her hands. "I'm so glad you're to be honored by another meeting with The Lord Magnate! Good luck to you both and I'll see you after the breeding!" She hugged Sarah and kissed her cheek and gave Sazar a little wave before fluttering off to a tall Alquon male with angular features and a disdainful look on his face—presumably her breeding partner for the night.

"Well?" Sarah slipped her hand into his. Sazar couldn't help noticing it was trembling.

"It will be all right," he said again, squeezing her fingers tightly. "Come on—let's get this over with."

Chapter Twenty

"Commander Sazar and the lovely Sarah! How good to see you again!" The Lord Magnate nodded genially but didn't rise from his golden chair beside a fireplace filled with blue and green flames. "Do come in," he said. "Guards, shut the door and don't bother us."

"Yes, My Lord." The Alquon guards bowed obsequiously and closed the door, leaving them alone with The Lord Magnate in the small but sumptuously decorated antechamber.

"Well, you're looking lovely tonight, my dear. Come a little closer." The Lord Magnate nodded at Sarah, his eyes crawling over her breasts just as Rando's had.

Sarah suppressed a shiver of revulsion and started to step forward alone—but Sazar wouldn't let her. He kept their fingers firmly entwined and stepped forward with her, partially blocking The Lord Magnate's view of her breasts.

A spasm of annoyance passed over the Alquon ruler's smooth, handsome features, but he smiled brightly the next moment and Sarah almost wondered if she'd imagined it.

"So," he said, speaking to Sarah and ignoring Sazar. "When I met you the other day I had no idea we had the answer to our ancient prophesy in our midst!"

"You…you mean the one about the silver fingers and the, uh, ivory mounds?" Sarah asked faintly.

"Indeed, yes." The Alquon leader nodded decisively. "As you

know," he continued. "I am in the unhappy position of being the only male in our lovely society without the pleasure of a pair partner." He sighed in a melancholy way. "For I have never found a female with blood pure enough for me to pair with her." He leaned forward, his aquamarine eyes fixed on Sarah. "Until *you* my dear."

"I...I..." Sarah didn't know what to say. She had an awful feeling in the pit of her stomach—the same feeling she'd gotten when Father Caleb had called her into his office to announce the "happy news" that he'd decided to accept her as a "Bride of the Prophet." Was that what was about to happen here? Was The Lord Magnate going to proposition her?

"What are you saying?" Sazar asked, his voice low and menacing. "Are you insinuating that you will take my mate as your own? Because I cannot allow that." The last word ended on a growl that made the short hairs on the back of Sarah's neck stand up.

"I'm offering her a great honor." The Lord Magnate scowled angrily. "The chance to become my pair partner and rule by my side while she bears me many pure-blooded children."

"Sarah is *my mate.* **Mine.**" Sazar's eyes flashed red as they had just before he'd attacked Councilor Rando. "I'm not sure you understand what that means to a Kindred, My Lord Magnate, but it is not a relationship to be taken casually. Kindred males form a bond with their females which cannot be broken. We will *kill* to protect them."

"Yes, yes—honor and duty until death." The Lord Magnate waved his hand languidly, as though such concepts were hardly important.

"And love." Sarah spoke up. She was amazed at her own bravery but she couldn't just stand by and do nothing while the creepy Lord Magnate tried to steal her away from Sazar.

"Love?" The Lord Magnate raised his white eyebrows as though this was even harder to understand. "What does love have to do with breeding?"

"Everything," Sazar growled. *"I love Sarah* and I will never give her up to you or anyone."

"Is that so?" The Lord Magnate rose, glowering at Sazar now. "Well perhaps I'm not *asking* you to give her up. I'm *telling* you. As ruler of Alquon Ultrea, it is my right to have any female I choose and I choose Sarah!"

Sarah's heart fisted in her chest. Part of her was saying, *I can't believe Sazar really said he loves me!* It was probably just part of the act he was playing but still, hearing that possessive growl in the big Kindred's voice sent a thrill through her entire body.

But she couldn't enjoy the pleasurable tingle for long because the other part of her mind was screaming, *Crap! It's Father Caleb all over again! He's going to try to take me and if we say no he'll feed us to the grike. What are we going to do?*

"If you try to take Sarah from me I will fight you until my last breath. And you should know, Kindred do not die easily." Sazar bared his teeth, letting the Alquon Leader see his double set of fangs which had grown long and sharp.

The Lord Magnate grew pale and the look on his face turned belligerent.

"You dare to threaten me?"

"No, I dare to tell you the truth," Sazar growled. "You will have to kill me to take Sarah from me."

"That can be arranged." The Lord Magnate smirked. "The *grike* is hungry tonight. I trust you saw it in the palace foyer?"

Sarah's stomach felt like someone had filled it with a bucket of ice cubes. *Crap, crap,* **crap!** What were they going to do? *Help!* she prayed silently, though she wasn't even sure who she was praying to. *We're in big trouble here – we need help!*

Suddenly a strong, warm presence seemed to fill her mind. ***All will be well, daughter,*** murmured a feminine voice in her head. It sounded familiar somehow but not like her own internal monologue.

Sarah opened her mouth.

"It won't do you any good to take me away from Sazar," she heard herself saying.

"Oh no?" The Lord Magnate raised an eyebrow and smiled at her coolly. "Is that because you could never love another besides him and you think I could never win your heart? Because I must tell you, my dear…" He leaned forward and deliberately let his eyes run up and down her body from her bare breasts to the tiny golden panties, clearly visible under her split skirt. "I'm not interested in your heart—I only want your body and your womb to breed my pure-blood babies in."

"My womb won't do you any good," Sarah said, still not sure where she was heading with this or what might come out of her mouth next. "Because of the bond Sazar was talking about—the one Kindred have with their wives, er, mates."

"What are you talking about?" The Lord Magnate glared at her distrustfully. But by this time, Sazar seemed to have picked up the thread of what she was saying—though Sarah hardly knew what it was herself.

"The bond between a Kindred and his mate is unbreakable and it also renders her infertile with any male but him," he said. "The moment I first spilled my seed into Sarah's channel, her womb was dedicated to me and my progeny only. She would never be able to conceive your child. She is mine, body and soul." He put an arm around Sarah protectively. "As I am hers. We cannot be parted."

"Is this true?" The Lord Magnate glared at Sarah. "I cannot believe it—is it really so?"

Sarah nodded, doing her best to look sincere. Inside she was praying again. *Oh please, let him believe us! Oh please let him believe!*

Peace, daughter. He will believe, whispered that same warm voice. Then the comforting presence faded but somehow Sarah knew that things were going to be all right.

"I'm afraid it's true, My Lord Magnate," she said. "I can't have anyone's babies besides Sazar's. So even though I'm, uh, extremely honored by your offer, I'm afraid I can't take you up on it."

A petulant look came over the Alquon ruler's face. The look of a spoiled child, denied something he truly wants and realizes he can never have.

"But this is not right! How can your people survive if your biology doesn't allow for interbreeding?"

"We have done well for millennia," Sazar said firmly. "Our biology precludes the type of relationships you Alquons are used to, but we do not find that we miss it." He pulled Sarah closer. "And may I point out that one reason the Kindred thrive is that we value *diversity.* We would have died off long ago if we had been too obsessed with the purity of our blood to make trades with other peoples."

"In light of what you've just told me, I don't see how we can possibly make a genetic trade with you," The Lord Magnate snapped, clearly still miffed. "Such a backwards race cannot be mixed in with our own fine bloodlines."

"Very well. I understand completely." Sazar made a low bow. "Sarah and I will leave at once so as not to importune you any longer."

"No!" The Lord Magnate rose from his chair and started pacing, his white and gold-edged robe and trousers swishing against the golden floor. "No, you cannot leave now! Not after causing such a stir by fulfilling the prophesy in such a public way." He turned on Sazar and pointed a finger at him. "I have given you the place of honor in the throne room. I had *hoped* to be breeding Sarah while you bred one of my concubines there. But as that is not to be, I will *not* have you ruining the ceremony by leaving without participating."

Sarah's heart sank. They had been so close to getting out of here! And now *this*. She looked up at Sazar who was nodding.

"Of course, My Lord Magnate," he said coldly. "We would never wish to cause you embarrassment or disrespect your customs. We will be happy to participate and we will leave directly after."

"See that you do," The Lord Magnate snapped, still looking sulky. "And see that you put on a good show during the breeding. Every eye will be on you. Now go!"

He snapped his fingers and the door of the antechamber popped open, revealing an expectant guard.

Silently, Sarah and Sazar left, their hands still clasped tightly together.

We have to get through this. We just have to get through it, Sarah told herself silently. She wished the warm, comforting presence and the soft, feminine voice would come back and help them out of this mess too. Who or what had it been? Maybe the Kindred Goddess? But the presence was gone and the little voice didn't make another appearance.

Apparently they were on their own.

Chapter Twenty-one

Almost all of the Alquon noble men and women were at their respective breeding couches by the time they came out of the antechamber and went back to their own bench in the center of the front row. The strangely androgynous attendants they had seen on Chandra's video were there too, moving from bench to bench clad in their floor-length white coats. Their hair was uniformly short and their faces were coated in some kind of white makeup. The strange uniform completely disguised their sex.

Were they some kind of subclass here on Alquon Ultrea, Sarah wondered. Or were they regular Alquons dressed up in a specific costume for this night only? It was difficult to tell and anyway, it wasn't the attendants' appearance that ought to worry her—it was how sharp their eyes were.

Will they catch us? Sarah wondered as she and Sazar took their places on either side of the bench and stood stiffly, as the Alquons all around them were doing. *How can we possibly get away with this when literally everyone in the room is watching us?*

Because they were. She could feel the eyes of everyone in the room directed at them and there were murmurs and whispers as some of the Alquons discussed her and Sazar, none too quietly.

"That's the girl—the one from the vid I showed you! Do you see how pale her skin is?" Sarah heard a girl several benches down from them whisper to her breeding partner.

He craned his head to look at her and Sarah pretended not to notice, though her cheeks were hot with embarrassment.

"She's pretty enough, I suppose," the Alquon male said after a lengthy inspection. "But her breasts are *much* too large. I mean, I like an ample bosom as much as the next male but more than a handful is *too* much."

"Think how pure her babies would be though," the girl whispered enviously. "I only wonder that The Lord Magnate isn't breeding her himself."

"Don't listen to them," Sazar murmured.

Sarah looked up quickly and noticed that he was looking at her, his face pale with anger.

"I…I wasn't…" she began.

"They have no right to discuss you like that," he growled softly. "If we weren't in this situation I would never tolerate it. I am sorry Sarah—I should have taken you away from here the moment we realized how you'd be expected to dress. The Alquons demean and objectify their females—it's clear to me now they would not make good trade partners, no matter how advanced their technology is."

"It's okay," she whispered, reaching for his hand. "I was the one who wanted to stay. But what if…" She bit her lip. "What if you have to, you know, actually—"

"Don't even say it," Sazar ordered. "I told you, I won't do that to you. Won't take your greatest treasure here in this ridiculous display of public breeding." His eyes softened somewhat and he cupped her cheek. "You deserve more, Sarah—so much more."

"Thank you," she whispered, her heart pounding. "But Sazar, what if…what if we can't fake it?"

"We'll manage," he said and there was a finality in his tone which brooked no argument.

Sarah started to say something else but just then the door to the antechamber was flung open and The Lord Magnate stalked out onto the dais—*like an aging rock star coming out on stage,* Sarah thought. At once all the whispering and muttering stopped as everyone gave the Alquon ruler their complete attention.

"My people, fellow Alquons, welcome to you all," he began, his voice ringing through the suddenly quiet throne room. "Tonight we have a special treat—a perfect addition to our Breeding Ball." He flung out an arm, draped in dazzling white and gold, and pointed directly at Sarah and Sazar. "Behold—the pure one and her pair partner," he proclaimed. "Sarah of Earth is the answer to our prophesy—

'When the silver fingers…

Find the ivory mounds…

There you may be certain….

Pure blood abounds.'"

There was an awed hush for a moment and then the murmuring started again as everyone in the room looked directly at Sarah.

At first she didn't know how she could bear it—she had spent a good part of her life trying desperately to go unnoticed. And now hundreds of people were staring at her and talking about her.

If this is what it's like to be famous, I don't like it! she thought. *I wish I could sink through the floor and disappear.*

Then she felt Sazar squeeze her fingers.

"You're beautiful, Sarah," he murmured in a low voice for her ears alone. "Don't hang your head in shame—*own* your beauty. Let them see who you are—let them see your courage the way you let me see it the very first time you walked into my office."

The big Kindred's words were like a shot in the arm.

I can be brave, Sarah told herself. *I ran away from the Compound even though I knew the consequences if the Controllers found me and took me back again. I ran from the only life I've known into uncertainty. And I had the nerve to interview for the job as Sazar's assistant, even though I knew my resume was terrible and he would probably want to bite me. He's right – I have courage. I can do this.*

Taking a deep breath, she lifted her head high and fearlessly met the eyes of the curious Alquons staring at her and whispering. Let them stare! She would not be frightened or intimidated. She would not be ashamed.

At last the murmuring stopped and The Lord Magnate spoke again.

"And now for the decision you have all been waiting for. For this year's Breeding Ball I will take Thessoly Tangood for my own breeding partner," he announced.

There was an excited squeal from one corner of the room and a girl who looked young enough to be The Lord Magnate's granddaughter ran up onto the dais. Her long hair was barely kelpy at all and her skin was such a pale green the tint was barely noticeable. Her gill slits and the webbing between her fingers were all but invisible.

"Oh My Lord," she breathed, rushing up to bow low before The Lord Magnate. "Thank you so much for choosing me! I will do my best to conceive, I swear it!"

"Yes, yes, my dear. I am certain you will." He tugged her breast chain absently. "Now then, as we are all assembled, let the breeding commence. The attendants will come among you to be certain all goes as it must. To begin, let us have a bit of cock worship, shall we?"

Cock worship? Sarah wondered. *What in the world is that?*

It didn't take long for her question to be answered. All around her Alquon females were dropping to their knees before their males, who were opening their trousers to allow long, thick shafts to poke out.

"Oh…oh my," Sarah whispered as she watched Chandra, a few benches down, lean forward and swallow the long, thin shaft of her breeding partner to the hilt. Did they expect her to be able to do *that?* Because there was no way it was possible. She'd had only passing glances at Sazar's equipment but if she tried to swallow it all like that, she would surely choke. He was much too big!

"Woman, why are you not worshipping your male's cock?" The cool, severe voice in her ear made Sarah jump in surprise. She turned her head and saw one of the white-clad, androgynous breeding attendants frowning severely at her.

"Oh, well…I just…" She looked up at Sazar for help but he was scowling. Clearly he was trying to think of a way out of this but Sarah was pretty certain there *was* no way.

"Well?" the attendant demanded. "What are you waiting for?"

"Nothing. I just…wanted to be certain I was in the correct position." Instead of kneeling on the floor, Sarah settled herself on the end of the breeding bench.

The white-coated attendant scowled even more fiercely.

"What are you doing? Drop to your knees as the female who services The Lord Magnate is doing!"

"But I *can't*," Sarah explained. "My, uh, pair partner is too tall for me to reach him that way. Look."

She reached for Sazar and for a moment she thought he

wouldn't come. He frowned at her so fiercely she was almost afraid. But then she lifted her chin again. They *had* to do this—there was no faking this part. Not with the attendant standing right over them. Besides, how bad could it be? She'd never touched male equipment before but from the few brief glimpses she'd had of the big Kindred's, his was rather nice.

"Come on, Sazar," she said coaxingly, tugging lightly at his trousers when he stayed stubbornly out of reach of her mouth.

"You shouldn't have to do this." His voice was a low growl.

"But I *want* to," Sarah protested and knew that it was true. She wanted to taste him—to know him as he had known her the other night. "You put...put your mouth on me," she reminded Sazar in a soft voice. "I...I just want to repay the favor."

"But you shouldn't..." Sazar shook his head and sighed as Sarah pleaded with him with her eyes. "All right," he said at last and stepped closer to the bench.

Tentatively, Sarah unfastened the magnetic tabs which held his trousers closed and reached inside. Something long and thick and hard met her seeking fingers.

For a moment she almost felt burned—he was so *hot*—hotter than she'd ever expected him to be. And so big too.

His skin was smooth and soft here, ridged by veins and his shaft seemed to pulse in her hand as she drew it out of the loose trousers.

"God," she whispered, looking at it, half in fear and half in admiration. It was a good thing he'd promised not to put this in her tonight—she didn't think her little virgin pussy could handle it. She ran her hands up and down its length and tried to circle the thick base with her fingers but couldn't. He was *huge*.

A muffled groan from above reminded her that the amazing

shaft she was exploring belonged to someone—namely her boss. She looked up quickly to see Sazar looking down at her, his eyes half-lidded and flashing from pale to red.

"*Ladara*," he murmured. "Your soft little hands…"

"Are not nearly enough," the attendant, who was still watching, declared, glaring as Sarah. "Well? When are you going to get started? You must take him in your mouth to worship him properly."

"Oh yes—yes of course. I'm sorry," Sarah murmured. She leaned forward, examining the broad, plum-shaped head which was darker than the rest of his shaft. There was a small slit at the top of it and a shining bead of clear liquid was welling from it.

Since there was no way she was going to be able to swallow him down her throat, the way Chandra had done with her breeding partner, Sarah decided to take a different approach.

Leaning forward once more, she put out her tongue and lapped away the little droplet. A salty flavor like the ocean filled her mouth and she felt her entire body respond. Her nipples were instantly hard and her pussy was suddenly liquid between her thighs.

Numalla, she thought, remembering what Sazar had said about females who make a lot of honey. Was a *numalla* also good at other things? Like licking and sucking cock?

Sarah decided to find out.

She swirled her tongue around the broad head, drawing a groan from Sazar. His big hands were fisted at his sides, she saw, and his big body was rigidly still as though he didn't trust himself to move—or maybe he just didn't want to hurt her.

She suddenly felt deliciously in control of the situation, despite the watching attendant. It was a heady sensation to know she had such power over the big, muscular Kindred—to know that she could make Sazar tremble with her touch.

She licked him again, starting at the base this time and dragging her tongue upwards, as though he was her favorite flavor of ice cream and she wanted to eat it all before it melted.

"Gods, *Ladara*." Sazar's deep voice drew her eyes upward. "Your sweet little mouth is so soft," he murmured. "Love to feel you tasting me."

Holding his gaze with hers, Sarah dared to take the entire broad head of his cock in her mouth. Licking and sucking, she worked the long shaft with her hands. She had no idea where she got the courage to act so shamelessly but somehow it seemed right...and felt deliciously naughty.

She'd never wanted to act this way before—for most of her life she'd been running from sex. But now she realized it wasn't really sex she'd been running from—it was the abusive males she didn't want to have sex *with*.

Sazar was different—she *wanted* him. Wanted to touch him and be touched by him...wanted to taste him as he had tasted her. His deep, male musk invaded her senses and she sucked harder, lapping at the tip to get more of his salty precum as she stroked his shaft.

Suddenly the breeding attendant was pulling her away.

"Enough!" he (or she?) proclaimed. "You will cause your male to spill his seed outside your pussy, which is sacrilege. You must not profane the ritual in this way."

"Oh...I'm sorry," Sarah gasped. "But how was I supposed to know? You asked me to worship his, uh, his equipment, so I was worshiping it."

"You must not profane the ritual," the attendant repeated. "Either through action or inaction."

"Seems to me you'd better make up your fucking mind," Sazar growled. "First you force her to suck me, then you say she's sucking too much. What in the Seven Hells do you people expect from us?"

The white-faced attendant's eyes flashed.

"We expect you to do as you're told," he or she snapped. "Now come—it is time for the breeding proper to begin." He/she made an imperious motion to Sarah with one white-clad arm. "Turn over and lie face down upon the breeding bench. It is time to submit your pussy to your breeding partner's cock so that he may fill you with his seed."

Oh God, here we go! Sarah felt a shiver go through her—a tremor of heat which started in her belly and moved outward. How were they going to fake this with the attendant standing right over them? But there was nothing they could do but try.

Taking a deep breath and shooting a silent look at Sazar, she turned over and laid face down along the padded breeding bench. Her breasts just barely fit through the oval hole in the upward curving end—clearly it had been made for girls with much smaller endowments than hers. She rested her chin on the padded curve and gripped the wooden cross-pieces which came off on either side, forming handles.

Then she spread her thighs.

When she opened herself she could feel a little breeze, like a chilly finger, invading the hole in the back of her breeding panties. Then the breeze was gone as Sazar stepped up behind her. Instead of a chill she felt the heat of his big body up and down her spine and especially between her spread thighs.

It suddenly occurred to Sarah that even though faking was better than actually doing the deed, the fact remained that the big

Kindred's cock was going to be awfully close to her unprotected pussy.

He would actually be rubbing against her and even though the breeding panties would hide the act, she would still feel his naked shaft sliding against her bare pussy lips—he might even slip inside her slick slit and rub right against her swollen clit. The breeding panties were tight and would hold him close to her as he thrust, simulating the breeding act.

It would be awkward to be so intimately close to her boss, especially in public with the attendant watching, but Sarah told herself she could handle it—could handle the feeling of his naked shaft rubbing against her bare pussy. She *had* to handle it, after all—there was no way they could get off Alquon Ultrea until the Breeding Ball was over and everyone thought they had participated in the ritual.

Soon enough, she felt his muscular bulk and the heat of his big body as he bent over her with his chest to her back.

"Are you ready, Sarah?" he murmured in her ear.

"Y-yes." She stammered the word and her voice came out sounding high and uncertain in her own years. Sarah cleared her throat and tried again. "Yes," she said more forcefully. "Yes, Sazar, I'm ready. You can…can breed me now."

"Good," the watching attendant said and motioned at Sazar. "Go on—thrust it in her, nice and deep. Fill her with your shaft."

The sounds of breeding were all around them now—the low groans of males thrusting and the higher pitched gasps and cries of the females being bred by them. The slap of bare flesh against bare flesh and the creaking of the wooden breeding benches. But somehow Sarah managed to block it all out so thoroughly she could hear the low rumble of a groan behind her as Sazar prepared to take her — or at least, prepared to *pretend* to take her, she reminded herself.

His big, warm hand caressed her inner thighs and stretched the hole in the back of her breeding panties. Then something warm and broad and slightly slippery was pressing its way inside the hole in the gold lame' fabric and rubbing against Sarah's outer pussy lips..

For just a moment the head of Sazar's cock actually lodged just at the entrance to her pussy and she wondered if he was going to thrust inside her for real. If so, should she try to stop him? But how could she do that without being found out? No, if the big Kindred decided to fill her pussy with his thick shaft, there was nothing she could do but spread her thighs wider for him and submit to his fucking.

The thought sent a shiver of illicit desire through her and Sarah berated herself. How could she *want* such a thing? It was wrong to imagine her boss's cock inside her pussy, thrusting deeper and deeper until he filled her with his seed. And yet somehow the mental image persisted, though she tried to drive it away.

After a moment of tense anticipation, Sazar pushed forward, though not inside her. Instead she felt the broad cock head parting her pussy lips and sliding deep within her furrow, rubbing against her swollen clit just as she'd imagined he might.

The jolt of pleasure Sarah got was beyond anything she'd ever imagined. Goddess, to think the big Kindred's cock was rubbing against her open pussy! The very thought made her that much wetter and Sazar slid against her with ease, his hands tight on her hips as he pressed against her, for all the world as though he really was buried balls-deep in her tender pussy.

They went on and on like that until Sarah thought she was going to go crazy with pleasure and need. Though she knew it was wrong, it seemed her pussy was crying out to be filled and she could feel herself building to climax, though she knew it would be shameful to come on her boss's cock.

"*Oh*," she moaned, unable to help herself. "Oh, Sazar—yes...*yes*."

"That's right, sweetheart," he growled in her ear as he continued to pump his hips, simulating fucking her. "That's right, spread your sweet little pussy wide and let me get deep inside you."

Sarah thought half-deliriously that they were putting on a damn fine show. Part of that was the fact that she wasn't acting. Every stroke of the big Kindred's cock against her open pussy pushed her higher and every time the head of his shaft accidentally came to rest against her pussy entrance, she wished he would enter her.

Everything might have been all right and they might have finished and gone back home to the Mother Ship without incident if only Sazar's shaft hadn't been so long. Unfortunately, it was—much too long to be contained by Sarah's low slung breeding panties.

As he pressed forward, rubbing his hard, throbbing length against her swollen pussy, the flaring crown of his cock was protruding from the front of the panties, clearly showing for anyone who dared to lift the side of his robe and observe their progress up close.

Unfortunately, their breeding attendant dared.

"Here now—what's this? What's this?" the attendant demanded, pointing to the offending sight. "Stop at once and explain," he/she demanded of Sazar. "Why are you not filling your breeding partner's pussy but instead only rubbing against her?"

Sarah was panting at that point, with a mixture of pleasure and fear of exposure. The *grike* was looming large in her mind and she was certain the big Kindred was thinking of it as well. It didn't help that when she looked around, it seemed that everyone in the room—including The Lord Magnate—was watching them.

"It...it's a Kindred tradition," Sazar growled at last. "We warm up our females first by rubbing against them. This enables a male to get his female wet and stimulated enough to take his large shaft. It also gives pleasure."

"That's very well," the breeding attendant said sternly. "But I'm afraid the purpose here isn't pleasure but breeding. You," he or she snapped, pointing at Sarah. "Take off your panties. Yes, you heard me—take them off. I have to make certain your breeding partner's shaft is going where it's supposed to."

In vain did Sarah try to protest about privacy—the strict attendant wouldn't hear of it. He or she commanded her to take her panties off again and Sarah knew there was no saying no—not if they wanted to avoid the *grike*.

Can't help it, she thought despairingly as she saw The Lord Magnate's aquamarine eyes narrow as he stared directly down at them from the golden dais. *There's nothing else we can do. I have to take them off...and Sazar has to breed me for real.*

With trembling fingers, Sarah slid down the golden breeding panties, leaving her pussy completely bare, completely defenseless. She wondered if it would hurt, trying to take the big Kindred's massive shaft inside her—or if the excessive honey she made would help ease his entrance. She hoped desperately for the latter.

"Very good." The breeding attendant nodded, clearly somewhat mollified when the panties came off. "Now," she said to Sazar. "Let me see you put it in her—for real this time."

Sarah glanced over her shoulder and saw the big Kindred giving her a look which was both unhappy and uncertain. She could almost hear his thoughts. Should he obey and fill her pussy with his cock even though he had promised not to? Should he take her virginity though he had sworn he wouldn't? Would she hate him if he did this to her?

Sarah could see the indecision and self-loathing on his face and suddenly she wanted to reassure him.

"It's all right, Sazar," she whispered. "You can…can slide it inside me. I don't…don't mind."

"But I swore—"

"Never mind what you swore," Sarah murmured. "*I* swear I don't want to end my night in the belly of a giant fish with teeth as long as my arms. Now come on—do it."

He leaned over her and she felt the blunt head of his cock rubbing against her inner thighs.

"I'm only going to do it once, then," he murmured, his voice hoarse and rough. "Then, when the attendant turns away, I'll slide out again."

"And get us caught? No." Sarah shook her head. "No, you'd better just…just slide it in and leave it there, Sazar."

"But I swore I wouldn't—wouldn't take your virginity and breed you," he protested, even as he lined up the head of his cock to the slick entrance of her pussy. He was leaning over her as he did this, his deep voice no more than a breath in her ear.

"You can't…can't help the virginity thing. And it's not really breeding," Sarah insisted as she felt the broad head of the big Kindred's cock slide into the mouth of her pussy. "Not if you just hold it there in place. Breeding would be if you moved back and forth and…and came in me."

"I will certainly not do that," Sazar growled softly. "Thrusting inside you would cause me to fill you will my seed."

"Exactly," Sarah whispered, biting back a moan as he pressed another thick inch into her naked pussy. God, he was so big she wondered if her little virgin pussy could take him—but she had no choice. He *had* to be inside her—the attendant was watching.

"I won't fill you with my seed," Sazar said again.

"No, of course not. But, well…just holding it inside me isn't so bad," Sarah panted. "It's not…not really breeding—right?"

"I suppose…" Sazar still sounded uncertain but his cock had no such qualms. It was as though it knew exactly where to go as the big Kindred pressed slowly foreword, stretching her unprotected pussy with his thick shaft. There was a sharp little pain which made her gasp and tighten around him and then Sarah felt the broad head of his cock kiss the mouth of her womb.

"Oh, Sazar!" she couldn't help moaning as he finally bottomed out inside her. "God, you're in me so *deep*."

"You're so tight, *Ladara*," he groaned softly in her ear. "Gods, your pussy is so tight and wet."

But though he was in her deep, the head of his cock kissing the mouth of Sarah's womb, he didn't move but only held himself still inside her. She felt his big body trembling and knew he must be fighting with himself not to move, but he didn't thrust, not even a little bit.

They might have finished the Breeding Ball and have gone back to the Mother Ship with only that one awkward intimacy between them and tried to forget about it. Sarah really thought they might be able to get away with it, since the breeding attendant had suddenly become busy with the couple beside them.

As she and Sazar dealt with their own situation, the Alquon male had been pounding into his breeding partner's pussy and finally, with a low male roar, he finished inside her, pressing deep to fill her with his seed.

"Good! Very good," the breeding attendant exclaimed. Coming forward, he or she produced something from the fold of those long white robes—it looked a little like a clear cork to Sarah.

As the male pulled his shaft free and the first dribble of cum started to slide out of his female's freshly opened pussy, the attendant rushed forward and pressed the clear cork-like thing into the entrance of her sex. Sarah watched as the thing expanded, filling the Alquon girl's opening while still showing the massive amount of cum left inside her pussy.

"There." The breeding attendant nodded with satisfaction. "Not a drop spilled. Now, you know how it goes," she said to the Alquon girl. "The stay-tight will dissolve after twenty-four standard hours but until then it's going to hold all that lovely seed deep in your pussy and give it time to take root in your belly."

"Yes, thank you, attendant." The girl smiled as she climbed off the breeding bench with her partner's help. "I pray I shall conceive."

"May it be so, and may your child have blood as pure as our ancestors," the stern attendant said, coming in Sarah's estimation, dangerously close to smiling.

But when the happy couple left, the attendant turned back to Sazar and Sarah and frowned.

"Well, I see you've put it in her at least," the attendant remarked, motioning to the place where the big Kindred was buried to the hilt in Sarah's pussy. "But why are you just holding still?

Breed her! Go on—do your duty! Breed your partner and shoot your seed deep in her pussy!"

Oh God... Sarah bit her lip and looked over her shoulder at Sazar again. He had a troubled look on his face and she knew he was torn up inside about actually doing this. He didn't want to hurt her—didn't want to break yet another promise.

But again they had no choice.

"Just...just do it," she told him in a soft, breathless voice. "You're already inside me, Sazar. Inside my...my pussy. I guess it won't hurt if you slide in and out a few times."

"Sliding in and out is breeding," he pointed out, even as he slid his long shaft out of her pussy until only the broad head remained inside her. "And breeding you is wrong. I've already taken your virginity from you which I swore not to do." He thrust back in again, as though to emphasize his words.

"You also promised not to let me get eaten by the *grike*," Sarah whispered, trying not to moan at the delicious sensation of his thick shaft stretching her to the limit. "You're not the only one involved here, Sazar. But...I don't think we have any choice. Maybe you can just...just do a few thrusts to make the attendant happy and then we can pretend you came in me and get out of here. Besides, I don't think it's really breeding unless you, you know, come in me."

"You don't think so?" He sounded extremely unhappy but he slid out and then back into her anyway, thrusting that thick shaft deep in her pussy until Sarah couldn't help moaning with pleasure.

"Oh God, Sazar," she gasped as he pulled out and did it again. "That feels *amazing*."

"Feels good to me too, *Ladara*," he growled softly as he did it again, setting up a steady rhythm inside her pussy. "Your pussy is the sweetest and the tightest I've ever known."

"Feels right, doesn't it?" the breeding attendant asked, nodding at Sarah approvingly. "Feels right to spread your thighs and let yourself be bred by your male."

"I...I...yes," Sarah couldn't help confessing. "It does."

"That's good," the attendant said approvingly. "Now keep it up—press back to take your male's shaft and milk him for his cum. It's the only way to get yourself a big belly."

Pregnant by her boss...Sarah bit her lip at the thought of it. And yet, would it really be so bad, feeling Sazar's child stretching her belly?

Sister Hope didn't think so and look what happened to her. Father Caleb got rid of her as soon as she started to show, whispered a nasty little voice in Sarah's head.

She pushed it away. *I won't think of that now. I won't!*

"Don't worry," Sazar whispered as he thrust inside her. "I'm not really going to come in you, Sarah. I swear I won't."

"But how can you avoid it? Coming I mean?" she panted back. "The attendant's watching us, Sazar—he or she is going to expect to see your...your seed leaking out of me when we finish."

"Sarah, I won't—"

"Just do it," she moaned, completely lost to all reason or shame by now. "We have no choice, Sazar. You have to—*please*."

As she spoke she felt the peak of pleasure approaching again. Sazar's deep thrusts were rubbing the top of her pussy against the padded end of the breeding bench and sending sparks of sensation through her throbbing clit each time she was pressed against it.

"I shouldn't," he groaned but even as he did, Sarah felt his already thick shaft swelling even more inside her. She gave a little cry as something hot spurted inside her.

"Oh...*oh*," she moaned as the first spurt was followed by another...and then another and another.

Coming in me, she thought deliriously. *Oh my God, he's coming in me. If I'm not careful I'm going to get pregnant!*

Then the pleasure overwhelmed her and she felt her pussy clench around the big Kindred's shaft—milking him hard, as though her body wanted to get every last drop of his seed inside her.

"Sazar," she moaned and everything seemed to blur for a moment as her orgasm took her and shook her—scrambling her senses with pleasure until she couldn't see—couldn't even think—could only feel.

The next thing she knew a deep voice was saying bitterly, "There—it's done. I took what I had no right to take and finished inside her. Are you happy now?"

Sazar's thick shaft slid out of her but almost before she could cry out from the intense feeling of emptiness, the breeding attendant was pushing something else in place inside her pussy.

What are they doing? Sarah wondered hazily. Then she remembered the clear plug-like thing the attendant had called a "stay-tight" which he or she had pushed into the pussy of the Alquon woman who had just been bred. She wanted to take it out again but she didn't get a chance.

Sazar dragged her to her feet and held her firmly by the hand. He looked at the attendant, his eyes narrow and angry.

"We've done as you asked—are we free to go?"

"If you wish. But don't you want to attend the Breeding after-party?" the attendant looked surprised.

"Under no circumstances," Sazar growled.

"Well then, you might at least say your goodbyes to The Lord Magnate. It's customary to do so before leaving the ball, even if your duty is fulfilled," the attendant said.

"Very well." Standing stiff and tall, Sazar waited until he caught the eye of The Lord Magnate, who was breeding the girl he had picked in a leisurely manner. Sazar bowed once, stiffly, and waited until the Alquon leader had nodded in return. Then he took Sarah's hand and marched them through the rows of still-breeding Alquon nobles and out of the throne room.

"Sazar please…please, you're hurting me," Sarah gasped as he dragged her rapidly through the palace.

"Yes, I imagine I did hurt you—quite badly," he growled, staring straight ahead. "As well as lied to you and violated you—and broke my oath not to take you. For that I can only ask your forgiveness. But there's no time now—we must get out of here before The Lord Magnate changes his mind and decides he wants you after all. A male like that, used to getting his own way, won't give up on what he desires unless it's put well out of his reach."

"But…But…" Sarah wanted to tell him she didn't feel he had done any of the things he had accused himself of. But her head was still hazy from the aftermath of her orgasm and she could scarcely think he was pulling her along so fast.

Later, she thought. *I'll talk to him later — once we're on the ship.*

She just hoped he would listen and that she could find the right words to say.

Chapter Twenty-two

Bastard! Sazar thought furiously as he rushed through the glass tunnels of Idd, dragging Sarah along behind him. *Oath breaker…liar…violator!* He was all these things and worse—he had done everything to Sarah he had promised he wouldn't do.

And the worst thing was, he had enjoyed it—had gotten pleasure from the acts he was committing.

I took her virginity, he accused himself. *Not only that—I took her in public, in full view of the entire Alquon court. Then I filled her with my seed which I swore I wouldn't do. And all the time I was violating her, she had to pretend she liked it.*

Of *course* Sarah had pretended to like it—to like what he was doing to her. She'd played her part well, moaning for him to fill her when she was probably dying inside.

She ran from a forced breeding, escaped from the cult where she was raised at great danger and expense to herself and what do I do the moment she comes to me? Do I protect her as I swore I would? No, I abuse her—strip her of her virginity and breed her. I subject her to the hell she was running from in the first place. Now she'll hate me and want to leave me—she'll probably go as soon as we reach the Mother Ship and I don't blame her.

The fact that he'd taken her virginity was the worst, he thought. Among his own people, a female's virginity was considered all-important. And a male who took it without her permission—who violated her—was criminal scum—the worst of the worst.

That's me, he thought grimly. *The very fucking worst.*

There was only one bright point—at least for Sarah—in this whole dark mess. Though he had filled her with his seed, Sazar had managed to keep from biting her and injecting her with his essence during the moment of ejaculation. They might have fucked—well, *he* had fucked *her*—but they had not had bonding sex. So at least Sarah wasn't tied permanently to him and they didn't share the mental bond which all Kindred form with their mates at the moment of bonding sex.

Thinking of that bond of intimacy—longing for it—made Sazar even more aware of what he'd lost. He'd come to love his little human assistant—he saw that clearly now. But after what he'd done, he could never have her—never bind her to him permanently as he desperately longed to.

Once more he felt the sharp ache of sudden loss, just as he'd felt when he came home for lunch almost two years before and had found Malinda lying cold on the floor while Tsandor cried in confusion over her body. His young, lovely wife—gone in an instant. Exactly the way Sarah would be gone the moment she had a chance to get away.

And this time the loss was his own fault.

Goddess, he thought. *Why must I always lose what I love? Why does everything I touch turn to ashes?*

He had no answers—only a pain so deep he felt numb.

* * * * *

Why is he in such a rush? Does he really think The Lord Magnate is coming after us? Is he? Do we really need to go so fast?

Sarah's thoughts went around and around in a circle and she hardly noticed it when they found themselves in front of their room.

"In," Sazar growled, unlocking the door with his palm print and pushing her inside. "Put on some decent clothes and pack. We are leaving immediately."

Decent clothes...

His words made her look down at herself with fresh eyes and she winced at what she saw.

The decadent gold and diamond breast chain and nipple bands still glittered, emphasizing her bare breasts. Her split skirt was open, showing the fact that she was bare underneath it—her tiny golden breeding panties had been left on the throne room floor. Her thighs were still wet with her juices but not with the big Kindred's seed.

That's because it's up inside me, Sarah thought. *That cork thing—the stay-tight—is holding it in there.*

Suddenly the words of the breeding attendant came back to Sarah's mind.

"There—now you're set. The stay-tight will dissolve after twenty-four standard hours but until then it's going to hold all that lovely seed deep in your pussy and give it time to take root in your belly."

A big belly—pregnant. It's going to make me pregnant if I don't get it out!

And she knew from experience what happened when a woman got pregnant by her boss. She thought of Sister Hope's tear-stained face as she left the office with orders never to return. She had thought that Father Caleb cared for her—that he loved her. But the moment she was no longer pretty and sexy, he had gotten rid of her.

Oh God, is that going to happen to me? Is Sazar going to fire me now?

She had been about to go to the pink carry-all cube and start packing as he had ordered but she bolted to the bathroom instead, panic rising in her like a wave.

Get it out—I have to get it out! she thought frantically. But though she worked frantically between her legs and scratched herself badly with her own fingernails, the clear stay-tight cork refused to be extracted.

"Sarah?" There was a heavy knocking on the bathroom door. "Sarah we need to go. Get out here *now*."

At last Sarah gave up.

If I'm going to get pregnant it's probably already happened, she thought unhappily. *And if Sazar is going to fire me, there's nothing I can do about it.*

Feeling dejected and rejected, she came out and brushed past the big Kindred to go pack.

Chapter Twenty-three

"Oh, do you really have to go so suddenly?" Chandra was standing with them at the *tuve* station—by the numbered *tuve* leading back to their ship. She was still wearing her own pink and purple breeding gown and it was clear from the way she walked, she also had a stay-tight tucked up inside her.

"I'm afraid we do," Sarah said and suddenly she was fighting back tears. It wasn't just that she was sad to say goodbye to her friend, it was the way everything seemed to have gone wrong so suddenly. It had seemed to her that she and Sazar had shared a moment together while he was breeding her. The pleasure had been intense—overwhelming—and she'd been certain he felt it too—the sense of connection…the oneness…the rightness.

But apparently not.

He was angry and terse—wanting nothing more than to just forget about what had happened between them and go.

"Well…I'll miss you." Chandra looked like she might cry. "I had so many other activities planned for us to do together. So much more of Idd I wanted you to see."

"We've seen all we care to," Sazar snapped. "Sarah, finish saying your goodbyes."

"All right!" Sarah snapped back, her temper rising at his rough treatment. "Just give me a minute—I'll probably never see Chandra again."

"Oh dear, never?" Now Chandra really did begin to cry and Sarah felt her own tears rising as well.

"I'm sorry," she said in a trembling voice. "But it seems like…like a trade between the Kindred and the Alquons isn't going to happen after all. But thank you for everything you've done for us."

"Oh Sarah, I know I haven't known you long but I'm really going to miss you!" Chandra threw her arms around Sarah's neck and hugged her hard.

Sarah hugged back and then pulled away to swipe at her tears. She was aware that Sazar was standing there scowling at her, waiting impatiently so they could go.

"Good bye," she told Chandra. "I'll never forget you or the adventures I had here."

"*Adventures*," Sazar muttered savagely as though the word tasted bitter in his mouth.

Sarah looked up at him but the big Kindred didn't say any more. So she kissed Chandra on the cheek and left the weeping Alquon girl behind.

She stepped into the *tuve* which whisked her upward and out of the city of Idd forever.

* * * * *

"Get strapped in," Sazar ordered as soon as the hatch had closed and Sarah had stowed her pink carry-all cube in the luggage hold. "We're going home to the Mother Ship—at least I am."

"What…what does that mean?" She turned to face him, her eyes stricken.

"It means I'm sure you won't be on the Mother Ship for long," Sazar growled. Because why would she want to be near her violator? She would probably wish to go back down to Earth, to the shelter where she'd been safe.

"You...you're getting rid of me?" she asked in a quavering voice.

"You're going, aren't you?" he demanded. He didn't want to talk about this—didn't want to draw it out. "Unless you prefer to press charges against me once we get to the Mother Ship," he added. "Which is perfectly within your rights. I did, after all, violate the bounds of our professional relationship in the worst possible way."

"I..." Tears were spilling over the edges of her lovely hazel eyes—tears he had put there, Sazar told himself savagely. "No," she choked out at last. "No, I...I don't want to press any charges."

"You should," Sazar growled. "I won't fight them if you do."

"You...I..." She shook her head and then looked away, her shoulders shaking with silent sobs.

Sazar felt like his heart was being torn out. He wished like hell he could go back and change what he had done—wished he could give back her innocence and the virginity he had taken from her. But there was no way to turn back time—what was done was done.

He hated himself and he didn't blame Sarah for hating him too.

* * * * *

Why is he pushing me away? Why does he hate me so much? Sarah thought despairingly as she tried to control her sobs. *At least Father Caleb kept Sister Hope around until she started to show. But Sazar doesn't even want to wait that long. Maybe he figures I'll get pregnant for sure since the attendant put the stay-tight inside me. And he doesn't want the baby. Hell, he can't even take care of the child he already has — let alone one by me.*

The thought made her sorrow turn to anger. Poor little Tsandor! She'd wanted so badly to be there for him, even if Commander Sazar wasn't. She'd promised herself he wouldn't spend Christmas alone and now he would do exactly that, because Sarah was going to be leaving the Mother Ship — sent back down to Earth with no way to contact the lonely, love-starved little boy.

Sarah brooded about that and wiped at her eyes with the long sleeves of the red sweater she'd pulled on after taking off the Alquon breeding outfit. It wasn't fair — wasn't right. Not just to her but to Tsandor too.

As her anger built, Sazar placed a terse call to the Mother Ship to fold space for them. Before Sarah knew it, they were entering the fold in space — which looked like a bloody red gash in the endless blackness. When they came out on the other end, an incoming call from Commander Sylvan came up on the viewscreen.

"Commander Sazar," the blond Kindred said, looking slightly perturbed. "You are back more quickly than we anticipated. May I ask how your mission to Alquon Ultrea went?"

"Regrettably not well," Sazar said, scowling. "I did not see anything that would help us in our war against the Hive. And The Lord Magnate, ruler of the Alquons, has elected not to make a trade with us on the basis that we Kindred mate for life and object to trading partners and living a polyamorous lifestyle."

"Ah, I see." Sylvan's pale blue eyes were sharp. "I perceive that there is more to this than you are telling me now, but you can unburden yourself further during your debriefing, Commander Sazar."

"Thank you." Sazar stared to cut the communication but Sarah spoke up.

"Commander Sylvan, I have a favor to ask."

"Yes?" Sylvan raised an eyebrow at her. "Sarah, isn't it? My wife Sophia and her sister Olivia and their friend Kat will be glad to see you again. Would you like me to have them come meet you at the docking bay?"

"No thank you," Sarah said, although her throat got tight at the idea of leaving yet more friends behind, never to be seen again. "What I'd like to ask is that someone take me back to Earth as soon as possible."

"What?" Sylvan looked genuinely surprised. "Did you leave something there that you need to bring back to the Mother Ship?"

"No." Sarah looked straight ahead at the viewscreen although she could feel Sazar's eyes on her. "I just need to go home. I won't…" Her voice almost broke and she had to swallow hard before she could continue. "I won't be working for Commander Sazar anymore."

"And may I ask why not?" Sylvan asked, raising one pale blonde eyebrow.

Sazar started to speak but Sarah beat him to it.

"Just like the Alquon mission," she said, shrugging stonily. "It didn't work out."

"I am sorry to hear that," Commander Sylvan said gravely. "More sorry than I can say. But I know Sophia and the rest will at least want to come and say goodbye to you."

"Please don't let them." Sarah was losing it now, the tears filling her eyes. She blinked rapidly and took a deep breath. "Please, I…I can't take any more goodbyes right now."

"All right." Sylvan sighed. "But know that you're welcome back aboard the Mother Ship at any time."

"Thank you." Sarah lifted her chin. "I appreciate that, Commander Sylvan. And please thank Sophie and Liv and Kat for all their kindness to me."

"I will certainly pass on the message," Sylvan said gravely.

"And please tell…" Sarah took another deep breath. "Please ask Sophie to give Tsandor a hug for me."

"Tsandor? You mean…" Sylvan's eyes cut towards Sazar whose face was like stone.

"Commander, I must cut the com-link now," he said, his deep voice absolutely inflectionless. "We will see you in the docking bay."

Without waiting for an answer, he cut off the communication so that the viewscreen showed the huge white side of the Mother Ship instead of Sylvan's face. He turned to Sarah who mentally braced herself.

"Why did you ask someone else to convey affection to my child?" he asked in a low, dangerous voice.

"Maybe because you never convey it to him yourself," Sarah flared. She knew she was feeling angry and hurt and this wasn't the right time to discuss Tsandor but then, when *was* the right time?

"What is that supposed to mean?" Sazar spoke in a low growl as he began the landing procedure.

"It means I have something to say to you before I go, Sazar. And you're going to listen." Sarah stabbed a finger at him. "And no, it's not about what happened between us on Alquon Ultrea, which you seem to want to forget and sweep under the rug as fast as you can. It's about your son."

"What about my son?" His eyes flashed from pale to red, a sure sign he was upset but Sarah refused to back down.

"You need to go see him. You need to be a dad," she said, voicing her true feelings on the subject at last. "He's a sweet little boy and he's starving for love—the love of his father." She glared at him. "I had hoped while I was working for you that I could go and see him often and try to fill that gap. But since my employment is apparently terminated, I'm telling you that you need to fill it yourself."

"You are speaking of things you do not understand." His voice was low and dangerous but Sarah was too upset to worry about his feelings.

"Oh yes I *do* understand," she flared. "About a year after my parents joined The Brotherhood of Peace and dragged me along with them, my dad decided he'd had enough. I begged to go with him—even then I knew it wasn't right, what we were being subjected to. So what did he do?" She clenched her fists in frustration. "He *left,* Sazar. Left in the middle of the night and never looked back. He abandoned me the same way you're abandoning Tsandor by never going to see him, by not giving him the love that he needs."

"That…is…*enough.*" Sazar's voice was a low roar and the ship set down in the docking bay with a harsh metallic *clank,* as though to emphasize his words. "You will not speak to me so about my son. He is my blood—not yours. You know nothing of him."

"I know he loves you," Sarah said quietly. "But he won't forever. Kids grow up fast, Sazar. Spend time with him while you have a chance."

Then she unbuckled the flight restraint straps and grabbed her pink carry-all cube.

"Sarah," he began but she ignored him and climbed out of the ship. She was damned if she'd listen to one more word from the big Kindred bastard.

Sarah had had her say and she was leaving—for good.

Chapter Twenty-four

"I'm sorry to say that it doesn't appear things went well for you," Commander Sylvan said neutrally as they watched Sarah climb stiffly into a ship piloted by a Beast Kindred who had orders to take her back down to Earth.

"No," Sazar growled. "It' didn't."

"What happened?" Sylvan raised one blond eyebrow at him. "If I may ask."

"As my commanding officer, of course you can ask—though I wish I didn't have to tell it." Sazar sighed deeply. "We were put into a…sexual situation there was no getting out of. The Alquons demanded we attend and participate in their 'Breeding Ball'."

"They *demanded* it?" Sylvan frowned.

"On pain of being fed to a very large carnivorous fish," Sazar said dryly. "I…" He cleared his throat, wishing he didn't have to say this but knowing he needed to. "I took her virginity," he said to Sylvan in a low voice. As a fellow Blood Kindred, the other male would understand the gravity of the situation and the great evil Sazar had done.

Sylvan raised both eyebrows in surprise.

"So…you bonded her to you?"

Sazar shook his head. "No, thank the Goddess I at least managed not to do that. I knew she would hate me after what I did—I didn't want to tie her to me for life on top of it."

"I see..." Sylvan nodded, his blue eyes thoughtful. "And are you quite certain she hates you now?"

"You saw how eager she was to leave me," Sazar motioned to the ship which had taken off and was preparing to go through the permeable atmosphere dome.

"Yes, but sometimes with Earth females there can be...misunderstandings. Cultural differences can magnify arguments and grievances," Sylvan said. "Just because we learn their languages quickly doesn't mean we understand everything about our Earth females."

"Sarah isn't mine—not anymore," Sazar said bitterly. "And she never will be again. Commander Sylvan, may I be excused? I know we have to do a debriefing but—"

"We'll do it tomorrow," Sylvan assured him. "Until then, try to get a good night's rest. You must be weary."

"More weary than you know." Sazar turned away but not before he saw the ship bearing Sarah back to Earth pierce the atmosphere dome and disappear into the darkness of space.

Goodbye Ladara, he thought, his heart filled with sorrow. *I'm so sorry for what I did. I hope that someday maybe you can forgive me.*

* * * * *

The ride down to Earth was silent and Sarah thanked the driver who nodded casually and immediately took off again, headed back to the Mother Ship. She blinked back tears to see him go and wondered what Sazar was thinking—then pushed the thought away.

Forget him, she told herself. *He's probably already forgotten you.*

She set out determinedly for the shelter but she hadn't even gotten three steps out of the Tampa Human Kindred Relations building before she realized she'd made a big mistake.

Not by telling off Sazar or leaving the Mother Ship—she didn't regret that for a minute, she told herself. Her mistake had been telling him off and leaving *before* she got the big Kindred to help her take the Alquon nipple jewelry off.

She was still wearing the gold and diamond breast jewelry under her red sweater and she had no way to take it off herself. Not only that, it made her nipples poke out like two sore thumbs. She hadn't gone half a block before she noticed men staring at her, their eyes wide as they took in her large breasts and extremely prominent assets.

Sarah marched down the street, trying to ignore them. She also tried to ignore how hot she was. Up on the cool, temperature controlled Mother Ship the fuzzy red long-sleeved sweater had seemed like a perfect choice. Kat had talked her into buying it, assuring her that she looked fabulous in it. But there was a big temperature difference between the Mother Ship and Tampa, Florida.

Even though it was the day before Christmas Eve and the streets were decorated with holiday cheer, the sun beat down mercilessly. It was eighty-five degrees and humid—Sarah was drenched in sweat before she even reached the corner.

She turned down a small side street to get into the shade of one of the larger buildings and continued trudging along. She wished she could change into one of the thinner t-shirts she had also purchased on the Mother Ship but she knew her nipples would be even more prominent in one of those.

I guess I could try to wear a bra over the jewelry and put on a t-shirt over that, she thought doubtfully. But would a bra fit over the breast chain? She was afraid it was more likely that the compression of a bra would cause the chain to tug unmercifully and her nipples were already sore from wearing the gold and diamond bands longer than she should have.

Go back, whispered a little voice in her head. *Go back and talk to Sazar. Ask him for help. How are you ever going to get those bands off otherwise?*

But her heart was sore and proud and she couldn't bear the idea of going back to beg the big Kindred's help. He'd used her and tossed her away, the big jerk! She never wanted to see him *again*.

But how are you going to get them off yourself? whispered that maddeningly practical little voice. *Cut them off? Melt them off?*

Just the thought of anything sharp enough or hot enough to cut or melt metal near her sensitive nipples was enough to make her wince. But still she went on.

I'll go back to the shelter, she told herself stubbornly. *Maybe I can get some help there.*

Although from whom she had no idea.

She was just thinking that maybe she would duck into a fast food restaurant and at least *try* to put on a bra so she could wear a thin t-shirt instead of the stifling sweater when a big silver Buick pulled up by the curb next to her in a no parking zone.

At first Sarah paid no attention. She was too busy thinking about how her nipples were being rubbed raw by the rough weave of the sweater and how hot and miserable she felt in the too-hot clothes she had on.

Then a familiar face appeared in front of her.

"Well hello, Sister Sarah," a man said.

Sarah gasped and her eyes went wide as she recognized Charlie Dearborn, one of the Controllers from The Brotherhood of Peace.

"Is it really her?" Another familiar face poked out of the silver Buick's driver side window — Amos Hammond, also a Controller.

"It's her all right. Can't believe we finally found you, Sister Sarah." Charlie began stalking towards her. He had close-set eyes in a big, round head and his breath always stank due to his peculiar fondness for raw onion and mustard sandwiches.

The sight of him made Sarah sick. He was one of the men who might have taken her after Father Caleb was done with her. He only had one wife right now and he'd indicated to her on more than one occasion that he wouldn't mind having her as a second.

"Get back from me. Get away!" Sarah swung the carry-all cube at him, causing him to jump back.

"But we can't do that, Sister Sarah," Amos said coaxingly. He got out of the car and began advancing too. He was tall and skinny with big-boned, freckled wrists that always poked too far out of his coat sleeves. His long, skinny fingers reached for her, making Sarah shudder.

"Don't touch me!" She held the carry-all in front of her menacingly, wishing she had another weapon.

"Father Caleb sent us especially to bring you back to the Compound," Charlie said.

"I don't *want* to go back!" Sarah exclaimed, backing away from them. "And you can't take me! You don't own me!"

"Oh yes we do," Amos hissed, his thin, freckled face twisted in a sneer. "Once the Prophet's property, *always* the Prophet's property. You know that, Sister Sarah."

"Stop calling me Sister!" Sarah yelled. "I'm not your sister and I don't belong at the Compound. I *hate* it there—I always have."

"Well that's too bad because you're going back." Charlie lunged at her and she swung her case at him again, catching him squarely in his considerable gut with the heavy pink cube.

"Oof!" He stumbled backwards, his face going red. "You'll pay for that, *Sister*. When the Prophet is done with you I'll take you on as a second wife and teach you some manners!"

"Like hell you will!"

Sarah didn't waste any more words. She dropped the case and ran as fast as she could.

Back to the HKR building, she thought desperately as she pelted down the sidewalk. *I have to get back to the HKR building. I'll be safe there. The Kindred won't let them take me!*

She was just beginning to think she would make it—the larger street she'd left to get out of the sunlight was just ahead—when someone grabbed the back of her sweater and yanked hard.

Sarah was jerked backwards and the neck of the sweater caught her right in the throat. She began to gasp and choke as she was reeled backwards.

"Grab her!" she heard Charlie yell hoarsely.

"I got her—keep your voice down," Amos hissed. Long, horribly strong, skinny fingers wrapped around her arm.

Sarah did her best to struggle but she was still trying to get her breath back.

"Leave me alone. Help me! *Help*," she yelled, or *tried* to yell anyway.

But the small side street they were on was deserted. Where *was* everyone anyway? Probably at the mall doing last minute Christmas shopping. Or maybe sitting on their butts at home shopping online. Whichever it was, they weren't there to hear Sarah shouting—no one was.

"Help!" she managed to yell one more time but then Amos's other hand clamped over her mouth and she was dragged over to the idling Buick.

Before she could do or say anything else, Amos was shoving her in the trunk while Charlie took the wheel.

"Time to go, Sister Sarah," he said, smirking at her. "After all, you wouldn't want to miss your chance to be a Bride of the Prophet, would you?"

He and Charlie roared with laughter as the trunk slammed closed, locking her in suffocating darkness.

There was a jolt and Buick sped off down the deserted street, heading for the Compound and the nightmare Sarah had thought she'd left behind her forever.

* * * * *

"Commander Sazar, I'm sorry to bother you so late." The apologetic voice came from the 3-D viewer on the stand by his bed. A vaguely familiar female face was projected there, seeming to hover in mid-air over the small device. Sazar couldn't quite place her although he felt like he ought to know her somehow.

"That's all right—I wasn't sleeping," he said, sitting up and rubbing his eyes. In fact, sleep was the farthest thing from his mind. Though he had lain down and closed his eyes, he was too tormented by guilt and shame and regret to drift off. He kept seeing the tears in Sarah's eyes when she'd told him goodbye and wishing he had handled the situation differently.

I should have apologized and begged her forgiveness instead of getting so angry and defensive! I knew she would hate me after I had to take her virginity but I probably made her hate me even more by the way I acted. What's wrong with me?

His debriefing was tomorrow and he needed to try and get some rest but at this rate, Sazar felt he might never sleep again. So he actually welcomed the call and the interruption of his own tortured thoughts.

"I'm glad I didn't wake you," the caller said. "It's about your son."

"Tsandor?" A cold fist clenched his heart. "Is he all right? Did he hurt himself? What happened?"

"He's perfectly fine," the caller said—now Sazar was able to place her, she worked at the constant care house where Tsandor stayed.

"If he's fine then why are you calling me at…" Tsandor glanced at the clock. "Oh-four hundred hours?"

"I know it's early…or rather late, to be getting to bed," the woman said apologetically. "But you see, Tsandor's been having nightmares and calling for you all night. I've tried *everything* to calm him down and nothing is working." She made a worried face. "He's so worked up he can hardly breathe from crying. I'm afraid he's going to make himself have some kind of a fit if he can't calm down."

Sazar felt a stab of guilt. Tsandor had had night terrors in the past but only Malinda had been able to calm the boy down. He thought about telling the care giver that—telling her that the only person who could calm Tsandor was dead and there was nothing he could do.

But then he remembered Sarah's words.

"He abandoned me the same way you've abandoning Tsandor by never going to see him, by not giving him the love that he needs... Kids grow up fast...love him while you can."

The memory pierced deep.

I abandoned her and hurt her and pushed her away as surely as her own father did, Sazar thought ruefully. *The same way I abandoned Tsandor to the constant care house because I couldn't deal with how much he looked like Malinda...because I couldn't answer his questions about when she was coming home.*

Gods, he hated himself.

"I know you're a busy man and I probably shouldn't have bothered you—" the caregiver woman said.

"No." Sazar shook his head. "No, don't apologize. I'll come. Tell Tsandor I'm on my way."

He got up and threw on some clothing. He had no idea what he could do to calm his son down—he'd barely seen him lately and it had always been Malinda the boy adored anyway. But he had an obligation to try—he was Tsandor's father and it was time he started acting like it.

It was a short trip to the constant care house and he saw that the lights in the front room were on as he knocked at the door. The woman who had called him—Lola, was that her name?—opened the door holding a sobbing Tsandor in her arms.

Sazar's heart clenched when he saw the small face, twisted in misery. Tears were pouring down his round cheeks and he was crying so hard he could hardly catch his breath. He clung to Lola tightly, his small body wracked with sobs.

"Tsandor?" he said, feeling helpless and useless at the same time. "It's me—Patro." Patro was the Blood Kindred version of "Daddy" as Mamam meant "Mommy."

At first he was certain his son wouldn't respond. It had been too long since Malinda had died and Sazar had made too few visits, always running from his own grief, unable to bear to see his small son.

But then, to his surprise, Tsandor looked up, his crystal-blue eyes still filled with tears, and held out his arms.

"P-patro," he whispered brokenly and then he was in Sazar's arms and Sazar was hugging him tight.

Guilt flooded him but so did love—a love he had almost forgotten because it had been submerged in grief. A feeling of protective tenderness rose in his chest and he crushed the little boy to him, feeling the strong little arms wrap around his neck as Tsandor clung to him, still sobbing.

"Tsandor," he whispered, his own voice tight with emotion. "What is it? What has you so upset in the middle of the night?"

And then his son said something which froze his heart.

"Sarah," he said, pulling back to look at his father with wide, tear-filled eyes. "The bad men took Sarah. And if you don't get her back they're gonna do something *awful* to her."

"What?" He looked at Tsandor in disbelief. "What do you know about Sarah? How do you know?"

"It's a bad dream," Lola the caregiver said quickly. "When your new assistant, Sarah, came to visit Tsandor a couple of days ago he really took to her and he's been talking about her ever since. I think he just had a nightmare because he misses her."

"No!" Tsandor insisted. "No, it's *not* just a bad dream. I mean it is, but it isn't *just*."

"Tsandor, honey—don't you want to go back to bed?" Lola asked gently. "Come on now, I'm sure Sarah will come see you again soon."

"She can't come because the bad men took her!" Tsandor broke into fresh sobs. "I saw her, Patro," he said to Sazar. "I saw her walking down the street in her red shirt. And she was holding a big pink box. Then the men came and took her! I *saw* her!"

The cold hand that had gripped his heart when Tsandor first mentioned Sarah's name turned to ice. He remembered the red sweater Sarah had changed into before they left Alquon Ultrea. She'd been wearing it when she left the Mother Ship and carrying the pink carry-all cube which had all her clothing in it.

How could Tsandor possibly know that?

"I saw them take her, Patro!" The little boy's face was a mask of tears. "Please go get her—bring her back before they hurt her. *Please!*" He buried his hot little face in Sazar's neck, his words muffled but still understandable. "The Goddess sent her for you and me. And now she's *gone.*"

Sazar felt like a big hand had reached down his throat and turned him inside out so that his heart was beating on the outside of his body.

She's in trouble…the Goddess sent her…the bad men took her…

He remembered the things Sarah had told him about The Brotherhood of Peace. She hadn't wanted to talk about it much but she'd admitted it was a cult she had escaped from—and that they would be looking for her. It was why she'd wanted to take a job on the Mother Ship to begin with—to keep away from those she'd run from.

And I drove her away—drove her back down to Earth, Sazar thought, feeling sick. *It's my fault she left—my fault if she's in the hands of The Brotherhood right now.*

He had to go find her! He would call the shelter first—maybe she would be there. Maybe Tsandor's dream was just a nightmare, not reality.

But somehow Sazar didn't think so.

"Tsandor," he said, stroking the golden curly head gently. "I'm sorry but I have to go now."

"Are you going to go find Sarah?" The little boy looked up hopefully. "Please Patro—please find her."

"I'm going to try," Sazar said grimly. "Did you dream anything else? About where they took her?"

Tsandor shook his head.

"No—just that it was someplace bad she didn't want to go."

The Compound, Sazar thought. *It must be the Compound place she talked about, where the Brotherhood's headquarters are at.*

But where was the Compound? Somewhere on Earth was all he knew. Probably in the vicinity of Tampa.

Well that really narrows it down, whispered a sarcastic little voice in his head.

I'll find it — I'll find her. I have to!

He kissed Tsandor's flushed cheek and handed the little boy back to his caregiver, Lola.

She looked back and forth from Sazar to the quieted Tsandor uncertainly.

"So...you're going to go get Sarah to make Tsandor feel better? Isn't she somewhere on the Mother Ship?"

"I'm afraid not." Sazar felt his jaw clench and his hands fisted at his sides. "She's somewhere down on Earth. But I'm going to find her."

"Hurry, Patro." Tsandor's crystal blue eyes were wide and worried. "Hurry—they're going to do bad things to her soon. I know it—I saw it."

"I swear I'll hurry." Reaching out, he stroked the boy's flushed cheek. Tsandor's face was so like Malinda's but for once the comparison didn't hurt. "I...love you," he said, nearly tripping over the unfamiliar words.

"Love you too." Tsandor spoke with the uncomplicated sweetness of childhood and gave him a tiny smile. "Find Sarah, Patro," he whispered.

"I will," Sazar vowed. "I promise."

"And then we'll all live together and be a family, right?" Tsandor asked.

Sazar felt his heart lurch in his chest. Though he could promise to track Sarah down and keep her from harm (or at least try to) he couldn't promise anything like that. After what he had done, she would still hate him, even if he saved her. He was sure of that.

"I'll find her," he repeated. And with a last look at his son, he left the constant care house.

It was time to go hunting.

Chapter Twenty-five

"Well, well—so the prodigal returns." Father Caleb steepled his wrinkled, liver-spotted hands under his jowly chin and regarded Sarah with interest. He could look charming to the world when he wanted to but when he was at rest in his own office, he looked like a big old lizard sunning himself on a rock—at least to Sarah.

"Not by choice." She glared back, heedless of the way Charlie and Amos, standing on either side of The Prophet's plush leather office chair, were smirking at her.

"You look a little worse for the wear, my dear. If you don't mind me saying so," Father Caleb remarked.

Sarah was a disheveled mess and she knew it. After bringing her back to the Compound in the trunk of their car, Amos and Charlie had locked her in a small storage closet and left her there for the rest of the night. She'd been allowed out exactly once to use the bathroom and that was only after she banged on the door and threatened to go right in the closet if they didn't give her a break.

She was still wearing her jeans and the red sweater and the Alquon nipple jewelry under it. Her nipples felt sore and chafed but though she'd attempted to take off the jewelry herself—what else was she going to do while locked in a closet for hours and hours?—she hadn't been successful. The gold and diamond nipple bands weren't budging for anyone but Sazar.

And he's probably up on the Mother Ship enjoying his life and trying to forget me, she thought bitterly. There was no use hoping that the big Kindred would come riding to her rescue. She was on her own here—which was a very bad place to be.

"Father Caleb," she said, trying to keep her voice steady and even. "Please just let me go. I didn't join The Brotherhood of Peace by choice—my mother brought me when I was twelve and I've never felt like I belonged."

"But you do belong, Sarah—you belong to *me.*" He smiled at her, a warm, charming, televangelist's smile showing whiter-than-white teeth, but there was steel underneath it, like a bear trap waiting to snap shut.

"You can't *own* another person!" Sarah protested.

"A mere mortal cannot, perhaps. But I am The Prophet!" He rose from behind his desk, spreading his hands and displaying his immaculate white suit.

Dressed all in white and full of himself, just like The Lord Magnate, Sarah thought and choked back a hysterical laugh.

"Praise be!" Amos and Charlie said together and Amos added, "He is the Prophet—he shall purify!"

"Please, just let me go." Sarah's voice was shaking now, though she tried to hold it steady. "I swear I won't say anything bad about The Brotherhood! I just want to go live my own life."

"But it appears to me you've already *started* living your own life, my dear." Father Caleb came to stand in front of her. "For instance…what is going on *here?*" He nodded at her prominent nipples and Sarah felt her stomach do a slow flip.

"We don't know *what's* going on with her, Father Caleb," Charlie volunteered. "She was like that yesterday when we found her."

"But we didn't touch her," Amos said quickly. "We left her alone, just like you said."

"That's very good." Father Caleb nodded. "But now I want to see what's going on with my sweet little Sarah. Charlie, come and lift her top."

"No!" Sarah took a step back but before she knew it, Amos was behind her, holding her arms behind her back and Charlie was lifting the hem of her red sweater. She struggled uselessly but the gold and diamond nipple bands and the golden breast chain with its diamond charms was quickly revealed.

"Well!" Father Caleb's pouchy eyes grew wide. "What have we here? You *have* been living a separate life—far from the upright and moral one you were trained to." He frowned warningly at Sarah. "Is this some kind of Kindred thing? I know you got a job with those Godless alien heathens."

"No, it's not," Sarah said defiantly. "It was a gift from a friend on Alquon Ultrea."

"*Where?*" Amos demanded, shaking her so that her breasts jiggled.

"A planet I visited when...when I worked for the Kindred." Sarah wished her eyes wouldn't fill up with tears. But she couldn't help wishing Sazar was here now—even though she was mad at him, the memories of everything they'd been through together made her long for the big Kindred horribly.

"What kind of planet was that—a *whore* planet?" Charlie demanded and he and Amos laughed uproariously.

"Never seen anything like it. Look how big her tits are! How come we never noticed it before?" Amos marveled.

"Probably because she was always hiding behind those little glasses of hers and pretending to be all shy and quiet. Guess she's not so shy now."

Amos shook her again, making her full breasts wobble. The float dots were still in place beneath them, causing her full mounds to stand up pertly, putting on even more of a show.

Sarah was flooded with shame and anger as the three men stared at her bare chest. Even on Alquon, walking around topless, she hadn't felt so vulnerable…so helpless. Probably because on the alien world, she wasn't the only woman who was topless and also, she'd been certain that Sazar would protect her if anyone tried anything.

She had no such protection now.

"You should take that stuff off her, Father Caleb," Charlie remarked. "Bet it's worth a fortune."

"I'm sure it is." The Prophet eyed her speculatively. "But as sinful as the jewelry is, it's also rather lovely, don't you think?"

He reached out his liver-spotted hand and circled one banded nipple with a wrinkled finger.

At the feel of his hand on her, a wave of revulsion rolled over Sarah, so strong it made her nauseous.

"Don't touch me! *Don't you touch me you son of a bitch!*" she screamed, thrashing in Amos's grip.

Father Caleb backhanded her, hard across the face. The heavy golden ring he wore on his right hand—a symbol of his divine priesthood—cut Sarah's cheek and her ears were ringing. Pain sang through her and the tears that had threatened earlier overflowed and spilled down her cheeks.

"You *bastard*," she whispered. "I hate you. I've *always* hated you!"

"Watch that language, my dear—unless you want another," Father Caleb murmured.

"You better shut up and show respect to The Prophet," Amos snarled in her ear, shaking her again.

"That's right—keep it shut," Charlie echoed.

"Wise advice, Charlie…Amos. Our Sarah would do well to listen to it." Father Caleb smiled at her—an ugly, greedy smirk, much different from his radiant televangelist smile.

"Just leave me alone! Just don't touch me." Her voice came out in a dry croak.

"I touch what's mine whenever I want to, Sarah. You should know that by now." Casually, he straightened his immaculate white cuffs and used a fresh linen handkerchief to rub away the traces of her blood on his ring.

"I'm not yours. I'll *never* be yours." But the defiant words came out in a whisper. Her cheek was already swelling and she could feel blood running down her chin.

Father Caleb walked back behind the desk without even bothering to answer her.

"Now let's see—what else did you bring away from this Godless planet you visited?" he mused. "Bring it here, Charlie—let's see it."

"I think it's some kinda suit case." Charlie lifted her pink carry-all cube and placed it squarely on Father Caleb's solid mahogany desk.

"Open it." Father Caleb gestured impatiently and Charlie hastened to comply, unsnapping the silver latches and spreading the cube, which unfolded in six parts, open on the desk.

"Well, *well* – just look at all these sinful, worldy clothes you got for yourself in your 'new life'," Father Caleb remarked, picking through the modest shirts and jeans and business suits gingerly, as though they were piles of crotchless bikini panties and stripper gear. "And what is *this*?" he added.

He lifted something out of the suitcase – a *chample,* Sarah saw. She'd packed a few in her carry-all, mostly because she'd been throwing everything she could reach into it in their hurry to get off Alquon Ultrea.

"Tell The Prophet what it is!" Amos demanded, shaking her until her breasts jiggled again. Sarah could feel his greedy eyes on her every time he did it – it made her sick.

"Looks like some kinda kid's blocks," Charlie offered, squinting at the brightly colored cubes scattered through the case.

"No it's not – it's a fruit," Sarah said unwillingly. She didn't want to tell them anything but she knew they wouldn't let up until she did.

"A fruit, huh?" Amos remarked. "What, like a square alien apple?"

"More like the forbidden fruit, right?" Charlie laughed hoarsely. "Like little Sarah herself. Can't touch her – not yet, anyway." His piggy little eyes crawled over her bare breasts, making Sarah want to spit in his face.

"That's right – she *is* forbidden," Father Caleb said. "Your turn will come, Charlie...Amos. But first this little one's virginity is mine."

Sarah felt another surge of fear. What would happen when The Prophet found out someone else had already taken what he wanted? And he would – there was no way around it. The Alquon stay-tight was still inside her, holding Sazar's seed in her pussy.

Though it was only supposed to stay in for twenty-four hours, it showed no signs of dissolving yet. She had to buy herself some time—but how?

The *chample* in the Prophet's hand gave her an idea.

"Those fruits," she said. "Be careful with them—they're delicacies. Nobody but The Lord Magnate—the ruler of Alquon Ultrea—was allowed to eat them. They grew them specially, just for him."

"Is that right?" Father Caleb examined the brightly colored *champles* in her suitcase with considerably more interest. Sarah knew he liked to have things that were exclusive to his use alone.

"They have different flavors and textures," she continued. "That yellow one kind of tastes like lemonade and grape popsicles and the red one with green and yellow spots tastes like a cheeseburger."

"Like a cheeseburger? What do aliens know about cheeseburgers?" Charlie demanded. "You're lying!"

Sarah shrugged. "They don't know anything about them. That's just what I thought they tasted like."

Father Caleb looked at her suspiciously. "I thought you said only the ruler was allowed to eat them."

"He let me have some. I was an honored guest—an assistant to the Kindred diplomat." Sarah raised her head proudly as she spoke. The men in this room didn't need to know how her time with Sazar had ended. For all they knew, she had been treated like a queen on Alquon Ultrea.

"I don't believe a word of it." But Father Caleb was fingering the *champles* as he spoke, lifting them up and sniffing them with considerable interest. Sarah was certain he was going to try each and every one of them as soon as he was alone.

"It's true," she said and added, in an off-hand manner. "The brown ones taste like chocolate cream pie. I thought so, anyway."

"Chocolate pie?" Father Caleb's eyes filled with a greedy light. "You don't say."

"That's what it tasted like to me," Sarah said, shrugging again.

Of course she had never tasted the brown *chample* at all since Dod had warned them that it was strictly for medicinal uses. She remembered her thought that it might have the same properties as prune juice or laxatives and hoped fervently that she had been right.

She also hoped Father Caleb would take the bait. He had a sweet tooth which kept the sisters who ran the kitchens constantly baking. Of course, none of the women in the Compound were supposed to eat any of the sweets themselves—that might make them unsightly and fat. But The Prophet had *whatever* he liked whenever he liked and one of his favorite treats was chocolate cream pie.

"Well, we'll see about all this at the proper time." Father Caleb put down the brown *chample* but she noticed that he kept one hand on it possessively. "For now, I'm sending you to the women's quarters in the Compound to be dressed for our ceremony."

"What—*now?*" Sarah's voice came out in a panicked squeak.

"Yes, now." Father Caleb frowned at her. "You've been wandering far, my little lost lamb. It's time I brought you back into the flock. And after seeing your, ah, new jewelry, let us just say I'm quite eager to make you a Bride of the Prophet." His eyes flickered over her breasts again and Sarah thought she might throw up.

"No," she said, trying to keep the pleading out of her voice. "No—don't do this. I don't belong here!"

"Don't be ridiculous, my dear—the Compound has been your home since the tender age of twelve. Where else would you belong?" He made a motion to Amos and Charlie. "Take her to the women's quarters and have her cleaned up and properly arrayed."

"What about the nipple stuff?" Charlie asked. "Should we have her take it off?"

"No…" Father Caleb said thoughtfully. "No, I think we'll leave it on. At least until I'm finished making her my bride."

"You mean raping me," Sarah said in a low voice. "That's what you do here—you rape young girls. You can dress it up however you want to with holy names but that's all it is—just *rape*."

"Shut your mouth, you little whore!" Amos snapped, shaking her until her teeth clicked together. "You ought to be grateful The Prophet will still touch you after you went out and acted like a slut!"

"Yeah, shut it," Charlie shouted, poking a finger in her face.

But the Prophet's expression remained serene.

"Well now, I think Sarah is simply confused," he remarked. "She doesn't understand how holy the act of submitting herself to The Prophet can be."

"All I know is I want her for a second wife when you're done with her, Father Caleb," Charlie said. "I'll teach her some manners."

"No, *I* want her for my third wife," Amos protested. "Who knew she was hiding such big ripe titties? I should get her—I grabbed her first."

"Peace, my sons." Father Caleb raised his hands to quiet them. "What I'm thinking is, why should little Sarah here be a second or third wife to anyone? At least, not for a while. After I'm finished making her my bride, she can play the roll of concubine for a time. That way, *both* of you can have a turn."

"What? No!" Sarah gasped. "No, *please*."

"I'm sorry, my dear but you have no one but yourself to blame." Father Caleb's smile curled up cruelly. "You cannot expect to go around dressed like the whore of Babylon without inciting the lustful urges of the men around you. And for that, you must be punished. In fact…I think it will be good if every one of the Controllers has a turn. Spread the word, Amos, Charlie. It can be an early Christmas gift."

Sarah's mouth was too dry to talk and her legs felt like water. There were ten men among the Controllers the last time she'd counted. Was Father Caleb really going to give her to *all* of them?

I'd rather die, she thought, her stomach rolling. *Rather die than let that happen!*

"Please," she managed to gasp out but Father Caleb only smiled.

"Next time think a little before you decide to rebel, Sarah," he remarked. "Now take her away and get her ready for me." He made an imperious motion with one liver-spotted hand and Amos and Charlie dragged her out of his office and back towards the Compound.

As she was dragged, stumbling between them, Sarah suddenly thought of the warm, feminine voice that had come to her when she and Sazar stood before the Lord Magnate who had wanted pretty much exactly what Father Caleb wanted.

Had it been the Kindred Goddess? Kat and her friends certainly seemed to believe in her. Sarah didn't care who it had been—she only knew she needed help from anywhere she could get it.

Oh please, she thought, praying as she had when she was on Alquon Ultrea. *Please whoever you are, help me now! I'm in so much trouble. Please help me!*

But she heard no answer.

* * * * *

"She's not at the shelter or any other shelter in the Tampa Bay area." Sazar hung up the phone in frustration. "And no one at the HKR building has seen her since she left yesterday afternoon."

"What do you want to do?" Sylvan spread his hands. He looked somewhat rumpled from being dragged out of bed an hour earlier than usual but he was willing to listen and help, which Sazar was grateful for.

"I don't know." Sazar ran a hand through his hair. "But I have to do *something*. I have to find her!"

"Are you certain your son didn't just have a nightmare?" Sylvan asked gently.

"He described what she was wearing and the carry-all cube she was carrying. And..." Sazar cleared his throat. "He said...the Goddess had sent her to us."

"Ahh..." Sylvan looked thoughtful. "The Goddess is often close to children. Their innocence allows them to hear her more clearly than we can sometimes."

"If she's not in a shelter, she's probably being held by The Brotherhood of Peace." Sazar clenched his fists in frustration. "I know where their business headquarters is but I don't know about the Compound where they live. And I'm afraid if I go sniffing around there, they'll know something is up and move Sarah someplace else."

"We can get the local police force involved," Sylvan offered. "In fact, I think it would be a good idea, especially in light of some of the things apparently going on there."

"You call them," Sazar said. "I'm going to go down to Tampa and see if I can pick up a Blood Trail."

"You think you can do that?" Sylvan looked at him, obviously surprised. "I know Pitch-Bloods have a special ability to track their mates through the blood they've taken from them but you and Sarah aren't even bonded."

"I know, Goddess damn it! Now I wish I *had* bonded her to me." Sazar sighed. "But it's all I can think to do. Maybe the Goddess will be kind and allow me to find her."

"Let me know if you do," Sylvan said. "I'm going to speak to the human police and see what I can get from them."

"Agreed." Sazar nodded and the two males went their separate ways. But though hunting around Tampa was better than nothing, he still felt deeply uneasy. He kept hearing Tsandor's words echoing in his head.

"They're about to do bad things to her, Patro – hurry!"

He *had* to find her — *fast*.

Please Goddess, he prayed as he piloted his ship down to Earth. *Please let me find Sarah before it's too late! Even if she hates me now, let me save her.*

Chapter Twenty-six

"Oh my dear, I'm so proud of you! My daughter, finally a Bride of the Prophet! And within the hour, too! *So soon.*"

Sarah's mother fluttered around, as happy as any mother of the bride on the big day. The difference was though, Sarah thought, that she was being forced into this "marriage" and nobody at the Compound seemed to care.

Sarah had been told to wash her hair and shower and now Sister Maggie and Sister Judith were dressing her in the largest "bridal gown" they could find. It was a simple white dress with lace attached to the sleeves and bodice—not really a wedding dress— just a plain, nearly shapeless garment that had been sewed by the women of the Compound.

They had four of these gowns in varying sizes, for every young woman either born or inducted into The Brotherhood was expected to become a "Bride of the Prophet" at some point in her life. So it wasn't truly surprising that Sarah found herself in this position— the miracle was that she'd escaped this fate for as long as she had.

And now I'm going to pay for it, she thought dismally. *As soon as I'm ready to go they'll drag me into the chapel and perform a quick ceremony so Father Caleb can rape me. And then he'll pass me off to Amos and Charlie and the rest…*

The thought made her sick with fear and she tried to push it away. But pretending this wasn't happening wasn't going to help her. She needed to face the situation and try to think of a way out.

"My daughter—a bride!" her mother cooed excitedly, breaking into her desperate train of thought.

"Mom, do you realize what's about to happen to me?" she demanded.

"Why yes—you're finally going to become a Bride of the Prophet! How I have prayed for this day!" Her mother sighed in apparent bliss. "I remember the day *I* became a Bride of the Prophet."

"Yes, I do too—it's the reason Dad left you," Sarah said flatly. "And don't you think it's just a *little* bit creepy that Father Caleb slept you with and now he wants to sleep with me too?"

"Of course not, my dear. It's the way of The Brotherhood. All must submit to the Prophet."

Anger and exasperation rolled over Sarah like a stinging wave.

"But I don't *want* to have sex with a man old enough to be my grandfather! I'm not doing this of my own free will—they're forcing me, mom! *Father Caleb* is forcing me—he's going to *rape* me!"

For a moment her mother's eyes went wide and there was a shocked silence in the common room where Sarah was being prepared for her "wedding."

For a moment Sarah had hope. Maybe she had finally gotten through to her mother—something she'd been trying to do since the age of twelve when her mother had first dragged them into The Brotherhood of Peace and then had stubbornly refused to leave or see anything wrong with Father Caleb and the way he operated.

"He's done this to all of you—all of us," Sarah said, speaking to the room at large now. "Can you honestly tell me all of you *wanted* this? *Wanted* to have sex with an old man who controls your entire life and passes you off to someone else when he's tired of you?"

There was nervous shuffling of feet and Sarah thought she saw uncertainty and longing in the eyes of some of the younger women—women who had been used by Father Caleb and passed on to the other men of The Brotherhood. Women kept helpless and pregnant and ignorant, forced to stay in the Compound their entire lives until they withered and couldn't even imagine trying to break free anymore. If only she could get them to rise up—to revolt! There were many more women than men in The Brotherhood. Together they could—

Then her mother broke the heavy silence with a tinkling laugh.

"Oh my dear—for a moment I thought you were serious! But of course Father Caleb *can't* rape you—he can't rape *anyone*. He is the Prophet—what he says is law and what he decrees is always right and just."

There were relieved murmurs of assent from all corners of the room.

"Blessed be—he shall purify," said one of the Sisters and the others took up the chant. "Blessed be—he shall purify. Blessed be. Blessed be."

"So it's basically all right for him to do anything he wants because he *says* it's all right. Is that it?" Sarah demanded. "Are you hearing yourself mother? Do you understand how wrong and ridiculous that is?"

But her moment was over. The sounds of forced gaiety rose around her, purposefully drowning out her voice. The Sisters went about the business of getting her ready for her "wedding."

Sarah felt a surge of bitter despair course through her.

Why did I think I could make her listen – make any of them listen? It's always the same. She doesn't hear what she doesn't want to hear and she doesn't see what she doesn't want to see. None of them do. They're all blind and deaf to anything but what The Prophet says.

She was going to her doom and her mother didn't even care. No one cared.

Maybe I should kill myself, Sarah thought bleakly. She could say she had to use the bathroom and use one of the razors to slit her wrists. Or there might be a cord long enough to hang herself in the closet. *I should do it – it would be better than what Father Caleb has planned for me.*

No, my daughter. Do not think such things.

Sarah started and felt a surge of hope. Could it be? Was it the same person who had helped her back on Alquon Ultrea? Maybe…the Kindred Goddess?

Yes, my daughter – it is I. Do not be cast down or dispirited that your Earthly mother will not hear your pleas. I hear you and I care.

But can you help me? Sarah thought at the voice which seemed to come from everywhere at once, though no one else in the room showed signs of hearing it.

Help is coming. Hold on a little longer, the warm, strong voice promised.

Then it was gone but Sarah lifted her chin a little higher, hope filling her heart. All was not lost. Not yet.

* * * * *

Goddess, Sazar prayed silently. *Goddess, I've been a fool. A selfish, self-centered idiot. But now I need your help and forgiveness.*

He stood in the middle of an overgrown field outside the city limits of a town called Brandon which was on the outskirts of Tampa. This was where his search had led him. One of the police officers Sylvan had spoken to had said he believed the Brotherhood's Compound was located somewhere out here. But the overgrown wilderness was vast and Sazar knew he was running out of time. He had to find Sarah soon, some inner voice told him. If he didn't it would be too late…

Yet try as he might, he couldn't catch even a trace of her Blood Trail.

Once a Pitch-Blood Kindred was bonded to a female and had drunk of her blood, he was able to "feel" her presence and track down her location with deadly accuracy. But part of the Blood Trail was the bond that existed between a Pitch-Blood and his mate. Without it, he was like a blind man feeling around in a dark room for something he knew was there but couldn't locate.

"Please, Goddess, I know I'm asking a lot, especially after the way I acted, the way I treated her," he prayed, aloud this time. "But please…please let me find her. Let me—"

Your prayers have been heard, Warrior.

The strong, feminine voice nearly made him jump out of his skin. Suddenly the entire weedy, overgrown glade looked somehow beautiful and golden. The air around him was filled with a divine presence so strong and overwhelming that Sazar dropped to his knees.

"Goddess," he breathed.

I know you have had pain in your life, Sazar, the Goddess said, speaking both inside and outside his head at once. *I grieved with* you when Malinda died. But when I sent you another chance with Sarah, you threw it away.*

"Forgive me, Goddess—I thought she would hate me after I took her virginity," Sazar protested.

Was that really the source of your strife? Look within yourself, Sazar—look well and do not lie to me or to yourself.

"I..." Sazar closed his eyes. "I suppose that wasn't all of it. I pushed her away." His hands clenched into fists at his sides. "I pushed Sarah away because I was afraid of losing her—the same way I lost Malinda. I didn't want to take that risk. It hurt so much...too much when Malinda died." He swallowed hard. "I couldn't bear the thought of someday losing Sarah too."

Death is a part of life, my son. We all lose the ones we love at some point. The Goddess's voice was softer now. *But know this— death is not the end. You will see your Malinda again someday. Now, though, I call on you to be brave—to be courageous enough to reach out your hand for the new love I offer you. A love not only for yourself but for your son, who has long hungered for a mother's touch.*

"Yes." Sazar's throat felt tight with unshed sorrow. "Yes, Goddess—I understand."

Do not fear to love Sarah and do not fear to love Tsandor. Live bravely, love fearlessly—that is what I call you to do.

"I swear I will." Sazar nodded fervently. "I swear it, Goddess."

I am glad you hear my words. Your female is in danger. And you too will face grave danger to save her.

"I don't care," Sazar said fervently. "Please, I'll brave any danger. I just need to save her!"

Good. Then rise, Warrior. Rise and find your love.

Sazar stumbled to his feet and suddenly a wave of certainty crashed into him—an undeniable knowledge of exactly where Sarah was. It was like an invisible rope was tied around his waist, tugging him toward her.

"I'm coming, *Ladara*," he growled hoarsely and began to run.

Chapter Twenty-seven

Sarah wondered where the voice of the Goddess was as she was led down the aisle—more like dragged down it—by Amos and Charlie.

Goddess, she thought frantically. *Goddess please, I know you said to be patient and that help was on the way but we're getting down to the wire here. Where is the help you promised?*

She was desperate to do anything to put off the ceremony, which she knew was going to be short and perfunctory. The Prophet didn't really care about the wedding part of the whole business, his main interest lay in what came directly after—the claiming of his bride.

There was a "Bridal Bower" waiting just through the far doors of the chapel—really just a back room with a large four-poster bed in it. The bed was kept draped in white and fresh sheets were laid for each new Bride of the Prophet. Father Caleb liked to keep the sheets he used with virgins as trophies, after they had been stained with blood.

Only there won't be any blood from me, Sarah thought dismally. *And that's going to make him so mad!*

What would make him even madder was if the Alquon stay-tight still hadn't dissolved—which it hadn't the last time Sarah had checked in the shower. If he couldn't get to get what he wanted, he would doubtless take his anger and lust out on her some other way.

And it would be twice as bad when he learned she wasn't a virgin anymore.

Father Caleb would take any woman in The Brotherhood who suited his fancy as a "bride" but it was the virgins he liked the most. Especially young girls he'd watched grow up in the Compound. He often referred to them as "Flowers waiting to be plucked" or more crudely, when he was speaking only to the men—his Controllers—he might say, "cunts waiting to be fucked."

That was all women were to him, only that and nothing more.

Disgusting old monster! Sarah thought, remembering her own adolescence, hiding and shying away from The Prophet, praying he wouldn't see past her glasses and her bulky clothes. No one should have to live with that fear, that uncertainty. No little girl should have to look in the mirror and pray, "Please God, make me ugly so The Prophet doesn't want me."

And now The Prophet *did* want her and there was no place to run. No place to hide.

Though she tried to drag her feet, Sarah soon found herself at the front of the chapel, just below the raised dais reserved only for The Prophet.

Father Caleb was standing there, dressed as usual, in blinding white, with a benign smile on his face.

"Beloved," he began as Sarah was brought to a halt with Amos and Charlie both holding her arms to keep her from running. "We are gathered here today to bring this lucky young woman into the light by making her a Bride of the Prophet."

Father Caleb always performed his own "weddings." In this way he could get the inconsequential ceremony done as soon as possible and take his new "bride" directly to the Bridal Bower to enjoy her assets.

"We…" Father Caleb stopped for a moment and frowned, putting a hand to his belly. Then his face cleared and he resumed. "We know that such unions are right and just because The Prophet must purify."

"He is the Prophet—he will purify," chanted the congregation. The males were sitting on the left and the females of the Compound—of which there were many more—sat on the right of the small chapel.

"And the only way to…to purify." Father Caleb winced, as though at some internal pain. "The only way to purify a female is to…to take her as my bride." He winced again.

Sarah was watching him closely. What was going on? Usually he was smooth as silk during these ceremonies. He'd preformed so many of them he knew the words by heart. So why was he hesitating and wincing?

"He is the Prophet—he shall purify," the congregation chanted on cue and there were a few scattered murmurs of, "Blessed be."

"When I take…take a bride as my own…" The Prophet was sweating now and his face had gone red but he went doggedly on. "When I take her she is brought…brought to purity by my touch."

"By his touch," chanted the audience. "By his touch she is made pure. By his touch. By his touch."

"But I don't *want* you to touch me!" Sarah wasn't sure where she got the courage to do it but she heard her voice ringing out above the brainwashed murmurs.

"Shut up, you little slut!" Amos shook her but she didn't care.

"I don't want to be a Bride of the Prophet!" she shouted, glaring at Father Caleb. "And I bet none of the girls he's 'purified' wanted to be his 'bride' either!"

"Silence her!" Father Caleb made a chopping motion with one hand. He was shaking now and his face was more purple than red. Something was definitely wrong with him. "Shut her up!"

"You just don't want to hear the truth!" Sarah shouted.

"Shut up, bitch!" Charlie slapped a meaty palm over her mouth. "Shut up and wait for The Prophet to finish."

Sarah bit him and he screamed hoarsely, ripping his hand away from her teeth and splattering blood on her white "wedding gown."

"You little *cunt!*" he roared and lifted his hand to punch her.

He was too close to duck. Sarah closed her eyes...but the blow never came.

Suddenly a warm, spicy, familiar scent filled her senses and a low, dangerously soft voice filled her ears.

"How *dare* you touch my female?"

Sarah's eyes flew open and she stared in shock at Sazar. The big Kindred had Charlie's upraised fist held casually in his own much larger hand and he was glaring down at the smaller man.

Charlie was clearly doing his best to move but though Sazar didn't appear to be using any effort at all, he couldn't get free or budge his captured hand so much as an inch.

"Get away from my female...*now.*" Sazar spoke in a soft, measured voice yet there was so much rage in his tone it froze Sarah's blood.

"Okay, okay—just let me go, man! I wasn't gonna hurt her—I swear," Charlie gasped.

"You'll never hurt anyone again—not with this hand." The big Kindred's fist tightened and there was a crunching sound, like many small branches breaking.

Charlie's face went pale and he sank to his knees, moaning. When Sazar finally loosened his grip, the thing he released hardly looked like a hand at all.

More like a baggie of meat with a few crooked sticks poking out of it, Sarah thought, feeling slightly ill.

The rest of the Controllers had raced over by now but they stood uncertainly, milling around Charlie who was moaning and clutching his ruined hand.

Sazar ignored them and focused on Sarah.

"Are you all right? Did they hurt you? I swear to the Goddess I'll kill every last one of them if they so much as laid a single finger on you, Sarah."

"No, I…I'm all right. They didn't get a chance." Sarah swallowed hard. "That…that would have come after the ceremony."

"Kindred devil!" Father Caleb shouted, his voice hoarse and strained.

All eyes had been focused on Sazar and Sarah but now the entire congregation looked to The Prophet again. He was shaking and clutching his belly, his face going from pale to puce and back again. He pointed a shaking finger at Sazar.

"He is a devil and she…she is his witch! She has poisoned me! Poisoned the Prophet!" he groaned.

Surprised murmurs ran through the crowd. "Poisoned the Prophet? She poisoned the Prophet? How?" "How did she…?" "Why did she…?" "What did she…?"

The same questions were running through Sarah's head. She'd been so stunned by the sudden appearance of Sazar she hadn't had time to really question what was going on with Father Caleb.

But suddenly she remembered the brown *chample.*

"Tastes just like chocolate cream pie," she'd told Father Caleb.

Apparently he'd believed her—at least enough to take a bite. And one bite was all it took.

"You heard Father Caleb—this little bitch poisoned the Prophet!" Amos, who had backed off when Sazar entered the room, suddenly roared. He surged forward and so did the rest of the Controllers—all of them burly men Father Caleb had picked for their strength more than their brains.

"Stay behind me, Sarah." There was a light in Sazar's eyes—the light of battle…of rage. She saw them flash from pale to red and knew someone was going to die if they didn't watch out.

"Get back," she shouted at the Controllers. "Get back, you idiots! He'll kill you all!"

As if to illustrate her point, Sazar bared his teeth, flashing his double set of fangs which had grown long and sharp.

Sarah heard someone mutter, "Fucking vampire!" and then Sazar waded into the knot of Controllers, moving faster than her human eyes could see.

Everything was a mass of confusion. There were blurs of motion followed by hoarse screams and cries. Controllers dropped to the floor clutching wounded throats, broken arms, shattered ribs…Father Caleb was roaring from the front of the chapel and the rest of the congregation was too shocked to do anything but watch, though some of the Sisters screamed and fainted.

He really will kill them, Sarah thought numbly. *All of them…*

And then a new voice rang out.

"Sazar, stop!"

Sarah's head jerked around and she saw Commander Sylvan standing at the entrance to the chapel. He was flanked by four large, menacing looking policemen although not even Tampa's finest could look as big and scary as a Kindred warrior. Still, they were enough to make the males in the congregation—the ones Sazar wasn't currently fighting—look pale and start edging for the doors.

"Enough, Sazar," Sylvan shouted again. "Release the *Rage*—your female is safe. The human police are here to help us. You *must not kill.*"

Sarah wasn't certain if it was the authority in his commanding officer's voice or the pleading in her own voice when she whispered, "Sazar, please stop!" that made the big Kindred still his violence. She only knew there wasn't a single Controller left standing when he straightened up and his eyes gradually went from red to pale.

"What's all this about? How dare you come in here like this and interrupt a wedding ceremony?" Father Caleb demanded. He was still clutching his stomach but sick or not he was clearly unwilling to allow anyone else with authority within his venue.

"We have reports of a kidnapping, *not* a wedding," said one of the policemen.

"Yes, that's true," Sarah said, stepping forward. "Father Caleb had me snatched off the street yesterday. He planned to pretend to marry me today and then rape me in the back room of the chapel. Then…" Her voice got suddenly tight and she almost couldn't go on. "Then he was going to…to let his Controllers—these men…" She pointed to the fallen men, lying on the floor of the chapel groaning. "He was going to…to give me to them. And let them rape me too."

"Bastard!" Sazar's eyes began to glow red again and his big hands, already bloody, curled into fists.

"Liar—she's a witch and a liar!" Father Caleb shouted. He looked at the policemen and somehow managed to find his old reliable televangelist grin. "Jonathan Styles, I know you! We worked together at the last policeman's fundraiser. Now who are you going to believe? A man you trust or this little witch?"

"Well..." The policeman, who seemed to be the ranking officer, began to waver. "You've always seemed like a good guy before, Father Caleb," he said. "I'm just not sure what to believe here."

Sarah's heart sank. Was this all going to be for nothing? Would The Prophet get away with the evil he'd been doing for so many years because of his duplicitous charisma and charm?

"It's true—everything Sarah said is true." The new voice came from the female side of the chapel. Sarah whipped around and saw Sister Jenny standing there, her chin lifted defiantly. "They did it to me too," she said, speaking to the policeman Father Caleb had been trying to win over. "I ran away too—like Sarah did. And they found me and brought me back. And when they did..." Her voice started to choke but her eyes never wavered, though they filled with tears and spilled over. "When they did Father Caleb "married" me and he let the others do it too!"

"He did it to me too," another girl spoke up—Sister Lena who was younger than Sarah by several years and heavily pregnant. "He does it to all the young girls in the Compound—rapes them and then passes them off to the men who serve him best."

"Sister Lena and Sister Jenny and Sarah are telling the truth," another girl spoke up.

"It's true—it's all truth. He keeps us here—we can never leave," said another. "We're prisoners!"

One by one, they rose and spoke. Mostly the younger women, whose spirits hadn't been broken yet…but some of the older ones as well. Sarah was sad to see her mother was not among them but at least she now knew she wasn't alone.

"Listen to these women, Officer Styles." Commander Sylvan's voice was soft and intense as he gripped the policeman's shoulder. "Listen to what they're saying and see what has been done to them. This is an offense—an evil committed against those who should be protected and cherished. *Do your duty.*"

Officer Styles nodded and jerked his head at one of the more junior officers.

"Come on—up here."

They went up to the platform where Father Caleb was. The Prophet had gone white with rage—or maybe the after effects of the brown *chample*—Sarah couldn't tell which.

"Don't touch me!" he exclaimed, holding out his hands as though to ward the policemen off. "How dare you? Do you know how much I've donated to your organization? I'll have your badges if you try to take me in. I'll…I'll…"

Suddenly he doubled over, clutching his belly.

"Poisoned me—oh God, she poisoned me," Sarah heard him moaning.

"Come on now, Father Caleb. That's enough." Officer Styles grabbed The Prophet by the arm but the next minute he made an exclamation of disgust and jumped back.

Spreading across the front and back of Father Caleb's immaculate white suite pants was a large, brown stain.

As he sank to his knees, shouting and raving about how he'd been poisoned, Sarah turned away. It was enough. The Prophet had been exposed and his credibility ruined. The women of the

Compound would be free to seek their own lives and hopefully most of the men would be brought up on charges.

And most of all, she could finally be free herself.

"Come, Sarah—I think we've seen enough."

She looked up to see Sazar staring down at her, an unreadable look in his pale eyes.

"Sazar?" she made his name a question, though she hardly knew what she was asking.

"I've come to take you back to the Mother Ship," he said quietly. "Will you go?"

Not trusting her voice, Sarah only nodded.

A look of relief passed over his sharp features.

"Thank the Goddess," he murmured. Swinging her into his arms, he carried her out of the chapel, away from the Compound, and The Brotherhood and her old life forever.

Chapter Twenty-eight

Sazar tried to think how to phrase his apology all the way back to the ship, which was still parked in the dusty field where he'd prayed to the Goddess. But there was no eloquent way of putting it, he realized. He would have to lay his heart bare and hope that Sarah would accept his words instead of turning away.

He took her to the ship but didn't open it. Instead, he set her down carefully on her feet and then dropped to his knees in the long grass before her.

"Sarah," he said, taking her hand in both of his. "I broke my word to you. I took your virginity, which is extremely important to my people. I thought it was important to yours too, and that you would hate me for taking it when I promised I would not."

"It *is* important to some people," Sarah said quietly. "I was raised to think it was all important because someday I would…" Her face twisted as though she'd tasted something bad. "Would give it to The Prophet—to Father Caleb."

"That old bastard…" Just thinking of what Father Caleb had wanted to do to Sarah made the *Rage* start to return. He had to blink hard and take a deep breath to prevent the red curtain of fury from dropping over his vision again.

"He didn't get me, Sazar." She cleared her throat. "He would have if you hadn't gotten there right when you had. Well, after he finished dealing with the effects of the brown *chample*."

"Is *that* what was wrong with him?" Sazar frowned. "I thought he was having some kind of a fit."

"He was, I guess—in a way." Sarah's eyes turned fierce. "I hope they haul him down to the police station just like that with his pants all stained! I want everyone to see his shame!"

"You saw to that." Sazar looked at her with fresh admiration. "How did you trick him into eating it?"

"Told him it tastes like chocolate cream pie and that it was a delicacy only for rulers and leaders," Sarah said promptly. There was a twinkle of mischief in her large hazel eyes that made Sazar bark out a laugh.

"So you appealed to his vanity and his gluttony at the same time. So devious! You amaze me, sweetheart."

"I had to be devious to avoid Father Caleb for so many years. And you amazed me too, showing up like that," Sarah said softly. "I…I didn't think you cared. I thought you wanted to get rid of me after you had sex with me—the way Father Caleb always passed on the girls he was finished with to someone else."

"Never," Sazar swore hoarsely. "I would never do that, Sarah."

"So…you pushed me away because you thought I would hate you?" She frowned.

"That was…only part of it," Sazar said heavily. "There was more, which the Goddess made me see when I prayed for help to find you."

Her eyes widened. "You spoke to the Goddess? She talked to me too!"

"She is merciful to her children," Sazar said gravely. "She made me see that I was pushing you away because I was afraid to lose you…the way I lost my wife, Malinda."

"What...what happened to her?" Sarah asked softly. "I'm sorry to ask but—"

"A blood vessel burst in her brain." Sazar said the words quickly, wanting to get them out. "I believe you humans call it an aneurism. She was young and apparently healthy but such things can be invisible—hidden for years—until they finally..." He shook his head, unable for a moment to go on.

"Oh, Sazar...I'm sorry." The look on her lovely face eloquently expressed the sorrow he'd kept locked inside for so long. "So sorry..."

"When you lose someone like that...so suddenly and for no apparent reason..." He looked up at her, his throat tight. "It makes you aware that we're all living on borrowed time. That anyone you love can be taken at any moment. And that...is a difficult realization to live with."

"It's a really scary thought," Sarah agreed softly. "But Sazar, you can't live in fear."

"I know that now." He nodded. "I know I pushed you away because I love you. The same reason I've been pushing Tsandor away." He bowed his head. "You were right, Sarah—I have been a bad and neglectful father since Malinda died."

"You were grieving," Sarah murmured and he felt her soft, small fingers carding through his hair soothingly. "At least you made certain he was in a safe environment with people who cared for him. And Sazar, it's not too late. Tsandor still loves you—he still wants to be with you."

"I'm grateful it's not too late to be part of my son's life." He looked up at her. "Please tell me it's not too late to be part of yours too. Please forgive me for the wrong I did you, Sarah."

She nibbled her lip, uncertainly.

"Are you asking me to come back to the Mother Ship and be your assistant again?"

"No." Sazar shook his head firmly and her face fell.

"Oh, I just thought—"

"Sarah, I'm asking you to come back to the Mother Ship and be my wife—my *mate*," he said earnestly. "I know we haven't known each other long but so much has happened between us. And the Goddess..."

"The Goddess put us together," Sarah murmured. "You know, Tsandor told me he had dreamed of me before he ever met me?"

"Did he? It was his dream of you that let me know you were in trouble." Sazar smiled. "I think the two of you already share a special bond. Will you come back with me and be a mother to Tsandor and a wife to me? Please, *Ladara,* say you will."

"Yes..." Sarah whispered the word but it had the intensity of a shout. Her eyes were shining and her lovely mouth was curved in a trembling smile. "Oh Sazar, *yes!*"

"*Ladara!*" He rose from the ground and took her in his arms but to his surprise, Sarah pushed away from him. "What is it?" he asked anxiously. "You haven't changed your mind?"

"No, of course not!" She tried to laugh but it turned into a wince. "It's just these...these damn Alquon nipple bands I'm still wearing. I've had them on for over twenty-four hours now and they're *killing* me!"

"Ah..." Sazar shook his head. "I have to confess, I didn't even think of those. What a bastard I am, letting you leave the Mother Ship without helping you get them off."

"You can help me now," Sarah murmured, looking up at him.

Sazar felt his shaft harden in his flight leathers.

"I'd be more than pleased to do that, sweetheart. But can you wait until we get up to the Mother Ship? I'd like to take you to my suite and take my time about it."

Sarah's eyes went wide and her breathing quickened.

"Yes," she murmured. "Yes, I can wait. As long as we go right up."

"Immediately," Sazar promised and opened the door of his small shuttle to help her inside.

He was going to take his sweet little human back to the Mother Ship and claim her completely.

And he intended to take his time.

Chapter Twenty-nine

Sarah couldn't believe it was possible to be so happy. She felt incredibly light and free and indescribably relieved that Sazar had saved her before Father Caleb had carried out his evil plan.

He loves me – Sazar loves me! she thought and a deep joy welled up inside her – a fountain that would never run dry. Sazar loved her and she loved him. The misunderstandings were all cleared up and they would be a family, just as little Tsandor had hoped.

She hummed contentedly in the shower as the warm water sluiced down her back. Yes, she'd just had a shower back at the Compound but Sarah had felt she needed another one. She wanted to wash the stink of The Brotherhood off her skin completely.

The Alquon nipples jewelry was still painful but she knew soon Sazar would help her remove it and heal her of any harm it might have done.

Just the thought of having him touch her and taste her again made her quiver inside. She'd been missing his touch in the time they'd been apart. And now that he had asked her to marry him – to become his mate as the Kindred said – she felt free to give in to temptation and do anything she wanted with him.

And I want a lot, she thought to herself, humming as she scrubbed gently around her tender breasts and then down between her legs. Suddenly she felt extra wetness between her thighs and gasped.

What the…?

Looking down she saw that the clear Alquon stay-tight plug had finally dissolved.

Well, I guess that's a good thing, Sarah thought. She'd been wondering if it would ever melt away as the breeding attendant had promised. It seemed that twenty-four hours on Alquon was a longer time span than twenty-four hours on Earth.

She was washing herself thoroughly when she heard a knock on the bathroom door.

"Sarah? Are you all right?" Sazar's deep voice asked. "I thought I heard you gasp."

Sarah finished rinsing and turned off the water. Wrapping herself in a towel, she went to open the door.

"You heard that? Even over the sound of the shower?" she asked.

He shrugged. "Sorry. I'm just…very attuned to you right now."

"It's all right. I did gasp. Because, well…" Sarah bit her lip and decided to tell him. "Because the, uh, stay-tight thing the breeding attendant put in me just now dissolved in the shower."

"The what?" He frowned, then his gaze cleared. "Oh yes—the little clear plug that was supposed…" He cleared his throat. "Supposed to keep my seed inside you."

"It did, you know," Sarah confessed in a small voice. "Until just now. I, uh, thought that was one reason you wanted to send me back to Earth. I thought you assumed I'd get pregnant and you didn't want a baby. That happened with Sister Hope, Father Caleb's secretary. He got her pregnant and then got…got rid of her."

"Sweetheart, no!" Sazar took her in his arms and hugged her hard. "No, I would never send you away to deal with a pregnancy on your own! In fact, it never even crossed my mind that you *could* be pregnant."

"It didn't?" Sarah pushed back from the hug, frowning a little. "How could it not? I mean after the way we, you know, had sex and the fact that the stay-tight was keeping everything up, uh, inside me?"

"I knew you couldn't be pregnant because we hadn't had bonding sex," Sazar explained patiently.

"What do you mean? Of course we had sex," Sarah protested.

"Yes and with some of the Kindred races making love and allowing the male to come inside you is enough for bonding sex. But not for Blood Kindred or for Pitch-Blood Kindred," Sazar explained. "With our kind the male must bite the female at the moment of ejaculation and inject her with his essence—the same liquid, secreted from my fangs, that I used to heal you."

"Oh." Sarah was surprised. "So I was worried for nothing."

"You didn't know." Sazar shook his head. "And I should have realized you would be worried about such an eventuality. It was damn inconsiderate of me to let you go when you were thinking you might be carrying my child." He ran a hand through his hair. "I was just so angry and upset I didn't consider it—just as I didn't remember the nipple jewelry."

"Well...you can make it up to me about the jewelry." Sarah shifted uncomfortably. Though she had wrapped the large blue towel very loosely around her chest, the nipple bands were really beginning to ache.

"It would be my pleasure, sweetheart." Putting an arm around her, Sazar led her out into the living area and sat her on a long, overstuffed brown sofa opposite the crackling fire in the fireplace.

Sarah felt her heart drumming in the cage of her ribs and her skin felt flushed all over. All this and he hadn't even touched her yet! God, she had really missed him! Missed his big hands and warm mouth on her.

And his fangs, she thought and shivered. Should she offer to let him drink from her again? It hadn't been that long so he might not need the blood but somehow she *wanted* him to bite her.

Maybe in a minute, she told herself. *After he gets off the nipple bands.*

"Drop the towel, sweetheart," Sazar commanded in a low growl. "Let me see what I can do."

Taking a deep breath, Sarah opened the dark blue towel, revealing her full breasts. The float dots were still working, making her breasts stand out as though they were being supported by a bustier and the gold and diamond nipple jewelry was still firmly in place.

"Gods, your poor nipples," Sazar murmured, cupping her breasts. "They're very red." He looked up at her. "I think I'm going to have to spend some time healing you, Sarah."

"That…that's all right," she whispered, almost tripping over the words in her eagerness. "I don't mind. Just please…get the bands off me."

"Of course." He ducked his head and took her right nipple into his mouth, sucking and laving the tight little bud, setting all of Sarah's nerve endings on fire.

"Oh…*oh!*" she gasped as the gold and diamond band wrapped around her tender peak finally came free. It hurt but felt good at the same time and her nipple was incredibly tender.

Sazar pulled back and examined her bare breast.

"Hmm...let me get some essence..." He opened his mouth and Sarah saw him run the tip of his tongue over the sharp edges of his fangs for a moment before leaning down to spread the healing essence they produced over her red and swollen peak.

"Mmm," she moaned softly. Feeling his essence heal her was hot but the sight of his fangs made her even hotter. She couldn't help remembering how it had been to have him drink from her breast...how good it had felt when those sharp points slid into her tender flesh...Her pussy got wet just thinking about it and she had to squeeze her thighs together tightly.

"Feels better now?" Sazar raised an eyebrow at her questioningly as he pulled back from her breast.

"Yes," Sarah whispered. "Much better. Thank you."

"Then I'll do the other one." He sucked the left nipple into his mouth and repeated the process, ending by healing her again. Then he sat back. "There, *Ladara* — all healed."

"Thank you. They...they don't hurt at all, anymore." Sarah smiled at him shyly. "But...what does '*Ladara*' mean? I've been wanting to ask you ever since you started calling me that."

"Oh, well..." He cleared his throat and looked uncomfortable. "It's a...nickname of sorts. A tern of endearment among my own kind."

"But what does it *mean?*" Sarah persisted. "Is it like sweetheart or baby or honey or what?"

"Well actually it means sweet-*blood*," Sazar explained a bit stiffly. "I'm sorry if that offends you and please know that while I love the flavor of your blood, that's not all I love about you. I—"

"I like it," Sarah interrupted him. Reaching up, she carded her fingers through his thick black hair. "Sweet-blood. It's...sweet." She laughed.

Sazar looked relieved. "I'm glad you don't mind. I have heard of other Pitch-Bloods who mated with human women who were not so pleased to be nicknamed for the flavor of their blood."

"It doesn't bother me," Sarah assured him.

She was still feeling hot and wet between her thighs from the way he'd healed her nipples and she wished she could think of a way to get him to do more…to bite her again…to make love to her.

"Speaking of sweet blood," she said, trying to sound casual. "You look kind of pale to me, Sazar. Do, uh, do you need a drink?"

His eyebrows raised in surprise. "Are you offering? It hasn't been that long since I took blood from you, you know."

"I know, but…you look like you could use some. And I don't mind."

"I love the flavor of your blood," he admitted. "And if I bit you more often I wouldn't need to take as much at once time."

He could bite her every day as far as Sarah was concerned. But it was *where* he bit her that she was preoccupied with right now.

"That would be fine with me," she told Sazar. But when the big Kindred started to nuzzle her neck, sending a shiver down her spine, she knew he wasn't aiming for where she wanted him.

"Hey," she said, still trying to sound casual. "Remember on Alquon Ultrea when you, uh, took blood from me here?"

She traced her right nipple with one finger, shivering a little at the erotic feeling of touching herself in front of her lover. It was certainly something she wouldn't have done before but now she felt free…and extremely hot and needy.

Sazar's pale eyes went half-lidded and flashed red for a moment.

"Yes, of course I remember. Drinking from your breast was one of the most sensual experiences of my life."

"I...I liked it too," Sarah admitted breathlessly. "Did...did you mean it when you told me you could call a vein anywhere on my body?"

"It is one of my abilities as a Pitch-Blood," he rumbled. "Do you want me to drink from your breast again?"

"Not exactly. I mean, I love it but..." Sarah bit her lip, trying to think how to put her request. She wondered if it was kinky and wrong to want what she wanted. But kinky and wrong as defined by who? By The Brotherhood? The Prophet? They were out of her life forever—she was making her own rules now, she decided defiantly. She would do what she wanted.

"What is it, *Ladara?*" Sazar murmured, sensing her hesitation. "What do you want to ask me?"

"I just wondered...remember when you healed me between my, uh, my thighs?" She stumbled over the words but was determined to get them out. "When the, uh, pearl panties had been rubbing me too long?"

"Of course I remember." His voice was a soft, low growl. "Healing and tasting your sweet little pussy was one of the greatest pleasures of my life."

"Well could you...can you..." Sarah took a deep breath. "Can you call a vein and drink from me there?"

Sazar's dark eyebrows shot up again.

"Are you certain you want that? It can be very uncomfortable for a female unless she is a Fated Mate to the Pitch-Blood who is drinking from her there."

"Fated mate?" Sarah frowned. "What's that?"

"Any Kindred can mate with any female when the Goddess brings them together," Sazar explained. "But with the Pitch-Blood, there is a certain, special female with whom a perfect bond can be formed—complete unity."

"But how is that different from the bond a Kindred usually forms with his mate?" Sarah asked. Kat had told her a little about how it worked with Kindred and their mates, how they were able to pick up on each other's feelings and send each other thoughts. It sounded amazing. But how much better could it be with a Fated Mate?

Sazar took a deep breath and looked troubled.

"A perfect bond means that death cannot part them. Basically, it ensures a long, healthy life for both and it ties them together in such a way that they will die at the same time when their end comes."

"So if you find your Fated Mate you don't have to worry about losing her?" *The way you lost Malinda?* Sarah didn't say it aloud but she knew both of them were thinking it.

Sazar nodded. "But it's extremely rare. Not one Pitch-Blood in a thousand finds his Fated Mate."

"And how can you tell if the girl you're with is supposed to be your, uh Fated Mate?" Sarah asked.

"By the way she reacts to your fangs piercing her in…sensitive areas," Sazar said in a low voice. "A regular female will feel intense discomfort unless she is being stimulated during the feeding. The pleasure acts to drown out the pain of the bite. But a Fated Mate will feel the Blood Pleasure—the intense fulfillment of allowing her mate to bite her in such an intimate area—whether she is being stimulated or not."

Sarah thought of the intense sensations that had rolled through her when his fangs had pierced her breast before. But he'd been touching her at the time, stroking her pussy so she wouldn't feel any pain. What would it feel like if she let him bite her *there* between her legs without touching or stroking her at the same time?

"I want to try it," she said abruptly. "But what happens if I'm not your Fated Mate?"

"Then I will love you and cherish you forever," he said softly. "And only drink from you in more conventional spots. Malinda was not my Fated Mate yet I loved her to distraction." He closed his eyes for a moment. "Losing her almost killed me."

And wouldn't it be wonderful if he could never have to worry about losing me? Sarah thought to herself. *If I was his Fated Mate we would live a long life and die at the same time – guaranteed. That fear that he must have that I'll go suddenly, the same way his first wife did, would be completely dispelled.*

Of course, she probably wasn't his Fated Mate if the phenomenon was as rare as he said. But still, the idea of letting him bite her *there* continued to make her feel hot and shaky all over.

"I want to try it," she repeated. "Can we, Sazar?"

His eyes were half-lidded again.

"You have to ask me if I want to bite you? If I want to taste your sweet pussy again?"

Sarah felt her breath coming short and she bit her lip.

"I don't know – do you?"

In answer, he dropped to his knees beside the couch.

"Spread your legs for me, *Ladara*. Let me drink from you."

Sarah had been sitting there with the dark blue towel pooled around her waist. Now she opened it and lay back on the couch, cushioning her head against the thick leather armrest.

Sazar knelt between her thighs, running his big, warm hands up and down her bare legs.

"So beautiful," he murmured. "So fucking gorgeous when you're all open for me this way, sweetheart." He began placing slow, hot kisses up and down her legs, from her ticklish inner ankles to the tender insides of her knees…and then up the sensitive flesh of her inner thighs.

"Hey," Sarah protested breathlessly. "I…I thought you weren't supposed to, uh, stimulate me before you bit me? How can we tell if I'm your Fated Mate if you're getting me all worked up first?"

"Getting you all worked up, as you put it, doesn't do anything to prove or disprove the Fated Mate theory," he murmured. "It's only if I'm stimulating your sweet little clit while I bite you that negates the test. And to be truthful, even manual stimulation won't help you enjoy my bite between your thighs if you aren't my Fated Mate." He stroked her inner thighs and kissed her again. "So I can taste and lick and suck your pussy all I want to—it won't make any difference when it comes to biting such a sensitive area. Either you'll enjoy it or you won't."

"Well then, let's see if I enjoy it," Sarah suggested a little breathlessly. But to her surprise, Sazar shook his head.

"I want to taste you first, *Ladara*," he murmured. "I want to drink of your sweet pussy juices before I drink of your blood. Only after I've licked your hot little cunt and felt you coming all over my face will I sink my fangs into you there."

"Oh..." The dirty words spoken in his deep, growling voice were doing all kinds of things to Sarah's insides. "All right," she whispered. "I guess if that's the way you want to do it."

"It is..." His eyes were glowing red again with obvious lust and need. "So spread yourself for me, sweetheart—let me get between your thighs and taste you deeply."

"Yes, Sazar," she whispered and opened her thighs wider, allowing him easier access.

* * * * *

Sazar groaned when he saw her sweet, pink folds spreading for him. Gods she was so hot and sweet and perfect, his little human! And her pussy was already so *wet* – the hallmark of a true *numalla* – prized by the Blood Kindred because their wet pussies allowed a male's thick shaft to slip easily into the female's sheath.

He longed to lap up those sweet juices, to feel her quivering against him as he tasted her perfect little pussy. But first he had to mark her with his scent. It was something all Kindred, no matter what type they belonged to, felt the need to do.

Leaning down, he gripped her thighs and rubbed his cheek against her soft mound. Her sweet feminine musk filled his senses and his shaft was suddenly so hard in his flight leathers it ached for release.

Reaching down, he popped open the magno-tabs holding his leathers closed, giving his shaft some room to breathe. He thought of taking himself in hand but he needed both hands to touch and pleasure Sarah right now. Indeed, she was already shifting her hips against the couch and moaning though he had only rubbed his cheek against her. Gods, she was so sensitive...so responsive to his touch!

Time to touch her more, then, whispered a little voice in his head. Sazar couldn't have agreed more.

Ducking his head, he spread her outer pussy lips with his thumbs, opening her sweet, pink folds even wider, before placing a hot, open mouthed kiss over the tight little button of her clit.

Sarah moaned and bucked upward at once and her pussy got even wetter. Looking at how her folds were shiny with her honey, Sazar knew he couldn't wait any longer to taste her fully.

He nuzzled closer and let just the tip of his tongue slip into her entrance, finding the opening to her channel and the sweet treasure within. Sarah gasped and quivered, her entire body shaking, as he lapped upward, gathering as much of her salty-sweet juices on his tongue as he could.

"Oh," she moaned and he felt her small hands in his hair. "Oh Sazar, please…please don't stop!"

His cock surged again, making him feel hard enough to fuck through a brick wall. Gods, he loved her soft, sexy, curvy body and the way she begged for his tongue in her!

"Just getting started, *Ladara,*" he promised hoarsely. "Just lay still like a good girl and let me lick your sweet pussy until you come."

But of course she couldn't hold still. As he licked her again and then again and then sucked the bud of her clit into his mouth and circled it lazily with his tongue, she moaned and cried and jerked under his exploring mouth. Sazar had been right—he needed both hands to hold her in place as she writhed against him, her soft little fingers tugging at his hair as broken syllables of need fell from her lush lips.

Just tasting her was almost enough to make him come. Feeling her full thighs wrapped around his head, hearing her cry and moan, lapping away her honey while she made more and more, living up to her *numalla* name…it made him fucking rock hard and nearly crazy with lust until he didn't know if he wanted to bite her or fuck her or both.

Make her come, he told himself, holding onto his self control grimly. *Make her come first and then you can do both.*

"Sazar…*Sazar!*" She cried his name like a prayer, bucking her hips up shamelessly to ride his face until his mouth and cheeks and chin were shiny with her juices.

"Hold still sweetheart—need to eat your sweet pussy until you come," he growled.

Gripping her hips in both hands, Sazar held her down and lapped her, exploring her pussy thoroughly with his tongue and teasing her tight little clit. Every once in a while he tested her by pressing his fangs lightly against her sensitive flesh. But Sarah never jerked away or begged him to stop. In fact, she seemed to get even wetter every time he tried it. The Blood Hunger was teasing at his nerves even though he had drunk from her not that long ago. Gods, he wanted her!

He became aware that Sarah's moans and cries had turned into coherent words again. He lifted his head for a moment and tried to focus on what she was saying.

"Bite me, Sazar," she was begging, her bare breasts and tight pink nipples heaving as she panted with need. "Please, please bite me! I want you to—I *need* you to!"

Sazar told himself he should make her come first. If she wasn't his Fated Mate, the pain of him sinking his fangs into such an intimate area could ruin or derail her pleasure. But she was begging him so hard he couldn't help himself—he *wanted* to bite her as badly as she wanted to be bitten.

He had to do it now.

Pressing her down hard with his hands to stop her wiggling, he leaned forward, fangs extended, and struck.

* * * * *

The entire time he was tasting her, Sarah kept feeling the sharp points of his fangs brushing against her slippery inner pussy. Though she was well aware she shouldn't like this, it seemed to push her higher—further into ecstasy. She cried out and bucked against him, tangling her fingers in his hair as she rode his face shamelessly.

She began to want his bite—to crave it as she had never craved anything before. Every time those sharp points brushed her she felt closer and closer to the edge. Finally she heard herself begging him, crying for the pleasure of his touch—the sharp kiss of his fangs.

"Bite me," she begged, pressing up to get more of him—his cheeks scratching against her tender thighs, his hot tongue lapping from the entrance of her pussy all the way up her slit. "Please, Sazar—bite me *now*! I can't wait—I need it—need you. Bite me!"

At first she thought he wouldn't listen, that he would insist on making her come first. Which he certainly could—she was close already. But she couldn't help thinking that it would be so much better, so much hotter, if he would only bite her first.

And then, finally, she felt his big hands pressing her into the couch, forcing her writhing hips to hold still. His mouth came down, the fangs long and sharp, and she felt them pierce into her flesh.

Sarah nearly screamed.

The pleasure she felt was indescribable. It was as though someone had taken ten—no a hundred—no a *thousand* orgasms and distilled their pleasure down into two tiny sharp points applied to her pussy.

It felt like someone had set off a nuclear bomb inside her.

She grabbed the big Kindred's head with both hands and rose upward in defiance of the way he was holding her down. She only knew she needed more—needed it to never end as the intense sensation rolled over her, blotting out everything else except for the orgasm that gripped her and wouldn't let go.

"Sazar! Oh God…Oh please yes, *yes*," she heard herself babbling. "That feels so good…so right. Please…*please!*"

It was too much. Her toes curled and it felt like very muscle in her body had a current of electricity flowing through it. Her pussy spasmed, clenching hard though there was nothing to clench and she knew she needed him in her again, filling her…fucking her…claiming her.

"Please!" she moaned again. She felt like her heart might explode…like she might never be able to get a deep breath again. Like her body was made of light and was scattering into a million pieces.

Then Sazar lifted his head and licked his lips.

"*Ladara*," he whispered hoarsely. "You *are* my Fated Mate."

"Then take me!" Sarah demanded reaching for him. "Please—I need you in me. *Now!*"

She didn't have to ask him twice. With a low groan of need, he rose from the floor and settled between her spread thighs.

Sarah fumbled between them eagerly, pulling his shaft out of his flight leathers—too needy to take it slow. She needed his big, hard length inside her, stretching her pussy, filling her completely.

"Eager, aren't you, sweetheart?" He grinned, one corner of his sensual mouth curving up.

"I need you," Sarah whispered. "Please, Sazar—I feel so *empty.*"

"Put me inside you then, *Ladara,*" he growled softly. "Slide my cock into your tight little cunt...let me stretch you open and fill you with my seed again."

Again his dirty words seemed to flip a switch inside her.

"Yes...oh God, *yes,*" she gasped. He was thick and pulsing in her hand as she rubbed the broad head, already wet with precum, against her slippery pussy. He found his way easily into her folds and then the tip of his shaft was breaching her entrance and pressing inside.

Sarah moaned as he filled her. It seemed to her she'd forgotten how big he was, how thick and long. As he pushed deeper and deeper into her, she wondered if her pussy could take it.

But I took him once, she reminded herself. *Back on Alquon when I was still a virgin. This time I'm not, and I'm a numalla—I can do this. It's the only way to have bonding sex...the only way to be with Sazar forever.*

Besides she wanted it—wanted *him*—badly. Moaning eagerly, she tilted her hips upward and locked her legs around his waist as she pulled him into her.

"Gods, Sarah," he groaned hoarsely as he sank into her. "Your pussy is so tight and wet...you feel so good wrapped around me."

"I like...like the way you feel inside me," Sarah panted. "Like the way you fill me up. But I like it even better when you...when you move. When you thrust."

"When I fuck, you mean? You want me to fuck you, *Ladara?*" he growled. "Fuck you long and deep and fill you with my seed?"

Still panting, Sarah nodded.

"Please," she begged shamelessly. "Please Sazar, yes!"

"All right, sweetheart—I'll fuck you." He cupped her cheek and looked into her eyes. "But I warn you, I'll be breeding you for real this time. At the moment I shoot my seed in your pussy I'm going to bite you and inject my essence at the same time. That means I really could make you pregnant."

For some reason this made Sarah even hotter.

"Yes," she whispered, bucking up to get more of his thick cock into her tightly stretched pussy. "Yes, Sazar do it—breed me. Make me yours."

"Look in my eyes while I do it," he commanded, his deep voice filled with lust. His pale eyes—now a pulsing red—caught and held hers as he pulled almost all the way out. "Look at me while I fuck you, Sarah—while I claim you and make you mine forever, my sweet Fated Mate."

Moaning with the intense intimacy, Sarah obeyed, looking up at the big Kindred. Sazar held her eyes with his own as he slowly sank his thick shaft back into her pussy to the root.

"*Numalla,*" he growled softly. "Gods, you're so hot and tight and wet. Your little pussy is so slippery and sweet. I love that you can take all of me, right to the hilt. Love that you can open up and let me breed you."

Sarah thought she was going to go crazy with need. She could feel a second orgasm rising inside her—a deeper one this time. She didn't know how much more she could take after the intense experience of having him bite her between her thighs but she had a feeling she was going to find out.

"So sweet and tight and hot," he groaned as he thrust inside her over and over, pulling her close as he looked into her eyes. "I love you sweetheart—love you so much. Do you know that?"

"I...love you too," Sarah panted. And then suddenly the way he was filling her and rubbing against her clit with every thrust became too much. "Oh Sazar," she gasped. "Think I'm going to...I...I'm coming. Can't help it!"

"Don't want you to help it. Gods, I can feel you clenching all around my cock," he growled. "Bare your neck for me, *Ladara*. Let me claim you."

Sarah turned her head to one side, her pussy still spasming helplessly around his thick, invading cock. And then his fangs were sinking deep into her throat as she felt his shaft grow even thicker and something hot spurted deep in her pussy.

His seed. He's filling me with his seed. Claiming me – he's claiming me, she thought deliriously.

"That's right, sweetheart – I am" she heard his deep voice growling in her head. *"Now we'll never be parted again, my beautiful Fated Mate."*

Then the pleasure took over and Sarah couldn't think anymore but could only feel.

Chapter Thirty

Tsandor played aimlessly with the paint and glitter on his paper plate. There was a round, white ball to one side he was supposed to be decorating with the art supplies but he wasn't getting very far with it. It was Christmas Eve so he was supposed to be making a Christmas ornament according to Ms. Sophie but he didn't really understand what that was. Something to hang on a tree, she had told him. But trees already had leaves—why did they need a ball of glitter and paint too?

He didn't really understand much about the Earth holiday they were supposed to be celebrating tomorrow. Some of the other kids had tried to tell him about it. According to Shad a big man in a red suit called either Santa or Fanta—Tsandor couldn't remember which—would come tonight while he was asleep and leave him lots of presents.

Tsandor didn't know if he believed that and anyway there was only one present he really wanted—to be together with Patro and Sarah again. Ms. Lola had told him that his Patro had called to say Sarah was all right but Tsandor didn't know if that was really so.

Adults said things to make you feel better sometimes, even if they weren't true. The way everyone kept telling him that Maman was just sick for a long time after she went to be with the Goddess.

What if Sarah is still in trouble? What if the bad men hurt her after all?

The thought tied his stomach in knots and he didn't have any appetite for the red and green sprinkled cookies that were on the plate beside his juice box.

"Hey..." Suddenly a hand touched him on the shoulder.

Tsandor looked up and saw Shad standing beside him. The other boy's pale, almost white hair and big dark eyes scared some of the other kids. But Tsandor liked Shad—he had been nice to him even when he didn't know anybody after moving to the Mother Ship from Tranq Prime.

"Hey," he said listlessly, stirring a finger in the green glitter on his paper plate.

"You're thinking bad, sad thoughts," Shad said, frowning. In contrast to his light hair, he had dark eyebrows which made his frown intense.

"Yeah..." Tsandor didn't ask how his friend knew. Shad just...knew things sometimes. Like the way he'd known Sarah was coming. He drew more patterns in the green glitter. "Yeah, I guess so."

"Well stop," Shad said, so firmly that Tsandor looked up in surprise.

"What?"

"The Goddess told me to tell you Sarah is all right," Shad said. "And you're gonna see her and your dad real soon. Okay?"

"Really?" Tsandor looked at his friend hopefully. Unlike the adults in his life, Shad had never played him false.

"Really." Shad nodded solemnly. "So don't be sad, okay?"

"Okay." Tsandor smiled. "Thanks Shad."

Shad shrugged his thin shoulders.

"I only know 'cause the Goddess said. She doesn't like it when kids are unhappy, you know? So finish your ornament. You got to have something to hang on your Christmas tree."

"But I don't *have* a Christmas tree," Tsandor protested.

"Do it," Shad directed. "You will."

He went back to his own seat and Tsandor shrugged and went back to the round white ball and the paint and glitter.

He had just finished it when Ms. Lola came up to him. She was holding a bag and inside it Tsandor could see some of his new clothes and Lump-Lump, the stuffed animal Sarah had given him.

"Ms. Lola?" He looked up at her, fearful of this sudden new change. Where was she talking his clothes and Lump-Lump? Was he being sent away from the constant care house? If so, then where would he go?

Then he saw that Ms. Lola was smiling.

"Tsandor," she said, beaming at him. "I have a really great Christmas surprise for you."

Tsandor felt his heart give a strange little jump.

"Do you want me to guess what it is?" he asked.

She shook her head.

"No, honey. Just come with me. You'll see."

Wiping his hands on a paper towel and leaving his ornament to dry, Tsandor got up and followed Ms. Lola, wondering what was going on.

She took him out of the playtime area and around to the front of the constant care house. At first Tsandor thought the surprise she meant was inside the house.

Then he saw who was standing in the front yard of the house, looking at him.

"Patro?" he whispered, coming a little closer. "Sarah?"

His father grinned at him and Sarah smiled that beautiful, warm smile that reminded him so much of Maman's smile.

"Come here, Tsandor," Patro said. "Sarah and I have come to take you home."

At first Tsandor couldn't believe it. Then he remembered what Shad had told him—that he would see his father and Sarah really soon. And then Ms. Lola had said she had a surprise for him—was this it? Was it really exactly what he had been wishing for?

Joy overwhelmed him and he ran to them as fast as he could and threw himself into their arms.

* * * * *

Sarah laughed for sheer joy as she and Sazar held each other and Tsandor tight, in a big, family hug.

"Sarah! Patro!"

The little boy was wriggling like a puppy he was so excited. But after lots of hugs and kisses he settled down enough to ask a question.

"Is it true?" he asked, looking from Sazar to her and back again. "Am I *really* going home with you guys? Really-really?"

"Really-really," Sarah assured him, smiling.

"It's true, Tsandor." Sazar's pale eyes were suspiciously bright. "You're coming home with us and you'll never have to live here at the care house again."

"And...we'll all be together?" Tsandor persisted, as if wanting to be sure.

"We'll all be together—one happy family," Sarah promised. She felt a lump in her throat as she hugged the little boy tight. She'd felt a pull towards Tsandor from the first moment she'd seen him—

almost as though she was meant to be his second mom. It felt right to hold him tight—as right as it felt when she hugged Sazar.

"What are we going to do now?" Tsandor demanded, wiggling like an eager puppy again. "Where are we going to go? Are we going to go home?"

"I thought first we could get a Christmas tree," Sarah said, smiling at Sazar. "Can we?"

"I think they still have a few for sale at the open market," he remarked, smiling back.

"And we'll need some ornaments to hang on it," Sarah said. "And then I think we'd better get some ingredients to make Christmas cookies."

"You mean the red and green kind?" Tsandor made a face. "Because I don't know if I like them."

"Those are the boxed kind," Lola said, speaking up from the side yard where she'd been watching their reunion with a wide smile on her face. She shrugged apologetically. "I'm afraid they're not very good."

"You have to make them yourself for them to taste right," Sarah said decisively. She smiled at Tsandor. "Would you like to help me? I have to warn you—it might get kind of messy."

His little face broke into a grin.

"I *like* messy!"

"I do too." Sarah hugged him and pressed a kiss to his hot little cheek. "I have a lot of Christmas traditions to teach you and your dad because Christmas is tomorrow."

"Is that when the elderly overweight male goes to every house in the world in one night and brings presents?" Sazar asked, frowning.

"Exactly." Sarah grinned. "Come on—let's go. We have a lot to do to get ready."

They put Tsandor down and held his hands between them as they left the grounds of the constant care house forever.

Sarah had a warm feeling, like a glow deep inside that radiated outward as they went. She wondered briefly if Malinda, Sazar's first wife, could see her holding her son's hand from wherever she was. She wondered if Malinda could know how much she cared for Tsandor and Sazar and how badly she wanted to be a good wife and mother.

Then, for a moment, she had a brief flash of a slim, blonde woman standing beside someone else—another woman but one whose face was so beautiful it was hard to look at.

Was it Malinda and the Goddess? Somehow, Sarah thought so. And both of them were smiling at her encouragingly.

I'll take good care of Tsandor, she promised them silently. *I'll love him like my own, I promise I will! And I'll be good to Sazar too.*

I know you will, my daughter. That is why I chose you, the voice of the Goddess murmured in her head. **I will bless your union with Sazar with many other children but you and Tsandor will always remain close. And you and Sazar will grow old together in harmony and love.**

Then the brief flash was over and Sarah was left to blot the tears out of her eyes and smile at her new family. For the first time in longer than she cared to remember, she was going to have a happy Christmas—a family Christmas with the two new men in her life and she would never, ever let them go.

Epilogue

"So you're his Fated Mate? What does that mean?" Kat asked as she watched the kids running around the open park land of the Mother Ship's common area. Because of the season, the intensity of the green sun at the center of the Mother Ship had been lowered enough to permit snow to fall and the result was magical.

Everywhere kids were laughing and playing, making snowmen and throwing snowballs. In the center of it all, covered in the densest blanket of snow and undisturbed, was the Sacred Grove—the temple sacred to the Goddess. A few of the priestesses could be seen peering out from the snow-covered branches of their grove and smiling as they watched the kid's antics.

Sarah, who had been born and raised in Florida, was amazed by the gorgeous sight. She'd often wished to see snow as a child but this was her first experience with it. It made everything seem perfect and right and indescribably beautiful.

"Well basically it means we'll live to a ripe old age and then die at the exact same time," she said, trying to draw her mind back from the snow to answer Kat's question. She wasn't about to go into the fact that Sazar could also drink from the more sensitive parts of her anatomy and give her multiple orgasms by doing so. That was a little too embarrassing to share, even with her good friends.

"That's wonderful! Sazar must be so happy he doesn't have to worry about losing you the way he lost his first wife," Sophie said softly.

"We haven't talked about it much but yes—I think he's really relieved."

Sarah smiled as she watched her new mate sip hot cocoa and talk with Commander Sylvan and a few other Kindred warriors who were gathered by one of the many picnic tables set up around the perimeter of the common area.

"Right now we're just getting used to being mated and being a family," she added as Tsandor threw a snowball and ran away laughing when Shad threw one back at him. "But I have to tell you—I've never been so happy. Not since I was a kid myself."

"It shows." Liv smiled at her. "You're positively *glowing*."

"And what's that on your finger, doll?" Kat raised an eyebrow at her, looking at Sarah's hand.

"Oh..." Sarah blushed and laughed, looking down at the pear cut diamond solitaire on the ring finger of her left hand. "Sazar gave me that last night after we tucked Tsandor in bed. Kind of as a Christmas present slash engagement gift. He said that the other warriors told him Earth women liked them and he wanted me to be happy."

"I'm guessing that's not the *only* present he gave you, hmm?" Kat laughed and nudged Sarah in the ribs. "You don't have to tell us—we know how it is when you're newly bonded."

"Oh, well..." Sarah felt like her whole face must be red but just then Liv put her fingers to her temples.

"Oh dear! Baird just bespoke me—they want us to gather up the kids to start bobbing for *tam-tams*."

"They want to what?" Sarah asked, frowning.

"Oh, one of those weird Kindred Winter Solstice traditions we told you about," Sophie said. "They have this big tub of greenish-blue slime and they float little toys and prizes called *tam-tams* in it."

"You have to put your hands behind your back and try to grab one of the prizes with your teeth," Kat continued the story.

"But the slime is semi-sentient which means it thinks the toys are food—so it tries to keep the *tam-tams* away from you," Liv finished.

"It's kind of like bobbing for apples if the water in the tub was sticky and gooey and alive and kept trying to grab the apples away from you." Kat shuddered. "We hate it—the slime gets *everywhere.*"

"But the kids love it," Sophie said with a sigh. "And since we make our guys put up with all of our Christmas traditions, we really can't complain about theirs."

"*I* can complain," Kat exclaimed. "You know how long I kept finding little pieces of live slime on my triplets' clothes and in their pockets last year? War and Peace were *determined* to keep some of it for pets and the little bits of it were creeping all over—it was like having a house full of living blue-green boogers! Ugh!"

Sarah couldn't help herself—she burst out laughing helplessly.

"I'm sorry," she finally managed to say when she got herself under control. "But Kindred brides have…have the *strangest* problems."

"You're one yourself now, doll," Kat pointed out, grinning. "We'll see how hard you're laughing when Tsandor brings home a wriggling handful of blue-green ooze and wants to name it 'wormy.'"

"Come on," Liv said, hooking her arm through Sarah's and nodding at Kat and Sophie. "Let's show Sarah what she got herself into."

Laughing, the four women made their way through the Christmas snow to gather up their kids. As they went, Sarah sent a silent prayer of thanks to the Goddess. She had a man she loved, a little boy she adored, and a home she was safe and sheltered in.

Life was good and she felt overwhelmingly blessed. This was the happiest Christmas she could ever remember.

The End?

Of course not! There are always more Kindred books coming. I'm hoping to dive back into the main series and write Brides of the Kindred 21 in 2018 and I also still have lots of ideas for other Kindred Tales as well. Plus I want to write Alien Mate Index 5 and Cougarville 4 and the Goddess only knows what else.

In the meantime, I wish you all a very Merry Christmas and a Happy New Year!

Hugs to you all,
Evangeline
Christmas 2017

A Note from the Author about
Brides of the Kindred and Kindred Tales

This is the fifth Kindred Tales novel I have written and it won't be the last--I have lots of ideas for side stories set in my Brides of the Kindred universe. Each Kindred Tales novel is set in the Kindred world and has the recurring characters you've come to know and love, as well as new Alpha heroes and spirited heroines who have lots of hot sex.

However, good news! I finally have a handle on the plot of Kindred 21, Vanished, which I hope to release early in 2018. For some of you who have been asking, it's going to involve time travel and the hero is going to be Shad, Kat's little boy who is a Shadow Twin. But don't worry, you'll still get to see some of your favorite recurring characters too.

I have been teasing this forever and I am SO excited to finally write it! Look for it soon and in the meantime,

Hugs and Happy Reading!

Evangeline

Also by Evangeline Anderson

You can find links to all of the following books at my website: www.EvangelineAnderson.com

Brides of the Kindred series (in order)

Claimed (Also available in Audio and Print format)

Hunted (Also available in Audio and Print format)

Sought (Also Available in Audio and Print format)

Found (Also Available in Audio and Print format)

Revealed (Also available in Print)

Pursued (Also available in Print)

Exiled (Also available in Print)

Shadowed (Also available in Print)

Chained

Divided

Devoured (Also available in Print)

Enhanced

Cursed

Enslaved

Targeted

Forgotten

Switched (Also available in Print)

Uncharted

Unbound

Surrendered

Vanished (Coming Soon)

Kindred Tales series (side stories in the Brides of the Kindred which stand alone outside the main story arc.)
Mastering the Mistress
Bonding with the Beast
Seeing with the Heart
Freeing the Prisoner
Healing the Broken *(a Kindred Christmas novel)*

Born to Darkness series
Crimson Debt (Also available in Audio)
Scarlet Heat   (Also available in Audio)
Ruby Shadows (Also available in Audio)
Cardinal Sins (Coming Soon)

Alien Mate Index series
Abducted (Also available in Print)
Protected (Also available in Print)
Descended (Also available in Print)
Severed (also available in print)

Cougarville series
Buck Naked (Also available in Audio)
Cougar Bait (Also available in Audio)
Stone Cold Fox (Also available in Audio)
Big Bad Wolf (coming soon)

The Institute series
Institute: Daddy Issues
The Institute: Mishka's Spanking

Compendiums
Brides of the Kindred Volume One
Contains Claimed, Hunted, Sought and Found all in one volume

Born to Darkness Box Set

Contains Crimson Debt, Scarlet Heat, and Ruby Shadows all in one volume

Stand Alone Novels
Purity (Now available in Audio)
Stress Relief
The Last Man on Earth
Anyone U Want
Shadow Dreams
Hunger Moon Rising
Cougar Christmas
Planet X (Also available in Audio)
Deal with the Devil (Also available in Audio)
The Sacrifice (Re-Releasing Nov 18th in ebook and Audio)

The above books are just a small sample of Evangeline's work. For a complete list of books from all publishers, please visit her website at www.EvangelineAnderson.com **

About the Author

Evangeline Anderson is the New York Times and USA Today Best Selling Author of the Brides of the Kindred, Alien Mate Index, and Born to Darkness series. She is thirty-something and lives in Florida with a husband, a son, and two cats. She had been writing erotic fiction for her own gratification for a number of years before it occurred to her to try and get paid for it. To her delight, she found that it was actually possible to get money for having a dirty mind and she has been writing paranormal and Sci-fi erotica steadily ever since.

Find her online at her website: www.EvangelineAnderson.com

Come visit for some free reads. Or, to be the first to find out about new books, join her newsletter.

Newsletter – www.EvangelineAnderson.com

Website – www.EvangelineAnderson.com

FaceBook – facebook.com/pages/Evangeline-Anderson-Appreciation-Page/170314539700701

Twitter – twitter.com/EvangelineA

Pinterest – pinterest.com/vangiekitty/

Goodreads – goodreads.com/user/show/2227318-evangeline-anderson

Instagram – instagram.com/evangeline_anderson_author/

Audio book newsletter – www.EvangelineAnderson.com

Newsletter Signup

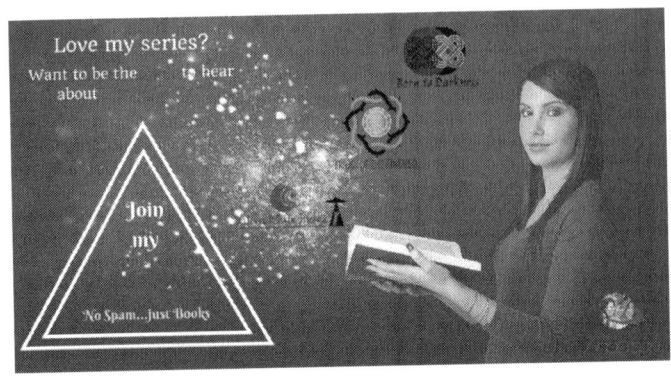

Join my newsletter at www.EvangelineAnderson.com

Or if you love audiobooks, I have quite a few of those too...

Join my audiobook newsletter at www.EvangelineAnderson.com

Printed in Great Britain
by Amazon

VILLAGE VIEW

A YEAR ON SYMI

Also by James Collins

Novels:
Other people's dreams
Into the fire
You wish
Jason and the Sargonauts
The Judas Inheritance

Non-fiction:
Symi 85600
Carry on up the Kali Strata

Screenplays:
The vessel
The Judas Curse

For more information on these books and James' other work see www.symidream.com/james

JAMES COLLINS

Village View

A year on Symi

First published in Great Britain in 2014

Copyright © James Collins 2013

The right of James Collins to be identified as the Author of the Work has been asserted by him in accordance with the Copyright, Designs and Patents Act 1988.

All rights reserved. No part of this publication may be reproduced, stored in a retrieval system, or transmitted, in any form or by ant means without the prior written permission of the publisher, nor be otherwise circulated in any form of binding or cover other than that in which it is published and without a similar condition being imposed on the subsequent purchaser.

Photography © Neil Gosling

Cover artwork © Sarah Bassett

Design and layout by Allan Robinson

Printed by CreateSpace, an Amazon.com company

ISBN 978-1497435889

Available from Amazon.com, Amazon Europe, CreateSpace.com and other retail outlets. Also Available on Kindle.

Foreword

James and Neil moved to Symi in 2002. Symi Dream, the website, started online in 2004. In those days James' contribution to the site was a monthly article called 'Village View' in which he wrote about aspects of life on Symi, a small island in South East Greece. Over time the website evolved into what it is today: a site about James' writing, his partner Neil's photography business, and their life on the island.

James has previously published two hugely popular books about Symi life, *'Symi 85600'* and *'Carry on up the Kali Strata.'* In this, his third collection of thoughts from a Greek island, he publishes a whole year's worth of blog posts from the Symi Dream website in which we find him, among other things, tap dancing for the mayor, attending name day festivals and making a feature film. Neil provides the photographs while the deaf and highly characterful 'Alarm Cat' Jack, makes several appearances. Village View gives us an upfront and honest account of James and Neil's eleventh year on Symi and includes some of the more popular typos that regularly amuse early morning readers to the Symi Dream blog.

Thanks

No book writes itself and I would very much like to thank everyone who has contributed to the creation of this collection. A grateful round of applause goes to: Jenine and Sam for keeping the blog going when I was away. To Neil for his on-going support in my writing endeavours and for his wonderful photographs. Allan for the sterling (and, I imagine, rather tedious) editing, layout and preparation of the book. My mother, Sarah Bassett for the cover art and Alarm Cat drawings. And our customers and supporters who keep the Symi Dream shop, and therefore our own dream, alive. And that includes you. (If you have bought this book.)

Contents

January 1
February 21
March 41
April 61
May 81
June 103
July 125
August 149
September 173
October 197
November 225
December 257
List of illustrations 283

January

Floods, storms, dances, dodgy Symi internet and a car that needs a push

Damp houses and what to do about them

Cold and clear here this morning, the house is misted up on the inside for the first time which means windows must be opened and the condensation must be removed before it encourages black mould.

I remember, years ago, working for a company that looked after properties, and getting in lots of complaints from tenants about black mould in bathrooms. Some of the properties were old conversions and the problem was bad because of some ancient and dodgy building design. But it happens in most, if not all houses, and that was something that was hard for some tenants to understand. It happens here a lot as well, and when people ask what Symi is like in the winter, the answer often is: damp.

The bathrooms get it the worst I guess, being the places most susceptible to moisture in the air, then kitchens and other rooms, particularly bedrooms as we breathe out 'about a pound of moisture' during sleep every night. The answer to the problem? Well, once it's in it's hard to get out but bleaching off any dark patches as soon as you see them, keeping windows open to allow air flow which dries the moisture before it has a chance to grow the spores, not hanging washing inside to dry, and keeping the heating on at the same time as having an air flow, all these things help. It was hard for some tenants to grasp the concept of heating a house while the windows were open, understandably so, but it really does help. I'm in the front roof-cum-fridge right now with the door open, trying to dry the condensation from the balcony windows.

All this internal damp is compounded by many other factors: the external damp of course, the leaky roofs, the gaps between windows and frames, or doors and frames, that let the rain in, the lack of damp proof coursing, the sternas abutting walls, the stone itself, the fact that many houses are now coated in suffocating 'plastic' paint rather than the asvesti which lets the walls breathe the moisture out, the heavy dew and the rain when it happens. So yes, in the winter, Symi can be a very damp place at times and you have to expect parts of your house to succumb to black mould. Get those rubber gloves out and get that bleach in the bucket, and get cleaning as part of your morning, exercise regime.

Getting back to normal

There's a definite feel of things getting 'back to normal' now. Neil's back at the shop for his full working hours, my old PC has finally come home and I intend to set it up again over the weekend and see how I get on. I've rather got used to the laptop these past few months so it's going to be strange to work on the old screen and get used to the quirks of the PC again.

This winter, so far, there have been more visitors to the island than usual. I don't just mean Greek people coming to visit families but more out of season visitors and tourists. Some came for Christmas, some for New Year, others have been here a while and are still here, there have even been day-trippers as late as December coming over from Rhodes. A good sign for the year ahead perhaps? I've noticed some sailing yachts in as well, and more adventurous winter wanderers than usual. Not hundreds of course, but some.

And here is the (Symi) News

Well, maybe not that much news but a few interesting notes and messages to leave you with over the weekend. Firstly, let's go back to those earthquakes…

Greek Reporter
Put out a piece a couple of days ago titled: "Volcanic activity suspected off Turkey's coast: A new submarine volcanic eruption might have recently started off Turkey's west coast in the Marmaris Sea between the mainland and the Greek Island of Symi near Rhodes. Scientists from Istanbul's Technical University announced that they have found evidence of two active vents at about 200 m water depth along a north-south trending fissure 2.5-3 km long." Apparently the temperature of the sea rose slightly, which might be good news for swimmers.

The Symi Gallery
Last night saw the opening of a new exhibition of arts and crafts made on the island of Symi. "Opening reception Friday 4th January from 5:30 to 8:00pm. Join us to have a look at the exhibits and enjoy a glass of wine."

Symi Best
If you have a business on Symi, or know someone who does, you may like to email Symi Best and check out that your details as listed on the site are correct. They/we are updating the site for the new season soon, so if you want anything added, changed or removed, drop a line to mail@symibest.gr or go through the website symibest.gr

A couple of words

Yesterday, in an idle moment, I was trying to remember which two words in the English language contained all the vowels in the correct order. I could only remember facetious for some reason, so I looked it up on the net. Naturally the one I could never remember was abstemious. Funny that. There are actually a few more and here's what the rest of the article said: "Oxford Dictionaries Online also contains the chemical term arsenious 'relating to arsenic with a valency of three', while the 20-volume historical Oxford English Dictionary includes abstentious 'abstinent' as well as the rare botanical and zoological terms acheilous 'having one or both lips absent', anemious 'growing in windy situations', caesious 'bluish or greyish green', and annelidous 'belonging to the phylum Annelida.'"

So now you know.

Morning trivia

According to my new desk calendar thing that came from Jenine at Christmas, 'This day in History': Crazy Horse fought his last battle on this day in 1877, in Montana, USA. There you go, there's an interesting piece of information you can share with your work colleagues today.

Work? Hmm. I have started on the new book (and if you are reading this, then I have now finished it) and intended to have a full morning of writing yesterday, but some kind of pre-man-flu symptoms kept me confined to the sofa. Feels a bit more like a head cold this morning and the drowsiness appears to have gone, so I might crack on with it today instead.

I also need to get to the harbour, check the post office, take care of a couple of other things and get the housework up to date. That's a lot of things on the to-do list for a winter's day.

And it does finally feel like winter on Symi today. Not as breezy as yesterday, there is still a chill in the air. The sky is a clear blue, the sea darker and the hills of Turkey opposite are very clear; sharp without any heat haze at all. I dare say if I was up high and able to see further across I would see snow on the peaks of the mountains in the distance.

Cold again today

Another rather chilly morning this morning involving a shower in a bathroom where the window doesn't shut. The weather forecast last night predicted 'real feel' of minus 9 degrees, though the wind dropped after dark. I still wouldn't have liked to have been out in it.

Talking of bathrooms: some visitors to Symi are still astonished that there are many houses here that have external bathrooms, but that is the way it is. In our house, the bathroom is inside (though it may as well be outside, it's not warm!). We have several friends who have to cross their courtyard to get to the shower; it's not uncommon at all. There was a time when several houses, in the village, would share outside facilities and there is still at least one outside 'facility' to be seen in the village, though it's not in use. Not for its original purpose at any rate.

Yesterday we had a jaunt to Yialos, walking down through the village, quiet at this time of year, with shop doors only slightly ajar to let people know they are open. The sun was shining, but we were both wearing five layers and still felt the chill. A brief discussion with the postman concluded that it was colder in Horio than it was in Yialos, due to the breeze, though the sun was almost felt on the other side of the harbour, when standing still in it.

Afterwards we walked back up the Kali Strata (which I can still do without getting out of breath) and headed to the windmills to help push-start a car; the kind of thing that happens around here at this time of year.

I'm away to get on with some writing, and I've just seen the Blue Star boat heading into Yialos for its twice weekly visit from Athens, it's got a calm, but chilly, sea to sail in on.

A naughty but flattering Symi community group

We were invited to dinner last night, to a house in a parish higher up in the village. We wrapped up in several layers for the short walk and took our new, handy, wind-up torches that came in Christmas boxes from mother. (They work perfectly.)

The air was cold enough to chill the lungs, the sky was clear and the stars bright. The company was good, the food fabulous and we had a great time. The point of mentioning this is to say how 'flattered' Neil was to see, at the house, a calendar produced by one of the island's local organisations. It showed various images of Symi, one per month, and was for sale in various places around the island. We looked through it to see what views they had used and were very interested to see the name of the photographer credited for the shots. (Someone whose non-Greek name I didn't recognise.) We were particularly interested to see the image he had used for November, mainly because it was a reproduction of the exact same image that we had used for November in our Symi Dream calendar a couple of years ago. It was one of Neil's images and there was no mistaking the fact. No mistake because it was taken on a certain day of the year from a certain place and shows an arrangement of boats and people that could not have been repeated unless the credited photographer was standing right there at the same time.

It's kind of flattering to have your work used in this way, though it is also very naughty as the product is for sale and the original photographer (who is the copyright owner I believe) is not credited. Had the proceeds not been going to a local community group, we would no doubt be seeking some kind of proof of originality from the calendar producers. I think what happened was that the Symi Dream image was re-photographed by the photographer from an enlargement someone owned, which brings up the question of who actually owns the image if it is a photograph of a photograph. I assume it has to be the original photographer: it's a bit like me taking a shot of something on exhibition at a gallery and then using it to make a book cover or a greetings card.

Anyhow, I just thought it was a bit naughty and rather flattering. Like when a local church used one of my images from the website on their publicity without permission. I was quite happy but it would be nice to credit Symi Dream for the work it does. You will notice that these days most of our online images are watermarked.

Things to do on Symi on holiday

There are heavy grey skies this morning and the sea is the colour of a battleship. I don't really have much news as I wake up and start to warm up in the very cold front room, so I thought I would point you in the direction of the 'Things to do on Symi' page on the website (it's in the 'Symi Holidays' section of the menu).

This is in case you stumbled upon this post while looking for your next holiday and wondered what exactly there is to do on Symi when visiting. The start of that page is, of course, about the things we offer including Neil's popular photo walks. He is thinking of adding another route to the list this year, perhaps the upper village and parts of Horio where many people don't venture. I expect he will also be doing his other routes on request.

There are also lists of beaches to visit, though not quite as comprehensive as can be found on Symi Best. Check the Things to Do page on that site for even more ideas and details.

There are plenty of places to walk to, there are churches to visit (when open) including the famous monastery of Panormitis. There are also a few museums on Symi; the Nautical museum in Yialos, the Folklore museum and the 'Sala' (mansion house) in Horio, though whether they are open or not depends on funds and restoration work at the moment. There are also museums at Panormitis and the Old Pharmacy building in Horio, again, this is not always open in these difficult financial times.

And then you've got all the bars and tavernas, the shops and the general café way of life where you sit and gaze and relax. Check around the rest of the site for ideas of what to do, look up the boat trips, the taxi boats, and the scooter and car hire, the woods, the hills to walk and the swimming, and you'll soon find there is much more to do on Symi than you first imagined.

Nothing much but some Alarm Cat antics

Another day of quietly getting on with things yesterday, until the earth shook and the windows rattled, again. That passed by and everything returned to normal.

I managed to get a piece of writing 'finished' for the moment so now I can get to work on the new book idea and start on that proper next week, all being well. Neil was at the shop, as usual and is off back to work this morning. There was a bit of a storm last night with high winds at times, and pelting rain, but things have calmed down again this morning, and we're promised 13 degrees tomorrow and Monday which will be good as we've been invited to a barbeque.

As you can probably tell, there's not a lot of news from the desk today, I had a bit of a lie in and so have started the day late. It's not easy to get out of bed when it's cold, and rush for a shower in the bathroom where the window doesn't shut, but at least I don't have to go outside to reach that bathroom. I do have to open the front door first thing though, the Alarm Cat insists on that.

He'll wake you up at whatever unearthly hour he decides is time to come in, then run away so when you open the door he's not there and you're made to stand in the cold for a few seconds until he decides you've learnt your lesson. Then he'll come pelting down the garden path from the roof where he has been waiting for the door to open (why the roof?) and then rush in shouting his head off. First breakfast must be served immediately and, if you are very quick, you can get a shower in while he has that. But more often than not he's at the bathroom door demanding second breakfast before you even get your hair wet. So then comes the biscuit course and then the hunt for the morning 'sleepery', his currently favoured place is the chair with the cushion that's by the front door, Ian's golf chair. That's where he is now and hopefully he will stay there quiet for a couple of hours. My next official duty is at around 11.00 when he will wake for elevenses. I'm looking forward to that.

Electric heating? Who needs it?

That was a very pleasant if chilly weekend with not a lot going on, for me. There was a wedding or two by the sound of the bells on Friday, Saturday and yesterday, plus the big bang of dynamite yesterday afternoon, and the weather stayed clear and warm during the day, though the temperature fell a bit last night to say the least, and it was a bit icy this morning.

I'm now trying to heat up by the small heater in the front room. The new (two months' old) halogen heater in the sitting room blew another bar this morning, so we're down from four to two. They really are a waste of money but cheap, so all that's available to us at the moment. Our 'old faithful' that we've had for nine years, an old electric two bar heater of the old school, also gave out this year. Well, not so much gave out as shorted out the entire house. Each time it warmed up to a certain point it threw the trip switch.

A bit like the cooker yesterday. We've long had one ring that doesn't work, or at least it works but it throws the electricity off. Yesterday I turned on the 'old faithful' medium size ring, the one we always use, and that cut the power off immediately. By some strange quirk though the big bad back ring that usually blows the house up was working fine after all these years, so I was able to make the dinner after all, but had to remember not to turn on the usual ring.

Apart from that, the piano playing up from time to time, my new camera paying[1] up, the socket in the front room occasionally blowing up the trip

---

1   Noticed this one on my read through. The new camera actually ended up going wrong not long after we bought it, second hand. So although it was meant to be playing up here, we actually ended up paying up through the nose for a something that didn't work.

switch when something is plugged into it, and the occasionally flickering light, our electrics seem to be in reasonable condition. Let's hope the heater keeps going as now is not the time to be doing without. And let's hope the sun stays out and warms us up for later in the day when we've been invited to a barbeque in the upper parts of the village.

Another late start

I went to a marvellous barbeque, as Noel Coward might have said had he not been to a party.

It was held in the square behind Agios Stavros, yesterday afternoon, as the sun went down over Turkey and the sea lay like glass in Nimborio bay, which you could also see from up there.

The event was, for us, followed by another round or three of golf, and I think I actually won one of those rounds, which is a bit of a rarity these days. As for other entertainments this week: the tap classes resume tomorrow evening and I've been practicing my steps (not) with vigour (never) and can't remember a single one of them. Well, I can remember the first three bits now after a reminder yesterday, but the rest as still a bit of an enigma. So that should be a fun time avrio, hoofing around.

And after all the fun yesterday I find myself missing the alarm, ignoring the alarm cat and not getting up until late, for me, so am already an hour behind schedule, which will now throw the rest of my day. So I'm not hanging around.

Live long and prosper, on Symi, Greece

We've had a couple of days of minor disruption in various parts of Symi recently due to margarine.

Well, so I've been told. There's been a film crew here making an advertisement and I was told that it was for one of those healthy margarine things that reduces your whatsit, so the more of its fat you eat the better and healthier you feel. Never been sure how that logic works but there you are. We passed the crew on the steps a couple of days ago, a few people we know have been stuck in their shops unable to come out because a take was in progress, they were filming outside Neil's shop yesterday (could be on the telly one day, again) and have been filming on the Kali Strata.

Maybe they are using the recent report from (I forget where, the BBC?) that suggested that people in Greece lived the longest out of all Europeans due to their diet of healthy foods, and hard work. There was an interview with a 90 year old man picking his olives, or cutting back his tree; he was saying that he had to carry on working or else he would not eat. I've read, in Symi guide books, that the island of Symi produces the longest longevity among the islands. (Not sure if that's how you write that, but there you go.) It must be all the steps and the walking up and down, the exercise to keep warm in the winter and the 14 hour working days in the summer, coupled with permanent ouzo intake, souvlakies and clean air.

Mind you, more and more these days people use their mopeds, quad bikes, cars, trucks, vans and lorries to get about. I used to know someone who would drive from a part of Horio that is accessible by car, down to Petalo to find the main road, then up to the village and to Kampos, then into the village by the main path and across the village square to get as close to the school as possible; it must have taken about 10 minutes to get there by car. The walk, taking a more 'as the crow flies' route, would have taken about five at the most. But then, if you've got a vehicle and can afford to run it…

So, natural, local produce in your shopping basket and walk to and from the supermarket, that's the way to live long and prosper on Symi. Well, I'm not sure about the prosper bit, not at these prices, but the live long is a good start. And I shall be watching out for the 'eat more fat and get healthier' advert when it comes out.

Happy name day Tony, Adonis et alia, from Symi

According to my list of Greek name days, today is the name day of ANTHONY (Antonia, Antonios, Antonis, Andonis, Anthony, Tony, Tonia), and also THEODOSIOS (2) (Theodosios, Theodosis). Which would explain the bells this morning, in part at least. Tomorrow is our Parish church's saint's name day, ATHANASIOS (Athanasios, Thanasis) and that of CYRILLOS (Kyrillos) and THEODOULA (Theodoula, Theodouli).

It's a bit blowy here today but not as windy as yesterday, and not as wet by the looks of it, though there wasn't much rain last night. It was spitting a bit as I made my way back from the tap dance class, the first of the year. Jenine and I had to leave on time so as to get back to her house for Ian's birthday party. His favourite dinner of lasagne followed by apple and mincemeat pie and custard (with candles) was a bit of a treat, as were the 'favours' of Lego models that we each had to build. Thank heavens for nine year olds is all I can say. My baby grand piano built out of Lego (or something similar) with keys and a stool and a lid that works and everything, would still be in pieces had Sam not stepped in to help. Harry had the various Star Wars machines built in seconds and Neil's frog, once reassembled and put back together correctly by someone younger, looked majestic.

But that was yesterday, today it's back to the usual winter 'grind' with writing, shop, housework, and keeping warm. The lunch is in the slow cooker; the second ring on the ancient stove has gone now and we're saving for a new cooker. We're down to the briki ring (the smallest thing in the world, intended for, I assume, making Greek coffee on, in the absence of gas), and the second smallest ring which is as good as useless on a good day. Inside, the oven half-works so that's also a bit unstable. Lunches are going to be more like 'Ready steady cook' in this house this winter, making whatever we can on whatever feels like working that day. But it will keep me on my toes as I practice my tap steps around the kitchen.

Getting to Rhodes this year, and on to Symi

There are also rumours abroad of more ferry problems ahead. I say rumour as I didn't hear this directly from one of the port authority workers, but a second party did. It looks like the Proteus has stopped running for the foreseeable future, but I don't know if that's due to maintenance or contracts or what; perhaps someone will let me know? And I also heard that there may soon be disruption on the Dodekanisos Seaways routes, but I'm not sure of the details. I suggest keeping an eye on the Symi Visitor Travel Blog where Andy will no doubt put up any news once confirmed. He's got some useful links to flights and info there at the moment. Flights to Rhodes from Germany, Netherlands, Belgium, UK and Switzerland. This also includes info on and links to flights to Kos, as that is our second nearest airport.

I could do with information on how to get from Kos airport to Symi, but I've not done that journey myself. I assume it's a taxi to the port and then the boat but I don't know how long that takes, how much it might cost, the name of the port and so on. If anyone wants to submit reliable information then please do and I can add it to our resource.

Right then; I've had my porridge (with water, yum) and the sky is set in and grey, the bells have been ringing for Ag. Athanasios' name day, the heater is on and I am all set for the day ahead! Well, as much as I will ever be.

Film making on Symi

Somewhere on the site there is a links page… goes searching for it… where did I put it? Ah ha! Found it: symidream.com/wp/useful/links/ And the reason I was looking for it is because there used to be links to various sites that were about films that had been made on Symi, in full or in part. The links page holds a little section that says 'Filmed on Symi' with links to titles such as "Anna's Summer" and "Pascali's Island", probably the two most well-known ones, along with "The Guns Of Navarone."

And the point is? Well, the point is: I have been contacted by a film producer who might be interested in making a small scale film on Symi. I can't give out details at the moment but what the company want to know is:

a) Does anyone have a contact who is a 'name' (films, theatre, acting) who would be willing to undertake a day's cameo shooting and be willing, in principal, to attach their name to a filmed-on-Symi project?

b) Are any of our readers and Symi-philes potential investors/producers?

Some explanation:

To be a producer and get a credit and/or slice of the profits you simply need to invest money or some other in-kind activity. For example, if you allowed your property to be used extensively as a location, or if you provided the accommodation for the cast on some low-cost deal, or free, if you acted as on-location go-between and so on… you can negotiate to be a producer.

And of course, all this depends on the film itself. Will a 'name' appear as a cameo and be 'attached' to any old project? Well, if I were a name it would depend on the nature of the film and how my attachment would be perceived. Those are the kinds of details that the company will go into if anyone does come forward as genuinely interested.

I think what they want first is the name, the 'star' who will be a minor player in a low-budget film in order to a) promote the film and b) promote Symi, but who will want to see a synopsis at least and know that they are being attached to a decent product. (Knowing this film company the product will be good.) And what they also want is contact from anyone who is genuinely interested in seriously putting something in to the project. We're not talking 'I'll be an extra and am on the island for a week in September,' and we're not talking 'I'm willing to be in the background drinking beer and you only need to pay for my beer,' and jokey stuff like that. We're talking "I have £5,000 to invest, what's my return?" Or, "I have a hotel/bar/boat/restaurant you can use free of charge, what's the publicity deal?" Serious stuff only please. (And all treated with confidence, at least until the contract stage.)

So, have a think over the weekend and if you are interested or if you know someone who might be, then get in touch with me in the first instance and I will pass along serious replies and enquiries to the company. You may not hear anything for a while but they will keep you in touch with the project if or when it starts to happen.

Vasilopita, Βασιλόπιτα, on Symi

Last night saw the celebration of Βασιλόπιτα on Symi, the event was organised by Η Ενωση Γυναικων Σύμης, the Symi Women's Association, and the Mayor of Symi, Eleftherios Papakalodoukas, cut the cake at the end of the evening. Here's an online definition of what this is all about:

"Vasilopita (Greek: Βασιλόπιτα, Vasilópita, lit. '(St.) Basil-pie', see below) is a New Year's Day bread or cake in Greece and many other areas in eastern Europe and the Balkans which contains a hidden coin or trinket which gives good luck to the receiver. It is made of a variety of doughs, depending on regional and family tradition, including tsoureki.

It is associated with Saint Basil's day, January 1, in most of Greece, but in some regions, the traditions surrounding a cake with a hidden coin are attached to Epiphany or to Christmas.

In other areas of the Balkans, the tradition of cake with a hidden coin during winter holidays exists, but is not associated with Saint Basil at all."

We went down to the Opera House for 5.30 yesterday afternoon and Neil made himself busy taking the photos.

After some words of introduction by Sevasti, and after several dances from the dancers of the Symi Women's Association, the Mayor made his speech and cut the cake. Other cakes and treats were supplied for the audience and the event finished just before eight.

We then took a steady walk but up the Kali Strata, having made our way down via 'ο καταρράκτης', the Katarraktis (waterfall), the original village access path at the back of the acropolis. This path joins Horio to the back of Symi, and is unseen from the sea which is why it was the original path; it's safer. At least it was then; now it is much as it was before, still a bit rough in places and uneven, with large cobbles and long steps. It's a good, healthy alternative to the bus and taxi, though we preferred the Kali Strata for the return journey as it is easier underfoot and has better lighting. Having said that, the Katarraktis does have solar street lights on it now.

January 22nd

Waking up to a grey and overcast morning this morning after a windy day and night last night. I was up during the night securing shutters and listening to the howling wind batter the roof. I was surprised to see the Blue Star in last night as I popped out to the shop in the early evening, but it was there at the clock tower with another boat waiting to come in. I could only see the lights of that one so am not sure what it was.

Ancestors and other rambles

It was like a spring day in the harbour yesterday when I went down to sort some paperwork things out. Lovely and warm, especially on the far side and in the sun.

I'm still keeping an eye on an unwell Neil today; he's spent two days more or less just sleeping so today he may have to be persuaded to 'get thee to a doctory', unless he's feeling better when he wakes up later this morning. Which is a long way of saying that the shop may well have to be closed again today.

I've been taking a few hours off from the usual day-to-day to check out some more ancestors. You may remember I was doing this a couple of years ago and compiling a book. Well, there were some lines, in Essex, that came to a standstill because I ran out of parish registers to check, because they weren't online and it's a long way to pop to the records office from here. Now those records are online and for a reasonable fee I can flick through them all when I want to. I've only got a limited access time though so am trying to get them all checked, for the relevant towns and villages, right back to the 1500's, while I can. I have already established my family name and main 'Collen' line back to 1694 in the Quendon/Chickney area of Essex, but can get no further back there until I find a certain baptism, or birth, of a William Collen (around 1694) who went on to become a wheelwright (as did the rest of his descendants until the 1970's by which time they were garage owners and mechanics). The search continues. And this is a separate search for the elusive Captain Arthur Henry Scott who may or may not have been related to Scott of the Antarctic; we're still stuck with him in Devon, possibly Croydon, between 1868 and 1942.

But I have no idea why I am telling you all that; it's just what's in my mind this morning as we start off on another day on Symi. Another winter's day where there may or may not be fresh produce in the shops. That, as you know, depends on boats..

A thought on the village surgery

I'm not too sure if this post will be up on time as there is a problem with the internet in our part of the village this morning, possibly elsewhere as well. It keeps cutting out. I seem able to get online for about a minute at a time and then it's off again.

There was a thunderstorm last night so I can only assume that has something to do with it. Perhaps water in a vital part, or a lightning hit on a tower on the mountain or something. But the storm appears to have passed; at least it is clear looking out that way, towards Turkey. Behind me, up over the mountain, it was still grey and gloomy just now.

For anyone following Neil's progress he is getting a bit better every day following a nasty bout of something akin to salmonella which came from we know not where. We went down to the village doctor on Wednesday after a couple of days of 'it's a bug, it'll pass' and 'there's lots going around at the moment' which you always hear. The doctor wasn't too busy (always go when there is a church service on, he's always got less customers then), so we went straight in. He gave Neil a good check-up, asked many questions, and diagnosed something along the lines of a nasty bug in the tummy. I fixed the resolution on his computer screen and we called it quits. The village pharmacy had the medicine and he's been on the mend ever since.

We're very lucky to have the village surgery and it should get all the support we can give it. As I understand it our doctor actually has his house and family in Rhodes but lives on Symi for as many days per week, or longer, as needed, because he likes his work so much. He's usually cheerful and always thorough and to the point. And for us, when you have a patient who can't walk very far without support, or if you can't travel too well yourself, it's so much easier than having to get down to Yialos. They also do a sterling job in Yialos of course and we do use that surgery when we have to, but without a car, and when not steady on your feet, it is a long way to get to.

Anyway, that's what's on my mind this morning. I'll battle with my spasmodic connection and try and get this posted and then go and see how the invalid is today. He was getting fed up with DVDs and cold chicken, scrambled eggs and water yesterday so there should be some improvement when he wakes up.

Yialos, Symi, flooded again

So far so good with the internet. This morning it was online for about an hour before playing up, this afternoon it's been fine. Fingers crossed, wood touched and so on. Strange though; the neighbours are all fine, and our phone line is completely off. If it stays this way a call will have to be made (from a mobile) to OTE to see if it's just us having the problem.

Took a walk to Yialos on Saturday and Sunday and walked back up both times. Both times the harbour road was awash thanks to a full moon, high tide, storms and heavy rain.

The walk back up the Kataraktis (καταράκτης) today was taken at a leisurely pace, as it must be. Gone are the days when I could walk from work at Takis' leather shop to Ag. Triada at the top of Horio in 14 minutes, in September. That was ten years ago now, how tempus fugit. But the views remain as stunning as before and the climb is arguably a quicker way home. If I am not stopping in the village for shopping at least, because the top of the kataraktis is close to the house.

It's funny, it was last Sunday that we walked down that way to get to the Opera House for the Vasilopita. This Sunday we walked back up. We also managed to dodge the big storms this weekend by being at home when the rain came. There was a downpour just now (Sunday around 3.30 pm) which lasted for about three minutes and then the sun came out again. The downpour included hail. Last night the thunder was rolling around again as it was on Sunday morning, and the night before that. Today I popped out around the corner and it was hot and sunny, for an hour or so. Crazy weather days.

Anyway, enough about that. Here's hoping the boat finally managed to get in yesterday as we're waiting for some medicine from the pharmacy, who are waiting for supplies to be delivered. Neil tells me he heard a boat, and there looked to be some harbour activity happening on Sunday morning. Other than that great excitement, it looks like it is going to be a standard Symi week ahead for me, with no plans apart from Golf on Monday, and tap on Wednesday, and cards on Friday, and quiz on Saturday… Tell me again, what do we do on Symi in the winter?

From a Symi ruin to You Tube in no easy steps

Neil put a photo up on his Facebook page thing yesterday and, by chance, I had taken one of the same building only the day before. And then I started thinking about the other pages on the site that you might not have seen if you only pop in here to read the blog.

He'd just had an enquiry about some limited editions and that reminded me that we have a page of examples: symidream.com/wp/symi-photos/limited-editions/ Also on that page is a video of a slide show showing some of Neil's work. At least there used to be. I just went to take a look and saw that the video box now read : "You Tube embedding disabled by request." This is one of those situations when you speak to your computer and say 'Oh no it wasn't!' and you start to get cross because someone, You Tube in this case, has made some kind of change to the way your account works without telling you. It may have told you, but you would need to be one of those users who spend 48 hours a day on the site to have picked up the detail. I am often embedding my Symi videos on the Symi Dream site, does this now mean that all the old ones will no longer play unless I go back to You Tube and change every single setting? Why has this video changed and not the others? Or have they? And why can't they leave things alone? It was working fine before, I've not changed anything myself so… and so on. You know how it is.

Anyway, I did some delving and discovered that if you come across a notice saying "You Tube embedding disabled by request" it means that someone (possibly even yourself) has asked YT not to allow embedding on your video. In my case it was embedded and playing one day and then not the next and I'd made no such request, so I imagine a lot of people will suffer the same thing. (It's interesting to note that You Tube is an anagram of Obey Utu, and Utu was the sun god in Sumerian mythology, and 'Sumerian' is an anagram of Main User, which was clearly not me when it comes to my You Tube account.)

What you have to do then is go to your You Tube account, find Video Manager, and find the video in question, and click on Edit. On the next page you have Basic Info showing, but you need to click next to it on Advanced Settings. At the bottom of this page is a tick-box (or check-box if you are American) and put a tick (not a check, which is actually a cheque) in the box. Your video should then be embeddable again.

How on earth I got from an old ruin on Symi to instructions on how to work You Tube when it decides to take over your decision making process I don't know, but there you go. Perhaps it has something to do with the magic of words in that 'Sumerian' is also an anagram of Same Ruin? Which is where we started. Spooky eh?

A quick post before the lights go out

Apparently there may be a power cut this morning, 8.00 to midday, so I'm dashing off a quick note just in case we 'go dark', as they say on 24.

There's no great news actually, Jack (the cat) put up a photo on Facebook yesterday in honour of the anniversary of the publication of 'The Raven' by Edgar Allen Poe on 29th January 1845. It's a cold and windy day here today, though dry, but it's not likely to get over about 10 degrees according to AccuWeather.com, so that's going to be fun if the power is off for the morning. What will we do? Chop wood, light up the real fire, keep warm by doing the gardening? Or just sit and read a book under the duvet? Hmm, I wonder.

Actually, all being well I should be able to use the laptop to work on, by some marvel of modern technology when there is a power cut I can also connect to the internet and have a few hours doing something online should I want to. I don't ask how it happens, it just does.

Διεθνής Έκθεση Τουρισμού EMITT Κωνσταντινούπολη

Symi is being represented at the International Tourism Fair EMITT in Istanbul. The chairman of our council Mihalis Tsavaris was in Istanbul along with the mayor of Symi, Lefteris Papakalodoukas heartily promoting the island.

That gave me an idea to look at the predictions for Greek tourism in 2013 and I found this interesting result: "Early signs suggest that Brits booking holidays in the Greek Islands next year (2013) could rise by 10-15%, according to tour firm forecasts." That was from Greek Islands Travel who also have a Symi page where I found a link to an article about the Symi Volcano. "Evidence of volcanic activity near the Greek island of Symi has raised questions of who would 'own' any new volcano that might emerge from the sea - Greece or Turkey. If a volcano were to surface in the seas between the Greek islands and the Turkish mainland it is unclear who would 'own' the new territory and both countries may well attempt to establish territorial claims on it."

Interesting question, but I gather a rather unlikely occurrence. That rather took me off the point but I didn't mind, I was getting bored with the point anyway, and the site was far more interesting.

Meanwhile, back on Symi, the power was off yesterday morning for the hours between 8.00 and 12.00, or just after in our case (and is due to be off again this morning for the same time). After the laptop battery ran out I had time to dust the front room, clear up all the unwanted computer cables that are lying around and tidy up my bookshelves. Putting some old, unwanted, leads up in the moussandra I was interested to note that I already have 16 monitor leads, five general, heavy duty adaptors, with leads, a couple of Ethernet cables, a few phone line connections (our phone is still not working), 101 red and black audio leads and several other assorted cables of no immediately discernible use. And I thought it was just coat hangers that bred when you weren't looking.

February

A Symi film, a Symi book, a Symi advert and Symi parish churches

Kalo Mina from Symi! February already

After a couple of power cuts, we think we're going to be ok this morning. We shall see any moment now as the power has been going off dead on 8.00 and coming back on just as promised at 12.00, roughly speaking. As for the telephone, that's still another matter. It's still not working so a call to OTE is in the offing. Not that I mind as I am not a telephone fan at the best of times.

It's another lovely, cold, clear day out there today and the wind of yesterday evening seems to have dropped. The sea is still a bit chunky by the looks of things, further out, beyond Nimos and it is blue and icy looking. I'm going to find another layer to put on.

New doors and a new film

Over the page is an image showing the new church doors at Saint Athanasios church, which is our parish church. Next Sunday (10th) is the name day of Haralambos (Harry) so we may well be attending part of the service with him and staying for coffee and cakes afterwards. A good opportunity to examine the new doors close up.

No great plans for the rest of this weekend though; I think we're out this afternoon and then tomorrow, if the weather is good, I might go out and do some filming around the village, if Neil will lend me his HD camera. We headed down to the post office yesterday and I had a go with the camera, then brought the data card home and tried some very basic and rough editing. I was seeing what effects I could get and also learning how to put music tracks underneath.

What I really need is some kind of professional editing suite; yesterday I spent a few hours with Real Player, Windows Movie Maker, Audacity and about two other programmes, in order to get the music on and the sound off and the images in… All very time consuming. But hey, that's what winters are for aren't they?

Maybe for now; I'm also supposed to be working on some new stories for a book and we've got the shop stock to start to organise soon and before you know it, it will be Easter again. I mean, we're already into February. So, I best get on…

More filming

I was out filming yesterday as well, doing some more experimenting with Neil's HD camera and getting some shots around the village. This is just for fun, a winter hobby you might call it, and I might share some results soon if they are any good.

Meanwhile: those waiting for Adriana to get back and pick up her Symi blog again may have to wait a few more days. I am sure I just heard on the news that there was a ban on all shipping, and that boats would be staying in the harbours until at least Wednesday now. If that's correct then we can expect no mail or fresh supplies for a further three days. Let's hope the water boat came in recently as we're starting to run low and the sterna needs topping up.

Boat strikes, Adriana, photos, Zumba

The wind seems to have died down and although it was very windy yesterday the Dodecanese Pride (or Express) came to Symi. I did hear that this was to bring emergency medical supplies, but I'm not 100% sure about that. I also heard that there will be a shipping strike from Wednesday, which will put our big Blue Star schedule out somewhat.

I also know that Adriana is back from her recent trip and has already started blogging again in her bi-weekly Symi diary. Yesterday's entry was from Rhodes. If you have been to Rhodes and explored the Old Town in the summer then you're going to be interested to see what it looks like in the winter; quiet, cold, long empty streets, all the T-shirt and tourist shops closed up… You'll enjoy the photos she's put up.

If anyone is on Symi and reading this and is looking for something healthy this afternoon, then Clare is starting up some Zumba dance classes from today.

Zumba, apparently, is "an exhilarating, effective, easy-to-follow, Latin-inspired, calorie-burning dance…" Sounds like a good way to burn off that still hanging-around Christmas excess.

Symi decline 1912 onwards, great photo, dark skies

Another great shot from Neil today which captures the desolation of some kind of aftermath.

Whether it be the aftermath of war or neglect, this ruin seems to say it all, particularly with the moody, brooding sky. This building is in the 'millstone square' (Alamina Square) in Horio and may well have once been a kafeneion I was once told by a relative of a previous owner of several properties around that square that this little area was once the thriving heart of the village.

Men would come and sit here for coffee after finishing work, after trudging back up from the harbour on foot, up the Kataraktis or, when they were built, the Kali Strata steps and Alamina would be the place to come to meet and do 'kafeneion' business. We're talking 17th to early 20th century here I guess. It's a bit sad that the square would have gone into a decline after 1912, when the island came under Italian rule, the first World War took its toll and then the depression and the second World War. Sad for 101 reasons of course but particularly sad for George Stavrou who opened the large kafeneion there in 1909 (April 1st). He would have only had a couple of years of good business before people started to leave and these buildings started to fall into disrepair.

But there we go, a little bit of history for a Wednesday morning. It must be the heavy skies and distant thunder that brought that on, and this dark, black and white image as well.

Lightening up, the news from home is that the non-working phone line has been reported to OTE and an engineer will be fixing it, sometime. No time, day or date was given but as the junction box is about six feet from our balcony windows and at the same level I will hear and see the ladder going up and know when attention is being paid. Then we should be able to phone out and in again and maybe the internet connection will stay on for longer than ten minutes at a time too. No other great news this morning except there may or may not be a shipping strike; the news was just telling me that some boats have defied the strike and loaded up. I assume they mean the crew rather than the actual boat, but that's news headlines for you.

Symi TV advert number two

Another little treat for you today if you're not in Greece, or not a Symi follower on Facebook where a short film has been doing the rounds.

It's a follow up advertisement from Becel, also filmed on Symi a few weeks ago. You might remember I mentioned that there was a film crew here, and at one point Neil was unable to come out of his shop because of filming? That's because part of this advert was being filmed, so if you know where to look, you can catch the Symi Dream shop in the background.

More importantly, anyone who now[1] Takis Leather will recognise Takis doing his piece to camera as he comes down the steps. There is also a fleeting glimpse of him working on one of his leather-art creations. It's a nice little plug for Symi [and probably still available on line if you look around].

Friday morning update

I'm going to be quick. There is thunder rolling around his morning though the sky is currently blue right overhead. Mind you, I can't see the coast of Turkey so perhaps there's a storm coming in from the… (works it out), northeast? So I'd better be quick as I don't want to suffer a strike and lose the phone, connection, computer, modem, as often happens when there is a storm around here.

I expect the Symi Gallery is hoping that the rain holds off as they have a poetry reading and barbeque planned for tomorrow evening, at the gallery on the Kali Strata. Everyone is welcome. We have a name day celebration to attend on Sunday as it is the name day of Haralambos (Harry) so we will be going to church and then having our own barbeque or something afterwards. And those are the plans for the weekend. Simple and straightforward.

We bit the bullet yesterday and headed down to Yialos to take care of some business; we went during a gap in the rain and were doing fine until it was time to head back up again. Heavy, grey clouds come over and dumped a load of rain on us so we waited it out under an awning in the harbour. Then, when the rain had calmed, we headed back up the steps against the tide, as it were. The runoff was still coming down but it wasn't so bad and it was possible to avoid most of it if you changed direction and did the occasional jump across the streams.

Symi Animal Welfare message

Today I have a message from Symi Animal Welfare.

"Symi Animal Welfare has made an arrangement with a vet in Rhodes to neuter feral cats free of charge with only the anaesthetic to pay for. Symi Animal Welfare has made eight or nine trips to Rhodes so far this winter taking a minimum of three/four cats per trip. So anyone wishing to help-out by taking local street cats and escorting other feral cats to Rhodes would they please contact Symi Animal Welfare so that they can make the necessary arrangements with the vet."

---

1 Oops, I'm always doing that 'now' for 'know' and in this case 'knows.' I new I'd do it again.

As we have had many new visitors to our (almost) daily Symi blog recently there may be some folk who are not sure who the Alarm Cat is. His mother was a stray kitten we took in not long after we moved to Symi. She was found parentless by the senior school and was tiny. She was named Slippers (we also had another stray kitten called Pipe).

Unfortunately/fortunately when the vet came to Symi to neuter the feral cats on his next visit, it was too late for Slippers, she was too far 'gone' to be operated on and a little while later Jack was found behind a spare mattress in the moussandra. This was at our previous house and it's all in the book. Symi 85600, plug, plug. A few months later, after Jack (he was named after the Greek word for 'fireplace' so there were Pipe, Slippers and Fireplace) was weaned, Slippers died and a couple of years later Pipe disappeared. So here we are, nearly 10 years later and Jack is still going strong. He has survived two emergency vet visits, one with a badly broken leg, two other major illnesses, which he pulled through thanks to Symi Animal Welfare, and now has his own Facebook page 'Jack Cat Says' and his own merchandising.

So now you know. Oh, and he is called the Alarm Cat because he wakes us up before the alarm every morning wanting to get back in the house after his nights out.

Χαράλαμπος name day on Symi

There were plenty of nice things happening over the weekend, apart from the thunderstorms and the rain.

The poetry event at the Symi Gallery was really well attended, lots of people turned up to read and listen, participate and share a barbeque on the Kali Strata afterwards. There were at least six or seven different nationalities represented, and poems were read in Greek, English and Urdu possibly other languages as well. By the time we were able to get there, inside was full and it was standing room outside only.

And yesterday was godson Harry's name day, and the name day of everyone named after St Haralambos, Χαράλαμπος, or Charalambos.

This year Harry got himself fully involved, helping to carry the icon around the church and standing with it as the bread was blessed and passed around. The boys were given a whole loaf to take home with them, and this was duly shared out among friends who came to the Harry house afterwards for coffee. That was after we'd had coffee in the church refectory, sweet, strong Greek style coffee, with milk and bread, and donuts, and truffles that Sam had made, and a chocolate éclair from the church. All very nice thank you.

And so the week starts and it's a big week for us: golf tonight in the on-going Symi golf championship[1] (I think I am currently ahead by a few strokes), tomorrow it's pancakes with the boys, Wednesday is the tap class (must practice!), I think Thursday is a 'day off' (for Valentine's Day), Friday will be the usual card game, Saturday quiz, Sunday is Jenine's birthday so there is a day out planned and we're hoping the rain stays away. There was another thunderstorm last night, the towels are down under the doors and windows, but it looks like it might be clearing up… famous last words as it is forecast to be "showers in spots this afternoon" whatever that means.

Kalo Wednesday in February to you!

Great pancakes last night; Ian, Sam and Jenine all took turns throwing them around the kitchen. The floor claimed three, there were 101 various things to go inside the many survivors, there was one burned hand and a Lego plane crash incident, but a generally fun night was had by all.

Today is a writing and tap dancing day, as they go so well together. And tomorrow is St Valentine's Day. I am not sure if there are any events taking place on the island apart from perhaps name day festivities for Dinos and the variations of Valentine. In previous years there have been a quiz and a music night, and other musical get-togethers, and suppers for the evening. But I have not heard of anything this year. A sign of the times perhaps? I am sure that Valandes' flower shop will be doing business though.

---

1   I should explain that this is played from the comfort of our sofa on the Xbox 360, none of that needless spoiling of a good walk for us!

Thinking about it, it has been a quieter winter all round this year. I've noticed less building work going on, though that might just be because I have not been out and about so much. There is a house being done up near us and I have heard some work taking place across the valley from time to time, but not as much as usual. There have been less people around; we had quite a few visitors right up until New Year and now things are very quiet. But then again they usually are around this time of year. It's too cold to be out in the square, working hours are shorter, and people are only just now starting to think about the start of the new season. Although that's a few months away yet, things soon creep up on you. Neil has to start thinking about 2014 calendars, new cards, new limited editions and new images CDs and DVDs at this time of year, and we're only just getting in last summer's VAT and tax bills. All seems the wrong way around really.

Topical trivia from Symi Dream

Here's wishing you a pleasant St Valentine's Day. Ημέρα του Αγίου Βαλεντίνου ευτυχισμένη.

I was second out of the starting blocks this morning, Neil got up to let the Alarm Cat in, so I wasn't first to get to the rose bush in the garden. I now have two roses and some bougainvillea on my table, in a vase. I'll have to look around the garden for something for later. An orange from the orange tree perhaps? Does one give oranges on Valentine's Day? No don't laugh; there is a connection:

In 1886, on this day, the first trainload of oranges left Los Angeles. And that's a fact.

At least it is according to my desk calendar of fascinating facts. The Spanish had established Los Angeles in 1781 to help colonise the region, then as the Anglo-Americans began to take over, they broke up the Hispanic style, large, ranches and grew various, diverse crops on the land instead. Oranges included. Then you had the railways so things could move around easier, and oranges grew well, and so the Californians started shipping their oranges east and the first batch left LA today in 1886.

So, happy orange day to you, especially if you are in California.

On Symi, The Dark Month Rises

It's one of those mornings where I have no great news to impart. February is very often a quiet month for us socially, for the shop, and for many businesses on the island.

It's known as a 'dark' month even though the evenings are staying lighter for longer. I think the name comes from the fact that it is often cloudy and wet, it certainly feels dark. Also because, in business terms, you're kind of in the middle of the tunnel; the long, lean winter period where the summer season is the light at the end of that tunnel. (I now have a song from 'Starlight Express' in my head; great.)

The Symi Dream shop has been open all winter, apart from Neil's trip to his daughter's wedding reception in India, and will be open now for the rest of this year, apart from a short trip in March. But the busy, social and hectic hot days of summer are still several months away and the days of being cold and damp, in layers of clothing, in the shop for the benefit of a couple of customers a week seem to go on for ever. Except they don't because already we're saying it will be Clean Monday soon and then Easter, and before you know it we'll be saying 'where did that winter go?' It doesn't help, and yet it does, that we have regular social activities during these winter months. It's Friday again today so that means another game of cards tonight and it only seems like a couple of days ago we played (and lost) the last one.

And so it starts to rain again. You see? There are dark grey clouds making February feel like the dark month. (Note to self: 'The Dark Month rises.' Possible film title. Maybe not.) It rained yesterday evening just as I went out with the camera to try and get some HD video footage for a possible project, so I came home and did some indoor shooting work. (Another note: must look up how to use this camera!) And later we went out to the House of the Rising Sun (Sunrise Café) for a couple of glasses. It had more or less stopped raining when I left the house but the water was still pouring down the steps. I kept dry feet all the way to the village square and managed to get just past the Rainbow without any infiltration, but there, on the widest part of the path, there was no way ahead without stepping in a torrent; this must be the place where the channels meet.

Anyway. Enough rambling, there's a day to be getting on with. One that will include a trip to Yialos to check the post and a game of cards this evening. I wonder if we will let the opposition win again this week?

A new novel set on Symi, Midas by Dominic Ranger

Today is getting off to a good start; early to rise, quick dash to get dressed as it's cold, quick to make a herbal tea and get a fresh juice on (beetroot, apple, pear and carrot) and quicker to get to the blog.

And there is a slight link there as I go on to pass on the news about a new novel which is set partly on Symi. 'Midas', by Dominic Ranger, poses the question: "If you suddenly discovered you were the richest person in the world, what would you do?"

Here's what the publishers, Troubadour Publishing Ltd., say on their website:

"Midas, Dominic Ranger's superb debut thriller novel, is a rollercoaster ride of revenge, intrigue, sex and money, taking readers from a quiet town in Hampshire to the tiny and incredibly beautiful Greek island of Symi.

"Newly-bankrupt and newly-separated Alan Marks discovers he has never-ending riches when he tries to use his cash card at an ATM in Farnborough, Hampshire. He's desperate for money, but has no hope of success – until £200 appears out of the machine. Then another £200, and another… Alan Marks is suddenly rich, and it's not come from his account. If this works in any cash machine, he is potentially the richest man in the world. What does he do now?"

"Garry McAllister, ex-cop, top fraud investigator and a lifelong lover of Scotch, arrives for work at his bank's headquarters. Glancing at his computer screen, he discovers his worst possible nightmare. Someone is operating Midas, a scheme which allows the holder to withdraw endless amounts of money, without the withdrawals attributing to any account. Now McAllister is on a mission; to stop Midas. And the bank doesn't really mind how. But what McAllister doesn't know is that he is not the only one trying to get Midas…"

"Dominic Ranger is the pseudonym of Christopher Lillicrap, a former teacher, prolific writer and composer, who is best known as a children's TV presenter in the 70s and 80s. He is still involved in writing for children and his educational series Numbertime gained the Royal Television Society award for Best Educational Programme. Christopher has also worked with numerous police forces over the last twenty five years as a media consultant and been an adviser on several high-profile cases, including the Millie Dowler murder in Surrey. It is this work which has inspired Midas."

People who know Symi and its characters should be able to identify locations and possibly some people. And if you think the author's real name sounds familiar, Chris and his wife have a villa up in Horio where, last year, his son Dominic was married to Joey; Symi Dream were the photographers and videoed the event as well; there are photos on the blog somewhere around last September.

Bricking up ruins

Funny how some things just happen. I am in the middle of putting together various video shots for a possible project that might possibly take place on Symi, possibly later this year. It's not 100% certain, but not impossible. Maybe.

Meanwhile, I was asked if I could get some shots of ruins, and a few of people, and some views from around the village. So, I have been out and about from time to time with Neil's HD video camera and found some perfect places. I found a perfect ruin for one perfect shot and arranged for a couple of friends to be there on Thursday to be the people who need to be seen in it. I even stood inside it and did some filming to get some background shots.

On Tuesday I popped around the corner, where the ruin is, to go on an errand, and lo and behold the council have been past and bricked it up. After what? Sixty years of it being open to the public, with no notices and a wide, open doorway, they decided to do something about it now. Did they know my intentions? I wondered that but no, it's pure coincidence. They are bricking up a lot of ruins around this neighbourhood at the moment. It is an attempt to stop naughty people from throwing rubbish into the ruins and then starting fires in them. It just so happens that the one I wanted to use was walled up on the day after I decided to use it. When I say bricked up, or walled up, they use the stones that are usually piled inside, the old wall stones, to fill the doorways and windows. Like I said, this is to stop lazy people dumping their rubbish bags in them. Let's hope it works.

Meanwhile I will be on the lookout for another location. That's after I've gone to Pedi with Neil to get some shots of 'quiet island bay' this afternoon. Hopefully. If it doesn't rain or cloud over too much. I was up during the night unplugging the computer and phone as a thunderstorm rolled over. And, looking at the forecast for the week ahead, my main filming day (Thursday) may have to change as there is more rain promised, or threatened. Mind you, they said that for yesterday and there was none until the night. Hey ho! That's the way it goes I guess.

Life in Pedi in the winter months on Symi

Continuing with our little filming project, Neil and I went down to Pedi yesterday afternoon to get some shots of the bay.

You might think that Pedi would be quiet at this time of year, and you would be right. But there were still a lot of things going on, in their own quiet way. Someone had been busy shoring up the supermarket against the sea, there is sand and shingle right up against the walls there, from high tides and strong winds, though the road has been cleared now, so that is passable. There were folk on George's Taxi Boat hanging out and chatting and there was at least one Panga heading out to sea for fishing or whatever.

And over in the boatyard we said hello to several people; George was working on his boat and he had an old mate helping him; you should pop into the boatyard if you are down there and see the wooden hulled boats that are being built. A few older ladies were paying calls, I had a chat with a tethered sheep which watched us go by, and the chickens were hurrying around being busy and clearing the road of grit by the looks of it.

Hebus[1] came down, there were a few younger guys on their motorbikes heading down that way for some reason we don't ask about, and then turning around and heading back up to the sports field. A few cars were going up and down the road, people were working in their fields and on their pieces of land. It was all very similar to summer days, apart from the fact there was no one lying on the beach, and the tavernas are closed. We headed straight out on to the main jetty and then went north, so I don't know if the Katsaras bar was open.

And then we walked back up the slow, shallow hill to Horio and Neil headed off to work. I came home, downloaded my filming and then went off to a rather good, if tiring, tap class, brilliantly led by Rhiannon. Jenine was complemented on the lightness of her taps and turns, I was not surprised not to be as I still hoof like someone from Stomp, and mine are not so much turns as 'graceless alternative movements' (European Directive definition 120:34a). But we're coming along. A bit worrying: the ladies were discussing

---

1   Ah ha! Another favourite, the 'missing T.' I think the T key on my keyboard doesn't work properly that's why I am always putting He for The and Here for There. But as you know, typos for me are neither here nor here.

costumes for the dance show in April, glittery waistcoats, tails, and even leggings were mentioned. The men will of course wear sensible suits and full face masks.

Weather halts shoot, Villa Papanikola and beetroot

It doesn't look like there is going to be much filming going on today. The wind has been howling all night and it's still going, rattling the shutters and the roof.

It's also raining now, the clouds are big and heavy and show no signs of going away anytime soon. I was due to be up at the Castro this afternoon with camera and my two actors of the day, but unless things change drastically this morning I'll have to make a couple of calls and reschedule the shoot. That's another 2M lost from the budget. Oh dear! (Only joking. What's a budget? We're only doing this for fun, and maybe February is not the month to be doing it.)

But we shot some ghostly footage yesterday with Harry and his dad around the corner. There were dark clouds about but they were moving and different shades, so looked interesting. This morning's lot are just plain dull.

Which is something you cannot say about Symi in the spring, which is almost here again. Walking down to Pedi on a hot and sunny day on Wednesday, there were cyclamen growing at the side of the road and things that people had planted in allotments were coming up. We've already had some totally organic and tasty beetroot from Adriana's farm this year, as well as eggs from her chickens: bright yellow yokes and actually tasting of eggs. So there are some positive signs that better weather is on its way and that the seasons are turning.

There was also good news being reported in the papers that there has been an upturn in tourist bookings for Greece for this summer already; manly from Eastern Europe. We have seen, in recent years, an increase in Eastern European visitors, and languages being spoken, as more money it seems, is available to people in Russia and former Russian states. We see them here as mainly day trippers, but every visitor is potential good news for some business owner, and the day trip visitors put some income into the island, so it's a good thing all round.

And the other day I met the people who have taken over Villa Papanikola, the 'Small World' singles accommodation (as was) that has been out of use for a while. It was the inspiration for a setting for my novel 'Jason and the Sargonauts' and sits overlooking the harbour on the south side.

There are plans to re-open this accommodation which will be great news, so I will keep you informed about that if and when I hear more. I just thought I would mention it as I believe it might be singles accommodation again this year and there isn't much of that around these days; places where you don't have to pay extra for a double room you don't need. I think it's going to be run through Symi Visitor Accommodation, but let me know if that's incorrect Yiannis, and I will re-post details.

Stocking up the Symi Dream shop

Storm did indeed stop play yesterday, and not just here on Symi. There were floods in Athens, the worst in many years, and there were high winds here, plus a thunderstorm overnight. Things have quietened down now and we have leaden skies and a flat, gunmetal sea.

So filming was postponed yesterday but a new schedule is being drawn up for tomorrow onwards. Hopefully we will have everything done by Wednesday and then I can start to see if it is any good, or if it is going to work, so more about that later.

Neil has drawn up his stock list for the Symi Dream shop, that's a stocktake I suppose you'd call it. Looks like he's got new limited editions coming along, there should be new cards as well as the popular ones, and a new calendar (for 2014). We've still to get in lots of other general stock, like paper and ink, and we have to redecorate the walls, and decide what will be upstairs in the gallery this year.

Later on this morning I have to head down to Yialos to the bank or else I won't be having a weekend, then I'll have to get back to make lunch which today will involve homemade baked beans (slow cooker recipe), we've already had our daily juice and today it was carrot, lemon, apple, pear and ginger, there is shopping to do and a quiz to attend later. It's all go.

Celebrating on Symi, it's Monday morning!

See if you can spot the word of the week in today's blog post.

It's Monday again and that's always a great time of the week as it means there's another week ahead to look forward to. This week should be filled with filming and dancing, afternoon walks, if possible, and writing. The weekend was full of exciting things done, such as a walk to Yialos on a Saturday afternoon. The harbour has a completely different feel on a Saturday afternoon than it does on a weekday morning, which is when I usually head down that way.

We bumped into Nikos and some school children who are preparing to present a play on March 9th (more details to follow). They were heading off to make the scenery with instructions from Fotini and Ian. As Nikos said: "Δάσκαλοι και μαθητές ετοιμάζουν το θεατρικό σκηνικό. Ενα μεγάλο μπραβο σε δυο καταπληκτικούς δασκάλους Φωτεινή Κρανίδη και Ian Χαυκοχ." (Children preparing to make the scenery; a big 'thumbs up' to two amazing teachers, Fotini Kranidis and Ian Haycox.)

Sunday was spent filming again, having fun learning how to use the Nikon properly (or learning about 20% of what the Nikon can do) and we were out with the camera quite late, until the day started to turn to night and became crepuscular, and filming had to stop.

Which reminds me, the roaches are back, and they are quite crepuscular in their behaviour. The traps from Australia are down and new sprays have been bought ready for the chase, and I have already found a few on their backs when I get up in the morning, presumably having partaken of the bait and gone legs-up just before dawn.

Sadly, they are a part of life around here, along with several other creepy crawlies that are not to everyone's liking but what can you do about them? But good news is that it won't be long before the ants are back; at least they get rid of the bodies.

Did you get the word of the week?

crepuscular

— adj

1. of or like twilight; dim
2. (of certain insects, birds, and other animals) active at twilight or just before dawn

[C17: from Latin crepusculum dusk, from creper dark]

More from the filming on Symi project

Today we've got a short video taken at the Castro yesterday.

The video is not as good a quality as it started out due to the fact that I have to change the file type, then use a programme which then saves it at a lower resolution, and then upload it to You Tube which also seems to degrade the quality a bit. Shame that, as it started out as HD format and now it is, at best, what they call DVD format. (Or something.) And it's also hand held as I had left the tripod down the hill a way and was too lazy to go back for it.

In contrast, here's a shot I took a couple of days ago, this is also from the Castro, and it is the cross which is lit up at night. This was part of the on-going filming project but the shot wasn't actually on my list of instructions, not on the script you might say. But I was so impressed with the Hammer Horror style clouds, and the silhouette function of the Nikon, I couldn't resist. The thing we're working on is a ghost story/horror/thriller anyway so it seemed quite appropriate.

Last night we did some night shot experiments, again using the various settings on the Nikon and some trial and error and, as long as it's not raining later this evening, we're going to do some more. It's windy today again and there is a bit of a haze over the sea towards Turkey which could be cloud, but otherwise it looks like it should be a clear day.

Visiting Symi parish churches when on holiday

Here's an experimental shot taken the other night as I was out on the balcony. Horio by night you might call it.

The church tower you can see is of Ag. Haritomeni, and above this, the lit-up cross of the church dedicated to Mary the Virgin at the Castro. I went to look up Saint Haritomeni to tell you a bit more about this Greek saint and the first page that came up was from Agia Marina Donkey Rescue in Crete, which I thought was rather wonderful. They tell us that:

"Derived from Greek χαρις(charis) meaning "grace, kindness". This was the name of a 1st-century Greek novelist. In Greek mythology, a Charis is one of several Charites (Χάριτες; Greek: "Graces"), goddesses of charm, beauty, nature, human creativity and fertility, and in Homer's Iliad, Charis is the wife of Hephaestus. Charis is also the Spartan name of a Grace."

The name day is September 28th

If/when you come to Symi and explore the village you will, most days, find the church of Haritomeni open. Petros is the caretaker and he lives next door. He is often there, looking after the building and welcoming visitors. If you see the gates open, pop your head inside and have a look around. He will tell you the various stories from the church: the soldier being shot (you can see the bullet hole in the screen), the story of the rescued icons, and you will be able to go up onto the ladies' gallery and look down at the icons, paintings, the Turkish grandfather clock, the pulpit and the splendour of the decoration. It's well worth the climb up and, unlike the churches you see from the harbour, this one is more likely to be open. You may have to buy some herbs on the way out and sometimes (often) it is very hard to catch everything Petros is telling you, unless you speak Symaika fluently, but you will be rewarded!

That's something to keep in mind actually. Often in the summer we have day trippers puffing their way up the steps and asking how to get to the Church; they mean the one that they can see from the harbour, with the big red dome, H Lemonitisa. We direct them of course but there is always a dilemma. Does one say: this way but it is not open (because it is only open for services), or does one let them take the walk and enjoy the view and discover its closure for themselves? I do the latter because along the way they will get a few stunning views to buffer their disappointment.

And I should be having my own glorious views this morning, later, as I head of down to the harbour again. Neil's planning to visit a dentist, I need to check some paperwork and the post, and it's a lovely day for a walk and some exercise and a tap class. An active day lies ahead.

Bills and the day-to-day routine on Symi in the winter

I found this photo that Neil had put up on Facebook, possibly even on his own photo collection blog.

I thought this was a really nice image as it shows the Island's mayor, Eleftherios Papakalodoukas, a couple of holidaymakers/visitors, the British Olympic Holidays rep in traditional island costume and local Symi ladies all dancing together. Nice shot. Nice message I thought.

The weather is turning (he says with fingers crossed) and the days are warmer again, the sun is out, it was over 20 degrees yesterday and things ahead are looking as if they are going to be dry and sunny; until Sunday at least. Spring is in the air, and the heating can be turned down. That's just as well as the recent round of electricity bills has started to show the increases being introduced. It looks like the best advice is to save, pay the estimated bills when they come in if you can and lessen the blow of the full bill when it arrives. Ours was, on reflection, not bad for four months of winter weather, but still confusing. The full estimated amount was paid, but the amount the bill shows as being paid as 'witness' against the estimated was €60.00 short, but then there was €95 added on for something untranslatable against the previous what'sit of the second imaginary thingummy, and so on. We're lucky that we have an all-year round business and so have a bit of cash flow during these months. Other people are finding it really hard this winter. And don't get me started on the unemployment benefit reforms that the government kind of tried to sneak in, and did, when no one was looking; or maybe they were.

Anyway! Back to more mundane and day-to-day matters; Thursday on Symi and what's occurring? Well, not a lot, not for me at any rate. The usual: some writing, some housework, a quick tap practice with Jenine later this morning, while borrowing some more DVDs, making lunch (maybe something with fresh eggs from Adriana's farm), then heading out for an after lunch walk or photo shoot or filming session, or a doze on the sofa, and then some more writing and staying in saving money while Neil is at work, hoping for customers who will help contribute towards the next round of bills. (Water bill needs to be paid today as well, that arrived a week overdue and hadn't taken into account the previously paid amount. I think there's a conspiracy happening around here…)

MARCH

Donkey parking, gigaflops, troubled by the wind and a birthday in Transylvania

Summer holiday? Got to be Symi

Here's an up to date photo from Symi harbour showing the on-going road-works around the main harbour road.

Over recent years it looks like there has been funding available for repaving and so the paths have been paved, and then parts of the road were repaved, and now this is extending around the north side of the harbour, past the famous Takis Leather shop.

Yialos a couple of days ago was calm and quiet, with businesses not yet quite out of hibernation. But it won't be long now before tables and chairs are out on forecourts, shops and tavernas get a sweep out and are made ready for the summer. There is a little way to go before then though, a few more weeks of quiet winter activity: walks and dinners, specializing, preparing stock lists, photos, writing, more walks, dancing, birthday parties, and so on.

And so your mind might be turning towards the summer holiday this year and where to go. Well, as always we can heartily recommend this small slice of the Aegean, and if you're after some ideas for holiday companies to investigate then why not take a look at our Symi Holidays page.

If you're coming to Rhodes and want a day trip to Symi then check out our 'Day trips to Symi' page on our website.

And if you are coming independently and want to know the best way to get from Rhodes to Symi after landing at the airport, then check out our 'Getting to Symi from Rhodes' page.

We also have one about getting to Symi from Athens.

As always, you will need to double check with travel companies, shipping lines, flights and so on to make sure they are working, and that this info is up to date.

So, stop hanging around here reading this and get to your travel agent, or online booking page and start investigating this year's summer holiday on Symi. It's going to be a good one. We're offering the usual wine nights and exhibitions, there will be regular photo walks, afternoons in the sun, evenings on the steps, chat and stories to catch up on, and that's just at the Symi Dream shop.

Τσικνοπέμπτη (Tsiknopempti) on Symi and gigaflops

The word of the week today, which has nothing to do with anything really, is:

Gigaflop.

n. | (Electronics & Computer Science / Computer Science) Computing a measure of processing speed, consisting of a thousand million floating-point operations a second

[from GIGA- + flo(ating) p(oint)]

I've had a few gigaflops in the past; that moment when you find yourself on stage in front of several hundred people, you tell a joke and no one laughs. Or that time when you are on the stage of the Theatre Royal Margate and the show should have started ten minutes ago but you're hanging on just in case a coach party miraculously appears to fill the balcony. (It doesn't but you still get presented with an award after the show anyway.)

There are other, naughtier definitions which I have not included here, but a couple that are printable:

"Geek slang for ultimate fail, derived from the term used to measure a computer's performance. The word is split into two parts to justify its meaning. 1. GIGA (meaning loads or 1,000,000,000) and 2. flop (meaning fail). Not to be confused with GagaFlip the act of discarding an unwanted Lady Gaga." Urban Dictionary.com

And if you were wondering why, or where from? It was a word that came up in yesterday's crossword, and the rest of the team decided it would be good to have it as this week's word of the week. And now for something completely different.

It will rain on Thursday. How do I know? Well, apart from the fact the online weather forecast tells me so, Thursday is also Tsiknopempti, and for the last two years (at least) it has rained on this day causing the cancellation of the souvlaki celebration in the village square. Instead, the event has been held at the school, or rather the council supplied meat-treats have been given out at the schools where the children have dressed up in costume, sprayed foam and silly string to their hearts' content without fear of ruining cameras, causing people to slip and break bones, or blinding passers-by. They've enjoyed the souvlakies and shouted until they were horse.[1]

Symi starts to get into pre-Lent mood

Lent will soon be upon us and so the island of Symi is already getting into pre-Lent mood, with the start of the various church services and carnival events.

This Thursday is Tsiknopempti, but I am still not sure what is happening for that day. Thursday is also the day the country celebrates the reunification of the Dodecanese islands, with Greece, following WWII. This is mainly a local celebration with bands and marches, parades and festivities on Rhodes, Symi and other Dodecanese islands. If I remember correctly it celebrates the day that the British forces handed back the islands to the Greek nation following their surrender in on May 8th 1945. And on 31st March the then king of Greece hoisted the Greek flag on the island and so there is another parade and celebration on that day.

And on Saturday there is a Carnival Party!

---

1   If they'd carried on shouting they would have eventually have been a supermarket ready-meal.

Full details for our local readers: Saturday the 9th March, in the Opera House, starting at 5 p.m. it includes a theatrical performance of "The Little Prince" by the 4th class of the Primary School. There will be a clown, a bazaar, music, tea & coffee, cakes, and lots of games for the children. This is being organised by the PTA of the Yialos Primary School.

I will soon be taking a two week holiday and so will miss things like the Independence Day parade on 25th. But we will be having a guest blogger looking after things while I am away. Maybe not every day but when possible you should be able to check in and get a different view of Symi island life. More about that later.

Today I am planning to do battle with a couple of Roland instruments, a sequencer, a midi port and the PC to try and get my recording system wired up to the computer in order to record more music. It's been a long time since I've done this so anything can happen. Frustrated shouts and bad words most likely.

Pollen is up on Symi; a short rundown of plant things

I happen to know that on this day in history Real Madrid was founded (1902). I read that off my daily desk calendar Christmas present, but I read it as 'the real Madrid was founded' and wondered what had become of the fake one. Apparently it was the best football team of the 20th century according to FIFA and, in 2011, the world's second most valuable one according to Forbes. Here endeth the annual mention of football on my blog.

There's a bit of sneezing and wheezing going on in the house today and has been these last couple of days. Many people are reporting a sudden increase in nasal activity and plants are being blamed. Even I, who have never suffered from hay fever*, am sniffing and sneezing and have cold symptoms. I took an antihistamine tablet two days ago and am still drowsy. For me they only work as sleeping tablets, though they do relieve the symptoms a bit I am useless for a couple of days after taking one. Neil had to have three yesterday, but luckily he is not affected in the same way as I.

But for sure the flowers and plants are out and budding. We have orange blossom in the garden. The Lemon tree is slightly confused as it has blossom and lemons. The vine is starting to grow back, the rose has been in bloom on and off through the winter, the apricot tree is starting to grow leaves again after its pruning in November, and so is the plum tree. I don't know much about plants but there is cyclamen everywhere at the moment, those 'Judas plants' are coming back up and the wild fig trees have buds on their sticks.

The sun is out, the sea is calm, there is more washing to be done and I am battling with a new piece of software on my PC. At least I will be later. I have rigged up my keyboard to the PC via a midi input and I now have Cubase 5 to load on later today. The idea is to get back to writing and recording music. It's been about 10 years since I've handled Cubase so I'll need to go back to basics, and it's bound to have been updated since I used whatever it was I used, on a Mac, in a cellar back in the UK. All I know is that my sound box (Roland JV 1010) is now so out of date it doesn't seem to be compatible and I can't remember how to wire it up to make the sounds anyway.

But that's an adventure for later on this morning. If anyone knows how to do all this midi-Cubase-Windows 7-JV 1010 - recording, please drop me a line!

*Hay fever: I once suffered a very nasty bout aged about 11 when playing on a friend's farm, in the hay barn in all day, making tunnels and generally unknowingly being dangerous. And I suffered another bout of it in my twenties when I went to see a particularly bad production of it at the Savoy Theatre (before it burned down). Oh, and I didn't burn it down because of the production, though the man who lit my first musical in London was head electrician at the time. Coincidence.

Τσικνοπέμπτι on Symi, March 7th in Greece

Today is Tsiknopempti in Greece (Τσικνοπέμπτι) and also the celebration of the day the Dodecanese Islands were reintegrated back into Greece following WWII and a lot of time under other occupations.

Τσικνοπέμπτι, which is variously knows as 'smoky Thursday' or 'sooty Thursday' and other names, is the day when meat is consumed, clearing out the stocks ready for Lent which will be starting in a week or so's time. This day is usually celebrated with barbecues, parties, sometimes free souvlakies from the town council and a carnival style party in the village square. In recent years this has all happened at the schools due to the weather. I am still not sure what is happening today, if it is a school event only or if there will be a party in Horio. But it looks like the weather might be an issue as it is cloudy today and not very pleasant out there.

But the parade must still go ahead and the school children have already taken their wreaths down to the memorial. There will be a church service and a walk-past later on this morning.

At the Symi Dream house, I'm not sure what's happening. I'm still under the weather, to such an extent that I had to miss a valuable tap rehearsal last night, the throat is still painful, the head isn't working correctly or painlessly, and the ground is spinning when I move around. I've got things to do though, so the self-pity stage will have to come later after: blog, working on a script, working on music for the possible film idea, making lunch, and putting the washing away. Hardly great chores but already I am looking forward to a couple of episodes of Friends, an afternoon doze and a quiet evening in. I've already had my juice for the day so that will help (beetroot, lemon, ginger, apple and carrot, with the lemons coming fresh from the tree and into the juicer in their entirety. Vitamin C coming out of my ears now.)

Anyway, enough waffle. Here's wishing you all a happy 'reintegration day' (there must be a better world for it) a happy Τσικνοπέμπτι and, to my mum: Happy Birthday! Symi is holding a march and a meat feast just to celebrate for you, knowing that you're a pacifist vegetarian. The island is preparing for your arrival in June. Have a great day!

A weekend of parties is planned

Carnival Party! Saturday the 9th of March in the Opera House at 5 p.m. includes a theatrical performance of "The Little Prince" by the 4th class of the Primary School; A clown; a bazaar; music; tea & coffee; cake; and lots of games for the children! Organised by the PTA of the Yialos Primary School.

And then there is Harry's school party at Bloom Café Bar (Aletheni Club) on Sunday.

Now then, you know I am always doing something: writing stories, films, music… well, I am pleased to say that I now have Cubase 5 on my PC and was able to set it up really easily. There were none of the problems I had when I first started using the programme on a Mac 15 years ago, though to be fair those problems were not because the machine was a Mac. (The programme would freeze for no reason, or crash, and work would be lost. This was completely random and I got into the habit of saving the files after every command, more or less, as well as having an auto save running. Calls to the company, a friend with his own studio (a bit of a genius) and me (not a genius) spent hours trying to fix the bugs. It finally, after about three years, went back to the shop because we had exhausted everything, and there we found out that it had a cracked motherboard from birth; after that, Cubase, which was the only programme I ran on it, ran perfectly.)

There was no point to telling you that long rambling story except to say that I started using it yesterday to record some more improvisations. I was supposed to be getting a new book together this winter, and I did make a start, who knows I may even make a finish one day. But meanwhile, while there is a musical muse in the air, I might record some more piano music so I will have something new available in the shop this season.

Neil will have plenty new, he's putting together the new Symi calendar, he has some new limited editions to get printed when we are in Rhodes in a couple of weeks, and new cards to make.

We will also be having our popular wine nights, a different exhibition in our gallery, and a choice of photos walks, if I understand the plans correctly. There will be more on that soon.

Big winds and lots to do

It's a bit windy this morning as we make a start on the week. I was awake half the night with things rattling and banging about, and it was even worse outside.

The sea is being whipped up and the olive tree opposite is having a hard time staying still. The shutters are hanging on and the roof is rattling a bit, Jack Cat was very eager to be let in as it's turned a bit colder in the wind, so he was actively alarming from around 6.30 and I distinctly remember hearing the 12.30 bell last night. So I fully intend to be deservedly bleary-eyed later in the day.

Later this morning Neil has an appointment down in Yialos to check out a new hotel for its publicity and online photos. He's going to check location and views and set dressing, what exactly will need to be done for the shoot and so on, so let's hope he doesn't get too blown away en route. And suddenly there's lots to do for the season and not a lot of time to do it in.

Partly that's because of our holiday which starts in 10 days. We're going away for my 50th birthday and while we're away we will be leaving a special guest blogger in charge of Symi Dream. More about that nearer the time. Before then though, for our loyal readers on Symi: if you are around on Saturday at 7.30 pm there will be a special quiz night at the Sunrise Cafe and the first drink will be on me. Everyone's welcome. My birthday isn't until 26th but by then (wind willing) I shall be in the Carpathian Mountains on a quick tour or Romania.

And before then, there's a lot to organise for the shop. We've got to get things ready for the Rhodes leg of the journey, prints to order, lists of stock to buy and so on, there are other things to be made up and made ready so when we get back there isn't a sudden, last minute rush. Already other businesses are starting to prepare for the summer season; painting tables and chairs, inside and out of buildings, stock-taking and generally getting ready for a what we all hope will be a good year.

Wednesday morning update

The high winds have passed. They passed yesterday afternoon actually, and left behind a misty, murky and warm afternoon. I couldn't see the coast of Turkey only a short distance away because of what looked like fog. It's still pretty hazy through the front windows, though that could be to do with the fact that they need their spring clean. Oh, no, it's not the windows. Just looked up and the coast is starting to come into view.

So what's happening on Symi at the moment? Well, this time of year it's all about getting ready for Lent which starts next week and also getting ready for the start of the season. Depending on when Easter falls there can sometimes be a lull in business. It works like this: Everyone gets ready for Easter and the season has a kind of mild start-up as people come for a visit. If Easter is early, March/April, then there is a quiet period before the summer flights start in May. But if Easter is late, as it this year when it is in May, then this lull is less noticeable because the flights have already started. This makes the winter period feel longer because there is a longer time before any business is done, a big gap between October and May, but it also means (hopefully) that when business starts up again at Easter, it carries on.

I know that a fair few regular visitors will be here for this Easter and so we're hoping that the season will start and stay started, if you see what I mean. It also means that there may well be visitors here when Rhiannon and the dance school put on their performance in April. I'm still not sure of the date yet, but I will let you know. The 16th or 23rd has been mooted for the show which will happen at The Opera House, Symi. Watch this space.

Right, best be off to clean those windows and practice those shuffles. (That earthquake, 8.16 a.m. wasn't me!)

A windy night on Symi reminds me of Cairo

I expect there are a few blown-about properties around this morning. The wind yesterday was huge. Neil said that from his place at his desk at the shop yesterday evening he could hear things breaking and smashing outside and around. I was woken at 1.00 a.m. by the sound of someone using the front room as a playground and went to investigate. Somehow, the outside door that is wedged shut due to 'winter expansion' had come open a little way and Jack had managed to squeeze his great bulk through the little gap. He was happily turning the camera equipment, tripod and space under the desk into some kind of midnight playground. He was soon chased out.

And then at some point during the night, I was woken by silence as the wind has suddenly stopped. I don't mean died down, but stopped completely.

That reminded me of a not very interesting thing that happened to me in Cairo many years ago. I had just arrived for the start of a holiday and was on the umpteenth floor of the Sheraton Hotel (Thomas Cook escorted tour, rather posh). The noise of the traffic was non-stop, a continuous underscore through the evening and well into the night. I hadn't heard of ear plugs in those days so I lay awake for hours listening to car horns and yells, the constant hum of traffic and people calling. And then finally I managed to drift off. Only to wake with a start at around 4.30 to realise that there was no noise. It was completely silent out there, and very eerie. I went out onto the balcony to have a look (this was pre-vertigo days) and there in the distance were the pyramids lit up, the lights of the city, the other hotels and down below, no cars. Nothing. Silence. No traffic. I went back to bed.

The moment I got back in, it started up again. I reckon I'd witnessed Cairo's three minute break in traffic. It must happen every night at the same time. Everyone stops for three minutes for a silence break, and then it starts again.

But the wind hasn't started again today, as yet. Instead we are shrouded in a grey cloud once more, not cold, not yet wet, but still and mysteriously misty.

An interesting way to start what should be a fun weekend: a day off today, a card game tonight, a 50th birthday quiz tomorrow evening, a Sunday with the godsons and then a couple of days of packing before heading off on holiday on Wednesday. Only four more blogging days left until I take two weeks off and Jenine takes over. Don't worry, she won't ramble on like this, not with two boys to get ready for school.

Temporary parking Symi style

Today it's like one of those mornings when: "You know when you live on a Greek island because…"

You wake up in the morning to discover that someone parked their donkey outside your front windows during the night.

She's out there happily munching away on the weeds (I could borrow her for our garden), and over to the right of our view I can see the Pedi valley. Some of it will soon be obscured slightly by the house that is being renovated.

The sun is just starting to break through and it feels like it is going to be quite a warm day today, though the forecast is still for rain. There's a carnival on tomorrow in Yialos, and Monday is Clean Monday which heralds the start of Lent. Bells have already been ringing for church services this morning.

There's not a lot of other news today; the birthday quiz is this evening, there's no blog tomorrow, being Sunday (I sometimes write one on a Sunday during the summer), there's golf on Monday, packing on Tuesday and then

Jenine takes over the blog from Wednesday. I need to nip down to Yialos at some point before then and buy boat tickets, Neil has the shop to pack away ready for doing it up on his return, I've ordered the 2014 calendars so we have some in the shop ready for the start of the season.

Καθαρά Δευτέρα, Clean Monday and a non-birthday weekend

Am having a slightly later than normal start today thanks to a rather wonderful non-birthday weekend.

It started with a quiz at the Sunrise on Saturday, so a big thank you to Peter for arranging that, Kevin and Claudia for the hospitality and to everyone who came along and joined in, and brought cards and presents. Neil had arranged various photo displays showing pictures of me through the years that I'd forgotten we had and I think it's safe to say that everyone had a good time.

And then yesterday we had a quiet lunch with the godsons next door, just a light lunch of homemade steak and ale pie, sausages (as a second course) and all with peas, carrots and five different potato dishes. I've always been a bit of a potato fan, something to do with the Irish side of the family escaping the famine in the 19th century I think. And it was St Patrick's Day yesterday as well, so that could have had something to do with it. A big thank you to Jenine, Ian and the boys for making yesterday so special.

After lunch we all took a walk up to the top of the Castro to get some fresh air circulating around, and to prove that we could all still move after such a feast. Down in Yialos the stage was being set of the carnival festivities which took place there later in the day. Today being Clean Monday in Greece and the start of Lent the carnival happened yesterday. Today, the shops are shut and families will be going out with kites to fly and having barbeques of seafood and salads. I'm not sure what we are doing; getting some things up to date before we leave for holiday on Wednesday I think, and warming up left over sausage and mash, new, jacket, dauphinoise and roasted potatoes.

So, I'm off now, see in you in two weeks

It's the last day before my holiday today and as usual there are 101 things to be done before I can finally relax and set off to distant shores.

Well, not that distant and not shores either. And not that much to be done: finish off a piece of writing, pop down to town to get boat tickets and check the post, pack, a bit of washing, make sure everything is in order and that's it. From tomorrow (or as soon as possible) Jenine will be starting on the blog and looking after Symi Dream for us until around April 3rd or so. That's going to be fun and will give you a different perspective on Symi life. I think she might be planning blog posts about what it's like to get the family ready for work and school, a day in the life of Sam and one in the life of Harry; giving more of a family perspective on things.

And meanwhile we will be:

Rhodes tomorrow for the night (some business to do, things to start organising for the shop, so a bit of a working day as well), Athens on Thursday night, Bucharest for the weekend, meeting Neil's brother and a friend, then up to Sighosoara for a few days on Monday, sightseeing and so on, then Brasov, Bran and surrounding area for a couple of days, back to Bucharest, back to Athens, back to Rhodes (to complete the shop orders and business) and then back to Symi on the Dodecanese ferry on April 1st, wind and weather permitting.

And we've decided not to take the laptop with us; the only equipment will be phones (for the time and alarm clock) and cameras of course. None of this sitting in a café on 'tablets' (not that kind anyway) and emailing each other or telling each other good morning through Facebook and Twitter and LinkedIn and TimeWaste or whatever they are called. Internet free for two whole weeks; can't wait. If we need to be on line to check flights or whatever then we will make do, if anyone needs us then we have the mobiles and if they don't work in that part of the world then it will be back to the old fashioned way of… well, waiting until we get back I guess.

So, that's my plan for the next couple of weeks. When we get back it will be straight into dance rehearsals for the show on April 20th and then into the summer season, more or less.

Anyway, have a good couple of weeks and thank you for keeping us going through the winter. It's always nice to know we have so many people keeping in touch with Symi through the Symi Dream blog. And, if you've not already discovered it, then on a Monday and Friday you can also catch up with island news through Adrianna and her famous Symi blog.

Testing, testing from Symi

(Jenine takes over the blog for a couple of weeks)

So, just a quick blog post today from Symi whilst I make my way through my very comprehensive, "How to be the Symi Dream Blogger" instruction sheet left to me by James.

I watched from the Olive Tree terrace as the Blue Star left on Wednesday with Neil and James aboard, headed for the land of Dracula. The idea was to take a lovely panoramic photo of the ship sailing peacefully away, surrounded by blue skies to make you all jealous of our wonderful spring days. In reality my camera battery had run out so I failed in my first attempt at blog reporter extraordinaire!

Anyway, I wish them kalotaxidi and a safe journey and hope they have a wonderful time. I did receive a few texts as they travelled through Rhodes and up to Athens.

I can tell you that they had a great meal at the Chinese Burger just down the street from the Plaza Hotel in Rhodes. They safely survived the flight up to Athens which I would imagine would have been a bit bumpy, as here we were experiencing force 9 gales for most of the afternoon and evening. Last night's text from the travellers read, "at airport hotel, v posh, v expensive but a choice of 3 showers in the bathroom. Jazz pianist in bar where cheapest glass of wine is 6 euros and tiny!"

This morning I was woken by the church bells at 6.15am as the Lenten services start to come into effect, followed by torrential rain and thunder. Sam left for school in full wet weather gear and Harry and I were pretty much drowned rats by the time we reached his school. I then could have really done with a canoe to white water raft down through the village to the Olive Tree. Unbelievably, I am now sitting looking out of the window at clear skies and a flat calm sea, it is amazing how it all changes so quickly here on Symi.

The children are finishing school early today and will parade down to the harbour where each school will lay a wreath at the memorial in anticipation for the Independence Day Parade on Monday. We are very excited as, for the first time, both Sam and Harry will march in the parade – a proud moment for any parent!

Saturday Symi Kitchen

It's Saturday and our favourite day of the week for cooking and making a mess in our kitchen!

This winter we have had all sorts of culinary experiments going on in the Spalding kitchen; chocolate truffles for Harry's name day, Jamie Oliver's carbonara, homemade bread which you have to knead until your arm falls off to make it perfect, lemon curd, pancakes, waffles, Christmas cake, gingerbread men, meatloaf and our favourite… Homemade fish fingers.

Thanks to my lovely Nan, I have always been a huge fan of homemade, wholesome food and now that I have children I have become somewhat of a fanatic. Nothing that I make is rocket science, it is all down-to-earth common sense eating. I suppose living on a tiny Greek island in the middle of the Aegean does steer you towards this type of living anyway. After all, it is only in recent years that you can find a ready made frozen pizza, frozen meatballs and fish fingers in the freezer of your local shop. If, like us, you are on a fairly strict budget then these types of food cannot really fit into the daily shopping basket, so you are pretty much forced to make everything from scratch.

In fact, feeding your family becomes a bit of a daily "ready steady cook"

1. go to the supermarket,
2. buy a few staple ingredients,
3. add some fresh fruit and veg depending on if there has or hasn't been a boat and
4. take it all home and concoct a nutritional dinner.

For this reason, meals tend to be simple and wholesome and usually pretty damn tasty as the ingredients are fresh and E-number free. If, on the other hand you are craving for a chick pea stew or falafel ball then plan a couple of days ahead as you need to buy the dried variety, soak them for at least 4 hours, boil and then turn into the chick pea dish of your choice.

We don't tend to eat a lot of meat, as again it takes a huge chunk out the budget, but what we do have is bulked up with plenty of vegetables, pulses and beans. I know that traditionally children, and sometimes husbands, are not huge fans of these food groups so sometimes a little disguise is needed. My family love anything with my homemade tomato sauce incorporated inside and, unless I tell them, they will never know it's full of courgettes, aubergines, red peppers and olives! Another trick is to get them interested in the preparation, they are much more likely to start to taste new foods if they are involved in the chopping, mixing and stirring!

So for anyone who is sat there thinking, "What can we have for dinner tonight?" Here is our fun to prepare and tasty fish finger recipe:

Ingredients

    800g chunky white fish fillets [bone free][defrosted if frozen]

    couple of handfuls of plain flour and good pinch of salt in a big bowl

    2 eggs whisked up with a tablespoon of water in a big bowl

half loaf of bread whizzed up in a food processor with a handful of parsley, good dose of black pepper and good grating of parmesan cheese and then put into another big bowl [put left over crumb mix in bag and freeze for next time].

at least 2 children

What to do

1. Cut up the fish fillets into strips about 2 cm wide along the length of the fish. Sit them on some paper towel for an hour or so to soak up excess moisture.
2. Prepare you and your children - roll up everyone's sleeves and stand small children on a chair.
3. Arrange yourselves along the table, first person with the fish fillets and bowl of flour, second person with the bowl of egg and the next with the breadcrumb mix bowl with a lightly greased oven tray to the side of them.
4. Take your first fish stick, cover it in flour, lift and shake off the excess and drop into the eggy bowl. Next helper give it a good swish around the bowl to cover completely, lift and drain and put into breadcrumb bowl. Next helper roll it around until it is all covered, lift and shake and put onto the oven tray - first one done!
5. I then cook in preheated oven on 180 degrees C for 20 minutes ish as our fish is fairly chunky. Turn them over half way through. When they are browning and slightly firm to the touch they are ready. Don't overcook them as they will go all chewy. Serve them with a tray of potato wedges [potatoes cut into wedges, tossed in salt, pepper, sweet paprika and olive oil - placed on a baking sheet and roasted for about an hour in hot oven.]

There you have it - your own fish and chips and you know EVERYTHING that has gone into them, happy cooking and have a good weekend!

Greek Independence Day, Χρόνια Πολλά

This day was purposely chosen in 1821 to pronounce freedom to all Greek Orthodox Christians and so began the War of Independence against the Turks, which would eventually end their 400 year rule in 1832. It still amazes me how, after being under the Ottoman rule for so long, Greece was able to keep its autonomy and retained its strong Greek traditions and culture that we still experience today.

Last night would have seen the harbour side road lit up with oil lamps as the evening Vespers took place in the newly painted and decorated church of Agias Evangelismos which sits above the boatyard area of Harani.

As for us, Sam has already left to join the rest of his school at the church of Agias Yiannis in Yialos where the Independence Day church service will take place. Harry has donned the Symi Traditional Dress [ηστολή] and will join his nursery school class mates to parade later this morning. I will be one of many proud parents attempting to catch a quick snap shot of the children as they march past. In fact, I always feel quite emotional at these events as they give me that feel good factor of belonging and comfort to the country that I have made home for me and my family.

Have a good day everyone and I expect you all to be standing to attention whilst you sip your morning coffee whilst listening to our National Anthem. Happy Independence Day!

Happy 50th birthday to James

Had a phone call from a very excited Neil last night to say that they had arrived in their Transylvanian Spa Hotel to find that the booking had been messed up. So by way of an apology they had been given the two storey Presidential Suite complete with 4 fluffy dressing gowns! Knew we should have gone with them!

The text earlier in the day said that they were sipping hot chocolate with temperatures of 5 below, eating too much and having a fab time!

Think he deserves it though. He is one of my very best friends in the world - kind, intelligent and always guaranteed to make me laugh, snort and reaching for the Tena Ladies. In the 10 years of knowing him he became ordained on the internet to officiate our Wedding Blessing on the beach, became one of Harry's godparents, convinced me that tap dancing is our shared ambition and educated me in the world of musicals and the Golden Girls. Basically him and Neil are ab fab and I love having them as part of our family.[1]

A little bit of sunshine and it feels like spring

It is a lovely time to visit Symi as the island slowly wakes up from its winter slumber. Local business owners have their doors open to air their properties, tables and chairs are being rubbed down and repainted and generally there is a buzz in the air. Just up from the Symi Dream shop the flower shop has been given a makeover by Valantis the owner, who, in the last week, has swapped his floristry skills for a drill and hammer. On the opposite side of the Kali Strata the small one storey building is being renovated. It is going to be a shop selling herbs, spices and teas which will add to an already thriving village community. Today the building was attacked by the electric sander and has been prepared ready for a fresh coat of paint.

In the Olive Tree I am ready to go inside, the spring clean is complete and I am open for business. Still lots of work to do outside, including the whole terrace floor which needs a new coat of paint but the weather is too unsettled for these types of jobs. For me, it is a time for stocking the larder, so today I made a huge batch of spicy beetroot and apple chutney with fresh Symi beets from Adriana's garden and lemons brought to me by Yianni Rainbow. Tomorrow I plan to start homemade ketchup production, no Heinz for us! Next will be "How many things can you make with Symi lemons?" Starting with preserved Moroccan lemons plus lemon concentrate for the gallons of homemade lemonade we get through.

---

1   Now I know what it is like to read one's own obituary. (JC)

Wind, potatoes and flying the Greek flag

It has been another windy day here on Symi. I had big plans of washing all my windows but with the wind and the rain forecast later in the week it is not really worth it yet.

A quick Google of Romanian potato recipes and potato salad seems to be the most popular - might give it a go as a welcome home treat.

So The Symi Dreamers were due to arrive back to Symi tomorrow evening on the Panagia Skiadeni but the timetable has changed and she is due to do her first run on Thursday, not Monday as originally scheduled. A couple of unplanned nights in Rhodes on the cards then. They should just relax and make the most of them because once back on Symi the summer work begins and there are virtually no days off until the end of October.

Talking of boats I will leave you with this week's journal entry that Lyndon sends regularly to his friends. Both the Dodecanese Seaways and The Blue Star make journeys to the tiny island of Kastellorizo throughout the year. I would love to visit one day as it is meant to be extremely picturesque and peaceful with amazing hospitality. His journal tells us the amazing story of one of Kastellorizo's old inhabitants, enjoy.

I am awake early this morning and sit on the balcony watching a light show that dances its way across the island and on the mountains beyond. The air is perfectly still and cloudless but full of chattering swallows. Behind me on a telegraph pole a blue rock thrush sings a sweet short song, a shy nervous bird that flits from one perch to another every few phrases. A small colony of house sparrows has made their home in the bell tower of Agios Stavros and the males are busy trying to out sing each other. At three minutes past six the sun comes over the headland above St Nicholas and bathes the remaining houses that sit under the mountain at the top of the village.

Much later, one and a half hours late I watch the big ferry "Diagoras" come into the harbour. Today, Friday, it is running to Kastellorizo or Megitsi which is the furthest island away from Athens tucked into the Turkish coast almost halfway to Cyprus. I think it is some three weeks since the Diagoras made it there, due to the bad weather conditions.

Lady Of Ro

Achladioti's most renowned deed is that every day she would fly a Greek flag over the island even though the island was not formally part of Greece (as with the rest of the Dodecanese controlled by Italy) till 1948. This made her a Greek hero, especially when Greece nearly went to war with Turkey in the 1970's, because the flag would be easily visible from Turkish soil. She raised the flag every day, regardless of the weather, from the time she arrived on the island until her death on May 13, 1982 at the age of 92. Despite not having veteran status, she was buried on the island with full military honours.

A Greek military unit is now based on the island, with the main duty of keeping the tradition of raising the flag.

April

Extended holidays, internet playing up again, tapping, anniversaries and a Symi protest

(Jenine still in charge of the blog.)

Sam's Day

Dedicated to Sam, aged 9:

I woke up and I was really tired because we had changed the hour yesterday. I really wanted to go back to bed but it was time for breakfast. After my cereals I got my school bag ready with my books and then got dressed.

On the way to school I called in to see Jack and give him some food. He hissed at me again so I quickly left. When I got to school I played with my friends before the bell rang at ten past eight. Before we go in we all have to stand in the playground in our class lines. Kiria Thoukissa, our head teacher, talks to us and then we have to all make the sign of the cross before we go into class.

At 20 minutes before 10 it was break time. We played chase and a kid got hurt. Next we played war games and then went back in after 20 minutes.

Next I went for my extra lesson with Κυρια Βούλα for language. We did some reading and then questions about opposites.

Then I joined the rest of class for English. We followed a little story about a policeman having an interview about where he works and what he does and if he likes his job. The teacher asked us lots of questions.

Then break outside at 12 o'clock. We played war games again for 15 minutes.

Then Μελετη / general science lesson. We talked about vehicles and how they are destroying the planet.

After that our last break for only 5 minutes so we played chase.

For the last lesson we made picture frames from clay, stuck pasta on and painted them. I checked and watered my bean plants that we are growing in the class room - now they are about half a metre tall.

At 1.15 I left school and came to the Olive Tree. I had some pasta salad and an ice lolly which I froze yesterday from my left over iced tea. Now I am helping mummy paint the terrace in her shop with terracotta colour on tops of the walls.

So there you have a normal day in the life of a nine year old boy on Symi. Probably pretty similar to most children of his age with the exception that his parents are raising him on a remote Greek island. I still watch with fascination as both boys develop in their bi-lingual world. I love how they directly translate many words from Greek to English and vice versa and sometimes I have to really think what they are trying to say to me. The Greek language tends to have a fairly descriptive vocabulary with words being made up of two or three smaller words. For example Το Σαββατοκύριακο - literally Saturday-Sunday meaning the weekend. Whereas in English we have specific words for every item, in Greek one word can cover a multitude of similar things. For example, το καρότσι in Greek can mean virtually any type of trolley from a push chair to sack trucks to a wheel barrow. Το πόδι is your foot but also a leg. And we have almost given up correcting the direct translation of κλείσαι τοφως - close the light. No! Turn the light off!

Sam, especially, is looking forward to summer. He tends more towards creative activities rather than sports but his passion is swimming so roll on the warmer weather when he can spend endless hours diving and snorkelling. Cycling comes a close second but the village is not the most bicycle friendly place. One of his dreams is to go to a big park in England and cycle around and around all day. He will be doing that while Harry spends the day on a big red bus!

Shouldn't have washed the windows

The forecast was right. The wind really got up in the night and we have misty horrible rain. You can blame me as this week I washed all my windows and doors, now they are covered in red dust again, great! I should have taken a bit more notice of Adriana's blog post a few days ago.

My view from the terrace is a grey murky harbour with Nimos island just visible.

The Symi Dreamers were due to return from Rhodes this morning on the Dodekanisos catamaran but this has been cancelled. Looking on the shipping tracker, The Blue Star Diagoras is on its way down from Kos and is due in about an hour. Hopefully the shipping ban in Rhodes will be lifted this afternoon and it will be allowed to leave again so Jack's dads will be home tonight.

No painting for me outside today. Instead my first batch of homemade ketchup is simmering on the stove ready for your breakfasts this summer. This afternoon I am aiming to finish designing this year's menu. Perfect rainy day jobs.

Thank you for all the lovely comments you have sent whilst I have been writing the Symi Dream blog. I felt a little like I had been entrusted with the crown jewels so all your encouragement really helped. Have a good day and hopefully tomorrow you will be passed back to James, another year older but just as witty I am sure!

Back at last and (almost) raring to go

Just a quick blog this morning as I am running late and the head is still in a spin, and there's too much to say anyway. The photo shows why we didn't get back on Wednesday; it was a little bit rough to say the least.

In fact, we should have been back on Symi on Monday evening as there was a boat scheduled when we left, but not scheduled by the time we got back. Not a problem, these things happen, so we stayed in Rhodes and booked a ticket for the Wednesday morning boat. Which didn't happen due to rough weather. But we still walked down to Kolona harbour with our bags to check, and then back to the hotel again. Back at Plaza Travel, Irini was dealing with several folk who were trying to get to Symi and beyond. There was a baptism due to take place on Thursday, and a small group of us bonded during the morning as we waited for updates about the Blue Star which was on its way down. Apparently that didn't call into Symi in the morning as planned, due to the weather, but it was saying it was going back at three that afternoon. Then later it wasn't, then it might be but it may not stop at Symi; there were no guarantees. Then Ian phoned and said 'don't get on that boat' as the sea was blowing in waves directly into the harbour, like a Cornish beach. So we checked into the hotel for another night.

Where we met a couple of Symi folk who insisted the boat was leaving at seven that evening and they were going to get on it. At seven we went for a walk around Mandraki, which is where the photo was taken, to see if we could see the boat heading off. We didn't know that at this time it had still not managed to dock, and people who were expecting to disembark at Rhodes at around nine in the morning were still out there sheltering off Rhodes and waiting to get in. It finally set off way after nine in the evening, by which time the sea had calmed and it was able to get into Symi. But we, and many others, were settled in for another night on Rhodes and all met up on the first run of the Dodekanese Seaways Panagia Skiadeni the next afternoon; and a very nice crossing it was too. We were even invited to the baptism (which had by then been put off until Friday) but were unable to go.

And if you were wondering where I've been, we went to Romania for my 50th birthday. There is a lot to tell, and hopefully the stories will come out over the next few days as I get back into a regular blog cycle again. And on that note, I am very sorry to disappoint all the latest fans but yes, I will be back at the blog now, but we could ask Jenine to write a post every now and then if she would. She's done a great job and so has Sam, telling us what it's like to be at school, and with the recipes and then View from the Olive and all that, it's been very popular. So, a huge thank you to Jenine for that and to everyone who sent birthday wishes. It feels like this birthday has gone on forever, what with a party back on 16th March, the holiday, and then last night being given two presents that hadn't arrived by the time we'd left… Oh boy! I think we've done the birthday thing now.

I was raring to go but…

I was raring to go this morning but then… No internet, the PC at home was playing up, then not, so I wrote a post for when we were back on line, then tried the laptop and that's playing up but then the PC was fine again, and Neil was back on line at the shop, so I came down here to update the blog and the piece I'd written is still at home, and it's raining and there's thunder around so I've got to switch off in a moment and try and get to the post office... Back with you, all being well, tomorrow!

Blogging live from the Symi Dream gallery

It was all bit mad yesterday morning what with computers working and then not working and no internet here but a connection at the shop. I ended up taking the laptop down to the shop and reconfiguring it for me (must get around to setting up separate user accounts on it) and then at least getting the blog online, and it looks like that will be the option until things are sorted out at home; I am here again this morning. It's not just us though, many people are off line (Facebook must be desolate) and an engineer was dispatched from Rhodes yesterday morning to deal with what must be some kind of server or hub problem at OTE.

I also took a walk down to the post office yesterday to pick up a few things. The harbour pavement was flooded all the way from the Pharmacy to just about Eva's bar and the corner, and the rain was on and off all day. At least that kept the pollen down. The day before even I had to take a tablet to stop my eyes watering and puffing and itching; very unusual for me. Unfortunately the tablets then make me drowsy for at least 24 hours so I spent the rest of yesterday fighting to keep awake or dozing when I lost the battle.

The picture today was taken during our extended holiday in Rhodes.

On the Monday we did little apart from relish a lunch at the Chinese Burger, where we had chicken satay and noodles as it's not just burgers, and where we saw our first Brit tourists, bright pink and white like some kind of ice cream and ordering hamburgers, bacon sandwiches and plates of French fries, which they then left because they weren't chips. We were also looking forward to eating at Napoleon's, near the Plaza hotel, but that wasn't opening until the next day. Back at the Plaza one of the waiters slithered up to me in the early evening while I was looking at the menu in the foyer. 'We can do you a buffet at a discount' he whispered through clenched lips, as if he was proposing something rather naughty from under the counter. 'OK,' I whispered back and then later, working together as some kind of resistance movement we wangled two buffets with a four euro discount. My god you can eat at that place! You basically have a four course meal on offer for €15.00 a head, though after the ten days of Romanian food (meat and potatoes) we just overdosed on the salads and veg.

It wasn't all about eating, though there is not a lot else to do at times when stuck in Rhodes. We walked a lot, doing the beach walk one day, the old town walk the next (where we were regularly pounced on as there were only about eight other tourists in circulation, apart from those hospitalised with sun burn that is), we did the harbour seafront walk, we shopped, well, window shopped and dreamed on, and we enquired about some excursions, well, local bus trips; but the butterflies were not open and Lindos was also still half asleep and we saw it last year anyway. So, a few days of wandering and eating was on the cards, and plenty of sitting in the Plaza foyer with coffee watching the world go by.

More about that another time no doubt, now I have to go and organise yet another pile of washing and do some more dusting while Neil carries on painting up the shop and getting it ready for the season.

Back to basics: no internet on (some of) Symi day five

April 11th is a day of anniversaries in our house. As well as being the date on which my father died, it's Neil's daughter's birthday, so happy birthday Charlene, 25 today! (She was only Sam's age when I first met her, nine) It's also the day I gave up smoking two years ago, and I reckon that's one stone for every year. And, most importantly in our house, it's Jack the Alarm Cat's birthday. So he'll be getting something special this evening. A worming tablet, or a squirt of ear mite cream or something. Anyway. On with the blog.

I'm told that the parts of the island without the internet could be without the internet for up to 10 days. So, if you are waiting on an email from a Symi holiday business or similar, it may be a good idea to phone them instead. I also heard it won't be that long, that OTE are improving the system, things are being upgraded and also that no one knows what's going on.

Here's another blog post written the night before it happens as I will have to go to the shop in the morning to post it, by the looks of things. If so then this will be the fifth day without access to the internet for many people on Symi. I know it's not as bad as no water, or no boats, or no doctor, but it's also very frustrating.

I've set up temporary camp in the Symi Dream Gallery among the exhibits from the Symi Gallery which were stored there for the winter. I was doing some work there on Tuesday during the day and in the evening, and as usual, storing it all on an external HD, so I could transfer it to the PC at home, which currently isn't working. For some reason last night I thought I would also copy the work onto the laptop's main HD, and start having a backup that way too.

So, after finishing the piece on Tuesday I went to upload it to someone's site for them only to find that site wasn't working properly, so I let them know. I looked at it again this morning and it was still not working correctly so I carried on writing something else. A couple of hours later and one of my everyday programmes suddenly stopped working. So I rebooted, hoping that would clear the problem. It didn't and what's worse the laptop (I'm in the gallery again, the PC is still not working) wouldn't actually shut down. I forced the shut down, rebooted in safe mode, checked the programme and that was fine. While I'm about it, I thought, I would transfer the morning's writing to the laptop like I did the night before. Only to find that the folder I'd been storing it in was 'empty'.

Investigations showed that the portable HD, the backup (the *new* backup) was malfunctioning and everything on it is now inaccessible. Luckily I had Thursday's work saved, but I was then another two hours at the gallery re-writing everything I'd been writing in the morning and seething a bit under the collar. The laptop works fine now without the HD plugged in. Ah, I thought, perhaps that's what's been causing the fault with the PC. Dashing home hopefully I turned the PC on and it was fine. But still without internet.

After lunch I tried the PC again and… nothing, so it's still bust and there's something wrong there and there's no external HD with all my work on it, a repeat of what happened last year. I'm going to only use 'cloud' storage like Dropbox in the future. But I can't do that at the moment as we are still not able to connect to the internet.

That's it! I've had enough! Tomorrow, after posting this, I am going to go right back to basics and have nothing more to do with technology. I'll draw water from the well with a bucket, darn socks, and keep chickens, I'll build my own generator and plough the garden, I'll barter for food I can't grow and go to bed with the dusk, get up with the dawn, and never even use electricity. Mind you, I have no idea how to do any of these things so I will have to Google it all to find out.

Symi by night, village walk, new Rainbow and things

I'm getting ahead of myself again by writing this morning's blog last night. And last night (that's the night before I am writing this, so two days ago from today, which is actually tomorrow…), on Wednesday:

On Wednesday, after an exhausting but rewarding tap dance class and rehearsal for the show on Saturday 20th April (more about that in due course no doubt), I tapped my way down the steps to meet Neil in the harbour; we had a photo assignment to finish off, pictures of a new hotel and some night shots. And more about that in due course as well. We had a drink with half the town council and the mayor, well, we sat beside them and all but joined in the discussion, before taking some shots of Yialos by night. And then, at sometime around ten, we walked back up again. The bus is in Rhodes at the moment.

Here's a Symi thing: we dropped the equipment off at the shop and thought we'd call in at the Rainbow for a nightcap after our long climb. The only two people to whom I owe money were sat there. (Our landlord, the rent was due today/yesterday, and the computer fixer.) Owing money is clearly not an issue as they bought us a drink.

The Rainbow bar is being painted up at the moment by Ian Spalding painting and decorating Ltd. And regulars will notice a few subtle changes when they next call in: new bamboo (no idea what happened to me old bamboo, I think someone wrote a song about it, it got big headed and left town), and new doors where the curtains used to be, and a new air conditioning unit, mainly for the winter I think. Everything else is, as far as I know, going to be the same.

And today, the boss and I took a walk around the upper parts of Horio, checking out a new photo walk route or two and getting some general snaps which will be appearing here over the next few days and on into the future as I replace my 'spare pics to post' folder. Jack had a good birthday, getting cream rubbed onto his nose to get rid of a black spot and lounging in the sun or under the clothes horse.

Symi protests against education reforms

Breaking news from Symi! Yesterday, April 12th, teachers, parents and children from Symi schools gathered to protest against proposed changes in the education system in Greece. The government are planning to cut the number of teachers by combining classes. But also by combining the years, so children of different ages will take the same classes together. How would that work? No idea.

Rachael Papacalodouca of the PTA writes:

'Today's demonstration was a big success the two Primary schools and the two kindergartens were closed and even the High School came to support our cause. We marched around the square twice and then went up to the Mayor's office in the Town Hall where phone calls were made to the local minister of the area who is supporting us. Our video coverage has been sent to the major TV channels and should make the news. Apparently we are the first to make such a demonstration so let's hope we have set the example for other small islands and villages. Let's hope our small island has made enough noise to be heard!'

Neil had some shots up on the wonder web by midday yesterday. We also took some video.

Meanwhile:

Here's some important news for all British Ex-pats living in Greece.

From 15th April 2013, British nationals in Greece will submit passport applications to IPS in the UK for processing. All the information needed to complete the passport application process will be available on the website.[1]

The last time I renewed my passport it was from Symi. I'd heard that things were changing and there might be issues around what kind of photo paper was used, how the image was taken and so on, so I consulted the Embassy in Athens and the department who then dealt with applications. 'Are there any specification for the photos?' I asked, to which the very nice lady replied, 'We don't really mind dear, as long as they don't look homemade.'

Those were the days eh? Since then there has been a period where applications had to go to Spain for some reason, but now we're back to sending them back to the UK. Neil has to send his off soon, a year ahead of schedule but it's getting a bit worn, so we should be able to report back, one day, on how this new process works. Sending mine to Athens in 2006, I think it was, took three weeks during which time the nice lady phoned me up to apologise for the delay.

New shops, old shops, Kali Strata new piazza

I really am getting ahead of myself today. It's Saturday. I know, you are reading this on Monday, but I am writing it while I wait for Neil to finish in the shop. I'm still working from here as there is still no internet on at home. And, last night for the first time, I used the 'scheduler' on my Wordpress dashboard: Saturday's post was written on Friday before the tap dance rehearsal, and the scheduler was set to publish it this morning. So I was blogging in my sleep, literally. And that's what happening with this post too.

The tap class went well. Actually it was more of a run through for running order and so all the cast were there. (Was there?) There are 16 dance routines and a finale all choreographed by the rather talented Rhiannon Wheeler (who also has the Windmill Restaurant in Horio) and danced by some also rather talented dancers aged from about three to an age we don't ask or assume. And then there's me, the only man in the company tapping around like something out of Fantasia.

In the Symi Dream shop, Neil is now making up cards and has already taken bookings for his photo walks, so this year is getting off to a nice start. There's a wedding booked for Easter Monday (so no wine night that night, I'll let you know when they start), and the shop is now painted up and the new stock is in. The calendars are on their way, as are new copies of Symi 85600, and Carry on up the Kali Strata is also in stock.

---

1 Note to readers: this information may be out of date by now, so don't take my word for it.

The shop opposite us, which has been a store room for several years, is also now being done up by its owner. It is going to be rented out as an herb shop apparently. A source of herbal teas and maybe coffee beans, natural herb products perhaps? It's looking good and the folk on our part of the steps are now saying 'we are turning this little area into a piazza.' I thought he said pizza and perked up, but then I worked it out. So, on a Monday night while supping a wine from our gallery, and purchasing exclusive photo-things from our shop, you will also be able to stock up on your herbs while you get your PC looked at by Kon before popping up to the Olive Tree now only a few doors up, buying some flowers from Valantis en route. We're not sure what's happening with the Kali Strata Bar (the bar with the view) this year, but if it doesn't open you can also get a view from the Olive Tree terrace. And soon, thanks to a cross border agreement between Symi Dream and The Olive Tree you will also be able to send a fax from there. The only place in the village where you can fax from, apparently.

Babbling on so will get on with the rest of the weekend: walk to town for exercise, chicken salad dinner, crosswords this afternoon, housework tomorrow, barbeque in the afternoon, back to work on Monday at the shop if no internet. By that time this will have been published automatically and we shall see how it all worked out.

The Alarm Cat's nose and other gossip

The wind died down a little yesterday, though there was no ferry in on Monday night due to storm force winds out at sea. I was at the Opera House for a quick tap rehearsal, which I didn't do very well, and I am back there tomorrow in the hope of doing better. The show is on Saturday evening at 6pm if anyone is around and wants to come and see.

Meanwhile, I'm still trying to work out what's going on with the royal nose. That's the Alarm Cat nose. He's had a small black spot on it for a while and I read that it was a fungal thing. I put some Lamasil on it for a day or two and it started to get better. I carried on with the treatment, as you're told to do, you know, even when it gets better you finish the course, and the thing came back again. Apparently these things go away on their own sometimes so unless I can think of any other ideas he may just have to sit it out. It's not causing him any problems though, he's still his cheery old self. At least he is happy when he is being unhappy, complaining about the lateness of breakfast and wanting to sit on laps all the time. Mind you he is getting on.

Do cat years work the same as dog years I wonder? Seven to one is it? If so, he is 70 now.

Meanwhile: people are starting to return to Symi; the ferry did come in today bringing Tina back to the Olive Tree and Gerrie and Sue for six months, Penny arrives soon and others are on their way for Easter. Before long we will be saying 'where did that winter go then?' Mind you, it was back for a while this morning. I went to put the washing out and there was a definite cold snap in the air, just like you notice in later November.

As you can probably tell, I spent Tuesday at home so haven't seen anyone and don't have any great news. There are still plans afoot for the 'film to be made on Symi' idea to progress. More news on that will follow, and it looks like (at the moment) we may be able to make an announcement within the next few months. The company will be asking for people to put their money where their dreams are and help towards raising finance; that's if the project gets the go ahead from the production company. All a bit shrouded in mystery at the moment, but then it is a thriller/horror we are working on. More news in due course.

Tap, things to do on Symi, festivals, Bouzouki…

Another day of being at home yesterday (apart from another rehearsal for the show on Saturday) so not a lot to report.

I can report that I only discovered yesterday that the floor in our front room is very similar to the floor at The Opera House hall, and the tap shoes don't mark the tiles, like they do in the sitting room. I don't know why I didn't try it before. But I was able to clack trough the routine a couple of times during the afternoon. For some reason my shin muscles gave out half way through and I was unable to move my ankles. Don't know why that should suddenly happen now when it's been fine for months. I warmed up and everything… Hmm. Will keep working on it.

On a completely different note: Don't forget that if you are planning your summer holiday and want something special then Symi is the place to visit. Just thinking ahead to what there will be to do in the village (that's aside from the beaches and boats and Yialos and walks) there will be: Photo walks from us of course, plus Monday evening wine nights at the shop and gallery, live music nights at the Taverna and probably at kafeneion such as The Secret Garden where they regularly have live bouzouki music, and Manteio's perhaps, no doubt there will be events at The Sunrise as well, and I am pretty sure the Olive Tree will be hosting all kinds of things again. I am not sure if the museum is open again this year, or if the repair/renovation works have been finished, I will enquire when next heading that way.

All happening in Yialos

More businesses are preparing for the summer. I was down in Yialos the other day and evening and there were stacks of chairs being painted up, tables being washed down, plastic awnings from the winter being taken away, signs being painted and even day trippers coming in on the Dodecanese Seaways ferry for the day. It's all starting to start up again; Merekles is open, as is Vasilis' Dolphin Pizza, Bella Napoli too (did that stay open all winter?) and loads of other places as well.

There are also some new shops open, like the garden centre that has put down roots in what used to be the benefits office – best not ask what happened to that office. OK then, so it moved into the public toilets. But they did get rid of them first and put up a new building. I have no idea where you go if you want a loo now, probably the old tinker's shop 'cos he's now where the PC shop used to be, and I have no idea what happened to Christos.

So, it's all go in Yialos. And it's all go up here as we prepare well in advance for the 'Symi Festival 3013.' My mind, however, is on my shuffle ball changes and five beat riffs at the moment. I will be back on Saturday with news of how the dress rehearsal went. And on that note: The waistcoat is here (many thanks to my couriers, mwah!) and it's looking blue.

Dance show dress rehearsal, all tip top tap

Last night's run-through and dress rehearsal went well, and everyone is in good spirits and ready for tonight.

It was raining yesterday, good for the plants but not so good for the €8.00 trainers which have more or less come to the end of their useful life, after one winter's constant wear and a long walk around Romania. That was all

I expected to get out of them of course. By the time we got to the Opera House last night my feet were soaked, but I'd brought a pair of dry socks, and the tap shoes were also dry so that was OK, not too much slipping about on the tiles.

We stopped off for a bite to eat afterwards and then, having decided that there would be no taxis at 9.45 on a wet Friday night, we walked back up the hill to home, which, surprisingly, only took us 15 minutes.

So, today: we've had our morning juice (lemon, orange, beetroot, apple, pear and carrot) and Neil is singing hits form the '80s as he gets dressed next door. The skies have cleared, there is still a breeze so I should be able to get my outfit washed and dried, pressed and ready for tonight. Time for a bit of a warm up this afternoon and then back to the show around five.

Shock Symi news alert: Mad Brits sweep Kali Strata

I'm absolutely done in today thanks to '50 things to do when you're 50' number three.

Number one was, obviously: wake up in Transylvania, on your birthday, in the snow; see photo.

Number two was tap dance with the ladies in the Symi dance show, done. (Rewarded with a handshake from the Mayor). And number three? Well, I'd always wanted to sweep the Kali Strata from top to bottom. Done.

We helped out with a few others yesterday in the Mayor's clean-up campaign. Yesterday it was Horio and some members of the council and other volunteers went out from the village square armed with brooms and bags and did a litter pick and general tidy up. Neil volunteered us for the Kali Strata as we had to pop down to the bank anyway. Mad!

We weeded it from Georgio's down to the Kali Strata Bar (as was, it's closed now) apart from outside the Olive Tree which Jenine, who was working, did. And then we realised that to do the whole lot would take several days, so from just by where the Symi Gallery was we started doing only the major weeds and rubbish. Stinging nettles and a few other odd bites and stings put paid to that idea by the time we got to Maria's house. She made use of our rubbish bags and did her side of the street as we passed, and from then on it was major rubbish only. It took us three hours and we rewarded ourselves with a beer and a lunch in Yialos when we got there. We saw the mayor and waved our brooms at him to show we'd finished, and got a thank you, and then we had chicken fillet and a pork chop (not one each) at To Spitiko by the taxi rank.

The next treat was a taxi ride back up the hill, having done the Kali Strata four times in the last few days (five times for Neil) and still having brooms and stuff with us we didn't fancy the walk, besides, we didn't want to get it dirty. And so to Kevin's birthday party at the Sunrise and the last quiz of the winter season. I think that all went well, I bailed out and made it home though I am not sure when, but I do know I left my PG Tips and a broom behind; I can collect them later.

A post about brown rice

Well, not just brows rice, but brown rice, beetroot and other veg, with the occasional tin of tuna. That's the new regime for the next week as we give ourselves a bit of a detox after the winter.

We did this 13 years ago (OMG!) for a whole month, and that month included a week in Lefkada, where I still managed to get to the end of the sentence, I mean, time period and yet be on holiday. Not so tricky in Greece where there is lots of opportunity for salad, fish and potatoes, all of which are permissible. I can't remember the name of the book we used then but the ingredients are stuck in my head. This time round we are only doing a week, and some items may creep in, like tomatoes and oranges which I remember we weren't supposed to have, but we've got some so may as well use them up.

The hard parts will be the usual staples like wine and bread, bacon and all things nice really, but we will manage I am sure. So far today the order of the day has been:

Herbal tea.

Fresh juice: pear, orange, lemon, carrot and beetroot.

A bit of work.

Taking delivery of a new cooker (Neil and Ian did most of the heavy work).

Shopping (Neil).

Getting over the worst of a head cold (Me; bad sleep last night fever and raging throat which then seemed better in the morning).

Then the highlight of the day, lunch: Brown rice, peas, carrots, beans, garlic, herbs, cucumber, tuna all mixed up with itself.

And, as I am writing this late afternoon yesterday, the evening plans are to have the rest of that rice thing if hungry.

Only problem is the only brown rice we can get is Uncle Ben's and not the really rough raw stuff we like. But we will press on as best we can. Looking forward to the caffeine withdrawal symptoms later today but as I have to take an antihistamine later I shall be well and truly knocked out. That's why I am writing this now as I'll never get up early tomorrow after an 'X-tab.'

Symi is warming up and it's getting hotter

We took a walk yesterday in the late afternoon, through the village, up to the Castro and around, and then followed the path around to the square. I think it was having this cold but even the Alarm Cat couldn't rouse me this morning, and the church bells tried but they failed as well. I finally dragged myself out of bed and to the desk though, and found this wonderful wildlife photo from Neil.

On the domestic front, the new cooker is in, slightly bigger and deeper than the old one so a new worktop needs organising, but 'the man who can' has that in order. Not tried the oven on the cooker yet as we don't yet need to, but it has a fan and all kinds of variations and images on the control. There's one with a fan and what looks like a drip coming from it, if anyone can tell me what that means I'd be interested. (There's no instruction book as it's second hand, though hardly used.)

And so, after that quick ramble I must catch up on the day and what a day it looks like being: more brown rice and veg on the menu and with some big beans as well, yesterday I spring cleaned the bathroom and today… I may not bother with cleaning as the weather has suddenly become so hot and pleasant. But there are jobs to be done and mail to answer, washing to sort out and all those chores to do. I will just pause a while and have my juice first: lemon, orange, carrot, ginger and pear this morning, and a herbal tea to follow. Joy!

Leading up to Easter, and Easter events

So, a weekend is on us and not a lot is planned in the run up to Big/Great/Easter.

In fact, we seem to have very little going on now, after the dash around that was last weekend, the dance show, the sweeping up and all that. There's a possibility that the garden might get cleared this weekend, if the hay fever tablets work, otherwise it will have to stay as a jungle for a bit longer. I did try planting things but the snails made off with them and no amount of pellets seems to get rid of them. But the chilli plants might be making a comeback, hard to tell at the moment. The cat went out there recently and wasn't seen for several days. He came back with this chap who had been hiding out and didn't know the war was over, so we really should get something done about it.

The fruit trees are doing nicely and have really grown since their cut back last winter. The lemons are going in our morning juice and the orange has done its blossom thing; the apricots should be getting ready to flower and the surviving plum tree is far more accessible now, so we may even get something from that later in the year.

Meanwhile, out and about, the fig trees have fruit on but I think that's the early variety that you can't eat? I did have a talk once from a man who said something about birds, bees and the gender of a fig tree, and I got mildly confused. But there is still plenty going on in the valley to make for an interesting photo walk.

The Great Week:

Holy Thursday, make your tsoureki, dye your eggs red, Holy Thursday evening, church services include a symbolic representation of the crucifixion, and the period of mourning begins.

Holy (or Great) Friday, a day of mourning and no work, not even cooking is allowed for the very devout, there is the solemn service on Good (Big/Great) Friday morning, but this is the only day of the year in church when the divine liturgy is not read, the bier, the epitaphio, is decorated, the death bells sound during the day and you hear that 'silence of the lambs' effect (see Symi 85600).

On the **Saturday,** the holy flame is brought to the country by military jet ready for the late night service and the dimming of the lights, followed by the passing and sharing of the flame. Meanwhile the μαγειρίτσα is made, ready for breaking fast after midnight. (Ingredients include: About 2 pounds of lamb or kid offal (liver, heart, lungs, and other organs), intestines from

2 lambs or kids, juice of 2 lemons (as if that's going to help!)[1] and several other things.

And then on **Sunday** you can eat the nice parts of the animal, have barbeques, spend time with the family and celebrate… with a Symi photo walk!

Warming up, cruise ships arriving, holidays are happening on Symi!

Over the weekend Neil weeded the garden and I gave the kitchen a spring clean, we took a walk through the upper part of the village and out to the donkey track and took some photos. Neil intended to paint the steps outside the shop on Monday morning but arrived to find it had been done for him by the owners of the new shop, opposite. That's the one that is getting ready to open sometime this season selling herbs and teas, coffees and other 'spicy' things.

On Sunday the first cruise ship of the season called in, or rather anchored off a bit and ferried people ashore, there was a buzz in the village square in the afternoon and evening with some of the first of this year's visitors leaving already. Leaving? I know! The season hasn't really started yet and some people have called in had a break and gone again. There are more arriving soon and spaces on the photo walk for this Easter Sunday is filling up fast.

---

[1] It doesn't - Ed.

May

A Symi Easter, a birthday, a letter from the mayor, some pomegranate rain and a little bit of goon news

Tomorrow will happen avrio

Sitting at home yesterday, at the desk in the afternoon: door to terrace open, balcony doors open, still warm, little breeze, listening to the birds have a good old chinwag out in the olive tree. Someone exploding bangers down the lane, the church bells announcing various parts of various services for the crucifixion; the sea flat and grey in the haze across the way. The Alarm Cat taking up his position under the piano stool that I'm sitting on, giving the occasional squeak as he asks to be taken back to the kitchen for the fifth time today. Me refusing as there's no reason at all why he can't go on his own. Watching the ferry glide gently towards harbour.

Reminding myself to pick wild flowers on the way home as it's May Day and a tradition. Not leaving the house all day. Staying in, writing, making lentil soup for lunch; where did that idea come from?

Neil staying late at the shop to take some customers through some photos, coming home for lunch of lentil soup, dozing slightly in the heat afterwards, then back to the desk.

The night before: popping down to the square again, needing something to eat, calling in to Georgio and Maria's for a light dinner; lentil soup actually, there's the inspiration for tomorrow's lunch. Putting away the newly washed blanket, watering the garden, listening to the neighbours' music, and then lying in a blanket-less bed listening to mad laughter ringing out from somewhere across the village.

The afternoon before: washing the huge blanket from the bed, in the bath, good old fashioned way, dragging it outside dripping wet, laying it across the clothes horse and chairs, drip dry, ready in a few hours. Checking out the garden and a few shoots from cuttings growing in jars, chasing away a stray cat found investigating the kitchen, watching the Alarm Cat stare at a roach outside, wondering what it was and should he be doing something about it; being hot, sitting in the sun for a few minutes reading; wondering why I am reading "The lair of the White Worm" again after all these years.

Wondering about nothing; it's nearly summer, it feels like summer, no need to think about tomorrow, tomorrow will happen 'avrio.'

Why is Greek Easter at a different time to western Easter?

An oft asked question explained on this Holy Friday:

The first factor, the calendar, has to do with the fact that the Christian Orthodox Church continues to follow the Julian calendar when calculating the date of Pascha (Easter). The rest of Christianity uses the Gregorian calendar. There is a thirteen-day difference between the two calendars, the Julian calendar being thirteen days behind the Gregorian. The other factor at work is that the Orthodox Church continues to adhere to the rule set forth by the First Ecumenical Council, held in Nicea in 325 AD, that requires that Pascha must take place after the Jewish Passover in order to maintain the Biblical sequence of Christ's Passion. The rest of Christianity ignores this requirement, which means that on occasion Western Easter takes place either before or during the Jewish Passover.

[From The Greek Reporter.]

Easter celebrations continue on Symi

We are right in the middle of the Easter celebrations today here on Symi with tonight seeing the ending of Lent.

Yesterday the bells were tolling for most of the day, there were many people heading to church at various times, and several shops and businesses were closed for the day. Tonight there will be the procession of lit candles coming back from church after midnight and the traditional breaking of the fast.

Our island life continues as per: Neil is working this morning and this evening, we may be going to the church service tonight, Astrid's bar is reopening this evening, we have the photo walk on in the morning, now fully booked for this weekend, and the wedding to record and photograph on Sunday, and then the post Easter routine will set in, with, we hope, plenty of visitors and fun summer times ahead.

Goon[1] news and Bad news

The good news is that 1066 Productions have released the 'teaser/trailer' that we worked on a few weeks ago. Our three weeks' of filming is reduced to a minute, but there should be a longer film about Symi coming in due course.

The bad news is of a different curse, that of refugees having to seek a better life. This is a translation from News Now of a story that broke over the weekend.

'Arrested Saturday in Symi, by men of the Police Department of the island 30 foreigners, of whom 23 were Afghans (22 men 1minor) and 7 Syrians (4 men, 1 woman 2 minors), for illegally entering the country, as they were not in possession of valid documentation. As a result of the police investigation so far, the arrested departed from the Turkish coast by boat(inflatable boat), which sank after they landed on the island of Symi. The preliminary investigation was conducted by the Police Department of Symi'

Stay tuned to Symi Dream for more images and updates, and no doubt more chat about Easter. It's a busy time with the start of the season, Greek Easter, May Day holiday, May 8th parade on Wednesday and our first wine night next Monday. I'm surprised any work gets done.

The sounds of a Symi Easter

This is a piece I was asked to contribute to a USA based Greek newspaper.

As an ex-pat British man my first Easter on Symi, Greece was something of a surprise to say the least. I remembered the Easters of my youth as to do with chocolate eggs and holidays, time off school and peace and quiet.

I had no idea what to expect from my first Greek Easter but people kept telling me about the noise. Assuming they meant the singing and celebrating from one of the 16 churches near to me in the small village where I lived, I went about my new life undaunted. The house was within 50 feet of one of the main parish churches, Agia Triatha, and so close that at night I could hear the mechanism of the bells as they clunked into action, ready to strike the hours. After six months on the island I was adjusting to the chimes, though when a wedding or baptism was celebrated and the peels rang for half an hour, there was no point in trying to hold a conversation, or watch the television. So yes, I was ready for the noise of Greek Easter on Symi.

Little did I know.

---

1   Ah ha Mr Editor, you missed this wonderful typo! (And so did I, clearly)

In the build-up to Big Week and through Big Week particularly, the local children delight in throwing bangers, fire-crackers if you like. They are meant to be warding off evil spirits as I understand it, but what they seem to be doing is warding off hapless passers-by, and each other. These crackers range in ferocity from a small pop to a heart-stopping bang, and are often enhanced by being put into tin cans. But boys will be boys and no one actually throws them directly at anyone else, so I was able to get used to that sound as well.

The next new sound came in the last few days of Big Week, the sound of sheep and lambs. Symi is a rural island and before Eater the lambs are brought down to graze around the village on whatever is left to be eaten. In this case, the patch of ground outside the house. I woke one morning to the sound of a contralto profundo ewe seemingly bellowing in my bedroom. Well, she might as well have been. Her complaining went on through the week, through the day, though the night and through the tragically sad peels of Big Friday. Until, on Saturday morning, I awoke to the silence of the lambs, literally. Having grown used to them, it was a stark reminder of what was happening when they suddenly weren't there anymore. The occasional gunshot from the hills reminded me of why.

And then the biggest surprise of all; Easter Saturday. We attended the church, standing outside as there was not enough room inside, and avoided the many bangers that were being thrown about with passionate abandon. We witnessed the lights going out, the candle flame being passed along, and then I had my first taste of Midnight.

The bells were fine, many and loud, and there were fireworks, rockets set in bottles that wobbled on the church yard walls, flares from lower down in the village were sent up and coming down right on the roof of my house. That was a bit worrying but my mind was suddenly distracted from this health and safety disaster by the dynamite.

'Keep your shutters closed and the windows open,' had been the advice and I had luckily followed it.

I am told that Symi and Kalymnos, being 'Sponge Diver's Islands' are unique in the amount of dynamite used to celebrate Easter. The mountains of Symi shake and crumble at the noise and vibration on a yearly basis as barrels of the stuff are set off. One year I was told that we had 200 barrels of dynamite going off over Big Weekend. Why? Because it was the 200 year anniversary of the use of dynamite on the island.

Yes, well, not sure about that. But what I am sure about is that if you want to be on a rock that rocks, then you need to be on Symi for Easter.

One of my busiest Symi weekends ever

I am finally getting back to a normal routine following the Easter celebrations which were followed by The Judas Curse celebrations, which were followed by the wedding celebrations, which were followed by Allan's birthday celebrations.

So, a bit of a catch up might be in order, if I can remember everything that I've been doing on Symi these past few days.

Easter Saturday: We were invited to Ian and Jenine's house, and to attend church with the godsons later in the evening. We bought Lambadas (candles) from the shop and decorated them at home, and then gave the boys one each to take to church. While there the entire congregation was given a decorated candle each, with which to light the holy flame that had been jetted in from Jerusalem that morning. What was really nice to see was the number of visitors who were invited in to the church for the service, each given their candle and a cake or two for after midnight. The lights were dimmed, there was a rush to light candles from Papa Lefteris' flame and then the dynamite and bells started. The congregation moved outside for the final part of the service and then everyone dispersed to write X&A beneath the lintel of their doors at home.

Easter Sunday: Neil was up and bouncing around early, preparing for his first photo walk of the summer. He had a full complement of guests that day and they set off from the shop at 9.15 to walk through the Pedi valley and end up at Pedi. The sun was out, there was certainly plenty of wildlife to see and by all accounts everyone had a great time. These walks will continue through the season.

And then, on Sunday evening it was back to the Harry house for our Easter Sunday roast lamb. I eventually remembered that I was in charge of mint sauce so grabbed some from the garden and found a recipe from the BBC, concocted the thing and took it with me, along with Easter gifts for the boys, cards, and a rather cheeky red that had been a gift from Sotiris at the supermarket. We sat on the terrace, Sam cooked the lamb's testicles and he and Neil ate them while I admired the view and kept quiet, hoping that they wouldn't pick on me for audience participation. Luckily they didn't and we were able to move on to the main course before watching Jesus Christ Superstar on DVD and missing the fireworks from the harbour.

Bank Holiday Monday: was taken up, for us, with a wedding at Panormitis. Andreas and Christina from Sparta, and families, had come to Symi for the wedding which was conducted by Papa Staphanos. We were there an hour beforehand to take 'the bride getting ready' photos and background shots and clips of Panormitis.

The wedding went well and Neil took care of the photos while I took care of the video. I'm not supposed to do this as he hasn't finished processing the images yet, but here's one shot from the ceremony I thought you might like to see.

And then back to Horio for a birthday drink with Allan and a meal at the taverna Georgio & Maria where Nondas and Lefteris were providing the music. After a couple of weeks of lentils, brown rice and vegetables only, it was good to get the rickety old teeth into a chicken souvlaki, while others had the beef in Metaxa and lemon roasted chicken.

And while all this was going on the news was breaking that a British film production company is keen to take one of our screenplays and make it into a feature film, and better still, film it on Symi. "The Judas Curse" kind of an appropriate piece of timing for a story with that name. If (and it's still an IF) the project goes ahead there will be all kinds of opportunities for Symi lovers to get involved; either by donating money from £5.00 upwards in return for a sliding scale of 'perks' as they are called, or by offering services, property, filming rights and even 'talent' as actors are apparently called. I know that the company is already in touch with the town hall to establish legal and licensing matters.

And I also know that I had a deadline of Tuesday evening to present the first, rough, draft; a deadline that my writing partner and I managed. Now we are waiting to hear about re-writes, which will depend on, at this stage, the thoughts and input from the producer and a director.

But, all in all, a busy weekend was thoroughly enjoyable and very productive, if a little hectic at times.

May 8th parade and film project update

Yesterday saw the May 8th celebrations, the signing of the surrender of the Dodecanese islands at the end of WWII, an historic event which took place in Yialos, on Symi. Neil was there to record the parade and ceremony, and there is one of his images on the blog today.

There is only one because he's not been able to process them fully as yet, as his shop PC is still under the surgeon's knife; but it should be back in the shop today. And he's not had much time at home to catch up on any work on the home PC, which is also in the same shop, though the laptop is working. But I've been using that, and he only has three hours at home in the afternoon anyway, now the season has started, so not much time to do anything apart from have lunch and relax before getting ready for the evening shift.

While he has been doing that I have been doing what I can to get "The Judas Curse" further forward, working with the publicity manager for 1066 Productions. Still nothing concrete yet but they are moving forward, getting ready for the fund-raising push which will need to be the next big thing to happen.

For those worried about the weather: the rumoured thunderstorm has not happened yet, today is cooler than of late, the sky is grey and there are clouds, but it feels fresher than yesterday which did feel like a rain storm was coming: so it's so far, so dry

Expecting to be mobile today

Apparently, today, a representative of my mobile phone provider is going to come to visit me at some time between nine and five. We shall see.

The contract for my phone ran out a couple of weeks ago. Before it ran out I was sent a text message saying something like: 'your contract is about to expire, please call in to your nearest branch and renew your contract and choose your new phone.' OK, but for me to call in to my nearest branch means a walk to Yialos, a boat trip to Rhodes, a day in Rhodes and a boat back, approximate costs €70.00 including a cheap lunch and loss of earnings, so that's not going to happen then.

I sent an email asking for someone to email me back and asked that we did what we did last time: they send the new contract by courier to the bookshop and, when convenient, I pop down with my passport for ID and pick it up, collecting a new phone at the same time. Nothing happened. So, at a particularly inconvenient time at work the other day they rang me. 'Are you Mr Collins James?' (Sounds rather good hyphenated.) 'I am from your phone company and am here to talk to you about your new contract. And would you prefer to speak in Greek or English...' All this in Greek.

The upshot of it all was that I chose to have a new phone, rather than a discount, as the new phone was worth three times the amount of the accumulative discount. The end of the conversation was the best part: 'Someone will come and call on you between nine and five on Friday at your address… oh, you don't have an address… Someone will give you a ring when they are there.' Where, I have no idea, but I am half expecting someone to arrive on Symi today, with a contract and a new phone (Black, they called back later to check which colour I'd like) and to then phone me to see where I am. This is probably going to happen at the most inconvenient time of day possible, so I am really looking forward to that. Or else, someone will have worked out that I am not in a suburb of Athens and will phone and say 'we will put your phone and contract with a courier and send it, like last time.'

Meanwhile, Neil is looking forward to having his computer back up and running at the shop. The marvel who is Konstantinos from the computer shop opposite worked for two days to convert my non-working PC and Neil's non-working PC into one hybrid working PC and then spent a good hour or so last night in the shop updating drivers and making sure it worked, mouse and all.

And as a PS, there is a festival at the monastery of Agios Konstantinos on Saturday, the bus leaves at 7.45 in the morning and they promise to try hard to get everybody back afterwards. Not sure what that means, but it's not a long walk if it doesn't come off. The festival of St Christopher was at Zoi's family's new church yesterday, and as far as I know Koukoumas is still scheduled for Saturday at Agios Athanasios.

Symi mayor welcomes filming on the island

An update on the film news: The Mayor of Symi has responded to 1066 Productions saying:

'We welcome your proposal to film on Symi and we are glad you have chosen Symi to make your scenes. If the filming takes place at the village or at any other place on the island, there is no need for any special licence. If your filming takes place in museums or any other archaeological monuments, then it is necessary to ask for the permission of the Archaeology in Rhodes.'

So that's great news for the production, and the company office is now in contact with the Archaeologia in Rhodes as they are interested in filming at a couple of local sites too. The shooting is not definite yet of course, that is going to depend on finance and there will be a fund raising campaign starting up shortly. I will keep you informed about that. The company want to employ as much local talent as possible, which will be good for the island and, at the same time, promote Symi in a positive way, bring it some publicity and possibly even boost the visitor numbers.

All kinds of things to mention after a very nice weekend

On Saturday we had a visit from Carol Dunning who runs The Greece Property Buying Guide. We've met Carol before, last year when she came over from Rhodes for the day to conduct an interview with us and see a little more of Symi. This time we had lunch at the Olive Tree overlooking the sea and the view. And she brought us a gift; a copy of the film 'Pascali's Island' which I'd never seen before.

This film will be of interest to everyone who loves Symi and/or Rhodes, as it was shot on location on both islands. Symi appears at the beginning as the port of arrival for Charles Dance, and it is also used for the location of Ben Kingsley's (Pascali's) house. The film was released in 1988 and is set in 1908, shortly before the end of Ottoman rule in the area. It's very hard to get on DVD, or even VHS now, so was a great gift.

Also this weekend the 'clean up Sesklia' day took place. The Poseidon boat gave free rides and lunch to around 30 volunteers who went down to Sesklia and collected 30 bags of unwanted jetsam and stuff that had washed up there over the winter, improving the look and appeal of what is already a very appealing place to go. You can take trips on the Poseidon and some of these include a stop off for lunch at Sesklia. When in Yialos, you can see on the board what trip the boat is doing on what day.

The weekend also saw Jean's birthday party at Manteio Bar, which followed the live music at the Taverna George & Maria which has started again and which will be happening each Friday during the season; book a table early.

Sunday was Neil's photo walk and he set off for Pedi in the morning, a morning that was sunny and clear when I woke up at six, after an early night and a good sleep. And this morning I am off to town later to collect my new mobile phone and contract. You remember I said they were sending someone to call on me on Friday and I thought that may not happen? Well, it didn't. But, as expected, the phone and details have been couriered over so I now have to trudge up the hill, half way to Nimborio to collect them from the courier and pay my €5.00, show my passport, hand in a copy, sign some forms and walk back again. I'm not mentioning the name of this mobile provider, but once I have jumped through all of those hoops I shall, I hope, be Free To Go.

A day of collecting things and getting wet

The first wine night of the season went well last night with around 50 people turning up to meet, browse, mingle and chat.

It came at the end of a busy day: after catching up on some work in the morning we headed off down to Yialos to take care of some business: seeing the accountant who wasn't there, calling up to the courier conveniently placed half way to Nimborio up the steep slope, paying the shop phone bill after half an hour of queuing, picking up one pair of sandals from an order of two, both dispatched at the same time and one still on its way, and then calming down with a lunch at To Spitiko before heading back up to arrange the wine night wine with Sotiris.

And then, after putting together my new phone (a smart phone apparently, but it's not that smart, it doesn't have a keyboard suitable for grown-ups so my texts yesterday were all in code), and after putting on my new sandals I slipped down the hill to look after the bar for a bit. There was a thunderstorm yesterday, which I was caught out in, and so I arrived to soggy orange chairs and Yianni sweeping rain water away like mad. I got there quicker than I would have liked thanks to the slippery new shoes. 'Oh, what's on the Syllogos menu todaaaaaaaaaaaay. Phew, no one saw me.'

And then the thunder returned during the night, waking the Alarm Cat nice and early so it was a bit of a sleepless one. Not a late night though, even though I did listen to the other new arrival last night, a CD of Rick Wakeman and Tim Rice's 1984; great to hear that again after all these years.

Ready for your close up?

Today I thought I would share one of Neil's images from his photo walks.

When on a photo walk with Neil, not only do you get a nice walk, a good chat and the chance to meet some new people, ask Neil what he does on Symi in the winter and buy him a beer afterwards, but you also get to find out how to take photos like these. And you can do them with more or less any camera these days. Macro lenses are used, and someone recently asked why the lens or function was called 'Macro', what does it mean?

So, public service being one of my occasional hobbies: I looked up Macro on Wiki-dodgy, or whatever it's called and got off to a flying start with: "A macro (short for 'macroinstruction', from Greek μακρο- 'large') in computer science is a rule or pattern that specifies how a certain input sequence (often a sequence of characters) should be mapped to a replacement input sequence (also often a sequence of characters) according to a defined procedure."

Clearly I had typed in the wrong search string (also often a sequence of incorrectly inputted characters I assume), so I tried again and found this:

'Macro photography (or photomacrography or macrography, and sometimes macrophotography) is extreme close-up photography, usually of very small subjects, in which the size of the subject in the photograph is greater than life size (though macrophotography technically refers to the art of making very large photographs). By some definitions, a macro photograph is one in which the size of the subject on the negative or image sensor is life size or greater. However in other uses it refers to a finished photograph of a subject at greater than life size.'

I just think it mean you get nice close-ups of pretty butterflies and characterful bugs.

Wedding bells and weather

I had a 6.30 alarm call from the Alarm Cat this morning which I wasn't very impressed with. Mind you I needed an early start as there are thing to be done today.

I have been asked to work on the text for a speech for a promotional video about Symi, this is to go along with the fund-raising appeal that the production company will be putting out to try and get funds in to make "The Judas Curse" on the island.

Meanwhile, back on the island. The weather is trying to settle down, a bit breezy this morning, warm again yesterday after an unsettled week and a storm or two, but the week ahead is forecast to improve until it becomes, and I quote: 'Beautiful with plenty of sun.'

Neil has been busy in the shop, I have almost finished the wedding DVD, there is a photo walk on this Sunday, wine night to look forward to, more visitors arrived on Wednesday, and yesterday morning, we may have to re-visit the accountant today, take care of some business in Yialos and I must remember to water the garden. It's that time of year again.

The photo today were taken at a wedding last Sunday. Petros from one of the village supermarkets and his bride met, in the traditional way for the village, at the corner of the village square. Her party came up and his came down, they met, with the priest and the guests, led by musicians, before heading off up to the very top of the village and the church of Agia Triada for the ceremony. Traditionally the church bells ring from the moment the bride leaves home to the moment she arrives at church; they rang for a long time last Sunday.

Busy harbour, quiet weekend

It was busy in the harbour yesterday with day-trippers from Rhodes coming over. That was good to see, many of the tavernas were doing good business, as were some of the bars.

We were down there around lunchtime to visit the accountant, check the post office for Neil's new sandals, which had arrived, and to do a couple of other business things; all successfully taken care of I am pleased to say.

The wind was up and café advertising boards were being blown over, the sea was whipping up and the walk back up the hill felt easy enough as it wasn't too hot. There's still a cool breeze around this morning and the day still has a bit of a grey feel to it, but it's supposed to be brightening up later.

I am just starting today with a beetroot, apple, lemon, orange and ginger concoction from the juicer and have very few plans for the day other than writing some text for a promo video for the island. Neil has his walk on tomorrow and we have friends coming up for something to eat on the terrace in the late afternoon, so some shopping event needs to happen today. Other than that, and a Eurovision Song Contest party at Astrid's bar later (we have already sent our enthusiastic apologies), it looks like it's going to be a standard kind of weekend.

Symi roundup

Just a couple of news items this Monday morning to keep you up to date with what I've found out. Thanks to the wonder of modern science I can now sit on the steps outside the shop of an evening and connect to the internet while watching a view that, apart from the odd telegraph pole, has not changed for hundreds of years.

And while doing that I can check in to the darker reaches of sites like Facebook and discover what's going on just around the corner. Or, failing that, I can overhear gossip and pass it along the line. One thing I did hear recently was that The Symi Gallery will soon be opening after the winter with a couple of exhibitions lined up. One will be showing the artwork created by the children and students of the art classes organised by the Symi Women's Association and led by Ian Haycox, the Gallery proprietor. The other exhibition I heard about was to be of work from a Cuban artist, but more details will follow.

Symi calendars, spiders and missing history

Trying to get ahead of myself again today (Monday). I am working on the wedding video and putting the final touches to it, adding some music and some extra Symi Videos of ours that the wedding party requested. And then turning it into a DVD. The making of the DVD takes time and I can't have very much else running while it does it, so I thought I would use the time and get today's blog done today which is yesterday. I've been doing a lot of this recently.

While Neil was out doing his photo walk I was working on the film script and the Kickstarter pitch script; much more about this to come in due course no doubt. And I was also getting the house ready for visitors who came up on Sunday evening. We had a lovely time on the terrace chatting, and the Romanian chicken dish I made seemed to go down well. So did the attention the Alarm Cat received from some of his fans.

Monday morning I was back at the desk working on the video, and noticed that my day to day 'This Day in History' diary that Jenine gave me had not been attended to for a few days, so I flicked through to see what I had missed. Tearing off the pages since 13th May to 20th I found out I had missed: Pope John Paul II being shot (1981), the departure of the 'Lewis and Clark' expedition (1804), the start of the seven years' war (1756), the first Academy awards ceremony (1929, it's a very USA based desk diary), Washington criticising 'taxation without representation' which sounds kind of apt for anyone paying a Greek electricity bill these days (1769), Randy Johnson throwing a 'perfect game at 40' which meant absolutely nothing to me (2004), and Pete Townshend writing 'My Generation' in 1965. So quite a lot goes on when you're not looking at your calendar.

Which could be a bit of a local-news-TV style segue into the Symi Dream calendar 2014 which is now for sale in the shop and on line. (It's never too early to be thinking about Christmas presents.)

Art gallery events and a starting season

Not getting ahead of myself today, the blog this morning is being written 'live' at 07.27 thanks to an early morning alarm call from…

No, not the Alarm Cat, from (I suspect) a mobile phone company phoning the landline well before seven. On the second call back I got up to answer it only to have the phone put down on me, so it could have been a wrong number. Either way, we were up early and the juice was made well before either cat or alarm.

Monday's wine night was well attended, many people came for a browse, a 'glass' and a chat on the steps and we noticed many of our guests later in the taverna as we passed. The fans have gone back up at the Rainbow Bar and yesterday Yiannis next door was putting up his. The temperature has risen again and the reports are showing figures in the 30's for the coming week. The round the island boat trips have started with the Poseidon going out and some of, if not all, the taxi boats are up and running again. Today, Olympic Holidays have something like 63 new guests arriving for their holidays; things are starting to get into the summer season swing.

It's raining pomegranate petals

A bit of a mild morning this morning, cooler than yesterday, with a slight wind and some cloud; no rain forecast on my weather station but that's not always accurate. And the morning juice is also milder than of late with less ginger in with the apple, beetroot, pear, lemon and orange. One of each and we've got about half a litre of juice each.

Not that we are trying to be healthy or anything, but the main meal of the day (lunchtime due to shifts and work) has recently been consisting of brown rice and salad mixed together with something interesting such as halloumi or tuna. The supper snacks have moved from crisps (unless cheese and onion are found on the island in which case it's open season) to, for example, a small tuna salad at Taverna Zoi on the way home, or some of the leftover rice and salad from the fridge. And still no smoking, in fact I've not had a cigarette for just over two stone now.

Today's photos are from Neil, taken outside the shop where the neighbour's

pomegranate tree is in full bloom.

It produces so many flowers that it has to weed itself out so I am often standing there, or sitting on the step, leaning against the wall, when I find myself being showered by red petals and getting the occasional tap on the head by a bud, such as these gathered up in the morning. Neil then sweeps up what the tree doesn't want every day to clear his little part of the Kali Strata.

A weekend on Symi, what to do?

So, you have a weekend on Symi, what are you going to do? As far as I have heard, the exhibition at the Symi Gallery is opening tonight, but the poetry reading has been moved to the following weekend, due to the exams taking place at school.

That's the news out of the way. Weather report for those heading this way soon: Cloudy again today, clearing up later in the day, set for sunshine all the way through next week, less windy today; always warm and smiley at the Symi Dream shop. Which is where I spent yesterday evening after attending a birthday cake party, or rather, a party with a birthday cake.

And as for things to do this weekend, well, the weekend starts on a Friday night with live music at Taverna George & Maria (Georgio's) in Horio. Very often in the village over the weekend there is also live music at 'The Secret Courtyard' in front of Anastasia's apartments, that might be happening on Saturday; Manteio's also has musicians from time to time, but I've not heard anything definite about those two places as yet. And there is often music being played in Yialos, in Kantirimi and other bars; there's certainly no shortage of music on the island.

There is a boat trip to Turkey on Saturday (but you will need to have organised your ticket already; the point is: if you're heading this way and wondering what there is to do, then there is often a boat trip to Turkey on a Saturday, but places are limited). There's the photo walk on Sunday, be at our shop at 9.15 a.m. for a stroll to Pedi.

And there are taxi boats to beaches (have they started running now? I'm pretty sure they have), and plenty of walks which are good to do while it's still not too hot. So, plenty of ideas for things to do on Symi there. As for me, well, I have a rewrite session ahead of me so I am not sure if I will be doing anything this weekend apart from unpaid writing. So, no change there then. Whatever you do, have a good one.

More live music in the village, a Symi Saturday ahead

Scary happenings indeed. I went to the first showing of the "The Scary Show" exhibition last night; this is work made by the children who attend the art classes during the winter. The theme was picked by the children who had used all kinds of recycled materials for the pieces. If you are passing and see the gallery open, call in for a look.

There was indeed a lot of music taking place up here last night, as I suggested yesterday. What I didn't know then, but found out later, was that taverna Haritomeni also had live music playing, and there was a gig by 'GMT' at the Sunrise. (That's my name for them: George, Marcus and Terri.)

The Sunrise often has music on, and it's easy to find the café; it's along the lane from the Village Hotel. If you stand looking at the Village hotel (you will eventually get run over so don't hang around) and look left, you will see their sign, lit up with a lantern at night in the style of 'the Ghost Train'. You'll also probably see a few cars there, just walk with the cars on your right, follow that lane a little way and there you are.

Haritomeni is a bit more complicated to explain, though you can get a taxi to it from Yialos. From Horio, walk down the steps from the village and you will see the Symi Dream shop on your left. Stop there, call in, buy everything and then you will have something to discuss over dinner. Carry on down the Kali Strata (with the signed copy of 'Carry On Up The Kali Strata' you just bought) and when you get to the main corner carry straight on; rather, do an S bend around the six foot drop so as not to break your leg, or the glass covering the framed limited edition photo you just bought. Carry on down the slope past the school and then diagonally right through the collection of cars.

There you come to a road/lane which you follow. And keep following until you think you have gone too far, and your arms start to get heavy under the weight of all the Symi Dream purchases you have. But keep going, around the zigzag bend until you see a road coming up to join you on the left. Cary on, keeping right, a few more yards and there's the taverna. Great views, great food, great place to admire your original Symi gifts, and I assume great music. (Not had that pleasure yet.)

OK, off into Saturday we go: scriptwriting this morning, then housework, walking to Nimborio tomorrow and having a 'day off.'

So what did you do this past weekend?

It started for us on Friday night with a visit to the shop by Dutch singer and star Manuela Kemp, which was a bit of a treat for us.

With her were the folk behind the film "Camp Kickitoo" – we saw some of the clips and trailer and heard about the fund raising and making of from the writer/producer Ric Sternberg. We all had a glass of wine and a good old chat and then Neil and I headed home, via just one more at the Rainbow Bar.

We had a bit of an attempted break in on Saturday night which was unusual. Part of one of our shutters has fallen away, it's been reported to the landlord, it's been looked at, discussed, thought about, much coffee has been spilt over its repair programme, and three years later it's still there. And, as we like to have the window open during the warmer months, it's now an 'in' route for any cat who fancies himself as a cat burglar.

I have no idea if it was Jack or the black and white one who thinks he lives here too, but someone was trying to clamber in through the missing shutter panel and open window at some hideously bleak hour of the night. They were unsuccessful and found the window firmly closed in their face. In the morning I noticed that someone had also slept on my potted chilly plant during the night, breaking off a stalk or two as if in a fit of pique. So vandal cats and burglar cats; what is the world coming to? And they were brawling outside (probably over the chilli plant) for a long time after, keeping me awake for longer. But finally they settled down and I was able to start to drift off again. Until someone stared snoring in an operatic tone.

Symi 85600 book review

A great wine night last night made all the more special by the arrival of this email from a photo-walker, Symi visitor and Symi Dream viewer which I am going to share. Not just because it made us feel very warm inside, but because we're rather proud of it. To hear people say they want to come back to Symi gives everyone hope for the future of the island's prosperity.

"Hi Neil and James,

Just to say Hi, and how we enjoyed the Photo walk and wine night recently. It was great fun, and now I feel that I am actually thinking a little before taking a photo, which is no bad thing. I have returned to New Zealand for a while, but missed Symi as soon as we got on the plane. I would love to come back and maybe buy a place there in the future.

Tell James that I loved his book, read it on the plane to London and just posted a review on Amazon.

All the best for a great summer

Maria"

Promoting more local businesses via Best and Dream

It was a bit of a harbour day for us yesterday.

We had to go down to run a few errands: get the new photo walk posters copied up and a few laminated, visit the bank, buy some boat tickets, check the post office… The usual kinds of things.

Yialos was busy when we arrived, around 11.30, with various tour groups being led around. Some day-trippers had broken away from the pack and were wandering the streets on their own, free yet slightly in awe, some were heading up the Kali Strata as we were coming down and it was a glorious morning, the sun bright.

After several cheery hellos from fellow business-folk, friends, and even some strangers, I went to get the boat tickets; all successfully organised by Symi Tours. A little while after I was approached by a nearby business about Symi Best, and Symi Dream. Seems we'd been recommended as the place to put adverts, Symi Best being free and Symi Dream having a big readership (and being free). Anyhow, the point of all this is to remind other local businesses that we're more than happy to list on Best for free and also make a blog post about the business here, where several hundred readers will see it.

So, all that done, we then decided to have lunch at Meraklis, the Taverna at the end of the same street, as we've just been sharing their Facebook page. Here we were greeted with a friendly wave and a complimentary jug of wine, which was rather good, followed by a plate of lamb chops, for me, and the lamb in the oven for Neil, plus a salad. All very nice I have to say, and very reasonable.

We also managed to fight our way through the crowds to see Takis, popped in to see Anna at Soroco, pick up some cat food for a currently very fussy Alarm Cat, collect a package from mother from the post office, and even managed to remember to collect the new posters before heading back up. A taxi-treat in this case which included a good old chat about things with the driver.

And all that before 2pm.

More good news about my film script project

We are aiming to get the script for The Judas Curse finalised over the next few days. As you may know when you write a script for a film it's not a case of saying 'here it is' and then putting your feet up, there are all kinds of collaborative stages to go through. The current one is what I call 'producer input' and in this case the producer is also a scriptwriter, so that's a very useful process for me.

But we have had some interesting news back from the snappily titled Government department: 'Hellenic Republic Ministry of Education & Religious Affairs, Culture And Sports General Secretariat of Culture 4TH Ephorate of Byzantine Antiquities' about shooting footage in the catacombs of Nimborio and on Symi generally.

No permission is needed to film in Horio, or Pedi apart from inside churches (where church permission is also needed), but to film inside the catacombs, or 'Dodeka Spilia' as they are formally known, permission does have to be sought, and when asking for this in writing the film company would need to submit a full script, exact dates, and exact list of props and 'other means affecting the site.' And there is also a fee set out in a piece of legislation with such a long title I shan't repeat it here.

But that's great news; though we probably won't be able to afford to use the catacombs, and it was only for one minor scene. But it does mean that 1066 Productions now has the blessing of the Mayor of Symi who has welcomed them to film here, and the 'Archaeologia' in Rhodes has also said exactly what is necessary, and where we want to film is covered in the 'needs no special permission' area. Now we simply need to find a few locations and houses, ruins and lanes that are suitable and seek permission from a few house owners.

That's my main news, what else? I'm doing a couple of cabaret songs at The Symi Gallery on Saturday night, 6.30 onwards, as part of The Scary Show which is based around the artwork the children created during their winter art lessons, run by Ian Haycox and organised by the Symi Women's Association. I believe there is live music tonight in the village and possibly tomorrow night as well. The weather has gone from windy to still and misty all day and the view this morning is a bright silver sea mist with Nimos half hidden and no sign of Turkey. Calm and still though and looks set to hit 30 degrees at least.

June

Entertaining Ma, hunting Henry, signing Midas, a visit from the Keystone kops, and odd goings on at the bus stop

Symi Gallery event, birthdays, clouds, spiders…

There were all kinds of scary things happening on Saturday night at The Symi Gallery, not least of which was my vamping out a couple of Tom Lehrer numbers. There were also poems, a drama piece and some video, plus readings and participation from local folk, Greek, English, French and Danish alike. I think my highlight of the night was Lynne reading 'the Raven' by Edgar Allan Poe, one of my favourite poems of all time (though I still don't understand it all).

Saturday was also Dawn's birthday so there was a lunchtime gathering in the square and then later, I believe, an evening one as well. We were home early on Saturday night as Neil has his photo walk on a Sunday. A day which was rather windy and grey I have to say; gusting to 33 knots at nine in the morning according to 'windfinder.com' (who also have Symi as being in Turkey, but whose weather reports are usually pretty accurate, after all, we are closer to Turkey than we are to Greece). Luckily it looks like things will be calming down after today.

Apart from that, and a barbeque in the evening on Sunday, it was a pretty quiet weekend, oh, apart from another Symi spider making itself at home in the house on Friday night, I am sure they are breeding in the old armchair by the fireplace, or more likely they are dropping down the chimney. Or even more likely they are abseiling down the chimney in full climbing gear. There's probably a platoon of the things living in there and each night they send one out on manoeuvres to worry the humans and snaffle supplies: food, something from the fridge, the X Box…

Enough of that, on with the week ahead, highlights of which will include: Wine night, Monday, 5.30 a.m. start on Tuesday for the 7.00 boat to Rhodes, a day in Rhodes, meeting mother and her friends at the airport, a night in Rhodes, a day trip to Panormitis on Wednesday, a Kalodoukas transfer up to the village, and another photo walk, at least. Should be a fun week.

From Symi to Rhodes in a couple of hours

I'm not sure what time this post is going to get online today, but it will probably have to do for Tuesday and Wednesday as I am currently on my way to Rhodes.

Actually, I'm not currently on the way to anywhere as the Panagia Skiadeni hasn't left yet, and I am sitting in its rather plush lounge with my first coffee since Romania (March) and a bottle of water. It's 6.47 and I have been up since 5.30, due to set off at 7.00. An early start as I am heading over to Rhodes to take care of a few bits of business during the day and to meet Mother and Co. from the plane tonight. Tomorrow will be taken up with the return journey, via Panormitis. (If heading this way, buy your boat tickets early, the day trip sailings on the Panagia Skiadeni have been selling out; I bought our tickets last week.)

Knowing I had to be up early today I had an early night and was happily drifting off when someone in the neighbourhood decided to build a chicken shed from scratch. Well, that's what it sounded like, in the darkness, through approaching sleep. Someone with a hammer and some wood knocking up a quick henhouse at 10.45 pm. I did wonder if it was the builders who had been working on a nearby roof all morning, but doubted it.

Anyway, managed to get to sleep for a while before being woken up by the loudest alarm 'tune' in the world, with the phone right next to the bed, managed to get down to the harbour by 6.40 and am now (6.55) feeling the engines start up beneath the carpet. Yup, we've started to 'shimmy' so I'll switch off as my coffee is now dancing perilously close to the laptop and getting closer.

9.24: now at the Plaza Hotel, Rhodes, walked around from Akantia, straight to hotel, straight to check in, a room is ready and here I am Wi-Fi and fancy free. A quick blog post and out I go to take care of some business. Have a good day!

L. O. L. O. A. Q. I. C. I. 8. 2. Q. 4. A. P.

Just very briefly this morning, as there's a lot to be done at the house before I head out for the day to meet Mother & Co. and see what today holds in store.

A day and a night in Rhodes felt like a holiday in itself, though I didn't actually do much. I took a couple of photos but they all seemed to be 'views from a dining table.' Breakfast: by the old market, on the seafront, looking across the road to the Symi II. Lunch at 'Napoleons' where you can get a spaghetti Bolognaise for €5.00. And dinner at the China Burger where the chicken and veg went down well. Between meals I was at the Plaza, reading, dozing and generally hanging around.

The bus to the airport was the usual adventure and I headed up there early just for a change of scenery. It wasn't until I got there that I realised I could have come and had dinner at the taverna opposite for a change, and for a new experience. But instead I went to the café in the new building to investigate a glass of wine.

"Can I have a glass of wine?" I asked the young lady behind the counter.

"Are you sure?" she replied, and then went on to persuade me to have a small bottle as it would be safer. "When I pour a glass for people they all complain," she explained, looking at the tatty old box in the fridge. Fair enough.

I sat and sipped and wondered at the name of the café. It's in the new international departures area where you can sit and watch huge long lines of grumpy holidaymakers stressing up before heading back to Moscow, Vienna, Glasgow and other exotic locations like Manchester. You can see how, on occasions, the lines stretch right back and out of the doors, you can have a front row seat on other people's misery.

The name of the bar is rather provocative, I thought: "Qu." I'm not sure if that's meant to be just "Queue" or Q-U, as in "Queue-you Jimmy!" Either way it seems a bit of a mickey take for all those people waiting with cases, small children and sun burn who are dying for a drink but can't actually leave the Qu in order to fetch one from Qu in case they lose their place in the queue.

Anyway, must get on; things to do and adventures with family to be had.

BTW: L. O. L. O. A. Q. I. C. I. 8. 2. Q. 4. A. P ('ello, 'ello, a queue I see...)

An early start again

Another early start after another busy day yesterday: meeting the family at the Olive Tree, taking a walk through the village, showing the guests the house, walking up to the Castro and around to get the views, then down to the village again.

In the evening heading off down to Yialos to look around, seeing Takis and his latest leather artwork, ladies buying bags, and natural products from Dawn's shop, taking a look at the sponges for gifts to buy, dinner at a taverna and a bus ride back up the hill. To meet Neil at Manteio, have a nightcap and finally head home.

This morning will be a similar event except I have to go and see the accountant and the guests are planning to "head to Nimborio, or perhaps not, will see how we feel when we get up." Quite right too, you're on holiday.

And as for the weekend ahead, the usual village events are planned: live music at Giorgio's, and other venues I expect, and the photo walk on Sunday. Wine night on Monday… which makes for an opportune moment to mention the following Monday: at the wine night (on 17th June) there will be an exclusive book signing by author Dominic Ranger, signing his new book 'Midas' which is partly set in Symi, I understand.

A day on holiday

Yesterday was a bit of a being on holiday day (after getting up at six and writing for three or four hours).

A cup of tea at Village HQ (The Olive Tree), a walk down the steps to the accountant, "come back later", a browse around the shops – how many new shops are there in Yialos this year? A coffee at Eva and then nip back to the accountant, "I didn't do the papers yet, come back tomorrow."

A wait at Pacho's while mother gets fish to do her feet and has a foot massage next door at the Fish Doctor, and then finally a taxi back up the hill.

Do the shopping at Sotiris', "hello mum," and wander home with bags of healthy stuff. Make a salad, have some nice ham with it, sit on the terrace for lunch. Visit the Rainbow Bar and watch the annual hanging of the awning; Fanouris was up and down his homemade ladder with frightening speed, arranging the wires and cables and tying the knots. This must be about the ninth year I've watched this event. Luckily it passed off with no accidents.

And then the afternoon slips into evening as we all meet up, Guests included, and head to Taverna Zoi for 'a bowl of soup' which turns into several starters, a main course each and probably too much wine. And then finally heading back to the Rainbow to listen to the live music from next door only to find out that both bars are playing a football match and you can't hear anything but the occasional near-miss sound effect and a commentator; oh, and the fans blowing those strange horn things. A nightcap there and then home to bed.

And all that under a cloud or two which produced about 16 spots of rain in the afternoon and which seems to have passed on by his morning. And as for today, well, who knows what lies in store, apart from a trip to the accountant, again.

Various places to eat on Symi, all tried and tested

Things are a bit hectic when there are guests around. Only really in terms of getting up earlier to get house things done before meeting people for the day. But this morning (Sunday) Neil has taken Ma & Co. on his photo walk with some other walkers and, as I write, has just phoned me. Always a worry when your seventy-something mother (who is fitter than I am, I should add) is out there somewhere in the valley and Neil phones you up. Luckily he only wanted to know the Greek word for butterfly. Did you know that in Ancient Greece a word for 'butterfly' (πεταλούδα) was 'soul' (ψυχή), or mind or psyche… depending on which website you get your answers from.

Fascinating. Anyway, while he is out doing that I have a couple of hours to catch up on bits and pieces around the house. I've just dug some holes in the garden and put in some plants, and Jack has just come back in from a walkabout with suspiciously dirty paws. I will need to go and see if my lemon thyme (or whatever I bought) is still in place.

We've done nothing but eat and drink the past few days. It sounds like we can afford to eat out all the time, but we can't; that's only the first flush of holiday excitement. We're staying in tonight and ordering Dolphin Pizzas. They will deliver to the village, if you can explain to Vassilis where you are, or arrange a rendezvous.

That's tonight (last night actually). So far on this visit we have tried out: Taverna Giorgio and Maria in Horio who gave us an extra wine and a rather nice loyalty bonus discount; great food as always, lots of different mezethes and some 'plates' as well. We've had two lunches at the Olive Tree, all healthy stuff there with homemade quiches and juices and cakes with cream. We've been to Taverna Zoi for dinner, well, just a bowl of soup or something, which turned into two courses each as it's all so good (plus loyalty bonus wine jug and fruit). And we've had a meal at Meraklis in Yialos complete with loyalty bonus sweet, a sandwich at Café Eva, a huge array of snacks at Manteio in Horio (where you don't need a loyalty bonus as it's all so reasonable to start with) and two lunches at home. Good Lord! In return mother has offered her feet to fish in Yialos and fed them at The Fish Doctor. We've also bought plants from the new 'garden centre' by the town hall, loads of shopping from Sotiris 'Hello Doby's mama,' and helped out Yianni-Rainbow's retirement fund a little.

And all this while also having a G&T on a terrace at the insanely wonderful Kyriaki Apartments in the care of Kalodoukas Holidays; and a huge thank you from Ma & Co. to everyone who helped get the water pump under control. You really do get an excellent service from Frances, Michelle, George and everyone else involved.

So, enough of all that. I now have to tidy up a bit before having a shower and heading off down the Pedi road to meet the walkers at Katsaras on the jetty and have a quick bite to eat before racing back up the hill (hopefully by bus, or else the shower was redundant) by three.

Tuesday morning catch up

The thing is, when you have guests, there's never enough time in the day to do everything that you want to do; I'm worn out!

Not that we have been busy, but since I wrote yesterday's blog (on Sunday morning) the following has happened:

I walked down to Pedi (in 20 minutes from door to door) to meet the walkers after their photo walk with Neil and we had lunch at Katsaras, on the jetty. They do a very good meze plate for around €16.00 which is a bit of almost everything, for two people; they also do loads of other nice things as well. Then I caught the bus back up later in the afternoon, and in the evening, after some piano playing, we ordered pizzas from Vassilis and had a delivery at home.

Monday: Ma and I went into Yialos, bought a pair of steps, had them delivered later, paid the water bill, did some shopping, stopped for a Coke Light, caught a taxi back up sharing with Michaelis from the kiosk, did some more shopping, went home, did some gardening, made lunch, pottered around and then it was time for the wine night. Harry's end of school play was on but we were working and I had a meeting with an actress as well. Later we had a bite to eat at Giorgio's. The wine night was well attended and I forgot to take a photo, and now Harry has finished nursery and next term will be at the junior school. It all happens when you're not looking doesn't it?

And today, Tuesday, there is nothing planned at all, apart from meeting Ma & Co. at the Olive Tree later this morning. The Co. went to St Nicholas beach yesterday and totally loved it so they may be heading that way again, while Ma has her eye on some vine and tree trimming in the garden, hence the steps purchase yesterday. Me? Having been woken up very early by the Alarm Cat breaking noisily into the front room and trying to get into the bedroom, I have my eye on a long sleep somewhere.

Around Symi in the rain, perhaps?

Looks like it's going to be an interesting day for a round the island boat trip: "A shower in spots this morning, otherwise sunshine and a few clouds…" says the weather forecast. Ah well, not to worry, if you go in the sea you get wet anyway so there's no problem there.

Last night's treat was a visit to the Windmill restaurant for a few dishes. The restaurant was quite busy, early on particularly, and we'd like to thank Kerry and Steve for the departing gift of the jug of wine. They will be on the boat now, crossing to Rhodes and heading home. The stray cats of Horio are going to miss them and their daily attentions.

The rest of yesterday was a kind of 'at leisure' day as they say on holiday itineraries. Ma came and did some gardening and pottered around outside with a broom while I tried to reformat Carry on up the Kali Strata for a novel sized and shaped publication. The current landscape one is all fine and still available from Lulu.com, but I want to put a version on Amazon and they don't have the same layout, so I have started putting a 9 x 6 version together.

Not as easy as it sounds. For a start the original Word files went with the PC crash, so I downloaded the PDF from the Lulu file storage area. Then had to find a programme to turn the PDF back to Word. I found loads of 'convert for free' offers and programmes which I tried, one after the other, only to discover that 'free' actually means 'you have to buy this to get it to work properly' and you only get three pages free and then nothing. Why can't these people be more honest and tell you that before you end up with unwanted programmes on your machine? Argh! Anyway, luckily I was able to send the file to Allan who already had such a programme and he promptly sent me the Word file back, compete with all the images.

So, I thought I'd just change the size and orientation of the thing and there we go, but no. This is Microsoft we're talking about so that's not going to work. 'Your margins are not right for what we think you should be doing so we're not going to let you do it at all,' and similar kinds of error messages came up, so I started from scratch. I got a template from Amazon and copied the whole thing into that. Except Microsoft knows best and it wouldn't let me keep the Amazon page size and simply gave me a replica of what I already had, in landscape format.

So, page by page and image by image I am copying the text and pictures across bit at a time; the page numbering doesn't work (always a nightmare) and a few other odd things are creeping in, like the occasional landscape page comes with the text even if I run it all through notepad and 'clear out' the formatting. But I will persevere and get there in the end. Then I will look at the page numbers and probably have to call on someone to help.

So much to do on Symi this weekend

If ever you hear anyone say "There's nothing to do on Symi," don't believe them. We now have two invitations to two separate events on Saturday evening:

The Symi Gallery has an exhibition of work by a Cuban artist opening on Saturday at 18:00 until 21:00, at the gallery on the Kali Strata.

Fotini's wine shop in Yialos is hosting a wine tasting at 18:00 on Saturday. Everyone is welcome at both events and we are certainly going to try and get to each in some kind of order.

Sunday is the Pedi Valley photo walk and on Monday we have the book signing at Symi Dream at 19:00 where Dominic Ranger will be signing copies of his debut novel 'Midas' partly set on Symi.

As for the guests: '& Co.' set off yesterday afternoon to Rhodes to spend a day exploring there before the flight home tonight, leaving Ma in charge of the apartment, and us. We spent the evening on the balcony watching the boats come and go, and I was particularly excited to sit and watch the Blue Star coming in from the high vantage point. (Note to self: must get out more.)

Today, after our morning rendezvous at Village HQ at 10.00, we're coming home for a home day of gardening and pottering around, and staying close to home to watch some films this evening. Tomorrow we have a full day to ourselves which might include time in Yialos, a walk, some wine tasting, some art, who knows. It looks like the weather might have calmed down after a couple of days of cooler temperatures, and my forecast shows things heading off into the 30s during next week.

We also had coffee in Yialos, browsed the shops, and Ma bought a new dress from Fredericka's shop at the bottom of the Kali Strata (just up from the Kalodoukas office), which came with its own matching bag; she was very happy with the price too.

So, all in all, it's been a busy week for us and the guests (with Neil working all week, including a night shoot in Pedi) and it looks like it's going to be another busy week after this rather relaxing weekend. Have a good one.

Carry on up the book signing success

Well, I think we can safely say that last night's book signing and wine nigh was a bit of a success, with every book, bar one, sold and signed and over 50 people attending.

There was a bit of a strange start to the evening though with a drive past by a digger of some sort, that was making its way up the Kali Strata. I believe that this was on its way to the main road from where it had been working for several weeks. Just to the south side of the harbour and up the hill a little way, someone has been terracing the ground, rather than building a house. Looks like they've finished with this machine now and the only way to get to the road was by driving slowly, and carefully, up the Kali Strata, much to the amusement of us and some visitors and the annoyance of some neighbours.

The busy evening came after a busy morning in the harbour where at least two day-trip boats unloaded their passengers as Ma and I were out and about. We managed to leave them behind after getting our jobs done and headed back up the hill for a quieter time at home before heading to the shop in the evening.

Dominic Ranger (aka Chris Lillicrap) was on hand to sign his books for those who wanted to buy a copy, and we spent a couple of hours in the company of many visitors who came up to meet him and buy their copy of his thriller 'Midas', which is partly set on Symi. I have a copy but, as yet, have not had time to set about reading it.

And today is the last day of Ma's Symi holiday this year. We have a quiet day planned ahead of an early start tomorrow morning; the boat is at 7.00 a.m. which is perfect for a 14:00 flight, apart from being so early in the morning of course.

And, another piece of Symi book news, I am about to order the first copy of the new edition of Carry on up the Kali Strata to test drive it before making it available for sale in the shop. This is the same as the original landscape edition, but with slightly fewer photos, and, all being well, it should be in the shop in a few weeks. It seems quite appropriate to announce that today, after the digger going up the Kali Strata and past the book signing. Perhaps, when I have some copies, I shall organise a book signing of my own and a drive past of… what? A forklift?

Waiting for a bus on Rhodes

Settling back into a more usual routine now; a bit of this, a bit of that, an early night and early start to today. The sea is silver and a slight mist is rising from it out there towards Turkey. Outside, the birds have been tweeting for an hour or so now, and I hate to think what they are saying in their 140 characters or less…

My mind wanders back to something I saw at Rhodes airport the other day. I was waiting for a bus to head back to Rhodes town and so I checked the timetable: 13:00, 13:15…. All seemed well; it was 12:55.

A group of Greek ladies with suitcases were chatting in the shade, it being about 39 degrees that day, and a young Russian pair arrived, a boy and girl, about 20 years old, complicatedly chatting in Cyrillic. They were obviously on a 'do it yourself' mission as they turned down an offer from a rogue taxi driver for 'Five Euros each to Rhodes town.' I'm pretty sure that's illegal and that his mates in the queue of about 30 taxis ahead would not have been happy with him. But no, they were going independently 'спасибо' (thank you). She even checked the timetable to make sure she knew the time of the next bus: 13:00. (Один O'clock)

We waited, and at about 13:02 a bus came along the road and pulled into the airport. Ladies with luggage prepared themselves and everyone ignored the queue rule and went to stand where they thought the bus doors would open, so they could be first on. But it's not like the London underground where you're pretty sure about where the doors will be, a bus can stop where the driver fancies. They were wrong and the Russian duo was correct. Except they were not allowed on. The inspector who barred the doorway told us that this was not the Rhodes bus, and sure enough it drove away.

There was some grumbling from the baggage ladies who told the inspector that the timetable said 13:00 for the next bus, and look, it was now 13:03. The inspector wasn't having that, 'it's at 13.05' he said gruffly, but the ladies directed him to the timetable that the Russian girl was again studying, and, through her rather over ambitious, bleached, hair-do, he squinted in at it. He made that noise best described as 'hurump,' and, as if by magic, produced a new timetable from his pocket and stuck it over the old one.

The next bus was due at 13.05, so the Russian girl checked again and reported back to her other half, 'одно Опяти' as the bag ladies gathered in a conspiratorial group and gave the inspector sideways looks.

13:05 came and nothing happened. The Russian girl went back to the timetable and read it again, as if, by some miracle, it had changed itself, or time, or something. I mean what's the point? You only read it two minutes ago, will it have changed? But that's what we do when we want to be reassured that we are indeed late.

13.09 and the bag-conspiracy confront the inspector re: the timetable, 'it said 13.05,' they now conceded, 'but still no bus.'

'You just missed it,' the inspector explains, taking a bit of a gamble; some of the ladies look less than happy.

Before blood is shed another bus pulls into the airport and rumbles up, at 13.11 which seems nicely, Greekly, equidistant between 13:00 which was actually 13.05 and 13.15 when the next bus was due.

'Can I help you with your bags?' I ask one of the bag ladies as they have two huge red suitcases a piece and I have nothing.

'Thank you,' she replies and we line up to have our tickets inspected by the inspector as we get on.

'Can we buy tickets on the bus?' I hear the lady ask as I climb aboard, dragging her suitcase behind me. (It's at least 40lbs. She is clearly transporting gold bullion. Possibly dead bodies.)

'No, tickets at the café,' the inspector replies with just a little too much glee in his voice. (It's now illegal to travel on a Greek bus without first finding a ticket from somewhere.)

The suitcase is wrenched from my hand as if I were trying to make off with it and the ladies, now as red in the face as their cases, tell the inspector to hold the bus while they go back inside the terminal and collect their tickets from the QU Café. Remember that one?

Anyway, I got a seat on the time travel bus and the ladies didn't. That inspector wasn't going to wait, he had a timetable to be not kept to. He was a job's-worth; by the time we were leaving the airport he was re-inspecting every ticket he had just inspected as we got on, smiling to himself at the ladies he'd left behind.

As we left the airport another bus, presumably the alternative 13.15, came in so the ladies would not have waited long. You never have this trouble with the Symi bus, sadly.

ΤΑ ΣΥΜΑΙΚΑ ΝΕΑ

It's all about news today as Symi is in the news locally, and now has another new news site.

Locally there was a piece in the Rhodes based Η ΡΟΔΙΑΚΗ about the waiting time for boats arriving at Yialos. Due to under-staffing it seems that even boats carrying VIPs have to wait in turn to moor up and have their paperwork completed. Well worth the few minutes wait I say.

But more interestingly to everyone who likes to follow what's going on, the island has a new and completely free online newspaper ΤΑ ΣΥΜΑΙΚΑ ΝΕΑ. The title translates as 'Symaika News', Symaika being a proper noun for the island's people.

Konstantinos Papatheodosiou, now runs the Facebook page for the new venture, says:

"ΣΥΜΑΙΚΑ NEWS: the new electronic and interactive journal of Symi!

Here you can read all the latest news of our island as readers, but you will have the ability to publish news, reviews and announcements through interactivity tools like Facebook. For those who do not have a profile, you can create a page through networking and to become a member of the group.

Our goal is the free transmission of news, greater interactivity and full transparency in the use of tools. Here we are, starting a new, revolutionary, online activity where the reader can become a journalist and reviewer!"

At the moment it is a place where posts from online newspapers, social networking posts and other sites are being pulled together, as long as they have the common thread of 'Symi', but as the announcement implies: the more you get involved the bigger it will grow. There is a button to link to Symi Radio, and some other links of a Symi interest. Used properly by people who love Symi and want spread the island's popularity, this new site could do very well; it is certainly well worth taking a look.

What did you do on your Symi holiday?

I spent some time out and about with Neil and his brother James yesterday; a few hours with 'The Booze brothers,' you might say.

Actually, we were heading off to the wine night which turned out to be a very sociable affair. This week we had red, white and retsina on the steps to give away a 'glass' or two to those folk who came to visit the gallery and shop.

It's been quite a busy week already: Neil took his Sunday morning photo walk to Pedi as per usual, he was asked (but couldn't make it) to photograph the football teams taking part in a match that was taking place at the same time as his previously booked walk. His brother James arrived, we all went to Manteio for supper, and had an early night as the flight from Vienna was a practically over-night one. There was live music at Giorgio's last Sunday evening because it was Pentecost weekend, but we didn't go. Yesterday was all work and wine night, today looks like it might be a trip down to Yialos, work in the shop, and then maybe a quiet evening in, for me at least.

Oh, and I wanted to say hello to Hilary, Lin and everyone else who has just got back from their trip to Symi and is catching up with what went on while they were here. It's always good to hear that people enjoy reading my early morning, half-awake rambles about 'what I did in the holidays (yours)', the kind of thing I never got marks for writing at school. So many people seem to take a sneak peek at work, or log on first thing to catch up on Symi 'news' (my news on Symi is a better description). And many people say they can't wait to get home from their Symi holiday in order to read what's been going on while they have been here. That all sounds suitably the wrong way around for my liking.

First day back in the office after a fortnight away: 'How was your holiday?' asks the colleague. 'Give me a minute and I will tell you,' replies the returning worker, booting up her computer.

I hope you've all now found out what went on while you were here. It's not everything that went on of course, only my view of what I see and get involved in or hear about. And this morning, from the desk, I see: bands of grey and silver-blue on the sea, no movement in the fig or olive tree outside, I can smell bread baking at the bakery around the corner, and I hear the birds starting up, the fan running up in the moussandra and the church bell strike seven. Already? I best get on.

Yialos twice in one day

Feeling sympathy for those who are on the 7.00 a.m. boat this morning; I know what it's like. Not only an early start but also leaving Symi after a holiday. Here's wishing you a safe journey.

I was in Yialos twice yesterday, which must be something of a record for me. After a healthy breakfast of fresh juice and a couple of cups of tea, some writing and a quick tidy up, I headed down to take care of a few jobs. First off: a visit to Kristallo to discuss Hoovers. A couple of variations in stock but no Henry, in fact when I asked if they were able to order me a Henry I was asked 'Who's Henry?' and our exchange was in our best of each other's languages, so it wasn't a communication problem. The other possible Hoover supplier was out, so the Henry-hunt continues.

Then to Antoniardis' hardware shop for two light bulbs, you know, the old fashioned sort with bayonet fitting. Actually the very old fashioned sort: ones that actually fit your light fitting. Not these 'last forever' ones that don't fit anything you happen to have in your house. The two old energy-guzzling extravagances are for the bathroom cabinet. The only light we have in our bathroom comes from a wonderfully 1980's celebration of plastic, a cabinet with three lights in it, and when it is no longer possible to buy bayonet light bulbs we will either have to spend a fortune on changing the bathroom lighting around, or will ablute in the dark.

Then to a supermarket (or a Super Market as many are called) on a beetroot hunt. 'None to be had at the market sir, not even for ready money.' And then to the bank to pay no less than two electricity bills; shop and house. And that brings our bill-paying right up to date, apart from a couple of things outstanding at the shop. Then there was time for a quick Coke Lite at Pacho's with Neil's brother James before walking back up the Kali Strata.

My way was dampened by a water escape from somewhere and the steps were glinting in the sun as I sweated up at 11.00. It was a bit unfair of them to glisten so and looks so cool and refreshed as I dripped along. (Dripped perhaps but not gasped for air; I can do the whole lot without getting out of breath, which is something of a medical mystery.)

And they were looking warm and golden as we made our way down again in the evening at sunset. We went for our now traditional pizza at the Dolphin Pizzeria and were very well fed for a very nice price thank you very much. That was followed by a taxi ride home for Neil and I while James raced up on foot. Don't ask me why. It's probably one of those being on holiday things. After having a big Mexican I am hardly able to walk, let alone scoot up the steps. (It's an incorrect use of a verb and a kind of pizza, before you say anything.)

So, here comes Wednesday, it's just past seven, the boat will be pulling away and several people are taking their last look at Symi for a while. But, as I always say, you have to leave in order to come back.

What did you do on Wednesday?

Why on earth do you wake up with random songs in your head? And why are they never straightforward ones? 'I remember you.' Is today's tune, but not the original, not the usual one; but the Bette Midler and James Caan version from "For the boys." No idea where that came from.

Nothing to do with yesterday which was a very pleasant and very hot day. The Henry-hunt continued with an email suggesting finding the name of the company who make them, and their suppliers in Athens. That was followed literally two minutes later by the website address of the company from Kate, that led me to finding two suppliers in Athens. Both have email addresses so I have emailed the first one to see if they supply individuals, or if not, if they can tell me where the nearest outlet is.

Neil had a usual day at the shop where we all met up in the evening after James and I had gone for a completely gratuitous walk to Yialos. My idea was to head down past the school, down the steps there and then immediately back up from the zigzag. There's a handrail down those steps, the ones that run up past the music school, and that was actually too hot to handle yesterday. We reached the zigzag and then, for some unknown reason decided to carry on right down.

I picked up a bottle of water, and we headed back up past the new Thea Apartments, joining the Kali Strata on the corner where the donkey stop is. (If you're a regular Kali Strata walker you will know where I mean.)

After work we nipped around to the Sunrise Café for a light supper and a chat with Delphi who has recently had a haircut; she looks a lot cooler now. Which is just as well as it looks like today is going to be a hot one as well; July temperatures already. New visitors were arriving, and included first-time visitors, which is good. Let's hope they enjoy Symi and catch the famous 'Symi bug', the one that makes you want to come back again and again. Finally: walking home, past the Windmill Restaurant, which was doing good business, and deservedly so, and through 'the gauntlet', the part of the square through the two bars, stopping to chat with just about everyone on the way… a very pleasant end to a pleasant day.

The Henry-hunt continues and the Keystone Kops invade

Who would ever think that buying a vacuum cleaner could be so much fun, and such an international affair?

I received a reply from the suppliers in Athens last night. They explained that as they are mainly importing 'for the professionals' they prefer to import the 'strongest' machines, and then go on to explain that we're talking kind of industrial Henry's here, and not the friendly yellow James I was hoping for. In fact, the model they recommend was so industrial it wasn't even christened yet and was called a 'NVP180-2 with by-pass motor of 1200', which sounded a bit worrying from a cardio-health point of view. Also, having looked at the cost of these things online and getting an idea of what to expect to pay had I been in, say, London, the cost of the machines from Athens was twice the price, two and a half times the price in the case of a baptised Henry, and that's before shipping through 'one of the transporting companies between Athens and Symi.' I dread to think how much extra that would add on to the price, but it is nice to know that not only the vacuum cleaners have human names. "Laurie" the transport company presumably ships supplies in a surrey with a fringe on top. (Oklahoma! fans will get the reference.)

But all is not lost. Thanks to the power of the Symi Dream blog, I am not hunting Henry alone. Yesterday lunchtime Neil's phone rang (he'd left it at home by lucky mistake). I answered it and it was Chrissie from England, a Symi visitor and blog-reader. She had called me to give me the phone number for Numatic International, the company that makes Henrys, and suggested another online company I'd not thought of checking out. So, a huge thank you to Chrissie! I'll be looking into those leads later today.

A rather spooky aside: I wondered where in the UK the call had originated from, just out of an interest in detail, and so found the area code through a Google search. A little map came up and some details and then some of those adverts that get put on pages, and they were all for… yes you guessed it, vacuums. I can't get away from them now.

But, just before that phone call, the house had been invaded by the Keystone Kops. I'd been taking an inadvertent siesta on the sofa thanks to an instantly forgettable book I was reading, when I was woken by the sound of a cat hissing. The door was open and Jack was on his chair right by it, hissing at the television. He jumped down and started hissing at something under the table that the TV sits on. Snake perhaps? Large spider? No, either of those two and Jack wouldn't be seen for dust. It was a stray cat that hangs around, 'Silent Movie.' (It's black and white.)

Silent made a dash for it, scooting out the other end of the table and into the hall. Jack followed, great yells and kitty-swears fouling the air. I could see where SM was heading and just stood back to watch; Jack could sort this out. SM scooted into the passage way, did a 360 turn, his paws pounding the air rapidly in the same place (to the sound of a xylophone), he took a run up and then headed for the window with a great leap.

The window was closed. Cue: cymbal crash, slide-whistle and tweeting birds. SM landed with a crumpled thud, but his paws were still going as Jack was still hot on his tail. A few bitch slaps were thrown, one connected, some black, and much white, fur flew up and SM was off again, back through the sitting room and out of the front door. Jack hot on his heels, waving a truncheon and shouting 'come back here and take this you menace!' as he raced in hot pursuit through the living room, He aimed for a short cut under the table and ran straight into the table leg. Cue stars and slide-whistle as a big pink pump[1] raises on his head. Then he turned and hissed at me! As if I'd put the table there to thwart him, as if to say 'whose side are you on?' And then he was off, outside and over the roof in a cloud of dust.

Never a dull moment in our house

On the Symi news front; there is going to be a concert next Thursday, 4th July, in the evening, at the newly refurbished cultural centre in Yialos (opposite Hatzipetros supermarket). Everyone is invited. The Symi Music School are organising this, with musicians from Rhodes coming over to play and also with musicians from Symi.

And the Symi Shrimp Festival is going to be held towards the end of July, but again I'll let you know. Justine has been to dance rehearsals already; I

---

[1] At this point my editor gleefully points out 'Typo!' (which I decide to leave in) and then questions 'raises' as the correct use of the verb. Never having had a pump on the head I wouldn't know if it raises or rises, thus the use of 'pump' instead of 'bump' seems justified. But all the same I thank him for arising the query.

don't know how she finds the time or energy. As usual Symi Dream will be there to photograph. I am not sure if this is part of an unofficial Symi Festival, which appears to have petered out this year, I don't think so as it is a festival of its own which is held every year. I did try doing a search online for any more info about the Symi Festival 2013, but the only information that came up was from Symi Dream, saying we hadn't heard any news yet.

Meanwhile: Last night's hefty breeze, which is continuing this morning, should take the heat down a bit; it certainly feels a bit cooler this morning, though I am still sitting here at 6.45 writing the blog topless, ooh-er missus.

There were two scary boys about the shop last night, and I don't just mean Neil and James his brother. Harry and his friend were making fangs out of snacks and being ghosts on the steps behind us for a while, as we sat and watched the boats coming and going. Mainly coming in actually, some with sails up, proper sailors I call them, heading in on a tilt/lean/list/all of the above in the strong wind. One was coming in as the Blue Star loomed up behind it and it reminded me of that famous painting of the Titanic going out from Southampton, with a small sail-boat of some sort dwarfed alongside it. I was watching this through gritted eyes thanks to the wind blowing up everything from the steps.

Also yesterday evening, Neil had a Skype chat with his daughter and grandson in Edinburgh. We (James and I) both managed a lean in to the camera and a wave.

The good news of yesterday, concerning the Henry hunt is that one has been found. After days of searching the Amazon and trawling through unexplored parts of the Bay of E, after hours spent among the unknown tribes of Online Shopping, calls from England, emails to Athens, a helpful chat with a Viking, some time with the missionary John Lewis, and even a look at something called Argus, I received a message from Jenine at Village HQ. She sent me a link and more or less said 'here you go' and lo! These was a place on Amazon that I'd not found where they would send me one and where the postage was less than £9.00. And, checking my in-box this morning, I find that my new vacuum cleaner has already been dispatched. Would you believe it? The wonders of modern science. (And Jenine.)

We thought it would be far more confusing all round if we had another James in the family, so we've gone for one of them; he will add to James (me), James Neil's brother and his son James, and Neil's other nephew who is also called James, and it will also fit better in our house where there is no storage area at all. So, thank you to everyone who was involved in that particular hunt.

And so, on with the weekend. I have two clear mornings of writing time, I am expecting Judas Curse news any day now, either good or bad, and will pass that on, and Neil has a boat to meet this morning as more copies of Midas arrive on the island. He has a walk booked for Sunday morning and his brother will be accompanying him before heading off back to Vienna in the afternoon. It's still all go around here. You have a good weekend!

July

Parties, concerts, pumps, shrimps, tweets, dives, petitions and a little syncopation

Jack Cat snack, bells and giros

Getting ahead of myself again as it is Sunday, which actually means that I am writing today's blog last month. Kalo Mina! Happy month and all that.

Neil is off on a photo walk, I have done the housework and I still have an hour before I need to get ready to go and meet him and James for a light lunch at Manteio.

I am also bouncing around emails to do with the Judas Curse film project that 1066 Productions are interested to make on Symi in October. They have announced that news on casting should be available in ten days, so I'll keep you informed.

Yesterday was the feast day of St Peter and St Paul and today, Sunday, the bells are ringing out loudly as I type. Sounds like the morning service has all but ended, there will be coffee and cakes in courtyards very soon.

Last night we stopped off for our own feast, well, to collect some giros from George on the way home. One each for us and one for Jack. Jack's a real grazer, as well as being a bit of a bruiser. He rarely sits down to eat a meal, he's always been like that. He'll have a bit and then wander off, then come back later for a bit more, then wander off. All well and good but we have to keep an eye on the food that's left to keep it away from flies, bugs and now Silent Movie, who will creep in cartoon-like at any moment and snaffle away any Whiskers that Jack has left on pause. (Accidental pun. Oops.)

Jack also likes to be taken to his table which means I only get an hour at a time of peace and quiet in the mornings. He'll snack, find a place to bath and kip, wake up after an hour or so and come and stare at me silently. I have to go with him to the kitchen, where I usually make myself a cup of tea while he snacks a bit more. Then I get back to work and he goes back to sleep, usually, in the summer, on my feet. The process is repeated often throughout the day. I wonder if it is to do with his deafness, not liking to eat on his own? He'd rather have company, or are all cats like that? Must track down a book on cat psychology.

Much to do about nothing but fugu, fogy, fogou & foggy

This is one of those mornings where I wake up with absolutely nothing in my head. After a good, solid, nine hour sleep and still feeling like I could have a few more hours, I'm putting virtual pen to paper with no idea what to write about.

A quick run-down of yesterday would be rather dull: work, a bit more work, watering the garden and then an early night; it's all suddenly rather quiet and 'back to normal' after a month of guests and visitors. We did have cause to send off a bit of a grumpy email to suppliers as we are still waiting for certain stock for the shop after five weeks. (It usually only takes two to arrive.) So we're hoping that is resolved soon. But that was about the highlight of our yesterday.

It's Wednesday again today so some folk will be heading off home on the early ferry and, at 6.41 a.m. the Marine Traffic site shows me that the ship I can see far out beyond Nimos is the Artimis heading to Bodrum (and, therefore heading in the wrong direction), and the Diagoras (which usually calls in to Symi today) is currently between Kos and the Datca peninsular and is about to run straight into 'Fugu.'

Now here's a thing. I thought a Fugu was an ancient underground chamber, for burials or storage or something built hundreds of years ago just so that Time Team could investigate. Looking it up online I find that a Fugu is actually several things:

The Japanese word for the pufferfish, 'A Compact Reference Vertebrate Genome (no idea!), a 'graphical front end for the text-based Secure File Transfer Protocol (SFTP) client' (well, of course), and/or a company that makes 'illuminated inflatable furniture' (I dread to think).

I was thinking of the word *fogou* which I had to look up in my trusty old Oxford Concise because it completely stumped the online dictionary who asked me if I meant fogy. No I didn't. I may be feeling a bit foggy this morning as my mind might be foggy after such a good sleep, but I know the difference between 'an underground, dry-stone structure found on Iron Age or Romano-British defended settlement sites in Cornwall', and 'an excessively conservative or old-fashioned person, especially one who is intellectually dull.' Or maybe the online dictionary knows something about me that I don't.

Anyhow, this stream of semi-consciousness has taken us from Marine Traffic to old fogies via inflatable furniture and Roman Cornwall, and I still have nothing in my head to tell you. Oh, yes I do!

I had a message yesterday from my friend and editor who is helping me put together the next book. It will be a compilation of and most of this year's blog posts, edited together in a smooth and subtle blend of reading material, and made ready for sale by, we hope, next April. The end of June marked the half-way point, so we are half way towards a new book. No title as yet, I am still waiting for the muse to slap me about the head and face, but there is still plenty of time. Another six months of this kind of early morning nonsense and we'll be there.

And, a quick update from Marine Traffic and the passenger craft Artemis bound for Bodrum is now heading directly into Symi (ah, maybe it is a cruise ship, it is flying a Malta flag they say), the Diagoras is passing the Datca headland heading in the right direction, and the pleasure craft Fugu is still 'underway' with no apparent destination (or clear meaning).

So, do Symi tweets equal Sweets?

You know how it is, I came home yesterday evening to do some writing and turned on the machine to pick up some notes and was still on it an hour later having written one paragraph of a new story.

First of all there were some email messages about The Judas Curse. Now, I can't say very much as the project is now out of my hands, apart from any rewriting that I might be called on to do, and any production and location managing I may volunteer for later… But there are two directors very interested to direct, a British actor I am a great fan of who wants to take a part if the schedule fits, ditto a German actress not a million miles away, and the production company are very soon about to launch the Kickstarter appeal for the funds.

Secondly I received a message from Neil saying some visiting friends want to know if we are out tonight (Wednesday). So I'll be heading back to the village a little later to be sociable.

Thirdly, Neil has now started his own Twitter page and I wanted to get something out about that as I am sure you would love to follow his tweets, if you are a Twitterer, Tweeter, or whatever the word is. If not, I am sure you would equally love to pass on the news to your friends who do tweet.

Up until now we have had a Symi Dream Twitter page with a small following and the account was called Neil Gosling Symi Dream; makes sense? Now though, Neil has one as a photographer in his own right and so created his own account calling it Neil Gosling Symi Dreamer, but our original one was showing as being called Neil Gosling, as is Neil's new one, and so it was all a bit confusing. Bottom line now is:

To follow Neil go to: twitter.com/symidreamer

To follow Symi Dream: twitter.com/symidream

The astute and slightly balmy among you will notice that the only difference in addresses is the 'er' bit after 'dream', so I can now say that Neil is 'er indoors' ho-hum. Actually, if you search for him on Twitter you find he is in good company: Up come Sam Neil, Neil Diamond and Neil Gaiman in the same list. Mind you, so does someone called Neilytodd which puts me in mind of a certain Sondheim musical: "Attend the tale of Neily Todd…" Mind you, the rest of the lyrics are not flattering so I won't go on.

And a final odd observation from my desk, at 18.30 on a Wednesday night, with all doors and windows open; I can hear the chef at Syllogos playing on his Euphonium from here and there is not a breath of wind. Well, there's quite a lot of it going through his brass tube but not much to carry the sound up, so he must be blowing pretty hard.

Symi music school concerts

Yesterday evening Neil and I headed down the Kali Strata just after five to attend the end of term concert given by the students of the Symi Music School.

The concert took place in the newly refurbished Cultural Centre in Yialos. As I understood it, the building has been repaired and improved by the municipality, and the mayor was there to see its first concert.

There were actually two concerts last night. Firstly the music students from the Symi school, who gave us 25 pieces in total, on piano and classical guitar. The evening was introduced, blessed by the Patriarch, the cantor students then sang some prayers and blessings, and then the concert was underway. Each music student took his or her turn to come to the front, take a bow, present their piece, take another bow and return, always to great applause from the audience. The children (and one adult) all performed brilliantly and did their teachers proud.

There was then an interval during which we had time to meet friends before returning to the concert hall for the second programme, a concert of piano and classical guitar from music students from Rhodes. There was a great turn out of visitors and residents and the hall was full.

The artistes were aged between 17 and 23 and the programme included incredible performances of Chopin's Scherzo No.2 (piano), and classical guitar works by Rodrigo, Roland Dyens and others. Classical, modern, jazz, all kinds of techniques were used by these gifted guitarists. Again the standard was simply stunning, the performances were mesmerising and the evening a huge success. It was an evening that we shall remember for a long time.

Money was raised for the Symi Music School by way of €5.00 entrance fee (to the second concert) and you'd be very hard pushed to find such a concert for such an entrance fee anywhere else. We were honoured to be there.

Our evening was finished off with a dinner with friends at Trata Taverna, and then a slow, cool-ish, walk back up to Kali Strata to home, which at 11.30 at night is not so bad.

So, a very big thank you to the Symi Music School for inviting us to their concert and to all the hugely talented musicians who entertained last night.

Is there too much going on?

There's a fair old amount of catching up to be getting on with, and it's only Sunday morning, as I write this.

We've been 'doing the Kali' a bit in recent days. Neil has been up and down those steps like the right hand of the concert pianist playing Chopin the other night, while I have been a bit more Bartok about it. Friday: down to Yialos to make an appointment at the dentist, then back up the steps. Saturday, down to keep the appointment only to find out there's nothing wrong (and that a crown these days costs €200 for porcelain and €500 for enamel, in case you were wondering), and then back up those steps again.

On Saturday night there were at least two birthday parties and a night of traditional dancing in Syllogos square organized by the blood donor group. Actually, that was badly written. On Saturday night there were at least two birthday parties but they weren't held in the square. The one we attended was held on the Poseidon. We sat and watched as it came back from its day trip and the crew set about cleaning it. Yiannis took Yiannis off on his motorbike and then, a little later, came back to help unload pots and pans and trays of food from the back of a car. Then the guests arrived and Yiannis came back, freshened up and ready to go out again. We headed over to Taviri Bay on Nimos, but there was already a party going on there so we then headed over to the islet at Agia Marina. Music, dancing (I think Neil was the cabaret) and great company made for a very pleasant evening.

Sailing back from Ag. Marina at night, with the lights of the boat turned off, apart from the essential safety ones, and there's a great view of the stars. The Milky Way was clearly visible and the stars were so bright they looked like you could light your candle from them, if you had a candle to hand, which I didn't, but you know what I mean. After a lift back up the steps (in a car, thank you to Paul and Melanie) we stopped off on the way back for a nightcap in the village square where the music was just winding down; looks like there was a great night had by all.

Coming up this week is a celebration of 100 years of sponge diving and I'll try and get more details up on the blog in time. There are events being held at the Nautical Museum which, if I read the poster correctly, is being inaugurated after repairs (?) this week. More news on that to follow.

And now, as it is Sunday morning, I have a few hours of housework and cooking to look forward to. We have guests coming for dinner tonight, so I need to do a bit of tidying up and get something in the slow cooker later.

Symi's Alarm Cat update

You will have to study the photo very carefully here and then you can join in the game 'hunt the Jack Cat.'

Somewhere in the image there is an Alarm cat taking a snooze… Answer at the bottom of this post.

He's had quite a nice weekend actually. Apart from dozing for most of it we had friends around for dinner on Sunday and Jack was on hand to provide some attention seeking behaviour. He isn't normally allowed on our laps due to his habit of shedding a pillowcase worth of fur a minute, but he is allowed to indulge his guests and came in for some serious petting. It was a lovely evening guys, thank you for making it so.

There really have been a lot of things going on recently and more are to come. Tomorrow's post will contain details of an event being held on Symi next week: "Hadzis Stathis, 100 years of modern apnea" which is celebrating a dive made by a Symi sponge diver 100 years ago, a record breaking dive using the free dive technique.

But that is for tomorrow, and I know that because I have already scheduled the blog post and have it written.

But today is mainly about the cat for some reason and so here is the answer to the question Where's Jack? You probably saw that he was in his favourite place, between the pillars of the balustrade and the scrolly thing on the other side. (Clearly I failed O Level architecture.)

And now for some local news: the street light outside our house was repaired on Monday morning. We are lit again.

Well, how 'local' do you want your local news to be?

Symi filming project update

You will have to get used to these 'The Judas Curse' updates as it looks like things are soon to progress to the next stage: the fundraising stage.

I'm still in an odd position where I can't say too much about things as 1066 are waiting until everything is in place, and then they will make the announcements in the proper fashion. It's not up to me; I am only one part of an increasingly expanding team. A team which now includes known director and actors… who I can't name just yet.

At the moment we are looking at the third week in October for filming (16th to 23rd) if the money comes in. We have already had offers of help and volunteers for certain jobs and locations, and these people have agreed to give their time and properties and services for free in order to help the film get made here, and thus help get Symi some more positive publicity. Some volunteers have agreed to get themselves here and will make being part of a film-shoot part of the annual Symi holiday.

A quick catch up, running late

Well, I knew I was tired yesterday but I didn't expect to sleep for nine and a half hours. The blog is a little late getting online this morning, not that there is a set time or anything, but I already feel as if half the day has gone and it's only 8.30.

It's probably the heat making me tired as the temperature has been rising and the humidity going up with it in recent days. It is a very still morning and already I can feel the heat of the day. Yesterday was around 35 degrees I'd say, and not the kind of temperature in which to celebrate the arrival of a new vacuum cleaner.

You may remember the debacle of trying to find a certain kind of machine a few weeks back, well, he finally arrived at the house and yesterday I put it all together and gave the old floors a going over. We had to get a 'James' of course. The Alarm Cat was interested to know what this little yellow round thing was and gave him a close examination. I spent a good half hour hoovering up cat fur from all manner of places as it gets everywhere, and then decided I might as well pick it up at source, which Jack rather enjoyed. I dare say that had he been able to hear the machine he wouldn't have been so keen on being hoovered.

And so, on to the weekend. A visit to Yialos this morning to collect a package from the book shop; either a new office chair or a set of calendars for the shop. And then another quiet night in followed by Neil's photo walk tomorrow morning. And then the highlight of this weekend, Sam's 10th birthday party at The Olive Tree in the evening. We have our invitation and now only need to find something suitable to wear and we are all set.

Next week sees the celebrations of the 100th anniversary of a record breaking dive by Stathis Hadzis with events in Yialos, including dancing in the square on Tuesday night, so I am told.

Kali-Monday from sunny Symi!

What a great weekend that was! Not only a lunch in Yialos on Saturday, but a birthday party last night at the Olive Tree.

Back to Saturday. After spending some time working on the stage version of 'Shocking the donkeys' I nipped down to the shop to cover for Neil while he went and delivered a photo job around the corner. We then headed down to Yialos as a package was waiting for us at a courier's office and we were expecting both a stock of new Symi calendars and an office chair, which was potentially heavy. It turned out to be only the calendars so that was nice and light. Neil conducted more photo business by phone outside of St John's Church while I waited in the shade, and then it was time for a decision. A quick beer at Pacho's while we made up our minds where to have lunch. Or not?

Time just watching the world go by, as you can do for hours in Yialos, and watching the boats come and go while sipping a cold beer is no time wasted at all…

Lunch, a walk around the harbour, back to the village, a quiet evening at home, a really good night's sleep and Sunday working on my script with the balcony doors open, the church bells ringing and the cat sleeping in the shade, Neil guiding a photo walk to Pedi, stopping for a beer on the jetty afterwards, then home for salad lunch (standard summer fare at our house). A perfect Sunday morning.

Symi's record breaking dive with a "kampanelopetra"

In the celebration of Stathis Hadzis and his record breaking free dive, today sees the reopening of the Nautical Museum in Yialos. Neil has been asked to go down and photograph this historic occasion so he has his work cut out for him today.

If you were wondering what "kampanelopetra" was, is or are, it is the flat, round stone that the 'naked', or free, divers used to use. The technique was pretty simply, though I'd not like to try it. The diver would be attached to the boat by a rope, he would dive in, holding his breath, with his bag, knife and kampanelopetra (also attached to the boat by a rope) and the weight of the stone would pull him down. Once at the right depth he would collect the sponges, put them in his net and then, when ready to resurface, would let go the Καμπανελοπετρα and swim/float back up to the boat. The 'bell stone', as the rock is known in English, would be pulled back up afterwards. You can see some of them at the museums on Symi.

So, that's Neil off photographing this morning's event, and possibly even staying for the memorial dive, with stone, but probably not taking his underwater camera. I'll have some photos of that on the blog before long.

We had a quiet but very pleasant wine night last night and Neil has a few people booked on to his morning walk tomorrow. On Sunday we went to Sam's 10th birthday party, before calling in to Astrid's party on the way home.

Yesterday the Alarm Cat was malfunctioning and I'm hoping it doesn't lead to complications. After his (first) breakfast of the day he started having trouble with his mouth, like something had become caught in it. Breakfast was, as usual, some very expensive sachet of alleged tuna, beef, or chicken, in sauce, so there should have been no bones to get caught up in his throat. I reckon he had a blade of grass or something stuck at the back of his mouth, and into his throat. Poor old chap was trying to get it out by heaving and then sticking his claw into his mouth. He had calmed a bit by the evening and this morning he seemed fine; charging in off the roof, straight to his table, didn't even put on his linen napkin before diving in to something that's apparently genuine rabbit. So, hopefully he is fine again; we'll keep a watch and see as the last time his happened he went and got an abscess on a tooth.

Nautical museum reopens, a petition to the town hall

Neil was at the reopening of the Symi Nautical Museum yesterday, followed by the demonstration of free diving which was held around the headland on Nos beach.

Looking through some of his photos, it looks like many people attended the blessing and the opening, and it looks like the museum is now housing many interesting artefacts, photos and items from the history of Symi's sponge diving. In the evening there was dancing and food in the town square.

While up in the village I was tied up for most of the day in discussions about the film project, but I did manage to pick up on this piece of local news: A petition is being organised to ask the town hall to do something about the many ruins in which, over the years, rubbish has been dumped. It is asking the powers that be to clean up the ruins and make them in some way inaccessible to the lazy people who throw their rubbish there rather than take it to the skip or bins. "We call on the members of the Town Council to take appropriate action in accordance with the law and their conscience to relieve the Chorio area of Symi from this Third World type of situation and regain the reputation it is worthy of." Says part of the petition.

Some work has already been done on this, in the area around Alamina Square (near Ag Athanasios) but the problem still persists in other areas.

Dancing the 'Michanikos'

It was a cooler day yesterday thanks to some stray cloud that had wandered in from somewhere. It looks like it's now wandered out again and passed by, and already the day feels July hot.

Part of the celebrations of the 100th anniversary of a record braking dive by Stathis Hadzis was a performance of 'Michanikos', the 'sponge diver's dance' which is often danced on Symi (and Kalymnos, the other sponge diving island).

The dance tells a story of a proud, handsome and able bodied man who goes to sea, dives and later becomes crippled after suffering 'the bends.' Originally divers used the 'naked diving' method, which is what the demonstration of diving showed us the other morning; we would call it 'free diving' now. These days it is a sport, in the sponge fishing days it was work, a means of staying under water by holding the breath. Because of this held breath, there was no danger of the 'bends' on the way up. Then the Skafandro came into use; what we would now call a 'traditional' diving suit. Divers were able to stay under for longer, harvest more sponges, go deeper… but were not aware of decompression sickness, 'the bends', or its causes and effects. Many divers became crippled because of this, many died. It became known as the diver's disease. The dance, the 'Michanikos' tells that story in dance.

There is a description of the dance in Faith Warn's book 'Bitter Sea.' This book tells 'the real story of Greek sponge diving' and is a fascinating read.

Water pumps, a Symi tradition

The end of this week has become quieter, following a slightly busy early half of the week where Neil was out and about doing his work; photographing the diving events and church repairs for the 'Archaeologia' while also keeping the shop open, hosting the wine night and doing the usual day to day. I've been working on new writing projects, doing my own usual day to day, being at the shop, and keeping an eye on the Alarm Cat (seems fine now after his minor ailment the other day).

Yesterday was the feast day of St. Emilianos as there was a festival at the famous church around on the west side of Symi. It's now 7.15 and the church bells are ringing out loud and strong for the festivals of DIAS (Dias, Zeus), GARYFALLIA (Garyfallia) and MAKRINA (Makrena), according to my list of Greek name days.

I've got another quiet but productive day planned: working on a new story, catching up on film project emails and news, and pumping up the water pump which is once again low on air. The pump draws water up from the sterna below the sitting room and directs it into the pipes which then run across the flat roof right to the back of the house where they either drop into the kitchen or turn back on themselves to the bathroom. It's got something to do with a vacuum (not the new one, 'James') and a red metal chamber that sits beneath the actual pump. That chamber has air in it.

Only, at the moment, it doesn't, so when you turn the water on the pump runs continuously. It's only meant to run for a while, once the pressure has dropped, and while the pressure rebuilds. The lower the pressure the more it runs, in the case of our pump and thus the quicker the thing will wear out. So, about once every six months there's a procedure to follow. The last couple of times Ian has done it with great success as our foot pump leaks, which means you're pumping in air at a rate of two steps forward and one back out. But I'm going to borrow his foot pump and do it myself later this morning. This involves:

Turning off the pump from the house fuse box. Opening a tap and draining off all water from the pipes. (Into a big bowl for use later on, so it's not wasted.) Heading up onto the roof with the foot pump, attaching it to the red chamber and pumping a bit of air in to help flush the last water from the pipes. Going back downstairs and inside to check the flow of draining water as I am doing this on my own and there's no one to tell me when the tap stops dripping. Waiting for that to finish. Remembering which way is 'off' for the taps and turning the tap off even though there is nothing coming out of it. Heading back up on the roof, attaching the pump and, in the full glare of the mid-morning sun, pumping the air into the chamber for a minute or two (about 60 pumps by foot) and blocking out visions of the chamber exploding under the pressure and embedding my leg with shrapnel. Unattaching the pump, going back downstairs and throwing the switch back on. Listening to the pump start up (and waiting for it to stop when it's reached pressure) and making sure we still have water. It usually works fine.

If not, I go and find Ian.

A little syncopated in the village on a Friday

I spent some time out in the village last night, trying out a little syncopation. It went down very well.

I'd been at home doing some work on the stage version of 'Shocking the donkeys' when Neil sent a message suggesting a beer, as we'd not really been out all week. Well, apart from Wednesday when we'd popped to the Sunrise Café for a glass of wine and a sausage sandwich. So, having reached a point in the script where I needed to stop and plan how I am to rewrite, it sounded like a good idea. I'm getting towards the end of the story which, in the film version, involves our ancient heroin racing to save the day on a motor bike and then a jet ski, and requires at least two of the cast to dive in the sea, a boat, a helicopter and a large crowd. Drury Lane could probably cater for it but not your average house.

So, I headed down to the square and sat chatting to Lyndon, then Peter, then Justine for a while, and watched the tables and chairs of both kafeneion fill up. Neil arrived and we headed off to the Sunrise again at around nine, just as Nondas and Lefteris were starting their music at the taverna.

You never know what's going to happen around here, especially at the Sunrise, and so it was we ended up having a conversation with Amanda in the UK via a ladle in the courtyard. Apparently, putting the phone in the ladle aids reception (something like a satellite dish effect perhaps).

That done, and another (highly recommended) sausage sandwich devoured out of sheer gluttony, and it was off home again. But with one quick stop at Lefteris' kafeneion at the invitation of Allun & Andy, for a catch up chat and that last glass of wine. The syncopation was really starting to show so we just had the one, and then headed home to sleep in the 30 degrees of the bedroom. The fan is going all night every night at the moment. It was 37 degrees on the terrace in the shade yesterday.

And today has dawned remarkably bright and early and uncluttered by the wine. I am still faced with what to do about my jet ski and moped riding yaya, but no doubt, when I wake up, something will come to mind.

(Syncopation. n.) Syncopation, my music teacher David Purvis used to tell me was 'An irregular movement from bar to bar.'

Happy Monday from Symi

I don't think I did any of the things I'd planned to do this weekend just past; things just kept getting in the way and plans just kept changing.

A quick trip into Yialos to take care of a bit of business turned into a long lunch, which kind of threw the rest of the day out of kilter. While we were down there and passing by the Alegrito Café, Neil was called in to do a quick photo job. Actually, he was called in with a 'take a photo of us for your blog' request, which of course he did, quite happily.

Yesterday was the photo walk to Pedi which went down very well again, everyone enjoyed themselves, I am told. And tonight is our wine night, so we're looking forward to that. The portrait layout version of 'Carry on up the Kali Strata' is now out and there are some copies in the shop. This is a new edition, with a change of layout but with all the same text, and about 90% of the photos there were a couple that wouldn't fit, but you'd hardly notice. The next one I am going to get into the shop is 'Jason and the Sargonauts' we've not had copies there for some time, but now there is a new edition of this as well, via Amazon, and a new kindle version too.

Wine night on the steps of the Kali Strata

It was something of a long day yesterday, starting at 6.00 a.m. (for me) and finishing at around 11.30 pm.

Not that very much happened for me during the day, apart from managing to get some more work done on the stage version of 'Shocking the donkeys.' The first draft of this is nearly complete, then I can go back through it and cut down the number of characters as, so far, there are about 30, which is a lot for stage, though fine for film.

I also had an email yesterday asking if I could write some songs for a new children's theatre show that's in the planning for 2014/15, over in the UK, which was flattering to receive. So, talks have opened up in that department. There were also emails in about The Judas Curse which, apparently has already started to attract attention from the British press due to the lead actor; but I've not seen that in detail yet and am still unsure of what's happening at the moment.

Most of our work yesterday happened at the wine night which was surprisingly busy for July, with around 35 to 40 people stopping by at some point between 6pm and 9.45 pm when we finally closed. It was a great evening, we nearly sold out of Dominic Ranger's book 'Midas', which will be the second time we've sold out, and the bookshop in the harbour keeps running out as well. It's turning out to be a very popular read, and rightly so. More books will be ordered. Cards, calendars and limited edition photos also went well, and we met and chatted with many friends both old and new.

Afterwards it was good to see many of the wine night 'cast' had settled in at the tavernas, the Windmill and the two kafeneion in the square. We stopped 'for one' (as I'd not actually had more than one glass of wine at the wine night, bravo me) at Astrid's bar on the way home, had a chat, and were just thinking of leaving when the rest of the wine night cast came in, in twos and threes, and before we knew it, it was half eleven and one had become three;

so, straight home, no nightcap but water, and straight to bed in order to be up and fresh at 6.30 again (well, 7.30 actually, a bit of a lie in today).

And on to Tuesday with nothing planned apart from more work, writing, and watering the garden. It looks like it's going to be still, and hot again, and I've just received a wad of emails about all kinds of interesting things, one of which states: "[the actor down to pay the lead in The Judas Curse] had an urgent message from Ridley Scott telling him not to shave off his beard." Why I should need to know this I have no idea, but it's all rather fascinating; apparently there's a new film being planned called 'Vatican' and our leading man is up for a part in it; if he gets it, it won't interfere with our film project – if the project goes ahead.

Writing projects, Shocking the donkeys & Dracula

I've finally finished the first draft of the stage play version of 'Shocking the Donkeys', if anyone is interested.

This, as you might know, started out as a screenplay and reached the stage of being developed with a potential director a couple of years ago, but then ran out of steam. Well, actually, ran out of money, and then producer. It's been sitting there for a while, had some interest from a few companies, but no one took it further despite radio interviews and press coverage, and its topic still being relevant now. So, I thought I'd re-vamp the story to fit the stage and see if any theatre companies might be interested in staging it. It will come with a built in publicity machine and publicist in the UK, and its theme is still very relevant. Particularly as the UK now allow same sex marriages, and yet Greece has not even addressed the issue of civil partnerships, let alone anything else and still takes a backwards stance on such things.

Meanwhile, the new Symi book is being worked on and should be in the shop for next season. This one is going to be a collection of blog posts from Symi Dream that will take us through a year in a life on Symi, with some photos. It's going to be interesting to see how it comes out and at one point, like, today, we're going to get to what I call the 'Dracula moment.'

OK, so you're wondering what I am on about. Well, Dracula (the original Stoker, not any of the not-as-good copies) is a story put together from journals and memos, letters and diaries, etc. As the story unfolds the characters realise that they can catch up on what's happened to each other by reading each other's journals. There comes a pretty surreal moment, about half way through the book, when you suddenly realise that the characters in the story that you are reading now know as much about the story as you do because they have just read the same pages as you have. In effect, they are reading the same book as you. I'm not sure if Stoker intended that, or realised he'd done it, but it has always struck me as being a great piece of plotting. This isn't quite the same thing perhaps but, if you are reading this in the book, then hello, and welcome to July 24th 2013 when I am writing about exactly what you are reading.[1]

And as for the other writing project, The Judas Curse. There is still no definite news on when the funding campaign will be launched (the producer's wife is currently in labour, so there's an understandable pause in proceedings), but I do know that a top name has been arranged for the lead, there is a website in the making and, as far as I know, we're still looking at October 16th for a start of shoot date on Symi. But it's not definite yet. I'll keep you posted.

Symi filming project: the countdown starts now

I am going to find the next week very difficult (and August extremely so).

It's going to be difficult because I have to keep a secret. "Can you know a thing and never tell it." (The DaVinci Code) No! Yes, I mean, of course I can, and I must. And it is all about the film that might get made on Symi in October, The Judas Curse.

I am co-writer, but my job now is more along the lines of production co-ordinator, but more about that later. The exciting news is that the company, 1066 Productions, have set a date for launching the Kickstarter campaign, and that date is July 31st.

From that date onward there will be four weeks during which time they must raise a certain amount of money through the Kickstarter scheme. It's called crowd funding. Basically: Individuals pledge certain amounts of money, on a sliding scale, and in return they receive a sliding scale of rewards, or 'perks' as they are called. *If* the target is reached (or even better, exceeded) then Kickstarter collects in the pledges and distributes the money to the company; the film gets made and everyone gets their rewards in due course. If the target is not reached, no money is collected at all and the company still has to pay Kickstarter for their services, and there is no film.

That will all be explained in full on the Kickstarter site when it is up. So, I will now be counting down to Launch Date while keeping secret the star names who have agreed to come to Symi for the filming. Here's a clue: One of the actresses "…..was famously caught in bed with Sam Neill by Superman star Henry Cavill….."

---

[1] And, incidentally, welcome also to December 10th 2013 when I am rereading this as part of the editing process.

If you work it out, please keep it to yourself! 1066 want to launch the campaign and official website at the same time as releasing the news to the press. Hence why I must keep secrets for the next week.

But I can tell you that we have already had some great offers of help from local Symi folk that are going to save money from the incredibly tight budget: free accommodation for some cast and crew to stay in, locations, translations, assistance to the crew and so on; but we still need more. I, in my role as Prod-Co, will have to find good accommodation for "…an actor and musician who numbers Coldplay and Snow Patrol among his fans…", at least one BAFTA nominee and a director whose latest film has just had a mainstream release in the USA. We will also have to transport them, feed them, and generally look after them for an intensive one week shoot.

Neil has been brought on board as the official shoot photographer, taking images for one of the 'perks' (more about that later too), and for any publicity shots that will be needed for print and online media, TV etc. He will also be acting as Assistant to the DoP, if needed – all for free of course, well, in return for a credit on the film and a listing on the IMDB for himself, as Assistant DoP is a creditable title.

So, more news will no doubt be leaked out by me when 1066 are not looking. We are all hoping for a successful campaign so that we can get Symi in the news, get those 'names' over here, get a brilliant film out there and get some more location tourists coming over to see, stay, spend and fall in love with where 'The Judas Curse' was made. And, the best bit, everyone reading this will be able to play a part in making that happen. Watch this space.

Shrimps a-coming, Русскиена Symi

Saturday morning and a whole weekend off, for me at least. Neil has the shop open today and has his photo walk on Sunday morning.

It's the Symi shrimp festival this weekend, 9pm in the village square, with free Symi shrimps for anyone who wants them, live music being played and dancing by the Symi Women's Association. (Funny how we say live music rather than just music. I very nearly wrote 'music being played and live dancing' which would not have sounded quite right.)

Yesterday we made one of our excursions to Yialos, to check the post office and the bank, and to buy Jack some special cat food as that's all he will eat at the moment. It's not that we mind, but he is becoming more and more fussy, and there's no point giving him stuff he won't eat and then seeing it left there tempting bugs.

We saw a few friends, Neil picked up a couple of jobs, so simply wandering around the harbour is time made use of, and we took a photo or two of the new moped hire shop 'Back Street Bikes' which is behind the smart looking new wine shop that is what was once the Harani club. The club has gone now, so no more late night dancing is to be had there; I did hear a vague rumour that another one was going to open up somewhere else, but I am not sure where.

Later, we had lunch at Xaris Taverna and watched the world go by. Tuna salad followed by some Symi lamb with lemon potatoes; very nice. Good view of the boats coming and going and people walking past, a good place to people-watch. It was interesting to hear so many local people now meeting and greeting in Russian, or some other acrylic language. There was a large party of Russians in the taverna, at one huge long table, all digging in to fish and shrimps and having a great time. I've noticed many day-rippers now from that part of the world, some make it up to Horio for a quick look at the church before dashing back to Yialos again; I wonder if they will come back next year and spend their whole holiday on Symi, that would be nice.

And then, after lunch, back to the village and an evening in, for me: Managed to watch Into the Woods, and Hairspray and, for some reason, some of the dances from Bombay Dreams. It was a bit of a musical end to a very nice Friday.

Ps. Yes I did mean to say acrylic, it was a gag. Kind of. However I didn't mean to say 'day-rippers' but left it in for you to find, I of course meant day-trappers. до свидания!

This could be an interesting week

I am doing one of those 'getting ahead of myself' things today, as it is actually Sunday morning as I write this. I've done all the housework, Neil is out on a photo walk with guests, and I have an hour to spare before making lunch.

Also, as tonight is not only the Symi Shrimp Festival, but also Tina's birthday pizza bash, Monday morning may not be the best time to be trying to string words together. Sunday, around midday, with the fan on, the balcony doors open, the cat asleep under the dining table and a calm sea in the distance seems like a better option.

Meanwhile: the usual Symi summer continues with work at the shop, returning visitors, dinner at Taverna Zoi last night as a treat, and a baptism to film and photograph in Panormitis next Sunday. Editing that will keep me busy for a couple of days afterwards.

But my other news is that I have, finally, finished the stage play version of the story 'Shocking the donkeys.' It is currently on its way to one theatre company in England, and may be on its way to a couple more before long. First come first served.

So, here comes another week, another wine night tonight, perhaps the launch of a Symi film project, and a week of Symi sun as we head towards August.

Symi Shrimp festival, and a catch up

So, today really is Tuesday, as I write, and I can catch up on what happened after I wrote Monday's blog on Sunday.

In the evening we were invited to a party at the Olive Tree, Tina's birthday, where, along with a homemade salad, pizza was on the menu; delivered from the Dolphin pizzeria in Yialos. These were followed by a banoffe pie with a candle in it. And that was followed by a visit to the Symi shrimp festival. Unfortunately Neil had to miss that as he hadn't been feeling too good all day and so went home early, and slept for 14 hours. He was feeling a bit better yesterday evening when we held the usual wine night at the shop, but still had an early night, and so far today is still in bed. Mind you, it is 6.47 so that's probably where most people are.

The festival was very well attended, probably the most amount of people I've seen there in many years. All the chairs were full, there were lots of people standing and both kafeneion were also full as I passed by at around 9.45 in the evening. So that was good to see and made a right old change from how quiet the square and steps have been on most other evenings during the week, but then it is late July, nearly August and things tend to be quieter at this time of the season, picking up again later on. We hope.

News on the film is that the process to get the fund-raising appeal ready has started, with the director and producer filming pieces to camera, the editor starting on putting clips together and the administrator starting the online process: registering the company on Kickstarter, filling out the forms. They are still on target for having it ready by Thursday, but then the online company will probably take a couple of days to check over everything before making the appeal live.

The end of July

The end of July already, and August tomorrow. Already! It's 6.40 and the air is still, the sea calm, a slight haze hangs in front of the Turkish coast, and the only sounds are the early birds, my keyboard keys and a neighbour's first-thing cough. I pause to chase a mosquito around, and a moped comes down the hill behind me, outside, and a long way off.

I saw the first of the 'Kickstarter' appeal video 'rushes' last night; the first clip of the director being interviewed and talking about the story. It was very strange to watch someone I've never met talking in depth about a story and characters I have created, owning them and enthusing about the themes and ideas. I then went to the site and into the 'backstage members' area where I could see the page that is being built up, the page that was due to be online today/tomorrow. (It won't be, not just yet.) It's coming together very well, and shouldn't be long now. Again, strange to see faces and biographies of cast and crew and knowing that they may well be over here, on Symi, in ten weeks or so, if we can pull in a small (for a film) amount of investment and donation. All rather surreal really. Let's just hope it happens.

Meanwhile, don't forget to keep hitting the Judas Curse trailer as the more hits that has before the campaign launch the better. It's on 2,276 as I write this; I wonder how much we can boost that by in the next 24 hours. Just a click, won't cost you anything, but will give the project more credence to anyone who sees the campaign page, when launched.

Enough about the film project for now though (I just wish I could give you the full details, it's a hard secret to hold on to, especially from you!) What does today hold in store? Well, who knows? That's half the fun isn't it? I know what I intend to do. (Pauses to chase another mosquito.) Some writing on a new story. Meanwhile, now the 'Donkeys' play is written and the possible film is out of my hands, I have time for something else; and it's got nothing to do with Symi!

August

A month of festivals, celebrations, birthdays, dancing and stars of the silver screen

Work starts on a new Symi medical clinic

This from Rhodes Report yesterday:

"Today the excavations for the new Multipurpose Clinic of Simi started. The new clinic will function like a hospital in the village of Horio, Symi (parish of Agios Eleftherios), and will be 800sq.m.in area. The project has a budget of €1,100,000. The feasibility study was done by the Municipality of Symi in collaboration with the Region of Southern Aegean and the project is funded by the NSRF. Estimated time for completion of the project: May 2014."

That was my understanding, roughly, from a translation. I noticed that our village doctor had mentioned this on Facebook yesterday, which is how I found the news. As I understand it this is being built near the current clinic, and car park in Horio. I'm not sure if it will replace the Yialos clinic and/or the current Horio one though, but hopefully it's all good news. Let's hope it gets finished. Not being funny but the sports centre…?

And on another note:

"Dear Neil. Morten and I have now returned to Denmark after the most wonderful 3 weeks on Symi. We didn't get the opportunity to say a proper goodbye to you and James, and especially thank you for the inspiring Photowalks and your kindness! Looking forward to see you and Symi again at Easter."

Exactly the kind of message we like to get at Symi Dream and share with everyone who reads the blog. Keep those messages of support for Symi coming in folks; we need all the good publicity the island can get, we need more visitors, we need more day-trippers who come for a day out of curiosity, and then come back to stay for a week, and then come back to stay for two and then before they know it are addicted and come and stay for a month. We need tourists, the lifeblood of the island, and the country. And we need to do all we can to publicise Symi (and Greece) in the best light possible. Down with negative thought I say, and up with creativity, good ideas and creative ways to bring people to the island.

And rather pleasant day it was too, in the hairdryer

It's certainly doing that warm thing to start off August here on Symi. But there was a breeze around last night which raced through and around the house slamming doors and rattling shutters. It was a bit like sitting in front of a big hair dryer.

I have to say I had a rather pleasant day yesterday. I was up reasonably early, and headed off down to Yialos at the same time as Neil went to open the shop; 8.50. I checked the post office (no Golden Girls series six as yet, but it's on its way), I won a little at the cash machine, enough to buy Jack some of the special cat food which is the only thing he is interested in eating these days; the expensive stuff from Taxas of course. He seems to know when I buy it from the 'American' (exactly the same stuff) as he doesn't like that. These days I have to actually walk to the harbour and back in order for him to eat.

After that I had a short wait for a shop to open so I had a cup of tea at Medeteraneo. Actually I had a pot of tea, more than two cups and for only €2.00, which I thought was a very good price. The new DVD machine was also a good price, from Spacephone Symi, and so small! I remember the first time I saw a 'Video player' at school back in 1832… or was it around 1973? A huge machine with great clunky buttons that were a joy to press, assuming you had the strength. And the first one I owned back in 1983-ish, where the remote control was connected to the machine by a cable. And even the DVD machine I am replacing now (it won't even play CDs), is twice the size of this new little box which fits on one of my (1980) Pioneer speakers. Incredible. Imagine if the same thing had happened to cars. You'd be able to fit three Toyotas on your dining table. You wouldn't be able to drive them of course…

I even enjoyed the walk back up though it was still early, not too hot and I stopped for a chat with Petros from Australia en route. The last time we'd seen each other was in 2011, in Botany Bay where he lives. Actually, he gave us a lift back into Sydney, so I last saw him in the Oxford Street area I believe. But we'll be seeing more of him during his stay as he's visiting his family who live next door to our shop.

Got the DVD machine working, tidied away the tape deck we never use and the Mini Disc player we never use, and plugged the DVD into the amp and TV so now we have BIG sound for the DVDs I borrowed from Ged (big thank you as always, such a generous chap!) and will be blasting Jenine and other neighbours away with Sherlock Holmes doo-dah of shadows and other films over the next few evenings.

And talking of films: still no launch date for the Kickstarter campaign, but it's almost there; the video was being edited yesterday, the 'perks' were being tweaked and the producer was in the hospital with one of the cast (his wife) having their second baby, so a bit of a reason not to be at work I guess. More news in due course.

What's all this ear then?

It's a warm morning and it's only early still, but we are in August of course. The fan has been going all night and I can hear the neighbour's air conditioning humming away as I sit with all doors and windows open trying to catch a non-existent breeze; at 06.43.

There are two baptisms happening this weekend that I know of, both at Panormitis. We're photographing the one that is tomorrow. Today, in an unrelated event later this evening, we have been invited for a middle-eastern curry which sounds very interesting. It's a 'bring a small desert' party so I thought I'd bring the Carcross desert, which covers only 240 hectares of the Yukon in Canada. I will also, of course, check my spell checker and take a dessert as well; I am making a lemon cheesecake this morning.

I'm not very with it due to a sleepless night, so I have no idea how the cheesecake will turn out. Apart from the heat, I've got this ear thing which plagues me off and on and has done for several years. Seems it's quite common and irritatingly untreatable. It's not tinnitus but it's a clicking sound, like a soprano Geiger counter with no sense of rhythm. It goes off 24/7 in the left ear and nothing seems to get rid of it apart from Sudafed. I have some on order (other similar things don't work) and have some anti-inflammables to take meanwhile, which help slightly. (I know, but it's what Neil calls them.) It's not so bad during the day as I am concentrating on other things and there are other sounds going on, but trying to get to sleep with something tap dancing badly in your head is a pain in the ears. So, not much sleep has been had over the last few nights. Hey ho.

And on to the weekend. What are you up to? I am planning a writing and cheesecake making session this morning, very little this afternoon and a curry tonight. Neil has a walk on tomorrow morning and we're off to film the baptism tomorrow evening. Somewhere in between I need to water the garden again. Things are getting very dry now (there have been forest fires on Rhodes and in other places) and I must also get the housework done. It's so much easier now we have James the vacuum cleaner, but still not too much of a joy in 40 degrees plus.

Two days later:

We had a quiet but very pleasant wine night last night after spending the day working on the baptism photos and video. Neil also had a family portrait session yesterday and had those images to process.

In local news: although there is no Symi Festival as such this year, some local events are being organised. There is a dance show on the main stage in Yialos on Wednesday, around 21:00, with children from the modern dance school. And there is traditional island dancing on the same stage on Sunday, again around 21:00 as far as I know. I will let you know if that changes. Hopefully we will be there to get some photos, and perhaps have a pizza as well.

Another hot day looks to be on the cards, last night's welcome wind has died down and the day is starting with a light sweat settling in from the south…

Festival at Megalis Sotiris

We have just had the name day of Sotiris, and the annual Festival at the church of Megalis Sotiris, up in the middle of the island. Here is a post worth repeating, it is from 2011.

Last night, as I sat in the back of a flat-bed truck watching the Milky Way and bouncing over the mountain roads, I reflected on how wonderful it is when there are no barriers.

I don't mean the crash barriers at the side of the road, I'm always grateful for those when being driven across Symi at 12.30 in the morning (no offence to Ian's driving which is always safe), I mean cultural barriers.

We went to the festival at Megalis Sotiris last night, but we didn't go alone. The Olive Tree Charabanc had been mobilised, and fifteen of us set off in the truck at nine in the evening. English, Italian, Welsh and Irish alike, all heading for the same place as were several hundred other people on mopeds, in cars and on foot.

The church courtyard was already thronged when we arrived, the band had started playing and was still going strong three hours later when we left, and the air was already heady with the smell of barbequed fish. Our party headed straight for the small church to donate, light a candle and, in my case, have a quick think about the ancestors. Today is the feast day of Sotiris, and is also the Transfiguration, and you can see the event (if that's the right word) depicted in the icons in the church.

Outside, it was then time to mingle and chat, with many a 'yasou' and 'yasas' and 'welcome' and 'good to see you' and time to try and find a seat. Actually such events are a mix of standing and sitting, and dancing and it wasn't long before the dancing started. The mayor was handing out beers at the fridge, the plates of fish and bread were being passed around, and the children had a great time charging about, crashing into each other and then sitting and eating.

And what really came across last night, as it always does when we attend these cultural events, was how welcome everyone is. It makes you realise that there simply is no 'us and them' unless you chose to invent it. Resident or visitor, islander or off-islander, Symiot or not, Greek or non-Greek, local born or ex-pat, it actually does not matter; and not just on a special night like last night. Whether people knew us or not, and many did - other business owners from the village, neighbours, friends we meet at church on name days - we were made to feel welcome, as were the many other visitors and holiday makers who came to the festival.

The night carried on, more people arrived, the children started fighting sleep, some of our party joined in the island Sousta (which came around with alarming regularity, a guaranteed way of getting everyone up and on the floor), and later Neil and Gerrie leapt up for a tango. Several couples took the floor for this number and George II (the younger butcher) applauded wildly, having just led one or two very long and complicated dances himself.

Midnight came and we went, we had work in the morning and small children to get to bed. Up there in the middle of the island, with very little by way of light, the stars were magnificent. The Milky Way streaked right across the sky and guided us home through warm air and the scent of herbs. The coast of Turkey twinkled across the sea, and the village glittered below us as we came back down the mountain and were dropped off back where we started. And the best bit? Somehow these events draw into focus a fact that is easily overlooked: You don't have to go out of your way to feel part of the community you live in. You're in it every day.

Symi modern dance school and 'nearly there' news

And this means, all being well, the actual campaign to raise the funds to make this film on Symi should (might) be live by tonight. I will let you know when it is. If that's the case then we could be looking at the cut-off date being 7th September, a day before Neil's birthday. Wouldn't it be great to have something extra to celebrate on the 8th September (apart from Neil, Justine and Claudia's birthdays)?

Meanwhile: yesterday was a bit of a busy day for us both. Neil had his photo walk which took up most of his morning and which was very well received, I was at home writing and working on a script, as you can imagine. I came back for some more catching up in the evening and then, at eight, we headed down to Yialos of the dance show presented by Σύγχρονων χορών της Ειρήνης Μυλωνάκη, Irini Milonaki's dance school. There were 25 dances in total, with children and adults taking part. The town square was soon full of spectators who were treated to a wonderful evening under the hot stage lights on a hot August night.

The harbour was crowded with boats and yachts, the streets were pulsing with people, I've not seen it so busy in a long time. Mind you, I've not been down in Yialos after dark for a few weeks. We had dinner at the Dolphin and very nice it was too, and getting busy (people came up to me to wish me luck with The Judas Curse, which was a bit surreal), and then we watched the show and took some photos. Then, to top it all off, we walked back up the Kataraktis, which is no mean feat at any time of day or night; although it's less distance from the square to our house, it's probably a slower route.

More dancing on Sunday

There is another dance show on Sunday. These will be traditional Greek dances from various places in the country and will be performed by the Women's Association of Symi.

I was chatting to Justine yesterday; she is the Olympic Holidays rep and also takes part in the dance group. I couldn't help but take my hat off to her, even though I wasn't wearing one. She was on the 7.00 a.m. boat on Wednesday taking guests across to Rhodes to meet their flights, spent a day at the airport and harbour, came back with her new guests and settled them in, and finished work around nine in the evening. As if that day wasn't long enough she then spent Thursday meeting and seeing guests, having welcome meetings and catching up on paperwork before heading back to the harbour for a dance rehearsal. I also know that she has a couple of other very long days during the week and only manages, at the most, one day off per week. I just thought we should raise a hat to the holiday reps who work so hard to make visitors' time on the island so perfect. So perfect that they come back year after year.

And of course, it's not just Olympic Holidays and their rep who work this hard. My hat is off and on and off again to all reps who put in the hours. I know they don't get paid nearly half enough for what they do, particularly in the heat of August.

And this August also saw the end of Ramadan, on Wednesday night, which is why, apparently, there were something like 50 boats that could not get a parking space in Yialos the other night. Many people coming across from Turkey to celebrate the end of Ramadan, so I was told. The harbour was absolutely heaving on Wednesday and again last night. Great news for Yialos. If they could just send 10% of those visitors up to the village then every bar and taverna up here would be full as well.

It's finally time to launch the Symi film project campaign

Well, there we go. The Kickstarter campaign for The Judas Curse film project has been launched. We only need to raise £19,700 in order to hit the target. If we go over that then fabulous! If we can get more than we will be able to pay some of the volunteers who have already stepped up to offer time and skills, we could employ more local people on the project, we can ensure greater distribution and so on.

I thought back to when this project started and the earliest dated file I can find in my records is from April 2012, so that's about 17 months I've been working on this story. We're very close to making it happen; we just need the promise of donations from the public in return for the perks. The good thing about this system is: if the film gets made, any return from it, from DVDs, VOD, Cinema releases etc., will go straight back into making other films, and won't go to any fat-cat producers. 1066 are very keen to use Symi as a location for more films and they've not even been here yet. Imagine what could happen when they, like us, fall in love with the island.

First weekend's fund raising on target

Stats in from the production office: "The total now stands at £1,265 which is 6% funded, and only £48 short of our target for the first two days." A long way to go but still 27 days to go.

I spent most of the weekend in re-write mode, as we are aiming to 'lock down' the script by the end of the month. That means me coming up with a final draft based on notes and ideas from all concerned. This is then given to the director who will map it out in his own visual language, putting on paper what he sees in his mind's eye. This will then be used by his art department to draw up a storyboard, so that each scene is broken down into shots, and each shot is agreed by him and his director of photography well in advance. This in turn will mean that when filming starts, there is little time wasted; as we won't have very much time.

Neil spent the weekend at work too, with his usual Saturday hours at the shop and his usual Sunday morning photo walk to Pedi, and back. Yesterday evening he was in Yialos photographing the traditional Greek dances in the main square. This was due to start at nine in the evening by which time I was more or less ready for bed; I think I lasted until 9.45 and then had to give in to sleep. Today also looks like being a busy day; he has to go and collect a delivery from the courier who is half way to Nimborio, sort out a couple of things in Yialos once the shops open, order the wine for tonight's wine night, process the images from yesterday and host the wine night tonight. I have to carry on rewriting and also finish the baptism video from last week ahead of another baptism to video this weekend.

Oh yes, it's all quiet and peaceful on his laid-back Greek island today.

Day four; Symi wine night, Symi dancing, concerts…

Neil was up and down the Kali Strata again yesterday collecting deliveries from couriers; a photo order we'd made, things for the shop etc. Strange thing is, there were two parts to one delivery, from the same company, by the same supplier and through the same courier; one part ended up half way to Nimborio at the car repair shop and the other part ended up in Yialos at the motorbike hire shop. Seems ironic that both went to businesses with vehicular interests and yet neither could deliver to the village. Also seems a bit odd that two places share the same courier service; I think there was an error somewhere. But the things finally arrived, on good old fashioned shanks' pony, and all is right in the state of Symi Dream once more.

I spent a couple of hours at the shop, before the wine night, finishing off last' week's baptism DVD, in preparation for this weekend's baptism filming and photographing. The wine night went well, and was well attended; thank you to all our visitors for coming.

From September 9th this year we are going to be hosting an exhibition of photography by island resident Ged Horton, and so our gallery is currently empty while we get things ready. Everything that was on show is now in the shop, and outside on the walls of an evening, so our own work is still there to see. There will be a gala opening (wine night) on September 9th so make sure that is in your diary.

Last night there was, as I understand it, a radio roadshow and band on in Yialos, by way of entertainment. Not officially part of any Symi Festival 2013 as, again as far as I know (and news doesn't always reach the village, it's a bit like door to door delivery services in that respect) there is no Symi Festival 2013 this year; not officially at least.

The image of dancing today is just one of Neil's from Sunday evening's 'Traditional dances from Greece' performance. Dancing are Thanos Zanis and Thoderis Lerias. Very impressive.

And talking of impressive, I see I have been sent some casting information for the film; there are three main roles still to fill and, it seems, a great deal of interest in all of them. Although I have only today in which to finish my last draft of the script, I am still interested to see some of the names I might actually be writing for, so I'll get on and have a browse through before settling down to work.

In other Symi news… Well. I have spent the last four days at the desk, getting the final draft tidied up for the director, Neil has been busy in the shop, outside has been hot and very dry, some places have been very busy while others have been quiet. It's a real mixed August as far as I can see, but then I haven't been seeing very far!

I think though that I am now going to be able to slow down a bit, which is good news in this heat. My new Xbox game is still sitting there un-played, so that might get an airing tonight. I've got a baptism to film on Saturday evening in the village, so that will keep me busy on Sunday; Neil might have a photo walk this morning; Ged is preparing his exhibition for the gallery for early next month and the sun is coming up over a flat, silver sea, with and orange sky promising more high temperatures and fine, hot weather.

Now, if a gentle breeze would just blow in from the balcony, and if a few more generous souls called in to make a pledge (in any currency), the day 'would be complete for me', as Tom Lehrer would say.

Symi Animal Welfare Update

"The summer heat-wave continues when the evening lows don't offer much respite either; as the sun begins to go down from around 8pm, the cats decide to venture out from daytime shady sleeping-places found during the hottest hours. The hunt for food is left until evening and street cats congregate at traditional feeding-places, part of their daily routine - but during this meltdown period, rubbish skips are emptied very regularly for obvious reasons; as the desire to eat is much less, the street cats sit around at the bins anyway, relaxing in the slightly cooler conditions, without much interest in any new food-scraps delivered. Those of you who have already visited the island recently will have noticed how thin many of the street cats are, be assured that this is 'normal' during high summer. Even house-cats have reduced appetites. Drinking however is essential for survival, so please can we ask you to leave and top-up a plastic container of water, in a safe, shaded location where you've noticed that cats are. Insects & lizards are attracted to the water too, so don't be surprised if the old ice-cream container becomes your personally donated Symi oasis! Many of the owners of rental properties don't want cats on the premises, because not all guests like our feline friends unfortunately, but a suitable place for a water container can be found easily enough nearby.

Sadly, some sad news – Mickey passed away last week, he had not been well for a long time. His presence around the harbour area will be missed and our thoughts are with Pat who will miss him so very much.

Delphi continues to be fit & fully recovered, she is as gentle & sweet as ever after a frightening attack of Tic-fever.

The collection box at the Sunrise has been emptied mid-season - donations and monies received for animal medications totalled over 300 Euros, thank you for your support.

At the end of October, we plan to start up our veterinary programme once again, dependent on the boat situation of course. The system seemed to work last winter when we took 28 cats to Rhodes for treatment and/or neutering."

Melanie

August 15th on Symi, Panagia and pledges

Here's my quirky offer to you all for this week. It's Friday tomorrow so I'd like to combine Friday 13th with The Omen and call tomorrow 666 Friday. Whoever pledges £666 to the campaign tomorrow will get (on top of all the other perks) a special surprise from me personally. No, I won't be abseiling in through your window when you least expect it, I have something even better in mind. You remember the teaser-trailer we made? Well, what was used was only one minute out of about 30 minutes of Symi footage, including out-takes; I'll make you up a personal DVD of all that in return for your pledge. Or pledges; get two, three or four of your friends together and make individual pledges that add up to £666 (or more) as a group, and I'll make you up a DVD each; just for you and no one else.

I'll leave you to think on that one while I tell you that it's busy in Yialos! Whereas the village is not so cramped and crowded, the harbour is doing its usual, good, August business. I am not sure if all business owners would agree, I've not spoken to them all, but it's certainly the time of year for French, Greek and Italian visitors to be filling the tavernas and bars of an evening down in the harbour.

Many are here for today's celebration of the Panagia of Mary and the village churches were alight last night, the evening service rang out across the village and there were even fireworks from the Castro for a while. Today the many churches on Symi with a dedication to Mary will be alive with service, and some shops may even be shut as it's a bank holiday.

666 Friday for the Symi project; join the crowd

The Symi film project crowd-funding total is at 19% today, that's £3,776 with 23 days left to go. Not sure if that's on target or not, it would be great to end the first week at £5,000.

This in from the production office yesterday, before we hit 19%:

"80.13% of the total raised so far has come directly through people arriving from the Symi Dream website. So by far the biggest constituent of backers so

far are those reading your blog. Four backers (total £195) have come from Facebook. Three backers (£65 between them) from the widget, which is probably the one displayed on Symi Dream but could also be from other sites now carrying it. Three are direct traffic (people who had the link and just clicked, probably in an email) – that's £120. Three arrived after searching and finding it on Kickstarter itself (£135). And two people, each donating £50, came to us through Kicktraq."

Meanwhile, life races by here on the rock. The harbour continues to be busy, especially of a night time, the village too, the afternoon in the square yesterday was also a fairly busy one when I was there, which is always good to see. Today I am charging batteries and checking tapes for another baptism we are photographing and videoing tomorrow evening. This is to be in a small church in the village which I've never been into before, so that's going to be interesting.

Neil has some people booked on his Sunday morning photo walk so he will be having a busy weekend, and we're planning to head down to Yialos later to check in with the accountant (keep calm and carry on) and then to find some of the gold-dust cat food that is more or less the only thing the Alarm Cat will eat these days. And then it will probably be back to the PC and the email list. Apologies in advance if you receive emails from me, or see Facebook posts from us, or even get fed up with reading about our film project over the next couple of weeks, but for us it is probably the most important thing that's happened since we moved here 11 years ago and we're very keen to make it happen.

New shops in Yialos, 'Spago', new shops in Horio too

There are quite a few new businesses either up and running, or about to be up and running, on Symi. So many that I think I am going to need a day in September with the camera and a notebook; I need to update symibest with several new shops. Like 'Spago' which has very recently opened at the side of the town square, beside Neraida Taverna.

There is work going on at three properties in the village alone. Opposite The Olive Tree, what was the Grande bar is now being done up to become a paint and fishing tackle shop store room; George who has the shop in St John's Square in Yialos is moving into this building. Further up the lane beside the Old Pharmacy the house is being done up, and I believe is going to be just a house. And further along still, by Taverna Zoi, the old cake shop that was then Kon's computer shop is going to become a School of English.

There is a new sign in the harbour as well. Only the other day we saw several people head towards the comedy prat-fall slipway to cool their feet; they all did a slip, slide and bottom-land complete with slide-whistle sound effect. Now the town council (or someone) has put up a helpful, though rather fun-spoiling, sign.

Now we are six

It was a very warm night on the steps last night, with no breeze to speak of and although the humidity was only around 45% or so I was told, it still felt pretty airless. It was the same during the night when I had to get up for a 'cold and flu' tablet; not the best time of year to catch a cold. I didn't really get back to sleep so have been up since very early o'clock today. I'll have to try and manage a mid-morning siesta or something, after all, I need to be fresh for the big party tonight. Party? What party?

Happy Birthday Harry! Six today. I remember when I was six I had a book called 'Now we are six' by A. A. Milne, so, for Harry, here's *the* poem for when you are six. See you at the party later!

Now We Are Six - A.A. Milne

When I was one I had just begun

When I was two I was nearly new

When I was three I was hardly me

When I was four I was not much more

When I was five I was just alive

But now I am six, I'm as clever as clever;

So I think I'll be six now for ever and ever.

The Symi Film Festival – a possibility?

The film project has been getting support in from all over the place recently.

These messages are from the Horror Mansion chat pages:

"Thanks for the tweet guys. I'm proud to be a backer of The Judas Curse and I wish you all the very best in achieving your target."

"Am loving the location shown in the concept trailer I watch lots of horror from around the world a big appeal is to get a glimpse of the different countries and cultures. I have just been looking at images of the Greek island of Symi & one thing that's for sure, if you get these films out they will have a very distinctive look."

And also, at the other end of the spectrum, we were sent a link to Skopelos News, with suggestions for sponsorship. So Greek islands and horror fans alike are following our progress.

Which brings me to the question a few people have been asking: why a horror film, and set on Symi? Yes, I know, you don't immediately think 'horror' when you see the island do you? The thing though is, in the world of low-budget, high popularity film making, the horror genre is the one that sells the most. So, we're much more likely to make a decent return on a horror film that we would be on a romantic comedy, a drama or even a thriller. Strange but true.

So the idea is: we make this film, we release it (I say 'we', I mean 1066, after filming my role is zilch), it starts to generate an income from the horror fan community, and that income is put back into a slate of more 15k films, and so the ball rolls on. The Judas Curse, if we get just 15k more in pledges, could be the start of many a new film, and one or more of those will be, in the future, made on Symi. Who knows where it may lead?

The Symi Film Festival? The Symi Film School? The Symi Scriptwriting School? The possibilities, dear friends, are endless.

Meanwhile: Harry's birthday party was great fun last night. I tried to get a snap of Harry but he was kind of on the move a bit for most of the time. As one guest commented, you don't need air conditioning when you have children and chocolate cake – the air around was kept constantly moving.

As of last night we were at 27% and the statistics show that over 70% of that has been pledged by Symi Dream readers. Fantastic! If we keep this up, and do a little more pushing we should be able to get to the target and get the film made in October. Keep spreading the news and the links.

Holby City could be coming to Symi, kind of

28% and rising as of last night, £5,670 with only 17 days to go.

The new book is based on a year in the life of the island, or a year of my life living on Symi. It was suggested to me by friends one wine night last year, I am being aided and abetted in the project by Neil, who is supplying photos and Allan who is editing it; though we are leaving in some of my classic typos just for fun. It is based on the blog; a year long diary based on blog posts. I've mentioned it before. So, when you get to read this entry in the book you can think to yourself: 'Oh, I read that on August 23rd last year. How odd.' I've still not got a title for it yet though, I am still waiting for that particular muse to flutter down and land.

Meanwhile: In the wonderful world of film-making;1066 have an announcement:

We promised you news this week of further principal cast members and we are delighted to announce the first of them.

Many of you will recognise Rebecca Grant as the actress who played series regular Daisha Anderson in 97 episodes of the Bafta award-winning BBC1 medical drama Holby City from 2008-2010. She has also been Shaheen in the second series of Prisoners' Wives, Dr Stamford in an episode of Emmerdale last year, and Dita in the BBC adaptation of Trollope's The Way We Live Now (2001). She has been in several other television series and films and has appeared in London West End productions such as One Flew Over the Cuckoo's Nest and Bombay Dreams.

Symi gets a mention in Neos Kosmos in Melbourne

Only a short blog today due to a combination of cold, hay fever, cat, sleepless nights and the after effects of an antihistamine tablet. Am late getting up, have script work to do, the Alarm Cat broke in through the bathroom window during the night and announced his triumphant arrival noisily several times, and on top of that we've got no hot water as there is a leak in the hot water tank. We've told the landlord and someone is supposed to be coming around today to take a look.

It's not going to be an easy job. The hot water tank in our house is in the kitchen, and I know it is leaking because there is water dripping down the wall, luckily it is only dripping and not gushing. This means the pump kicks in every hour or so, so we turn it off when we are not at home. But the tank is behind the wall; a false wall of wood that has been constructed in part of the kitchen for the sole purpose of concealing the tank, I guess. I reckon all that is going to have to come out for a new tank to go in, which will mean no kitchen for a length of time, and possibly no water. We shall see. It might be just a leak on a pipe or a joint; there's no way of knowing until a plumber comes and… well, takes a wall down.

Meanwhile: there's a breeze this morning and things feel fresher. Not as hot and clammy as it has been. I have no plans for the weekend apart from some tinkering on the script and trying to drum up some more pledges, taking a cold and flu tablet, trying to shake the thing off – it's been on all week – and then doing as little as possible.

Now Emmerdale could be coming to Symi

Waking up to 31% pledged today and I wonder if this will start to get more interesting now that the name of the leading man has been revealed.

Kurtis Stacey is best known for playing the heartthrob character Alex Moss in the British TV soap 'Emmerdale' since 2011.

Saturday was a great day, despite this head cold (which is still hanging around, I can't believe it!). We were invited to dinner by Yiannis Agapakis and Eleni Paramixalopoulou. (Eleni very kindly translated all the English press release for 1066 Productions, into Greek, in a very short space of time- hence the mentions in the Greek press.) A birthday surprise for Yiannis was held at Haritomeni taverna overlooking Yialos. As always, great food and a wonderful atmosphere. You must go and pay a visit when you are here, they now have a special top terrace with large table for groups, and probably one of the best dinner views on the island.

Afterwards we headed up to Astrid's for 'just the one' and passed by Giorgio's Tavernas where a party was in full swing. There was a birthday to celebrate and the music and dancing went on well into the night.

Sunday was a quieter day with Neil catching up on some work at the shop and Ian fitting a new light for him in the gallery, me working on film stuff at home and then us popping out for one (and it was just one) at the Sunrise Café before heading home, watching a film and heading to bed early for a long sleep… until sometime around dawn when a stuffed-up nose kept me awake. But enough about that!

We're still without hot water as we need to source a plumber. Like I said, we mentioned the leaking hot water tank to the landlord who simple smiled sympathetically, nodded his head and bought us a drink, so we're kind of on our own now. A friend can look at it next week, if we can manage with the slow leak, wasted water and no hot showers until then. (The last not so tricky at this time of year, but what is the leak doing to the walls?) But we may well ask Valantis or someone to come and have a look sooner.

Exclusive Symi Dream interview with Kurtis Stacey

There is a good buzz about the film project locally and further afield. There have been reports and discussions in Rhodes and other newspapers which are helping to spread the news. There was talk about the project at last night's wine night too (thanks for the pledge Lyndon).

And today we have an exclusive interview with Emmerdale star Kurtis Stacey who, if we hit our target, will be coming to Symi in October to take part in the film:

I first visited Greece many years ago with my parents. It was Corfu, though, so it was very touristy. I can't remember a lot, but I know I loved it. So, I am really looking forward to coming to Symi. The island looks beautiful and I think the location will be the biggest character in this movie because it just looks amazing.

I will one hundred per cent be taking in the whole Greek culture, food, dance etc. I like to take as much as I can from every experience and I'm really looking forward to this one.

The first thing that attracted me to The Judas Curse was the plot of the story which was very different and unusual, and as a huge horror movie fan it sounded exactly like something I would be interested in going to see myself. And then, as soon as I saw the location, I knew this movie was going to be interesting.

Although I was born in Liverpool and brought up there, I much prefer the countryside over cities. I don't like really busy places. I'm a big fan of stress-free places with interesting history and culture.

My advice to young people who believe their dream is out of their reach would be to see themselves as a business. The more time, money, and effort you invest in yourself and your dream then the more likely it is going to happen. And it will happen if you make it the most important thing in your life. I really believe in that. I always say, think about "what can you sacrifice now for what you can become" and basically focus most of your time and energy on your dream and it will happen. Oh, and work your butt off!!

If I was to become an inspiration to people I would like to represent the belief that good health and hard work will get you what you want, so I would like to inspire young people to focus more on their dreams and living a healthy lifestyle.

It's very hard to think of my happiest memory, but I know I am at my happiest when I am a on film or television set working. Acting is my fun and enjoyment. And I am just happy to be in the position I am, doing my dream job, which I owe to my family and close ones who believed in me and supported me.

Day 10 of the summer cold, day 19 of pledges

34% today from a total of 92 backers – a real crowd is building, and these include some pledges made by people who came straight from reading about the project on Adriana's Symi blog. Thank you for the mention!

The money we are raising is going to be spent mainly on three things: being on Symi for the shoot (accommodation, food, supplies, local workers etc.), getting the core cast and crew here, and paying only a few of the cast and crew the very basic union rate per day. We are getting some pretty high calibre actors for very little money and the latest to sign up, to complete the cast, is Richard Syms whose film and TV credits include Gangs of New York, The Iron Lady, Secrets and Lies, Johnny English Reborn and Mrs Henderson Presents, among many, many others. Even if the film doesn't get made I am more than flattered that such names and talent should find my script worthy of their commitment.

Meanwhile, in the real world: we're in that strange, quiet, two week period as the southern European visitors start to leave and return to Italy, Athens, France, and just before the northern European visitors start to come in. Today is the Wednesday of the year that Neil and I would usually be flying out to Symi for our holidays, back in the late 90's when we were visitors, so this is the two week period that we would usually meet up with everyone, including other regular visitors who came at the same time. And some still do, so we're on the lookout now to see who else may be around during this next two weeks.

We are planning an evening out tonight to celebrate our 16th anniversary, which is apparently the Peridot anniversary (if you use stones) or Silver 'holloware' which sounds very much like a correctional institution to me. I think we will go to the wonderful Windmill Restaurant to have something delicious cooked by our makeup artist specialising on horror effects, Rhiannon, and served by our hopefully soon to be star of screen, Michaelis. It is also the 11 year anniversary of us leaving England to come and live in Greece. Where did that time go then?

Symi Visitor back The Judas Curse

A great leap up to 41% thanks in great part to Adriana's blog readers and Symi Visitor Accommodation.

Symi Visitor is the first business to take up one of the higher-end pledges and secure themselves 'producer' status for the film. In return the publicity will be good: mentions in the books and on the credits, exclusive photos with the cast and crew to do with as they wish, and of course advertising for their properties and businesses that will last for the life of the film and its distribution. Individuals can take these higher pledges as well, and one wonderful person already has taken one of them, but for a business there is the chance of all the extra publicity too, if they want it. So that's all rather brilliant and puts us over the £8k mark with 10 days left to go. If we can make it to 10k by the end of this weekend I reckon we will reach, and get past, the target. We have to do that by Sunday 8th September 10pm (UK time) or else all these pledges are lost and the only money that will change hands will be 1066 paying Kickstarter for their trouble. So it just goes to prove what we already knew: We need more Wendys! (Wendies?)

Meanwhile I am quoted in Greek Reporter today, *"Greece is going through a very difficult time at the moment and I wanted to do something to help*, said the screenwriter of the film James Collins." To the point eh? Not like me.

There were a few familiar faces out in the village last night, some regular visitor returning for the start of September, and more on their way next week. September is a popular month on Symi because of the temperature, it's cooling off, the sea is warm, the days are not as scorchingly hot as in August, and the evenings are still warm too. It's a good time to be here. Well, anytime is a good time to be here in my opinion. (Unless you have a summer cold when it is 30-odd degrees outside.)

Thanks for the anniversary wishes. This time 11 years ago we were in Athens on our way to live on a Greek island. But which one? You can read all about it in the new edition of *'Symi 85600'* if you've not already followed that adventure. And 16 years ago today, after my first ever visit to a Brighton nightclub (the first of only three as it turned out), I was waking up on the floor of a new/old house in Brighton (the removal company lost the nuts and bolts for the bed) and looking forward to my first real 'date' with the person currently still asleep next door. (Not on the floor.) 'Time,' as the Alan Parsons Project once said, 'keeps flowing like a river to the sea.'

OK, so what lies ahead for the next few days? Neil has a delivery to collect in Yialos today, that may or may not happen. As far as we know Neil has a photo walk on Sunday, and I am planning to get some work finished at home and maybe even pull some summer weeds from the dry earth that was once the garden. Wine night Monday and on towards the festival of the Virgos next Sunday. The combined birthday celebrations of Neil, Claudia and Justine which are flanked either side by those of Ian and Alex. It's that time of year again.

Backing update

This is looking encouraging, 47% that's £9,400 pledged by 107 backers and there are eight days still to go. Yes, I know, that's over 50% to be found in eight days. Let's aim for Friday night and see, this time next week, if we are going to be making a film or not.

OK, so a week to go and lots of work to do. Meanwhile, as I keep saying, life goes on here in Symi. We were down in Yialos yesterday having a quiet drink after doing some shopping, paying the water bill, collecting new calendars for the shop and stocking up on Jack's cat food from Harrods. Quite happily sitting there when comes a call from inside the kafeneion, 'Hey! I want to play the killer!' and such like; great support from our Greek friends in Yialos who are as caught up in the excitement of the countdown as we are. Thanks for the support guys!

Oh, and thanks to the mayor's brother for his message of support and for spreading the news –hopefully we will be able to give some Symi youngsters their first experience of working in film.

And once more, to the few who have said 'we don't want a horror film made here' and particularly to those who add 'we don't want to attract the wrong kind of people' (excuse me, what?!) Remember: we're making a psychological horror because that's the genre that brings in the most sales, which means more investment which means potentially more Symi films.

Lordy! And onwards and upwards back to the village where the square was slightly busier in the later afternoon as the breeze got up and the temperature cooled to more manageable levels. There is still a breeze today, blowing the flowers from the bougainvillea and rustling the vine, blowing the dust from the wasteland straight through the open windows and right up my nose – which is less sneezey I have to say. It actually feels like that cold has gone away at last. Fingers crossed.

September

A bar for sale, a film to make, a fake knife to find, an odd day off, a live rabbit and a dead goat

Welcome to September on Symi

We're starting the month with an announcement of a one-off photo walk. It's Neil's birthday next Sunday (8th September) so he is going to be running a walk, if you see what I mean. Not to the Pedi Valley for a change, and not through the lower village, not his usual walks, but to some unexplored parts of the upper village. Same price, same starting time of 9.15 from the shop, but this walk will finish at our house for wine and coffee for anyone who comes on the walk. You never know I might even make some sandwiches by way of a birthday treat. If you're interested just arrive at the shop, or better still, book a place by calling in or by email and we'll see you there.

Meanwhile, the great news about the film project is that we are 52% funded this morning and standing at £10,400 which means we have six days left to raise only £9,300 – that's only a couple of producer level pledges needed. It's all looking so much more possible even though it's a short period of time in which to raise a fairly substantial sum of money.

And on that note: you will remember last Friday's special promotion from Symi Dream, the 'Freaky Friday' pledge? Well, there were spookily 13 pledges or changes of pledges that fitted the bill. 1066 Productions gave each one a number and then asked Kurtis Stacey, who is our leading man, to select one number between 1 and 13, inclusive and he chose number six. And that was Linda M –no full name here as I've not heard from her yet as to whether she wants to be known publicly or not. But thanks to everyone who joined in, it really helped push us upwards and onwards towards the goal, and Linda will be getting the calendar, book, cards, and CDs sent by post as soon as I hear from her with an address.

The weekend saw some very high winds here on Symi, especially on Saturday, but they calmed yesterday and this morning has started cooler and fresher, with only the very calmest of breezes. I went for a stroll around the back of the village and towards the square, getting thoroughly blown about as I went, and took some snaps on my phone camera. I met up with Astrid who was taking Ginger out for a walk, though it might have been vice versa, and then met up with Neil at the shop. Sunday was spent at home, for me, while Neil was out walking and then we spent a few hours relaxing in the square in the evening.

This week should be fun: there's a portrait shoot at the shop this morning, we have the wine night tonight, to which everyone is, as always, invited, we are being treated to dinner on Tuesday, I must call into Yialos on Friday to see if Neil's birthday present has arrived, and then there is the special photo walk on Sunday, followed in the evening no doubt by a joint celebration with Justine and Claudia. This is where they all gather together and celebrate their birthdays around a lump of roast beef; it's a joint celebration. Hohum.

Travels with my camera, a new exhibition for the Symi Dream Gallery

54% with five days to go and £9,015 needed to get past the target by £1,00 and secure all the pledges made so far, or else lose the race (and the film).

There has been a lot of talk recently about the wind forecast for today and tomorrow, and people have been wondering about the boats and if they will be running. Some of the local boats, going around the island or around to Tolis have been a bit hampered by the recent high winds, though there hasn't yet been a total ban on shipping. This morning it's calm again, well, down to 15 knots, rising at six this evening to 26 kts, and then down again over night and repeating the pattern tomorrow, reaching a high of 26 kts again tomorrow evening.

(I sound like the BBC shipping forecast now. 'Variable Southwest backing three or four. Viking-Fitzroy continuing to Dogger Shannon Bailey. Variable Sole…' And so on. I'm only reading from Windfinder.com – and I am only really doing that because we are going to the windmill tonight, but not until later and the forecast for then shows 24 kts…)

It was blowing a bit at the shop last night for our wine night, the walk poster in the frame was lifted from the wall and dumped on the ground, the books were flapping around a bit, and there was dust in the wine, and yet we still had a great time with some very nice guests, thank you all for coming.

Next Monday there is the opening of a new exhibition at the Symi Dream gallery; Ged Horton is showing his photography in an exhibition called 'Travels with my Camera.' This will start on Monday 9th September and run until the end of the season, entrance is as usual free, and on a Monday night it will come with a 'glass' of wine.

Starting the final countdown…

This morning we need exactly £7,000 to put us £1,00 over target and ensure that we are able to make a feature film on Symi; we are suddenly at 64% thanks to a very generous pledge from Mr. Gray in Canada.

In related news, Symi has been receiving quite a bit of attention thanks to the press releases from 1066 Productions. The BBC were trying to get hold of the Mayor, the Daily Telegraph want to do an interview (with me) next Monday, Enetenglish have an article titled 'Spooky Screams on Symi', Dodekanisos News, To Vima, Rhodes Times and several other papers online and in print have been reproducing the story, so if nothing else, Symi has been getting some press coverage.

Here the wind is blowing but the boats are going. And I am slowly waking up after a wonderful meal at the Windmill (thank you to Alun and Andy for the treat), and looking forward to a quiet day ahead.

As you can see from the photo, Jack was in charge of housework yesterday. He really does love his broom.

The other image today is from Neil. He has worked on it in Photoshop (or similar) to produce a mirror effect, but the original image is of peeling pain[1] on a ruin in Horio. Just the kind of photo you can take on one of his village photo walks.

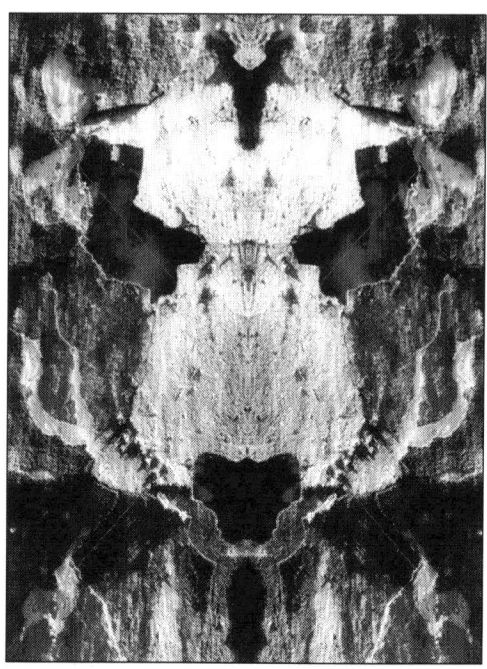

Three days to go – 20% to find for Symi film

Starting this morning at 80% funded with only £3,745 to find before the time runs out on Sunday. We have 130 backers now, that's 130 people behind us who all like the idea of a feature film being made on Symi. 130 people who believe, as we do, that this could really help the island in the long term.

Don't worry, there are only a few more days of this kind of talk to go and then it will be either a case of forgetting about the project or we will move into a blog that will be more about what it is like to be making a film. I'll try and keep things Symi-based ether way.

I am a bit tied up in the film fund-raising at the moment and have little other news as I only seem to be seeing the PC monitor, the kitchen and the shop, which is pretty quiet at the moment. Let's hope that also picks up for the last few weeks of the season; lots of winter bills still need to be saved for, including the VAT and rent and other fees.

---

[1] Spot the typo?

The gallery is nearly ready for Monday's opening night, Ged and Ian (from the Symi Gallery) have been busy up there setting things out; last I saw it looked really good. I know that yesterday saw more people arriving on the island than leaving, Miss DJ should be back from her UK and France visit, old friends are coming back soon, and some younger old friends too. Laughter still rings out from The Olive Tree all day long, Yiannis is still arranging his tables just so, the wind blows empty water bottles down the steps and neighbours do with them what they have always done, brush the detritus down one more step so their neighbours can brush it along in a kind of pass-the-parcel game that culminates, I assume, at the harbour. The wind is less today, the sea calmer and despite the high wind yesterday the boats still managed to get to Rhodes, so no one's flights were missed, as far as I know.

And so it goes on. A quiet, September Symi style of life set against the nail-biting final three days of the campaign to raise money for a feature film. I am actually looking forward to Monday despite the looming interview with the Telegraph. We will at least know one way or the other what is going to be happening. It would be so much nicer to tell the Telly-G that we are going ahead and making Symi's first feature film for many years.

64 hours and counting, now's the time to act

83% with only Two days and 16 hours to go until the win/fail deadline, and it really is all or nothing. We need another £3,240 to get us to the target and secure all the pledges made so far. £1,00 under that and there's no money/film, anything over that is a bonus.

It's Friday again, and it's the final Friday of the campaign, and we've kind of run out of goodies that Symi Dream can give away for increases in pledges or for new pledges made today. But thinking about it, just about everyone we know had made a pledge and we really can't ask any more from our friends, family and Symi Dream followers. Now we can only hope that others, people who support independent films, horror film fans, fans of the star Kurtis Stacey, and others who want to support Symi by bringing a film and publicity and hopefully more tourism here, will put in lots of small pledges or one large one which, as we have seen, will also really benefit the business. (The £1,000 and above pledges carrying with them great advertising opportunities.)

So, tomorrow will be the last day that I start the blog with X% and only so-much needed, as I don't usually write a blog on a Sunday. I wonder what that per cent and total is going to be?

The wind has died down so I assume the ban on shipping that was in place yesterday has been lifted. In fact, thinking about that, I did hear a boat come in last night so it must have been. Let's hope everyone got home or to the island on time yesterday and the starts of people's holidays have not been delayed by the wind.

40 hours to go for the Symi film project; will we make it?

91% funded, £1,669 to find in the next 40 hours. The way things were going last night it looks like we may even make our target today which would give us a whole day to go over target and raise extra funds which would be extremely useful for the post-production work needed. But let's not count chickens.

There was a great buzz online and also around the harbour and village yesterday, seems that everyone is talking about this project. Let's see what today and tomorrow bring and see what we wake up to on Monday morning's blog.

As for our yesterday, the trip to the harbour was successful, except the accountant wasn't in so we weren't able to hand in some receipts and things, but they weren't urgent. We had a pleasant walk down; at this time of year you can't help but stop to chat with returning friends. We picked up some post, both items were presents for Neil's birthday tomorrow, and we managed to get a couple of bills paid. We walked back up the steps later, slowly, though now things are cooling off the walk is actually rather pleasant. The wind has died down (so you should be fine for your crossing tomorrow Allan and Julie) and the sun is not quite as scorching as it was in August. Already the early mornings feel cool and fresh, just as I like it.

I was at home for the evening again, checking in to Facebook and checking emails and the progress of the fund-pledging while watching a DVD. I've been spending quite a few evenings at home, to save money and also to recover from a bout of vertigo that I've now got tablets for. They are having a strange effect and making me feel better (I can stand up with my eyes closed without falling over now, almost) and yet making me slightly drowsy and 'out of it', but the strange thing is, no one else seems to have noticed a change. Maybe I am always drowsy and out of it. But, it's getting better as I get used to the tablets. I think it all goes back to a bout of 'labyrinthitis' when I was in my early 20's. I was off work for a month, couldn't walk for two weeks and had to use a stick for about six weeks. I remember the morning it hit followed a night out at a club with some friends. The next day they all assumed I had a huge hangover as I crawled to the bathroom and stayed prone unable even to move my head, but I'd only been able to afford two bottles of San Miguel beer the night before. Anyway, I am in danger of sounding old now, talking about my ailments, so:

Saturday morning, the church bells are clanging away in a call to service, the sea is calm, the air is fresh and I have a house to clean. Neil has several people booked for his walk tomorrow, with room for more.

Film to be made on Symi thanks to Symi fans

This message from the producer of 'The Judas Curse' says it all:

"I'm probably going to destroy what little credibility that I had with this confession, but I was in the middle of cradling my four week old son and watching the Celebrity Masterchef Final when I heard that we had finally hit our target on The Judas Curse. I can also admit to a wild fist pump and a loud cheer at the news, which scared the Bejesus out of my baby boy who is now probably scarred for life (and will forever have a fear of loud noises!)

It's been an amazing experience and rewarding in many different ways. My motivations to make this film initially being purely artistic, the level of enthusiasm, loyalty and support shown by those connected to Symi has been a genuinely humbling experience. I don't think I've experienced anything like it in my entire career. So much so, that it's no longer simply about wanting to make a great film for creative reasons, but I really want to do everything I can to say thank you to everyone who helped us (in word and in deed) and to reward the incredible faith they have shown. The best way I can do that is to ensure that this is an absolutely cracking film that everyone can be proud of. And from here on in that will be my primary goal and motivation.

Let's make a movie!"

And from the office:

Now that the Kickstarter is over I can give you some stats for the blog:

We got a total of 207 backers of which:

46 came from Symi Dream producing £6,512 of total (32%). This is anyone who pledged having clicked a link on the blog page.
40 from Facebook producing £3,193.60 (16%). Many of those are probably Symi Dream readers too.
39 clicked the Embedded Widget (which appeared on a number of sites and blogs) producing £2,331 (12%).
30 from Direct traffic (emails probably) producing £989.60 (5%).
5 from readers of Adriana's blog producing £390 (2%).
1 from the Symi Visitor Forum at £40.
3 from eKathimerini producing £120.
1 from XpatAthens producing £20.
1 backer through Twitter worth £100
1 through YouTube worth £10.

Kickstarter itself (random searchers on Kickstarter) brought us 34 backers producing £6,106. Two of them came from having discovered us on Kickstarter's "Ending Soon" page.

So, now that that stage of the film making process is over we can get back to some semblance of normality. Which, after Neil's photo walk and birthday yesterday (20 people went on the walk with him, and then came to our hose for wine afterwards), followed by an afternoon in the square and then dinner at Zoi… now takes on the form of a very unusual day, for me at least:

11.00, friends of friends arrive on the island to be taken to lunch and looked after for a couple of hours. 15.00, Rainbow Bar. 17:00, telephone interview with the Daily Telegraph while, at the same time, being at the Gallery for the launch of Ged's photo exhibition followed by said exhibition and wine and food courtesy of Symi Visitor and… well, you can see it's going to be a bit of a busy day. I'll let you get on with it, add my HUGE thanks to all blog readers and Symi fans who have pledged for the film funding, and catch up with you tomorrow.

Another non-stop day yesterday

Dealing with emails first thing, then down to Yialos to meet friends of friends and take them for lunch on behalf of said friends, and show them a little of Symi while they were here. A delightful bunch of very talented people, one of whom, Sam, had worked with our friend Kinny Gardner on the recent revival of the Lindsay Kemp show Variete. Kinny had directed this at the Riverside Studios, Hammersmith recently and Sam had stepped up to be MD. So, despite being strangers we all had plenty to talk about and got along like burning houses.

We had lunch at Merakles as it's Kinny's favourite taverna in Yialos and after all, he was going to be paying, and then we all took a walk up the steps to show the guys some more of the island. They'd sensibly taken the Panagia Skiadeni across from Rhodes so as to spend as much time on Symi as possible, without the use of a guide, and so were not being herded in a pack and had much more free time. We walked up, had a drink at Rainbow, they went off to explore the village, found the kataraktis and walked back down to the harbour again. Then realised they'd not said goodbye so they walked back up the kali Strata for a second time to find us and say goodbye, then walked back down again. Oh to be young again.

In the evening Ged opened his exhibition in the Symi Dram gallery. We reckon that well over 70 people turned up to see the first night and share some wine and the food put on by Wendy and Adriana. It was a busy wine night on the steps and a great success.

So that rounded up a rather hectic and celebratory weekend, what with film funding and five birthdays, and exhibitions, and lunches with new friends. I feel quite worn out now as, for me, it was all done without the aid of a safety glass of wine. (Still on those tablets.) I am hoping that things settle down a little bit now, while at the same time hoping for a busy time at the shop to see us through the rest of the season and into part of the winter at least.

Back to being a typical Wednesday

There is this strange sense of getting back to normal after the excitement of the fund-raising campaign, now successfully finished, and now that the birthday/anniversary weekend is over.

The great excitement of the day is that a 'man who can' is coming to check out our hot water tank and see whether we can get the old one out and put a new one in without having to take down half of the kitchen wall. Ian has been and turned off the water feed to it so that it's no longer leaking and he tells us that it is large tank, presumably so as to fill the bath (which we never do). He also said that we probably didn't need one so big and then added 'but don't ask me to take it out,' which didn't bode well. But we'll wait and see what our other expert has to say about it later. Meanwhile the cold shower thing begins to be less attractive now the temperatures start to cool as we head into September.

While all that is going on, I am receiving email after email from the production office. They are trying to square up flights and accommodation now. We have had some very good offers of accommodation for cast and crew from individuals and two holiday companies in particular, and they will be getting credits and publicity in return, and maybe even a small film about their businesses on the DVD when it comes out. Flights are another thing, made difficult to schedule without knowing the full boat timetable, as the Blue Star ferry times for October are not yet available. Andy from the Symi Visitor Travel Blog has been very helpful in this respect. (Hope your shoulder gets better!) My job now is to be a kind of coordinator on the ground. If the director wants X I have to find it, if he wants Y I'll have to ask why and find the best match I can, that sort of thing. It's a bit daunting to think that they should be here and filming in five weeks.

It's Wednesday and despite the fact that people can come and go on any day of the week these days, Wednesday still remains a typical change-over day. Many people leaving, more coming in, and we usually expect Wednesdays to be the quiet days, the better day for going on around the island boat trip, as there are generally fewer people about. That's not always the case though so don't all rush to the Poseidon or Diagoras.

Right, Jack Cat is in, had his first breakfast and it washing his paws as he makes himself comfortable on my feet, so that means it's time for me to get on with the rest of the day.

A bit of a nothing happening morning this morning

A calm, quiet, cooler but still warm morning is breaking out there; the sea is flat, the olive tree is barely moving, the birds are twittering and the Alan Cat has, as usual, made himself comfortable at my feet under the desk.[1]

I know you love to follow these things so: the 'man who can' came and had a look at the hot water tank yesterday. He climbed up the steps, opened the inspection hatch, shone the torch in, found an old light fitting that was dead with rust and dust, and did a bit of 'Ooh and ah' and 'Hmm' and tutting and then declared that we have a dead 60 litre tank up there. Far too big for our needs and probably too big to come out without some of the wall coming down (it's boxed in behind wooden slats), and with the water feeds on the top for some reason. But not impossible. He's going to order us a 40 litre tank (or was it 20?), and then come back and swap them over when he gets it. 'Swap them' sounds far too simple but we shall see. I have every faith!

As I'm writing, something just blew up outside, and I've no idea what. We just had this flash of light and the sound of a fuse switch tripping out on the wasteland opposite, which is silly as there are no fuse boxes out there. All our power is still on, the phone line is still working and I can't for the life of me think what that was. Maybe something the other side of the ruin opposite, but it sounded like it was in the room. Spooky goings-on.

Ah well, whatever it was it's not affected the Alarm Cat. Having had his wash, dug his claws into my feet a few times and had a roll on his back for no apparent reason, he has now decided that it's time to have another round of breakfast. Better go and see that he gets served.

---

1   Clearly I meant to write the Alarm Cat. I hope.

Production news (get used to it) five weeks to go

What was I saying yesterday about it being cooler? It's suddenly gone warm again. Even now at 7.40 I am considering putting on the fan over the desk.

My mornings these days are being taken up with emails from the production office re: Flights for cast crew and executive producer, questions from directors and producers about this and that, can we X, Y and Z? And 'he wants to fly from Heathrow to Symi in one day, on a Monday,' and replies such as 'don't make me laugh', seem to be filling my time suddenly. But then we do only have four and a half weeks until the crew will be here and the cast and filming will be starting.

This morning's emails were about an Art Director, what we can change inside a property (nothing) and can we find a room that will look like a British schoolroom to use for a morning. Doubtful. But then I thought of the new English language classroom in Horio, and said I would ask next time I find the proprietor at work, at a suitable time as that room does look a little like a British primary school class.

The Blue Star ferry has just turned the corner and is starting to head towards harbour as I write this. The ringing in my ears is getting less each day and I saw the doctor again last night who has given me some different tablets for the problem. I've been on something with a very yucky name for the last 10 days, they've been fun; making me permanently drowsy and with 'avoid alcohol' attached, which I've done. These new ones don't say they can cause drowsiness but they do say avoid alcohol. So that's another 10 days without beer to look forward to. Hohum. Mind you, I can now do my belt up another notch even though the last lot of tablets gave me the munchies something dreadful. Ah well, if it stops the Geiger counter in my left ear I don't mind.

What to do on a day off on Symi?

This actually feels like a weekend off, with nothing to write or re-write and not too many emails in about production things to be dealt with this morning. What shall I do? The possibilities are endless.

Things to do on Symi when you have a day to yourself:

Take a walk up into the mountains and through to the forest, maybe right up to Stavros Tou Ploemou the highest monastery on the island, or up to Kokimides, or St George for the views and the exercise. Or in the other direction and over to Nimborio, over the top road through the country path and down the donkey track, and then back around the headland to see the sea views. I could head down to Pedi for a free sun lounger at 'Tolis' before lunch and then get an afternoon bus back after a swim. Or head around to St Nicholas or Ag. Marina by foot or boat for a day on the beach.

I guess I could spend a day in Yialos watching the world go by, sipping a very long slow coffee or having an ice cream. Perhaps a bit of shopping and a wander around the lanes at the back to find all those new and different shops? By the same token I could stay in the village and take a walk up to the Castro to see the views, or up to Ag Triada and around the upper village lanes and back streets to see the ruins and soak up some lost history. Or take a taxi boat out to one of the further beaches, like Nanou or Marathunda, to have lunch there, or even take a day excursion on the Poseidon or Diagoras.

Alternatively I could hang out at home and read on the terrace, while watching the boats coming and going out in the bay. I could potter in the garden, read a book or two, or draw something, tidy up the house, play the piano or write something profound.

Or I could just play it by currently rather noisy ear. I am starting on new tablets today so will see what effect they have on me. The lot just finished were like sleeping tablets and I have to say I've not slept better in years. But they also made me rather 'out of it' during the day which wasn't so clever, so we will see what this next lot do and if they get rid of the noise in the ear.

Actually, I think I will stay at home today and do nothing, just potter around and do a bit of this and a bit of that.

A Sunday walk

Yesterday I managed to get myself away from the computer for a while and went for a stroll around a part of the village I've not strolled around before.

We headed westwards from the shop, along the lane towards Villa Papanikola, down and along, further and further until we were beyond the west end of the harbour, under Lemonitisa, and then we zigzagged back and down until we arrived at the Kali Strata by 'the doctor's house', that large ruin that everyone admires. Here we headed back east slightly to look at the huge terracing that has been done overlooking the harbour, before finally heading back up the Kali Strata a little way and then heading off the main route again, and upwards. It's a bit complicated to explain the route and will make no sense to anyone who doesn't know the area anyway, but I found some interesting sights I'd never seen before and took a few photos.

After that it was home for a Sunday lunch and later some time in the square. The wind was blowing a bit yesterday and, dare I say it, I was feeling a bit chilly for a while. The house was still warm inside when we got back for the evening though, and things look calmer out there today, though having just said that I can see the trees moving about and hear the wind on the roof; but the sea is not as flecked with white as it was. That's just as well as we have the wine night to look forward to this evening and then, for me, the rest of the week is going to be taken up with pre-production arrangements as far as I can see. We may well be looking for a few local 'extras' before long, a few people of all ages to play some non-speaking, non-paid parts in a few scenes. I'll post more about that in due course, when I know more myself. All I know at the moment is that a couple of the crew, the director and his director of photography are due here in less than four weeks now, the script is, again, going through some changes, and we need to find accommodation for seven people for ten days; I have an idea about that and will be sending out emails very shortly.

No rain but clouds and a busy wine night at Symi Dream

Well, no rain, as had been promised though walking home around 10:30 last night the sky was heavy with looming cloud covering and then showing the moon, and some of that cloud did look dark and rain-full.

But this morning, a cool breeze, the scent of dampness in the air but no rain on the kitchen floor so I know there was no downpour last night. At least, if there was, there was not enough to come through the roof, or mark the outside furniture at our house. Some people can tell when there's rain because cows lie down or sheep stand on the head or something; round here we know if it's been raining as our feet get wet first thing in the morning as we make a cup of tea. Ah well, perhaps in a few more weeks.

Feeling much better this morning actually, thank you, though I did make the mistake of having a Coke 'lite' on the way home so didn't stop buzzing until around 1.00 a.m., shan't do that again.

Today holds what is starting to become a bit of a routine: the blog, 101 emails about the production, some with questions that need answering, some with jobs that need doing, others that are for information only, and then the usual day-to-day things that have to be done followed by lunch and work and the more emails in the evening. Less than four weeks to go and the director will be here and then a few days after that, the main cast and filming starts. (The Judas Curse, IMDB page is starting to fill up.)

It's one of those mornings with parish announcements

A new exhibition opened at The Symi Gallery on the Kali Strata last night and that will be running for the next few weeks. (Sorry I left the full details at the shop!)

Tonight, 18th September, there will be music in the village square "Rock & Rembetiko" at 21:00.

And Symi is in the Daily Telegraph (online) with a piece about The Judas Curse:

"A British expat hopes to boost the economy of a small Greek island by shooting his horror movie on location there."

Well, mine and many other people's.

And in Film News: we (the UK production office actually) are now firming up the flights and equipment hire, the cast and their dates. We (the island production office (Rainbow Bar)) that is Wendy, Neil and I, and Allan and Julie, were starting to square up some extra accommodation for cast and crew; plus ideas for extras and locations. It's all starting to happen but I've not yet got the final shooting schedule to work from so it's still all rather 'in principal' at the moment. We know that the shooting will be between 17th and 27th October in Horio though and that the Kalodoukas property 'Kyriaki apartment' will be taking a role.

Luckily my ear problem appears to be leaving me (for the time being at least) and I'm nearly back on an even keel. Just as well as my head is already fair busting with ideas and things to remember and things to do, emails to send and things to check. The more organised we are in advance the easier it will be for the cast and crew when they get here. That's the plan anyway.

Oh – does anyone have a couple of hand-hold sized identical old pottery urns that look like they have been buried in the ground for a few hundred years, one or both of which can be smashed? (Mum: thought about your box idea but need to be pottery.) As you see: the props list has started.

Production emails, concerts and exhibitions

Talking of water tanks, the 'Master' is in the house. (That's the name stamped on the tank, so who am I to argue?) He's come from Rhodes, spent a night on the Panagia Skiadeni, been back to Rhodes, and then come back to Symi where he was collected yesterday by Ian and brought up to the house by Ian and Neil. He's now camped out on the sitting room floor waiting for the man who can to put him up behind the wood panelled wall in the kitchen.

I'm pretty sure some of that wall will have to come down in order to get the old, retired 'master' out and this new one installed, but we shall see. Meanwhile, the sun grows weaker on the exposed pipes on the roof, and the hot water coming from the cold water pipes at shower time grows cooler as the season runs on and we start to turn towards autumn.

16 emails from the production office this morning, I've not started on them yet but will do after writing this and posting it. I see I have emails from the other two producers, the director of photography and the director, all of which I look forward to opening to see what new questions and ideas have arrived. Less than four weeks to go and we shall be starting on filming. Let's hope the weather holds.

Is Kos possible? And Jack on guard

Jack was on guard yesterday standing (sitting) watch over 'The Master' and keeping an eye out for Silent Movie the black and white opposition who slinks about trying to break in and snaffle leftovers when he can. He stood (sat) no chance yesterday.

I've yet to go through this morning's production emails, but there was a lot of talk 'on the wire' yesterday about flights and boats and how the two things don't match up. If I get time later I'll have a quick look at Kos, the destination not the actual island, and see if that's a viable alternative.

You see, in October, it seems that you can get off Symi more times than you can get on, somehow. That can't be correct of course, but trying to find an afternoon boat to the island from anywhere nearby with an airport and sensible flight times is virtually impossible after the 12th or 13th of October; I am hoping that the Blue Star puts on the same schedule as it is currently running. If not we will have expensive Rhodes stopovers for certain cast and crew.

While that is all going on I am now trying to source some pretty rare commodities and some common ones. Not only the earthenware jars, but now two goats, one dead and one alive. Neither should be a problem, a word with one or two local friends and farmers should source them easily.

Anyway, I had plenty of time to mull this over during the night following an unwanted mosquito attack sometime before sunrise. I was lying there, swatting away at my ear and tutting, wondering what I was going to put on the blog this morning and all this came into my mind, so at least I had a chance to rehearse the post today.

But now, after sunrise here on Symi, the bells are ringing and I am being treated to my morning broadcast. The Afghan guys who live across the lane always play half an hour of 'getting ready of work' music on their radio, and with their window open I get a light lilt on the morning breeze. It comes in through my open balcony windows bringing baking smells from the 'German' Bakery with it; it's all very charming here between 7.30 and 8.00 each day. Out on the street there is still a bit of a buzz about the concert the other night.

Changing seasons and retractable knives

Yesterday went nice and smoothly; just popped out for a bit of shopping at 11.30, didn't get home until 22:00. But did sort out cast accommodation, makeup and several other things. Mind you, I think we are still looking for a retractable knife with which to stab someone, but there are several emails in that I have not opened yet, so there may be a fake knife in there. If you see what I mean.

Today is going to be given over to making up the props list and list of 'things' needed for the film, based on the final script. I already have some ideas of what is need for certain things, and ideas of who to ask to help me find or make them. But there may well be a long list of odd items appearing here before long. Thank you to everyone who has volunteered to bring things over when they come- I will certainly be asking if we need to your help. The main crew arrive on 13th October and there might be up to seven of them, so they may be able to bring some things along with the lenses and lights they will be carrying, and then the rest of the cast arrive from 17th onwards; assuming the airline tickets can still be booked.

Emails, a rabbit, Wine Night, Golden Girls…

A few tiles from this morning's emails: Props, Church, Stage/screen knife, Completed schedule – draft, sound design, location photos, Gaffer, transfer times, accommodation. Yippee! There's no room for spam.

So, a quick 'welcome to Monday' from me, a photo of a rabbit, and some other silly things and it's straight to my voluntary work. That should more or less fill up the morning leaving my evening free for the Symi Dream wine night, from six to eight as usual on a Monday night; everyone welcome. The exhibition is still on in the gallery and the shop is still open. We've run out of 2014 calendars at the moment, the new stock is being rushed from the printers but has not arrived yet, but other than that we're fully stocked and all the usual things are available.

So, this rabbit then? Yes, well, he's (she's?) been there for a while now and is being looked after by the guys at the shop I guess. She's (he's?) not penned in, there are a couple of crates to give it some protection, it has food and it seems quite happy being there. It's in the alley between the old Olive Tree and Sotiris' 'super market' (it's absolutely super actually, you can now find PG Tips there). I don't know what his name is but maybe someone will tell me - I'm talking about the rabbit again now, not Sotiris, I know his name. (Note: ask Sotiris about borrowing a goat next time I call in for PG.) He was sitting there all bouncy and fluffy and happily munching away when we passed last night. (Same rule applies: talking about rabbit not Sotiris.)

We called in to the Sunrise to pick up Neil's birthday present as he'd left it there a couple of weeks ago. Then it was home time and a couple of episodes from series seven of The Golden Girls before bed.

Going to be a busy one: mail, mayors and mumbles

Today looks like it is going to be a bit hectic. Apart from things I have to do at home, work starting on installing our new boiler, and… let me count… 33 emails about the film so far (and a couple of spam this morning, I love the one headed 'RIP camera with Poe' which I will bounce straight back as the text starts with 'Dear Manager Vivian hope you blooming business,' to which I want to reply 'Dear Edgar Allan, mind your own blooming business'), apart from all that, I think I am heading to the mayoral office around midday to ask about stage lights, followed by a dash back up the Kali Strata to make lunch before my afternoon work, followed by (and this is where I can switch off a bit) dinner at Haritomeni.

Actually, that's not so much to do in one day though I do have 4,000 words to write this morning as well, I can see that going out of the window; and that's all after writing and posting the blog.

I'd just like to add, in all this madness, a quick word of thanks to whoever left the candlesticks on the shop door yesterday morning; they will do very nicely on the film set I imagine. And I would also like to thank everyone who has come past the shop, or wherever we have been, and who has taken the trouble to say thank you for the blog. Thank you for reading it! I am now going to post it.

Well, I would if I could find my internet browser; Firefox was absent without a note this morning. It's usually on my task bar, but when I switched on this morning it was still out in the playground and I had to go and find it. Detention for that little helper today I think. Why do computers do this kind of thing? Hide icons and programmes, and change things around overnight? Word is the main culprit, always opening up with the zoom on, or the page settings wherever they want to be not where I left them. And who on earth wants to have a default page set with Calibri 11 point font with double spacing? What's 'Normal' about that? Anyway, can't stay blathering about all this, there's too much to do today.

Wild goat in oven – live goat on set please

This is more like it; time of an evening to get a blog post ready for the morning so I don't have to rush first thing.

Now then, a few notices and requests: Let's talk goats. My favourite taverna sign is 'Wild goat in oven' to which I always want to add 'furious lamb in fridge.' I will of course be speaking to some local goat owners we know vaguely, but if anyone local knows or is related to any Symi goat owners who might be free every now and then between 14th and 27th October for a stand on part in the film, we are now definitely looking for a live goat to use. No harm will come to it, it just needs to stand around looking sheepish. No actually, looking suspicious. Can anyone help with that? If the farmer needs to be attached too that's fine.

We also need bits of dead goats like the skulls with horns you see on fence posts, if anyone has any on Symi that we can borrow, please let me know.

And back to the real world.

Where we are now missing a bit of kitchen wall which we had to take out (I say 'we' but actually I was nowhere near) in order to get the old boiler out. (No quips about who that might be referring to.) That was managed after a lot of undoing of pretty ancient, er, craftsmanship and found to be about a quarter full of lime scale. It weighs a ton which is why Neil helped out and not me. The new one is in place but yet to be joined up to the pipes. What with a new heating tank and a new oven I wonder if our electricity bills will show a difference? Probably not as that seems to be one bill that's going up each time regardless.

Most of yesterday's tasks were completed, but I can't comment on the evening meal as we haven't had it yet; it's still Tuesday as I write, so I have an evening off to look forward to once I finish this and a few more emails. So I will finish this now.

There you go. Finished.

Asteropi's Jean and Tonic Bar, Symi – want it?

People often say to us, 'you are so lucky to live on Symi.' We know what they mean, but actually it's not about luck.

We didn't just drift in on the tide; our move to the island was planned. Or rather, our move to Greece was planned; a couple of other locations were looked at and tried first before we decided to try here and stayed. It is, as they say, all in the book. 'Symi 85600'. The book also includes a short 'How To' section on moving to a Greek island.

And where is this heading? Well, you may be sitting there thinking that you'd like to move to a Greek island, but what would you do? How about run a bar? There can't be many regular visitors who don't know that Astrid's bar is closing at the end of next month, and that the business is up for grabs. 'The Jean and Tonic' was (and I will be corrected here if I am wrong) the first (non-Greek/ late night/cocktail/all of the above?) bar in the village and was very well established when Jean retired in 2007. It has carried on in popularity under Astrid's captainship as 'the Two As Bar' or 'Asteropi's' and will do so, but only for another month or so.

It's a great opportunity for someone: a manageable size, already established, popular and on everyone's way home, it would be a shame to see it close and go. I don't know all the ins and outs of what's up for sale and so on, but a quick call to Astrid will put you in the picture there.

So, there's an opportunity for you. In just a few months time people could be saying to you: 'You are so lucky to live on Symi'. How would you reply? 'Actually I planned to be here and looked for a business opportunity?' Or - 'It's not luck it's hard work?' Or - 'Actually we saved up so that we could take a few years out and try a business before we got too old/settled/scared/all of the above?' Or, like me, will you smile and agree but really know that if any luck was involved it is only that we are lucky to have a place like Symi to live on.

Quick blog today

I think mornings will start to become increasingly more like this before long: can't hang around too long, over 30 emails to take care of this morning (re. film) before getting on with my normal day to day jobs.

Many familiar faces are back on the island for their holidays and we had quite a busy afternoon in the square yesterday before heading home to finish off the last series of 'the Golden Girls' which we have been ploughing our way through of late. Yesterday was also a special day in that we had hot water back in the house for the first time in several weeks. Wonderful. The smart new hot water tank is now installed in the kitchen; all we have to do is get the wall put back up, something which will happen in the winter months.

The weather today is calm and looks like it's going to be warm, the sea is flat and the olive tree outside my window isn't moving, a sure sign that there's no wind out there. I'm just waiting to see the Blue Star ferry come around the headland and disturb the glass-flat sea; it should be here any second. Actually I can't wait; I have too much to reply to this morning.

Today's props list and extras needed

I am getting even more ahead of myself than usual today as this is a Sunday morning post. Well, written on Sunday morning while Neil is out on his photo walk.

I am doing this because we have had a wonderful invitation for an evening boat trip for tonight (Sunday) and I have a feeling that a lie in on Monday might be a good idea. So as this is loading itself up to the wonder-web, I will be happily asleep next door. Either that or fighting for the covers now things have started to chill down a little. Mind you, only a little and only overnight, Sunday's sun was wonderfully warm and I even had time to stand out in it for a few seconds.

Not looked at Monday's emails yet, obviously, as I am still writing this post toady, and today is still Sunday, but there are bound to be several emails tomorrow now that we are only two weeks away from start of production. Just to keep you all in the loop:

I have Peter on the trail of the lonesome goat (living).

Gerrie, Sue and Neil have been hunting out dead goat skulls and bones – we still need many more.

I am just in the process of checking with the production designer about props, as many will have to come from Symi, but if you are local please start collecting twigs, dead plants, any yellowed newspapers (I must leave one in the sun for a bit), white sheets, half used candles, rope suitable for a noose (old), dead animal limbs (various), maggots, old urn (small-ish), dead flower wreaths, incense burners and one corpse wrapped in a sheet.

Actually, don't worry about that last one as it will be played by an extra who can keep a straight face.

So, back to my Sunday, which is rapidly running out – but still with the Poseidon boat trip to look forward to tonight. A night away from everything! No phones, no emails, no internet. So that is either "hurrah!" Or "horror!" Depending on how addicted to Facebook you are. (Not very)

October

A gaffer arrives, some cables are found, old goats are needed, a night cruise is had. It's a wrap!

An evening on the Poseidon at Agia Marina; perfect

A Sunday evening boat party is a wonderful way to get away from the process of trying to organise things for a film. Mind you, I did discuss salads with Debbi, props with Miss DJ, goats' horns with Ian, blackout material with Libby, slow cookers with Jean and general updates with several other people.

The trip was a private party to which we had been invited and there were around 30 guests on the Poseidon heading out from Yialos at 6.30 in the evening. The sea was calm and the evening was balmy. A breeze did come up gently as we pulled into Agia Marina island, with everyone commenting on the great super-yacht that was moored across the water. I say yacht, these things are more like speed boats; there's no sign of a mast, sails or good taste.

Having pulled in we disembarked and milled around the shore, the steps and the church yard. The church was opened for those who wanted to go and take a look inside, and the BBQ was soon turning away. You know that wonderful lunch they do on this boat? Well, we had that but an evening version, with homemade meatballs, roasted chicken, salads, pasta, bread and a decent supply of wines and ouzo – of which I had two. (Small plastic cups, not bottles.)

Dancing was taken care of, with Nondas and Lefteris playing the music and many people taking to the floor. Later I took a wander away from the sound and light and over the top of the island to have a look at the stars. It was striking to see how much glow here now is from the Turkish coast. When we first landed here (I mean in 2001) there was hardly any light over to the east, now it seems there is a whole town sprung up, and you can see larger towns throwing out light from over the peninsulas, and from Rhodes as well. But I could still see the stars quite clearly, and the Milky Way.

Heading back, Yiannis turned out as many lights as he safely could and we all gazed at the stars as we came around the headland. The sea, still flat, reflected the harbour lights perfectly giving long fingers of different coloured lights on the sea, sparkling in places as if someone had known we were coming and had sprinkled glitter across the waves. The clock tower was showing midnight as we glided in, and the kitchen clock at home was showing 12.30 as we walked in, warm from the Kali Strata climb and heading for bed.

Mad day yesterday:

101 emails: can't have fish, no dairy, no tomatoes, onions, sweet corn, potatoes, nuts, or milk, and not all diet things are in yet. Our catering crew will deal with it!

Can I find a cart so we can carry equipment through the lanes and up and down the steps through the village? (Hmm...)

Know any places on Rhodes that hire out X32 -34m double-adjusting, side-winding pole clamps? (Er, no, sorry. By the way, what are...?)

Oops! Rain a-coming in.

Can we get a dead goat? Well, you may have to wait until Easter, or get lucky. Perhaps this storm will strike one down.

Did you know there is no sailing on that day? (When did that vanish off the schedule?)

Any comments on script scenes XYZ? (Probably)

Getting very dark around here.

And so it goes on. Or rather off – as the power went off for some of the morning. But at least we didn't have a waterspout like they did in Rhodes.

Need your help with cables, a trolley and an old man

It's all about: I can see clearly now the rain has gone on Symi today, yesterday – Thursday! Normal service will be resumed as soon as possible.

But on film news, I am still looking for a few basic things. These are for use between 13th and 27th October:

A sack trolley (that is not otherwise in use). I have the loan of one, another would be great. This is to transport lighting equipment around the village lanes.

Extension cables of any length, but the longer the better. Again, I have one that's not in use –lots of us have them but most are in daily use.

Socket boards – have one I can use (never liked the phone being plugged in anyway) but could do with more.

Another couple of folk to volunteer to cook for a couple of days. I just found out that my job as production manager will continue once shooting starts, and I am already down for being cook as well. Would be nice to let that go if possible.

An elderly Greek man. There is one particular non-speaking role in the film and the director would like: "Someone with a very characteristic face and stature (picture him as small, small eyes, big smile, someone funny even). Someone who doesn't mind taking on an important part in the film, getting drenched in blood and a bit of a wrestle with the lead (no big moves at all)." This person would need to be free for a day (not sure which one yet) and would be shown exactly what to do and how to stab himself without actually stabbing himself. Some spoken English would be useful.

And all that is without reference to the props list which is now in the capable hands of Miss DJ.

Lots of news from Symi today

There is a new exhibition opening in The Symi Gallery on the Kali Strata on Tuesday. "The Examined Life – drawings by Ian Bishop" opens at 18.00 and runs to the end of the month. Entrance is, as usual, free. Ian has a house on Symi and is the brother of Michael Bishop who is composing the score for The Judas Curse.

Which is a neat little link in to the next part: On today's list of things we need to find is a rope. A good old, hemp, rope suitable for making into a noose, rather than narrow nylon rope, this needs to look like your classic noose rope on the big screen. We could buy some, if we have the money, but it needs to look old and worn. So, if you see any lying around please pick it up and deliver it to the shop.

You could do that on Monday evening if you want and stop by for the wine night while you are about it. The evening events are still happening despite the chill in the air. But I have to say, the wind died down yesterday and the TV weather is forecasting 22 degrees for Rhodes and we usually get the same if not slightly warmer. The Windfinder site shows no wind to speak of until later in the week, with the air temperature rising to 23 on Tuesday. So I may be able to put the sandals back on for a couple more days. Saturday night it was boots, trousers and fleece time, Neil set off for his Sunday photo walk in trousers and shoes.

So, the week ahead is going to be another mad one I expect, so apologies in advance if the blog is sometimes brief, or even not here at all. We have the 'Gaffer' arriving on Friday on the Blue Star, so the work starts then, and the rest of the crew come in on Sunday with some of the cast. If you wondered what a Gaffer was on that list of credits at the end of a film, apparently it's the person who lights the set/location, so our lighting designer is arriving ahead of the rest. This is because he's coming from Spain and is collecting the lights from the man in Athens who equipped Captain Corelli's Mandolin; this guy is even letting us use his van as part of the very reasonable deal.

But that's all technical, for my part I have a meeting with the catering team on Monday at 17:30, and then the rest of the week is going to be about collecting more props, and set dressings, helping Miss DJ make strange looking charms from bones.

Last wine night and last photo walks this season

Yesterday was a bit mad, a Monday morning of emails and scheduling. The new shooting schedule arrived so I had to go through and make up call sheets for extras and non-speaking parts and players. There was also some fiddling about to be done with the 'drop box' online, shared storage facility we are all using, I had to send an image of a funeral pyre to Ian, and check various other arrangements with various other departments. I think, hope, that today might be a little less hectic.

October is the time to film on Symi it seems as yesterday at Polish film crew were out and about scouting for locations. They are here to make four, one minute promotional adverts for a company that advises travel; 'the company knows best' is the bye-line for this campaign. Apparently they are shooting four different 'best of Greece' ideas and they've chosen Symi to shoot them on. Bravo to them. It does kind of show the difference between advertising companies and crowd funded independent projects though; they have something like 30 in their crew and seven days to film four minutes. We have a crew of seven with just 14 days to film 80 minutes.

The first of our crew leaves his home in Spain tomorrow to start his journey to Symi. His journey will involve a night in Athens and a night on the Blue Star Diagoras heading down to Symi for Friday morning.

Meanwhile, we realised that although we wanted to keep our wine nights going while the shooting was happening, it's not going to be possible. So last night was the last wine night of the season. Next Monday Neil is playing the part of 'body in a barrow' and the shop will have to be closed for two weeks.

Making things from old goats

One of those blogs on the go –Tuesday night, gone seven, ready for tomorrow morning at six when it will go live.

Neil is at the shop printing off shooting schedules for makeup and Michaelis, I am answering emails about everything from extras to bedrooms and baked beans to IMDB. And meanwhile Miss DJ is in the front room with me and Jack making strange things out of the goat bones that Sue and Gerrie and others have been finding lying around the hillsides.

I've had a meeting with the catering team and this afternoon with Sue who is going to Rhodes tomorrow to do some bulk shopping for us while she is there. It's all hands to the capstan at the moment, or whatever the expression might be.

Anyway, must get on and see to several more emails. Miss DJ has just dropped her jawbone… no sorry, a dead goat's jawbone which she is connecting to a leg bone, and so on. It's all rather mad here; the first of the crew arrive in two days, the rest on Sunday and I still need:

Three drawings by a five year old child

Candles – used is fine

Church candles

End of candles, any kinds of candles

Dark, brown, cream or dull yellow coloured bedspread that looks old and knackered (and can be thrown away after)

Theological looking books –leather and dark, bound?

Old fashioned Greek telephone, any age pre-1980 (cradle and handle, not modern)

Rusty and faded tins of food (please don't tell me to go and look in ruins- these are unopened!)

Buckets

A crucifix on a chain to go around the neck (Man's)

Normal Symi blogging will be resumed as soon as...

The season is starting to wind down on Symi now, with only a week or so to go for some of the holiday companies. From our point of view of course things are starting to liven up, though Neil is doing his last photo walk this Saturday (not Sunday) and then the shop will be closed for two weeks, opening again after Oxi Day.

I have a few odd notes on my scrap paper pile of notes. The top one says 'blog' so I guess I am seeing to that now, and the next one says '3 x rev' and I have no idea what that means. Three revolves? Three vicars? No doubt it will come to me. Meanwhile, Note to self: leave self clearer notes.

Have to get on now, today is already filling up. I still have 3,000 words to write, €300 worth of food arriving from Rhodes around 09.30, Su coming to make charms out of old bones and grass, a boat timetable to check and various things to email.

Symi film, pre-shoot: lights!

If you are one of the Kickstarter backers who are eligible for the private access to The Judas Curse blog, you should have received an update email with details. It's only just starting off and is run by the UK office. What you read here at Symi Dram[1] is, as usual, my own personal blog.

Up early this morning to get at least a short blog post up for you and then to check where the Blue Star ferry is, then to get ready and dressed and out in time to meet it at Yialos.

The lighting gear arrives today with Rodrigo. He left his home in Spain two days ago to start his journey to Symi. He's come via Athens where he picked up the gear in its own van and, hopefully, drove it onto the Diagoras yesterday afternoon. Checking out Marine Traffic.com I can now see that the

---

1   One of those subliminal typos creeping in. As they say in Scotland, "Ye'll take a wee Symi Dram the noo?"

ship is… currently docking at Tilos. Which would mean it is late. Due in Symi 09.15 and Rhodes 10.45, and the traffic site now shows Rhodes ETA at 12.40, which is two hours late. If I see it coming around Nimos while I am still sat here I will know I am late, meanwhile I'll keep calm and carry on.

Rodrigo isn't the first of the crew to arrive; Chris Flagg (1st assistant director) is already here, Neil who is now associate producer (which means doing all kinds of helpful things), me, and now Alex Cullen who is going to act as Data Wrangler. As far as I can translate that job description, that means taking the memory card from the Director of Photography (DoP) and transferring it to a computer, checking it for errors and then backing it up, cleaning the card and handing it back. While he's doing this they are filming onto a spare card, and so it goes on. And one of the actresses has arrived, Wookie Mayer is here and has her script and schedule. A schedule which keeps changing so I've given up printing them and won't contact the extras again until Sunday when the rest of the crew will be here and everyone would have settled on the final schedule; I hope.

Yesterday Sue, Lena and Michelle got back from Rhodes with six heavy bags of supplies which I carried from the car park to the kitchen (shoulders now a bit stiff), Su L came around to spend a couple of hours making more charms from twigs and bones, Neil started negotiations with the language school about using their room, Miss DJ was out on a props hunt (I myself had a conversation about an old phone while out and about) and in the evening I met up with our technical religious adviser, catering assistant and general support person (all in the form of Alun).

Meanwhile: Blue Star Diagoras hasn't moved which makes me think it's going through one of those 'black holes' in the satellite thing and is probably on time. So I should get ready and head down to the harbour in half an hour just in case.

A quick rundown of yesterday's activity:

After writing the blog we set off down to the harbour. It was a lovely clear and calm morning and the steps as far as the shop were dry. The Olive Tree ladies gave their cheery hello as we passed and there were some people sitting at Rainbow even though we it was pre-Yiannis time. The steps around the corner were still damp from the dew, where the sun had not yet hit them, and there were folk out and about on the steps as we headed down.

We called in to Elpida's café for a frappé and to collect the sack trolley from Jeanette which had been left there. People in the harbour must feel very at home when they stay there. One lady, clearly on some kind of camping holiday, was heading off to find the shower block in her dressing gown. Or maybe she lives on one boat and washes on another, I don't know. Do we have a shower block for sailors in Yialos? I know they do at the harbour in Leros. Anyhow, Elpida heard the boat coming in before we did and we headed down to await a van full of lights.

This arrived; we leapt in, the sack truck just fitting in the back, and headed up to the village where we met Chris. A coffee later and the guys got to work unloading the equipment and moving it to the store. We visited the locations and I am sure I saw Rodrigo blanch when he saw the steps and paths involved – I had shown everyone the walk-around video a while back. But if he went white then, he went whiter later in the day when we climbed up to the hill to look at another location up near the Castro. Lovely view mind you.

Between all this, Neil was busy at the shop and I was sorting out the sitting room. It's now set out for serving dinners, there's a huge pile of plates to my left on the desk, the old trunk is covered in bags of props and things and the music stand is well protected from evil by the assortment of charms hanging from it. In the afternoon there was a gathering at the square with people discussing how many white sheets they could find, who'd been offered this and that, Neil had been to pick up books and things from Jean, Michelle called to ask how many Greek ladies we needed, and there was generally a buzz of anticipation in the air.

Shopping done (more to do today to finish the breakfast bags off), signs to put up giving directions, new schedule to arrange the extras and children for, power tests to be done on the electrical supplies (not my department) and lunch and dinner to get ready for the couple of crew already here and working. The rest of the crew set off from home today and should be in Rhodes tonight.

Symi film shoot: Day one

Met the boat at 09.20, whirlwind getting everyone off and into vans; Kalodoukas Holidays and Symi Visitor side by side on the quayside waiting for the arrival. All went very smoothly of course and then it was up to the village in various shifts and vans, into accommodation and back to Rainbow for the start of the adventure after everyone has had time to get into their houses.

There was a walk around the various locations, finding some new ones, checking the insides and outsides and what we have available, and then lunch at our house arranged wonderfully by Gerrie and Sue, the volunteers covering our first two days of catering. Much of my day was spent making sure everyone had what they needed, answering calls, trying to discover who owned which ruin now possibly needed for shooting, and processing Neil's photos.

It was a very tiring day, especially for the crew who had been travelling since the day before, as it was a case of: off the boat and straight to work. In the evening there was a slight moment of realisation from everyone as to how much there is to do, how much equipment to move and how hard that is all going to be given the layout of the village and the lack of crew. Our main volunteers, Neil, Peter, Chris, Miss DJ, have all been appointed a crew member to report to and work with full time now, but we are still very short of full time help. We will have to see how today goes.

Symi photo shoot, day two; and help from Rhodes

The news this morning can start off in Rhodes where our leading man arrived safely yesterday. He was met and entertained by our Rhodes agent, Josephine Kelly, author of "From Lindos With Love." (This is a novel set in Lindos, Rhodes, and it is a story in which Neil and I play a very small part.)

While we are on the Rhodes side of things I should mention that Josie and her Rhodes contacts have saved the production a large amount of money. She was able to secure sponsorship for the transport and that's a huge saving: you know how much it can be to get a taxi from the airport to the Old Town? Well, she organised several, and a van for the luggage and equipment, and yesterday for Kurtis, later for Rebecca and Richard, and then the same things again in reverse. So, I'd like to say a thank you to Rusticao Taverna for their generosity. And also to Romeo Restaurant who also helped provide transport and sent over some meals for the crew when they arrived the other night. The Greek hospitality vibe spreads far and wide.

And help and assistance is coming in more locally too. Last night around 10.15 one of our neighbours popped around to offer his help, for free, any evening after work, which was very kind of him.

Kurtis Stacey arrives on Symi today; Neil and Wendy will be going to meet him and then the poor chap will have about an hour to get settled in, come for his lunch and then get on set at Astrid's house. Meanwhile, Astrid will wake up to find her courtyard full of equipment before she takes her rescue dog Ginger across to Rhodes for the night and on to the plane tomorrow. Ginger is off to live in Scotland with Vi and Co. who already have a few dogs, so she will be happy, though I think Astrid maybe a little sad for a while.

For my part, I am making tomato soup and sandwiches and a packed lunch for everyone to take up to the Castro later, then I'll be coming back to work on dinner. Gerrie and Sue have done a fantastic job in setting up the catering and getting it running smoothly. I have a feeling all their carefully laid plans might now start going to (cooking) pot as I take over, but hopefully not. For Neil, having become a 'wafter' yesterday he is now going to carry on his duties as Assistant DoP, stills, equipment mover, publicity photographer and everything else. He, like the rest of the crew, has a very busy day ahead.

Symi film shoot day three; Kurtis Stacey arrives to work

I expect there are a few bleary eyes around this morning as the shooting didn't finish until very late last night. Luckily it was an indoor setting so hopefully no one in the village was disturbed too much.

The day started easily enough, a late call for crew which meant they had time for a lie in and a leisurely breakfast (not that they did, I expect, too much to do). But then the work kicked in with transferring the equipment from the store up to the location, and that's a lot of transferring; from the square to the Castro area, especially when even a battery (for the camera) can weigh half a ton, or so it feels like.

While all this is going on I am at home cooking up a huge pot of soup, and Neil, Wendy and Chris H are down in the harbour to meet Kurtis Stacey who is on his way over from Rhodes, via Panormitis. He arrives, photos are taken, chats are had between the three producers and the leading man, and then he's taken to his house. Meanwhile school turns out and an *inquisitiveness* of school children hurry past the house chatting and laughing. Strange; don't usually come this way. A few minutes later and they are back, they stop for a chat.

"Where's the thriller?" they want to know.

"Ah," I say as I think on my feet, "not here."

"Where?"

"Para pano."

"Where?"

(I can't actually tell them as it is in internal location and the crew are setting up heavy equipment and can't be disturbed. "I don't know," I have to say (and actually at that time, I don't). "This is only the kitchen."

"What?"

"I am only the cook," I say.

Several disappointed faces look at each other, there is some disgruntled murmuring, "Hmm, only the kitchen," and off they go.

There will be time to see things happening over the next few days.

Then the crew, hungry as always, start to arrive at the house. Joe and Jackie, and Alun, have already arrived to check out catering arrangements for their shifts in a few days, and to help, and very soon the men have started on the sandwiches. That's making them, not eating them, and before you know it there's lunch, there's 20 people on the terrace and Kurtis has arrived to meet everyone else for the first time.

But there's no rest for a working actor and soon after he's up the Castro with the crew and director while the first of his scenes is set up. There is one particular moment in the scene that requires a darkly dressed figure to be lurking and Peter steps up for the job. Rhiannon does an amazing job on his makeup, and it's very humbling to see local people bringing out their talents, for free, for our little film, and being so professional about it.

And so the shoot goes on. I pop to the shop for more supplies and am once again stopped in the street; this time by one of the guys who is bringing four friends to the 'funeral scene' on Sunday. It's actually a kind of 'Burning of Judas' scene they want to do and they do need some extras. And then, actually in the shop, I'm approached again by some of the younger villagers to ask if they can play in the film. ('Play' being as in, play a role.) That's a bit tricky due to their age and I still don't know what Navin has in mind for the scene, so I say I will let a certain friend know and I hope she will pass on the message. Everyone seems happy with that.

Back to the house to get the rice on for the dinner and Chris H phones. "Any chance we can have dinner on location tonight as they don't want to break." Of course, we're on Symi, anything is possible. So Ian, Chris and I carry the tub of chicken something up the hill with bowls, plates and all accessories, and everyone gets fed at some point.

I finally got to bed around 01.00 when I shut down the production office, and I still haven't sent all of yesterday's photos to the UK office for their blog. That's my next job after posting this. Then it's out for more shopping.

Symi film shoot day four; Alarm Cat has a new fan

Awake in a storm this morning, as promised by various weather stations, and with a phone call from Josie in Rhodes telling us it's pretty rough over there. John Gray, one of the executive producers, is booked onto a boat at 09.30, due to arrive here at 11.00. At the moment the weather has calmed and the clouds may even be breaking up. The storm has passed over but I am not sure where to. Let's hope he has a smooth crossing. It's not particularly windy, here, so he might be OK.

Jack the Alarm Cat met a new fan yesterday (Kurtis), or it might have been the other way around. He's actually been pretty well behaved since things became very hectic around here and now he feels confident enough to join in the group meals, sit on people's laps and let them rub his tummy. He's gone from being a bit wary of groups of up to 20 people around him at meal times, to being perfectly confident in everyone's company.

Jack of course has just carried on as normal.

Not sure how normal today is going to be. The scheduled days have been swapped around so that the indoor filming takes place today, but everyone still has to get the equipment from here to the Lambros area, as we call it. That's not far across the middle of the village, but on slippery steps with lots of equipment to carry, well, let's just hope everyone goes slowly and carefully. They are all due to meet here in 45 minutes.

It looked like everything went well yesterday; from my point of view it did. I made lentil soup and sandwiches, with Alun's help, and then sausage and bean thing in slow cookers for dinner. The water bottles turned up, or at least two packs did (we use about two packs of 24 small bottles each day), and nothing electrical blew up in the house, so that's a bonus. And this morning the kitchen floor is dry, which is another bonus. And while we are on bonuses, Jackie and Joe are taking charge of the kitchen today so I don't even have to think about the catering unless I am called upon to help out.

Symi film shoot day five: Executive Producer arrives

This morning? Cool, calm and with a hint of cloud - I am talking about the weather of course. A morning for not wanting to get out of bed after the most sleep I've had in a few days. Everyone else must be even more tired,especially after a long shooting day like yesterday. Nine o'clock: meet at house, quick chat, piece of toast, everyone off to the location to start, lunch delivered to the location and then, finally, stop for dinner at seven thirty.

The scenes yesterday were all shot inside and concerned Chris and Helen (Kurtis and Wookie) and included a deep hypnotism scene, a childhood regression session if you like. I watched the rushes in the evening and was completely mesmerised by the performances, I meant totally: 'did we write that?' And the way it all looked, the lighting and the angles, how the director had developed the scene to that level. Something pretty special appears to be happening out there.

And while they are out there making magic, I am at home being Mr Producer and my roles & tasks recently have included: discussion about contracts, post production and percentages, ordering enough water, doing the washing ('Hmm, I wouldn't have put him down for being a boxer shorts man'), tidying the house, finding extras forms, dealing with emails, emptying the bins and mending the toilet. Such is the heady world of show-biz.

Today is another quieter day for me as Joe and Jackie are cooking again. Everyone was treated to some incredible lasagne last night and, thanks to a particular donation, we are all enjoying some 'beer' of an evening (actually wine – and very much appreciated). Today is day six (already) and as usual there is much to do. I need to have a discussion with my co-writer about a scene scheduled for Sunday morning, and then sweep the floors, so best get on.

Symi film shoot day six: body count

A bit of a mad day today so only a few snippets of news and info.

The good news is that we are on schedule, which is apparently pretty unheard of in film making circles. We have one scene to pick up today, the one with Sam and his friends and the wheelbarrows, but we swapped that for another scene yesterday so that still means we are on schedule for the number of scenes in the 'can.' Though these days the 'can' is not a can it is a 'drive.' So, so far we have 22 pages in the drive.

Sounds good but that's only about a quarter of the script and there are only seven days left to go. But a lot of what has been filmed are the small 'here and there' pieces. Next week seems longer and more in depth scenes that are more static. So hard work for the actors but less lugging of equipment for the crew.

Today should also see the first appearance of Sotiris' goat. It is being brought down to graze in the village so it can be in the background. Hopefully it will look at the right place at the right time and say its lines only when asked.

Don't worry! He will have an animal handler, someone to look after it, a nanny you might say and it will be well cared for during the hour or so it is required.

I had a shock the other night when I was tidying up after lunch. I saw a transparent plastic jar on the piano and thought, 'who's left that there…' Mutter, mutter. 'Why don't they just put things in the bin?' So I picked it up to do just that only to find a Symi spider in it. Nice idea for a prop but please don't leave it in my house!

Mind you. I hope the production designer remembers that he has the head of a goat in his fridge this morning.

And I shan't tell you what Neil asked me when he came out of the bathroom just now. The answer, though, was: 'It's fake blood.'

Symi film shoot day eight: Neil becomes the high priest

It looks like the director got the 'big scene' in the drive yesterday with a very ritualistic event up in the square below Ag. Triada. Several locals turned out to watch the strange goings-on which included some local lads and Neil being sooted up in coal black and burning the body of a character in the story.

There was no real fire of course, just damp leaves on charcoal to produce smoke (I still smell of it) and a few well-placed lights.

Yesterday, Rebecca Grant and her husband arrived and Neil went down to meet them with 1066 producer Chris Hastings. While he was doing that I was setting about organising my usual lunch items and then called in to the schoolroom to see how that scene was going. This scene takes place before the main character (Called Chris) leaves England to come to a faraway Greek island, so we had Kurtis, from Liverpool, talking with Pantelis, from Symi, in a Greek classroom that looks remarkably English, because it is actually a Greek school of English. They are being watched by the designer (called Chris) and the Cypriot sound guy, Lefteris, was there, the Spanish gaffer and German cameraman, and the director, who I think is from Essex. Everyone would get ready for the take, the assistant director (also called Chris) calls for quiet, the crew say certain things so everyone knows they are ready to go, the clapper board claps and then action is called and a motorbike goes past, as we were right next to the 'road' by Taverna Zoi. So, reset and start again, same process, Pantelis and Kurtis share a joke, someone checks the clock, the light, the focus to pull, makes the most of the interruption to double check and then off we go again and Action! And my tummy rumbles. I let myself out after watching three takes and went to sort out lunch.

Sadly I forgot to sort out dinner but luckily we have a super-Rhiannon in reserve. So, after she's spent the day making blood with the SFX makeup artist, and after she and Michaelis had been up and down the steps 100 times to the set and dealt with the guys and the makeup and the lights and just about everything else, they popped down to the Windmill and made dinner for the whole crew and cast. A pretty nice day to finish off week one. Only six more days to go.

Symi film shoot day nine: Joe the Jam ends it all

One if the nicest things about this project so far has been the involvement of so many local people, people from Symi, and Symi visitors. Not only in terms of time and money and backing, lending of properties and props, but also of effort and enthusiasm and talent.

I mean where else in the world would you be able to say, when asked, 'Yes, we can do that,' or 'yes we have one of those' knowing that you can and you have. A trained makeup artist, and electrician, a goat, a huge bag of feathers, a hot water bottle, experienced extras, a million dollar film set, a data wrangler, and so on. It's all coming together nicely but it would not have come this far without the help and generosity of a lot of people.

People like Joe who arranged to be here so that he and his wife Jackie could help out. Joe was also the competition winner from the Kickstarter campaign. The competition was to work out the cryptic clues of the names of the perks. He was chosen at random and the prize was to name a character. In this case he named the character of the schoolboy Kurtis is talking to near the start of the story and he named him after his son. So when you see the film and hear the name Joseph you will know how that name came about. Joe was also asked to play the part of the 'Smiling Doctor' a non-speaking extra in the film. Being a professional extra he was perfect for that as well. Then, after sitting around the Rainbow bar for a well-earned beer yesterday, he popped home, got changed, came back and he and Jackie cooked for the rest of the day and night getting today's meals ready.

Meanwhile Tove was making the cast and crew homemade bread, pizzas and other wonderful things for lunch and dinner and everyone worked right through up until about 9.30 when they collected back at ours for supper. A lot of shell-shocked faces and tired but happy people milled around for a while and then went off home to rest. I hope!

My duties yesterday were quite simple: blog, breakfast things, sweep floors, wash the clothes, hang out the washing, tidy the kitchen, do the catering accounts, buy in supplies, rearrange the kitchen, order water, approve minor script change,visit locations, deliver snacks, liaise with other producers, answer the two way radio (while actually in the bathroom), collect and deliver food, check the square had been cleaned, answer emails, arrange a ferry ticket, process and send photos, back up photos and washing up. All in a day's volunteer work on Symi.

Symi film shoot day ten: This feels odd

What feels odd about today's blog post is that it is 11.53 on Tuesday morning and I have nothing to do. Well, apart from get ahead of myself and get at least some of today's post ready for the morning.

So far today I've put up yesterday's blog post, had a production meeting/breakfast which as you will see from my photo was chaired this morning by Jack. It was a case of perfect timing for Jack really. Navin Dev, the director, had rightly taken the central chair on the terrace, not for any kind of hierarchy thing but simply because you can see everyone more easily. He then checked around to see if everyone was present, "Rodrigo, Felix, Neil… (a shout from Jack) and Jack of course." Then he stood up to go and fetch something and in the two seconds it took to find it, Jack had taken the chair. Thus this morning's meeting was chaired by The Alarm Cat.

After that, I had a meeting with one of the Executive Producers, did some emails arranging what I could about flights and transport in Rhodes for

Sunday, checked about transport here, came up with one or two good ideas, arranged for some voice over recordings to be done, did the washing up and then had time to pop out to buy bin liners, have a cup of coffee at the Olive Tree and stare at the sea for five minutes. Lovely.

And then what was really nice to see was day to day life going on outside of the production office. One of the fishermen selling his fresh fish outside the supermarket, and chatting on his mobile phone. Nice how some things never change (apart from the mobile phone bit).

Jackie and Joe are in the kitchen cooking lunch and making me feel hungry, everyone else is up at the shoot working hard and I am wondering what to do next with this quiet time. It's like the time (parents who work at home may know what I mean) when everyone has gone off to school and to work and the house falls quiet after a mad rush of morning activity. It was like that yesterday as well, when all I could here was the peace and quiet, broken only by Kurtis shouting his lines up at the Castro.

Symi film shoot day eleven: Richard Syms on Symi

The British actor Richard Syms arrived on Symi yesterday for his two days of filming for The Judas Curse. Neil and Chris met him from the boat, Symi Visitor organised his taxi and his hotel and Wendy and Michaelis met him at the Hotel Fiona.

After a coffee and chat at the Olive Tree and a chance to unpack, he came up to the house to meet everyone for lunch. Later the crew did their first night shoot at 'the hanging tree' and finally wrapped for the day and came for some of Astrid's wonderful spaghetti bolognaise around nine, or it might have been later.

This morning we have the big group photo to take. This was one of the Kickstarter rewards a limited edition signed photo of cast and crew. Only trouble is: Neil has to take it and print a certain number of copies, and then have them signed by Rebecca and Lorna before they leave on the afternoon ferry, so he has a busy day ahead.

I have dinner duties today, my last ones of the shoot, and Richard and Kurtis have big emotional scenes to film up at the house beneath the Castro. I reckon it's going to be a lunch on set day so I am already trying to think of something portable to make. Sandwiches and… pizza delivery? If only we had the budget.

So, have to get on now as the boys will be arriving for their breakfast and Neil needs to get himself ready for the big shoot.

Symi film shoot day twelve: Group photos and things

Every day it becomes a little harder to get out of bed in the morning. The phone alarm goes off, playing its light classical melody which, after a few repeats, ends on an unfinished cadence, a dominant seventh chord, left hanging there as if threatening you in some musical way. I feel like heading straight to the piano to thump out the final resolve.

But I don't. I head for the shower, slightly bleary eyed from the waking sleep otherwise filled with strange dreams. Last night it was to do with the servant's stairs being blocked off and having to go all the way down again and through the front of the house to come up the main stairs to get to the place I was just in, only this time I could see out of a window and all kinds of people were heading into town, which was a modern, British looking town with people riding mopeds… I have no idea what that all means! And actually, I don't think I want to know.

After staggering through a shower I feel a little better and so set about writing the blog. While the PC is warming up I clear any debris from the front room to the kitchen and remind myself of my daily duties. Today they are: blog, tidy, empty rubbish, clean floors, take in water, order water bottles and see to company emails. Yesterday they were to do with getting everyone to the photo shoot on time (achieved) followed by cooking lunch and dinner (achieved) and then dealing with return journeys and onward arrangements (almost achieved).

It was another strange JC coincidence that, once we had put in the three boys in an insert, the group photo had 30 people in it. 30 pieces of silver?

The crew have only two more days of filming. Today is all indoor shots, apart from one I think, and tomorrow is picking up on all kinds of bits and pieces that need to be finished off; establishing shots, views, Michaelis attacking Kurtis, and then Harry and Ian. Definitely counting down the days now, everyone is running down and looking tired, and after nearly two weeks of non-stop hard work, I'm not surprised.

Symi film shoot day thirteen: Winding down

Talk about strange dreams. Why, I wonder, was I cooking in Wendy's house with water dripping through the ceiling? There was a nice piece of steak in a bowl that I thought I would chop up for dinner but sadly I dropped part of it into the cat bowl and another part into the sink. But, as others started coming into the kitchen and milling around, I was able to rescue it from both places. But then Ged came to cook dinner so I slipped away pretending I had never been there.

And then, at sometime during a troubled night, my 'staff' (whoever they were) were gathered to hear a message from someone else on high, the boss I guess. Trouble is, the message wasn't written down it was contained in the flavour of a cup of soup. As I couldn't remember all of the message I had to sip the soup line by line and translate it into words.

Discuss and explain.

Thank you for that couch session, I feel a lot clearer now. Actually, I quite like the soup idea; messages in flavours. Now there's a code that's not been used before. Or has it?

So, the final day of shooting today, after all this time. As has become usual they pressed on and got more scenes on the hard drive than was originally planned yesterday, leaving today free for a short scene with Richard and then some voice over work, and any other pickups that might have been missed. We are expecting a slower, calmer day with attention now being paid to packing the lighting van, collecting props, checking locations to make sure they have been left neat and tidy and preparing for the homeward journey.

Yesterday was actually a pretty free day for me as Gerrie and Sue did the catering. I was able to check a location, tidy up a little bit, get some of the kids' washing done, spend some time in the sun sitting and chatting, visit the doctor (all's well, just checking), have a glass of wine or two at Rainbow with Richard, Neil and others and then spend a very pleasant evening on the terrace with the older members of the team, and later with two of the boys. My old cabaret partner, Kinny Gardner, used to refer to younger members of any company we were in as the 'kids' and now I know why. It's not because they are younger and you're talking down or anything, it's simply because after a while you start to feel paternal towards them. Tomorrow our 'boys' will be leaving home and going back to England (and Spain).

But the nice thing for me today is that I am not cooking today. Ged is preparing us curry for lunch and a rabbit stew for dinner.

And dinner tonight will be at the house opposite the Rainbow Bar so everyone who has been involved with the shoot can come and have a drink at the bar, then dinner at the house and can mill around and then go to Astrid's last (ever) night at the Two A's Bar. Yes, it closes tonight, under Astrid's ownership at least. What will happen to it after that? You'll have to wait until the next reel to find out.

Symi film shoot day fourteen; it's a wrap

As they say. Just have to get the remaining cast and crew safely off the island and onto the coach in Rhodes, very kindly donated by George Kalodoukas, and our work here is done. For the moment at least. The final piece of work was completed yesterday, early evening, strangely enough in our bedroom/sound recording studio where Richard was recording some whispers for the audio. His final words were 'Judas.'

There were three parties going on last night: the wrap party at The Rainbow, the birthday party for Gerrie at The Olive Tree and the last night of the Two A's Bar. I was home and zonked out by midnight.

And finally, normally[1] can return to Symi

Well, actually, with the wedding of the year taking place at Agios Athansios, with the chairs being put out in its square early in the morning and the dancing and music going on well into the night, yesterday wasn't really that normal.

---
1 Nice chap, normally. Meant to write 'normality' I guess, but had no idea what normality was at that time: end of filming, end of 18 months' involvement with the project, all rather un-normal after 3 parties and a film shoot.

The day even started strangely, for us, with no crowds of people coming for breakfast, Jack, who at first didn't know what to do without his recent team of admirers, finally settled into a rather disgruntled doze on the chairs outside just in case someone turned up. We started tidying the house, counting the number of tubs of margarine in the fridge, wondering what we are going to do with six kilos of lentils and ten of pasta and then finally, Kurtis surfaced and came for a cup of tea.

Seems it had been a long wrap party with cast and crew heading for Astrid's own wrap party which went on into the early hours. Eventually though everyone was awake and accounted for, boat tickets were given out, goodbyes were said and Ian started collecting people in the Kalodoukas mini bus and ferrying cast and crew to the harbour.

Down there the send-off committee made sure everyone was aboard the rather busy boat (I was still at work) and the ship, as always, left on time. Later, as we assembled for a drink before dinner, Jackie sent a message to say that the bus, arranged by Kalodoukas Holidays, was there to meet them in Rhodes and they were on their way to the airport. I sent a thank you and with great timing the battery on my phone passed out. I've not heard a thing from anyone since, so I am hoping everyone got home safely. They should all be there now and probably sleeping.

Today is Oxi Day and there is a service and a parade in Yialos. I'm not sure if we will get there this year, there is still much to do here. But the weather is still perfect, hot in the sun and cool in the shade. There's washing to catch up on, a house to put straight and clean and then it's back into the normal rhythm of life while we wait to hear what happens next with the film.

But, as everyone kept saying, 'we did it.' And the thing that really registers for me is that this day would not have happened had it not been for Symi and the island's connection to so many people.

The summer season slipped by

It was a kind of 'getting back to normal' day for us yesterday, though today is much more like it, except for being awake and up and about at six, and that's thanks to being asleep by nine last night, eight in Neil's case.

But Neil is going back to the shop today to start working through his photos so that he can send over those needed for the books, as promised to the Kickstarter backers. I have some things to do at the house, there are props to sort through, and Miss DJ is coming to do those later, Rhiannon has some makeup things to collect and I have some writing to get back to.

Yesterday saw the Oxi Day parade in Yialos and a bank holiday though some shops were open as usual. The village square was quiet in the afternoon, at least to start with. Yiannis and Lefteris both now have their winter chairs out, not that it is wet, though there is a lot of dew around of a morning. There were a couple of visitors around, some day trippers and there are still some longer term visitors here. But it does rather feel like the end of the season has passed us by in all the turmoil of the last couple of weeks. Before you know it there will be golf on the Xbox, tap dancing and quizzes as we settle in to the real winter routine.

This year though I am currently determined to do some more walking we've already been promised a lift in a car with Manolis, or Yiannis, to go and visit a couple of churches in the mountains. Not exactly walking I know, but it's a start. But now, for a start to today, I must check the emails and then get some typing done.

Music and musicals – spot the actors

This morning's 'earworm' contains the lines: "I took a walk past the old Saxon well, down by the cathedral I heard the chapel bell." No prizes, but who knows what song that is from?

The mornings are sunny and silvery at the moment, everything remains clam and the sea flat. There's a mist in the Pedi valley and across the hills and the low light is turning more to winter with each day. I am still going to bed very early and waking up early to the sound of the Alarm Cat and coughing; that's Neil coughing as hay fever lands on his chest again. He takes tablets for it. The Alarm Cat too is taking medicine albeit reluctantly.

He's got some drops for his ears which we need to administer every day for five days; he doesn't like that one bit. But it should stop him scratching himself so much. We need to arrange some 'Advocate' for him somehow or some Stronghold and, we are reliably told, he needs to go on a diet. And I am not looking forward to telling him that.

The village square is quiet in the afternoons, it's like we suddenly missed the end of the season. Well, we were rather tied up with other things. But it's still just about warm enough to sit out, with a jumper on later in the afternoon, and watch the world go slowly by.

November

Long walks, talking clouds, a celebration or two, a tortoiselet, a closing down sale, some shopping, a brownie and a tart

Happy first of the month from multicultural Symi

Kalo Mina. 1st November, 07:40 there's the smell of a bonfire in the morning air, the Afghan boys who live around the corner have their music on early, giving me half an hour of Indian tablars and long-necked lutes to listen to as I write the blog, still with the front door open.

I think it was warmer yesterday than it had been for the last couple of weeks, and still felt reasonably warm in the late afternoon and evening. Which was when we met Jean, out for a walk with her cat who is called Tart, so I had to be very careful what words I chose to describe that encounter.

Yesterday evening we were invited to dinner at the Harry house to celebrate Neil's birthday again. There was a present, a cake and a Cornish Pasty pie which was rather well received. Neil had the boys in fits of laughter playing the part of 'silly old grandpa' which he does so well, we all ate too much and had a great time.

It wasn't a late night by most standards but for us who have been falling asleep by eight this week, following the filming, it felt like a late night. And then to be woken by the Alarm Cat at 6.30 I'm not quite feeling fully awake so I'll stop rambling on and go and dance to some shashtar on the terrace.

Alarm Cat strikes again

Late start to due to farewell party for friends last night. Not a late night as such but more of an early morning thanks to the Alarm Cat.

06:30 constant shouting at the door to be let in. Grumble my way out of bed, still worn out from the two weeks of filming, still needing loads of sleep. Open door, let in noisy cat, give him breakfast, head for sofa, sit. Doze off.

06:40 constant shouting at the door to be let out, grumble across room, open door, let cat out, close door, back to sofa, doze.

06:45 constant and rather annoyed shouting at door to be let back in again. Blaspheme my way across to the door, open, close, sofa, semi-doze.

06:46 very close and louder shouting about something right by my ear. It's a good job he's deaf, the amount of names he got called. Manage to ignore it for a while. Shouting stops, becomes a grumble and then there's the sound of biscuits rattling in a bowl in the other room. Check door is still open (through one half closed eye) it is, doze.

07:30 wake up with stiff neck and realise the cat has once again escaped his ear drop treatment, will have to try and catch him later.

So that's got today off to a rough start and I have no idea what else to say, so I think, when Neil has gone to work in a few minutes, I may go back to bed.

Things to see on a Symi walk, part one

Our first long walk of the winter yesterday left Neil hobbling about on his bad foot for the evening, but hopefully he will be able to walk this morning. No accidents, just the usual 'seizing up' after three hours of hill walking.

Yesterday: Up early, chicken in the slow cooker, cat fed, rubbish to bins, cameras from shop and off we go at 09:00 towards the upper village. Out along the path to Agia Paraskevi.

First odd thing to see en route: the Tardis from Dr Who masquerading as an outside loo for the small church. Locked, unlike the church itself.

Second odd thing to note a few yards further on is a bench facing the hillside, not exactly the greatest view but a nice place to stop and wait for the conveniences to be more conveniently unlocked. Carry on up to the road and turn right.

We're heading for Tolis, or at least in its general direction, and along the way we pass Tassos the donkey-man with his wife and child. He is loading firewood into his truck, they are watching and enjoying the hazy sun. The haze made for some interesting images, and also gave us some cover, but I still caught some sun on the back of my neck.

Down to Roukoniotis and we can hear people on the other side of the valley over at one of the Saint George churches, and remember that there is a festival happening there this morning and we were going to go, but it's too late now so press on down the hill and pause to take a photo of the old motorbike that's left there near the windmill. 15th century like the older monastery perhaps?

Carry on down the new road (well, new to us; last time we came this way there was no road, there was no Tolis actually, only a rocky beach and a ruined hut) and the sounds of revelry from across the valley continue. We wonder should we head back, it would only take an hour or so, but decide to carry on. We pass the exercycle by the side of the road and think 'that's a long walk to get to the gym' and then carry on carrying on.

Things to see on a Symi walk part two

There's a bit of a storm rumbling around this morning, one of those ones where it comes in and goes out and then comes back again, perhaps caught in the semi-circle Bay of Doris between us and Turkey.

The lightening is striking out at sea at the moment so I thought I would take the chance and plug things back in, put up the blog and then be ready to close down if it comes back at me. I can't actually see the sea of course, it's all grey out there but the heavy rain has stopped, for the time being at least. I was up during the night unplugging things and putting down towels, but so far the inside of the house has remained dry, which is a bit unusual but nothing to complain about.

I was going to carry on with our Sunday walk today, and I think I'd left you at the exercise bike on the way to Tolis. Well, that's still there but from there we walked on, heading towards the bay and following the signs for Taverna and the more colourful ones put up to guide tourists to the beach. Eventually we came to Ag. Dimitrios and from there were able to look towards both Tolis, and towards Ag. Emilianos; we decided not to walk on to either of them but instead, after consulting with some turkeys, decided that we had enough time to head off to Nimborio instead of taking the same path home.

But then we thought it best to check in with some real walkers and so rang Sue and Gerrie to check which path led where. After receiving our instructions we returned a few paces to 'the barbeque' and started following the red and blue dots across country towards Nimborio.

The things you see on a Symi walk: a bite sized tortoise which narrowly avoided my boot as I walked; luckily I was looking down at the time.

A strange hole in the path with twigs arranged around it, clearly not man made but animal made. But what kind of an animal lives in a hole in a path?

And some kind of ancient wine or olive press (or, as Neil suggested a spaceship landing beacon, yeah right) lying by the path. Placed there or always been there? There are signs of an early settlement around it: old terraces, shaped walls, semi-circles of stone. Wouldn't it be great to have some kind of Time Team investigation on Symi?

And so on to the hills above Nimborio and around back towards Yialos.

But the storm is heading back so I need to be ready to shut down and unplug for fear of being power-surged and losing our modem. Have a dry day!

Things to see on a Symi walk part three

The third part of our walk takes us from behind Ag. Dimitrios and towards Yialos, via the hills above Nimborio. The things you see on this stretch are mainly longer landscapes, rocky views and the sea.

This path is still well marked by the red and/or blue dots that guide you when following the 'Walking on Symi' book as released by Kalodoukas Holidays and Frances Noble. As far as I know you can still get copies of it from the office when you're here. These markers are a great help, even if you are not following the book. Should you be out and about and not sure where you are going, then look out for small daubs of red or blue paint and follow their trail. You will end up somewhere eventually. OK, so it may not be where you intended to go, but it will be somewhere.

We knew where we were going and marched on, the path was mainly smooth but high up on the hills, where more goats pass than people, there can be some tricky patches to manoeuvre around. The views more than make up for the effort with outlooks to Nimos and the haze beyond, across Nimborio Bay and down into the still, blue sea.

And then, passing above the church of St. George you start to see Yialos, Horio, the Castro and Symi, both harbour and Ano. If you have never seen the island from this angle before then it is well worth the walk up; you can get to a good vantage point by following the road out from the back of Yialos towards the cemetery and then walking up the hill and looking back. In the dusty mist of last Sunday it all looked rather magical, a kind of Rivendell in the Aegean.

But then you realise you are coming back to Symi normality when you pass the ever expanding farm at the end of the path, the front adorned with original paintings, chickens and dogs, goats and donkeys playing in their paddocks. When you see the horse, having time off from pulling its carriage around the harbour, frisking in its field and then you really know you've hit reality and come back down to earth when you see the ostriches. Two of them, camera shy and inspecting the ground as you pass by.

And so, back down into Yialos and time for a Sunday morning beer. It's taken just over three hours to do this circular walk, there are a few aching joints but nothing a couple of hours of rest won't sort out.

A bit of a damp day on Symi today

Late getting started this morning due to a thunderstorm which is still threatening to return. The rain has been lashing down since the early hours, and that's following an evening of if it last night.

At one point last night some kind of lightning struck something important nearby as, when we returned home from a dinner party, the electrics in the house had blown. Luckily the computer and phone had been unplugged and all seems well this morning. But some water had crept in under the balcony doors, under the front door and mysteriously also into the bedroom about two feet from the window, with the floor between being perfectly dry, as was the ceiling overhead. The kitchen has one towel and one bowl down still but the house is, so far, holding up remarkably well. The garden is certainly enjoying a good drink after the long, dry summer.

I wonder how Jenine and the boys, and Tina, are getting on over on Kalymnos where they have gone on holiday for a couple of days. They set off on the Blue Star into the gathering storm yesterday afternoon and I imagine the weather is the same up there as it is here. Let's hope it soon clears. The forecast was for sun today and tomorrow.

We are/were/will be planning a long walk to Kokimides tomorrow as it is the feast day of St. Michael, otherwise known around here as Panormitis Day. In fact, the festival starts today and runs for three days. I imagine there are some rather damp market stalls being set up down there at the moment, or else people are waiting until the skies clear before risking it.

The sky is still heavy out there, I can see flashes of lightning over Turkey and the thunder has started rumbling back so I best go and get his posted before unplugging everything again. The winter starts here it seems!

Panormitis Day, Symi

Today it is the name day, the feast day, of several saints. Most importantly it is the festival for St. Michael Panormitis, patron saint of Symi, and other things. Also included in the list of names celebrating today are: Angelos, Gabriel, Raphael, Stamatia and Taxiarchis.

We're collecting Ian at nine and walking up to Kokimides, another church dedicated to St Michael. We last did this walk several years ago now and it took two hours from house to church turning down three of our offers of lifts along the way as we wanted to do the whole journey there on foot. Coming back was a different matter of course; after lunch and a few drinks, all offers of a lift are welcome. Today the sky is clear and the sun is back, so it should make for a good, calm, steady walk, with that long winding road and steep hill at the end of it.

Yesterday's exercise came in the form of a walk to Yialos to the bank machine and then back up the steps, followed by an evening at home watching films. I didn't get much writing done and will start again in earnest tomorrow, or on Monday. I am working on the novel of The Judas Curse, telling the original story based on my first draft of the script. This should be ready early in the New Year, all being well. I am currently on chapter four, or around 9,000 words. Whether those are the right words is yet to be seen.

Anyway, breakfast is nearly ready, apparently, and I need to stock up on energy before this morning's hike, so I'm off. Xronia Polla to you all, and happy name day for 'Panormitis Day.'

Kokimides, a church of the Archangel Michael

Another long walk yesterday. The weather was perfect, cool in the shade, warm in the sun, my face is slightly tanned today, but none of me is aching. We covered the distance to Kokimides in around two and a half hours, including a lift for the last part, up the hill to the church itself.

We arrived just after the service, due to a delayed start from home, but were in time for coffee and a cheese pie. Lots of neighbours from the shop and customers from the Rainbow Bar were there, plus a few people called Michaelis of course, and everyone was very pleased to see us, to have their photos taken and to make us feel welcome. We were invited in (to the courtyard) for lunch which was made up of salad, bread, kritheraki and lamb served up with a jug of wine. This was after the Grace had been said (sung) at the table.

After lunch, which was served early, around 12.00, we set off down the hill again. Kokimides is a high church, set up on the top of a hill which is between St George beach and Nanou Bay, very roughly speaking. It is a very old church with fading frescos inside and wonderful views of the island's hinterland looking one way, the coast of Asia Minor all the way around, the sea, and right across to Rhodes and other islands when looking the other way.

It was tempting, on the way down, to head off towards the ridge over Pedi and come back that way, but we decided to head back to the main road and the way we'd come. It always seems quicker heading home, and heading down hill it certainly was quicker. It became a very speedy journey home when some neighbours stopped and offered us a lift in the back of a flat-bed truck. There was a pallet to sit on, bars to hold on to and scenery to watch as we were driven from Ag. Konstantinos back to Ag. Lefteris, everything to do with the day's journey being measured in churches. The two glamorously dressed ladies in the back with us had made themselves comfortable on upturned crates with cushions, their backs to the cab, and sat, quite unfazed by the speed and wind, chatting away about the church, the weather, the views and several other things as we headed homewards.

A great day out, well a morning really as we were back by 14:00, followed by a couple of hours in the evening in the square with friends and general chat. Back to work today though, there's a book to be written and it's not going to get itself onto the page.

Heading towards Nimborio

I think that after the walk last Friday and the house cleaning yesterday we've had quite enough physical activity for a while. Except that later today we're going to walk over to Nimborio for a visit. After that… Maybe we'll calm down.

Actually it's not far to walk over to Nimborio and it is a very nice walk, either way you go. You can head towards the town square and follow the road past Iapetos Village and the Grace Hotel and up the hill and then, once you get to the top, pass Manos' farm on you right and keep going. This is a path that reminds me of a country walk through certain parts of England, and probably other countries, with fields and stone walls, and it also offers a nice view back to the Castro. Keep going and you come to the church, St. George, and then follow the only path down to the road and you're there, almost.

Or you can follow the coast road, around the harbour, through the boatyard, past 'Paradise' Beach, up the hill and all the way around. Just keep going. When I first came here this was a rough path/road, Paradise beach was half of what it is today, there were no handy steps down to the rocky crags that we now have; if you wanted private swimming you had to risk life and limb to scramble down. And of course there was no mainline train service cutting through like there is now. Ah, progress.

Regular Symi visitors will know all this already but others may be thinking about taking your next year holiday here (and you should) and wondering what there is to do. Well, had you been at our house yesterday you could have involved yourself in the art of house cleaning. I even bought a new mop and bucket to celebrate the event. Neil did most of the work while I busied myself with other matters like dusting the piano, he was sweeping and washing floors, bathrooms and kitchens. I did manage to get outside, tidied up the terrace and that did include carrying the old 80 litre water tank complete with crud and lime scale away, down the steps and to the appropriate collection point. Not an easy job. We passed some guys surveying Villa Hani on the way and wondered if that was being sold.

Later we celebrated our clean Sunday with a few drinks and crosswords at the Sunrise which was, as always, good fun and cerebrally challenging. Almost. And so, back to today: some work at home and at the shop, a visit to the accountant, if he is in, and a visit to various places in Yialos before walking across to Nimborio. A full day planned and so far the sun is still shinning and it looks like a good day for a walk, though rain is forecast for later.

Walks, Kodak box Brownie, shop closed from Sunday

A nice walk, no rain, so that was a good thing. Actually it was a pleasant day all-round. We set off from the shop in the late morning, and then reached the harbour in time to deliver some photos, collect the post, phone bill (note: must pay today) and pay Neil's health insurance. We were met near the bridge by a lovely couple from France who had with them an old Kodak Brownie camera which they gave to Neil for his "Camera Museum" at the shop; very kind indeed. By way of thanks we showed them where the dentist surgery was. No really, they wanted to know. And then we set off up the hill towards Nimborio.

The walk over the top took us less than an hour, more like 45 minutes, even though we did stop to try and photograph the ostriches, there was one and she was very shy, and we did stop once along the way to open the water and have a drink. The views, as usual, were pretty special, as was the lunch and the lift back which was followed by a couple of glasses in the village square.

Next thing you know it's about nine at night and you're ready for bed. Up early today though, bells clanging for church (07:37), typing to be done, shop to be opening, and another trip in to town later, possibly, for Neil to find the accountant if he is in.

The Judas Inheritance

Just when you thought you'd heard the last of 'The Judas Curse' I start working on the novel. Well, actually I started on it a long time ago, now I start trying to finish it. To completely misquote Agatha Christie: I have the characters, I have the plot, all I need now are the words.

We are going to be in Rhodes for a few days next week, Monday to Wednesday for me, so I won't be here to blog, but what I think I might do is put up the first chapter of the book so you can have an exclusive first read, at least of the opening.

I will have to point out in advance that this is the first draft and it won't have been run past the editor, my little typo-fairy, so there may be some errors in the typing to amuse you. I can get that ready on Sunday and have it scheduled to appear while I am away.

I should also mention that when you get to see the film you will probably say 'It's nothing like the book' and that's because it won't be. The version I am writing is the original, the story I wanted to tell, the first ideas which

I think are more suitable for a novel. After this draft was written another writer became involved as did the production house and then later a director and then later still, actors. All have a creative input into the process of putting a film together whereas with a novel there's just the author, and later editors perhaps.

There's also the case of structure in that a film has a different structure to a novel and with a novel you can bounce around all over the place in the telling of the story, but a film needs to be more, well, structured. And you can put more words in a novel and more pages, you can tell how a character is feeling, what they are planning, you are more restricted in film and that all has a bearing on the way the story is told. So, the original will be the book. Which will be titled something like The Judas Inheritance, which is closer to its original title.

So, that's this morning's pre-warning and minor ramble, stay tuned for the first chapter which should be starting on Monday. Meanwhile: A quick Symi update with not much to report from up here as I spent the day at home yesterday. The Alarm Cat is still on his diet, the garden will soon need weeding, the Olive Tree is open again, the weather remains calm and clear, we've not got any big walks planned this week, we've still to track down the accountant, there's another bill to be paid, the heater is down from storage ready to be switched on and we watched 'The Ghost Train' last night, the old Arnold Ridley play made into a film. I'd forgotten what fun it was and how simple films were back then.

Symi weather update, a cloud on the horizon

A bit cloudy today, hazy out to sea, slight breeze, and a chill in the air. Rain is forecast (again) though this has been promised for a few days now and the day keeps changing.

Imagine being rain clouds, hanging around up there, chatting as they form: "Where you off to today Trevor?"

"Me? Oh they want me over Symi later this afternoon, I'm covering some of Sunny's shift."

"Nice place, Symi. I was there once."

"Yeah, so you keep telling us. Tell me again Luke, what's it like there in the winter?"

"Hang on!"

"What's up?"

"Typical. Just got this memo, they've shifted me to Thursday."

"Wish they'd make up their minds, they're having a laugh!"

"Ah well, never mind, what you say we go and find someone's parade…"

And so on. So, we may have rain today or we may not. Although the garden could do with it, I am rather hoping we don't as we have an appointment with the accountant later this morning. How posh are we eh? An appointment. Let's just hope he's there. There are bills to pay, finances to work out (or lack of them), things to collect and boat tickets to buy for Sunday ahead of my annual holiday in Rhodes.

I've already got the blog posts ready for those three days and have set up the magic blog machine to post the first chapter of "The Judas Inheritance" starting on Monday. I bet you can hardly contain your indifference can you?

So, here comes another Thursday on Symi with a trip to Yialos to look forward to for me, followed by an evening at home. I popped out last night and stopped for a glass in the square. It was good to see so many people out and about, keeping at least two local businesses going, people sitting outside the bars, and the taverna open and in use. We're not quite into deep winter yet and everyone is making the most of the stable weather while they have the chance.

Last chance to take away a piece of Symi history today

The Alarm Cat didn't get me out of bed until 7.30 this morning, so a bit of a late start today.

As you may know, the "Two A's, Asteropi's, Jean & Tonic, Late Place, Bar with no settled name", has closed, for ever. That's it. Gone. Almost. Today, between one and five in the afternoon there is a sale, at the bar, where anything not wanted on voyage by Astrid is going to be sold off. Mirrors, glasses, tables, memorabilia, keepsakes from a past era, all up for reasonable offers; and if you turn up a free glass of wine will be included.

Glad to report a successful trip to Yialos, stocked up on tax bills and the like from the accountant, picked up something from the post office, found the departmental department that I needed shut and now open only four hours per week, so that will have to wait until next Thursday, got some shopping, paid some bills, had a quick beer and decided to head back home as the skies were darkening and it didn't look like the day to be sitting out having lunch.

No great plans for today except Neil must start to get his packing ready for Sunday and the shop ready of closing for a month. May pop to the "Two Tonics Jean & Place Late Asteropi's Bar" this afternoon, otherwise, a day of writing. Lunch is already in the slow cooker so I have from now right up until 13.00 free to do what I want.

Leaving a Symi house for three days: a check list

We called in to the Two As closing down sale yesterday and came away with one of the coffee tables; sentimental and practical. We've sat around that table off and on for the last 15 years, I've even played a 'piano' on it, and now we have it in our sitting room where it has already proved useful. There's life in the old thing yet.

Today is about packing up the shop ready for its month off; taking the pictures from the walls to avoid the damp, bringing home anything needed here for the duration and tidying up ready for later in December when it will open again. Meanwhile at home I have washing to get done, and things to get ready for going to Rhodes tomorrow. Harry and Sam are going to look after Jack and make sure he gets fed, so I need to make sure there's enough food for him so the neighbourhood Alarm system doesn't break down. Monday, Tuesday and Wednesday blog posts are already done and in the queue so they should get posted on their own while I am away, and all being well with the weather, I'll be back here on Wednesday night ready to settle into a routine again from Thursday. A routine which is already disrupted as I need to go to the town hall on Thursday morning, but we'll worry about all that later.

Check list for leaving the house for a few days during the wet winter months: Towels down to collect rain water coming in under the balcony windows, front door, bedroom window where there shutter is still half missing, window behind TV, hall and in kitchen below the skylight. (We have a lot of old towels.) Tickets, money, passport. Unplug TV, computer, phone and piano in case of lightning strikes. Leave out cat food, water and bowls. Make sure all windows and doors are shut and that cats can't get in (double check bathroom). Finally, turn off water pump in case something goes wrong there and you return to no water in the sterna, but plenty of water inside the house.

The Judas Inheritance (The Judas Curse)

The story was inspired by the ruins in Horio and is complete fiction, but I was captivated by the mysterious dates, numbers, and names that appear on many of these hauntingly strange buildings that seem to conjure up a curiosity about the lives of the people who once might have lived there. While the story is set on an imaginary island, visitors to Symi will recognise a number of features which I have borrowed.

As promised, here is the first chapter of The Judas Inheritance:

You are in darkness. Your eyes are closed. You can't see but you can hear. A strange kind of whispering sound, like voices from another room, frantically chattering, excited, hushing each other, gasping, begging, all mixed up. And behind all that but close to you, some kind of motor is whirring away, a small, tiny motor driving something on, steady, slowly. What is it?

It's getting louder.

There is something in the room with you. Something or someone. You just need to open your eyes. You just need the courage to open your eyes.

A quick glance. Open. Shut.

You saw a photograph. A man. A priest was it? Something old, a bit faded, the colour draining, the edges tatty. And an album, the photo was going into a photo album, a small one, a red cover, a plastic wallet of old memories. Who was doing it? Whose hands were those?

Eyes still shut, ears still aware: thumping sounds, what is that? Sounds like books being dumped one on top of the other, a pile of heavy books being stacked and... Someone crying? If the whispers would die down you could hear better but that's definitely someone crying. A man. An older man breathing fast, desperately, trying to control himself. A whimper of fear.

Another quick glance.

The crying man is pushing the red photo album into an envelope, his fingers are trembling. There is a name on the envelope. You can't see it. You don't want to know what is going on. You close your eyes again.

And hear the whispers rise in excitement, tumbling over each other madly, a crescendo, incoming chatter down an unseen telegraph wire, and the sounds of whimpering and the old man mumbling. You just wish it would all stop, all go away, leave you alone. Your eyes screw up tighter, your eyelids actually hurt, your face is distorted. And then:

A scream that holds within it all the horror and desperation of a man with no way out.

'I can't do it!'

You have to look.

You see Frank, a man in his sixties, in the darkness of a small, closed room at night. A candle on the table lights papers and books, and his face. It lights the lines on his skin as if his face is made up of crumpled shadows wet by the streams of his tears. His hands are over his ears.

The muffled thump-ker-thump of a heartbeat within a body. The rhythm of life or the sound of approaching death.

He takes his hands away. The whispers have changed key. Lower now and more conspiratorial. They have something planned.

Shadows jostle on the walls of the room like keen spectators as Frank looks down to the table before him. A small metal chest with its key, a small silver pill box, an envelope, a roughly drawn map and a book, one of his journals. He places his hand on this book as if he were about to swear an oath. It is a journal, 'The Judas Curse' and it is his life's work. Beside the book a Dictaphone whirs as it records.

Frank picks up the envelope now and quickly slips it inside the journal, this he throws onto a pile of other books in an old box, then picks up the pill box. It rattles. There's something heavy inside. He clutches it tight in his hand for a moment, drawing it towards his chest and then he throws it, as if it just burned him. It rattles into the box of books.

And then he slumps down. Deaf to the sounds around him, or immune, he looks slowly at the map. Hand drawn, rough, tatty, it makes no sense to anyone but him. But it will. It has to.

It's useless. All of it. Desperate and useless.

He hesitates, picks the map up and is about to rip it in half when:

Sudden screams shatter the gloom and the chattering falls silent. Frank stands still his grip poised to rip the map ready to destroy the clue. But a deep, low growl rumbles through the room and the sound of frightened children pulls him to his senses.

'No. Please,' they say, close enough that he can feel their ghostly breath.

'I am sorry,' he whispers back and his grip on the map relaxes.

'Help us.'

'I can't!' And with that he swings around and grabs the candle. He thrusts it into the darkness lighting up the walls, the shelves, the locked cupboard, the shuttered window, but no faces. He is alone.

The cupboard.

He unlocks it, puts the map inside. He knows he cannot make this too easy. Too easy and it will not happen, it will not be finished. He has to make it a challenge or it won't work. It will not end.

He locks the door and pockets the key.

The voices are calmed, but the shadows loom up, crowd in closer. Frank spins, something darker than the rest stands in the corner, something with the stench of evil about it, death in the air. He staggers back, knocks a picture from the wall, upsets a small table as he thrusts the candle to the corner.

'He will finish it!'

The light burns the shadow away. Nothing there. No one there.

'He will,' he says, quieter now as he lowers the candle and looks at the desk.

It is finished. Words from a book he read once and believed in always. Into thy hands…

His work is done, all but the chest. The final clue to leave. Tears now pouring from his eyes, his heart beat counting down his last moments of life, he drags the chest from the table and walks to the door.

The whispers follow him from the house as the Dictaphone blinks its red recording light on the table in the darkness. In the silence.

Soft silver clouds scud by a faceless moon as Frank falls from the house and into the narrow, cobbled lane. Hard stones under foot, uneven, passing light, gathering night, he clutches the chest and half runs, half lurches his way along the path.

He stops at the corner, a church tower bears down on him, challenging, disapproving and he shakes his head at it. He cannot explain. He will be there soon enough. He will tell his story in person.

He runs on; he knows where he is heading. Windowless ruins of a dying village look down on him like buildings blinded by history. He reaches out to the walls for support as his breathing becomes tighter, his vision blurring from the tears. The warm night air a stark contrast to the cold stabbing in his heart.

As he passes a gaping doorway he reaches for that key.

'It must be a challenge,' he mumbles to himself. He takes the cupboard key and throws it into the ruin, it clatters on a stone and then is swallowed by the undergrowth.

Frank staggers on, turns, follows the twisting path until he reaches a door. Metal, creaking open, clanging back as he staggers into a large lobby and towards an arch.

Clouds part showing him the way as he enters the apothiki, the store room.

'This house,' he whispers. 'He will know this house.'

The store is a large stone cellar smelling of damp and things long dead and best forgotten. The walls crumble as Frank attacks them with his fingers, pulling the mortar away from the rocks, freeing one large stone.

He looks back over his shoulder. No whispers. He is alone, and yet he knows he is not.

He can see it in the corner. So near and yet so impossibly far. It would be so easy to take his last few steps that way. Over to there, to that in the corner.

'Why?' He shouts out. 'Why can I not do this one thing?'

But he knows why. He has always known. This is not for him, this was never his to finish and that's the punishment. That's what he deserves.

The rock falls from the wall revealing a hollow. The chest slides in, the rock is replaced, he crams crumbled mortar around it.

'So close. So near.'

Near enough that he can feel the presence behind him, laughing at him, invisibly grinning and wringing its hands and winning, gloating, sneering...

Frank looks down, sees a length of rope amid a pile of clutter, work tools, cans of paint, a dusty baseball cap that reminds him of...

He picks it up. Places it. A smile creeps onto his face and then rushes away as, with his other hand, he picks up the rope and clutches it tightly.

Behind him, in the cellar, that thing in the corner starts to breathe and stir.

The night darkens with the slowing of his heartbeat, the rope swings and the noose waits.

'It has all come to this,' he says, quietly, resigned. 'I did what I could, but I could not do enough.'

'You could not give enough,' the unseen children whisper back inside his head. 'You have betrayed us all.'

Frank falls to his knees. Sobbing, he claws the earth, digging, his fingers catching on rocks and stones, bleeding, he pulls up the ground and frees a stone.

'I didn't know!' He shouts and dumps the heavy stone to one side. 'I didn't mean this to happen!' Another stone, another rock, another step, the pile grows higher.

Until it is high enough and he stands. He places one foot and then the other on the stones and steps up. He balances on the stones and looks down over the edge of a wall. It's a drop enough.

He takes the noose and places it around his neck.

A flickering light like hope steps out from the shadows and lights the pale face of a young woman. She watches with cold eyes as Frank looks up and across.

'I can't,' he says again, and she knows.

She just stares back. There is nothing she can do, not now. But all the same, she must try one last time.

'If you take this path,' she says and her accent is as rich as the night is black, 'then he will slowly possess you. He will grow in you and thrive.'

Frank tightens the noose around his neck, the coarse hairs of the rope scratching his stubbled skin.

'Only you can end this.'

'Not only me,' he counters. He looks away from her now. 'Not only me.'

The rocks beneath his feet shudder as he edges forward.

She watches him, her eyes impassive, the candle dancing yellow across her face.

'I am sorry,' he says, and he is.

Frank's feet slip from the rocks and the rope burns into his neck as the noose grows tighter.

She watches and then silently blows out the candle and disappears back into the darkness.

The Judas inheritance and other James Collins books are available for sale from various outlets.

See symidream.com/james for details

Shopping in Rhodes, a thought or two

So, back from three days in Rhodes, Neil safely in Vienna as his brother's guest, me back at the desk, and later the harbour if it doesn't rain, and then the shops. Not that I have not had enough of shops for a while.

I can now see why people regularly go across to Rhodes to get shopping. And I can see how easy it is if you have a car. It's like popping 'up to town' from Brighton or the countryside once a week for essentials, or like driving an hour or so up the road to visit the nearest Sainsbury's, if you live in a rural place. Symi is, after all, a pretty rural place.

You get on the number 10 bus (in this case the Blue Star Diagoras) when it calls in on one of its twice weekly visits, and you socialise across the sea for an hour or so, drive off and within ten minutes you're at the shops. I don't mean the collection of ladies fashion shops, shoe emporia and pizza slice bars in the new town, but out a bit further towards Faliraki and other places where you find the likes of Carrefour and Jumbo.

There were aisles and trolleys to push down them, tacky music, car parks, you name it, all those things I've not seen in a supermarket for many years. No screaming children though which was a nice touch, everyone seemed quite happy and content to be doing their shopping.

Many things were so much cheaper than on Symi you can actually make up the cost of your transport in savings very quickly. Some things cost the same, which is interesting to see and makes you wonder why are some items more expensive here and others not. Some are in fact cheaper on Symi (if you know where to look).

But mainly there is so much choice. As soon as you walk into one of these huge stores you realise how much has been missing from your life. Or at least your kitchen. I mean, how did we survive all this time without a day glow orange potato peeler and blue plastic bottle opener? No wonder our bathroom has never felt complete, we don't have the stylish luxury of a wooden hook-rail that reads 'Bath', and as for our garden shed! It must have felt so desolate all this time without its handy hang-and-store shelf unit and lawnmower cover. Hang on, we don't have a lawn mower. We don't actually have a garden shed.

So you do have to stop yourself impulse buying but when you can get six steak knives for under €5.00 and they are good quality, new Christmas decorations, several Christmas gifts, new notebooks and all kinds of other stuff that completely fills a large bag or two, for around €30.00, well, you have to go a bit bonkers don't you? I mean: last week I bought 10 blank DVDs in a local, Symi, shop that sells such things. They cost me €9.99. I bought exactly the same item yesterday for €3.99. Someone's having a laugh, as they say.

But still, mustn't ramble on: there's work to do, washing to be done, an unsettled Alarm Cat to settle back in, a trip to Yialos to deal with and a book to start writing in earnest.

Sign of the times; winter money queues

06:15, the wind is blowing out there in the dark and it has been raining overnight. I am having an early start after an early night, the Alarm Cat is safely inside and having had his breakfast is already looking forward to lunch, I'm setting about the blog before a day of writing and being inside, dry and warm.

The weather yesterday was warm, still, and dry as I went to Yialos and back in the mid-morning. There was nothing at the post office and my town hall visit wasn't very successful, but never mind. I had some exercise and got some fresh air before returning to the desk and the task in hand, the new book. Or rather, books. The Judas Inheritance is coming along slowly, I'm trying to get the first draft down along the lines of "Don't get it right get it written" and then can go back over it in more detail and with more care. And the 'Untitled, new Symi blog book' is still coming along bit by bit. I am now up to the month of June in my checking through of the editor's edits and the original texts as typed here at this time of day. So you could say we are half way through the first draft of that and, as you are now reading it, we can also assume that we must have managed to get to the end of the editing stage too.

Random thoughts: I guess this is one of the first signs of the cutbacks on Symi that I have noticed. Austerity measures finally kicking in down here perhaps? In previous years, at the end of the summer season, people finishing work and signing off employment would go and find Irini at the appropriate office. She would be there ten until two, five days a week and people could call in during those hours and check their paperwork, get their forms filled out and have their claims sent off to Rhodes.

This is for the winter payments and it used to be that you could work for a certain number of days in the summer and then claim winter money for the rest of the year, a system which, to me, never really added up as some employers were putting in less than their laid-off staff were then being paid back, and that money was also going towards funding the national health care system.

Last winter some people were suddenly told that there was no winter money for them because they had had too much in previous winters, and were left high and dry, end of story, nothing, and without warning in many cases. This year, apparently, everyone is to get three months' worth and that's it. All very odd. But the sign of the times is that Irini (and others) who now deal with those claims are only available between ten and twelve on Tuesdays and Thursdays. And their office that was in the converted public toilets building is now in the council chamber at the top of the town hall.

Now, instead of calling in and being able to go and pop back if she was busy, there's a ticket system and of course, long queues. If you go and wait for two hours only to find you've not got the right photocopy of this or that piece of paper, it makes for a very frustrating morning I expect.

There were several people waiting in a line, on chairs, outside the council chamber yesterday and it reminded me of a school scene with pupils waiting outside the headmaster's study. Not that I was ever told to go and see the headmaster you understand. (I did once but that was to demand he hired a drama teacher for the sixth form. 1981. Fat chance.) But the point is that it is the first time since the great economic collapse a couple of years ago that I have actually noticed, on Symi, the kind of queues and frustration that I've seen on TV in other parts of the country.

Anyway, social observation over with, the sun is starting to turn the black beyond the windows to grey, the Alarm Cat has settled into his chair by the desk and a second cup of tea is now needed.

Wet and windy Symi ahead, a quick quiz, books…

Let's get the week off to a quizzical start:

Something first appeared on this day, the 25th of November, in 1952. What is it? Winston Churchill was Prime minister of Great Britain, Stalin was the Soviet ruler, and D.D. Eisenhower was president-elect in the USA. This mystery 'thing' was originally intended for Queen Mary, wife of the late King George V. In 1974 the 'thing' moved to its present location where it can still be seen. What am I talking about?

Answer at the bottom of the page.[1]

It's a windy, grey morning here on Symi, the olive tree outside the house is blowing in the wind, the sea is choppy and flecked with white, the cables are swinging from their poles down the lane and the skies don't look too blue at all, a bit grey in fact. The forecast is showing rain for the next two days with a thunderstorm tomorrow afternoon.

Winter is settling in on the island and my diary is starting to fill with regular winter activities. Apart from the daily writing of course, the usual housework and winter chores, such as mopping up rain, drying towels, clearing dead vine leaves, weeding the garden and keeping the place warm, apart from those things I also have tap classes starting up again tonight, invitations for a birthday bash on Thursday, crosswords and kafeneion quizzes, card nights and, when Neil gets back, golf to play.

The book is coming along. I had a great writing day yesterday and feel quite proud of myself. The new Symi book is about 50% through the first draft, 'The Judas Inheritance' is about 30% through the first draft, and an old idea for a story, a comedy, is finally coming together in note and plot structure form in a new notebook I bought from Jumbo last week.

So, as you can see, no great news to report here, no new photos either, I've not been out much this weekend apart from Saturday afternoon when there was a lot of laughter (can't remember the funny bits now), and apart from a short walk yesterday just to stretch the legs and rest the brain. Apart from writing, I have been reading, I've just finally got around to reading 'Death in Venice' and next on the lectern is James Herbert's 'Haunted.' I've sorted out the bookshelves in the sitting room, so there are a few other odds and odders waiting to finally be read before being passed on or sent to the great literary graveyard in the sky, aka, our moussandra.

That's it for today. Well, I may not be funny but at least I'm quick!

---

[1] Yesterday in 1952, *The Mousetrap* opened in London.

House getting damp, sky clearing up

The sky is clear this morning and the windows are misted up on the inside, which means I will need to open at least one and a door for a while this morning and let some of the condensation dry out. If you don't do that regularly you speed up the growth of condensation mould on the bathroom and kitchen walls, and elsewhere that moisture settles.

You can't really avoid the walls 'going black' at this time of year, not unless you are willing to make a full time job of drying them down every morning, keeping the house warm and ventilated at the same time, and not breathing while inside. It's a combination of cold stone, moisture in the air and warmth from bodies inside the house. The bathroom is usually the worst, though since the widow decided not to close properly it's not been so bad as it has a constant supply of cold air (and snails) from outside.

But at least it a clear sky today, unlike yesterday when another storm threatened, with distant thunder during the afternoon. It never appeared though, just turned dark and cloudy for a while with mist and low cloud settling over the Vigla for a while.

I nipped out to take a photo and realised that the rose bush had roses on it. (I would have been even more surprised had they been lilacs). The rosemary bush is in flower, which I am sure is a bit early as usually she's covered with bees when there are flowers (maybe they last a long time, through the winter and into spring? Can't remember), and the lemons are slowly starting to turn yellow. It will soon be time for lemon and hot water every morning.

So, highlights of today? Perhaps I might indulge myself in a little washing to use up some of the extra water caught in the sterna during the recent storms. That's something else that will have to be dried outside (the washing, not the sterna) to cut down on the inside damp. Trouble is, it's just as humid and damp outside as it is inside, so the washing has to eventually come in for drying. But I've still not had to put the inside heater on. I am leaving that for as late as possible due to the increases in electricity bills. (Just put an extra jumper on and you'll be fine.)

Listen to Symi Radio – Radio Symi

Today is the first day I've woken up and found the house noticeably colder, cold enough to consider putting the heater on. But no, just another layer for now.

Today is also Miss DJ's birthday, so happy birthday to you and I'll see you later for a walk into Yialos. It's not going to be very exciting: paying the water bill, seeing the accountant (if he is in), checking the post office, but at least it will get me out of the house for a while.

I went out yesterday afternoon actually, for a short walk up to the Kastro and around. I thought the clouds might be of interest and there were some nice views. Coming back down I had one of those Symi winter moments; passing a friend's house I was discovered by a small party and invited in for a glass of wine. Thank you! Nice to catch up and I hope the fairy lights worked in the end.

Neil has left behind his old Nikon so I had a decent camera to take with me, except that there has been a polarising filter left on this lens for ages now and we've not been able to get it off. I thought it had been knocked and become cross-threaded perhaps but, after getting a decent grip on the thing (having taken if off the body first) I finally managed to get it to come free with a bit of brute force. Well, maybe not Brute, more like Aramis force, but it came free and now the lens is back to normal so I don't have to run every shot through an anti-polarising filter in post processing.

I've got Wind, it's multiplying, and I'm losing control…

Saturday, all jobs done and up to date, a day ahead for writing and relaxing, calm, clear, cold, perfect.

Well, maybe not. We will have to see, but another wander down to Yialos may be in the offing. You see I have Wind and I made a mistake with my Wind a few days ago and now I think my Wind has made a mistake with me, and I may need to go and see the man who has Wind in Yialos and ask him to help me with mine.

Wind is my mobile phone network provider, in case you were wondering. When we first moved to Greece in 2002, Neil and I both bought mobile phones and then the provider was called Telestet, which has a nice, telephonic ring to it. In 2004 we were crossing the English Channel on a ferry, heading to St Lô for a family funeral when suddenly my phone beeped and I received a message saying 'Tim welcomes you to France.' I had no idea who Tim might be, let alone how he knew where I was, and it was all rather worrying until I looked into it. As it turned out I wasn't in a spy novel, my phone network had changed its name. And then, a few years later, Tim got wind of the fact that Tim wasn't a good name for a phone company and so became Wind, and I've been windy ever since.

Now then, I am on a contract and Neil is still on pay as you go top-ups. Every now and then he gets a message saying, 'dial this number and you will get three years' free calls to all people whose name starts with the letter Z and 100 SMS for the next month' and stuff like that. Consequently he only has to top up every now and then, or during times of high demand like when he is making a film. Me, on the other hand, pays up a certain amount each month and hardly ever uses the phone. But I do get a new phone every 12 months or so, and this time they gave me the unintelligent smart phone on which I can connect to the internet.

But only when there is an open signal, I don't pay for internet connection through my contract. So, in Rhodes last week for a few days and there are loads of open signals, Rhodes Town Hall has one, and it seems Rhodes generally has one, so I am online pretty often. While there, having lunch, I receive a message from Wind saying something about internet connection and how I can get a better deal if I dial this number.... I idly do, interested to see what will happen. After all, Neil does this and gets a lifetime's free chat with both great-grandparents and 2,000 free SMSs a day. I vaguely wonder what I will get in return, and then get on with lunch.

Next day I have a text message and take a look. 'Oh it's from Wind, another offer I don't want.' I ignore it. The next day another, I ignore it. The next day another, and so on until one day (Thursday) I realise it is the same message and wonder what it actually means. I translate it to discover it is telling me that yesterday I was charged €1.00 for internet connection on my phone and I can call and get a cheaper deal up to 20Mbs a day. What?! I realise my rouse to save money has backfired on me (and I have now spent half my monthly allowance) and call Wind immediately. A very helpful chap understands, and confirms he will remove the feature, but it will take an hour or so. No problem. There, that's put me back on track.

Next day, yesterday, I get the same text message and again phone Wind. Helpful lady there understands what's happened and says she will put me through to the right department (I didn't speak to a right department the day before) and so I hang on and wait for 20 minutes listening to some obscure cantata by a rap band called Nosey-Mutt-T (featuring Screecher), or some such. I gave up in the end and decided that, if I have another text this morning (they come in around 11.00) then I will go and share my wind with the Wind man in Yialos and ask him to cure it.

So that's why I may be going to Yialos today. Thrilling eh?

December

Multiplex, shipwrecks, mysterious pins, Christmas shopping, closing banks and the office party

Weekend activity, a grey Sunday walk

Here we are off into another week. I was woken during the night by one of the shutters banging as the wind rose again during the night.

It had been grey and cold and windy all day, apart from some time in the late afternoon when it calmed. I made the most of that and went for a walk. I'd already made two trips to the rubbish skip after doing some clearing out in the house, tidying up the front room and finding loads of old paper and junk to get rid of. On Saturday I'd weeded half the garden and taken a shorter walk, so by the time I was back from my Sunday walk towards 'To Vrisi' and back I felt as if I'd done enough exercise for one weekend.

The rest of my time was spent writing, making notes and having ideas (always much more fun than actually sitting down and typing up), going to parties, (Wendy and Ged had a joint birthday bash at Manteio's on Saturday night), and watching some old films on TV. I also managed to get in some shopping, though not much was needed, some incidental housework, and some reading. So, all in all, not a bad weekend.

There's not a lot in the diary this week, which is nice in a way as it keeps the channels clear for the book typing, but I am due to be at a tap class this evening at seven, and I will probably go and check the post office again on Thursday and see if I can catch the accountant in his office once more. Most things depend on the weather as they do at this time of year. A rain storm can keep you housebound for safety reasons, and the cold and wind can keep you from only the most necessary of walks, and according to my forecast it's going to rain through until Wednesday; I better make sure there are some spare towels to hand just in case of window or roof leaks.

Two Screen Yiannis, or welcome to the Multiplex Symi

Passed by the Rainbow Bar last night on the way to the tap class and Jenine called in to get some water for us.

"Yiannis Two-TV" could well become a new nickname for "Yianni-Rainbow." Symi is an island of nicknames, or so it was once described to me by a Symiot lady who lives around the corner from the shop. There are so many people with the same name that nicknames are often used to differentiate between them, even people with names that are not so common get them. Neil is still, locally, the 'little ducky' on account of being a Gosling. I hate to think what they call me.

But Yiannis now has two televisions in the bar, showing simultaneously. This might be because he has two satellite installations now, one running Nova and one running the newer OTE service, which also has the British football on it – and probably other things as well, I don't profess to understand such things. So now, on a quiet winter evening, you can go and sit, sup a drink and bounce back and forth between Animal Planet on the right and the national news on the left. Or you might catch Manchester United Vs Folkestone Utd. on one side and A.E.K. Vs Rhodes Park Rovers on the other, or whatever it is. (Actually I saw the MU Vs Folkestone Utd. And Folkestone won 4/1)

After that excitement the tap class went… well, it went rather fast actually. Before I forget:

(r) tap, toe, heel, (l) heel, pick-up, (r) heel, (l) toe, (r) heel (l) toe. Is that right – and then repeated on the left?

And then:

(r) step, (l) shuffle, (r) ball, (l) change, (r) step, (l) brush (1st two times: (r) step and repeat, third time) (r) hop/toe, hop/toe, hop/toe (while turning) and repeat on the left?

Not much to remember really.

And here is the local news:

The Blue Star from Rhodes has been cancelled due to bad weather further north so will not arrive today. It is scheduled to leave Piraeus tomorrow at 15.00.

Anne Zouroudi has her first Kindle publication out titled "Butterflies in the rain" she writes:

"I have at last ventured into the arena of eBook short stories with my first Kindle Single (I'm very late to the party, I know). It's a story I wrote for a national competition, set not in Greece but the western USA. It's a total bargain at only 99p, and if you do download it and enjoy it, please consider doing me an Amazon review: good reviews are good news on there. And don't ask me if Rosita is angel or devil, because to be honest I'm not sure. I just write the stuff. Your views are welcome."

The weather: There was a thunderstorm in the night, but outside now grey clouds are passing by and the forecast is for sunshine later.

And not so local: On this day in history (1872) the Mary Celeste was found abandoned.

Neil has arrived safely with his daughter in Scotland for this part of his family tour 2013.

Shops and stuff

I didn't take a walk yesterday, apart from to the shops, due to the weather, but today looks clear. Talking of shopping; we use a couple of the 'super markets' (sic) that are available in the village, and we use them because they are on our way to and from our own shop, and we use both as they have different opening hours, and different prices on certain goods. Yesterday, for example, I used Sotiris' supermarket because I was out in the early evening, and the day before I used the 'American' because I was out during the afternoon when Sotiris is shut.

There is a marked difference between the two on a few counts. The American has things that the other doesn't have, and vice versa, but I find Sotiris is always more of a madhouse, more noise and laughter. His is also on one level and you can usually have a conversation with whoever is at the till as you browse around. The American is on two levels and once upstairs you're on your own. It's recently had a sort-out up there and now has a different system on the shelves, and I always think it's much more of an Aladdin's cave. I spend ages looking at all the interesting bits and pieces and wondering if I can justify buying things I don't need. Everything from camping stoves to tin oven trays; you never know what you will find.

Prices are a factor as well, but you have to keep on top of price-watching like you would keep on top of a daily diet (not that I would know). Some things are cheaper in one than the other, some things are the same, others vary, some things are even cheaper than that were on a recent trip to Lidl in Rhodes (baked beans are an example). You also have to go where the supplies are; sometimes Sotiris will have something people want (exhibit 'A', last week's fresh parsnips, though not for me), but then the American may have onions which don't squash when you squeeze them, and perhaps a few fresh cabbages. At this time of year you take what you can get.

There is also the shop at Campos which I don't use very often as I am too lazy, but I can't comment on it without knowing it, so I won't.

No idea why I started talking about that. Anyway, the typing is calling me, the Alarm Cat is in and at my feet, he has a routine of being there for about ten minutes before he starts complaining that it's not good enough and shouts at the various rooms in the house for 15 minutes before finally and quietly settling into a chair somewhere, and there are things to be done around the house, so let's get started.

Metal pins hold Symi together but what are they?

If you wander around the village looking down at your feet all the time, you may avoid tripping up, but people will think you very antisocial. However, while you are walking that way you may notice some things on the ground and wonder what they are.

I don't mean the ever increasing amounts of, shall we say, left over Chum that more and more dog owners seem to think is someone else's problem, and ditto the occasional bag of household rubbish that never made it to the skip. (Perhaps the carrier was mauled by a loose and wandering hound and never made it, that might explain it.) You will, of course, notice lots of steps and stones, and looking at one's feet is often the safest way to travel around these parts, especially at night. But also, you might notice small pieces of metal embedded in the stone at irregular intervals.

What, you may wonder, are these? They appear in odd places, one right outside the Rainbow Bar, there are several around a house opposite us where some surveying work was recently done, and there are more all through the lanes in Horio and possibly Yialos I haven't noticed. What are they?

I have no idea. I wondered if they might be to do with where cables ran underground, but then cables don't run underground around here, and the water pipes are also over ground. They might be to do with drainage I suppose. The big house near us was recently surveyed and, after the guys had clambered around on its roof, stood with their theodolites and other equipment in the streets and looked up at the building tutting and shaking their heads, 'It'll have to come down guv,' and after they'd made notes on clipboards, they circled some of these metal things in red. Why?

Alien landings? Underground streams? Theodolite markers? Surveyors' tools? I am sure there is an obvious, and probably rather dull, explanation and when I mention this on Facebook there will be some sensible (and silly) suggestions. So, my thought for the day is: what are they? I will let you know if I find out.

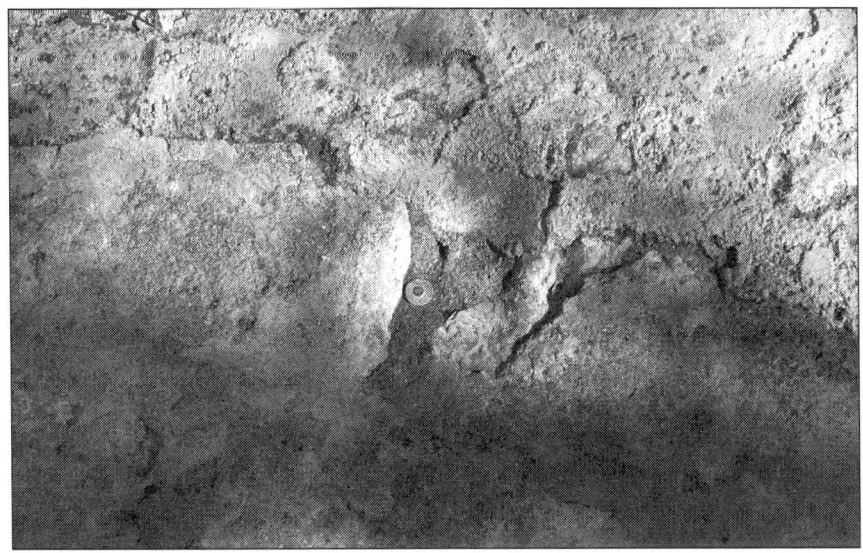

Cold, clear, big wind a-coming, and an explanation

As Victoria Wood said in one of her skits, 'By 'eck Ma, it's parky.' It's suddenly very cold out there (for us) and made even more so yesterday by a strong wind.

A wind that blew the front door open during the night on Saturday giving the Alarm Cat a chance to break in and start playing noisily at five in the morning. On these occasions the only thing to do is get up, let him come in, give him an early breakfast and then try and get back to sleep for an hour. Trouble is, when he's finished eating he has half an hour of vocal training exercises to do, which tends to jolt you awake just as you're nodding off. If he finds where you are sleeping he will knock off early and catch forty winks on your head instead, which also makes it hard to get back to sleep. No such luck for him this morning though, the door was firmly closed, but his Reveille was still early this morning at just before seven.

Over the weekend I did manage to find out what those metal pins in the ground are all about and they are, it seems, to do with surveying. We had a few comments in from people who know about these things including:

"They are survey bench marks." (David)

"Yes, survey points." (Allan)

"It seems that Greece did not have up to date Ordnance Maps and some 15-20 years ago Symi was chosen by the EU as the prototype for Greece. A team of Surveyors arrived on Symi and measured the whole island inputting this information into a computerised form. A copy of the Completed Map is available in the Notary's Office in the Harbour." (Jean)

"So, points and bench marks = reference markers for a land survey, 'put your measuring instruments here and be consistent with other records' kind of thing?" (Me, for clarification.)

"Yes that's it. They measure the contours of the land by measuring the distance and the elevation angle between points." (Allan)

So we can put that mystery to rest now, if indeed it was a mystery to you. I always wondered what they were about. I'll look out for more later when I head out into the cold to do some shopping. I have a busy two days ahead as I want to get everything up to date and three bog[1] posts ready in advance so I can head off to Rhodes on Wednesday and do some (Christmas) shopping, meet Neil and try out the Indian restaurant. That is, if the boat sails on Wednesday. I keep checking the forecast but it doesn't change: very strong winds scheduled for Wednesday, up to force eight or nine, and that might well mean no boat, which will mean no trip to Rhodes until Friday morning, which is when Neil should be coming back, so there'd be no point in me going unless we spend the day there and came back later in the evening. Decisions! Will keep watching Windfinder.com.

You could be running a late night cocktail bar on Symi

It's difficult to get out of a warm bed into a cold room, at quarter to seven in the morning, before the sun is up, and then go into a colder kitchen to feed the cat before heading to the even colder bathroom where the window doesn't shut properly for a shower; with warm water, luckily. But it has to be done.

I know it's colder in other parts of the world where you are reading this but it does feel as if the cold of winter has suddenly bitten in with no warning. Mind you, at least it's not raining, the air is very clear, the view across the sea is spectacular and there is no damp in the air. And, with two heaters on to warm up the front room and fingers, thing aren't so bad.

---

1   This is one of the typos I most dread making and I made it this day; about an hour later I had a message from Jennie saying 'three bog posts, ha ha,' and suspected something was wrong. So I headed back and made an addition to this blog post saying 'obviously I mean 'blog' posts there.' At least, I think that's what I meant to write.

At least it is not yet windy though that is promised for later. I am keeping an eye on it to see if the Blue Star will leave Athens later today and make its journey down. If it does and it calls in to Symi tomorrow and then to Rhodes, I shall be having another couple of days holiday across the water. A bit of eating out, a bit of shopping, and meeting Neil on his return on Wednesday night. If the boat doesn't run then I shan't, and if the wind is that bad (predicted force eight and nine), then there is a chance that Neil won't even make it out of Athens and will have to spend the night there. The joys of small island living in the winter - and you wonder why islanders talk about the weather and boats so much.

Another thing the islanders are talking about is the Jean and Tonic Bar in the village. This business /lease/license is still up for sale by the owner of the property. Although the previous owner has closed and moved on, the bar is still there and licensed as a late night cocktail bar. So, while you are sitting in, in the winter, wherever you are, and dreaming of living on Symi but wondering what you might do, here is a chance to take over something that comes, more or less, complete, and with good recommendations and publicity behind it. I'll leave you to think about that.

Noisy and windy on Symi, noisy in my ears

I'm still here. Well, I would be, it's 6.45 so even if I was supposed to be somewhere else I wouldn't have gone there yet. But I am going to be here even when I should be somewhere else as there is no boat today, or tomorrow, and I am coming back on Friday anyway, from where I can't go today, so no point in going there then when there should next be a boat.

Strong winds, up to force nine you see. Except I can't see, not yet because it's still dark out there, but I can't hear either, apart from the occasional blast and rattle of a shutter, but it is supposed to be very windy later, around 11.00, and very cold. It's not exactly warm now. But still, that's how it is in the winter when the weather is not always with you.

So, instead, I have a couple of extra days in which to get the house shipshape for Neil's return on Friday, which also gives me a couple of extra days working on the book and that is what I shall be doing later this morning. I was going to be in Rhodes seeking out an ear specialist to get some opinion on the tap-dancing that takes place in my left ear 24/7, off and on, but that will have to wait. I've seen doctors about this before, but not a specialist in Greece, so thought I might give it a whirl one day. It's been off and on for years now; a clicking sound that is sometimes low like a Geiger counter and inconsistent in its rhythm, and sometimes fast and high and stabbing, as it is now, but still a clicking and no pain.

I've trawled websites and medical advice sites and fora (that is the plural, I looked it up) and learned of other people's experiences and found all kinds of odd 'remedies'. Sinus tablets such as Sudafed is what the original doctor ordered, and it works for some people but not for me; hanging upside down is one of the more advanced breakthroughs in medical science apparently, and is actually used in some hospitals. (More for the junior doctors' amusement than anything else perhaps.) I tried lying on the bed with my head hanging over the edge but that only succeed in making me look silly.

I've seen a You Tube video of a doctor treating someone simply by laying the head on one side and then other, and sometimes leaning to the left for two minutes will settle it down, though I look pretty foolish when waiting in the post office or walking in the street. Some say it is tinnitus, some say it is not as it is not the same frequency and sound all the time, but the sound comes back with such regular frequency it might as well be.

Meanwhile, I'll click on and try and ignore it. I just thought I would share all that with you in case you are a fellow sufferer and didn't know exactly what it was, or in case you did happen to have a miracle cure and fancied emailing it to me. And now, with the Alarm Cat shouting around the house (having shouted me awake at 5.30 this morning) I must get on. That wind is definitely picking up and I am wondering if I should go and shut the shutters before it's too late.

Greetings from a very cold Greek island

The front room, where I have my desk, really does feel like a fridge today, it has recorded some of the lowest temperatures I can remember in here, and it's not much better outside.

The talk yesterday was of the bad winds and the two small wooden fishing boats that sank in the harbour, the sea was that rough down there. Apparently one was swamped and the other hit against the harbour wall so many times it was holed and then sank.

The sea looks calmer today, but there is still a breeze and it still feels bitterly cold. Neil, arriving back in Rhodes last night, said that if felt colder there than it did in Vienna and Edinburgh, where he has recently been visiting family.

So, the heaters are on, both of them, around the desk, the cat has taken refuge in the depths of his armchair, and I am going to do what work I can before my fingers seize up and I am forced into the sofa with vegetable soup and a good book. (I am aiming for that to happen around midday, though I have yet to make the soup).

I did nip out yesterday to have a quick decaf at the Olive Tree and pick up a few supplies from the shops, and also thoroughly enjoyed a chicken pie at chez Harry in the evening where not only was I well fed but also very well entertained by the boys and came away with a complete set of Thunderbirds drawings from Harry, now in place on the fridge. The real fridge.

All being well, Neil is back on Symi tomorrow and will be back at work on Monday, mornings and evenings (except Saturday eve and Sundays) through the rest of the winter. He's had his holiday, I am planning mine for this afternoon.

12 hour trip from Lindos to Rhodes? Not sure about that

The last I heard, which was yesterday, the Blue Star was on its way down and the Dodekanisos Pride, which is due to leave Rhodes this morning at 08.30, was stuck at Lindos, sheltering from the winds. But that was last night.

As so often happens on Symi at this time of year one has to keep an eye on various tracking and weather websites, or an ear to the phone of the port police, to know what is happening with our vital supply links. The port police in Rhodes are not yet answering their phone but the Marine Traffic site shows me that the Diagoras (Blue Star Line) was last tracked at Kos, so that is getting closer and the pride is on its way from Lindos to Rhodes, so that sounds like good news. For Neil that is, who is hoping to get that boat in an hour and be home by ten this morning. If the Pride doesn't turn up then the Diagoras will leave Rhodes tonight but not until 21.00 which would mean another long day in Rhodes.

So, my morning should, all being well, consist of a quick tidy up of the house and a walk down to Yialos to assist with Jumbo bags, then shopping to restock the house with provisions as I was down to my last vegetable soup last night. I was aiming to empty and defrost the freezer, but there are still things in it, so that's not going to happen.

Another quick check of Marine Traffic and the Pride is currently heading from Lindos to Rhodes, ETA 18.30 UTC, which is clearly wrong, either that or the boat is very sick indeed. I am told that current UTC time is two hours behind what I am actually in, so it is now 5.39 UTC (07.39 GMT (Greek Maybe Time)) and that means that the boat is going to take over 12 hours to travel up the coast of Rhodes; unlikely. More likely a glitch in the Marine Traffic site). There is no wind out there, and the Windfinder site tells me it is way calm enough for a sailing from Rhodes, so that's more good news.

So, a slight break in my usual routine for an early morning hike to Yialos, rather than a later morning one which is usually the norm. I shall go and do my odd jobs around the place to make the house look presentable and await the text that says Neil is finally setting off and on his way home. Then I will wrap up warm and head down the steps.

Symi Saturday

All went according to plan and Neil arrived home yesterday morning, weighted down with Jumbo Bags (like everyone else getting off the boat) and happy to be home.

On the way down I spotted what must have been one of the boats destroyed by the high winds and seas the other day

I also noticed a huge grey cloud that looked like it was being drawn across the harbour like some kind of covering; a straight line to the south, cloud stretching back to the north and west, it was like we were being covered over. It's gone today though and it's clear and cold again this morning.

The Alarm Cat had been at work since about six, and I finally gave in at seven or just after; he's in the house now but still going off, as he does. I'm never sure who he is talking to or what he's trying to say when he sits there looking at the room and then suddenly stands up and shouts and moves

to a different position. The other day he searched the whole house like this before finally deciding to sleep on the bed, but it did take a lot of shout and stare, explore and complain before he finally settled down.

Anyway, what does the weekend hold? Well I have some work to do this morning and I want to do some writing tomorrow, Neil is probably going to go to the shop today and check it out, make sure everything is still in one piece and the things haven't become too damp; give it an airing ready for reopening properly on Monday for the run up to Christmas. I expect he will be open most days now, though will close again for three days over Christmas, and a couple for New Year but, apart from maybe closing for a few days at the end of winter to have a spring clean and re-paint, he's open now every day except Sunday right the way through until the end of Summer next year, all being well.

But that's a long way off, we have Christmas to get through first and more presents for the boys to be wrapped up and put under the tree.

Slow start to a Monday morning

Well, that was a Sunday of doing very little, for me at least. I wrote some more of the book, The Judas Inheritance (The Judas Curse) and watched a lot of films on television, ate a large Sunday lunch and did little else.

And there's not much planned for today either apart from, perhaps, a walk to Yialos at some point and a tap class tonight, and some more writing and pottering around at home of course. For a moment yesterday I did think about going out and weeding the other half of the garden, as I have still not done that, but then something got in my eye and it caused a reaction, so I had to take an antihistamine which meant I was not fit for anything else all day, and I am still drowsy this morning after a very good night's sleep. The eye is getting back to normal though and I don't look so much like Marty Feldman anymore.

But all that nothing might give you an idea of just how exciting things can get around here at this time of year; there's not much else for me to talk about after a day at home. Cat's fine, Neil's fine and back to work properly today and already has a customer lined up at nine for official photos, the Blue Star did another Sunday call in yesterday, but when it does this on a Sunday it doesn't come back again, and there was an extra Dodekanisos boat put on over the weekend as well, apparently. That's the news from my view of Symi!

Closure of Co Op Dodecanese Bank

In the end, no tap class last night as Rhiannon was setting off to England for a holiday. So a quiet night in watching Time Team and then some films, all courtesy of You Tube. I'm not sure if they are meant to be there or not, but they are so I don't mind converting them and putting them on to a data stick and transferring them to the Xbox and TV; it's cheaper than getting Nova or the new OTE equivalent satellite service that we can't afford. If we got that we'd only spend the day channel hopping.

We did make it to town in the morning though, for a quick delve into the post office where all Christmas orders have now arrived (for us that is) and where I am only waiting for one last package to be delivered; a pair of shoes. And then it was on to the Alpha bank to take care of some business but, er, no. The queue in there was so long I decided to leave it for another day.

It transpires that the probable reason for this activity at Alpha is the closure of the Dodecanese Bank, the Cop-Op bank on the corner by the bridge, and its branches elsewhere as the business itself has stopped trading/functioning – you will need to check out a news site for the full and proper report, I'm not a news service. This is obviously bad news for anyone who had money in the bank and who had paid for the obligatory shares when they signed up for an account.

The good news is that Alpha Bank took over the business (again, check the real press for accurate details) and now those who had a Dodecanese account can get their money from Alpha. All that seems to have happened pretty quickly, which is good, but the downside of it all is (apart from losing your initial shares, your job, your livelihood and all just before Christmas) you will need to open an Alpha Bank account if you don't have one already; or so we were told. I assume there's no hassle if you already have one but if you don't you need the usual paperwork needed to set up a bank account. It's been so long that I can't remember what that is; passport, ID, proof of address I guess. I advise checking with someone who knows, i.e. the folk at the bank, hence the queues, the above is all based on what I was told by people who had been told by people who…

Dodecanese Co Op bank and our Christmas tree

Update/clarification from Peter about the Dodecanese Bank situation as mentioned yesterday:

"All banks and building societies in Europe have had to increase their capital base (i.e. the basic free cash and buffer zone in case something goes wrong).

The main banks in Greece have done it and in the UK the Co-Op bank has had to sell new shares to an investment fund instead of remaining entirely owned by its members.

The Dodecanese (and two other co-op banks in Greece) were unable to raise enough extra capital from the existing members (by offering new shares) so their license was withdrawn by the relevant banking authority on 8thDecember and Alpha Bank have taken over the deposits. Alpha announced it would take about a week before people could access their accounts to allow for the necessary information to be gathered and loaded onto their systems.

Any money paid for the offer in new shares is ring-fenced and will be returned. In any case up to €100k of deposits in personal accounts is guaranteed under European law."

I knew it was something like that; thanks for putting it so clearly Peter.

Today has started off grey and wet so a photo of our Christmas Tree might brighten things up.

I spent a few wasted minutes trying to get a decent shot of the thing, did some messing around with turning the focus as I clicked the button and even got the tripod out to try and get some atmosphere with slow exposures, but this was the result. I had a theme this year: blue and silver and, unlike the previous five years, I didn't simply drag it down from the moussandra and stand it up. I took it apart, took the last five years' worth of stuff off it, started again and made it up in blue and silver with only a couple of deviations. A paper decoration from Vienna that is made out of an old music manuscript book, and a white angel and star that arrived in the post from Lin, thank you for that Lin, and we wish you a merry Christmas too.

Symi photographs and copyright

One of those days when I have no idea what to write on my blog so I sit and write, 'one of those days when I have no idea what to write on my blog.'

I keep meaning to put up another gallery of photos as we've not added any for months. There's been no reason for this, apart from laziness perhaps, and the fact that I've not been out and about very much. I have a collection of photos through the year and I may put them up towards the end of the year. But I just don't seem to have had much time to sit and sort through photos and resize them, watermark them as you have to do these days and then send them all up.

We started watermarking our photos, even the little ones from my phone, a couple of years ago. It's not so much of an issue for me but when Neil, a professional photographer, started finding his photos all over the web with no credit, and even finding them reproduced on a Symi calendar carrying someone else's name as a credit, we thought it was time to do what we can to prevent such copyright theft. So now all the photos are embedded with copyright data that can easily be extracted but which can't be seen, and also we watermark them all, or at least most of them. These can be cut off of course, but the digital data is still in there if needed.

Symi, the only place for Christmas shopping in the world

Yialos! I am thinking of heading that way tomorrow for some Christmas shopping, anything that I didn't find in Jumbo or on Amazon will have to be sourced from Yialos and if I can't find it there then it won't be found at all. I have been collecting things since September and now have suddenly run out of time, but we still need a couple of things for a couple of people and I need to find some presents for the Danish Christmas present game we play.

There are also the wine requirements to source which means a visit to a couple of 'off licenses', or rather, wine shops, for things like port and sherry because these things have to be done correctly after all.

I am planning to have a rest next week, and to only write what I want to write when I want to write it and to do very little else apart from relax.

It's been a strange year writing-wise, and no doubt I will wax lyrical some more as the end of the year approaches, but there are only a few more days to go, and that means only a few more pages left in the book which you may find yourself reading and which should be out by Easter next year. Still no title though, so that's something I must turn my mind to over the next few weeks, what to call 'the Symi book number three'? Allan has been beavering away on the edits and cuts, Neil has been finding the photos to act as illustrations, I only need to carry on as normal with the blog (which will make up the text) and find a title, and an intro perhaps. Maybe inspiration will strike over the next week, possibly after a glass of port or two on Wednesday after lunch. No, maybe not; the title would then be something like 'Zzzzzzz'.

So, will spend today tidying up bits and pieces I want to get out of the way before my week off starts with a lazy morning tomorrow and a walk into Yialos for that last minute Christmas shopping. Perhaps I will find something at the Symi Gallery craft fare on Sunday afternoon? Oh the thrill of excitement!

Father Christmas visits Symi - official

It's official, Father Christmas will be coming to Symi. For children of all ages who have been good he will be making house calls on Tuesday night, and then, as a special bonus, will be appearing in Yialos, in the town square at 16:30 on Thursday, Boxing Day, if you have a Boxing Day.

So, it's not too late to get your skates on and whiz across to Greece for a quick and adventurous holiday. Christmas on the rock, fancy it? Sounds like I am going to give away free tickets as a prize or something, which sadly I am not, but I did just wonder how easy and possible it would be to get here in time for Christmas Day if you decided on a trip right now.

Obviously if you live here and you are reading this then you have an instant advantage, but if you don't then you will have to hurry and get yourself to Rhodes by Monday morning as the last boat to Symi leaves at 08.30 on that day. The Next Blue Star leaves Piraeus on Thursday afternoon so you won't get here until Friday if you come via that route. So that leaves you today to find a flight, Sunday to travel to Rhodes, via Athens more than likely, and after a night in a hotel you could still be here by 09.30 on Monday.

Assuming you are coming from London you can do the trip with Aegean Airlines for £356.10 on the way out and £228.10 on the way back, well worth thinking about if you ask me, and if you have the spare cash. You could have Christmas lunch at Pandelis in the harbour as I believe he is open on that day, you could take a long, bracing Christmas walk and, if you contact Neil, I am sure he would organise a special Symi photo walk for you.

And if that sounds a bit rash then while you are looking at the Aegean Airlines site, you might think about booking for next year. June (he says randomly as he's rambling) is a nice month here, not too hot and usually reliable for weather. If you flew on June 2nd, for example, and stayed two weeks you could currently book flights for £109.10 out and £110.10 back, all taxes and standard baggage allowance included.

Now wouldn't that make a nice Christmas present for someone? And talking of presents, I have my list of things I need to buy on my Christmas shopping expedition this morning, or rather this lunchtime as I am not going down the steps until later. I must remember to add on the cranberries (the fruit not the group) and Depon, paracetamol; that's not for me that's for the cook who needs them around about lunchtime on Wednesday when the sherry kicks in. Those few items and some more gifts for 'the game' and I should be set up and ready to celebrate.

Merry Christmas Symi medical team and thank you!

I just wanted to start this week of with a thank you to the Symi medical team and in particular Dr. Xanthos who is currently running both the Yialos clinic and the Horio clinic, as far as I know, on his own.

You might think that a small island is ideal for a practice, but remember that should an emergency occur then the doctor must accompany the patient to Rhodes, which would leave the island without a doctor and also, being on call 24/7 can't be much fun for anyone, no matter how much you love your job. There are some islands in Greece that have no doctor at all and the residents, if needing treatment, have to journey to Turkey and pay all those associated bills. So, Merry Christmas Symi medical team and thank you!

As for us, well, our Symi Dream Christmas party went off very nicely thank you. This year it was a chicken giros delivered to Pacho's kafeneion. Don't say we never do anything classy.

There is not a great choice of places to go for lunch these days, as most of the tavernas in the harbour and the village are closed for the winter, especially at that time of day. There are more open in the evenings but we had an appointment at the Sunrise for a quiz or two on Saturday afternoon/evening, so a lunch event it was.

By the time we'd walked down after Neil had closed the shop, had a walk across to the bank for some spending money, and then been to various wine shops and others (for Christmas things), time was moving on so we stopped for one quick beer at Pacho's, which turned into a couple more and then met up with Ged and Wendy, had a nice long chat and finally managed a taxi back up slightly late for our next event and weighted down with several goodie bags. Another quick shop yesterday and the monthly allowance, neatly saved, has all now been accounted for.

Last day in the shop today for Neil until Friday, only a few more things to wrap up and then the annual festival of lights is upon us; the lights being those at Jenine and Ian's house which is, even now, draining of the national grid as it illuminates, flashes and twinkles. You can actually see it from Pedi this year after dark; I kid you not.

Christmas Eve greetings from Symi

As far as reaching targets goes, I'm almost there, but will probably miss one.

Between us (that's myself, Allan the editor and Neil the photo person), we almost have this new Symi book gathered together. I have two more months' chapters still to re-read and check, Neil has a few more photos to put forward, we all have December's chapter to work on which we can't do until January, and then it will need to be set out, proofed and the cover created, by Sarah, and then that will be ready for the shelves and Kindles, so that is on target. Oh yes, and I need to find a title and an introduction.

The second book, "The Judas Inheritance" (The Judas Curse), is now up to 50,000 words of draft one, about 60% through the story and almost on target, the original and rather ambitious target being the end of the year; more likely to be the end of January now as a couple of things got in the way; mainly being a bit lazy and choosing to watch old episodes of Time Team of a cold afternoon rather than sit in the front fridge and type away.

Targets for the next couple of days include: No work, tidy house, wrap last present for our Christmas game (find it first, then wrap it), bit of shopping, haircut, visit a couple of friends to deliver something trivial, meet others for a drink, watch Polar Express and not have a late night tonight.

Have a great day tomorrow (that's my aim and also a well-wish to you) and try not to over indulge, while also remembering what this time of year is all about. I for one am not giving in to this gradually emerging Americanism of "Let's not offend" by wishing people at this Christian time of year 'Happy Holidays', but instead I am wishing everyone a peaceful Christmas.

Back at the desk, back at the blog

Good morning! And here I am back at the desk, though slightly later than usual and after a day off yesterday. I had intended to put something up on the blog yesterday, but Christmas Day turned out to be rather a long one, the Alarm Cat had me up very early the next morning and I dozed off again on the sofa; by the time I woke up properly, it was half way through Boxing Day morning.

Christmas Eve was a round of wrapping and shopping and tidying the house and doing domestic things. We did pop to the village pharmacy and to one of the supermarkets and this was early on in the morning. Already, at that time of day, the children were out with their triangles singing 'kalanda' (carols) at the shops and businesses. There were even queues of children at some shops, and I think this year brought the largest number of carol singers I've ever seen; or maybe I was just out and about earlier than usual.

After that it was vegetable peeling time at Jenine's house, doing our small bit for the next day. The boys were fascinated by their sticks of rock that Neil had bought from Scotland that turned their lips blue. And after that we spent the afternoon at home before making a couple of house calls to drop off presents. The day finished off, for us, with a glass or two at the Rainbow

Bar where, if you sit in the right place, the two TVs now afford you the chance of watching the same two football matches twice in one go thanks to the mirrors behind the bar.

Christmas Day was a riot of food, children, wrapping paper, games and more food, and also included carol singing at Wendy's house, and a walk to the village square. Some of the party were still in their slippers as the day was all about being comfortable and having fun. It wasn't wet, as the forecast had suggested, but was very windy, in fact it has been since Christmas Eve and still is now. Grey, overcast for some of the time, the sea was rough and still is, and the wind is howling. (But I do notice that the Blue Star Diagoras is on its way from Tilos to Symi as I write, so that is good news.)

Yesterday the boys came to visit us and we had a round of James Bond films, turkey sandwiches, soup and chocolates, and a viewing of the new arena performance of Jesus Christ Superstar, Neil and Sam's favourite musical; a bit 'Easter' perhaps, but then why not? A great day, a lovely three days actually, and now it's time to get back to work, as best as one can after such a nice break, and time to put the house back in order.

Neil is off to the shop today, and tomorrow morning before taking the rest of the weekend off, and I have a story or two to be working on and a 'swing of things' to get back into.

Starting to look back at the end of the year

So that was the last weekend of 2013, and passed by enjoyably, though rather lazily: a couple of chapters of the books written, crosswords and quiz at the Sunrise on Saturday, a day at home with dinner and games on Sunday.

A lot of rain last night, clear and cool today with calm seas and unruffled olive tree outside the window, and a day at home planned. I suppose, at the end of the year, thoughts should turn to what we have done this year, how it went, who has gone, who has stayed? But I was also wondering, as we are also approaching the end of the book that I might think a bit further back. (If you are reading this year's blog posts as the book you will understand; if you are just dipping in and have not picked up on that thread you will be wondering what I am going on about.)

I'm not going to flick back through 'Symi 85600' or even 'Carry on up the Kali Strata' but instead, might try and flick back through my mind as to how things have changed since we moved here in 2002. Thoughts and some feelings, some events and anecdotes are contained in those other two books, and the rest are contained on this blog which was started… some years back now. But what's changed? Someone asked me this in the summer and I can't for the life of me remember what I said.

What has changed on Symi in 11 years? Trouble is, when you're here every day you don't notice the change as much, it creeps on gradually like a waistline or wrinkles. There are more streetlights now than before, not all of them work all of the time but they are there, and there are fewer visitors. I remember the summer evenings when the steps opposite the bars in the village square were as full as the tables. I haven't seen it like that since Greece won the Euro-football thing during the Olympics' year; you no longer see a queue at Giorgio's of a night, in the summer. Sad but true.

We have half a marina in Pedi now and most of the outside of a sports hall. There's a big hole in the ground where a small hospital might one day appear, and the village surgery is no longer in a museum but in a rather smart clinic. Some shops have changed, up here; the hardware store became a cake outlet and then a bar and is now a paint store. The taverna opposite changed hands, was left fallow for a while and is now a thriving Olive Tree café. The other chocolate shop closed, became a DVD rental shop, a computer shop and now a language school, and so on.

The lopsided old tree in the village square lost a major bough and hazard to traffic, several more ruins had life breathed back into them, people we first met as children have got married and now have children of their own, other people we knew have passed on. Friends have been made and some have now left the island, usually for mobility/medical reasons. And of course we have our business. One of my books lists the things we arrived on Symi with and then lists what we had expanded to at that time in our 'back to basics' lifestyle, it starts with two rucksacks and a laptop, and gets up to date with computers, pianos, shops and cats, and that's pretty much largely the same, except now we can add another book or two and a film. Or at least the filming of a script I worked on. We helped write it, get it funded and get it shot and there our involvement ends.

So, there is that to look forward to in 2014, there is a new, hopefully, busy season to get ready for, the usual round of festivals and celebrations, birthdays and parties, the hot weather, the cold winter weather yet to come, visitors, a new novel and, all being well, more blog posts that will thrill you with the mundaneness of our life on Symi.

And that's just New Year's Eve-eve, what might I come out with tomorrow?

Here's wishing you a Happy New Year from Symi

Well, here it is the end of another year. I'm not going to get all reminiscent about the past 12 months, mainly because my laptop's thesaurus states that reminiscent also means Evocative, Suggestive, Redolent, Meaningful, Important, Indicative, Significant and Resonant and I am not sure that I can be all of those things at once, if at all. But looking up that piece of New Year's Eve nonsense did make me wonder about how words are linked (via my electronic and rather limited thesaurus).

So, from reminiscent we get Resonant and if I right click that and find an alternative word suggestion I find Rich (things are looking up already), and if I click again for a word to replace Rich I find I can use either Annoying or Amusing, so although I may be the first I'll try the latter and then from Amusing I click to Diverting (which is what I am doing with this post after all, I mean, surely there must be better things for us all to be doing). And then from Diverting I can click to Fantasy to Fictional to Fantastic which seems like a nice place to leave myself. I came in to this post with the idea of being a bit reminiscent about the year and will leave it on the thought of Fantastic, as that seems to sum up the past 12 months quite succinctly.

Afterword

Having just read through this collection of blog posts, I thought I should say something insightful and meaningful to finish things off with. But then I couldn't think of anything so I will just say this:

Thank you for buying this book and reading it. Thank you for following Symi Dream and my (almost) daily blog online and thank you to everyone who appears in here in either word or photograph or implied deed, by which I mean those who contributed to the Kickstarter campaign for the film, and everyone who has been a customer of our shop.

Don't forget that you can keep up to date with the on-going adventure at www.symidream.com

We'll see you there!

James Collins & Neil Gosling March 2014

List of Illustrations

January

2 Windmill house in Horio
7 Jack the Alarm Cat gives a high-five
10 'Little Michael' Statue in Yialos
14 Traditional dances at the Vasilopita celebration
17 Flooding in Yialos

February

22 Church door at Agios Athanassios, Horio
23 Ruin in Horio
26 Jack being comfortable
32 Boat in Pedi Bay
36 Spooky cross
37 Horio at night
38 Dancing in the village square

March

41 Road works in Yialos
45 Tsiknopempti celebrations in the village square
50 Parked donkey
56 Harry dressed in traditional Symi costume for the March 25th Independence Day parade

April

63   Storm in Rhodes
65   In the moat of the Old Town, Rhodes
67   Neil and Charlene in India
69   The harbour at night
70   Education reforms protest
74   Dance class
75   Transylvania 26/03/2013
76   Clean up Symi volunteers
78   Flies making more flies

May

84   Church congregation at Easter
86   Symi wedding at Panormitis
87   Music at Georgio's
88   May 8th parade
92   Insect on a flower
93   Symi wedding, traditionally meeting in the village square
96   Pomegranate petals and buds

June

103   Symi Gallery interactive exhibition
105   Town square in the early morning
107   Horse and carriage
112   Digger on the Kali Strata outside the Symi Dream shop
113   Book signing, Dominic Ranger and Jeanette
117   Wine night
119   Wet Kali Strata
120   Boats in the harbour

July

126   The harbour in the morning
129   The Symi Music School concert
130   Music School guitar recital

131   Guests on the Poseidon for a birthday party
132   Jack hiding
133   Jack located
135   Divers celebrating the records of Stathis Hadzis
137   Nautical museum blessing
140   Alegrito Cafe customers
146   Cooking Symi shrimps
147   Symi shrimp festival dancers

August
150   Ruin on the Kali Strata
154   Dancing at the festival at Megalis Sotiris
158   Traditional Symi dancers on the town square stage
161   Tourists in Yialos
162   Symi health & safety alert
163   Harry at six
165   Rebecca Grant
169   Zoe's taverna
170   Village square

September
175   Jack doing housework
176   Peeling paint
178   Fishing boats in the harbour
180   Photo walkers on Neil's birthday
181   Friends of friends for lunch
184   The harbour with Nimos in the background
186   Terracing overlooking the harbour
186   Yialos, the harbour
189   Jack on guard duty
191   Rabbit at Sotiris' supermarket
193   Wild goat
194   Expensive yachts in the harbour

October

- 198 Rain clouds obscure the Turkish coast and Nimos
- 201 Another Symi Dream wine night
- 202 Making props for The Judas Curse
- 205 Looking for a morning shower
- 206 Welcoming committee for the film crew
- 207 Kurtis and Josephine in Rhodes
- 210 Jack and Kurtis
- 212 Joe and Jackie cooking for 25
- 213 Filming at Agia Triada
- 215 Dead Joe (still in costume)
- 216 Jack chairs a production meeting
- 217 Fish seller in Horio
- 218 Richard Syms and Wendy at Hotel Fiona
- 219 Rebecca, Jackie, Kurtis and Joe on location
- 221 Cast and crew at the wrap party at the Rainbow Bar
- 222 Cast and crew leaving Symi

November

- 225 Tart (in Jean's shoulder bag)
- 226 Sam, Harry and Neil, because you can never have enough laughter
- 227 Tardis or toilet facility?
- 228 Exercycle (well, you'd have to push it)
- 229 View towards Tolis Bay
- 230 Wild baby tortoise
- 230 Carved stone
- 231 Nimborio
- 232 Rivendell of the Aegean
- 234 At Kokimides
- 235 View from Kokimides with Nimos and then Turkey
- 237 Nimborio from the donkey track
- 239 Storm clouds over the harbour

242	Cross at the Kastro
243	Richard Syms, as 'Frank' filming The Judas Curse
245	An inspirational spooky ruin in Horio
247	Richard prepares for the hanging scene
248	Jenine shopping, happy as Larry
252	Garden flowers in December; roses, rosemary and lemons
254	Yialos, looking towards Milos, the disused windmills on the ridge

December

261	Survey marker
263	Fishing boat
265	Rough sea
266	On the Kali Strata
267	Neil returns
268	Boat damaged in the storm
268	Strange cloud drawing a veil over the island
271	Christmas tree 2013
273	Yialos in December, boats moored further out for safety
275	Neil at our Christmas party (and getting a hand from Ged)
276	Fotini wraps the Christmas wine in her wine shop
278	Ian, Jenine and Neil, at Christmas

Printed in Great Britain
by Amazon.co.uk, Ltd.,
Marston Gate.